The
New Yorkers

The
New Yorkers

HORTENSE CALISHER

WEIDENFELD & NICOLSON
New York

Published by Weidenfeld & Nicolson, New York
A Division of Wheatland Corporation
10 East 53rd Street
New York, NY 10022

Originally published by Little, Brown & Company,
Boston, Toronto, 1966

Library of Congress Cataloging-in-Publication Data

Calisher, Hortense.
    The New Yorkers / Hortense Calisher. —1st Weidenfeld &
Nicolson ed.
        p.   cm.
    ISBN 1-555-84195-3 (pbk.)
    I. Title.
PS3553.A4N4   1988
813′.54—dc19   87-22492
                                                   CIP

A portion of Chapter 6 originally appeared in
Evergreen Review.

Manufactured in the United States of America

First Weidenfeld & Nicolson Edition, 1988

10 9 8 7 6 5 4 3 2 1

To
HEDWIG LICHTSTERN
and
JOSEPH HENRY CALISHER
who were married in a house
on East Seventy-ninth Street

Contents

I
The Crime Circle

1 The Judge's Evening Ride
January 1943

Passersby often remembered the house. Even on such a good street, where new young trees, carefully wired against dogs, wind and anarchy, are regularly set out to spindle, a house still occupied by a single family is a fireside glory to all. Such houses are against the natural design of cities, and from the time of the Dutch here were unlikely to be poor ones. After the Second World War, even the rich had lost interest in them. But trees were not enough to signal to the cold, pure heavens far above this particular city what was still single and humane down below. So, on those brilliant winter nights when the stars came out over the gas fumes, rich and poor, alike on the way to their hives, walked slower at the sight of the Mannix house, four stories above the stoop, all softly Florentined from within by light which seemed to come from another clime. Or, on those swathed, semi-tropic nights which rise out of New York harbor at any odd time of the year, they lingered past the deep, flower-ledged windows. The house was one they had once owned or visited, or dreamed. And afterwards, they thought they remembered it.

The street, a cross street, as side streets are more often called in a city built so much on the square, was in the borough of Manhattan, which meant that any house on it was in full view of the city, however much its own prospect might seem restricted to the houses opposite. On the northeast corner of the street, facing both it and the avenue, there was what at first appeared to be either a large mansion or three brownstones joined by the removal of stoops and the use of dropped entrances. Actually, its turn-of-the-century builder, dazzled by the Diamond Jubilee over the water, had conceived of these houses as "mansion-flats." By means of extraordinary rentals to his estate, these were still so maintained, with cream-and-brass foyers, leaded bow windows, and occasional glimpses of one of those fashionably confused interiors where old, coffered ceilings are lit by the bright, stark lamps of the latest transient. Center rear of "the old Ralston houses" as these were now called, an enormous iron-enclosed elevator cage, scrolled as ponderously as its era could manage, and topped by a water tower, rose to a height which once had dominated the land here, and still stood out against the flat rears of the avenue's apartment houses. When erected, it had at once curtailed the space, light and value of the plot adjoining on the cross-street side; no mansion could be built there. But on the next plot after that, going eastward, someone, a parvenu perhaps, had put up a French imitation, a narrow, sour-faced limestone château with a green dunce-cap roof, gone early to institutional use and for as long as anyone now knew inhabited by secretaries who were slipped through its door in the first fall mornings and not seen again until the six o'clocks of spring.

Between this and the Ralston houses, in the despised plot, which had lain empty for some years, "the Mannix house" had been erected. An ordinary brownstone except for its larger frontage, solidly conventional from service entrance to fanlight to fourth-floor salon, it was hard to imagine now as the young couple's enterprise it had been. Once built, it had inspired — both on the other side of "the French house" and opposite it — whole terraces of smaller ones of its kind, now no longer singly inhabited, their continuous stoops twice interrupted by one of the low, six-story apartment houses of the twenties, after which the street dwindled, much as it had in the beginning, to the tailor-shop and picture-framer crannies of a discreet or shabby small commerce.

All this lore, mixed with family ecology, European tours and Sunday afternoon anecdote as suited to the age and relationship of the hearer, was known in various degrees to all the inhabitants of the Mannix house. Most thoroughly perhaps not to its supposed inheritor, its mistress — but to her husband, its master. Already resident in the house for some twelve years, when he returned to it tonight — though as yet unaware — he would make his first real contribution to its history.

"Yes," said the Judge. "That's our house."

Across the banquet table of the best of those midtown men's clubs whose auxiliary dining-rooms had become so familiar during his scant year of political dinners as a trial judge, he answered the lady's question. With the sharpness his nearsightedness had at this range, he noted her emerald eardrops, almost as large as seckel pears, and the ermine coat she'd carried all the way to the table. Also checked was the French face of his schoolboy's watch — worn on the right wrist, under a cuff custom-shortened for that purpose. Although coffee cups had already been gently tapped with knives for the last time, cigars were well on, and some chairs had even been emptied with the usual excuses, he wouldn't be able to leave until things broke up — since this particular testimonial dinner was for him. Soon, as a member of the appellate court, he would be able to ignore these dinners. Putting on his distance glasses, he was reminded again how often the apparel worn to these occasions was more oddly agreeable than its wearers — as if some very superior cloth, jewels and furs whom one wouldn't at all mind meeting had been brought to dine by various rednecks and vaseline blonds whose acquaintance one could well spare. As on so many recent evenings for months prior to his appointment, he deeply wished to go home, out of a more urgent worry than had ever attacked him down all the years before. He was also aware that two men, on the other side of the table and a few chairs down the line, were commenting on his answer to the lady.

"*Our? Our* house?" one had almost certainly said — and he knew what they were saying, whatever the exact words were: that he was here without a wife; he was here alone. And that he had *his* particular wife. Meanwhile, the lady opposite, returning the flat, dark gaze, almost a miniature one, of the guest of honor — "Like a Japanese," she said later, "or like, if you could imagine it, a Japanese Jew" — gathered from the Judge's glance only one of these things. She touched an earring. "You like?" she said, smiling. "But oh — that house! I've been passing it for years. Those marvelous old écru lace curtains on the parlor floor, where did your wife ever —!" She shook her head at him. "Why . . . until the brownout — why, I bet I knew as much about that lovely room as anybody in it. As *you*."

At the age of twelve, the Judge had been a black-haired monkey who was mirror-writing champion (ambidextrous and simultaneous) of his modest West Side private school, a fiend at "points" (a ball game of the era, played mostly against the cornices of residences which were not singly occupied), a collector of Daumier prints (as inspired by his own father but not too much relished by the latter), a fast beginner at chess (which he had since made himself forget), and — thanks to a math teacher's explanation of compound interest — an incipient money-lender. An innocent one too. He was probably the only boy who had ever sincerely tried to teach himself math by the use of money. As a reward for coming out with the right answer (better than even), he was also probably the only boy on the proper Jewish West Side who had been flogged, at least for that reason, his father considering himself a Sephardi sensitive to any ingrowth of what he chose to think of as "Polish" practices.

The son was after that sent to a Massachusetts private school, where he learned how not to be a champion — though he remained a prodigy. For having been cured afterward even of this latter, he was grateful (with a few minor reservations, like hate) to the French school which he'd attended between the ages of sixteen and eighteen, during a family stay in Paris because of his father's practice, which was occasionally that of private international law. Thanks to the school's habit of ostracizing foreigners, particularly Americans, he never did learn much spoken French. At nineteen, therefore, he was normal, even scruffily dressed (a not quite five-foot dandy would have been too much), and ready to enter, first Harvard, which he left after two years, and then — via his father, who was a trustee — Columbia, which he left after another. There had never been any real trouble, merely mutual bewilderment, at times. Perhaps *his* only trouble, it had sometimes been said, was that he was small. "And lively," said his first school. "And inscrutable, of course," said the French one, in some surprise at having been asked. The Massachusetts one said nothing, merely referring his father back to him. His own answer was on record in the family humor-book, and until well past his majority often in use. "I don't *want* to be coxswain," he had said. Subsequently he had studied for the bar on his own, and allowing his precocity only that far, had passed, after which he had at once settled down to hard work — for he had an ambition which he concealed as jealously as if it were a soul — and to the business of forgetting how to play chess.

But the possession of all these talents still didn't explain how he could tell almost literally what those two men down the table were continuing to say about him — though the explanation was a simple one. While he gave the lady the ritual answers and cues in this house-dialogue which he had played so often, he watched that other pair — the elder a long-retired Justice of the Supreme Court of New York, the other a trial lawyer — both of whom the Judge, still Daumier in his preferences, thought of as "advocates."

The younger and heavier of the two, who had heard the Judge's reply while walking past him to greet the other, was smiling. "If that isn't like Simon," he said. " 'Our' house. Never *my*. Though surely it couldn't be *more* his —" He sat down.

"And you couldn't be more wrong, Borkan," said the elder, a non-agenarian who'd known both the Judge's father, and the Judge — who was now fifty-two — as a child. "Not that it isn't typical of Simon. It is. To say it that way." His wrinkled, silvery face looked as if it were retreating from life back to substance, but at its own pleasant-man-nered rhythm, the eyes hooded, the mouth still flexible and strong.

"Oh Chauncey, so it was the old Mendes house once of course, but —" The younger man shrugged, his heavy, sleek head to one side. Like many of the larger men here, Borkan had a look of the bruiser well barbered; actually he was a Grand Street boy who had come up the hard way, but from a strict, immigrant home. A "theatrical" lawyer, with a professional reputation as fleshy and night-owl as some of his demimonde clients, he knew all the ropes, and must have swung on a good many of them, but at home kept a good wife (upper Park Ave-nue, acquired the easy way) who had given him a late-begotten son — and many dull dinner parties for judges.

"Mirriam's father left the house specifically to him," said the elder. "Not that she would care — no, the house is his in every way, one can be sure of that. No, this is another attitude, and one of the things I admire him for. When you people say 'our house,' Nathan, you mean more than a family or even a clan, something biblical still. A moral entity is what Simon or any of you means. In a howling world."

"And what about *you* people?"

"Holding on by a feather," said the old one, grinning. "A few deposit boxes, and St. Thomas's Church."

The other laughed with the professional ease of a diner-out, but looked uncomfortable. "Don't romanticize us, Chauncey," he said. The consonants would have a slight heaviness, if one weighed them. "I pick up the papers these days, I don't know where I am. Don't even single us out." He spread his hands to signify he gave up the subject, folded them between his knees and pursed his lips, thick ones but mobile, a speaker's mouth, like so many others here. "Specifically to him? Not to his own daughter? Well, what do you know." Then he turned his back and the rest of the conversation was hidden.

The Judge leaned forward to light the lady's cigarette. "I grew up in a different house, one my father built, on Riverside Drive. My father-in-*law* built the present house, as a young man. Had to fight his whole family to do it."

He gave her the very deferential but firm nod which ended cross-table conversations and turned to his lefthand neighbor, who he already knew was hotly engaged with a man on his other side. This released the Judge to himself, since the chair on his right had for the moment been deserted, and also kept him turned away from the two whose colloquy he had been following. Then, to make sure he had removed himself from a talent which sometimes came over him inadvertently, he took off his glasses. He would have known what his friends had been saying underneath, anyway. They'd been saying — or thinking — that he was here alone, and that he had his particular wife. But the explanation of how he'd heard their words at some distance was simpler. He had once, long ago, acquired this trick for a good reason — to help him understand a child. His own hearing was ordinary, but he could lipread. He had a deaf son.

Left to himself, as guests of honor sometimes were after these functions got rolling and the real drawing card — influence — magnificently emerged, he preferred to look at the room in the large, as he was fairly well able, his glasses being mostly for driving and the theatre. To go on using that other trick would be to feel as a paranoid must — for there was always a certain amount of filling in to be done. No sane man would choose to live in such an eavesdropper's world. He had to live his mental life untinged, except for the timeworn exchanges men made face to face or in the saving reflections of print. No confident man would choose to live among the abysmal whispers from that underworld of what people inevitably said about each other. To him, face-to-face talk wasn't the morass it was to some; it was a natural, Talmudic game — though the Talmud itself was all but unknown to him. To him, the reflections of men as embodied in print were also no burden, but the natural lipreading of men and nations. Otherwise, he meant to keep his mental life unhampered except by the *considered* judgment — odd as that might seem for a man with a wife, and children too. He had to be able to feel this way, for the sake of that private ambition which he well knew to be a paraphrase of a much meeker biblical one, not from his part of the Testament. *Judge not, that ye be not judged* — that was the Christian twist of it. The Semitic interpretation was simpler: *Judge, that ye may be.* He wanted to judge — yes, in the courts, and yes, in the highest one. And he wanted to do it so that in those far, ancestral courts or heavens which even Jews like him — third or fourth generation assimilated reform Jews — still listened to, he might be judged.

Otherwise, Simon Mannix didn't count himself too self-conscious a man, and took a strong delight in such scenes as the one before him. Where else could one sit as onlooker, club member and actor too, before such relatively bloodless seats of power, and yet, unlike in the synagogue, the study or even the university, find oneself so much and heterogeneously in the world? Those presidents whom universities had directly or indirectly given the nation had either been nonentities or warped into excessive action by their own sudden immersion in the world of it. Business had plenty of color, dirt under its fingernails and — scratched from armaments contracts here and there — a little blood, in spite of which not even the rabbis mixed among his own merchant ancestors had denied that it was a necessary pursuit and could be an honorable one. But no one nowadays, even in America, or in the paid-for biographies anywhere, could give it any philosophy of the ultimate. Whereas in these city haunts of the law — from the district clubs of the police judges to these secondhand Vaticans of red velvet and marble where higher jurisprudence gave its dinners — one saw every jowl and paunch, nape and nose of male humanity, and of power too. Here was his boyhood collection all over again, not Daumier but Veronese, and with all the thronging, kneeling, bowing men in black tailored suits. One virtue of democracy was that potentate and retinue alike wore dinner jackets, which brought out the man inside. "In a monarchy," his father used to say, "coats-of-arms make themselves known when you go in to dinner; here, it takes a little longer — until dessert."

He gripped the leonine arms of his chair, whose high seat didn't allow his patent-leather toes to meet the floor. He was used to such suspension, often privately amused at its effect on others. The lady opposite, just ready to talk to him again, thought that he looked like a doll sitting there with that black pate, pale face, and the tiny hands so tight on the carved heads — or like a potentate.

His eyes crossed hers, unseeing. He was vain enough to hope that some day, hopefully under his tenure, the *New York Reports* would have a certain mastery — if not become a part of his country's judicial heritage. What had seduced him to the bar went even farther back than to Paris — when, at his father's elbow, he'd been permitted to share the latter's deference to a man who had served their nation in the Bering Sea controversy. Even in those earliest evenings on Riverside Drive when, still in knickerbockers, he'd been shunted away from young men arriving for their colloquies there, he'd already begun to sniff out what he now knew for sure. The public thought that the law was logic. Blackstone had said that the common law was the perfection of sound reason. Many of the men here, when they didn't think of it as influence and chicanery, might think it was wit and knowledge. But he — and most of those who had risen where he hoped to — knew better. The law was experience.

Opposite, the lady gathered her wrap and leaned forward, smiling. "Good night!" She paused. Since he had mentioned children but no wife, he might like herself be widowed. "And I'll look for you!" she cried gaily. "Behind those curtains."

The Judge, standing up, rescued the thumb of one opera glove which extended dangerously over her coffee cup, and gave it back to her. Women sometimes deplored his fussiness — which came from the same narrower range of vision which children had — or were excited by it. His wife had once been. Tonight he didn't notice. He bowed. "Good night."

Going down the long room took him some twenty-five minutes, stopped as he was at every hand. At this hour the ones who knew him best had gone — various associate judges of the courts of appeal who had perhaps helped make him one of them, still others from the Federal courts, from Albany, whom he knew from his own practice more than from the courts, which had never really been his sphere, and from dinners more exclusive than this one. These who delayed him now were men who came under that peculiar term "well-wisher," politicals who clustered at every appointment or election and greeted with a squinted eye and a limp, neutral hand. The party of reform had them as well as any other. How like they were, whether Irish or Jewish — in the old entente of state politics once called "the Sacred Heart of Israel" — or some of the new Italians who since the depression had been coming up very fast, filling the lieutenant-governorships, the state assemblies and the lower courts with graduates of the Catholic law universities. The German influence had begun to wane even before the war's outcry against the Bund in New Jersey and an ugly putsch or two in the hofbraus of the city, but here and there they still showed. The Judge, tapped for the bench almost straight from his own office into the relatively removed courts of appeal, still savored the unholy-holy mixture of sincere ward heelers, crafty law deans and faithful constituents which made up an everyman's land between politics and law.

"Thank you," he said, moving along hand over hand, "thank you very much." No doubt some of the same influences would align themselves at the resurrection or the advent of the Messiah, whichever sphere then found itself in charge. No one denied that these pressures still obtained, even in the highest court of the land. True, Cardozo had been appointed to that court when there was already another Jew there. Sainthood, great mental elegance and a wisdom almost exquisite had done it for that candidate. Mannix's own practice, of a barrister kind rare in America, had been in early emulation of this man, though he hadn't flattered himself with any personal resemblance to him. For one thing, the other hadn't married. "Oh yes indeed!" he said, to a surprised old jurist within whose hand his own had suddenly tightened. "And a very good night!"

Besides, his own admiration had long since passed on. For a while, like almost everyone else of his professional acquaintance on either side of the Atlantic, he'd wanted nothing better than "to be eighty again," with Oliver Holmes. Still thirty years away from that, he now considered himself fit as any man to be his own mentor.

"Well, *Simon*."

"Well, McAfee!" He smiled up at the flat-tongued Boston Federal judge who not two months ago, talking of the war in Europe, had asked him what none of Mannix's own kind had ever bothered or dared to: "Simon, why aren't you a Zionist?" They smiled at each other now, both remembering his answer. He'd considered quite coolly before he made it. McAfee's forebears had probably come to Massachusetts during the Irish potato famines of the 1840's — which about coincided with the half of his own which had fled the European revolutions of 1848.

"Why is it, Francis," he had said, "that you aren't Sinn Fein?"

But later comers of his own kind would never honor any such answer. Now that Jews were dead or dying in thousands which left the head numb, he was no longer as sure as once that he could. Before the war, though one couldn't hope to explain even to a man like McAfee all the hierarchies, envies and fears which beset the Jews themselves, among themselves they could be funny enough about it. He could have recounted to almost any of them how when he had brought home his schoolboy crony Abe Cohn, his mother had whispered, *"Russian?"* — even as, thirty years later, he had revealed it to Professor Abraham Cohn. Capping it with the story of how his mother, with her eighteen carat German-descended conviction of superiority, had had at last to sit in one of the vestry rooms on a Sunday afternoon in the Spanish-Portuguese synagogue, to hear one of her own daughter-in-law's relatives warn his congregation against their snobbish condescension to the Ashkenazim — the German Jews.

But now, all his legal rescue work for these many scholarly or humble refugee Jews for whom he had often made himself responsible in purse as well, couldn't convince certain of his "co-religionists" that — unless he was also for Zion, a Zion he was sure would end in the political — he was not a renegade. What strange tightropes a Jew like himself — a lace-curtain Jew and a lapsed one — had to walk! Now that a suffering not yet his had made his honesty suspect, and the whole history of his family's "assimilation" (which latecomers had perhaps coveted) traitorous! No wonder he yearned to escape into that larger court of justice for humanity at large, which they would see only as an escape. To them, if he was to be a lion, then he must be a lion of Judah still.

Strange path to walk for a man brought up to be as stiffishly proud of his race as he! To have to wonder now whether it was only pride — and to be damnably sure meanwhile that probably fifty percent of the "Americans" who might be fighting over there for his kind would still have reservations about them, over here. But perhaps this too was the strange, yeasty working of what one day might be humanity in the large. His own wife, one of whose family was in history books on the American Revolution, and another in Queen Victoria's government (and whose first husband and what other prior lovers he preferred not to know, had been Christians) had once whispered to him in one of "their" drawing-rooms, "Do you really ever feel comfortable with them? Not me. *Not me.*"

"Why — hello, August, Mr. Manken," he said to a man looming beyond the several around McAfee.

"*Gut* evening, Simon. You see, I come to your dinner."

Here was one feeling he could be sure of — his anti-Germanism —

even if he secretly knew its roots to be deep in familial dislike of those maternal cousins and uncles of his youth who had been as assimilatedly Teutonic as if ghettos had never been heard of, down to the dumpling creases in the neck, the Bavarian blue-green of the eye. A subtler tragedy of the later wave of well-to-do cousins who were coming over now — he himself had sponsored over twenty-five of them — was that they had *not* been alien to the German spirit but embedded in it, and hadn't ever conceived of themselves otherwise. August Manken here, this huge walrus of a man with his Hindenburg whiskers, was no relative. As the Judge's maternal grandfather's next-door neighbor, Catholic of course, in the brownstone to brownstone "German" enclave of Yorkville, he had been the grandfather's lifelong friend, in a way; certainly their wives and daughters had been almost as deep in the kaffeeklatsches as if all went to the same church — almost, if not quite. As a boy, Simon had been much in this maternal grandfather's home, whose circle had even then been referred to as "the Germans," his mother taking on the habit of his father's pro-English side. He and his father had seen eye to eye on them. "Even when a German takes a *friendly* pinch of you, Simon, he has no real feeling under the thumb." It was this lack, a kind of gross stupidity of the emotions, which would have kept old Manken ignorant of how the German-American stance on the war had ruined Yorkville as a political force forever, or of why its street of bierstubes was now all but deserted. And it was their Christmas-annual sentimentality — a sweet always saved in the end for themselves — which would have brought Manken here.

"Zo, little Simon. I come to see your triumph."

The Judge could have chortled aloud at this prime corroboration of his thoughts. He caught Borkan, the Grand Street boy, staring curiously at this encounter — let him. "Thank you, Mr. Manken, August. And how is Mutti?"

And Gusti junior, in his white linen Sunday knicks and sailor-ribboned hatful of nasty jokes to play on the girls — how is he? And Putzi, the *elder* junior and aptly so, in tennis blazer, cream-vanilla pompadour above its blue, in one hand his racquet, the other at the keyboard of a piano bevied with girls whose hourglass waists had seemingly sent the laced-away inches to their full cheeks — how were all they? Maitzie Manken, hot in a hall closet — *Simon, do this!* — had technically been his first woman, girl. How indelibly those afternoons on that Seventy-ninth Street block of about 1905 came back to him, the

tall kitchens looking out on the laundried gardens, the younger children, clip-necked, smelling of cough syrup and powdered down to the
navel, set out on the front stoops but forbidden to kneel, the brown
living-rooms, their mantels marching with steins, *verboten* the rugs
thick as cranberry sauce, coffee pouring like sap from every corner
where an aunt knitted, the beds' blue clouds of comfort forbidden in
the daytime too, the cakes and the sips of kümmel, and the ripe indi-
gestions of dusk. It all came back to him from the awful concaves of
those Sunday afternoons.

"Oh, the Mutti has her bad legs — and how are the girls?"

The "girls" were the Judge's maiden elder sisters, who lived now in a
large apartment house built on that very site; August himself must live
somewhere near it.

"Very well, thank you. Just the same." And indeed they were — like
the Mutti's legs, which even back then had been varicosed with comfort and her own mutton fat. Friendship between the two families,
mostly on the distaff side, had really been a matter of housekeeping
sympathies. The Judge's grandfather, as thick in his own way as his
neighbor, had never seemed to see that beyond an occasional glass of
Manken schnapps, the society of the editor of the *Staats-Zeitung*, the
German consul-general, plus the Rupperts and Piels, the Heides and
the Muschenheims, those brewers, candy millionaires and hotel operators, was — very politely — not for him. But young Simon had only
had to be with the women and children, and the maids too, to hear
another undercurrent already, perhaps in the same way that only
yesterday his own twelve-year-old daughter had claimed to see a Hitler-
face in the small, pugnacious scowl of a rose.

His grandfather had stood by the Mankens during the 1914 wartime,
when whole blocks of "Kraut" windows had been smashed, the Mannixes' own along with theirs, and everything German from Wagner to
knitting from the left had been removed from the repertory of living.
Whether or not August remembered this, tonight he had come to stand
at attention, even to bow as he had been taught — at a "triumph."

"And how are things in Yorkville, August?"

"Not so good. Business going down, riffraff coming in the Turn-
verein, the district club too. Why you don't come down to the neighborhood, one day? We could use a smart man like your father was, like
you. You were a smart boy, Simon. You had better luck than our
Putzi."

To compare the Judge's "luck" with Putzi the forger's could still be a father's pathetic arrogance. To claim a share of that luck was no old man's naïveté, but the bluntest statement of what was felt to be sentimentally owed. Taken together, these could well be the beginnings of just that German national character which now and then had to help the world militarily to an understanding of it. But Manken's other sad, city-park phrase — the neighborhood — could still strike a chord. "The girls, my sisters, live in that house now, August, did you know? The one which was put up on the old block."

The big head inclined deeply, its gray hair brush-cut in a mode which had long preceded the GI's. Manken's wing collar and black silk tie with gold-headed stickpin, a mask of comedy with a diamond in its stretched jaws, brought back other segments of that majestic household — fanged bearskin rugs, beetling cupboards and the snarling Orientalia which was thought to be imperial. "Mutti likes the elevators too. We share rooms not far from there, with Gusti. He has a fine wife." He sighed, for whatever contradiction? "You do not bring yours?"

The Judge, eye level with the stickpin, raised his glance sharply. Nothing had been intended; it was just a question of thumbs.

"Regards home, Mr. Manken," he said gently, and was about to thank him and move on when a disturbance at the gold-and-red-portiered end of the ballroom drew his attention. Down at that end, heads were turning from some rumor. A hollow-eyed servingman in green livery was coming toward him, carrying no salver but the very emissary of disaster; before the man came near the Judge had raked through most possibles in their likely order — first Mirriam, in a smashed mirror of alternatives, then David, hurt from behind by a car, then little Ruth, so poised but so vulnerable to people — but just then Borkan spoke from behind him: "It's Chauncey. He's had bad news, will you come?"

Beyond the curtains, across the club's central hallway, the door of a library closed except to members was now open, revealing floor lamps equidistant along the moroccoed silence, each glowing down on its table and leather chair, forming an island for the financier's solitude, the divorcé's meditation, the octogenarian's brandied sleep. The Judge had never seen it before, not being a member of this club or likely to be, though he knew its more public rooms well — since the depression, clubs like these had opened them to certain functions where some members were also involved.

He ran forward now with the short steps which from the rear made him seem like a boy in a dinner jacket, or like a quick-flying little prelate, if he had had a cape. A small group of men halfway down the room parted to let him through. Chauncey Olney was sitting in one of the chairs. He must once have been very tall, this man who would never see ninety again, his head still high and Venetian against the wing-back, his knees angled sharply, cloth-gaitered feet easily touching the floor. A silvery quiet surrounded him, an invisible weapon from which the other men had fallen back. The Judge had seen old people in his own family use their age like this. They lacked embarrassment. This was all they had. A house doctor, who had just come forward with his black bag, was motioned away.

"A body this age doesn't shock, Doctor, don't you know that? It just sits down." Olney saw the Judge and gave him a rueful grimace, as if asking to be rescued from his own incontinence. "Simon." He reached for a daily paper folded back on a pile of others and handed it over — a London *Times*. The Judge glanced automatically at the date: December 10, 1942 — two months old.

"Read it aloud," said Olney. "He might at least have that."

The paper was creased to the obits page. The Judge read where Olney pointed, an ordinary family notice, not the casualty list.

Died in action, last October 23rd at Alamein, Geoffrey Edward Audley-Taylor, only son of Lucretia Olney and Charles Audley-Taylor. Services private.

"They thought I mustn't know," said Olney. "My granddaughter Luce and her husband. Old people must be spared — that's natural, isn't it?" He stared at the circle of men. "They were hoping to smuggle it under. What's unnatural about it? Even in war, the middle-aged have time for conspiracy. A natural disrespect for youth *and* age." He seemed perfectly all right except for his little spate of talk. "I was too young to go, in '61," he said, conversationally. "Not yet twelve. But my mother, who was already a widow, bought my elder brother Julian a substitute; that was what was sometimes done. There's that to be said for those of us who stayed at home in those days; we didn't just pay for a walkie-talkie collection of wires and TNT, we bought us a full-grown, full-blooded man we could see. Oftentimes, it was somebody we knew." His accent had Southerned; up to now, the Judge hadn't recalled he was from there. "Wasn't anything on the battlefield he couldn't see by the dawn's early light either, that substitute," said

Olney. "Or so they tell me. I was the wrong age for all the wars, all down the line. Like my father before me."

There was a whispering among the men around the doctor. "He'll wear himself out. Can't somebody get him home?"

"There's families that breed like that," said Olney's old voice, pursuing its thread. Whether he had heard them wasn't clear, or was merely answering from the generalized determination of old men — to break in on events with what they thought *they* had. "Families that go on breeding behind the lines, or in the intervals. Or have men that for some reason or other get saved out. Or have daughters. Parlor breeds, you might say — but there's no shame to it, when it's accident. Somebody has to sit and talk. And breed."

The Judge understood at once what he was getting at, if not why. His own father had been the wrong age for all the wars of his time and had often talked about it; he himself had been the right age in 1917, but the wrong size. His own son, too young now, in any event would be saved. And he had a daughter. He wouldn't mind hearing what further the old man had to say — but pushed by the glances of the men around, he placed a hand on Olney's shoulder.

"Mostly people say 'at the front,' don't they still, Simon?" Olney looked up briefly, and — Simon would have sworn it — shrewdly, then began counting on his fingers. " 'With the Blue' or 'with the Gray' I b'lieve we said, or else the names of places, like you do in any war. Then, in the Spanish one, maybe we'd say of a man that he was with the Rough Riders, or yes, 'with the Fleet.' Wasn't that it? And then —" He began chanting, nodding with it too. "Over there, *o*-ver *there* —"

"Chauncey," said Borkan, coming up on his other side, "don't you think you better —"

"But what's it they say *now*, Simon?" said Chauncey, ignoring the other. "It escapes my mind." He rat-tatted impatiently on the death notice. "What's it they say now?"

The Judge thought a moment. " 'Overseas,' do you mean? But they'll still say 'at Alamein' about your grandson, or 'in North Africa,' Chauncey. Things don't change that much." It was always best to bring the old back to the concrete. In spite of all, they appreciated it.

" 'Overseas.' That's it. Thank you." He patted the newspaper gently. "Not my grandson. My *great*-grandson. But thank you for understanding what I was after." Even seated, the old man was almost eye to eye with him. "In my time, we always sat up with a man, as we called it.

Something like a wake — but at any time the news came to us. Two months or two years later, we always sat up with a man's spirit. Or tried to. And I thought — what better place than with all these men here?"

The doctor came forward with a glass someone had passed, and held it out. "Have some brandy."

Olney took it with a nod. "A toast to him? Or for me?" Glass in hand, he looked from face to face slowly. He was grinning, eyes, brows and that flexible mouth, as when first he had spoken to Borkan. He'd probably never looked less confused in his life. He seemed now to note the turkey wattles of one man, the lemon-shine of another's nude head, the red and mauve cheeks of sport, or of alcohol. "Just for me, I think. No toast. There's nobody young enough here in this room, have you noticed that?" He tossed off the brandy, and set the glass down so hard that the paper fell to the rug. "Nobody! There's nobody here young enough to mourn a young man — as he should be mourned." He stood up.

Borkan was just in front of him, not disheveled with the evening, consciously the darer, the carefully irreverent, as his section of the profession affected to be. "Some of us were counted on in the last war, Justice Olney. I don't know what you're driving at. And some of us will send our sons to this one." How rhythmically the men talked here, when they chose!

Olney looked delighted. He had broken in. "Just so, Nathan. I'm sure you will. I wasn't trying to asperse. And the middle-aged will always do their duty, Simon said it — things don't change that much. But that's what I — Guess I was trying to say that too. Something about the way it always is." He looked very old now. "You see, I wasn't ashamed of not going, when I couldn't. Young men don't really want to go, no matter what *you* say. Not in their heart of hearts. And I've enjoyed my life, all the ages I ever was." He paused, bewildered. "The middle-aged are nowhere though, are they, if they're not in power? And now I'm — this age." These words were a thread. His voice strengthened. "But I still wonder and think about it, how it is to be that particular breed. How it is, that . . . all that to-kingdom-come and awfulness is always — *over there* — to some people. Why, I could talk to my granddaughter in London during an air raid not long ago. And *we* were in the parlor. Here." His voice softened again, and he looked truly faraway and bewildered now: he was back not to youth but to childhood. "My brother Julian. That's it, that's it. Go back to that. He'd come in my room sometimes those leafy Virginia nights it was so aching hard to sleep, for all the things that must be happening some- where, and I'd clutch my knees up in bed and listen hard for he was my elder brother that was speaking. He was eighteen. Always had the map and pins with him, that he'd carried along to the back farm in the Piedmont where my mother'd brought the eight of us. We knew where the regiment was of course, and in which campaigns that particular division had figured. Even had an old head-by-head list. Hopeless acourse; we'd no news but what came from the old men at the court- house, that they had from an occasional runner. But every night we put the pins in and made out our pitiful little gazette, that hadn't any more . . . any more connection with the central howl of it — than *that*." He looked down at the newspaper on the rug. "But by the light of the moon that must be shining on him and his bivouac somewhere, we put the pins in and followed him. The substitute."

In the respectful silence, the men around him glanced uneasily at each other. In their lowered eyes, the Judge saw they'd already written Olney off, not just for his age or for that fishing in the past which was to be expected of it — but because he was now too good to be true. There was light for all men in the truly finished life; the saint burning round his own agony was daily knelt to by some here. For others, like Borkan, the criminal great coiled round their instructive crimes. But a life which was formed, finished, and still vocal — and only on the ordinary level — was not bearable. Olney drew a perspective tolerable only in the dead.

But when he shivered and seemed to falter, they moved, sympathetic to a man. Again he anticipated them. "Simon'll see me out, won't you, Simon. My man's outside with the car." He nodded gently to all round, as once he might have done to the court, and left, head bowed, thumbs linked behind him. The Judge followed, making his excuses silently here and there with a nod, a shrug, a salute. As the two left the room, someone thrust the newspaper into the younger justice's hand.

Outside in the hall, the younger man watched while the porter helped the old man with his coat. Olney took out a pair of earmuffs and a muffler. In the doge's-palace illuminations of the club, the face between the brown muffs could have been taken for old Maine, Rome or Virginia; odd how the prototypes which men made of *virtu* sooner or later merged. Olney's grin broke up that mask of it. "Had TB as a — younger man. It's served me well."

The Judge smiled and they waited in an easy silence for the car to be brought round. From the many old people in his own family in his youth, he'd got used to the worst of them and formed a taste for the best. When the old weren't idle chatterers it could be infinitely comfortable to meditate at their side. He knew he ought to go home with Olney, for that wake. But he also knew he ought to go *home*.

No, what was the need or good? The habits and defenses which two people made of the years could become an emotion of itself, serviceable, and always added to, added to. When and where had it been that her personality and his could have stood aside to point fingers or wring them, to say, "*This* makes it. We are separate now" — in lieu of saying, "We were never joined"? Her friends traveled in crowds, the women by day for causes or for company; they were social — and who was it after all who had met her in these circles, he as worldly as any in his own way, or more? They, her friends, went "everywhere" together, and what of it if the everything was anywhere, by night? Which of those complaisant, not so young young men — the good dancers, the escorts, the *cavalieri servanti* — would have the singularity, the energy to stand out — and be a lover? — the crowd asked the world. On his own side of the matter, when was it that he'd begun to be unlikely to be home of an evening, because he was never very fervently expected to be? And in time — so is a nest feathered against the cold — had more and more planned it so? None of this had ever been said. How powerful that was! He looked up from that morass to the face hatted like a sentinel's beside him, the woolen mittens crossed, the cane for a sword. It was a mistake to think that the unneurotic, like Olney here, lacked sensibility.

"Judge . . ." said Mannix. He liked to hear the title on someone else, it was a natural uplift. "Judge . . . for the worldly these days . . . where does the demimonde begin?"

Olney stared. "Why — Simon." He half laughed. "Expect me to answer that question from — from the heart? Why, I believe you do. For people like us, you mean?"

"Like — " If he said *us*, it would mean Mirriam as well, which was what he had meant but shouldn't ask, having forgotten until now that lipread conversation, and what it had held back. Like her — where does it begin for *those*? "Like — me."

"You've answered it. Isn't it a question of — for whom? And how far in." The older judge looked vague. "And for women or for men? For a man, you mean."

"Yes," said Mannix, lying promptly but almost inaudibly. "Men . . . and judges," he said, as the old car drew up to the steps. He put a foot on the running board. "I'd like to go with you, please. To sit up . . . a little while."

As they took off at about fifteen miles an hour, Chauncey slid half the lap robe over the Judge's knees, then lifted his profile attentively straight on, in an old motoring stance Mannix hadn't seen for years; his father had had it too. The car itself, a black Packard high as a jitney, padded with amber leather as soft and creased as an old wallet, might have been one of the hansom cabs in the park now or in his youth, the visored chauffeur up ahead a coachman, the hood of the car the back of a horse hoof-slipping on the yellow-spattered cobblestones of the avenues the Judge had crossed on his way to grade school — Columbus, Amsterdam, obscure out of the city rhythms to him now — the West Side. "Lower" East Side, "upper" — all cities had these directional signals which rang like tocsins in the mind of the dweller, conjuring up whole sociologies that even the stupid knew. Tonight, for instance, at his own dinner, he hadn't had any sensation of triumph, but in any year after — or now — he would recall how a triumphal evening moved through the streets, swam like a fish past its clubhouse of friends, colleagues and onlookers — and rode home.

At his side, the old man's nodding silence soothed him. As the car crept north, the dark-and-light of Central Park on their left wheeled slowly by exactly as in his childhood. On their right, the reaches of "upper" Fifth Avenue advanced on them just as fixed and stationary as then. Of course this wasn't so; a host of associations did this for him, or perhaps only a lamp, a passerby and a balustrade. In the same way, even when he went casually to a store, the lower and mid-avenue had somewhere in his mind another and fixed topography, in his case seen on red-and-blue parade through the flag-draped, smoky regimental haze of the 1914 war (though the armies were elsewhere) — a bond drive perhaps, with steeples and façades pressing closer through a heraldry that stained the sunlight with hurrahs. In the museum there was a Childe Hassam like that which he always wished he owned.

Not that owning it or anything else in this city — even a house — would ever change the city dweller's conundrum: was there any meaning to these assaults of memory that he carried willy-nilly in his breast, and if so, to whom could he charge them? Even if this whole mass of sea-scurfed islands, bridge-interlocked, heavied with people, were to be enumerated street by street, family by family, person by person down to the last stoplight and beyond, ninety miles out to the last beacon-buoy off Montauk — who would audit the single story of each? Again, again, to whom could it be charged — did a man even live out a single life story, so far from his own graveyard? Was this why, when old August Manken said "neighborhood" to him, the something in him that begged an entity from these streets, an audience to his life, cried out in response, "Hold. Hold"? Was a city, especially this one, ever an entity? Was it ever really audience? And why should the riddle never depress him but always exhilarate his tissues, his sense of living? What was attached to the key ring, chill as a piece of outer cold in the hand, when one said to the cab driver outside the Empire State Building, as one left it, to the red western sun behind it, "I believe the Waldorf once stood here"?

He still had the London newspaper in his hand, as they drew up to a house not twenty blocks from his own, nor from Manken's, nor from any kind, if one pushed the radius only as far from this side of the park as the rat-nested piers of its own river, the East. As the chauffeur went to open the door for them, Mannix suddenly recognized the house, one very narrow for a vintage residence on this avenue, with bowed iron window grates and an iron-scrolled glass door. It was in fact like many on the West Side, like the one he'd grown up in; even on this gilded frontage it was a part of all that other printless undercurrent of city life. "So this is *your* house, Chauncey."

"You were here once. With your father. You wore a school cap, I believe. Yes. And Mrs. Olney, my wife, was outraged because we gave you a sip of beer."

He should remember it, but didn't. Later, he must scratch up some tribute memory to Mrs. Olney; they had been a famously devoted couple. He laid the newspaper softly on a small half-moon table, for calling cards once, and let his hat and coat be taken, glad to let that other nihilist city stand back and wait, until once again in an off moment its vision would grow again, a timbre of death-excitement in his bones.

Olney lived alone now except for his servant and a daily. The man brought a tray with whisky and brandy, then left them in the library that fronted the house; his steps could be heard going to the rear, comforting as those of servants always were, then perhaps making his way downstairs to a room off the kitchen — not at the top, above but near children, like the Mannixes' own faithful Anna. In this house the fourth floor was more likely to have been the ballroom.

At the window, nursing a whisky he had given himself while Chauncey went off to change, he stared out at a park not plangent-voiced as in summer but stern in the black cold which to his mind became it better. It was never so New York a park as in the five-o'clock winter's tale of the electric lights on the sky and the sky on the snow, mauve as the chapped lips of the children one had brought there and must now take home to soup and cuddling, home against that un-earthly light. Or as it was now — a great strip of the city-fear, but warmed by a window, made Roman.

He drew a great breath; his chest expansion, like his sex, was large for the rest of him. Tonight, everything he saw was variegated, ex-panded, refined. Ambition made it so, rising past what would have satisfied another man, had satisfied Chauncey — a man whose admira-tion he returned severalfold. Behind him, the house was so shabby-nice — how good of it to be so frugal of the worst of wealth, so lavish with the best, so excellent and just a house, and here, on this avenue, halfway between the mansions of Carnegie and Frick, such a small one — and how good that he was here this night to talk with a man like Chauncey, even of what they had come to talk. What secret, beautiful houses and stories lay in this city! He drained his drink, its other ingredient rising from ankles to crown — ambition, ready for him as whisky in a glass.

"Well now, Simon," said Chauncey behind him, "don't you want to phone home?"

Without the earmuffs, the old man's temples were cockleshell frail; he wore a smoking jacket of a cut the Judge had last seen in his schoolboy's Paris of his father's day. Suddenly, without effort, he re-called his long ago afternoon here. It was to his father, and to Mrs. Olney, whom he now remembered wore pince-nez perched on a face too pretty for it, to this whole expectant house that he supposed he must answer, like a boy remembering his manners, or told to. There was no need to report in to a waiting wife. All his family knew that the Judge never spoke idly on the phone.

"Through that door and off the landing. You'll find one in the study." The old man had already turned away, rummaging in the bench in front of the concert grand at the far end of the room, its surface not littered with photographs like the rest of this grave, nineteenth-century chamber, but opened at keyboard and lid — did the old man play, at his age? Mrs. Olney had sung; Mannix recalled this to the pattern of some boyhood knickers he had loathed and must have stared at throughout. She hadn't sung badly, but the song had been that awful Victorian drawing-room effort — what was its name? — which went on forever with its one note. There'd been someone else beside her — only a draped portrait-shadow against Mrs. Olney's clear form with its neck jabot and glassy twinkle — who had also sung. He hesitated, about to volunteer all this, but the old man clearly expected him to go — if gossip about the Judge's wife was known to him, then perhaps all the more.

"Thank you," said the Judge, with nineteenth-century obedience, and went to do as he was told. He hadn't been born until 1890, the century's end, but its trust in manners at all costs, or at least at some, had persisted in him. To the latent ridicule — never expressed in words of course, only in actions — of his wife, born in 1896.

In the study, he rested chin on hand. Where would she be now — at that Club Savoy in that Harlem ballroom where her crowd had once taken him, the crowd itself as strange as anything there, with its pale, chicly drooping men out of Covarrubias and its parrakeet women, one of them in a black satin Pierrot cap and egret feathering the air? Or would she be at the Roseland ballroom, which, as a nimble dancer himself — although, as with clothes, he would not extend himself to the dandified in the cheek-to-cheek tangos — he could have understood as a kind of good dancer's slumming? But the Savoy, and the taxi-dance places, that was years back, fifteen years ago and more — before his marriage — and the crowd was no longer dancing but sitting, not from age but preference — meeting in what they now called bistros, or "Dixielands" or "Birdlands," listening to what he was sure was the same rhomboidal music — to which it was now gauche to dance. Or was that too now passé? The crowd, now that he thought of it, wasn't much of a crowd any longer, or else unknown to him except for a few tea-drink-ing strays met after one of his office days when court wasn't in session, or one or two of Mirriam's late-night escorts. That too, for almost a year, had been passé. Only one of those escorts was still known to him. One.

As he made the call, the thought of Anna, who would answer, came stable and comforting through the night air; good servants did this for their masters. Usually he took her for granted, faithful to them as she had been for so long, past even her own dim marriage, which Mirriam knew more about than he. Tonight he saw her plump, hair-netted image leave the two-room, top-floor suite given her on her return just as if she were a governess and not just a cook, and go straight to the phone on the landing. The phone had already rung several times, but he was unworried; she would come slowly, careful to tie the padded dressing gown he'd sometimes seen her tend a sick child in, though the house was all hers tonight. She knew all their prescriptions and needs, and no doubt tallied their satisfactions also; she would know more of Mirriam than he, though not through confidence; she was their Greek chorus, Czech version, who never spoke — beyond that calm "My hosh!" the children teased her for, and had adopted. David wouldn't hear anything, unless the electric mechanism, which had been rigged to a bedside light and a percussion block, was set going. Ruth, aged twelve, wasn't yet expected to hear. In the daytime, Mirriam, if home, might or mightn't answer; daytime calls she was languid about, as with most things — she herself said it — in the daytime. At night, when such a call might be from her rackety friends, she might answer from anywhere in the house, even, if she were passing, from his study, taking the phone with an indolence not quite insult either to him or the caller. Insult was never intended — she wouldn't bother.

"Hallo, hallo," said Anna. "Oh, Mr. Mannix, yayss." No wonder they'd all adopted her soothing patois, which saw so much in life answer-able with its "yayss." "Oh, you don't need to worrit," she said, before he could go on. "She be all right. I give her some hot milk."

"Oh . . . ?" He smiled into the phone his recognition once again of how anything this child did worked out well — even her stomachaches. He did not dote. But she was the perfect one, or rather, in a family of two children, not the imperfect one. Even nature seemed to realize it, in the flow of her luck. Anna took Ruth to be his natural excuse for calling; he recalled now that the child had been slightly indisposed. As simply, his call was no longer subterfuge. He nodded back at her. "Hot milk."

"I get it out of her, what dey have downtown, dose girls!" said Anna. "Bahninna split, she had. And before dinner, mustard sandwiches! No wonder she can't keep nothing down."

"I'm sure you did, Anna." Her literalisms were in their humor-book; tomorrow he would whisper to his daughter, I hear she got it *out* of you — meanwhile savoring too the child to whom one could whisper. "Well, I'm at Mr. Olney's, Anna, and I'm going to stay a little while. If Mrs. Mannix is in, tell her he's had a little upset." Surely this was reportable. And might get the proper reply.

"Aw," said Anna. "Aw." Once in a while Olney was their dinner guest — his and Anna's, now that Mirriam was almost never his hostess. The "Aw" was for Olney's impressive age — if Anna didn't volunteer soup for a man's ills, then he was done for. But suddenly, she was strictly the servant. "T'ink I hear somebody come in a while ago, Mr. Mannix. You want I go down and see? You want her call you back?"

"Oh no," he said. "No, that's not necessary." He understood her dilemma well enough. The downstairs rooms all had doors in the old-fashioned way; Mirriam, in the same way or from her English heritage on the Mendes side, kept them closed. "Close the door after you" — the children knew it as well as "Wash your hands." By the same protocol, well-bred persons opened doors without knocking; servants knocked but immediately entered — both on the proud assumption that no one in this household was ever to be caught naked, or in flagrante delicto of any other kind. Upstairs, on the bedroom floors, one knocked of course — but this was not the question here.

"Oh no," he said, almost as equably as until a few months ago he had learned to feel. "Don't bother Mrs. Mannix, if she has company." Until then, no matter how noisy or exotic, that had been all it was.

"Yah, I heard somebody," Anna said vaguely, as if people as casually swam like shellfish through their respectable, alarm-protected doors — which at times might be the way it seemed to her. "Yah, I tell in the morning, then." She expected him home, but unlikely to see his late-sleeping wife next morning. Or perhaps not at night either, through the connecting door which bound their bedrooms; no doubt she had calculated that too. All the threads of their life were in her capable hands — and quite safe there.

"Thank you, Anna, and good night."

"You tell Mr. Olney," said Anna. "Tomorrow I bring him soup."

He chuckled at Olney's rescue. "Good night, Anna," he said, warm in the glow of his household, tended, threatened less than some, and more regular than many — and about to hang up, heard with the slight freeze her phone-voice always gave him — his wife's voice.

"Soup?" said Mirriam. "What's this?" For the nth time he marveled at how, at forty-six, her voice, darkly suited to her as it was, had kept its debutante slouch.

He let Anna hang up, then explained briefly about Olney. And got one of Mirriam's intense answers; her late-night answers, he always thought of them.

"The war," she said. "The war." She laughed, not for his benefit, he was sure of it. "What some people get away with!" she said. He could tell she had turned away from the phone, to another person no doubt.

"You'll find the record player works again," he said. He had fixed it himself, though he had no bent for such things. Her company were always dancing — or had used to be.

"Oh, did you?" She neither expected him to nor would praise him for it. She was disorderly in the most practical way, he had once told her, at a time when this had seemed only charm to him; she was easily and fatally moved from person to person — yet always lightly, too; the years since their marriage must be littered with her discards of either sex, though none had risen to lovers, he would have sworn, until now. She was intensely questioning and expected the intensest answers, never herself giving back any. Night-blooming, physically reckless, her particular bent was perhaps the worst possible for a woman who, to the eye, lived so superficially.

"Nick asked to see some of the old Cosmos Club pics,'" she said. "We're upstairs." No resolve or inverted moral made her speak the truth at all times — though he would know that the "pics" of an old river club she had once belonged to were in her bedroom. And her company, for whatever reason, would have asked to see them — of that her husband could be sure. Long ago, when he was marrying her, he'd thought it beautifully ideal for his ambition that her only vice should be truth-speaking; now he could see how it was that she mightn't even particularly value the truth. Her vice was simpler, like rabid aspirin-eating in a woman who, like her, never drank or took drugs. She could not lie.

"Oh, Nick's there, is he," he said as swiftly as he could manage. "Well then, you'll have company" — as if she ever lacked it. "I'll stay and chat with the old man awhile. He doesn't sleep much any more anyway."

"Of course," she said. "I remember last time. How late he stayed, I mean, Anna said. Four." She spoke indolently, stretching even her usually lazy accent in a way he somehow recognized but couldn't identify, except that she wanted to keep him on the phone. She would be standing near the chaise, or lying there, crossing ankles too slenderly perfect for the rich weight they now supported, regarding them absently. "Oh yes" — again the voice sounded turned away from the instrument — "oh yes, I expect to have company, for a long time." Then she must have turned her head back to the phone; he could hear her breathing — heavy, intent. With a flick, he got it, just as if she'd shown him a picture from the pile of old ones between her and her company; his wife, for her own reasons, was flirting with him. She'd used to show him off like this in the old days. And he'd felt as foolish as now. But *only* foolish. "Ah well, yes," he said. "Well, good ni — "

She cut in. "How was your dinner?"

"Oh, the usual," he said. Then that other whisky, which he had added to Chauncey's, rose in him again. "No, matter of fact, it was — fine." Other possibilities rose with it, older ones — renewed. Why not? There were courses in life which dragged everything up with them. "Tell you about it. If you're still up when I come in."

"Oh, I'll be up," she said lightly. "But I may be out. We just came by to see that picture. One of Nick's old — clients." She gave the last word an emphasis. She *was* flirting. "Or tomorrow." She said that on a sigh.

But the daytime was never good for such renewals as they had managed. Funny, when most people would think it was her nights that separated them. "Well," he said again, "I'll say good night."

"Simon — "

"Yes?"

"Why did you call?"

The whisper, slow, almost harsh, made the phone rasp. He remembered where he was, in this good, old-fashioned house. "Is that so strange?" he said, from a reserve of bitterness he normally never let open. But so much was opening tonight, and perhaps better for it.

"Because we — never — you know —" Her voice drifted softer, even bewildered, although if he could have seen that high profile with its profusely artful, piled hair, or had had before him the almost un-lined forehead, those hooded Spanish eyes — he knew he would think otherwise. What had she ever had to be bewildered about? Her certainty, far beyond possessions, or insouciance, on the way to insulting the world's fears, was what attracted all her fly-by-nights to her — and drew him yet, in the part of him which was still the mirror-writer. It was the way she stayed in her society, her world, yet slanged it, which still got to that innocent, money-lending boy.

No, they no longer pursued each other's whereabouts as most couples did, but until now they had never acknowledged it either. Again his spirits lifted, irrationally light, as if tonight there were frail openings, portents everywhere.

"I'm dizzy with success," he said carefully. "You should have been there." And that was the slip he always made.

"You're the champ," she said.

"How's Ruth?" he said at once, in repartee — and sorry for that, too late.

"Ruth? She was all right when she and I came home." He heard her turn aside and call up to Anna from the landing, no doubt carrying the phone out there on its long cord — and this intimate house-bawling as always reassured him. His house.

She returned. "She's all right, Anna says —" He couldn't tell whether she was being distant to him or merely nonchalant in the way the Mendeses always were about health and children, both of these always acceptable and glorious — as theirs — even when afflicted, and neither ever paramount in their lives. "Quite all right, Simon." She was a good mother, but unable to conceal that she was a better one, a more natural one, to David. Her clarity got through the muffle around David as if it were speech. But their quiet Ruth, who could speak up for herself well enough to her father, could only half adore her mother in silence; Mirriam kept herself at an eagle's distance from this dove they had hatched between them. "You didn't call about that," she said, not severe, teasing — and again as if she'd turned from the phone.

"No." His truth-telling was different from hers, not a rash freedom but an abstention — from biblical wrong. "Matter of fact, Chauncey assumed I'd phone. He told me to go do it." He could smile at himself. "So, I went."

She burst out laughing. Her laugh was very slightly on a scale; if it charmed one, *she* did; all her friends were of that persuasion. She had charmed him in spite of it. The "lady's laugh" he used to call it, in the days when they spoke in lovers' bowknots flung one to the other — and he feared it yet. All her intensity — or imbalance — was there. At times, in place of this elegant shake of the bells, he wouldn't have minded the harridan parrot-screech that some men got, or a bit of good old Xantippe-nagging like his mother's. But Mirriam at her most reckless was always elegantly on chime.

"Oh, *Si*." This was a nickname even long ago used at rare times, seldom except at the best ones. "I can just see it — see you," she said. "Oh, Si." And she'd stopped laughing.

"Mirriam?" he said. "Wait up for me." There was a long pause. Then he said, "It's been an extraordinary evening. Night, I mean." He had no idea why he added that, tribute maybe to the window's cold blue even here in this tiny study, and to Chauncey waiting.

After a longer pause, she spoke. "I'll . . . wait up," she said.

"Good. I'll ring off now." But he waited for her to.

"Give my love to Chauncey." She said it as if it were soup.

"I will."

"And . . . Simon —"

A minute later, he could have sworn that he had already closed his eyes in reflex when she spoke, that the spot between his eyes had already tingled, prepared. The aim was in the way she said it, so softly, indescribable — unmistakable. "Nick wants to be remembered to you," she said.

As he stopped in the bathroom on the way back to rejoin Chauncey he had to look down at his hands, they were trembling so — for him a new experience. He had just learned something: his and Mirriam's habitual under-acknowledgment of the crosscurrents in their lives had become next door to the most powerful communication. So that when time came to acknowledge her lover, a system with its own language and cues, quickly interpretable, lay ready for it. This was the way it had been done. It seemed to him that if he concentrated on *this* thing he had learned, an insight on life, and not on the other, his hands would stop their trembling. He washed them thoroughly, as if they had blood on them.

On his way back through the rooms which led to the front of the house, he stopped and stared at a velvet wall, a framed engraving here, a greenish old hanging there, as if he wanted to scrutinize the style of decoration, or name its period. It was the least identifiable period possible, the mixture he'd been brought up in, loved and knew.

A wild idea assailed him — to ring back and ask the two of them over. *Come on over* was a constant phrase of the callers on Mirriam's evening network, between any two of whom the phone acted as stimulus, a connective between that same afternoon — when they had last seen each other — and the hours to come, when they must again meet. After school, his children often did the same. He would ask those two to come over here, his wife sure to be dressed in one of those marvelously unglittering ensembles in which she believed the riches of her pocket and of her body, that long monolith, could go "anywhere" — and her escort, one Nick Pecora, or Padona or Posloty, quondam detective-sergeant or captain of the New York police force, whether forcibly resigned not known, though retirement was out of line either for the man's age, less past forty than Mirriam, or for one with his physical cast. A man almost a head above her five-foot-seven yet too thick-bodied to seem that tall — his was the type which got its energy from do-nothing days plus the beefblood of sports arenas and late cabaret steaks, with a body which took its workouts in sexual exercise, slept off these bouts in some haven of mother or landlady unknown to its other women, and got its money in some manly form of underworld squeeze. If there'd been an urge to know the man's name precisely, to get a line on him in one of the means open to judges, the Judge had not allowed himself it. Mirriam referred to him as Big Nick. Though he might not be a gangster, this suggested environs and precincts; he had probably grown up as a big Slavic Nick among a lot of little Italian ones. From a certain cast of blondness, he was probably a Pole. The Judge had met him once in his own hallway, once on the phone, and increasingly on the fringes of Mirriam's conversational silences. This man, as instructed beyond a doubt by Mirriam, had wished to be remembered to her husband. And the Judge, equally instructed, had remembered him.

The phone would bring them. Mirriam, like the Judge, had been taught to honor age. She would come, this wife who in girlhood had been taught all the old-fashioned compassions, and still held to them as to an etiquette. She would stand here in the hallway of this house antecedent to her own, with the assured, half rebellious manner she always had in such houses, even in her own. The man with her would stand at her side as he had in the Judge's hallway, his eyes shrewd yet offhand; he'd been in places like this before, let nobody think otherwise, and his attitude, yes, would be just that: he was *with her*. Everything in their connection would be brought a step further, by one of those improbable social impulses a telephone made possible. What then? Would she and the man, looking about them here, see how impossible a couple they were, or would Mirriam alone see it, as earlier she must have seen it for herself and Simon — meanwhile aware even that this mutual impossibility of them for her, her for them, was what had brought the three of them together here?

He saw that vision and certified it as wild. For a minute only, he'd entered that mad, modern telephonic world of hers where everything was viable.

At the library door, he said, "Sorry I took so long —" and then paused. His host, bent over the piano, on the closed lid of which there were now ranged dozens of photographs taken apparently from the open bench and the wide drawers of an old breakfront, had his back turned to him, poring over them.

"Everything all right at home?" said Chauncey.

The Judge took a shallow breath. It was with these, not the expansive kind, that one lied. "Everything."

He went and stood by the old man's shoulder.

"Can't find him," said Chauncey. "Damnedest thing. Can't find him anywhere."

The Judge put a hand on that shoulder, reaching up to do so, and not only to console, to give him one of the few real gifts the old could use, to say — it's not only you need me; I need to be here, with you. Family had taught him this, his mother tucking his grandmother's specs into his five-year-old fist, saying, "Ask her to read to you"; his father taking him along on a visit to *his* father in the nursing home, to see the old man blush with pleasure at his son's laying the firm's books on the bedspread, his "Papa, I hate to bother you, but could you give me a word or two on this?" His father had needed the help; those needs, not the pretended ones, were the best. And he did, now. He would stay here all night, and welcome.

"Damnedest thing!"

On the piano, at least three generations stared in the wistfulness of all dead sitters — hoopskirted and muttonchopped, bustled and nautical-jacketed, after these the platter hats and bowlers, a little sprightlier from being still perhaps in the land of the living, then a scattering from the latter-day twenties and thirties, alive and crude. To see Chauncey's own visage, recognizable all down his long span, was the familiar shock one always had.

"There —" Mannix indicated a young man among the moderns, not in uniform but with a British haircut. "Isn't that your great-grandson?"

There was no reply. Chauncey, turning around, mightn't have heard, though his faculties, if performing variously, were keen enough. "How's that handsome son of yours?"

The Judge flushed, an often regretted reaction to mention of his son, not due to the boy's affliction, or not directly. "He's — thank you, he's doing very well. Actually, one tends to forget how well he's doing — it's almost no problem to him, any more. Except that he doesn't hear from behind or a distance, you'd never know."

"Still an athlete?"

"Yes. Track."

"Well, now. Your father'd have been mighty pleased at that."

"He was the one hauled him off to the Garden, Madison Square, by the time he was four." Why must he grudge that so? Or that David had never had the usually despairing tantrums of the deaf child but had seemed to know at once, long before the special school, that everyone was trying to help him, even in babyhood taking it in with grave, alert eyes?

"Favors old Mendes though, doesn't he? Got his long bones."

"Keep forgetting you knew my father-in-law, as well as Dad." As always, he was glad to get off that other subject.

Chauncey chuckled. "Don't know why I call him old; he was younger than me — except that he's dead." He turned to his pictures, alert on their easels or against vases or books he had stuffed behind them. Like a class of recalcitrant pupils they stared back at him, with all the inflections of willingness to learn except the one he could not teach them — how not to be what most of them already were. Behind him, the Judge once more wanted to reach up to that humble curve of back which was still marvelously, intricately alive. Then Olney, with a handsweep, sent the ranks down before him like ninepins. "Want my brandy. Let's sit down."

They settled themselves in two armchairs near the bow windows on the avenue and park. The Judge always liked to know where he was angled in a house, a farmer's habit but curiously the New Yorker's also, in these squared streets easy to see why. Settled here, able to look west, and north-south with a bit of stretching, they were to his mind in the very center of the city. By now, far from the Piedmont as Olney was, it must be his city also.

"Didn't rightly know your father-in-law Mendes; only saw him once, as a young man. In the upstairs ballroom of one of the Ralston apartments, the one the owners kept for themselves."

"Must have been way back. Never knew Meyer saw them socially."

"He didn't. He went there to buy the land for your house."

"Oh, I've heard his story of that night — many is the time! But he never said . . . whatever were you doing there?"

"It was *my* father-in-law who represented the Ralstons. Didn't you know that?"

"By God —" The Judge sat up, slapping the arm of his chair. "No." He leaned forward, the way he did when about to affix to his collection of stamps a rare one, lost and turned up again, that he hadn't known existed any more. "Chauncey —" He felt as if Olney was himself a jar of rare memories that he must very gently tip. "*My* father-in-law was in his thirties then, about to marry," he said eagerly. "It was the year before he broke with the family firm in London, threatened to set up an American branch of his own. Got one of the rival music publishers, Rinaldi, I think it was, ready to subsidize him. Told his mother and uncles that as the heir, if he was expected to run the business some day, he was going to do it then or not at all. So they gave in." He prized all that history, as much as if he had inherited it along with the house.

"Oh?" Olney said politely.

"Excuse me, Chauncey. It's just that — years later, to have another facet on what I always thought was cut and dried by now —" He poured himself another whisky. "Go on."

"Pour me one. The brandy. Thanks." Chauncey drank, coughed.

"Well, after the War, I was the poor widow's mite you know, got through the university somehow, University of Virginia of co'se, came up here just like any carpetbagger, only in the other direction, to see what I could squeeze out of the North. My folks had connections here and I renewed them for all they were worth. I was a sweet-talking young sinner, back then. The time we speak of I wasn't but twenty-three or so, clerking with another firm entirely. If my father-in-law knew he was going to be that to me, he hadn't said so, and I sure hadn't asked him. I was simply at an evening party there at his home. When we left the ladies for the cigars he said, 'Come along with me later, young fellow, to an appointment I have. Show you something interesting, you might never get to see.' So, I went."

"That ballroom," said the Judge. "It was like Venice, my father-in-law said, it *was* Venice — copied as a matter of fact from a room in the Ca' d'Oro, walls painted to look like marble, and the floors like terrazzo, but done in wood. Unfortunately the pictures, hundreds of them, were copies. But the fountains were real."

"That so?" said Olney.

"Didn't you — notice?" The year he inherited his present house he'd gone next door° to the Ralston houses to ask the tenant of that flat to let him see if he could find a scrap or two of all that trompe-l'oeil, but the room had been cut up, the walls painted over, the legendary fountains sunk beneath the floor.

"No, I didn't," said Olney, sharply for him. "Studied what I thought I'd been brought there to. I studied Ralston, the balky seller, and how his own lawyer and the buyer helped each other, how they checkmated him from opposite sides of the table, each for his own reasons, two men who'd never met before, our respective fathers-in-law. I studied young Ralston particularly. And I studied — the law."

"Ralston was one of the young aesthetes," said the Judge. "My father-in-law Mendes had seen his kind back home in London. Dressed plain, he said, all black and white, but everything as if it'd been knitted on him. An aesthete, but a young blood also. Lisped by intention. Boxed at the Athletic Club. And had his hair dyed gray."

"He was a builder's son, Simon," Olney said gently. "American. Lemme tell his principal characteristic as I saw it, that evening." He leaned forward and pointed a thumb, giving each word its burden. "He didn't . . . want . . . to — sell."

"Ah, well." The Judge backed away from that thumb, laughing, throwing up his hands before it. "Ah, well. The minute he saw the man, Mendes said — Mendes began to talk opera. You agree to that?"

"Opera it was," said Olney. "And how my future father-in-law abetted him, just by knowing nothing about it! I can see the rapscallion's head shine yet, turning from one to the other — he was one of those men with a bald head all one big freckle, nasturtium color. Puh. And I had to sit there, mum too — felt as if I was in knickerbockers. Which I was."

"Mendes happened to have the score of *Aida* with him. Had just been produced the first time, in Cairo, year or so before, 1871. By this time he was already an entrepreneur. He promised to introduce Ralston in opera circles — seems Ralston had a protégé." It had taken innumerable renditions of the story before Mendes had happened to mention the protégé had been a castrato, a boy. Mendes was no prude; he'd simply had his mind on another point which had seemed to him the final one.

Olney nodded. "Maybe so." He smoothed his chin, staring forth. "My prospective father-in-law didn't give a damn about the lot itself, or who his client Ralston sold it to, if persuaded to sell at all. It was Ralston's business agent he was after — fellow'd been asking too much baksheesh on the side. My father-in-law wanted him out of estate matters. This was one of the ways to get at him — and still keep Ralston under his own thumb."

He decided not to interrupt again. After all, was there anyone who knew *all* of it? "So that was it," he said. "And the end of it, do you remember that? What Ralston said to Mendes, after they'd agreed?" It had been Mendes's climax, half the reason for his telling the story at all, even to Simon, and when he was telling it out of the family, all of it.

"Not so's I could say."

"Why, Ralston said, 'Well, at least this time I'm not letting in one of those god-damned Jews.' And then Father Mendes had to tell him. Never occurred to him that people sometimes didn't know what a Mendes was; he was so proud of it. 'I think I should tell you, Mr. Ralston,' he said, 'that I am a Jew.'" The Judge paused — here was the part that had always tickled him. "Mendes always said he also offered at once to let the deal go. I'd like to be sure of that. But I'm not."

"Heh," said Chauncey appreciatively. "Well — and so —"

The Judge lifted a finger, forgetting about interruptions — Olney's recall seemed sturdy enough, almost impenetrable. "So young Ralston stared. Then, Mendes said, he looked around the room as if he were tallying it. Then back to Mendes again, with a kind of funny smile on his face all that time. Then he shook his head. 'That may be, Mr. Mendes,' he said. 'But at least you're not one of these god-*damned* ones.' "

"Heh-heh." Chauncey gave a heel-stamp. "Must say I've heard that same little twist from others of your co-religionists. So I'd say you were right about Mendes, maybe." He coughed. "Well now — want to hear the end of the story?"

The Judge stared. Then he said gently, "Yes, Chauncey. Tell me the end of it."

"Well." Olney sat with his hands on the curled paws of his chair, his thin legs uncrossed, the lamplight in the hollows under his cheekbones, the rest of him in shadow; he might have been gowned and in court. He was sitting in judgment, Mannix realized — in judgment on two quite other men than had appeared in Mendes's version. Seventy years later there was still satisfaction in it. "My father-in-law was rascal-rich, you know, I guess you do. And not used to all his own red velvet yet, slathers of it all over his drawing-room, gold fittings that I didn't know weren't brass till I touched them. So you understand why he said what he did. I've never forgotten it. 'So, Olney,' he said to me when we got out of there. 'Did you see?' And I said, 'Yes, sir, I think I learned something about the law tonight.' He gaped at me. 'You smart-ellicking me, Mr. Olney?' But he saw I wasn't, that I was serious. 'Why you young poop,' he said. 'The law? Didn't you watch *him* at all, *Ralston?* Didn't you see it?' When I said I hadn't seen anything special, that freckle of his turned bright red. 'Oh, so?' he said. 'Oh, so. Not so smart as I thought. Let me tell you something, mister. The way to be rich is the way that young man is rich, the way my own boy is going to be, if I can make him. My girls have got to take their chances; I can only do it once, and I'll do it for my boy. Only got one.' He almost choked on it, telling me. 'Can't do it for yourself. Has to be done *for* you. That boy Ralston is *miles away from his own money.* Don't know where it's from, scarcely knows that it comes. Has to be done for you — that.' He even shook me by the arm, as if to wake *me* up. 'Miles away,' he said, 'did you see it? *Miles and miles away.*' "

Into the dying fall of that other-century voice and Olney's silence, the Judge said, "Wonderful story, Chauncey. Wonderful telling, too. You're a past master."

"Damn well ought to be, in that one. Far as I know, he didn't pick me for his daughter's husband, she did, and I was already after her, I guess, that night. But I was always very careful, later, not to go into his firm." He sipped from his brandy and dried his lips. "Sometimes I wonder, though. He *was* rich enough after all to give his girls their own money, in the end. And I was a young carpetbagger. Didn't *I* pick *him?*" The old man made a sly face at him.

"Oh, Chauncey."

"Particularly fond of that story though, I must say," Olney said, smiling to himself. "Considering — the tail-end of it."

"You mean that wasn't?"

"Uh-uh." He let Simon wait, then cocked his chin at the ceiling. "Few weeks later — though I shore never got this from my father-in-law, and we never spoke of it later, b'lieve me — it came out that Ralston himself had already sold away, unbeknownst to anybody, the very room he was standing in that night; he'd sold the whole block of flats. For more money than a parcel like that had ever gone before. And he'd done it all by himself."

In the smallish room, so markedly plain for the prospect it fronted on, Chauncey's laughter rang loud and long, an elder's laugh and of its era; Mannix's laugh, though released specially for his friend, seemed of its own era, dimmer by habit, conserved in the chest. Looking around him, he could see yet another end to the story, a subtler one. The taxes on this place, in which one man lived with a servant, must be as high as any private one of its size in the city, for the land alone. The room's clever shabbiness, resembling some of Boston's, might be as characteristically Virginian, when there was money too. He smiled secretly, seeing his friend through the other end of the opera glass. Miles away from his money, miles away. And what of other sides to it, Chauncey's wife, the girl? A name suddenly connected in him — Father Mendes mentioning it, saying it with the honest Jew's high intellectual smile for Christian graft.

"Why, Chauncey, your father-in-law — wasn't he one of the attorneys for the Boss Tweed crowd — why, I've got a Thomas Nast drawing I think shows him."

"Have you?" said his friend, deep in the wings of his chair. "Yes, that was Mary's father. Thought you knew, maybe. Your father did, of course."

"He never said."

"Mirriam knows, mentioned it to me once. Seems there's lots of that crowd's great-grandchildren, still stepping out around town."

Mannix made no response. Forcibly, he kept his mind on the great double staircase of the city, up which went the thieves on the rise, the fancy girls, the peddlers Jew or Dutch, down which came the dowagers in their diamond dog collars, the race horse collectors and cart horse breeders — and the snake-hipped young men, the egreted women, who had danced at the Savoy.

"Pour yourself another drink, Simon."

"No, I've had enough." He got up and went to the piano, hunting among the pictures. There she was, Olney's wife, in the pince-nez and stiff bun of that afternoon forty years ago, not ugly even under the glasses, laborer in civic works, faithful helpmate in Chauncey's career, ever at his side. "She sang Tosti's 'Good-bye.' Your wife. The day I was here with Dad." He hesitated. "No. It was the other one."

"The other one?" said Chauncey. He had sunk all the way back in the chair now, hands folded.

A sister or sister-in-law? She was nowhere among the pictures, at least the silhouette of her as he remembered it. "A blond woman, I think. Hair in curls on top, one down her neck. Very quiet otherwise. Dark dress."

"You must mean my secretary, Mrs. Nevin, who lived with us. She had a daughter Lucy, about sixteen then maybe, who would have been away at school — or maybe not. Older than you. One of those two, it would have been."

He'd been ten, both older to him — how would he know? "Good-bye forever," the silhouette sang, in the dark of the generations.

"Luce, my granddaughter, is named for *that* Lucy — Lucretia Nevin. Her mother."

"Her —"

"I adopted Mrs. Nevin's daughter, since Mary and I had no children of our own. *We* did. My wife was a remarkable woman, Simon." Was there a deep twinkle in Olney's eye, a reminiscence at mouth, meant for Mannix to see? "No, there's no picture here, matter of fact, but you'll find a fine drawing of the two, mother and daughter, Mrs. Nevin and Lucy, on the upstairs landing, outside my room. Why don't you go see?" It was a command — or a wistful, ninetyish request.

Going up a stairwell heavily coddled in pictures far more luxe than down below, Mannix weighed his own father's odd friendship with Olney, never before seen as so out of their spheres for both — had he been the one to help with such things as adoptions? On the landing, he saw an indifferent line drawing, two laughing women intertwined in the simper of the period, in twin clouds of Charles Dana Gibson hair. In the agelessness of dull drawing they were identical. He tiptoed downstairs again, why on tiptoe, except for all the merged silences here, he couldn't say.

"Lovely pair; they must have been very alike." The Judge peered at his watch. "Isn't it time for me to go home?" He had spoken to an empty chair. Olney was at the piano, hunting fretfully. "Can't find him," he said. "Can't find him anywhere."

"Isn't that —" said Mannix, pointing again to the young Britisher's picture, but Olney, ignoring, walked past him to the window, recalling to Mannix how at their last dinner he had gained vigor with the late hour, only to fade, almost neatly, into doze — and a healthy rousing — and so off jauntily in the small hours with his man, who seemed used to it, in the car.

The Judge came and stood beside him. Nobody on the avenue now, not even a bus, and the planes of it, the lovely bones of light that were its trees, seemed to stand at attention, pressed forward by visions of it in other lights and at other hours.

"I like sometimes to see the young couples coming back from parties," said Olney. "Summers are better for it. I don't go away any more. Don't mind the heat now. Got everything here." He drew the curtains halfway, with a shy smile of guilt. "Once a girl saw me watching, ran up and knocked at the window, but nobody's thrown any stones yet." He chuckled. "Maybe they're waiting to see what happens to the Court." Very slowly, he bent over the tray, pouring out another brandy. "Yes, they were often taken for sisters, that mother and daughter." He was humming. "And Mary was a ve-ry remarkable woman." He'd poured the brandy, the Judge saw with a certain chill, into a third glass. It wasn't possible to tell whether he was wandering, or with the insouciance of his years was merely plucking down — as one might attempt the crystal plums carried by the wrought-iron maiden in the piano bay — all the themes, still fruiting, which inhabited this house.

"One for the road, Simon," said Olney. "And brandy's best, at evening's end."

"Is it?"

" 'Tis. And you've sat up with me long enough."

"Sure now?"

"Often sit up reading. Proctor's got a buzzer downstairs if I want a snack — he sleeps days, if I do. And there's always the window, even without girls. Five o'clock in the morning, it's a marvel."

Mannix took the glass.

"Your own little girl must be growing on, Simon. What's her name? Saw her with Mirriam once. Looks like you."

"Ruth. She's twelve." He could feel his face break into the sweet gape of fatherhood — and not only because she was an even smaller, femininely decent replica of him. "Off her feed tonight, Anna said. What girls of that age eat! — great big eyes and a bellyache, all of them. Used to get high fevers with any little thing, seems she's growing out of it." He heard his own babble, in this house of mourning.

"Luce used to ride. She made the three of us do it. Every Sunday morning." He pointed a long forefinger at the window. "Right out there, we used to come out of the park." The force of his glance and the gallery of pictures behind him all but drew that vision of riders through the French window, the three women on their mounts, girl, mother, and Mrs. Olney behind them, stepping through with the ease of apparitions, one by one, lightly equestrian. And Olney, behind them all, was still here.

"They grow out of it," said Olney, "all of it. And what about your boy — will he be for the law?"

"No," said Mannix. "Got some idea he wants to save the world."

"Heh. Won't ask how. Gather he don't think that process is synonymous with the courts . . . Simon — kin I ask you a question?"

"I know what you'll ask," said Mannix with a laugh. " 'Do I really think orderly process *will* save?' Yes I do, you old revolutionary. And you helped on my appointment, nevertheless."

"*Because,*" said Olney. "And because I — never mind. But if you find me going along with what's being done to the Court these days, I'm no radical. I b'lieve in a government of *laws,* not men, just like the founding fathers did — who got that idea from Harington's *Oceana,* by the way. And in the end, I plump for the men. Just like *them.* But what the hell are we talking about that for — after midnight?" He suddenly bowed his head. "I hope that boy —" he said, gesturing at the pictures on the piano — "I hope that boy had some women, in his time." Olney lifted his head, not lecherous, but as if poking toward some shrewdness he hoped was in his younger friend. Was he asking Mannix to note how all this evening's talk might now be seen as circling round that martial mourning they had joined forces for — that this was the way men properly sat up with the spirits of men? Or had Mannix's own evening, that nervous quick of private reflections, drawn everything from the other's to itself?

"What is it, Simon," said Chauncey, "that you hold against your own boy?"

He could feel himself shrink into the smallest corner — of not knowing. "I don't know," he said, from it, his voice a strangle of relief. Led like any witness into admission never yet made to the witness self, he stared at his clasped hands, seeing what advocacy could be.

"Not — because he's deaf?"

The Judge looked up, with a stiff smile. "I can lipread, Chauncey. I learned it with him, did you know that?"

Olney shook his head, as against a gnat. "He's *Mirriam*'s son, and I can understand how that could — but he's also yours."

He drew a shallow breath — and said nothing.

"Troubles you, I see it. I had no son." The old voice hadn't a quaver, strong with the evening's supply of life. "I'd have made do with a bastard, if I could've got one. But I can see how it would be between you, just now. Simon — we didn't fight in the wars of our time either, you and I. Are you agin that boy because he can't?"

"*Judge*," said the Judge. "Let us talk about *Geoffrey Audley-Taylor*." Then he was ashamed.

But the other held up a hand. "Haven't got the time to take offense — or to be polite." He grinned. "Nor, 's matter of fact," he drawled, "to wait out a bet I made with Borkan, about you. On reconsideration, I'd say he was right."

"What was that?"

"He gave you six years — to get there. I gave you ten."

He received this in absolute silence. There was no need to ask "Get *where?*" — any more than there had been to ask Chauncey what he had meant when he had said "the Court."

"I didn't know I was being mentioned for it," he said then.

Chauncey squinted. "Don't know's you have been, except by us. But *you've* thought of it. You just didn't know it showed on you. It always shows. Showed on me."

"I didn't know you ever — " The usual verdict on Chauncey Olney was that he had never cared to exert his endowment to the full — though there were those who contended that he was an unremarkable man, exalted into an air of endowment by sheer lifespan.

"You'd have known, if you'd been around. But I'll tell you something known to few, now all dead. I was offered it."

"You were . . . offered —" He counted back how many administrations that must have been, which President — never doubting that Olney spoke the truth. Vanity wasn't in that hooded eye. Perspective was. Even perhaps a surely inapposite — paternity.

"I turned it down."

"You . . . but in God's name, why?"

"I thought my . . . private arrangements — might not bear scrutiny."

"But — surely they already had borne —"

"I did not wish to bring them into full view."

He was stunned most of all, he thought, by the conversational difference between the two centuries — and by what the preceding one's mannerism could conceal, even from its successor's eye. Few in public life now would openly have dared such a ménage as must have been here, or made such a serene go of its "arrangement" — and this despite all the rapines of passion, and perversion too, nowadays so common on the cocktail tongue.

"That doesn't sound like you, Chauncey," he said, stern as a son who had expected better of his father.

"It wasn't," he answered. "You see . . . Mary convinced me. Yes, she was the one who persuaded me — that it couldn't be done. But not even the President knew that." Olney held out his hand. "Good night, Simon, and thank you. Confidences are tiring — you may find that out one of these days. And I have to take care of myself." He did look tired now, with dangerous hollows in his face that might not refill. But surely there was a glint in his expression still. "You see — that sudden bout of TB I had? Came on me as a middle-aged man. At just about that time."

While the Judge was taking this in, Chauncey pressed the buzzer on the wall. The man Proctor shortly appeared, wearing spectacles which gave him a clerkly look well suited to the house.

"Proctor'll drive you."

"Oh no, please. I'm looking forward to the walk. No, I really am, Chauncey."

"Grown bitter out." Olney went to the window, peering at an outside thermometer. "What do you know, down to twenty above. But no wind."

"I'll be warm enough. I need the walk."

Proctor helped him into his fur-lined coat and handed him the thick French-gray suede gloves which were his sisters' half-yearly gift, doing it with a measured approval as silent-footed as his service, and as much in evidence. Proctor and his kind held this world up, or what was left of it — which was a lot. He gave Proctor a nod of approval fully exchangeable.

"Proctor, give the Judge a pair of my earmuffs. Simon, you know that more than half the bodily heat loss is from the head?"

He submitted, even putting them on. "Almost forgot to tell you," he said. "Anna's bringing round some soup, in the morning."

"Anna's soup is always welcome. Not sure you can afford it though, Simon. Last time Anna brought round what she called a little meal, Proctor and I dined happily for three days."

So at last they came to the handshake, the good-bye, always at Chauncey's age to be thought of as perhaps eternal. Mannix took off the earmuffs, which made his own voice sound hollow to him, but dangled them ready, like the obedient child he felt himself to be. Soup, earmuffs and the like, fathers and mothers, aunts or sisters and the like — and always this silent, ceremonious third — how many hundreds of times he seemed to have undergone this ritual departure to the raw, unaffiliated outdoors! It was part of a background Chauncey and he shared in spite of race or against it, one of a sort that the Borkans, no matter how many bets they made with the Olneys, or how many Park Avenue wives they acquired, would never have — and it was more of a human sharing than the Spanish Mendes bunch, in their pose of non-assimilation, would ever admit. Chauncey too, looking down from his height, had a gratified expression.

Mannix turned to look long at the room, conscious that he didn't want to leave even now. And he was owed — one question. "*Is* that he on the piano? Your great-grandson?"

"Yes," said Olney's voice behind him. "That was Geoffrey. I scarcely knew him. Hard to b'lieve that like Christ, he died for me." He turned. "But that's not the picture I was hunting — Proctor!" But Proctor had discreetly gone downstairs again. "Well, never mind."

But Mannix, at the door now, had to know it — which end to what story, which lost silhouette?

"Who? Whose were you hunting?"

"They had it taken at the railroad station, just the two of them,"

Olney said, as if the Judge must know. "A barbarous custom. But it was often done."

The Judge saw them all falling through the water-curtain of the years — Luce, still a girl on her mount, and her grandson at Alamein, Mrs. Olney the wife, and the secretary singer, leaving together perhaps for the country in their wide platter hats — even the whole ménage of this house in a dogcart à la *Harper's Weekly*, with the father-in-law-progenitor in the center at the reins, his neck ruffed like a sunflower's as in the Nast cartoon. Then the door shut and he was standing outside on the steps in the steel-blue cold, the touch of his friend's dry fingers still in his gloveless palm, in his ears Olney's whisper, their last salute as he fled the drafts of the vestibule. "A picture of Julian. My brother Julian. And the substitute."

It was a quarter of three. He put on the gloves and started walking. As he turned north, he caught a glimpse, through a curtain still awry, of the wicker chair in the window, its sidepockets stuffed with reading matter, perhaps some of the *New York Reports*.

His steps rang exhilarated on the pavement; the city, solitary under its brindled welkin, was most his now, the breathless cold of its best season his element. Those curtains the lady had so admired were still eighteen blocks away, and the cold needled at the thin soles of his dress shoes, but if a lost taxi had passed him, out of *The Flying Dutchman* at this hour and on its way to Brooklyn, he wouldn't have hailed it. As a boy he had often contrarily slogged his way home on foot in the worst weather, the bus fare burning meanwhile in his pocket, a bet he was sure to win.

He passed a house on a northeast corner, a white marble balustrade; in those days it had been as high as his head. All one winter, his ninth, he'd rounded it on his way to old Basch the ear doctor, to have his bad right one lanced, the first year he'd been allowed to cross the city alone without nurse or mother. Even now, when he flashed by here in a cab, it was still old Basch's corner, the white mansion on it anonymous still, it being the balustrade that counted, memory floating a Piranesi still only that high. Though he himself now resided here on the "upper East Side," the phrase and the environs sometimes still had their early dream quality, half villainous too. So it had appeared in his father's conversations with the other elders — a mysterious stronghold, more than of Gentiles, of other morals and manners too and of course money, to which the old West Side families and their imitative mansions, the Ochses, the Meinhardts, the Littauers, the Mendeses — had themselves at last deserted. These currents were as strong as any that washed the city's extension, on far Montauk.

Here was Seventy-ninth Street, one of the old Astor places, wasn't it, or some other old fur peddler of the seventh-grade civics books, and here behind its balustrade a solitary rose of Sharon bush, left over from what new-century-green landscaping? Gaunt now, but bridging all the summers of his youth, the bush bloomed of a summer still. Such lore was what made a bred New Yorker, slum or upper, refuse even to sneer at those ten-twent'-thirt'-year migrants who presumed to know his city in a parade of restaurants, and who lived here, as they said — now.

His ears were as cozy as a child's in Olney's earmuffs. Above the park the heavens were as widening a scroll as on that wintry dusk when he and a chum had walked the floes on a lake drowning in its violet solitudes and snowy wastes, far across the steppes from the skyscrapers' lights — and, item for the biographies, two park attendants had rescued from its seal-cold waters a future appellate justice, and Professor Abe Cohn. "*Russian?*," his mother, who'd never before seen his chum, had managed to whisper, even into the steaming twin blankets in which she had wrapped them both — a kind woman, not vile, only wanting her son to stay in his society. And her son, if he had enlarged the society, had certainly kept the principle.

He was middle-class, of his particular proud race (and no one would ever make him ashamed of either), never servile to any of any race presumed to be above him, never consciously unkind to those whom, race apart, he presumed to be below him — even dedicated professionally to be of service to them, but not from any sloppy liberalism of the heart. His mother had also bequeathed him her shortness; there was a strain of dwarfism in her family — kept concealed and when found out unmentionable — from which he supposed his six-foot father had saved him, stretching him by a counter effort of the genes to a half-inch or so under five. Her Simon was supposed to have inherited her quickness also. Even now he could not quite bear to be slow. He had had an only son's obligation not to be. "You're the champ." But she hadn't been an honest person, his mother; like many women of her sort, behind a soft, Israelite amplitude of breast she was a person of many fiddling pretenses and not quite majestic fears. If he himself had the absolute honesty required of a judge, he'd got it from his father, that sportsman-innocent of the business world whom only the florid finances of the era had kept better than solvent, who had bequeathed him honesty general and uncontested, like the fact of always having a dollar in pocket.

There were only three more avenue-blocks now. The Judge took off the earmuffs. Kept the head warm maybe, but induced a simple, herbalist style of thought which would never do by day.

He stood quiet in numbing air already damp with a promise that came not to the eye but to the whole animal. He was well aware of that other guerrilla-haunted world of emotions, dissidences, opinions and temperaments which kept some men further apart from society than circumstance or money ever did. In that world too, he felt himself if not full-square at least somewhere near center, well within the balustrade.

His glance swiveled past the high clouds and down again to buildings west and south, in the radius of those beacons the city allowed to be played on it from dreadnoughts in the river. All his early life, lucky in his place and temperament, beneath both he'd felt that such a city had to be stormed by every man. By day, he'd credited himself with no longer believing it. Curious how at an hour dampened to most sound, freed most of men's atmospheres, the city rose again, in the dragons' teeth sown in its dwellers forever, once more, even to the solitary, conquering rider, an audience.

Three blocks on, he turned east, down his own cross street. Many times he'd walked toward many things down this street. Toward old Mendes's death and the vast clearings-out and movings-in which had left the house tribally fair to both generations. Toward Ruth's birth and the honeymoon closeness of those few after-months when all four of them had seemed to be fed on mother's milk. Toward that sub-life of his children in some mythical belowstairs he became aware of only when it erupted into real accident. To the rackety phonograph evenings which sat on the old rooftop like paper hats — and to his own study, below all activity and behind it, calm and free as such cells were. Always, he walked toward the power of his house. If the nature of this was biblical, it had taken a Christian to point that out to him — as was the habit of Christians with other people's testaments, and their agonies too. Though if he could have said this to Borkan and Olney, interrupting that lipread exchange, it would have been Olney who smiled.

"Don't single us out," pleaded Borkan, because he was Borkan, and in that was all one ever needed to know about the hierarchies of the Jews. "If we are not singled out," preached the rabbis, "we are nothing; all our history is nil." And that went for a man personally too if he had the brains and the bootstraps. Though of this the rabbis preferred to say nothing. "Otherwise, we in our turn" — so went a man's own secret addendum — "are nothing but the coral reef, the aggregate, the sediment of cities." This is the power of my house.

Tonight, what he walked toward in it was Mirriam. Even now, through all this, they weren't a divided couple, merely one not joined. Often, after their separate stimulations of the night, they met in bed, coupling with the excitement of strangers met in a dream house, in one of those exotically prepared way stations of sexual daydream which had somehow been legalized for them — and in the morning was seen to be their own. His six months of worry must stand, would be corroborated, if he spoke. But tonight's was an error, an over-subtlety of the nerves. Not to speak was merely the subtlety he and his wife had resorted to in these matters; why should she break it now that there was no need?

For all this time he had been going over their dialogue as in an examination; beneath the righthand flow of thought on which he walked, the left hand mirror-wrote also, to convince him that he understood her words on the phone as he understood her character — dark of motive until she chose to reveal it, jangled as a bacchante's when in action, but in utterance flashing pure. The fellow was leaving for the war, or war was his excuse — and in the brittle way she had when piqued, she'd been talking to the fellow all along. Dropping people, the privilege of it, was in her foolish, still debutante rationale, all hers. He'd so often before seen it exercised in her vague, demi-primrose wanderings from his house — which she would never leave. She'd used him, her own husband, out of pique. And now it was over or soon would be, and there was no blood on anyone's hands. But in the core of the bedroom, between the sheets when he had got her there — if he did not strangle her, he would speak.

A strange image, which he'd never had before, or not admitted to — and wasn't frightened of. A judge could also comprehend the motives germane to the strangler, and why a man might reach for the voice-box instead of the knife. Lawyers like Borkan made a virtue of this kind of criminal understanding — and a large practice. Only Mirriam's laugh wanted killing, and all it signified in her — her elegantly neurotic mockery of the edifices other people made. Even the children were sometimes seen to flinch from it with him, or for themselves — even David, who could after all *see.* But all the life-thrashing rest of her, her purebred compassions inherited the way royalty had its horses, they — and he — loved, in strands dark or light. Just so Chauncey, in his own way, hot under the façade of hypocrisy his wife had helped him with, might at times have wished — surely when he was offered the Court — to reach out and tear off that pince-nez which had allowed her to see so tolerantly double.

There was the house, across one avenue and down one house. Bulwark beneath all other feelings, he felt the paterfamilias gratitude that all his family was safe abed there, from Anna at the top, in the quarters she preferred even though four flights above the basement kitchen, to the children's floor below her, where slept the one child with his large affliction and the other with her small, winning frailties, and down again one floor — to his wife. There were bright lights on that floor. He glanced at his watch; not quite twenty after three. She was waiting up for him, as promised. Except for a dim permanence of hall light, the rest of the house was dark.

He crossed the avenue, passed the gnarled side wall of the Ralston houses, whose doors were all on the avenue side, and stopped in front of his own. Behind it, to the rear and above, the water tower still loomed. His house still had its high stoop which led into the parlor-floor level in the old-fashioned way. There were the curtains — taken from an attic stock of them bought with the house, which Anna washed and laid away again yearly — and still veiling the windows of one and a half times the usual frontage, which Mendes had supplied for all these thrifty, château habits. Through their ancient netting, which by day caught the south sun and drew it inward a little more yellowed than it came, he could see that elusive underlay which strangers saw. A vague claret-and-water light came from lamps invisible. Chairs and tables were blotted, in a furnishment which needed forms moving between to identify them further, but nobody was downstairs now. Because he knew where the stairwell was, he could see the twinkle, far above, of a small, prism-hung light. The young Mendeses had had no extra money for chandeliers, or for the cushioned grossities of their era. But could the lady of the earrings, or any stranger, see the fine French touches with which the present mistress had reset old rooms already proportioned for music? On the fringe of his vision, something made him turn aside. A lone car sat at the curb, in front of his stoop. Exhausted at last, he averted his eyes from it, climbed his steps and let himself in. If she could only *lie*. If she could only lie.

At once, with an animal motion, he closed the street door behind him, to shut out — though the block was deep in its reserved slumbers — all that other audience. From the long ell of his wife's bedroom just off the first landing at the top of the stairs, a single, singular voice was haranguing, behind a closed door even now. The doors in his house were heavy ones, to normal sound. But this sound went on in arcs, at an even height of passion or altercation which he had never before heard that voice describe. His wife's voice discharged steadily, at gasped intervals, like the nasal anguish of a dog injured or pursuing at the height.

In a flight which had no memory of itself, he found himself on the landing. He was held there by the sound of a man's laboring answer, shameless and deep, no words in it at all. He put his hand on the doorknob, must have crossed to it, then dropped the hand. At that moment he heard a slight, sharp crack, like the spit of a palm on a cheekbone. Gunshot. *Gunshot*. From a gun he knew well. Then, from the room's shorter ell, which led to his own room, a soft shrilling came, and stopped, as if his wife had made an end of lament — or of sex.

How slowly, quickly, he burst through the door.

At first he thought it was only passion which confronted him — that this was all. His wife was clasped by the man, from behind. He must have just caught her. The big man held her arched, falling weight as he himself could never have done, the man's great fists clenched and guiltless under her breast. He knew that already. All of her, wide-open eyes, stretched mouth, black-red bubbling over that throat and breast, was turned toward her husband — faced him.

"Mirriam. Ah-rr God." He felt the worst, the bottomless, a sexual deprivation which must last forever, the truth which couldn't lie.

Above her, the man's big blurred head shook itself sideways, lips smirched back from the teeth as if to a god they must both understand.

They got her to the chaise, the Judge's empty hands crooked under her, only guiding, at her hair, at the throat still intact, at her wrist. How quickly she had gone, leaving this behind her. The wound was — impersonal.

"A doctor!" he said nevertheless, his hand on the phone near the chaise.

The blond beef-face of the other man broke into a grimace too tender for its own hacked lineaments, the head shaking again — the fearful glance gliding away toward the room's shorter ell, signaling — what more could it warn him of now?

Before he could fully turn from the phone, a gun dropped to the floor, not from those big, stained fists the man was pressing round a handkerchief, not from the warm, dead hand. It had been dropped yards away. By whom?

He was afraid to turn; had already done so. Lines of force drew themselves forever, into the triangle ceaseless, they three. The man was an outsider.

She stood there, his daughter, in her old laundered-out pajamas, fuzzy with a sleep just come from, yet wide awake. This was all that could be said, now or ever. Like the young of any animal, her clear, limited face couldn't yet express what was inside it — or know? Her hair fell in a clipped round on her forehead. As always before she was sent to bed, a long strand from either temple had been tied together with a ribbon at the crown. She'd been cleansed with soap after her vomit, her mouth chubby still with the lost innocence of mustard sandwiches, still the sweet babe's mouth, rarely doleful, staunch not only for him, he knew that now forever, but for brother and mother too. Only he could see behind it — as a father would know from childish mishaps — her bewilderment. Only he would ever see her as a baby again — his Ruth.

As he went toward her, this upbore him. Her knees buckled in answer. Though she was almost as tall as he, this helped him take her up to him. It was an enormous relief to carry her, his arms grown to iron. He lifted her away and out of there. On the landing, bawling for Anna, this action of itself came to him like an answer. He held on, leaning against the banister, hearing Anna call "What, what?" from that eyrie where she heard nothing of their lives unless rung for. She called again, from the children's floor above, and again when she saw him, "My hosh, is she sick again? You naughty girl, at the icebox yet, what you boddering down dere?"

And then he thought: Only I. But Anna too. This came to him like a jewel of deduction he might have polished for years. Or like one Anna herself had picked up and handed him, in the trust which ready servants gave ready masters'. Not only he: *Anna too*.

"What, what?" she said, reaching them. She took Ruth from him easily, not an ox-strong woman but solid, in David's teens able to best him in their fake jousts, until these had stopped for his dignity's sake. Had she already glanced covertly aside for a moment, at Mirriam's door, wondering why no response there — and then loyally back to him? But Anna had been trained to expect these nocturnal comings and goings of her mistress — any notion otherwise was his. It was in *that* minute — and from his lipreading — that he became aware of how careful he must be. Always to remember the gap, even in the most normal lives, between what was said and half believed of most people behind their backs, and the way in which most — against their own knowledge not only of what might be *said* but of what *was* true — walked steadily, steadily on! From now on, the worst of his dangers might be the temptation to create his own whispers. This would be the chess game he could never lay down.

He gave Ruth up to her. He had a babe, a jewel he must keep hidden, but in the best place — exposed. Everything he did now came to him like a choice made after long thought — as if, twelve years after his daughter's birth, she'd been born again out of a dead mother, and he was carrying her into the maw already opening up for them, saying, "I choose *her*."

"Take her back upstairs," he said. "I think she's fainted." He wasn't sure of it. "Mrs. Mannix has had an accident." He put his hands on Anna's shoulders. It would be best if he shocked her with the other news, the final news — already and forever not the worst. "I'm afraid she's dead, Anna. And Ruth saw it." He heard his own voice dexterous. "Do you hear, Anna? Mrs. Mannix has — shot herself. It was an accident. I found her dead. And Ruth came in on it. Ruth *saw*."

He helped Anna up the stairs with her burden, hearing in her broad chest deep labored moans almost sexual.

At the door of Ruth's room, the child herself slipped to her own feet, as if to aid them. Her eyes remained closed. She swayed there for a second, fists clenched, heaving — then came the spout of vomit. He caught one sight of her eyes — incredulous, seized from behind by a shame not theirs, as the eyes of children in vomit always were — then Anna bore her off to the toilet, soothing, "Hold it, darling, hold it," as if this was any ordinary evening with a sick child. But from behind, he had seen that the seat of the child's pajamas was stained too, with the dark pink smirch of blood.

He looked down at hands which might have transferred it to her from her mother's wound, but his hands were clean. Then he went down a flight again, entering that hothouse double room as his daughter must have, through his own half, for its door was open. The connecting door to his wife's room was open also. Across the dressing-room ell between the two rooms, he could see his wife lying waiting for him on the chaise as in a French boudoir photo, the pompon of one high-heeled slipper trailing the floor.

In the center of her room, looking down at her, he was beset with a terrible itch to close his eyes. By one of the brain's shameful commemorations, he was seeing the room not with every worn corner of its familiarity, or from old spatial habits his body knew in the dark, but in that initial whirl of the senses — pleased at these assaults of silk, and transfusions of color — of the day he had first slept here, before their marriage, at the beginning of his affair with the widow whom "everyone" — her phrase for it — had still called Mirriam Mendes, by her maiden name. It was her eyes he must close.

"It's — why it's all Sardou and roses," he had said, standing right here. He recalled his lurch of inner delight when she had picked up the reference. And he his first intelligence that this woman would be the extraordinary being one waited for, full of references for him. "Oh Sardou, yes!" she'd said — "but there *aren't* any roses."

He'd seen then that there weren't, merely a flower-silk Parisian confusion of walls and hangings, in this room so faithfully maintained for her in her father's house, closed for the summer, that she'd been showing him. Patterns which, if he could only look away from her, he would still see. That day, he'd fingered a tall screen, the one over there, had sat in that chair. And the idle way she had identified screen and chair, in two luxurious words, had lingered in his head like an open sesame, token to the mysterious wealth — not of money but not dissociated from it either — to be found in her flesh. In whose roses not roses he'd bitten and swum his way, past fragrances only teasing in other women, toward an orgy of spirit altogether uncommon for him — and had made lapse with pleasure those Spanish eyes. "Coromandel," she said again now, like a music box — "brocatelle." In the international diffusion of love on a morning yellow with summer, he had declared peace with everyone — "Even," she'd said with her laugh, listening to his biography at her breast, "even — with the French?" It was those eyes he must close.

He moved to do it, but couldn't force himself, until, like a tug at his coat skirts as used to be done to him, he remembered his daughter. I choose *her*, he said to himself, and did it. The eyelid resisted. In a horror to get this underground and away, he picked up the phone — and only now remembered the man's grimace, rubberized on that blond head of male meat like a bought expression, forcing him, the father, to turn — and see her. The pistol was still on the floor over there, where it had been dropped. But the man himself was gone, no doubt skulked off from a police scrutiny his life couldn't afford. Yet he'd have been seen with Mirriam somewhere, this evening.

Very cautiously, a left hand in the Judge's brain picked up a chess piece marked *Suspect: Murder* — and was immediately checked by the right hand, which set down another marked *Blackmail*, or *Truth*. A course of action must lie somewhere between the two. Before he phoned police or doctor he must know it. A sedative for Ruth, create as much stir as possible, even wake David? — and in the melee put his own prints on the gun, even be seen to do it? Or do that now, and go quietly. A small thing to do for one's daughter. But not enough. It was not enough to leave.

He walked over to the chaise again, and stood looking down. The eyes were still wide, brown. Or do one final thing to this, his wife. Almost murder again, it would be, to tie the soft, voluminous, bittersweet cloud of the suicide around that head forever. Much could be hidden in that sticky ectoplasm. Enough? The wound was a possible self-wound. Even he, absentee from wars which informed men more clearly of their own gristle and bone, knew this. Surely her past life too was now its own disadvantage. He saw how it could be used, that evening life. Again, a hand countered, rigid as a stylus, to show him how this could be used against him — the husband, returning from his evening ride.

But the gun, blessedly the gun was Mirriam's, blessedly. He fought down that hysteria and walked to the window for air. For the world, perhaps the more confusion the better, but he knew his own limits. Whatever he did, and no matter the consequence, he must talk to that man after — get his version of it. He had to know what he lived *by*. There must be no more loose ends. He flung the window up, a front one overlooking his own stoop. The air doused his head, clearing it as if he were only a householder leaning out for his headache. At the curb, the single car was still there.

"Yes, Judge, I'm still here." The man came out of the bathroom — whose door was always closed — wiping his hands with a towel, its lace edge hanging lavishly. Just so this man would look when he rose from a woman's bed — raddled but stolid, not to be moved more than he had been, or an inch from his own world, but ready for more of the same.

By an effort which made him shake, he restrained the fists that urged him on the big man. He forced them down at his sides, in the discipline that all his life had left him no reserve for humor. All his life he'd had to know first, before others saw it, what actions would make him ridiculous. He walked to the phone.

"I wouldn't, yet."

He turned. "What would you do? What *did* you do?"

The man stared, an expert measuring a learner. He shook his head slowly, or rather, spoke with his face, again that pliable gesture; he must do this habitually. That won't wash, it said now; uh-uh, don't try that. Then he pointed to the gun on the floor. "Yours?"

"Mirriam's."

Again the face made its move. "*Your* alibi." He palmed his own side, brought the hand forward. A gun had formed there, held flat. "Mine." His pistol had a capable gray shine, long and thin. He put it away and stepped over to the other snub, dark blue toy, not quite touching it with a sleek toe, no cop's shoe. "A Beretta twenty-five, looks like, but—"

"Damascus. Any tourist."

"And any child can fire it?" He had thick brows, gray-blond like his hair. These now cocked faintly, the mouth drew down, the nostril dilated, and again the whole head negated firmly from side to side, a head one and a half times the size of Mannix's own. Pantomime on a face of such scale was unusual — it could be slum habit, pushcart expressive, but from the neck up only, the rest being required for the gun — and the voice kept neutral. "How *is* the kid?"

In answer, the Judge took up the phone. Waiting for his number, his eyes traversed the man unseeing; he was now absorbed in giving evidence — a mode of behavior he had observed many times. "Doctor, please . . . Joel? Simon. Please come at once." He waited for a question.

"An accident." As each question came, he answered carefully, "Mirriam . . . She shot herself . . . No . . . When I got in . . . Dead." The phone squawked to a silence.

The Judge hung up. He seemed to consider, then raised his eyes to those watching him. "*What* kid?" he said. It took all his strength, against all the tenor of his life. Turning his back on that, and on the dead, he grasped the arm of the brocatelle chair, and sat down.

"You make people talk, mister, don't you." The other was now on the far side of the big room, in the alcove where Mirriam's desk stood between a tea tray and the armoire where the "pics" were kept, both movie and "still" — all that adored film which best asserted the crowd's transiency, being kindred to it. The chaise was between him and Mannix. He stepped around in front of it, his bulk hiding some action he performed there. Then he walked to the window, shut it. The Judge saw that he had pulled a great oyster-white eiderdown over the body. The chaise reared between them like a shrouded piece of furniture, or a catafalque.

Bile rose in his own throat. He subdued it. He and the man were on opposing sides now, circling, each with a pink-stained guerdon of love in his pocket? His hands trembled. I choose her. "The doctor will be coming in twenty minutes," he said.

The other came toward him, his eyes direct and blue — and troubled? Up that close, it was clearer how the shadow of their hallway encounter had maligned this man or failed properly to reveal him. Everything in his style might still be as the Judge had appraised, but the face, handsome by any standard, lacked the expected thickness or coarseness; the nose was chiseled, the mouth brutally well cut under the kisses women would give it, but wreathed too in the complex lines of its own pantomime. The voice was a New York one, battered half a dozen ways. "*Her prints?*" He said it very softly, urgently. "On the gun."

The Judge considered that trap. Or proposal? "Why don't you go now," he said.

"You have to hear."

So the man knew that. Plainly he himself had no need to speak; he had a giant's phlegm.

"Later." The number was in the address book by the phone, under a dozen others in her sprawling script: Nick.

"Uh-uh. I go to be a hero, in the morning."

He had been right, right. "You're the champ." But how he still hated this, that even after she who had mocked his nature was gone, it could not forbear. "So I deduced. On the phone."

"Did you deduce she had a gun on me?"

"But — that was hours ago!" He glanced over his shorter cuff. It was only ten minutes of four.

"I got it away from her. And put it on the table over there." He nodded toward the dressing table in the ell, then hesitated. "Give it to you straight. I — don't normally sleep in other men's *beds*, whatever else I do. But it was good-bye. When the girl came in the first time, we were — pretty tangled up."

"The *first* time!" It was a statement. An admission. Maybe the other wouldn't notice.

But the man's lip twitched. He saw everything — that his kind would see. "Mirriam never saw her. I didn't want to welsh on the kid — she snuck out again. But I got up to go. That's when it really started." He thrust hands in pockets. "And that's the picture. Or nearly."

"Finish it," said Mannix. "Quick."

"You know . . . how she could be."

How innocent each man, somewhere. No, I don't know. But you're telling me. He said nothing.

"She knew I'd volunteered to go. In the service. And that I didn't have to. She said I'd done it to leave her. And that she'd see me dead first." He swallowed. "When the kid came in again, I think Mirriam was saying — I *think* she was saying, 'I'll get that gun, I'll get that gun' — over and over. I was having trouble holding her — she took me by surprise. And the kid, coming in just then — must have thought her mother was saying to her, to *get* it. The gun that was on the table. But Mirriam meant my gun. *Mine*." He glanced at the gun on the floor, still with a frown of puzzlement. "How she could have — Mirriam must have turned when I did. I don't know whether she saw the girl even, before the kid shot her."

"For you," the Judge said hoarsely. "The shot was for *you*." As he spoke, he saw what he had said. So witnesses, establishing what is unthinkable, establish it all.

"Well, there it is," said the other. "Quickly." But his face had suffered a change. Or to the witness, did they always? It had begun to look like a face liars might trust.

"A slap," said the Judge, looking down at the gun. "That's what it sounded like from outside. A slap."

The other nodded, shrugged.

"But Mirriam said something. After."

"No, that was the kid."

"A — scream?" It hadn't been, that third oddly trilling voice.

And again the man's face made that strange grimace with which it had begun its repertoire, an embarrassed gawk of pity trying to hide in its own lineaments. Involuntarily the Judge turned his own head, as at that first signal, but there was no pajamaed child there now.

"Ah, what the hell," the man said, in his roughest voice yet. "The kid must have been trying to tell her mother all evening. She said something about . . . she said like . . . "It's come like you said, Mummy. The blood.'" Then he turned on his heel, found himself facing that covered mound, and wheeled again, toward the other wall.

When the Judge finally raised his head from his hands, he thought his tongue had been sounding like a clapper in his throat. Save her. Save. But he must have said nothing.

"Listen, fella," said the man. "Before the doctor comes. Go down and get us both some whisky." He wasn't looking at the Judge.

It was several seconds before the Judge answered. Then, rising, he nodded, but faltering, like an old man. "Your — clients. Who are they?"

"I was in the force once, on the strong-arm squad. Now I — have a few concessions around town." And some swagger to it. But hesitation too. "There's a medical examiner I know, down at the morgue. Let me put him wise. From outside. Just to keep it quiet. That's natural. The wife of a man like you." He was all hustle now, the cheapness coming out in him after all. A bad time to see it.

He saw the Judge see it. There was that dimension in him too. "Listen, Mannix. I'm not as honest as you, your kind. But so help me, I'm honest enough for this. You'll never hear from me any more."

The Judge bent his head, and turned to go down.

"Mannix!"

He turned back.

"The kid can shoot, can't she."

He had regained himself. "Deaf children . . . often have target practice." He spoke as if instructing an interested world, to the air. "Any vibrational synchronizing . . . is good training. The school thought. She and her mother used to go with him. My son." Then he went down the stairs.

Downstairs, he entered the dining-room at the back of the house, and closed the door. Deliberately, he opened a sideboard, set a bottle on a tray and two glasses, and sat down in a chair beside them to wait, his eyes on his shorter sleeve. The doctor had a possible delivery to check on the way, in any case was always slower than intended; there was more time than had been said. And he had a bet on. It wasn't as certain as his boyhood bets with his own bus fare. But he had more chance of seeing its outcome than Chauncey and Borkan now would ever have, on any bet confabulated around himself. It vamped in his ear like a popular refrain. You won't hear from me, any more.

The floors of his house were well tended. He watched, while a great tooth splintered the parquet and grew upward, then another and another, until he was surrounded by them entirely, and the house, utterly rent by them, hung on its own transfixion, curiously stable to the idling wind. Though he could see the house like that — as if from the air above the city — nothing of the city, or of men alone, had sown them. These were the stalagmites of pure accident, in whose unearthly air he now must learn to live. Some accidents melted back into life after suitable mourning — from even the most honorable. But the cones of this one encircled a child, and with her, could only grow.

He watched for four minutes of the ten he planned to give the man upstairs. All night he had checked his wristwatch as if it were an hourglass. Yet enormity had occurred. If he believed in God, would he call it no accident, and himself Job? But even he, digging his heels back in the century he'd been born in, was too modern for that belief, and not in arrogance but in the humble, humiliated modern way. He'd been reformed past it, past even those well-meaning Jews who had helped their God reform himself. Of the cleft-foot humors of the Cabala, still faintly a-hoof in his grandfather's world, he now had little or nothing left. Yet he still believed that each man, out of his own accidents, made his own version of them, was indeed obligated to do so. Was it this made him a Jew? He couldn't get it out of his bones that each man had an audience in *some* city. And each a single story which — though there might be no God — only a god could understand.

On the seventh minute he heard the man he was waiting for, on the stairs like a new-hatched ghost of this household fleeing its own haunt, now out the door — which closed. A car revved up, quietly moved off, and whined away. He reached out and took one glass off the tray. It was still empty, like the other. He filled it, and holding it, opened the dining-room door. The house held that mysterious pressure of a familiar house at night, its routines laid down like brush and comb, but alive in the beating hearts of the sleeping, in the wing-beats of the absent, and in the soul of him awake in it like a hollow whistle in which these histories revolve. Half the bet was now won. Carrying the glass like a toast readied for the other half, he went back up the stairs.

On the landing outside the room, he paused. Higher in the house, on the children's floor, Anna was singing, in the Czech she had hummed them to sleep with as babes. Anna and he would never speak further of this night between them; this was the bond, unsure on her side, which would make them both secure. So that they could live with each other daily, this was the advantage he must take of her. Whatever the child said to her, she might keep for her own, as any woman might do with a child's delirium.

Beyond, David lay in his keep, where even in ordinary hours a father flinched to surprise him. So awkward, even now, the walking up from behind to touch him aware, the touch of flesh of one's own with which one was not intimate. In imagination, he now walked into that wire-devised room, in the dark (as he'd sometimes done in years past, always asking himself the same question), and looked down at his son. If he were sure this was not his son, could he then be free to hate him — or to love? And in imagination he walked out again, unable to bear to mouth news like tonight's — and watch his son slowly read it in his own face. A boy of seventeen was almost a man, and like men, must take his chances on the morning.

And now, here was the door of her bedroom, open.

He stood in front of his wife's body like a conspirator returning to a crime whose full plot he hadn't been given. Under the coverlet he traced the same curves of knee and hip, breast and head. The dangling slipper was hidden by the angle he observed from, but the covering hadn't been moved. A spurt of jealous shame made him lift it. Yes, the man, back turned, had done it while he himself only watched. The eyes were now closed.

Her one hand still hung down. But beneath it, to a point nearer but not too logically close, the gun had moved. Been moved. He had won his bet in full. Were the fingers above the gun more curved than before, as if newly held around it, and again let drop? He bent to observe, and found himself retching, on his knees. The glass he still held spilled on his hand. He looked down on that glass which held nothing but whisky, drained it, and let it drop to the rug. On his knees still, but with his back turned to that sepulcher, he clutched the deprived root of him, and guarded it. If a woman had been near, he would have thrust himself upon her, to prove that impotence. For he wished to mourn.

Oh man of Uz, he said to himself, wandering the stairs again, striking a hand here, there. But Job, once his kinsman, was dust. He prayed to the god he had deserted — how hast thou forsaken me? But he could mourn only her of his choice, or try. He saw his house as he must keep it for her from now on, a house with all the common drapery burden of houses of its kind, but bare as a birdcage to any piercing eyeball. And on such tremoring middle ground as even he despised. But he must keep it for her as one kept one's house for one's child. For all the coming treasures of the snow — and of the hail.

For there was one loose end that with all his talents he could never bind for sure. Though all he knew of war was what men and books told him, like all who live in houses he had an excellent knowledge of wounds receivable there. A lesion carefully wrapped away for years could split again in an afternoon.

Grasping the banister as if it were a Bible, he swore, resolved — and yet in the end only imagined — how from this day on he would never say a word of any of those happenings to the child, except in extremis, if she spoke of it, in which case he would answer: "You had a delirium." Reality came to children as it was made. There was a chance that this was no burial of the truth, but a strewing on the wind as one did with the ashes of the dead — a casting away into life. This was all he could do in that direction for his daughter, who was, ever would be — the loose end.

Afterwards, he saw how he had left his mark on this house. He saw the gougings on the banister, regular as from the tines of a rake or the close nails of some animal, and he inspected them as an animal did its own mark — as if another of its breed had gone before. Even if he gnawed off his own leg, he couldn't leave this trap, which he must make for her too. He prayed, this time without kneeling. Then he began to see the true abyss between one like him and one on her threshold, and began truly to mourn.

When the examiner and the doctor, meeting on the steps, rang the bell together, and he opened the door to them, he was silent. But they had already heard through the door the cry that rose up the stairwell. Afterwards, though no record was made of it, it may have puzzled them.

"That the Kaddish he's saying?" the doctor, who was a Jew, had murmured to the examiner, who was not, before they rang. "I only know it in Hebrew. 'Yis kodol.'" The sound, a whisper now, shivered again at the door before this was opened to them. "There's nobody young enough here to mourn her. There's nobody young enough here to mourn."

2   A Major Visit – *June 1951*

FROM the file cards which recorded all his visits to the Mannix house, Edwin Halecsy, long since dubbed the Judge's "law clerk," in sardonic tribute to his own youth and the Judge's lack of office, was noting before leaving for dinner there that this would be his seventh major visit, if other elements in it went right. He had no need to look at a card in order to know this or any other of the facts recorded on it either in the high-schoolish script of the earliest visits, dated 1944, or the typed ones beginning two years later, after the Judge's gift to him, on his receipt of a full scholarship to Harvard, of a portable typewriter — a machine which, in Edwin's whole life before, between Mott Street and the high school and his "jobs," he had never seen up close. To date, June of 1951, at the end of his first year in law school, the total visits numbered twenty-five.

His card files, however, dated from a period before the Mannixes had entered his life, from the day a bewildered eighth-grade substitute teacher had kept after school, to help her with all she didn't know about classwork, this brightest boy, a spectacled young snub-face of no particular age, who did. She had paid him the first time with a wad of "five-by-eights" — the very name of them, glib on her lips, was new to him — plus a nickel candy bar from her own worn purse, but after that, for the month she was there, at his own hint with the cards only; he was no gourmet. In that school, with its wooden, latrine-style toilets, its luxuriously crayoned decorations, so well matched to the waxy flesh tints of most of its students, she didn't have to ask why the broken bridge of his glasses, tied with string, wasn't better repaired, although she did put a finger up to the one cracked lens, with a "T-t-t-t-t," but only shaking her head, like the poor, powerless, soon to be jobless creature he already knew her to be, when he replied, "It's OK. I'm on the list at the clinic now. Here too."

It *was* OK for him; as long as he could see the means up ahead; time as yet meant nothing much to him. Down where he was with his mother, there wasn't much sense of time anyway and he had never much missed it, only later on getting the hang of what people scraped up and grieved over. He'd always known what it meant to be "on time" of course, this being required in his mother's life and very soon of his, at whatever his walking age had been — whereupon he had graduated from being left alone in the house to going along on the job with her, to help. But that other sense, of time past or lost, though it had got through to him like one of the luxuries he *didn't* want, even now never much bedeviled him. Nevertheless, it was after the girl teacher had asked him a certain question that he had started his file system. "How old *are* you, Edwin?" she had asked, on her face a puzzlement he had seen on others before. Many in the grade were taller than he, more patchily bearded than his blond cheeks were; some were eighteen — but none of these were that smart. She could see he didn't want to answer. "I don't know," he said, at last. This was true.

To her, a dumbhead as they both agreed, he'd seemed to know, in the line of lessons, about everything else, yet his school record went back, on and off, only about four years. She herself could have been only a few money grades above his, but in every other respect — little as she had in brain or hope or family situation — miles beyond. In her face, whose small range of expression helped him assess this new one, he began to glimpse, as she listened to his story of why he didn't know his age, that there was something very special about his poverty, even to her. Few could have expressed to him what that was, certainly not she. But she had situations, in the world and with it, that he knew nothing of; this he could see in her listening face — and that there was another kind of dumbness which surrounded him. "But you can't stay ... like *in* a cellar ... all your life — a boy with your ... *Bubele*, you gotta come upstairs!"

The "cellar" was literal, a reference to where he and his mother did live, in itself nothing unusual in the streets the school drew from, or even on her own Bronx one. But out of that patriotism toward life which teacher-study had brought her, she had made a metaphor to be proud of. Both of them felt it. "I tell you what!" she said in triumph. "*Pick* one. How you could come even this far without it —! *Pick an age!*" From cracked lens to clear, a faded, flag-pink feeling was exchanged, the way teacher and class did at the daily "pledge of allegiance," and with the same echo, as from an order behind. A day later he saw her go out of his life and felt neither gladness nor cost, not being much accustomed to either where people were concerned. These vanishings, shadowy replacements, were to him — except for his mother, who was in her own way a shadow — normal to all human constituents. A day or so later, he couldn't have told the girl's name. But the minute she had said "Pick!" he'd taken it as an order, from somewhere behind them both too. Until then, he hadn't understood what the hoarded 5x8's were for.

The story he'd told her was simple in its extremity. His mother, Marda or Marta Jalecsy or Halecsy — he didn't know the correct spelling — had come to the U.S. as the youngest of a trio of sisters, the two elder of whom had come first, later sending her the fare. A job had been lined up for her, and he thought perhaps a husband — at least a man had appeared at the immigration dock to claim her but had disappeared after; perhaps the man had been paid. She hadn't been very good at jobs. Neither Edwin nor she had much idea of how long ago this was. Here he'd hesitated, not out of shame but incapacity; it was always hard to explain to people about his mother, how she wasn't a moron or mixed up, and in some plodding ways very strong — merely how very simple she was. Perhaps this came over anyway, as he told how, after an indefinite time here, she had one night been attacked in a dark hallway, but never told her sisters of this or of her pregnancy — "She just let it grow," he said. When she came out of the hospital ward, the two sisters had already picked up and gone; among other things, because of the neighborhood, they had been afraid the baby might be Chinee. She had lost her papers, was illiterate, and actually couldn't say what country she was from, knowing only the name of the "small" town, the big town nearby, and the province. She had almost no stories of either. The modern names of the Slovak countries were unknown to her. He had no real knowledge of whether his own name was Edgar or Edwin. Only recently he'd discovered that the thick dialect they spoke together — he very haltingly, for she said little — must be Hungarian. He had found that out one night in a restaurant where she scrubbed — from a stray customer. The restaurant jobs were always the luckiest for them, since she could scarcely cook. He learned to. Earliest, she had worked "for the Jews," for a Jewish chicken butcher, until it was found she wasn't Jewish as assumed — this she did know and would have told them — and she'd been dismissed. Either because she couldn't learn the ritual for slaughter or because her presence was against it; she had never known which. But she was strong and knew a few good things — how to clean and to be clean was one of them — and she had found the cellar, passing meanwhile from one scrub job to another, mostly in stores, for she wasn't smart or "good" enough for the domestic trade.

It came out, in his brief summary, even to the girl listening, how very "good" his mother had been, at being silently poor. They had remained in the cellar, escaping censuses, elections, somehow all the numbers which bound most people to outside life. The relief bureau? — no, even if they had known about it, that depended on numbers too. Even if the two of them could have proved their existence, they had no way of proving, in the illegal hole where they lived for a small cash rental without receipts, how long they had been anywhere. No, he had never had anyone to stay with him in babyhood, as far as he knew. He must have picked up his first English when he had begun to accompany his mother; later he did it by imitation consciously, for a while from the priests. For, when he was quite tall, and had already had a few "jobs" on his own, he had remembered for her that she was Catholic, and they had gone to church — and under that influence he had been put in school at last, not the parochial but the public school. He had attended or hadn't, according to how he and she could manage. After it began to be understood — by him — how "good" he could be at school, he'd taught her that they must manage it, and recently they had.

The school — this grayish, battered trough for disinfectant, for a hard-mouthed staff climbed up from others like it, and always for the fleshy noise, weak or wild, of children — was to him, though he didn't say it, a dreamland. But it came out perhaps, to the teacher listening, how he'd acquired his dexterity with the stupid, with herself. For the rest — the neighborhood, mostly Chinese until one got to the pushcarts, had kept this couple to themselves, and him from the street life of his age, until he'd learned this too, at his "jobs." As far as could be seen, from his lightish hair and chub face, he was not a Chinee. "No —" the substitute teacher had sighed at the end of it all — "no, you really look *Hungarian* to me." This he had taken home with him too.

For he had no legend; obsessively this seemed to him the only differ-

ence between him and others, in the world that he knew. To him —
and this would be as much the measure of him as the intelligence many
found fresh and uncorrupted as an animal's — he was in every other
way in the prime and natural state of health, as much as any other boy.
The existence of riches, or even the modest lift of privilege which
would have raised him from the lowest, he bore with indifference, like
a moviegoer who had seen only two or three films (as was about his
score between school and parish house) to whom all Eldorado was
therefore the same. As yet he bore no grudge, for lack of a past for it to
spring from. But even in the bars where the Bowery bums got the 25-
cent shots and he and his mother sometimes scrubbed, he had heard
legend-scraps of family and nativity. In the rat-colored humidity of
these lowest depths, often such a brilliant rain of reminiscence came
over one of the clouded minds there, so much like a movie-flicker that
it was hard not to give it credit for being as real.

He had begun the filing system with his mother. Patiently as with a
cart horse, he had made her go over everything she knew, though at
first, seeing the "paper" ready in the shoe box, she was afraid, thinking
he'd somehow become involved with the police for whatever she and
he must have done wrong without knowing it. Slowly, she'd begun to
enjoy his questioning; he even fancied it had left her a little brighter
than she came to it. He made her describe over and over, for instance,
the man who had come with her sisters to be a pretend husband, since
this might after all have been a sort of father. He was pleased at the
slightest trace she could recall of the old country; once it was a pig-
sticking, which however stopped short of human detail, at the pig. He
began to hope, like the father of an idiot, that she would remember
more if she could only express it in her own language, of which, perhaps laid away somewhere, she might have more too. For a while it
was his highest ambition to meet another Hungarian, and bring him
home. (Instead, he was to find two — his aunts, known among the
Mannix retinue of suppliers, pensioners and hangers-on, all those
below the rank of guest but often fed and tended like these, as "the
Halecsy sisters," the Judge's sisters' dressmaker and milliner.) But all
that was to be later — and of course his aunts never came to the cellar.
Meanwhile, he had investigated everything he could think of, because
there was so little, and had stopped at nothing, even helped here by
what was special to him and his mother — that she had given him no

prior knowledge of what topics, in conversation with her or others, should be stopped at. But she remembered nothing about his father, her attacker. Nor was he able to make any more sequence of the years of their life than he knew for himself.

Then one night, he had a triumph. For as long as he could remember, his mother had worn the same coat, once black, once of a length and a shape, but now a kind of tireless no-garment suited to her looks and her losses; there was no telling her age from her looks now, but she was tireless too. When he understood that the coat belonged to her "upstairs life," in the days before the basement, he had to take deep breaths not to leap upon her to squeeze out the knowledge she must hold somewhere within, not to scare it away. The coat had been made for her, she finally said, by a sister — one of the two. It took him all evening to get the names of the sisters from her — her refusal ever to name them to him had been the only departure into emotion (other than her care of him, never expressed as emotion) that he had ever seen in her. He had never even been sure that it was a refusal, not merely that she was unable. But he understood at once that here was where he must probe. Something about the coat, now that she herself studied it, had affected her, perhaps only that like herself, after all the hours since that hallway — under all the morning haulings of water and the chapped candles of evening — it was still here. Before they slept, he had transcribed the two names from her guttural as best he could.

Another month or so lapsed before he did anything about it; he was possessed now by a strange inertia, the reluctance a fish might have before it made itself rise from the brown of the sea bottom, so soft with refuse it had paths through, into the blinding, rainbow air. He told no one about his inquiries once he did begin them, or rather no one of import, like the school registrar, who might help him too readily, with one grand push. Now and then, however, he begged hints on how to go about such research from people almost as low in the scale as he and his mother, who would be safe. For he had the wariest sense that he was meddling with life processes which had brought him forth into conditions which were meant to keep him where he was. And he had to do it on his own.

"Missink poyson, bureau vom missink poyson, dot's vat ya van," said a peddler for whom he sometimes "worked" — at sorting the rotten fruit down into the underlayers of the baskets to be sold, for which he was paid in kind. In an unguarded moment he had answered this with a statement of his own — then quickly taken up his pulpy earnings and gone on. Behind him, he had seen the peddler make a sign to his wife. "*Meshuggenah,* that little *goy.*" He wasn't used to being called crazy, but well used to the other — apparently the unknown half of him was neither Chinee nor Jew. For often he was called *goy* even by peddlers who didn't know his mother, and he thought of this as one more step along a path of elimination by which he might possibly present himself to all the nations of the earth one by one, so that he might get the answer "No — not us." Definition of what he *was* might even after that come hard, but he had one, of a sort. "No, *we* are the missing persons," he'd said to the peddler. And this he truly believed.

In the post office, on a rainy off afternoon, he'd inquired for a city directory. "My God, take ya till doomsday, even if I could give ya, kid!" said the idler behind the grating. "Whyn't ya try the phone?" The man had even held out to him, with a grand sweep of the arm, a last year's phone book, or he might never have looked in such a place. For several nights, after his lessons, he scanned slowly through the Y's, the J's, and at last the H's. When he found it, he had his first sensation of fear, mixed with awe. Somehow, he had never thought of anyone connected with him and his mother as having a phone.

Even if he had known for sure how to handle one, he wouldn't have used it for his purpose, and not only because his mother was as ignorant as he; if one rang in a restaurant late at night when the chairs were up, she continued silently scrubbing, or if it persisted, picked it up and listened, shaking her head at how the thing chattered at her. No, the only way to use what he had found was the straight method of the miracle, which was what he viewed it as, and what he told his obedient mother — they were going uptown for a miracle. He had never been uptown, but he committed to memory the line of print in the phone book, and never even put it on a card. It was too big a fact for one.

On the Sunday then, cleaned and buttoned as if for church, he had set out with her from the cellar, on directions obtained. The finding of the house had that calm rhythm which he thought must precede all miracles; after a smooth subway ride, a short walk and a steep climb to the fifth-floor flat, he rang the bell. The sisters were home — and in a way, all he had believed was true. The door opened, and the sisters recognized each other — three faces nibbled by life. His mother had fainted on the doorstep, tired at last.

It developed that the two old maids had always been ashamed of this sin of their "youth" — it was understood that they meant their youth in this country, since even at the time of their desertion, these two had not been young. Now that their sister and her boy were here — and he, from quick, sharp glance was certified as no Chinee but under his glasses a plain-featured boy, tall as a middle-sized man but wearing pants still too long for him — well, yes, the two had been missed. Hot chocolate was given them in atonement, and in time he would have his legend too, not too much of a one, as sifted through these two, but with its central fact, for him enough.

But by that time, the Mannixes, ever acquisitively generous — had him. Under their aegis, more had happened to him externally than a collegium of schoolmen expert at miracles could have chartered. Between then, which had been 1944, and now, June 1951, he had gone (with the aid of summer school and outside reading, in which the Judge had always been happy to guide him) from the ninth grade through Harvard, and one year into law school. On the very day he had met them he had already discovered — to be concealed from all but them until the oddity of those lost years faded — his real age. But the moment on the doorstep remained the miracle. It was the one in which he'd discovered what his true poverty was. Such a moment — in which emotion, only that instant discovered like a great valve, is at the same instant fulfilled — wasn't easily counterfeited. It remained the exquisite moment of his life. Despite this, he still kept on with the cards. From sense of duty alone he would have gone to them, the way a man would tend with rake and spade his birthplace, where personality had begun.

He and his mother lived now in affluence, in fifty-dollar-a-month rooms which the Judge's sisters had found for them near some of their own properties in the Czech-Slovak part of Yorkville, two rooms with an inside toilet, in a bathroom tiled with many remnant colors by a landlord who was also a housewrecker by trade, but still a tiled bath. By the accident of the city, the rooms, in a neat tenement between church property and the Mannix sisters', were less than ten blocks from the Mannix house itself. And because the place was his, whether he came home to it from that other house or from the ivied stone and bear rugs of the Harvard dormitories, it was still the ultimate in luxury. He'd already known about inside toilets of course, from the restaurants. Sophistication can only come to a man once. After that — as after his own first visit to the Mannix house — he can only be surprised.

The sunlight came in now on the wooden filing case, used as a desk also, which had supplanted the old, heavy-paper accordion files he used to steal; once he had taken a particular after-school job because on a man's desk in that office, he had caught sight of such a file. All change in him since had been his slow, natural reaction to circumstance. "If I had to choose an epitaph to put on your tombstone, Edwin, I know what it would be," the Judge had once joshed him. "Edwin Halecsy, a learner."

The Judge was a deadpan josher, with a great sense of humor, sour and raw, with flashes even of obscenity, all of which went with basics Edwin had learned too early ever to forget — and was part of why he could learn so well from the Judge. For there were certain kinds of fakery — the fake irony of many of his instructors was one — which sank to nothing the minute he remembered to test them against the badlands of his youth. Curiously, he didn't hate his early years; these remained to him his integrity, persisting alongside his pleasanter path like an always accessible reservoir, plumbless with monsters but *known,* necessary as water to life, and with the same taste to it as water — plumbless too, but what every man knows. He knew a lot about himself he never bothered with. If asked whether a learned honesty, acquired so late and so clinically, was different from the usual, his answer, to himself at least, would have come at once from that reservoir: "Yes."

The late sun was casting its beams through a window he valued, both for the colored reflections from the window of the yellow brick parish-house wing of the church next door, and because its own light, interrupted by the strong, ugly steeple, had a look of the view at the northwest rear of the Mannix house, blocked by a water tower, of whose influence on their history the Judge had told him. That same visit — on Edwin's declaring for the law — the Judge, silent but upright behind the desk in that study known to be the hallowed scene of all his days, had then said, "Reach up there! No, up there!" When Edwin handed down the designated volume, he'd been presented with it — an old calf copy of John Bouvier's law dictionary, dated 1839.

"*Devise* realty; *bequeath* personalty," the Judge said with a glint. "First thing I learned, though not from there."

In the room here, aside from a row of other presentation books kept separate from those he had acquired in Cambridge, there were small touches of gifts the Mannixes had given him unwittingly, bought at Woolworth's with his own money — a jar of cut flowers whose form Anna might have recognized, a green, tin-shaded lamp like the Judge's own tole. For the rest, the room was cleaner than the usual student's, kept so by his mother, but otherwise not elaborate, if one could forget — as neither of them ever quite did — that its light flowed never-failing from a meter, and its water ran.

His mother had changed little externally; internally much more than he. Cellar living had forced her intelligence, even as a caged animal could learn to walk a treadmill. Now, humanized by this unexpected warmth, giving herself over entirely to her sisters and to him, she had *stopped*. By day, she sometimes worked as a cleaning attendant in a nearby beauty salon — from which came the fiction given out by his aunts that their sister was a hairdresser. Often, there or at home, in the simple pleasure of being where she was she forgot what she was at, but since a very little push served to activate her again, she was never troublesome. In the evening, as she sat in the steam-heated apartment, her eyes, used to cellar cold, streamed continually. Sometimes, staring at her across the table, he wasn't sure that these tears were only rheum. In the early years of their partnership, her person had been a heavy blank to him, dependable hindrance as well as help. Now, in the way a good Catholic, or a half-one, might begin to over-interpret the heavy image of the Madonna lugged with him through the years, she began to seem wise. She had a new black coat.

It was time to shave and dress. He resisted — anticipation at these times was always part of the pleasure, and the recall also — then went into the bathroom to turn on and wait for the hot water, which ran slow. Seven years had made him younger only in what he thought of as the surface of his mind. Physically, he seemed to himself to have grown younger also, though this was mostly because of his clothes. In the slums, children's-size clothes were never as cheap secondhand as the tramp-trousers sold at stalls for under a dollar. For years he had lived in the anonymous crotch-smell of others, and had rarely seen, as other boys did daily, the gradual rising of his own knees. His hair, grown in a thick sprout from his crown, had been cut with scissors, one of their few tools, kept safe from the roaches with some bits of cutlery in a tin box, which the rats could knock over but never prise.

Now his head was clipped almost as smooth as a knuckle, and he wore army pants and the scuffed white sneakers which were beginning to be the other sign of his generation's youth. In the mirror, he could see behind him his jacket hung ready, to one side of a laden set of shelves. Sometimes in his dreams, dressed as of old, he found himself seated at an examination desk, on whose blank white paper he was being required to write down the names and uses of all the objects piled before him in a huge mound of human goods as high as the Resurrection — from shoe polish to tinned soup, to lampshades and coat hangers, even drawers with keys, closets with doors, step-on garbage cans and silver napkin rings — all the paraphernalia of the civilized, and all yet blank to him. Then he always woke with heart-knocking relief, and moving only his eyes, head still thralled to the stone pillow of this almost conservative nightmare, numbered each of these very objects in his shelter now.

It wasn't so much as comforts he saw them but as signposts, and faintly ridiculous, the product of elves. No wonder seven years among them had made him younger. Once again he rose from his cot in the cat-piss of the cellar, stuck his feet into his St. Vincent de Paul Society shoes, washed with a sliver of Fels-Naphtha, lifted the trapdoor and angled his neck out above the pavement seams, into a morning gray as yer grandmother's cunt said a bum just passing, or into a Saturday job's bright burden of sunshine on the noon soot of the gutters, or into a scrubwoman's midnight, luridly striped as his fondest fancy, a slab of Neapolitan brick ice cream. He sometimes thought that while others in his new world aged properly enough, he might spend his whole life growing ever more greenly superficially innocent, up from the maturity of those streets.

In this new world, crowded with ideas and objects of which he was daily still discovering the habits and names, people seemed to float calmly atop a wrack of these they had made peace with since the cradle. Fish-naked in his dreams, in his dreams he still walked toward these other denizens of the upper air, a man-fish flapping up the water-steps to *their* morning, in their own secondhand shoes. In his dreams they waited to receive him, and turn him back. But by day, they none of them seemed to notice what they had with them — the ancient young of the eel, colored with their own depths. By day, crossing Harvard Yard or ascending the Mannix stoop at a Christmas, he never mixed up their streets with his. Or better still for them, seemed not to grudge the difference. He could smile at that now, with an intelligence drawn from both sides; the differences *they* saw in him were so mild. But by night, by dream, a phone rang in the cellar — and his mother answered it.

He was knotting his tie when the real phone rang on the sunny desk.

"Hello —" he said. And as always as if his fists were up. Because he couldn't help that, but knew who was on the other end and why she mightn't like or trust him, he added blithely, just for the hell of it, "This is the Halecsy residence."

"Hallo," said Anna. "You don't say."

They were too near each other socially. She must hate to serve him on a par with her darlings (even though they might be his also) — the way nigger messboys in university commons disliked serving their own color when it ate on a fellowship.

"And how are you, madame, are you feeling the summer?" But he could never strike the right note of chaff with her, the way other young visitors could at once, Austin or Walter, on whom it was as easy as the leather of their shoes.

"I feel your backside for you, you come again late." He was the only one she sounded coarse with. If he hadn't known her secure position in that household, he'd have thought the footing he had there somehow frightened her.

"What are we having?" he asked, meaning "Who's coming?" or "Who'll be home?" By their favorite dishes, he could know. Not ham if David were already home; steak for Austin, a squash player as anyone would know, which Austin would laugh at himself. It might even be veal with olive — the dish of *her* choice; she had never had a homecoming until now. . . . Though he would settle for any of the "big" dishes which would mean the presence of them all.

"What *we?*" Anna said gruffly.

It was only what the others always said. But he wouldn't repeat it. In recesses he'd never known he had until he went to that house, he could now be hurt.

"Judge say you be here six." She knew well enough, when she bothered to consider, that the Judge was his law. And even she did bother to; they all did, without hierarchy, extending the gift of their solicitude to him who was as yet only a frequenter, just as equally as to Pauli Chavez, their old family friend, and to the Judge's first cousin Miss Augusta, who were among the solid habitués. His own knowledge of these gradations was even a sign of how they were training him to it. This was how it was when people lived not behind trapdoors but in houses. They all were concerned with what each other felt and did, down to the last and smallest thing. Happy families always were.

"But dinner's still at eight?" he said.

"Yah. Like always." But she knew his privilege, an hour and a half with the Judge. Tonight, it would be more.

"Anna . . ." His voice had lightened and he was holding the phone easily now. "Give the Judge a message for me, huh, a special one."

"Yah?"

"Tell him very carefully, huh?"

"So, yes?"

"Tell him — he wants a great copy of Fearne's *Essay on the Learning of Contingent Remainders and Executory Devises* — I know where."

"*Hah?*"

He repeated it joyously. He was learning their mischief, the younger Mannixes' of course; surely he was learning how to have a humor-book of his own?

She hung up on him, something he was unsure she'd ever do to one of them. But he was so pleased with himself and all his expectations — life ones, all fined down to the point of this evening, any evening with one or all of them — that he clicked down the phone as lightly as if born to it, and merely thumbed his nose at her, one of the politer gestures from his old repertoire. Since it was only five o'clock and a ten-minute walk, he opened the file again — then, with an affectionate sweep, as if he were dismissing a younger brother, he riffled the cards with the back of a thumbnail and closed the drawer.

The shadows were stealing in; it was going to be one of those fog-bound, all of a sudden mystery evenings in which he best loved to approach the house, drifting through the dusk on a kind of waltz time, toward that food, those lights, stepping past the areaways — even cel-

lars thereabouts were high-tone, though he would never live in one —
looking proudly about to see other passersby who weren't going there.
He picked up a case he had been studying, pleased to have it negligent
now in his hand — Cardozo J. in People v. Defore, 242 N.Y. 13, 21
(1926) — one of the Judge's favorites, he surmised, from its being so
often open there in the study; now that he was in law school himself,
the Judge never much talked law. Although the air was turning too
lavender for reading, he let it come without lamps, pushing its lilac
around him, letting him muse on his anticipations and over and over,
seven years over, on their source. He didn't need the file to remind
him; no matter how often he flipped the cards and stared, his first visit
was always the one returned to in the end. A major one, most major of
all, it had set a pattern for all the others. A major visit was one in
which all three members of the family, plus the two boy visitors he had
met there that day, were all there. . . .

The trouble with a miracle is afterwards — what do you do *then?*
Ever since loaves and fishes had once upon a time fed a multitude,
Christians had had to face this problem. In the first weeks afterward,
his mother, Marda, did it most primitively and best — she sat and
gaped. But the aunts were members of the church. Faced with this
awesome revisitation of the blood relative, there on their own frieze
sofa that mother and boy sitting upright, raw to the nails with laundry
soap but with the mordant air of that other district in every pore —
the aunts thought at once of jackets and coats. After all their own trade
was cloth — a covering.

For this occasion, Edwin's hair had been professionally cut, at his
request instead of his usual cash pay, in the barbershop where he was
sometimes a juvenile runner for the policy game whose headquarters
were in the back. The barber had done it for nothing in the end, and
Edwin, used to the benevolences of the poor, had accepted it as he
would later those of the rich — with the grace of an ignorance where
charity began. But though his schoolwork to date had barely warned
him of what distinctions life could make once it was able to raise
itself a minim above the need to eat and pee, he already could recognize smartness anywhere, and had seen at once that his aunts — only
more complex than his mother because there were two of them —
didn't have much of it. At first he had told them that he needed "the
facts" — as he called them — for school. The aunts' instinct, however,

after the first flush of anecdote, had been to measure him for trousers, not legend. His reply had been direct; unless they could produce what he wanted, he refused to be made respectable. Blackmail was known to him only in the jiujitsu of the gutter: use any lever handy. His mother of course did whatever he told her. On the sisters' tan sofa, hard from never being sat on except fleetingly by the soft parts of customers, the pair therefore sat, his mother in her heirloom black, he in his bankers' lice-gray.

By the fourth visit, a Jewish feast day when the markets were closed, all the tenants of the neat walk-up knew of this couple who "belonged" to the fifth-floor front, of the relationship (not cousins as the aunts had first let get about), and even, in such terms as they could understand it, of the boy's quest. A bachelor neighbor, a long, mild watchmaker named Schwer, was aiding the Halecsys in this, but old passports were not the easiest to find in the curly forests of a milliner's world, the other half of which specialized in "alterations." Had they even kept them, the sisters asked one another? "And what does the boy want from his bastardy?" whispered the oldest sister in Hungarian. "He can't get a *name* out of it!" To which the middle sister replied, "But maybe if we find it, we could ask *them*. Maybe they could get him one." This significant reference to the Mannixes, and their place in the minds of many of their acquaintances, went half unobserved. While feathers were sifted, plus the hat-and-hem scraps of many decades. Edwin sat on in his many layers of gritty sweater, his mouth full of cake like any boy, but otherwise refuser of the most delicate offers — Schwer's own discarded pea jacket, a newly bought pair of mittens — though it was on into the cold season outside. He sat primly, still unnerved by this comfort of real tables and chairs and food not scrounged for, and unable to see more than half of it at a time — the spectacle-string dangling on his nose.

Just before the cocoa boiled, the passports were found, along with a bunch of buckles which brought memories — "Remember these!" — and while he waited breathless, several inspirations for hats.

"Come, come — now we're in business," said old Schwer, and gave the boy a bachelor shrug he never forgot — even now, sitting here in his tortoiseshell rims, their twin lenses both sparkling clear, he treasured it — a first titbit of intimacy, extended the wolf-child. His mother's passport wasn't with the sisters', but those would do, as a beginning.

From then on Schwer would have to calculate the intervals — until Marda came over, until she was waylaid, until Edwin was born. . . .

Schwer sat them all down at the dining-table under the hanging lamp — milliners' memories were a feather forest too.

"No cocoa *now*," said Schwer. At last he had his considered entries, set as if in a Bible, on the black-lined guide-page of a school pad, in his spider script. The final interval was the easiest. "And now —" said Schwer, leaning back — "ask her if he was a full-term child." Schwer had conducted all the inquiry this way, very formally; the boy, watching, saw that he could never have done it that businesslike himself. He didn't help his mother with her answer, or help them to get it from her — fearful that he might affect its official value. Yes, she nodded, though with a shrug, when at last she understood what was wanted of her — yes, as far as she knew. And so, it was done. And Schwer, after a final calculation, the most workmanlike checking, and a last midwife flourish of the pen — gave him his age.

It was a moment less pure than on the doorstep only a few weeks ago, but more powerful, complicated with action, which for all his studies then and now was the element he best knew. The age itself, to a boy that young, was a revelation. Though from body manifestations he'd suspected he must be older than the "school" age by grade, which was all he had, three years more was a shock; at that age many boys in the district were already fathers, and though he had skipped another term just recently, he was still only in the ninth grade. The evening light itself, coming in the windows just as now but with the steel of winter in it, seemed to him biblical. Through his steaming lenses, the coarse glass lampshade of crude yellow, red and blue, blurred like the coat of many colors, though unlike Joseph, he wasn't being put out in the desert to die. His mouth was full of bread; he was being received. Around the table he saw the two sisters, more worried now, even aghast; he saw his mother as usual, dependent on him, waiting in her timid way for a cue to smile. Only Schwer, with some sense, put out his hand, with a sweep of accomplishment. "Like a christening," he said. "We get some schnapps."

After a moment, he gave his own hand into Schwer's, not understanding that allusion, but full of his own. Not to know one's name or one's father — this could happen to any foundling. But not to know one's age, and then, after this saints' supper of raised and lowered heads, to know it — was the difference between never having been born — and being born.

He was standing on the dais the aunts used for fitting customers, waiting to be measured for trousers, a Roman-striped kitchen towel pinned round his waist over his ragged BVD's, when Schwer came back with a bottle, letting enter in front of him a girl staggering under such a long, lumpy bundle of clothing that the only parts of her visible were her mittened arms clasped round it, and her head in its winter parka, above. Schwer, his whole lank personality blooming under the afternoon's accomplishment, moved forward with an air of having brought the girl along with his schnapps, and even said largely, "Here he is, the famous nephew"; each aunt said, "Miss Ruth!", then one muttered, "Our nephew — we found each other only a few weeks ago," and the other moved forward to take the bundle, saying "Miss Ruth . . . here . . . let *me*."

A screen had hastily been placed around his lower half and he was left to stand there, accepting this too as reasonable; things happened to him up here that he would have punched for or kicked out at, blindly or with vicious aim, in the district, but up here he merely suffered them, absorbed in every newness. The word "nephew" for instance. Of course he'd known its meaning and could spell it the way he could spell almost anything. But it had been years before he'd finally met all the relationships in the human family and could refer to them easily. This was only to be expected of a boy reared under such a scant list of them and three of those mythical: Mother, Son, Father, Sisters, Aunts. As for physical shame, his mother, dressing in front of him in the basement, and having to let him do the same, had given him what little differentiation she could; they had turned their backs on one another, they'd been as modest as hall toilets allowed, and never slept in their clothes if they had a change of them. Nose-picking, farting and belching, crotch-scratching and blowing the nose through the fingers, had all had to be learned away. As he once more cast back, he knew that although dozens of other novelties had over the years been tabulated, if he went deep enough the supply was inexhaustible.

Oddly, the girl, in her parka and with her bundle, enough resembled those at school so that at first she was merely another of a sex which had already given him his adolescent heats, but with whom as yet — as with all beings outside the fiercely sequestered circle of his and his mother's needs — he had had little to do. By rights, this particular girl, for her effect on his destiny, should have had a yellow nimbus scratched in the air above the white bunny-hat he didn't yet know wasn't fake fur like the others'. When she took her mittens off, the bitten nails, childishly swollen at the tips like half the kids he did know, made him feel, for the first time in this cocoa-and-whisper-soaked haunt of old-maid women, at home. Later, her sex itself would overtake him, but in her case almost inconveniently added to what else was already there.

. . . For, of all the people to come in the next seven years of his life, Ruth Mannix, in some central way he couldn't fathom, was the least strange. Recently, if she'd become at times dizzily sweet or light in his dreams of her, a modest pastel of gaieties and reflections, he knew this was more her environment sparkling down on him, molding her into manners and prettinesses whose style, met around Harvard, was the same as many girls'. Sexually, she was never the solitary occupant of his young man's dream. Something else, central to her, had made them at once natural with each other. She and he were not *like*. He didn't have with her the intellectual kinship he was as oddly to find with her father. Nor was it "sympathy" she gave him, unlike her brother David, who gave it too broadly to everyone.

Except for the seven years of his association with her family, what did he have in common with this calm, sweetly cool girl who hadn't even gone to college so far, and still spent her time at the ballet bar except when, in her lovely, filial way that moved even young people — she was companioning her father? Yet she, for all her legend, and he, Edwin the half nameless — shared. That was the feeling. She'd found him of course, and brought him home to that family for the afternoon, for seven years, for — he couldn't help hoping — forever. But the feeling antedated that; therefore he'd given up hunting for its source. He'd never before or since been met so intuitively. Therefore, what she and he shared must be something native to both their lives before. . . .

So Schwer had moved on into the room after her with his pint bottle. A pint, in the pocket or empty in the gutter, was what one had in the district too. "Come, come," said Schwer, who'd had a few drinks on the way, capering over behind the aunts' backs to broach the sacred china closet for its red-and-gilt glasses.

But the aunts too meanwhile were moving, peculiarly undulant, like the green fronds in the fishbowl at school, at the approach of the single, golden fish. Between them, the girl stared at him up there on his dais with his towel.

"So you're back, Miss Ruth," said the aunt who held the bundle, but still with that elegant sway, while the other murmured, "And how is it these days, on the other side?" The two backed up in horror at the sight of Schwer's laden tray, with a "Not whisky, Miss Ruth, Schwer, not for Miss Ruth," and a last "Watch the tray!" as Schwer, with a "Nonsense, babies get it for the digestion, it's only kümmel," handed glasses all round. He saw his mother receive one, with that hollowing of the shoulders which offered her unworthiness for all to see. He saw the girl see it. Then the girl, pushing back her hood, moved forward, holding up her glass. Behind her the aunts muttered in their almost unison, "We are fitting him for a suit, a fine suit of the best wool, Miss Ruth" — though a moment ago it had been cotton crash they had been talking about and only trousers. Then Schwer — with a "Happy birthday, Eric!" — put a glass in his own hand.

Schwer had misnamed him, but in every fairy tale there was a flaw. The light in the room declined to ordinary. He felt the burden of the three extra years. The aunts' faces looked foxy; even his mother's wasn't quite blank. What was the trap here? But then the girl came forward, all by herself now, and smiled, maybe to assure him that tales here had wonders past their own flaw. Normally he wasn't a wild-looking boy, only a meager one, but in the past weeks, to spur his aunts' search, he'd left his hair uncut, and now he felt himself to be that boy-beast, up from the street's bowels, of later dreams to come. She held out her glass, in a gesture he didn't know. His empty hand half moved out to take hers before he understood. He reached over his shielding screen as over a balcony; they clicked glasses. In the same flash, he said to himself, *She's smart*, meaning perhaps that she was good. Good was a word whose uses he had trouble assigning even now. But she meanwhile had seen, he was sure, how smart *he* was — meaning *smart*. She drank from her glass then, and he followed suit, tossing it down in the only way he'd ever seen men booze — and when the liqueur burned its way down, stood his ground.

"How old *are* you?" She was the first to ask, in the world of his new age.

"Eighteen," he said. The numbers were bright in his head: fifteen plus three, simpler than algebra, but whether loss or gain was yet to be seen.

"I'm fourteen."

He stared back, unblinking. "I was fifteen yesterday."

She widened her eyes, gray between lashes lighter than her hair, which made the face somehow recede and seem gentler than it was, but said nothing. The aunts, sipping with Schwer, hadn't heard.

Twenty minutes later, he and the girl were walking to the Mannix house, along much the same route he would walk tonight. This girl now knew all about him, at least what the aunts could tell, plus — between the lines, as she watched him listening to his own story — all he didn't say. If she now knew the reason for his last strange remark, she didn't mention it. Later, rarely as he saw her, he grew to depend on the reserve in her that was so much easier on him than other people's openness, particularly those who were as eager as social workers to talk with him about his rise in life, to clock his feelings and to insert their own sympathies, or rather their images of themselves as sympathetic people. Ruth, on the contrary, had a clued, trail-dropping way of assuming you knew she understood what you didn't say. Perhaps this arose from her own position deep in that family where, as the younger, the petted, the uncrippled, she was so dearly encircled — but they really didn't want to hear what she had to say.

Sometimes, with the Judge and Anna, and even with David, he had the strongest impression that they were afraid to hear — and not out of concern for her frailty, but for their own. More probably, this was merely one of the hundred and one ways in which he was still ignorant of the appearance of love. For at times he still couldn't tell whether his discriminations about people weren't the commonest in the world, his youth had had so few. The Mannix house had become the laboratory where he learned.

On that day he'd trotted after the girl down the four flights of the aunts' stairs, carrying for her a bundle of repaired dark blue dresses exactly like those she had brought. The aunts had maneuvered his going with her, why so greedily he couldn't say, over a delivery job for which, as they had carefully whispered to him, he must take no pay — later he appreciated better the role played in the affairs of men by the calculations of the most stupid women. He was willing, already addicted to the electric shocks of newness this world supplied. At the door, the aunts stopped the girl; like any of the old peddler-wives in the market, their most leading conversations took place at the door. From the girl's slight smile at him, she knew this too.

"Over there the other side, Miss Ruth sweetheart, how was it? You and your father had a good time?"

"Well, you know . . . the *war* . . ." the girl said patiently, as if she was teaching the word to them. "Daddy only got us over because of the refugees — you know . . . the people he brings here."

He'd listened dimly. They had the war in the district too of course, loudest in school and in barbershop, and in the Masses for the soldier-dead, in church. But he had to get to Harvard before he heard it much in conversation, and in the very overtone first heard in the voice of this rich young girl. The rich and educated — for so often these still went together, in spite of boys like him — always had the war more on their minds than the poor did. And it wasn't always because they had more time and perspective or even investment. The rich liked to be rich in conscience too.

"But the best thing for me —" the girl said eagerly — "was Daddy and Madame Fracca. Madame *Ninon* Fracca."

"Ah?" The aunts repeated the name, softly barring the door. "Madame . . . a lady?"

There wasn't a change in the girl's calm expression, no suspicion of a smile on her sugar-clean complexion — he didn't even know why he thought there might be, but observed that she could see through the two aunts as if their small, clockwork motives took place behind glass. There was a whole upper atmosphere of opinions, attitudes, intelligences in and around people, for which he hadn't the words yet but felt in the periphery of his skin, the way one feels a new countryside. This girl was the first to make him sense its existence. And that afternoon in her house — so quickly to become for him, as for all, the Judge's house — was to open up, like an avenue to be walked down, his place in it.

"Mistress at the Royal. The Ballet. She watched me try out. Maybe, when the war's over, they'll take me — if I keep on hard. Anyway, she persuaded Daddy to let me go on with it." The girl said this all in a rush, then drew back, as if she had given the aunts too much for their minds to hold. He watched, from his new and peculiar edge of distance, enthralled by the revelation that he could.

"Miss Ruth —" Both aunts shook their heads. "For why you want to be a ballet dancer, a girl like you?" Under her cool silence they retreated, then rallied, together. "Your aunts feel the same."

But this girl's aunts, no matter how much the Halecsy sisters invoked them as patrons or friends, would not *be* the same. He felt that, when the girl said merely, "Miss Halecsy — my bundle."

The bundle was brought at once, flutteringly. Here he spoke — forgetting merely to watch and learn, he was so interested — "But it's the same one!" — and everybody laughed.

"Miss Ruth belongs to a club," said the aunts. "To wear uniforms at school."

"Oh," he said. "Catholic." He felt brave to speak at all, yet knew somehow that he must begin to.

"No, not Catholic," said one aunt. Both shook a heavy frown at him — was it a disgrace to be? "No, the school don't ask uniforms. But the girls in Miss Ruth's club they all wear them, so the poor girls don't feel shame at what the other ones got." They appealed to him, wispy brows raised, under hair trodden to a brown grass by innumerable hats. "Now, isn't that ni-ice?"

He didn't get any of this, but he'd already begun to dislike this kind of whine. "Uh-huh."

It was then the girl blushed. "Well, thank you, Miss Gerda, Miss Ulla." She made them give her the bundle, then handed it over to him with a friendly smile — not to a delivery boy, to a boy. "Thank you very much, and good-bye," she said, in the same cool gush girls at school used, imitating maybe their mothers — and transcending accents. The aunts heard none of this, never would. He took all these soundings.

"Three inches at the hems!" the aunts called down the stairs after them. "How you girls growing! Every one of them had to be faced."

The walk was twelve blocks up and four avenues over. She led him. He clasped the bundle, dry-cleaned maybe, but it still smelled like much of the cloth his aunts worked on, cloth that had never really been dirtied, soft with its own worth. His trousers itched and crawled on his thighs from the yellow soap his mother rubbed and steeped them in, but there was nothing to be done with stale cloth. All the way to the Mannix house, he and that bundle exchanged smells. And on the way there, he, Edwin Halecsy of his district, and Ruth Mannix, of hers, had this exchange also:

"That woman they didn't introduce me to," she said. "Who was she? The one with — with a coat on."

"My mother." He shifted the bundle, and walked a way on. "They're going make her a new one."

At the next corner, she said, "Want me to take a turn?", and he answered no.

At the next, he said, "Your father — he need you to work? That he won't let you dance?"

She walked on a way before she too said no — and while they waited for traffic, " — Not to work, that is."

"Your mother work?"

She never answered that one at all. But they were just turning west, on the corner she indicated, when she said in that other imitative voice, "Your aunts and mine know each other."

He nodded matter-of-factly. "Customers."

She touched his arm. "The club, it isn't like that now, not like what your aunts said. It *was* — we were just kids, we had that idea. But the uniforms turned out too expensive. At first, that is. The cash outlay. Some girls couldn't always . . . pay all at once — and — we couldn't ask the Halecsys to wait. So it all ended up . . . social. And Diddy, that's my older brother David, said we had a better lesson in economics than we could even get at Dalton."

He never mixed up life with what he learned at school. But he knew the word "economics" of course. "Sure," he said virtuously, "and my aunts got what to work."

She looked at him cautiously, as if he'd made a joke. "But my *father* —" She gave a nervous laugh, as people did before a joke of their own. "He said, 'No, David, a *political* lesson. Because the girls still have their club.' "

He nodded, deeply, into that cloth. "Politics, that's the best mob." He slung the bundle to the other shoulder. "I wouldn't mind doing that, not at all." It was what the number runners always said.

Another avenue was crossed; they were going down a side street again. "Only two more blocks across," she said. "But long ones."

They were indeed long, for not talking. After a while, she gave that same laugh. "The Moka girls — that's what Diddy and I call my aunts and yours because they're always having cocoa together — they keep wondering about it. Whether he's going to 'bring another woman into the household,' they call it. My father. They talk about it all day."

From what he knew of Mott Street environs, and the vague, amoral world outside it, he considered which households might have two wives in them. "You Hindu?" he said.

"*What?* No, of course not, whyever why!" She peered at him again as if he was tucking back a joke or a riddle. "We're Jews." She said it proudly, the way all Jews did, the ones he knew.

"I know a lot of Jews," he said. "But I found out I'm not one by my father's side . . . No, I mean, you know — two wives."

"Oh," she said. And then, quickly — "No, they meant . . . another woman . . . after my mother."

"Oh." So she had a gap too. "Or they could mean you," he said. "Two women in one kitchen." He spoke with market-stall wisdom.

"You're funny," she said. "How could they mean me?" But she looked dubious. She glanced down at her knees, bare above their knee socks. For some reason, he looked down at where his own knees were, in their shuffling pants.

"Well, maybe not," he said. But this was a subject he knew well; in school conversation, mothers and fathers mythically arrived and went with rapidity, and replacements were made for known reasons: "To mind the kids, he did it," or "She's a widow but she can't get the pension," or, from the peddlers, "He got hot pants. Better he should have it at home." And there were often other considerations as discussable. "Well," he said, as reasonably as he had heard it said and believed it to be. "Maybe they're right. It's always another mouth to feed."

This time she did laugh right out loud. "Excuse me," she said. "I know that's not funny. But you are." Then she gave him a serious stare. "Diddy would like you," she said.

He didn't respond. Projections of that sort were not real to him. Ahead, at some distance, he could see green. "What park is that?"

"Central."

"I was there once. They took us. From school." He was about to walk on in that direction when she touched his arm again.

"No, we go one more block north now," she said. "I don't know why I always do it this way, but I always leave this one block."

This was clearly a ritual, like step-on-a-crack, break-your-mother's-back; he had them too. "I know. It's what called an o-bession." He read whatever he could get, understood only by osmosis or not at all, and had no dictionary. "It's like for me, revolving doors. Like when I meet them on some restaurant job. I always have to let it go twice around before I duck in."

She nodded, and for the first time they swapped glances, in some warmth, and walked on comfortably.

"Your mother," he said. "Which D?"

She moved her head very slowly. Her hands stopped swinging. "I don't — what do you mean?"

It was the common ordinary way in which his schoolmates asked one another about family gaps; to do it was a friendly sign — *Which D was yours?*

"Dead, divorced or disappeared," he said.

She stopped in her tracks. "It's this block," she said in a muffled voice, and made no move to go on. He didn't know anything to do but wait. Suddenly she reached over and grabbed the bundle from him, glaring at him as if he'd stolen it. Then she put her chin in it and started walking again, her face half hidden in it. He walked beside her, shifting pace so that they were in stride. "Dead," she finally said.

They went another half-block in silence before she said, "There, toward the end of the next one. Down there, across the street. Second from the corner. That's our house."

That brought him to. Before, he had been walking through a mist of streets, though it was a bright enough day. This was like the moment when he raised the trapdoor into a clear sky, climbed out of it, and stood erect. On some mornings, his flesh yearned backward, to his hole; cellar living wasn't all bad, even for the mind. But now he had come up into a street abandoned by the Saturday jostle he knew, or never entered by it. Here and there on both sides, parlor bays were set festive for robbery, curtains parted on the gleams of tables and silver pitchers; one showed a tall column topped by a stone bust. Down where she pointed, a continuous blur of high stoops and entrances paused at a peaked house, then the stooped one which was hers, and ended at a larger building on the corner, with a speared iron fence that made more sense. Above the park at the end, clouds flew like pennants. There were no pushcarts. The street had chosen itself, like a drawing. It had not been decreed.

"Give me the bundle back." He took it from her. It felt warm against him, a half hiding-place.

She looked sideways at him, as if she knew this. They were standing still again. She was meditating a question. Her lip trembled; he saw with a kind of relief that there was a smudge on it, of soot. She tossed her head. "Your father," she said. "Which D?"

Before then, he'd always answered, "Disappeared." Saying that had been a real convenience to him, like all the other phrases in which it was safest to converse. The truth, told once to the head worker in a settlement house, had come out in her face like a dirty word.

"Well, what?" said the girl. "I told *you*." She no longer looked hostile. "It can't be worse than —" A frown bemused her face, clouding it as if she were searching for a better word or a new one. "Than — *dead*."

He wasn't seeing her either, but that word, read but never heard aloud, which he now pronounced just as he had in the settlement house. "My mother, she was rapped," he said. "So about him, I don't know what."

"She was what?" she said, puzzled.

For fourteen, she wasn't wise to much. Or else he'd said it wrong, as often with the commonest word, from never hearing it at home. "Rapped," he said, like in a class spelling bee. "R-a-p-e-d, rapped."

She said it to herself in an undertone, "R-a-p —" then "Oh," and then "Oh, I see."

After a minute they began walking again, slow. He was having a trouble. The rich saliva of confession had backfilled his throat, making him want to cry there, though he did not want to do so in his *mind*. Already a lightness was there, and a rest. He stole a look at her face, but the word hadn't come out on it.

Almost at the steps of her house, the learner in him came to his rescue. "What school do you — attend?" he said. He could never get enough of formal language, even now.

"Dalton." Her tone reminded him that she had already said it.

He hadn't known it was a school.

"Where do *you* go?"

"Thirty-one," he said. He saw her doubtful look. "P.S. 31. On Monroe and Gouverneur." He was careful to say as they did in the district, "Goooverneur." "Before that, Number Four. On Rivington and Pitt." Suddenly he grinned at her. He had caught her expression. "Streets," he said. "They're *streets*."

She nodded swiftly. "And how is it? Number Thirty-one?" She was smart too.

"How is it?" He was playing for time. Right then and there at the bottom of those steps was when he learned it — that everything these people had and were must be under eternal scrutiny by such as him; it was this that helped overwhelm him a few minutes later, when she opened the door. "How do you mean?" He knew the proper answer of course — in the district: "You think *yours* is strict!" or the currently popular "They chop us in the morning, fry us in the afternoon." Mostly the word was its own foulest answer. *School.* He had never dared defend it.

"Do you like it, I mean."

The question disarmed him — that up here it was possible to ask. He thought truly of his loved haven, his adventure-place where people spoke in full words and sentences, knew times and places, where there was always a thunder-clatter of others like him, or nearly, up and down the pie-cut metal steps which went round and round like the days there, on the blissfully neat reassurance of "Hang up your coats" and "Fold your hands." In the church-warmth of the library, more than half the books were not too torn to read. And in the halls there was a great, breasting wind always blowing; this was the hall-sound of the teachers haranguing like peddlers, selling how to and what to — and the chance of — a thousand 5x8's.

But like the Jew vegetable brokers, he would never touch his luck with superlative. He hunted for one of their wry avoidances of even the shadow of the shadow of satisfaction. None came. In the Bowery, however, there had been a spoiled priest who went from one bar to the other in apostrophes to his bottle. (And years later he, Edwin, floating on this wreckage wisdom of the plebs, would gather a reputation for pith, with the people at the top of the stairs.) Now he shrugged. Did he like school? "Keeps the rats down and blessed," he said. He saw a mouse-flicker of interest in her eyes.

At the top of the stoop, he started to hand over the bundle.

"No, come on in." She produced a key hung round her neck on a ribbon. "Doorkey child," she said with a grin. "Daddy says he wants us to get a lesson in responsibility. Really Anna made him do it, to save her steps."

At his school the key on a string had been a mere fact of life. He glimpsed a difference, between his clear palace-hovel version of life, and theirs. These people were accustomed to instill in their children habits which his underworld of circumstance gave him for free.

"Who's Anna?" was all he said.

"She's our — housekeeper. But she's really a member of the family." And later he would understand too that while Ruth might have been taught this glibness in order to avoid the genteel "our maid," it was also a muddledly affectionate but exact judgment on Anna's place. So did they create their own murk. But at the moment, he'd taken the word in the double way the district did; sometimes a "housekeeper" was the helper briefly sent in by the welfare agencies to a motherless family in desperate straits — and sometimes it was what the men, very simply and accurately too, called any woman whom they brought into the home but didn't marry.

The housedoor was heavy polished oak with a mail slot; he thought they must have a good landlord. On the lower East Side — a phrase for the district he hadn't heard yet — there were plenty of brownstone fronts converted to tenements. The idea of a single house, here in the city, was farther from his ken than were palaces — of which he had heard. In the vaguest way, he knew that there was more money and comfort here than at his aunts' — by the way the aunts deferred to it. He'd never gone home with any schoolmate; though he'd now and then been asked, there were always the jobs.

So there he had been, worlding on their innocent doorstep, delivered there by himself, on as much of a birthday as he would ever have. When he didn't come right in after her, the girl reached out, one hand still on the doorknob, and gave him a patting push inward, with the other. She hadn't seemed to mind the corruption of his clothing, from whose dim, anciently inhabited checkers whatever soul he had shrank with recluse instinct, saying mutely and with all a foundling's urge, "I'm Hungarian."

So it had really been she who bent down and took him up and in under that lintel — and for her own reason. There was a reason, clearly as if he had seen it like a gold paper star pasted between her eyes — as the kindergarten teachers sometimes did for those destined to be their favorites. To date he hadn't discovered what it was — except that all of Harvard couldn't help him here.

"Welcome to the Mannix house," the girl said.

The Westclox on his desk was glowing; summer dusk had shifted on and he was in danger of being late for his precious audience with the Judge. Yet he lingered. The electric clock was their gift too, the first Christmas here; against sense, he still half-shared his mother's reluctance to buy too many electrical appliances, from a care not to bleed this witchcraft too far. Lateness was his own small independence in the new world — chosen precisely because it wasn't the wisest one. He had his luxuries. There was nothing he wouldn't do if he really *wanted* to — and in the performance, he knew he had something the Mannixes lacked. For, whatever his own newer, educated self would *not* do, the old one would — and vice versa. Any tension between, he tried to think of as "caution," a rope continuously extended between what intellect brought in — cargoes of sparklers every day! — and what his dark, homely reservoir already held. Up to a point, he liked to keep reminiscence within the old language and boundaries, like a horse that half-liked the dim sensation of its blindered days. But to report anything that had happened after that doorstep, and do it in the simple 5x8's of his old self, was now impossible. Once under that lintel even in memory, his brain now brought to him all its seven-year vision of it.

He picked up from the desk and pocketed a black leather notebook with attached gold pencil, in which after a visit he recorded the Judge's sayings, as well as anything else of value that might strike him after he had left the household. This he had bought himself. Only a fool wouldn't keep record of his life where he could.

Outside in the street he walked slowly; this was part of the visit too.

At first, inside the Mannix house, once the door had shut behind them, Ruth had gone ahead and up the stairs, assuming he would follow. But he literally couldn't. In the long hall and half-visible connected rooms before him, *down* was up, and *sideways* lurched against him in shapes which for all he knew might move on toward and through him, like whales on a ghost sea-bottom or dirigibles tethered in a room; there was everywhere a clutter of soft-hard furnishment which, if he touched his own filth to it, might sting. He saw his charity shoes at a great distance from him, on a floor more polished than any table he had ever seen. Fitted oversize, they helped bring him to balance; after any more than a few blocks walked in them, they made blisters. Raising his head, he saw in the hall mirror, of a greenish antique tint, which he took to be reassuring dirt, his jackstraw hair, his nose-string. Seeing it, he straightened himself like a dandy. Funds for a spectacle frame were still to come, but the fissured lens, always like a mist of error over his eyeball, had been repaired.

Above his head, several yards away and up, a light hung from a chain, its heavy glass pointed as an icicle, which should make any woodcutter's boy reluctant to go up that stairway. He stood fast, almost scanning the floor for a running brook or a mire, out of which would leap the stag that lured, or would burst the voice of a stone — after which he would plunge down through realms, to lift the buried haft of a sword. Then he saw the three boys, or young men, standing abreast under the stairwell, and knew that this was ambush indeed.

They were just such a queer triumvirate as was said to appear in other people's dreams and might now be in his own. On the left was a short, hunched creature, surely deformed, yet somehow pleasing in aspect. Then came a very tall middle boy whose good looks were made Frankenstein by a black box wired to his ear, and on the right, the shorter fair-haired boy, pure blond giant of the average — who seemed to have nothing else wrong with him. Seen together, the trio would always have a moment's staginess — the gargoyle, the ogre and the stooge — broken into at once by their amiable baritone chatter. If they were his dream, they hadn't yet noticed him or it. They were real.

Now, walking back through many visits to the greenish dark of that hallway, he could examine them as in the leisure of a dream. Nowadays, he always noticed Austin, the blond "average" boy, first. Actually, as he now knew, to be noticed first was Austin's and the whole Fenno family's propensity, all the more because they themselves did nothing to further this, and indeed gave no sign of knowing it. They all had a butcher-block solidity of fairness and bone, of rude health and yes, high-level averageness, all of which signaled at once — and especially to anyone with the black hairs of Latin inferiority in his nose — that the Fennos were everything normal to and beloved of the society; any Fenno child on a bus, in male or female navy blue with its schoolbag, was always so obviously the standard, the favorite, not singly but in dozen lots, which those in command of the comfortable and privileged life, or in service to it, had in mind. Brothers and sisters so resembled one another — or the type — in cheekbones and conventions, that this alone enhanced the impression, on meeting one Fenno, that one met the clan. Because of the heartiness of the type, the men stayed handsomer longer, but the girls, who wore their wheat-silk hair plain and their breasts flat, had no trouble getting husbands, solid sons of bankers, merchant owners, lawyers, old-fashioned publishers, public servants and occasionally doctors — who might have been their brothers. They were all so nice and pleasant that if one didn't like them — as

those who couldn't take the Anglo-Saxon Protestant ideal head on usually didn't — the world knew at once whose fault this was.

In fact, he'd seen the actual Fenno clan only once and unseen by
them, on campus one flying, sunny graduation afternoon — 1948 this
would have been, Austin's. But at Harvard he almost liked their sort,
perhaps not ever individually, but as a fine breed. He had fewer of the
inferiorities which prevented certain other onlookers from doing so;
this was the luck of having come from too far down even for that.
From there, he could better see that although physically the coarser
members of the breed sometimes declined to those snoutier stock-
broker types whose boys and girls were now spreading out into advertising and country club suburbia, underneath, they remained responsible to some norm of conduct, carried within them less flamboyantly
than among Jews or Catholics, like an informal household god. Much
of this the Judge had pointed out to him, as with so much else. For if the
law was experience, as the Judge so often said, then nowadays, all he
wanted to talk about, either with Edwin or the others, *was* that experience.

Austin's family, he'd said, were old New Yorkers in no need of the
shallower, new-style "house in Connecticut" roots, and of a sort which
had never lived with flair. There was therefore no telling, from the
somewhat shabby brownstone on Lexington, near Murray Hill but not
on it, whether they'd lost their money or merely kept it; Warren Fenno,
the father, who in Britain would have been an upper civil servant
perhaps but here was employed by various private foundations, had in
the decentest sense of the phrase made "good works" pay. Starting
with the Hoover committees, he'd been in on every famine and rescue
area of international charity since, the most recent being the refugee
distribution committees of the war period, on one of which the Judge
had met him, only to find that their boys, Austin and David, were
already school friends. There was even a third-generation tie of a
minor sort, a Mendes and a Fenno whose business offices had once
adjoined — "Never think, Edwin, that New York is a wilderness without connection; this is only the provincial view; even the sea gulls
know better, and have their patrons, and their lanes."

If clans like the Fennos, truly median ("Not so much the salt of the
earth, Edwin, as the sterling silver") were able to last, according to the
Judge it was because of a steadily reappearing intelligence which one

might never suspect from their stodgy to handsome exteriors, which never gave itself the racial airs of some, but rather persisted through generation after generation of all those navy-blue-clad children, like some stubbornly recessive but tenacious Mendelian pea. It was a special kind of intelligence, a Protestant one, not over-subtle but confident, on the sunny side of the street — and with this estimate of Austin, Edwin, and no doubt everyone else capable of it, agreed. Yet it was the Judge himself who had started the line, now a byword in the house, that Austin was "so handsome it's hard to believe he's that smart." Perhaps that came out of an envy which Edwin, in looks himself a fair, average sort, didn't share. Austin was good-looking of course, but what Edwin did envy was that assurance — when it talked to the Judge, or sometimes even talked back.

"Austin," the Judge had once said, during one of the topical dinner discussions he liked to foster among the young folk, this day on religion, "I'm afraid you're our pet Gentile."

Austin had replied at once, as graciously as if he were returning a compliment, "You must get over your prejudices, sir — after all, you're not *our* pet Jew."

For a moment, until the elder Fenno's profession was remembered, the table fell silent, then rocked with laughter — the Judge included. If Austin had been the least flashy of smile, it might have been insolent, but he had said it very steadily. Often Austin did answer so readily, one might think he'd already heard the Judge's remarks in private audiences of his own. But to do that and remain Diddy's close friend wasn't probable; more likely the Fennos had a clannish, collective memory of such remarks as the Judge's — from which the answers came pat.

Edwin himself had a question he suspected Austin might have an answer to — "Austin, what breed of pet here am I?" Yet the house itself, by admitting him to its affections, had released him from such questions. When there, to be dressed and clean in his present manner was enough for his vanity, though he disagreed with the Judge on the question of good looks in general. David, with his noble length of irregular feature presided over by the remarkable, intent eyes, was far and away his choice over Austin — but if intellect was to count, then everyone knew of course what the Judge considered his son's to be, or pretended he did. Perhaps this was why the Judge was always so careful to specify that particular requirement for total Adonis — intellect.

Back there, under the stairwell, the three young men had shortly gone on downstairs to the kitchen without seeing him, the new visitor, behind the corner of wall which kept him from their vision. But he still remembered every word of their paused confab before, how David's black box turned from side to side in their center, and Walter, half David's height, cocked his elongated spirit-face at a crow's angle to his humped body, emitting the heartiest laugh and the deepest at Austin's sallies, meanwhile clutching his own wishbone sternum with delight. Only past twenty, he was wearing the vest and cutaway jacket which best clothed his deformity; he had been a matter for the tailor since a child. College hadn't been his hope until David, almost nineteen and still to qualify, had persuaded him; encouraging each other on, they had gone, entering Harvard together the next year. Austin, not quite eighteen, was at that time already a freshman. And he, Edwin, waiting in the hallway, was to go last of all — to meet some of them there.

"Ran into him on the Merchant's," Austin was saying. "Coming down last night, walking through the dining-car. It was a first-class old Dr. Brace encounter. I wished him howdy-do and was about to go on down the aisle when he said, 'Good evening, Yortchley' — in class he always confused me with Biff Yortchley — 'And how's the girl?' "

"Yortchley's going in the navy, I hear," said Walter. "Instead of college. Got engaged."

"Engaged," said David, collating black box and lipreading in his usual shadowy, echoing way — to the oddity of which no one except his father ever paid the slightest attention.

"So I decided it was time old Brace knew I was Fenno, now that I'd graduated. Or maybe it comes of being a freshman all over again. Anyway — I meant to say, 'Dr. Brace, I'm Fenno, not Yortchley.' But there he was, looking at me with that goggle stare, and so help me God, I said, 'I'm not Fenno, Dr. Brace, I'm Yortchley.' "

The three collapsed in laughter on the bottom stair, David flat out on the floor — like many of the congenitally deaf, he let loose in gesture. Walter prodded him with a toe: "Save it for the rowing machine." David mouthed that too, grinning to show he'd got it. He had almost no hearing, even with the box. "Come on, let's go," he said, getting to his feet. His voice wasn't high or reedy, but his speech was careful with listening, as if he gave back accuracy to what he heard.

"Wait, you haven't heard what Brace said to *me*," said Austin. "He looked at me in that way of his, you know? I think he thinks he's twinkling. And he says to me, 'Quite all right, Fenno. I always knew you were.'"

This time, the three fell howling into each other's arms, which considering their various sizes was a feat that showed old habit.

In the hallway, the boy concealed from them by its angle and dark, felt his own chest as if it had a wishbone somewhere. The natural way these three were linked — there was plenty of this in the district, even if he'd never had time for it.

"Wait a minute, you guys, where we going?" said Austin. "You haven't even said yet."

"Didn't we write you?" said Walter. "I bumped into my rich uncle — they've got a swimming pool right in the house. Not in the basement either, right in the living-room floor. He married an Olympics swimmer. So, every time the butler goes for the phone, he has to watch out. All the help know how to swim. There's a rowing machine too, works *in* water. I told him about David wanting crew. So he lets us train. Anybody's welcome."

"Brawn or brain, for Harvard entrance," said David. "I'm teaching Walter to swim."

Walter stuck his thumbs under his armpits. His elderly clothes had dealt him the accompanying gestures. "*And* my uncle," Walter said.

Did they laugh like this always? He listened to them rattle down the steps to the basement, and prepared to slip outside the front door and be off. She'd forgotten him; that had happened to him before on a delivery. And he'd almost forgotten her, meanwhile. All the painful sortings and separations began again in his mind, as his gaze, freed now to wing out and over these rooms, darted here, there, helpless before all this foliage of matter. In his mind, too, one syllable clinked against itself like a glass wind instrument — *rich*. What did anyone in this house mean — or anyone even remotely connected with it — when he spoke of someone *else* as "rich"? Meanwhile, he rubbed one blistered heel over the other, propriety suggesting he would less contaminate these shining surfaces — the floor was now a floor — if he shrank into himself within his bag of offensive clothing, and perhaps stood on one leg.

Yet when the girl came back, he was still there.

"Thought you were behind me halfway up the stairs," she said, laughing. "Daddy's door was open, so I told him about you. Maybe he'll want to see you." She resettled the headband which held her hair from her ears, a style whose youth, compared to the extravaganzas of girls her age in the district, confused him also. "Did you see the boys?"

So they did still call them boys here. Yet he'd seen at once that these young men with strains of childishness in their confab had an awareness to the world's possibles which rarely came even to the elderly, in his. Not "maturity," not even "sophistication." By now, seven years later, he owned as large a vocabulary as any of them, yet he didn't think the world had a word yet for this quality which entered under their skin very early, from never having to fight, even in a depression, for meat, drink and shelter, from having so many avenues open to them, except where blocked by personal circumstance (like loss or deformity, which then were really *personal*) or by cataclysm or war. He would call it mobility — scope. The very quality of the human condition changed with its presence, a change in the vital animal underneath. He thought that the Harvard scholars of the social welfare or of men's economies hadn't enough noted this, or where they did, hadn't his opportunity to put the nature of it so precisely.

On his last visit, he'd tried to describe to the Judge himself the Mannix house and world as it had seemed to him that first afternoon. In order to remember his own former one with an émigré's passion. And with a growing fear.

"It wasn't only your possessions that I didn't know the names or uses of, that confused me." Not merely that he couldn't have told direction because of the very draperies, or that sometimes even now, in this world of marble and the airiest references, he'd had doubts as to which of its surfaces were literally hard or soft. "It was you yourselves, sir, in your heads and souls. It was like I couldn't even tell secondary sex characteristics at first, or what was the age of who."

"Well, Edwin, you were having a little age trouble yourself, back then."

So he supposed he had failed in the end to explain how sometimes, in this wizard's world, people in their silken approaches to each other appeared to him hermaphrodite, or one sex, or none — and even when he came to understand that they too had emotions — surely transvestite there too. "For a while, until I saw the sequence, you all scarcely *had* any actions. Just talk. Like magic powder — that explodes."

"And you, Edwin, were bare-assed, as far as the emotions are concerned. You scarcely had one to your name."

"They weren't freed." Sometimes he yearned to have their unfairness, the way they had their table manners. To have it — but not to know. They were in the Judge's study, where these interviews always took place. "I remember the day I first came here, when you made me step through this window. It was like a wizard's house."

The Judge bowed. "Public schools feed far too much on the fairy-tale literature."

"Well, of course!" cried Edwin, "And don't you see why?" How he had been led on!

"Tut, tut, Edwin. We are your romance. Just as we are. And I submit you understood it at once, from the moment I caught you buttoning your fly." He grinned. "But the poor understand us an edge or two less well than we understand them."

Back there, on that most recent visit, in one of the silences which were common with them, he'd thought long, while the Judge fiddled with the day's mail on stamps; with all his hobbies, welfares and philosophies set in action from this room, his hours were fuller, for a man without a job, than many a gasping executive's.

After a while, Edwin raised his head. To bend his face between his hands was a gesture he never used except here. A breeze was now blowing in the same window onto the garden through which, under the owner's gaze, sharp as a ruler on his knuckle, he had climbed. "Shall I tell you how the basement looked to me though, that first day?"

"Yes do. Always happy to hear anything which might help me understand what goes on in my son's world, not to speak of his mind. Even Ruth, who used to be like an open book, is beginning not to confide in me."

Edwin stared at him thoughtfully. One of his main reasons for not thinking Ruth an open book was that the Judge so often told people she was. The Judge's attention had wandered — though one could never tell for sure. On the stamp-wall side of the room, the beauties of his collection were affixed to a great relief map, made for him by an indigent refugee artist, of all the map pink, tan and green places on the dilute blue waters of a cartographer's planet.

"Well," said Edwin. "First off, it was clean. A whiteness which would've made my mother kneel. Clean is my mother's God, you know, all the one she has — maybe that's why I've never been able to get away from the idea that cleanliness must be stupid some way. I think the only thing upheld me in that kitchen was a pride in my own — dirt. Which I'd certainly never had before. And didn't want. For I saw at once that our basement was a burrow. Our floor had earth in it, where the cellar stone had worn away. There was no dark here, for my shoulder to rub against. There was no animal life here. They say that roaches appear even in the Egyptian hieroglyphs — man's company. I never thought I would think of a rat's rustle as something — *lost*."

"I see you're not ashamed of your origins, that's what I see. You can go far." He was no longer looking at his collection on the wall.

"No, it's physical," said Edwin. "The difference between us and you, between us as we were then, and even my aunts. Not just the condition of being warm or cold, starved or fed. Physical in the bloodstream of the mind. Like low blood pressure in the Arctic maybe, from many nights of cold. Or in what the soul expects."

The Judge said nothing, here.

"Anna had just shopped for the week," said Edwin. "For the *week*. That notion itself — My first thought was of how dangerous. Your house invited robbery everywhere." He swallowed. "Or trust."

The Judge had put his fingertips together. "And you were the marauder, perhaps? Now, Edwin. The poetry of one's early self is very affecting, isn't it. I gather that like every other student in the world, you've been reading Freud. My generation was the last, I often think, to read the poetry of the ages instead." He picked up a paper knife and held it, with a duelist's pause.

"I despair of ever saying it," said Edwin. "To you or myself. And that's because I'm losing it." Gnawing a knuckle, he was silent. Then it burst from him. "We were disorderly. But bare."

The Judge sighed. "I'm not built to be Socrates. Are you saying our middle-class clutter is the *real* disorder? Do you go on from there to consider your lost — simplicity — as art?"

"Not art, not down there!" said Edwin. "No, that's fakery. To say that."

The Judge quickly slid forward so that he could put his feet on the floor — he had the clearest, almost rhythmic sense of his physical self — Ruth had it too. "Hm-m, so you're from that burrow." He got up and walked about, looking out on the water tower, of which his study had the closest view in the house, across a patch of garden gone to yard. "So you don't go along with my two. You mean to say, you don't believe that art or social service is the answer — to all our guilts?" He swiveled quickly. "Middle-class guilts, I mean, of course. You surprise me, Edwin. Should've thought you'd acquired that up there, by now. Sincerity is every brewer's daughter doing rhythmics in a leotard, isn't it? And a billet in the American Friends Service for every banker's son."

Edwin looked at him with a dismay he hadn't learned to conceal. This man *would* be Socrates to him, if only he wouldn't let every one of their high dialogues finally crumble back into the personal. It had happened every time.

The Judge came up closer, still wandering negligently, in a professor's track. "Tell me — in one word, Edwin." Then he smiled. "Had French teachers made me do that. Unfair. But a good lesson in rhetoric — if anybody remembers rhetoric except the French — who are notably unfair. Tell me about that kitchen of mine, six years ago — in one word." He shrugged. "Maybe a legal one. I still remember some of my law."

Edwin felt the good pupil's rush of elated blood. He could do better; he could use a political word, which would please the Judge even more. It seemed to him he'd had the word in his head always. That first Christmas, when Ruth and David had taken it upon themselves to walk him and his mother — as if they were their children — through the chiming Fifth Avenue stores, as his mother and he had finally had it caroled into their heads, she perhaps never quite, that all this charade was for sale, could be bought by someone — then the word had begun to form in his head like a three-pronged bird ready to fly. Later, his mother had a new coat, but not a new face, or head. The word persisted. When they'd sent him to Harvard, the word became once more merely a word — yet telling the Judge, he had to rest his face in his hands again before he could say it as politely as was required by this house. "It was —"

He saw the Judge shake his head, raising a finger like a croupier. "Only *one*," said the Judge's lips; often he didn't seem to know that he talked like that, voiceless, watching lips opposite like a mute, or perhaps because his height prevented him from looking at most men eye to eye.

Edwin found his own voice, angrier than intended. "Anarchy!" he said.

By rights, the dialogue should have ended there. But the Judge chose to terminate it once again on the personal. "Why, Edwin," he said, "You're no longer calling me 'sir.' "

And on that same last visit — in the fall, just before he returned to Cambridge for his first semester of law — on their saying good-bye, the Judge had made him another presentation for his own minute library. That day he hadn't been made to climb up and get it down from the Judge's own shelves; it had already been waiting for him in the study desk at the beginning of their interview, one of the dark green packages of the British bookseller who was always pleased to hunt specialties for this prime American customer whose interests — philately, law, semantics, the history of the Jews from Zion to Israel and of religious thought in general, criminology, the psychiatry of women, and a touch of ordinary pornography — ranged so far. On Edwin's request, the Judge had inscribed each book according to his own dictate — *Simon Mannix to Edwin Halecsy, September 19th, 1950.* This time only two of the books had been older ones, Victorian editions and both American: Oliver Wendell Holmes, Jr.'s *The Common Law,* 1881, Boston, Little, Brown, and an early form book, Potter's *Every Man His Own Lawyer,* published in Poughkeepsie, New York, in 1834. The other two had been modern: Thurman Arnold's *Folklore of Capitalism* (which he'd already come across in college, along with Thorstein Veblen, Randolph Bourne and all that lot) and a current volume of essays, a number of these political, by a man named George Orwell, published in London that same year. "I'm bringing you up slowly, Edwin, eh, out of the dark ages where you were, into *our* anarchy." Nothing revealed by Edwin was ever left unused.

Nine months later now, walking through the summery evening at that point of city year and air when there were always country catches of green in it which even the island's lower tip, breath-fed on the rotten stews of the harbor, recognized and waited for, Edwin found himself following almost the same pattern of streets he and Ruth had done that first time. How much plainer it could have been if he'd had the nerve to say to the Judge's request, "There's *no* one word! Come down among us to the world of your children — that basement you say you never see, but which is full of you — and see me as I saw it for the first time." . . .

"Wait —" he'd said to the smiling girl back there. "You went *up* these stairs. But you came back from *there*." He pointed down the hallway, which conducted one toward the rear regions through brownish reflections of old furnishings, an aisle not quite shadowy, never brilliant, which he came to love. "There's a back way, huh?"

She nodded. Probably nobody before him had entered that house in such guerrilla caution over ingress and egress. Only a housecat, if they'd had one, would have taken for granted, as he did, a street training which sniffed at every old cul-de-sac and in new places kept its back to walls in which there were exits. But she said, with another little nod, "You like to — know how to get out."

It was the first small ripple of their peculiar sympathy. On her part it might be merely womanly — not like his market beldames and clam-lipped teachers, or even the warm dopiness of the junior substitute — but the way women were in the library books, and up here. Until he went to Harvard and met others of her kind who didn't have it, he wasn't sure it was unique to her. Quiet and cool as her face was, it was never sad, though its features — replica of the Judge but with hints of a larger-faced heredity — could have stretched to that, he grew to think, if there had been reason for it.

"Yes, I saw them," he'd said. "The — boys." If one has started the day aged fifteen and is ending it at eighteen, one can't be blamed for uncertainties of all sorts.

"Well, then, come on. Aren't you starving?"

Sometimes the locutions of this world still amused him.

"Who are they? The — the little one — is that your older brother?"

"Oh no, that's Walter Stern, our dear friend. He's the absolute dear of all time — and it doesn't even matter if I say so, it won't put you off, you'll like him just the same. You'll see. No, Diddy's the tall one."

"The one with the —" He touched his ear.

She nodded, courtly. "Just be sure to face him when you talk to him."

"And the third one? What's wrong with him?" He was used to seeing the lame, the halt and the blind hang about together for natural pro-tection.

"*Austin?*" She burst out laughing, clapping her hands — she always took full advantage of merriment, as if one should. "Yes, that's Austin to a T — there's nothing *wrong* with him."

"They all live here?"

"Walter used to, in the holidays sometimes; he's an orphan. Now he's got a place of his own, a whole apartment. They all went to school together, until Austin went away. Anna's putting on a feast, because he's back."

As she led him downstairs, he thought first, that it mightn't be smart to let himself in for three against one, second, that if Austin had been "away" — which in the district was a politer way of saying he'd been in jail, in jug, in stir — then there was already plenty enough wrong with him. It occurred to him that the house here might be a kind of placement home, on the settlement order but live-in style, for rich boys when they came home from their reform schools. With her stay-at-home father at the head of it.

The Judge and he had long since laughed together at this unilateral assumption — that the upper classes would have their own facilities all along the line. David and Austin had never been told it, both being uneasy laughers at any but their own kind — David because he couldn't bear to hurt, Austin from the depths of his own reserve. Walter, who could have been told anything, was always with them. Though the three, polite enough with Edwin, would have said of themselves that they did their best to be friendly, he knew they didn't trust his entente with the Judge. He himself had an upstart's jealous awareness that his standards of honesty mightn't satisfy theirs. Oh, he knew enough about the underskin forces between him and them to prove the Judge utterly wrong on who knew best about who! Back there, the succeeding ten minutes had been the most hated learning period of his life. Entering, he'd known at once that he belonged *here*, in *this* world — just as a natural designate of either heaven or hell, on entering either, would sense at once that this was where *he* belonged. They'd treated him tenderly, neither laughing at him nor with him. He was as bound to them, by then, brothers though they never would be, as if they'd scarred his cheeks like a committee of Abyssinian elders. And to the house also, beyond all its other enticements, because he had received his scarring there.

The kitchen as he knew it now was brown wood and stove-polished iron, with many seams of honorable use. The white dazzle of fixtures and floor had been mainly in his own mind. Anna had looked up at his approach, plump and in housewifely command, but in her eyes that dog's devotion to these others — which always betrayed her. That first time, she breathed him in and then out again, like an odor she recognized. As for him, he was grateful to her forever. Whenever he looked into her domesticated eyes he knew afresh that whatever else he might be, he was not a servant, here or anywhere.

The three young men stared bright-eyed at what the sister was bringing in. He entered chin lifted, like any male introduced by the female. Of his other braveries, in cul-de-sac and out of burrow, they couldn't know. The table already had a fruity whiteness of the sandwiches, milk and cookies Anna had provided; at their pleading she was just freshly studding it with delicatessen with whose window prices, black as iron bars, he was familiar; the three were nagging for beer as well.

"Yah, I know," said Anna to Austin. "I don't care where you been, you ain't any older than I know you are. Seventeen. And Diddy and Walter, they ain't even been away yet. It's milk. Or chincherale. No beer."

"Anna darling, Anna my hosh," said Diddy, his arms around her from behind, "we know you have it. You wouldn't want us to steal."

"Mr. Mannix didn't say for it." To Ruth only, Anna always said "your father."

"I'll go ask," said Ruth. She sat Edwin down at table next to Walter and left him. They all saw his wild look at her desertion.

It was at this point that David, as the host, came forward to greet him. Edwin, like the Judge, never thought of David under his nickname.

"Oh, the Halecsys," David repeated, but only because of his deafness. Still, there was a touch of the settlement house grandee about him — those boys so full of libertarian willingness, who came to the slums because it was good for *them.*

Austin, whose "haughty" looks would make him a dead duck to the hoi polloi before he even opened his mouth, didn't smile, from a reserve he extended to all. But he was the first to see that Edwin by intellect belonged among them. In the end it was he, whose extra intelligence was joined to a sensitivity of average thickness only, whom the protégé, the refugee, might best trust. Though at the moment Edwin took this as merely the result of Austin's having been in jail.

Walter was just as she said; he might have got his very hump from years of delicate scholarship on the subject of other people's feelings. In the long silences, he was filling everybody's plate. "We'll drown like logs," he said happily, passing the food with the lavishness of one of small, frailly dictated appetites. "They're going to teach me to swim," he said to Edwin. "I suppose you know all about that."

He saw Austin watching him, and gave the district's shrugging offhand answer, based on how it mostly did learn to swim, in a Y pool. "Oh, I dive for pennies," he said. There was another lengthy silence.

"Did the Halecsys stuff you with cocoa?" asked David. "I must say, your aunts make better cocoa than mine."

"We had kümmel," he said, daring pride — and meanwhile learning what courteous chitchat was, even from the mouth of the deaf — and how to be cavalier about food. For some moments the others ate busily.

"Kümmel?" said Austin at length. "For the bellyache?"

"No," said Ruth, returning, "it was his birthday."

He hadn't dared begin to eat yet, and looked up at her, waiting. She saw him — and didn't go on with her story. He saw that she had never had any intention of doing so. And from this he learned.

"Father *says* —" said Ruth. "*Father* says —" All heads arrested, including Anna's. "He says — Anna, give the boys *whisky* if that's what they want. But they're to eat your cake."

He'd already grasped the idea that they weren't hungry on demand, or at the sight of any dish, like him.

"A *cake*," David said at once. Anna was made to bring it; there were celebratory remarks. "Let *me* cut it, it's *mine!*" Austin said quickly, as if he, not Anna, were the child. In silence, like a mother who had misunderstood her children but not underestimated them, she brought out from the icebox an enormous bowl as well. "It won't keep," she said.

So, though they didn't eat much of the cake, he learned the delicacy — to a point — of master to servant. But that was minor. For, as he watched the four docile faces which appeared to be "against" no one, he had an extraordinary feeling — in the way even the young with nothing in common snatched these facts from one another — that if they lived somewhere a darker, deeper life than one saw, they kept their innocence not only for this kitchen, but for the whole house. He himself was already tethered to the house by its innocence, a mayfly vision seen from his own wintry basement lair, in the house above which every floor and wall was stained with the afterbirth, the death rattle, and the red hilarity of gangsters, and in whose garbage can only yesterday a withered, purple baby had been found, still in its slime. He had an idea that if they kept him here, it would be on both sides because of that innocence. He couldn't keep his eyes off the bowl Anna had brought out, in which there was a stiff Neapolitan hill of green, brown and pink ice cream.

"Want more," said Anna, watching him. He refused it, from her. The bowl was then placed in front of him by Ruth — because of his birthday. By the greatest effort, he didn't grab. In his ten minutes of darting glances he had learned where elbows should be, and the swan grace of spoons not clutched. In equal effort, he didn't finish the entire bowl, but uncorrected by any of them, he ate from it. Then he leaned back, replete, and, in token of their mutual interest, offered Austin a remark, like a cigar. After all, they were the hosts, and couldn't ask him anything. Where he had learned this, he never knew. He leaned forward. "Warwick, Otis — or Highland," he said. "Which one you were in?"

He'd been careful as a cat not to include Letchworth, the reform school for feebleminded only, and a common insult where he came from. Yet to reel off the big-time prisons, merely because from Leavenworth to Alcatraz he knew them all, would have been putting down Austin in another and subtler way, not the overture he intended. So if Austin was only seventeen, it would have to be reform school only — and probably one of those three.

Walter repeated the names for David, who echoed them doubtfully but earnestly.

" — Or there's that one in South something," said Edwin. "Way upstate. I knew a guy from there."

It was Austin who saved him. Kindness alone wouldn't have helped. Austin was brilliant as well — but only because it was practicable. "Uh-uh." He drooped an eyelid, clasped his hands and shook them, in the sign which meant "I'm rooting for you." "The best and biggest is none too good for Austin. *Sing Sing!*"

The three laughed dutifully, only David saying, "But that's a state *prison!*" and then, "Oh."

Across them Austin gave Edwin a business stare, concerned only that he get it: that his blunder had been passed off as a weak joke. Ruth too gave him a tremulous smile. He thought her born to be a sister.

It was all too much for him. In the dark center of all this learning, the kümmel suddenly burned. He had to go pee. He said it to himself like that, like a child opting out. He got up slowly. "Where's the hall?"

The hall, their faces said, what's the hall? He might have been deserting them. Once he had joined them, he learned this too. Anything he had lived, which they hadn't, might be a desertion of them.

Instinctively, he turned to Anna, who'd been watching it all; the role of the servant-watcher still gave him the creeps. She knew what he wanted — liking him no better for it because she did — but took him by the shoulders, propelling him outside the room to an alcove under the back stairs, where she flung open the door of a bathroom he now knew was hers. Her flat-set eyes — Polack, Hungarian? — scanned his Charlie Chaplin trousers, and she left him.

Inside the bathroom, he locked the door for the pleasure of it, but didn't think to look for a light. The room was brown wood like the water closets he knew, but varnished like an old master. A brush and comb lay ghostly on the porcelain tank, cleaving like a couple. Towels, carved out of alabaster, hung above. The narrow window, paned with a filmy, metal-patterned glass, shone bluish with early evening, from a prospect he couldn't see but heard. In silence he communed with it, the hall toilet silence of cities. In it he raised his head, like a stag. There was a mirror, but it didn't interest him. He wanted to butt his head, its new growth — which wasn't a miracle, but like teeth or hair — from within. He was an upper being, like them, like them like them. He found he couldn't relieve himself here. He dared not drop his dirt here. To contaminate them. Or to be stolen by them. This torsion, though he learned to deal with it, stayed with him always.

He opened the door, found the rear house door off the passage, and sneaked outside. A clothesline in the form of a tree stood there, its arms webbed with wash. Fog was rolling in. In the coarse crabgrass underneath his feet, a few bits of tinfoil glinted, a city confetti that he knew. A pigeon whirred up, then walked along a wall, over which a branch fretted a familiar ailanthus shape. The garbage cans were not so different. He let go against one of them. Above him, the iron water tower brooded its black arts, under the advance of the apartment houses' wave after wave of brick. It was more private here than in any of the yards he usually took advantage of, yet he'd never felt so naked. He knew he had come up out of his burrow for good. The city as audience confronted him, waiting for him to apply for his destiny — or not waiting. He prepared to run.

Behind him, a window in the house was raised. The silky light from it, as he whirled, watered his eyes, so that the man moving within its yellow oblong underwent a series of images, at first bending a monk's bullethead over the sill, then receding, against a confusion of book colors in the room behind him, into the worn silhouette of the second thief in the chapel at St. Boniface's — and ending up hands in jacket pockets, gently rocking, riding a howdah on the elephant night.

"Good evening," said the man. "I understand you want to go into politics."

3   In the Upstairs Sitting-Room
Fall 1944

In the nearly two years since his wife's death, the Judge had watched his own abnormalities with interest, and of course care. Abnormality was a better word than dishonesty, covering more.

During this apprentice period, the different shocks he had to learn to deal with came to separate themselves. The simplest was the loss of his wife in her social, household and maternal roles, even her sexual one. Compared to her abstracted or eccentric manner of filling these in life, convention now worked things back to a sadder but almost more manageable norm. As a widower, it was easier to sit at home of an evening than it had been not to be seen about as a couple, and now that the living woman no longer could get into bad company, the dead one left off provoking the small keen aches of half-mutilated loving; there was a convenience to the dead. In one simplest sense, she was safe now. Death had brought his wife out of the demimonde.

In the household too, where of late years Anna had been made far too responsible for a ménage which still had a mistress, now only his sisters, Athalie and Rosa, had a moment's qualm — at the propriety of it. This alone showed how far Anna had come. His sisters lived in the permanently thickened girlishness of maiden women maybe encumbered, but in the end toughened, by the presence of every family drapery well preserved, their highest task being to keep the chairs re-covered in identical patterns and the family sayings well oiled. Neither was unmarried because of ugliness or lack of offers, but because for each, to take the one necessary faltering step into the sea of the unrelated had been impossible. His father had never been able to get through his head how this could have happened to his pretty enough, petted darlings; his mother, fairly close to the asexual herself, an alien in that house where young men thronged, and the worst of matchmakers — must have known this about his sisters from the first councils

of the cradle, and had helped to make it so. Now sixtyish, they must
have passed through at least the heritable physicalities of women, yet
had managed to keep all fleshliness at the level of the cough drop and
the bowel. To think of servants in terms of sexes went surprisingly
beyond their narrow-curtained politics as well.

He'd barely stopped himself from remarking, "Why, I never knew
you two had a male thought under your beds" — but younger than
they, and an only brother — at one and the same time their "baby" and
closest protector — he was well aware that he himself was that male
thought, and in fact had been brought up to be. If this was "Freudian"
now, like so much in the *ancien régime* of families, then it had been
merely straight Jewishness once. So, on the afternoon, two weeks after
the burial, when they broached the question of Anna, he had sent them
back to their cocoa fast enough, not without a bit of brotherly mischief
first, very welcome to him in those first days. In some ways, these
menthol-smelling handmaidens of houses (the two had a joint and
antique sinus) could be helpful indeed.

"Well, why don't you two come and live here? Yes, why not?"

What a duet-round of stammerings then, reminding him almost exactly of how they had practiced their sisterhood at the piano, in their
teens.

Finally Rosa, who had always taken the bass, brought out, "What —
what — will we do with the *mahogany?*"

"And — with *Daisy?*" Athalie, the treble, immediately said.

Daisy was their factotum; the shift from white to black in this matter
had been a major event of their post-parental years.

But he hadn't realized how he'd frightened them. For they were
loyal. And though birth and death were rightfully their melodrama
(and to bring these properly to phone and table talk level their choral
function), they'd never yet had to deal with a death like this. If he
needed them this much, then it must be like the terrible month when
their mother had gone into pawn — and into veiled, cab-shrouded
black — for their father! They would *have* to.

No wonder both of them slid their eyes round to the fourth, up to
now silent person in the long room, where they were all clustered over
Anna's tea tray, in a book-shelved corner as far from the portrait over
the mantel as was decently possible. Miss Augusta Selig sat there im-
movably as usual: gray, rough-cut features good enough for a handsome man — she was a spinster because of them — over a vintage

tailored suit of any year but this. She must know that these suits, bought like a dowry on her final inheritance from his mother's brother, her fool father, gave her a first-glance look of a Lesbian — and that there was nothing else to be done with her. She was impoverished, independent. For the surer second glance, she was accustomed to wear a succession of heirloom onyx-and-pearl butterflies, horn-and-chalcedony scimitars, all as ugly and unmarketable as she, and on her pitifully feminine feet a round of elegantly custom-made shoes, for which somewhere over the years, she had found the ante. Well before the inheritance she must have decided upon what could and would be done with herself. When Augusta entered a room, the Judge always saw the shoes at once — always with the kindest intentions of including them as clues to her womanhood in his treatment of her — and never thought of them again until he watched their heels leaving it. Perhaps she had them made for this reason too.

The two sisters' eyes wandered, apprehensive of her, firm because of him. Since Augusta, from all their cradles on, had either known or suspected everything about him, these days he was wary of her too. During all the Mannix childhoods, even Augusta's succession of dogs, each one named Chummie, always knew, perhaps through some muscle communication, what had never been written on the walls of their well-ordered youth — that "Augusta loved Simon." This gave her the most minutely observant knowledge of him, satiric as from a concubine kept faithfully in attendance but never slept with, not to be feared for the sake of outsiders, for she was as loyal as Rosa and Athalie, but to be reckoned with for its sources of intelligence. The one thing she didn't know about him was that he knew of it. His sisters, in a more Oriental household, might have been made to marry, or under the more orthodox clan-to-clan surety, found themselves capable of it; even as themselves, they weren't too far from those dumb wives beloved of Jewish men in the folklore. But Augusta's good brain, already married to that exterior, would have evaded second-best in any age. Cynically amused now — for her only pose was to show exactly what she felt — she regarded them, the first cousin of them all.

"Augusta could come," said the sisters, characteristically to Simon. And then to Augusta, brave in having ranged him behind them, "You." Augusta said nothing. The sisters meant to be kind. Any remote affection of hers, clumsily adhered to their sacred brother, they assumed had vanished, like the ill-starred, crepe-backed satin ball dresses of their own untreasured youth. No one had ever been able to think of Augusta in terms of passion except herself, an early safety the sisters as girls would have rejoiced in, and saw Augusta as enjoying the fruits of now. No one could think it wrong if she and Simon lived here together — with Anna then clearly a servant. And for Augusta, what an accession, to come from what had to be called a "theatrical" hotel, back to the heavily beneficed air of all their childhoods, safe again in the orris root and beeswax of what was now the family house! Plainly they had talked it over, how to reoffer this poor daughter of an unfortunate uncle — for the annals of money, unlike those of love, were never to be let die from a family history — this chance at a destiny she had spent thirty independent years working away from.

"Eh, Augusta? Hah, Augusta?" said the bass and the treble. They smiled at her, deaconesses of a middle age they had worked toward also and now wore diadem, entrenched enough in its honors to spare some too. Then they couldn't avoid a quick, transparent look at one another. And *Simon*, whose taste in women had proved so tragic? They weren't certain what it would do for him (not liking to think too clearly on the needs of men or brothers) — but surely it would be safer than the dark freedoms of bachelordom, or those experienced candidates out to hook a man "in public life." They saw these in a henna-haired chorus line, pinkly presenting its widowed charms, maybe under some of the best banking names in the hierarchy, and from ball dresses worn all too well. Whereas Augusta, with a little coaching, might even be persuaded to keep an eye on his bowel. "She could be your hostess, Simon," they said.

Across their two innocent heads, Simon and Augusta exchanged their own smiles. He knew that these exchanges, even the sisters' presence to stimulate them, were the breath of necessity to her, silently confirming, like the secret looks between two cleverer brothers, her own image of herself as a personage independently spirited, and without sham. To him she was much too much like a good, gray elder brother whom the distaff side had almost provided him with, only at the last moment welshing out in the genes again, with a "Here's no dwarf in this one. But it will be have to be female." To his shame, he'd once made Mirriam laugh — she hadn't the patience to mind Augusta herself, but was always intolerant of the sexually starved — by saying, "Every time I offer Augusta the after-dinner brandy she's so devoted to, I have to restrain myself from also handing her the cigars."

Today he was careful to address his response to the sisters' aspersion of her — which they would never know as one — to those shoes of hers, on this afternoon a pointed pair of gray suede, with black buttons marching up their strapped fronts. "Oh, Augusta and I could never make each other respectable," he said. "No, if Anna can't do it, it'll have to be you two."

Miss Augusta — the *old* had just begun to be attached to her in the months since — kept her head lowered. Following her glance, he saw with a start — his reflexes were still nervous or numb — that she hadn't brought the current Chummie, absent only at funerals and marriages, the only other occasions he could recall being two — that first of these famous family conferences, thirty years ago, often detailed by him to the children, the one at which she'd declared her removal from Mrs. Delano's boardinghouse, last of the discreet ones on Irving Place, to her present West Forties hotel. The second time, never recounted to them, had been her first dinner here in Mirriam's house. Both no doubt had been acts of bravery. Why no Chummie then, today?

He had learned soon enough. The sisters, after his last remarks, were easily routed; besides, their Daisy, though she was more of a church-goer and teetotaler than her mistresses, had in all her twenty years of service never been given a key or allowed to leave the house without presenting herself, for check against the chance that she might "get into the jewelry drawers" or "take a nip from the sideboard" — the simple, republican reason for this being that Daisy was black. And that the sisters had to have some neatly controllable scare in their lives to make comfort all the cozier; his mother had made a similar use of servants too.

He closed the door on them, after a doorside duet of sighs and assurance from beneath mourning veils they must be the last non-Catholics to recall the uses of. In the past fortnight he'd learned to chew dread with his morning *Times*, gulp water with his midnight toothbrush despair, and trot obediently past the scarred newel-post all the day long. He'd dealt with police examinations — and with the clear and present evidence, even as he underwent them, that these were token, just as that proud owner of "a few concessions around town" had promised. He'd dealt with the morgue, whose "bullet in the left ventricle" had been matched to his wife's gun. That same evening, he'd undergone visitation from the rabbi who had buried his mother five years ago, and had now come (with the peculiar arrogance of

young rabbis to their elder laity) to extend to the bereaved "father"
first a discourse (on death by suicide as doctrinally set forth in what he
called "the literature"), then a personal lecture (on the felicity of being
left with children to console and care for), and finally an invitation to
return "before the high holidays" to the arms of the synagogue —
which he called "the temple." At the Judge's own door, the young man
had blessed him in Hebrew, which was gracious and acceptable, then
addressed him as Simon, which from him was not.

"Remember now, Simon," said young Dr. Hildesheimer, in a phrase
he might have polished in the study and would repeat to the wife,
"remember, hahr, that even a judge in his worst hour of loss must not
judge the Almighty. Today you are only a man." He held out his
hand.

"Learned *that* at my b'mitzvah," said the Judge, but remembered in
time that any authority had better be courted just now, and took the
hand. Watching the young twerp get back into his car, he caught
himself thinking "German. And reformed. How tasteless they are. This
would never have been the way of it in Dr. Pereira's time" — in dry
self-observance, of how apostates like himself, when in need of the
religion of their forefathers, quite naturally demanded that it be as
orthodox. Later, not knowing whether he meant it as bribe or blas-
phemy, he sent Hildesheimer a check.

In the next day's mail, the Judge had received a letter from closer
kindred — his companion at arms, competent concessionaire and closer
of dead eyes. And now soldier of fortune. The letter, dated a week
back and from Camp May, had read as follows: "So far, by the papers,
all OK. Knew it would be. You're the champ. Mirrie always said so.
You won't hear from me again. Even in the funny papers. So rest easy.
Take care of the little girl." The note was typed down to the yours
truly, and signed with a scrawl. He thrust it away from him, into
Mirriam's desk with her other personal papers, marking only that the
signature did begin with a P.

Otherwise, he'd had to learn, as one did every time, how few open
gestures surrounded a death, even death like this — and how little
these had to do with the long effect. To him, the worst were the
questions by telephone, from the army of Mirriam's evening friends, in
all voices and accents, bohemian slang and Harlem minstrel, musically
grave or hysterically juvenile, or contralto with alcohol, or glottal with
tears. On his instruction, he took them all. In two days of this, he

refined the art of what to say to people about her — to an art. (Though, at the next call, he never could remember what he had said before.) Answers to the somber lawyers, or to condolences from friends whose characters were there to go on, he could often remember afterward. Neighbors were not the easiest, being for the most part met by accident. Beyond any degree of worst lay the parried silences, from people who came not to ask but to brood, or who fell short of the question, or were careful in their turn. He could lipread any such silence blindfold.

The night before that helpful, emollient visit from his good, dumb sisters, when just about to retire in his own familiar bedroom — the ell to his wife's bedroom being closed, as often in her lifetime — he was for the first time in his life attacked by obsession. Often before in his fifty-two years he'd known despair, humiliation. Thanks to lively kidneys, he'd never been soddenly drunk, but had sometimes early in manhood been wildly so; he had several times smoked opium, in Paris, and had once spent three days there holed up in a convenience hotel with a tiger-haired *jolie laide* he had picked up in the Rue St. Honoré, emerging from that interlude blanched and smelly, trained to food and linen fed him through hatches, and to the most indelible images of a woman, nostril to armpit to labia to eye, which he thought he was ever to have — and in ten days had mislaid. But he had never before, in any situation, not been somewhere at the center of himself, in military control of his own nervous network.

Now, in his own leather and wood eyrie, with all the instruments of self-possession around him — drawers of shirts ready, ostrich collar-and-stud boxes of gear to clip them with, ranks of ties to thong him by the neck into reality, trousers in rows eager to make a man of him — he had stood naked, or what a minute ago he had thought was naked. There indeed were the whitish tufts of the Moroccan rug between his toenails. Yet he had the sensation, accompanied by a bottomless melancholy, that he was dressed again, and this time with the forced aid of invisible valets. Over and over, just as he got himself down to the skin again, he found himself hopelessly clothed. Under wave after wave of this, he began to form an idea of who they were — a vision of octopal arms walking sturdily forward on pad-flat feet, able to insist a coat over his shoulders by mere touch, to melt him into his underclothes with a whisper from horned mouths. Yet all the time he knew with some sanity that this was his own "vision," that to an even saner man they

were really there all right, but *in*visible. And all the time, like a third
and further vision of reality, he saw the tufts of rug, his own toes *really*
naked, each membraned nail. Then his valets would advance again, to
relieve him, but only for a second, of the suffocating intimacy of the
clothing which then once more formed on him. His pores felt the air
but were never slaked; his thirst for nakedness was never to be allowed.

Then, as sudden as the waving of a wand, he understood his obsession, found the so obvious key, and was free. To dissolve an obsession
one had only to understand it. It departed. And the second obsession
came upon him, in its place, saying, "So you've had that? Now try this!"
For he now *understood*: that if in his mind he now would search out
every one of the persons to whose questions during his trial of days he
had lied or prevaricated, and if to each he spoke a formula of the truth,
this second compulsion — for he sagely understood that it was one —
would itself be relieved. He was to say of each person — never directly
to him — "What would so-and-so say, if I were to tell him —?" and
then tell the truth as he could. He was not presented with any formula
for telling it.

Lying on his bed, he had spent hours or seconds of non-time fussing
lucidly over it, finding that although at first he had formulated the
names as they appeared in the death notice: *Mirriam Sheba Mendes,
wife of Simon, daughter of the late Meyer and Sarah de Sola Mendes,
mother of Ruth Zipporah and David Daniel Mannix* — he was not
required to do this, but could say simply: Mirriam, Ruth; my daughter,
my wife. And he wasn't required to say *kill*, for that implied intent of
which he was ignorant. When he comprehended that he was to say
only what he himself knew for sure, then the words were *given* him, as
in the Bible. *My daughter Ruth has shot my wife, her mother Mirriam.*
Next he was given to understand that he might drop the "has" — for
time passes, and the "wife and mother" also — for the dead must rest.
"Daughter" he must keep, as he would keep her. When all this —
watched by him like a biblical measurement of sevens and sevens —
was over, he began mentally compiling his lists, of every person, from
phone calls to the slightest encounter — to whom he had replied, implied, lied. Then to each person, ticking them off by category, he spoke
those words, understanding cannily that even in his mind he wasn't
addressing this person directly, not saying *you*, but only, "What would
he think . . . if I told him? What would *she* . . . ?" He had no fears of

omitting any of all these to whom he had agreed, "Yes . . . suicide"; he knew every one. And so finally he was absolved and naked, and slept.

In the morning, that same Wednesday of his sisters' and Augusta's visit, he searched his quarters to see whether in his seizure he'd written down any of this, but there was no signature of it anywhere, even in his face. Yet there had been a purging — or an increase? — for he was not the man he — was. He'd been let have a plunge into the nether-world of Faustian bargains, where a man of his temperament would not ordinarily go.

And he had never before in his life been so glad to see his poor dull sisters, and Augusta too, even if, in her having left the dog at home, he was warned. He'd glimpsed her at the cremation, and again in that surreal gathering afterward where, whether a body was earthed or burned, the peculiar demands of animal-human consciousness required all to tolerate that and afterwards eat over it. He thought he saw this sentiment too in Augusta's expression, also always to him, in any room they were in, the other critic intelligence. She too had the same sense of life as vehicle and as its own self-conscious creation, to what joys and ends neither could imagine of the other, though now and then she let him see its blue pilot-spark in the spinster's eye. Since the funeral, she had absented herself from the house, until this day.

Returning to the room then, where she still sat over the tea tray, he could imagine her in these past days, holed up in her hotel, sifting events through all her knowledge of him, then snapping her hands together like the Parcae their thread. He didn't fear her literal imagina-tions — who could imagine *this?* — and she was even often clumsily thick with others from regions where her own life-limits did not extend. He feared only her awareness, delicate as an elephant's lip, of him.

"You haven't brought Chummie," he said, returning.

She was hawked over the tea tray as if she saw fortunes in the four cups there, and made no reply.

"Is he all right?" he had said.

Nearly two years later, he could now remember that the current Chummie, still the same one as on that day, was a female, but no one ever bothered to distinguish between the dogs.

"Anna," his cousin had said, ignoring his question. "Whatever has come over Anna?"

"What do you mean?"

"She served the girls — tea."

"The girls didn't complain."

"No, but they noticed. Before you came in. She looks terrible too, Anna."

He wasn't afraid of his sisters, those eternal girls. He went to a decanter and poured brandy into the two silver déposé glasses which Mirriam and he had taken with them on their honeymoon.

"Brandy? At this hour?" But she took it. Probably she had never had brandy anywhere except here — at nine in the evening. He had another sense of her limits forever barricaded into the domestic, this competent woman — and of the sharply honed focus this gave her.

"How they jumped! Rosa and Athalie." The brandy had warmed her. "When you asked them to come live with you." She said it cruelly, for their other offense to her. "Brandy," she repeated, hovering her glass over the tray. "And tea."

"Can you wonder at what's come over any of us?" he said.

Such exclamations were the safest.

But she stood up, drained her glass, glanced down at her feet for the absent dog, and walked the length of the room away from him; he saw the high heels. At the mantel, she faced the large, florid picture, staring up at it. Reaching out, she touched the pair of gloves she was holding to the picture's nameplate — *Portrait of Mirriam Mendes Mannix* — added by the artist, and once a family joke. "No. No, I don't wonder."

Was she hoping to tell him that whatever had happened, Mirriam was still to blame? If so, he could be moved now by the sadness of her method. Outside, the world at large buzzed revolution and bloodbath in telegraphic whistles, crime blotted the single streets at eight and was news-of-the-world at nine, across continent or parlor people cried to one another "No bamboozlement!" — the whole century wrote what it thought on the sky. And here in Augusta, in a body which if male would have been more powerful for sports and war than his own, a minced emotion, hedged inflection, gesture with glove, were still preserved. She could always make him feel by contrast with her that he was still in the world. Even now, in wartime, she stood like some brass portcullis image refused to the metal collections, upholding the single story of his house.

"Simon." She was back at his side. "Don't — put too much on Anna."

He assented with a nod, not trusting speech.

"Simon —" Again she glanced at her ankles, for the dog. "Put it — on me."

He raised his head.

"I won't come here to live. Of course not. But otherwise."

If he could. He thought of last night. But he'd managed alone. Augusta hadn't been on his list of names to satisfy. As yet *she* had asked him nothing.

"Simon —?"

"Yes —?" he said, in great fear.

She had drawn on one gray glove, the pair a present from his sisters also, and another family joke. Now she touched his cheek with it. The house was full of jokes. "Simon," she said, in a voice so loud she must have rehearsed for hours. "Was it suicide?" At the far end of the room, the voice rebounded, a gauntlet thrown down. His nearer cheek she touched, with the real glove.

He couldn't move from under it. Slowly, waiting, he felt himself valeted by the unseen, clothed against her even to the cheek. Inside there, he breathed shallow, safe from all except the concealer's glee, which sometimes he had seen in the armored face on a witness stand, yellowing the eye.

"*Yes.*" He brought all the tonelessness he could muster to it. Then he walked away.

At the decanter's side again, he felt drained but revivified. He would not have last night's seizures again. "Another brandy?" But he checked his watch-cuff and let her see it. Born two years ahead of her, he could command some of the old inflections too.

"Time for the children to come home." Her voice was toneless too.

"David's gone off on a school field trip that was due. I thought it best. And he has Walter along." Dear good Walter, bemused by Mirriam herself as if for this hour — who believed everything he was told in this house.

"But you — kept Ruth here."

He drew breath shallow and easy; no, he would never be troubled again. "Doctor thought best. She still had the stomach upset."

"And the delirium?" She had the spinster's interest in symptoms, of course — or the whole clan's placatory-to-God, Jewish one.

"She got her first period," he said. His poor child — only Mirriam herself, always ready with a Marseillaise on any private right of wom-

anhood, could have kept that in the dark, from the clan. But he saw
Augusta flinch, as he had calculated. In a half-hour his daughter would
be returning from the ballet practice she had gone back to straight
from bed, as to a nunnery. She would be coming back as on every such
afternoon recently, brown under the eyes with the sweat of these lyric
hours, gabbling the Frenchy babble of those bacchae, and giving out
nothing else, *nothing*, even in her silences, which were offered too
bright-eyed to any observer. Speaking nothing else. He had to make his
cousin leave.

He saw her prepare to go, then turn back. "Simon . . . the girls are
letting out . . . that it was cancer — she did have that breast cyst two
years ago. Was it?"

He shrugged.

"But — the autopsy?"

"There was no full autopsy. They got the bullet. It was her gun.
They were kind."

She was thoughtful. "Kind." On that she prepared to leave.

But he had to give her something. He had better. "If *you* would say
it — take it upon yourself to say — that it *was* —" And it would help,
more than from the sisters.

He saw her turned-down smile — for all sham. But she was human.
And he was Simon.

"Another brandy?" he said.

She answered finally, but to which question of his questions he
wasn't sure; she had drawn him too into these mincings.

"No," she said, with deep, extended sadness. "No."

At the street door, he said lightly, "Don't forget to bring Chummie.
Next time." It was cruel, from him. One gawky, agonized glance, from
the girl of the boardinghouse, told him so. But he had done it. He'd
kept at arm's length that divination of him which reached from Augusta, from those antennae the ugliest beetles were often forced to
carry like queens — which would brush and brush over the old, known
part of him, to discover the new. He had prevented her from seeing
Ruth.

For already then, not half a month away from the death, his certain
duties had shut themselves in with him like lay figures, rising calmly

from corners to shut the louvers in on him and bare their effigy teeth in a silent ukase. He'd passed successfully through the special wake left by a suicide; now he had to bear only that nameless shock which was to last him for life, from the moment he'd carried back upstairs the bloodied child.

For the child herself — whom he meant to bear to a womanhood as protected from the worldly consequence of her act as if she were still in the amniotic sac — was safe from *him* only. He had to perform all his duties in darkness, without help from instinct, or from her. For he still didn't know what Ruth knew of her own actions that night. Therefore he was unable to ask her. He would never be able to. Ahead of him, a white cone at the other end of life's tunnel — and really only that mythical access-to-radiance of which all people kept an image — was the chance that one day *she* would tell *him*. Yet he knew this to be as unlikelier each day as if they two could grow old together — to mumble their secrets at exactly the same time. Yet he kept that picture too, gradually replaced by the most incontinent of all hopes. This was that in spite of all, she would somehow grow up maybe in the circumstances of a motherless child, an overfathered one, but otherwise in that state known to all but beggaring description, and therefore called normal. And would bring him therefore to a state of the same.

Things changed. Here — where he sat now in the dun dusk of an afternoon well suited to reading old correspondence and writing farewell letters — was a sitting-room once a woman's bedroom. Its flowered silks remained as always; her desk, at which he was sitting, still lodged its many pigeonholed archives between the same prettily niched confusions of pinks and greens. Yet the room now smelled harmlessly of chalk, crayons and cleaning fluid and the dozen other domestic tasks and interviews set to dry in the "extra" room. There in that chair the plumber had waited to sign his contracts; on that tall screen the dressmaker hung her cutouts; under their many fingerprints the room was now extra, rainy-day, characterless. Lack of drama was its job. How else could he have sat here, as had begun to be his afternoon habit even before he and Ruth had left the country?

Now on a week's return, the long summer just past already seemed a planet away, almost as out of logic for him and his daughter as those who had protested the trip, yet helped them to get there, had said. Actions which were altogether out of logic were different from the merely illogical. If only one could say for sure in all daily life — as easily as one could say it of taking a fourteen-year-old to wartime England — which actions these were.

Since their return, his afternoon habit here — as distinguished from the morning's professional hours in the study downstairs — had become fixed. Anna had made the changes in this room, whether in lucky fumbles that became tact, or in some exquisite knowledge which came of servitude, wasn't his to say. The chaise had vanished, replaced with a sofa come from somewhere in the house, since it looked worn and he had never paid any bill for it. The room's new name had evolved the best way, as perhaps the protective emotions and habits should also — through use. Opposite him, an ancient wardrobe, where he'd always stored any overflow clothing, from sailing gear to dress suits, still housed these, insuring his natural entry here from his own bedroom from time to time.

Since the death, his own illogic consisted in coming to this room for all decisions. These had been, in reverse order from the present: to write a parting letter to a woman (which he had just now done), to read and dispose of his wife's lifetime correspondence (which he had been doing all week), to go abroad with Ruth (accomplished), to write a memoir of his father (still unfinished), to give up his judgeship in order to work full-time at the rescue of legal scholars and others from the fascist countries (decisions not clearly connected but both undertaken that first six months), and — undertaken in that first hour after the death — to do what he had done, about Ruth.

Going upstairs to her third-floor room, he and the doctor had left the examiner in the bedroom — *here*. "No need for you to come in here again, Judge," the examiner had said. Standing in the doorway here, he'd spread his arms across it, barring it to the pair of them on the landing, but also meaning to be kind — and conspiratorial? He'd been a smallish man (though medium-size to the Judge), with a chin of incongruous length and a sidelong, putty nose. It was a confessor's face. The Judge had an impulse to lean on those arms, so spread for it, to cry Murder to that conniving, tweaked face. But the man turned his back on them. "I'm Ford," he'd said at the downstairs door, going past them and up to the death-room as if he had the ground plan of all murders in his brain. "I'll take care of everything."

And he had, even to the undertaker, who must have had a tie-in with that kind of trade. "Just leave the door on the latch for my men, please," he said, striding past the Judge, leaving Joel, the family doctor, on the steps, and except for that passage on the landing they hadn't seen him again. He had eloped with Mirriam, into the night.

"Wait a minute. You say she walked in on it?" said Joel, his hand on the knob of Ruth's door. His father had delivered her. He had inherited the same heavy, internist silences. All his patients were convinced they understood his simple personality better than he possibly could their complicated ones, and this arrangement was satisfactory all round; the magic could go into the medicine.

"She got her first period. She came to tell." The faintest sense came to him of how it must be to be female — an appointed day, a certain musk.

"She know about such things?"

"Of course."

"You'd be surprised," said Joel. "Even this day and age. I get commissioned to do it all the time. To tell them. Boys too."

"Mirriam was good about all that. Open. And I think they have a course at school." He'd never once made the mistake of the tenses, never again had said, "Mirriam *is*." He could observe that now.

"Give her something to rest, Joel." he said. "For God's sake, give her something." He'd inherited a family manner with doctors, or a Jewish one — abject, and imperial.

"Hold it, Si. Anna may have given her something." Joel's relationship here was mostly with Anna, over the children. Once it had been with Mirriam. The Mendes manner with doctors was more regal than the Mannixes'. They lived almost to their deathbeds without them — and lived long.

"That stuff you give her for her stomach — does it have a narcotic in it?" Or had she been delirious? He'd clutched at a last-minute faith in keywords, specifics which might explain everything.

"Trace of paregoric, peppermint." The doctor, listening past him, had had the same bovine stare as when he was auscultating. "But she wouldn't have heard that popgun anyway, would she, way up here." He knew all about the family target practice, having sent David to the ear man who'd prescribed it. Now he poked Simon in the chest. "You were still out?"

He looked down at his dress shirt. "A dinner for me. I stayed late with a friend afterwards."

"Oh?" The doctor had the conservative ethic of a man too busy for any but the good life; patients consigned their children to him but took

their own sins elsewhere. Any cynicism he had was reserved for the
bodies they brought back.

"He'd had bad news from overseas. He's ninetyish."

"Ah." In retrospect, Joel's I-wouldn't-think-otherwise smile reminded
him of Hildesheimer's — the same unction without imagination. A mixture widespread, for which he supposed he must give thanks.

For he'd made a slip then. "Mirriam was waiting up for me."

"And it was *then* she did it?"

The mind could be emptied. His had. His skull ached around it.

"I'm not surprised, Si." The doctor's words had been like a wand
drawing him to his feet again, from where he had sunk back. "I have to
tell you — that I'm not surprised at all." He spoke stiffly. "Ordinarily
I — Mirriam was not my patient, Simon." It was almost the worst he
could say. "She was unstable. I have to tell you it. Any medical man
could see it." Especially if he saw only children. "You better let me
handle Ruth."

"You mean you think *she* . . . takes after Mirriam that way?"

"No, Si. Not at all. I've been sticking needles into her long enough to
know what a great little kid you've got there, straight as a die. But
maybe she ought to spill a little before I give her anything. Especially
with the other business, or if she's in shock. You still are. Better let
me."

"David's still sleeping." And my son, what of him?

The doctor shrugged. "Let him, as long as he can, poor boy. David's
his own man, I could never break him down." So his own father might
have him. "Far's I know, David doesn't take after either of you, much.
But Ruth, you don't have to worry — she's all you."

So he'd given up, unknowing, his great opportunity. All his life
might have equipped him to be the seismograph here, and love as well,
but to the doctor, both his love and his shock disqualified him. Now he
could see where these might have been the talismans. The next night
he'd gone alone to her, prepared for honesty from her if that came, or
bewilderment. And ready for either with words agonizedly chosen neither to lead her on nor put in her mind things which — might not be
there. Could there have been such words? What he'd really done
was to leave it to her.

"I'll take care of her," said Joel. "As a patient." And so he had,
pushing in the door, that lightest of barricades.

A blue lamp was burning, though it was already day. Though the

Judge knew all the moods of the house, how it blended inner cloud and outer, he scarcely recognized this milky rain of light washing the window, above a horse race of clouds. The bulb of the lamp had been wrapped with the paper from a box of absorbent cotton, an old sickroom trick even of his time, of the women who made childhoods. Since the days of bedtime stories he had scarcely been in this room. Now he quivered for all fathers who meant to get to know their children in time. In an alcove, the enormous dollhouse still squatted in its dusty fairyland shrubbery, not to be got rid of except to younger children or one day to a charity; it had lights and linens on the beds and a doghouse, he remembered from the day of its arrival, and was the kind only a poor man like Pauli Chavez would give. On a rack to one side of it, a half-dozen school dresses hung in strict attendance. Ruth wasn't in the tumbled bed. Anna was sitting on the side of it, head bent.

"Dr. Choel." She seized on the doctor, yet was hopeless. "She has cramps yet. I give her Midol."

His own father used to give his sisters a little Holland gin for the same reason — had his father felt as clumsy, hangdog, as this? He wished he had only his father's reasons. Then Ruth came out of the adjoining bathroom in a nightgown, saw them, slid into bed like a truant, and closed her eyes. It wasn't a child's way of doing it.

"Are you in pain?" said the doctor.

She shook her head. Her eyes opened. Then she closed them.

"Is there much flow?" said the doctor in a stage whisper to Anna, who faintly signaled no. The doctor advanced to the bed and looked down on the brown topknot newly tied. "Ruth dear. What's happening to you happens to all women. You understand that."

Her eyes opened directly into her father's, to one side of the doctor. She kept them that way.

"We used to give Holland gin for it," he said. "To Rosa and Athalie." He smiled weakly, reaching for her hand above the coverlet, but the doctor's strong fingers, feeling for her wrist, barred his. The doctor spoke over a shoulder to Anna. "Was she delirious? Earlier?"

"I don't think —" said Anna. "I don't know."

"She was delirious," he said loudly, looking around him in each face. But no one regarded him, except the child.

"Going to put you to sleep," said the doctor. "Like an old office injection, that's all." He spoke again over his shoulder, as if she couldn't hear him, "I don't want to give her anything more by mouth." Then he turned back to her, but his double-speaking hadn't nullified her force, only his. "But Ruth darling, maybe you want to talk a little first." He meant that he did.

She would not answer. And he scarcely waited.

"The other that's happened to you. That's not ordinary; no one could say it. You've lost a mother, in a terrible way. But it should help to know your mother was sick, dear, in her mind. That can happen." The doctor's tenderness was like the rabbi's — for a large practice.

And he, the husband, did not deny it. Didn't say: "Not sick — angry, wild, intransigent, spoiled at forty-six, but until now never really despoiling!" (And maybe in your mother's flights of anger, my child, maybe even the spiritual assertion, against my calculating chess-ways, of the other beauty in the universe?) Would this have been a better legacy? But paralyzed, he couldn't say no to anything.

"Cry a little," said the doctor. "Be brave, but cry a little too." He offered a shoulder, but she refused it, with the same stare.

"Shall I leave the room?" said Joel. "Want to talk to Anna and Daddy?"

But her stare had been for them as well. She would take her sins somewhere else.

Then, downstairs, they heard the sound of that man's minions — the sound of stretcher-bearers — in houses with staircases, and maybe even those without them, one of the unique sounds of the world. He'd heard it three times before in a dwelling of his, the last in this particular one, when old Mendes had left it. In their sudden silence, the doctor gave her the needle.

"I go down," said Anna, hushed. There ought to be some respect paid, by someone from the inner house, as a body went out a door. He couldn't move, lulled into letting Joel take his place with his daughter, leaving it to Anna to find, between known limits and unspoken excesses, her anomalous place.

As Anna passed the blue lamp, she turned it off. On the half-drawn window shade, the red-penciled glow along its lower edge deepened. A golden blot of light ran like mercury to its center and hung there gleaming, moving on and off with the wind. Then a moan came from the bed, and Anna without comment turned the blue light on again and went out, shutting the door.

"Well . . ." said the doctor. "You've got them to live for, Simon. A fine girl and boy." He must announce births the same way.

Outside, the street was rising in beautiful health and clatter. The blue light seemed to melt, not quite to fade. The doctor gave a final pat to the girl, who lay with her palms upturned now, lids slipping. In the small profile, neat as marble, he saw his fatherhood. "Well, good-bye, old girl," the doctor said, in a voice like a punch. "You'll be all right. Come and see me later in the week." And to Simon, in the voice which ran back and forth between the generations — and got nowhere — "She'll be the bright little mother of this house, you wait and see. She's going to live to make you and David happy."

"And herself," he said — as if he gave and answered the responses here. To his sole credit he had said that, though her lids were closed now. "And herself."

The doctor shook his hand.

Downstairs, he heard or interpreted a murmur between Anna and the doctor at the door. The house had the acoustical whims of an old dwelling; sometimes he imagined it let each inhabitant hear only what he wanted to hear.

When Anna came up again, the smallish room, not dormered like Anna's fourth-floor quarters, but narrowing as brownstone third floors seemed to do against all actual measurement, was filled with the girl's regular breathing. They could marvel at how, in a sickroom, the patient's breath was consoling beyond anything else — and could leave her.

Outside, summoning all his failed strength, he said to Anna, "What did she say? Did she say anything more? When you brought her up." But Anna was weeping and he saw that she hadn't broken down until now. The red tears made channels in her face, ran from the corners of her mouth. Her lips swelled with them. He put his arms round her, for the only time in their history. He thought she made as if to put him off, but she was only finding room between sobs, to speak. "She ask me for the blue paper on the light," said Anna. "Dey were babies, Mrs. Mannix teach me how to do it. So I do it. Then she don't say nothing. She was being sick both ways, vomit and the other, but after we fix her and it was over, she creep to me but she don't say nothing, only one thing." The sob choked her; he could see it in her throat there, a red bit of meat in the throat of this red woman. From the skylight above, the sun in its great morning vibration shed for one passing minute a claret warmth straight down through the landings of the house. " 'Make it the night before this one, Anna,'" said Anna. "That's all she say to me. 'Anna, Anna, make it the night before.'"

And after that — he could go to his son. When Anna saw the direction his steps took, she said David's name and gestured she would come along, but he resisted the temptation to take her with him, to save himself from the ordeal before him — by David's one sight of her tear-blinded mime — and went down the hall alone.

David's room, allotted the firstborn, was much larger, and providentially so, since — from the moment his total deafness had been confirmed at the age of fourteen months — the room had begun to fill with apparatus, from all the electrostimulatory devices, wired and graphed and belled, which could be made to correlate sight and sound, to the merely practical audiovisual alerts and signals, plus a range of stereopticons and oscillators purchased on advices now lost. A sight of the room gave pause to any man who thought he knew the boundary between scientific and quack. David insisted on keeping them all, toy and grim; they were, as he said, his auditory memory. For this, their Smithsonian clutter, neatly as he tended it, was cheap enough price to pay. But these apparatuses had done even more. In the first years, for the Judge, rising early for a workout with the child as other men rose to cold showers and barbells, these devices had been the bridge to his actual belief in the deafness of the child.

Months past the diagnosis, he had remained unconvinced. There was no heredity of it for one thing; on either side, the hearing of grandparents, their collaterals, and even their parents had remained acute. Though he knew well enough that Mendelian laws allowed for this, to the end that anybody could inherit anything — including the will to disbelieve it.

But David himself had confounded the doctors. At times he appeared to turn at a voice behind him — or to the current of warmth behind it, as even now. In the physiotherapist's office of the school David had ultimately gone to, there was a sign *Use the tantrum — it is their way;* for it was a cliché that a deaf child was frustrate. And here came David, never saintly, not passive, but equable and busy even at two; from the first, his rage, if it was there, had refused to remain incommunicado with life. No child, even the handicapped one, it was said smartly to them, is ever average to his parents. But by what exquisite joinings of sight to sound, night to day, had this child taught himself not to be mute?

Going down the hall to his son's room that night, he wished for one of those mornings of uncertain agonies but happinesses too, both hallowed now. For, such exercises, with such a child, were a bridge to love also. Already he'd been unsure this boy was his son. By the time he had taught himself and them all, in these devoted mornings, that the boy was truly deaf, he had also convinced himself of the other thing. By exquisitely non-electrified communication with the past (Mirriam's) through the quality of the present he and she manufactured daily, or even with the boy himself (all means which he knew were suspect), he had decided it. The boy was not his son — if only because he could still think of him as "the boy." Doggedly he searched out stories of real offspring who disavowed real fathers, counseled his own ego once more to give up its games — and took up lipreading. It was possible that real fathers went through stations of trial like these to get to their sons; contrarily he himself had known fathers of adopted ones, who were to paternity born. There was ground for his doubts — one. He would *not* ask. If Mirriam had ever said, or hinted, late as it was he would have accepted either way, with lip, heart and loin. He even craved it. Meanwhile, as the boy steadily grew independent, the mornings lapsed, the bridges were left untended, the boy went to school to better tutors; he himself grew as used to a six-foot son as his own father must have done to one of his height — never used to it. Only the machines in David's room remained as was. And in the end, as often in the concerns of those who lived with Mirriam, he himself had been left unsure of anything.

At David's door that night, he did not hesitate. In spite of himself he slipped the knob as always, as if not to startle that deafness. In the dark, he stood by the bedside while the miracle of the retina took place, and looked long at that fine head, incandescent almost in its fastness. Men must take their chances with the morning. But this was only a boy of seventeen. On the pillow the fair head otherwise so aquilinely reminiscent of old Mendes on his deathbed grew clearer, at its ear the rigged telephone, center of other alarums here that would not ring but glow. There was something holy in such a trust in light.

He touched a switch, intending one lamp's softness. He knew all the wiring here — or had once. Or else his hand had expressed its real intention. The room flooded harshly, from overhead. "I'm sorry —" he said.

The eyes flew open, just as if the boy on the pillow had heard. The person behind them wasn't quite awake. It was that blank moment when the human returned to animal, tensing toward danger, or kin. Then the boy sat up. He slept nude. Large as the tendons were in that big brown shoulder, it was still a boy's. The Judge put his own small hand there, if not a father's, a man's. "I'm sorry," he said again. At once in the patient face opposite, he saw the monitoring begin — and found he himself couldn't go on. His mouth would not voice or shape. He was mute.

"Father, Father, what is it? Are you sick?"

At his own motion, a pad and pencil were pushed toward him. Sometimes he and David had done that in those mornings, though in certain exercises it was forbidden. He managed to write on the pad: *Bad news.*

But then, when he tried to go on with it, his trembling fingers also failed him, as if each member of his own body, when applied to, refused. He found himself staring at the boy's face, David's face, thinking in sacrilege that if it had been blind, then he could tell it the news, with his voice.

As if in answer, the boy knelt before him in the old posture and place, and put his own large but discerning hand against his father's lips — which again moved. But because they did not do well, the son with a half-smile closed his eyes, the better to feel the words, as performed by the blind and mute. And so to that face above him, grown longer and equine with youth, but still to the hand of that divining child, the Judge spoke. "Shot. Your mother. It was an accident."

Surely that was what his lips had said. In that order. But the hand feeling his mouth read otherwise, or like a true divining rod. He saw the shoulder at his own eye level shrink back in reflex. Then the hand struck him full across the mouth.

Bleeding from nose and lip, in the strangest sensation of having been *saved,* he watched his son flee the room.

Luckily Anna had been outside the door after all. For he himself was useless. *Now I can sleep* was what he said to himself. The concussion was nothing, its blood stanched with a handkerchief. Yet "Now I can sleep" he had said to himself with an exquisite lulling, cast back with a bit of hurt for himself. And staggering into his room, he had done so, fallen on his bed.

Where and how David had spent the few hours between when Anna left him for her own bed and the phones began to ring, could be seen from his track. He must have come first to this room where the Judge was now sitting, his mother's room — to find the body already taken from him. The smashing must have begun here. In here it had been merely a rending and a tearing — of the coverlet that had wrapped her, which the minions had dropped. The Judge next door, lulled, hadn't heard. Anna, upstairs in her fastness, hadn't heard it either, the steady frustrate rage of that descent through all the family rooms to the bowels of the house, grinding lamps to bits, stamping over chairs in a clean, methodical wake. The worst had been in the family rooms and at the front door, which still bore its grazings, irreparable in the oak. Neither Anna's kitchen nor his own study had suffered anything, nor any windows. In effect that almost silent raging had all taken place where it had always been — inside.

It must have been in the kitchen that the boy returned to his senses, for Anna had found food there on the table, gone after in the hunger reflex of that long bone structure, his own body, but scattered uneaten, the dish smashed. Then he had gone up to his sister's room, to find her sleeping beyond rousing, and across the bottom of her bed had sobbed himself to sleep. For the hour or so before the world advanced again, the house might have been Beauty's castle. When the two children woke, they were still alone. Together they must have heard Anna's first "My hosh, my hosh!", the trail of them as she went through the damaged house, and the Judge as he picked up and answered the first phone. Anna had found the two together, Ruth wan but the calmer of the two, David swollen to the eyes.

No one had ever spoken to David of what he had done. In the two years since, that track too had long since been overgrown. What the two children might have said to one another when they awoke wasn't known to the Judge either. He thought of this as part of the abnormality — his and the family's but ultimately his, which he had to deal with. In the alternately submerged and surface way that life took, he thought and did not think of it. The boy himself now kept a silent distance which had once been the Judge's only. Meanwhile, his own fathership, in no way more expressed, had secretly grown a little — as for a son adopted in youth, across old estrangements. Manhood might release them both. In the privacies of life, anything might burst through a door. But what those two children had said to each other remained inviolate. Upstairs, during these long afternoons growing toward winter, it sometimes seemed to him that if houses like his came to any value, it would be as among the last examples of a private life kept separate, untransfused either by its own public appearances or by what seeped more and more over the doorstep, or down from overhead— from the writings-in-the-sky.

Anna knocked now, but entered without waiting for the "*Come* in" he almost never gave anyway; he got so deep in here. Outside the study, where since his retirement he could never work himself deep enough in scholarship ever again to believe in it, she walked by hushed, fending everyone away with her own eccentric version of "in conference" — "De Judge is alone." But this room was her own partially created domain — and here, as she perhaps knew, he was never alone.

She walked by him now without comment — they rarely spoke on these occasions — laid on the bed his dinner jacket and trousers, unpacked from the Atlantic trip, and went out, again closing the door, so effigy a servant that one would have been undisturbed to meet her doppelgänger simultaneously on each landing of the staircase; indeed, that was the effect she often gave. She had nothing in common with that other red woman of a past morning. They never spoke of it.

She never hung his dress clothes away in the big wardrobe, but always left them in his sight, a hint against frowsting at home, from that outdoor philosophy which all servants fostered in masters. He liked to think that in this she was his ally, helping him do battle against what he thought of as "the self-pity of the wardrobe." A family inheritance of his side, huge enough to occupy the vision of anyone who sat at Mirriam's desk, it had once held all the retired sack suits, cutaways, patent dress shoes and collapsible opera hats of both father and grandfather. At the time of his wife's death it had held the thirty-odd suits of his own dandyism — and public ambitions. During those post-mortem weeks when his habit of sitting here began — with a never fulfilled intent to go through her correspondence — he often sat staring instead at this huge, hollow escutcheon, seeing himself in his true guise, a small man who only temporarily inhabited it. In his mind he had already retired himself. He'd never had to explain it to himself. Retirement, once effected, fell on him like the one suit of armor for which he had been born.

Now he got up, took up the jacket and trousers from the bed, hung them away, and sat down at Mirriam's desk, in front of its many dim slots for open secrets and improvidently brassed "secret" drawers. At her death, he had found himself as impotent to touch her private matters as in life some men were before their wives' flesh. But this had been his weeping for her, blood-sick and unnatural.

The old wardrobe held another kind of mourning — sweated, male. It mourned for fathers — and for all live burial. He knew that Jewish colleagues only less lapsed than he had said of his giving up his judge-ship that he was *atoning.* In their high holidays away from Mammon (and in the limestone Episcopal synagogues with which they replaced the puce Moorish of their fathers, or their grandfathers' slum-yellow, public-bath brick) they still kept a Day for it. But he wasn't too lapsed to know that privately a Jew atoned no better than anyone else — or just about the same. Now that the stench across the ocean was almost over, the world and maybe the Jews too both saw themselves moving into a new age of public atonement as one might move into public affairs. Not yet seeing how this too went against that jealous old God Jahveh, of whom, true, he knew little more than a spelling, yet like every born Jew felt he carried live in his breast. Inwardly he still fought the new Israel, or even the emotion that the six million martyrs were for Zion, not for themselves. But as a man with an obligation which there wasn't time to spell, he had helped. Maybe this was why he now could stare at the old escutcheon over there, at himself, the incumbent in it, and fight both. The man who would best have understood his retirement — long before he himself did — would have been Chauncey, one of the most Hebraic men he had ever known. How Olney would have relished being told so! But the second morning after their visit, Olney had been found peacefully in his chair at the window. Proctor, to whom the Judge had since spoken, had found him dead, early in the dawn hours, as Chauncey waited maybe for partying girls to peer in at his window, or wondered what had become of Anna's promised soup. Meanwhile, as yet the Judge saw himself buying no more suits. For the life he was expecting to lead from now on, those thirty would be far too many — enough.

But since his return from England with his daughter, he had at last been able to go through this desk and watch Mirriam rise again from her own mementos. Now that he and Ruth were safe home from their summer of war, he could be properly grateful for a trip even farther out of logic to others than his "giving up." He had elected to go to London and other points just at a time when all his work with the stream of refugees—from British children, to scholars and scientists trustfully waiting to be fitted into the world again, to the unswervingly romantic and handsome families of Polish airmen flying with the British — had been going the *other* way, as everyone said (meaning here). The trip was beyond duty, and to take a young girl impossible. Surely he and she had been a strange pair to be the first members of his family perhaps in a century to go to war, if only to attend it — and when a whole nation behind him was still freely choosing. Surely, he hadn't done it from the terrible connoisseurship which always sent some to sink their personal disaster in the common one. His work had needed jobs done over there. And he'd had to take her because of the decision which antedated all others — that she was not ever to be left.

Queerly enough, on the question of taking Ruth with him, Anna had been his ally too. Anna hadn't been present when, after the rabbi's visit, he went upstairs to his daughter. Sitting at the bedside where she was being wooed back from sedation with all the sweetmeats the women could muster, he carefully spoke the absolving sentence he had labored over like an essay: "Mother killed herself, in her own way. It was an accident." Gravely she nodded, giving back nothing, either of confession or assent. The school later reported their version of her, with rhyme as well: understandably his and their dear, bubbling girl had become *grave* — and "brave, dear Judge Mannix, so brave." Anna had been in the room again, with a custard, when he got up, hands hanging, said quickly, "I'll be with you always, *always*," and went out.

Once, as a young man still at home with his mother, he'd been involved in a dreadful weekend of harboring an old melancholic relative, while the red tape was being bound round the old man, for dispatch to a mental home. He and his mother, on instructions, had abstracted knives from drawers, drugs from cabinets, and kept the old man from windows, the hired nurse not having arrived and the registries being closed on a Thanksgiving weekend — he deserting his skis and a girl with a merry "Got to stand by some old loony in the bath-room and see that he doesn't cut his throat."

In the ensuing three days he'd felt closer to his mother than ever before or again, as they hovered in fealty, keeping the surface normal-ity going like a fire which never warmed *them*. For while they kept the old boy immersed in their smiling stability, theirs became suspect to themselves. His mother, drawing on a long record of literal-minded domestic service which for the first time shamed him into admiration, had revealed a similar experience, with an elder sister, before. Men had to go to offices; women had this sort of job oftener. He'd never forgot-ten that terrible housekeeping around a mental illness, that keeper's sense of himself, all day conscious of what the invalid was not, all day at his insane task of clearing up the leftovers of a sick mind more intensely at the task of life than his own.

He must take care now not to weave his own anxiety into such a situation. His own vigil over Ruth must somehow be relaxed.

"Does she ever . . . say anything to you . . . about *anything?*" he'd once asked Anna. The answer, "No." She too had her vigil. And when the trip under question had been mentioned in her hearing by Augusta (who now never further jeopardized her status with him, and always brought the dog with her, but in a budding entente sometimes took Ruth home "to see Chummie"), Anna had spoken afterwards, serving his solitary dinner. "I am maybe too nosy. But take her *with* you, Misser Mannix. *Go*." And in the damnedest way, had added a fatalism worthy of his mother — who if born to the servant class might have been happier. "De bombs," said Anna. "Dey watch over you."

Pauli Chavez had helped too, drawing from his ragbag of European friends-of-his-youth — all of whom seemed to have become famous in the years since without ever incurring Pauli's rancor — the name Ninon Fracca. At Mirriam's behest, Pauli, in youth an assistant conductor in European opera houses, had always supervised the selection of Ruth's ballet teachers, often happy to tag along with her to haunts of his own friendships and courtship, to any faintest detail of which Pauli re-mained fond; in the mind of such a man, when did "youth" formally stop? Pauli at the ballet school — as Ruth, who knew his mistress Leni, reported — was tolerably uncle-ish to the fauns there. "From having — you know, Daddy — an *old* sort of one at home."

These swift young verdicts were the only way Ruth's own character,

if one could call it that as yet, still peeped out as it used to. How the
Judge watched for it now, in joy and fear, recalling how once, for
instance, they'd heard her say of the school's fat boy, whose elder
brother had been drowned, "That's why his mother feeds up Billy."
Back then, he'd merely smiled over it — with Mirriam.

"Ruth is on the way to be a dancer," Pauli'd said, last spring. "Good,
Simon? Who knows. Not a dancer just in the legs, anyway. She has a
whole feeling for it, for that whole world. Leni says so too." And was
that why, in the end, her father felt he must stop her? For he knew the
fate of those who had only a feeling for art; Mirriam's crowd had been
composed of them. And of *their* hangers-on, of whom hadn't Mirriam
herself been one?

"And just *now* —" Pauli had said, with the silvery, pervasive innocence of advisers who are childless.

Agreed, though — just now. "Fracca," said Simon. "I seem to have
heard that name somewhere." Until he'd reached England and the
Dorset manor house, run like a close, where Madame and her troupe of
twenty of the King's best dancers guarded the votive fires of British
ballet — and now and then dared the blitz over London theatres to
douse them — he hadn't understood Pauli's smile.

"Yes, this is 'Thomas Hardy country,'" said Ninon Fracca, an im-
plicit "as you Americans would say" in her voice, though he and Ruth
had only exchanged light-struck stares at the house behind them in the
sun, and at the tiny royal figure, shorter than his own, advancing
toward them, in its brown wartime "utility" dress and silver-blond
curls, over the stage-green sward. Wessex wasn't in their minds, though
they were indeed not far from Dorchester. Ruth, who had photographs
of this lady in old *Dance* magazines at home, might have knelt, if the
seignorial brown façade at her own back hadn't reminded her of who
she and her father were, colonially.

Probably Madame had things she said to visitors. "Ours is a wartime
tenancy. The family is originally a Devon one — Stuccleugh." She
spelled it for them, her glance straying, but never abstract, toward two
of her nymph-troupe, in slacks and work boots, who had just pigeon-
toed their hoes around a garden frame. "Land girls, in their spare
time," she said briefly.

Ruth watched them hungrily. Since the trip across under the closed hatches of other people's losses, she had begun to be almost herself. Or rather, at what cost he couldn't believe in, had remained so. Always as long as her central mystery was not touched by transient remarks, never his of course. She bent now to the turf, her hair falling over her headband, and smoothed that electric green. She had never before seen turf, or England. "But you have no crabgrass!" she said. Afterwards, on the train back, explaining, "I thought an *agricultural* remark might help!" — and for that old glint alone, he would have let her stay there.

But coincidence had already interceded, like one of the long shadows on the lawn. "Any relation to the Stukelys?" he asked, spelling for Madame the name of one of his close associates in the refugee committee here. And of course it was the owner.

"Crebgrahss," Fracca said. "Whet is thet?" By habit perhaps tutorial, she never answered young people without a pause; older people were replied to on the double and often fliply — and might take the distinction to be Ninon Fracca's attitude toward life, youth and age, if they chose. Her voice was pizzicato, like her laugh and whole presence, down to the feet, now in stumpy court pumps, which might once have been that also. He supposed her to be perhaps forty-five. Though listed as French in the printed biographies, she spoke the best British. He never took her to be anything but Cockney, and did still, understanding also that, to the number of personalities she legally carried — *Madame, la Fracca,* and most divinely, *Fracca* — early perfidy meant nothing now. "And how is Pauli?" she said.

"You know *our* Pauli?" cried Ruth, who clearly found this mystically impossible, in spite of knowing it from Pauli himself.

Madame brought them into the house to await tea, along with — as she said crisply — "some locals" still to arrive. Meanwhile, she laid open for them a huge folio of manor houses of the region, in which the house took honors it didn't need, and even showed them its main glory, the free-hung, carved ebony staircase which led to her own oaken, fifteenth-century quarters, straight on in to the curtained Tudor bed which was as she said "too late" for the room, and to his pretty image of her in the bed — a small, jewel-winged, post-Tudor fly. Later, when he charged her with that purpose, it wasn't coyly denied.

In front of a Spanish mantelpiece which she told them had been brought over before the Armada, she said to Ruth, "Of course I know

Pauli, how else do you suppose you got here, at your age!" — and to
the Judge, "Pauli's *father* was our musical director, in my first opera
house engagement. And of course I knew Leni later on, a prima ballerina she then was. In the provinces. But even so. And in Munich," she
said. Madame's face darkened; minute as it was, it had scope enough
for the Germans.

Her intense silences were un-English, if not French, but actually
more a part of her style than of her opinions — a concertmeister's
emphatic of life.

"Is Ruth too young?"

They both looked at him, then Fracca at Ruth. "Fourteen?" she said,
with a swift, inclusive glance.

"Almost," said Ruth.

They examined one another. Their laughter sounded together, pretty
as bells in the vaulted room, and as chill.

"Too old," said Ruth. She said it first.

Madame smiled at her quickly, with interest. She leaned forward,
chin on hand, legs tucked back like a dragonfly's. "In Munich, two
years a ballerina, I was not yet sixteen. I was never a prima. Later on,
Leni was. At eighteen." She spoke yet more softly. "Here in England
before the war, at the theatre we sometimes had apprentices, who
help. Later they assist the directress, study choreography, or the costume. And of course they dance too, like everyone here. For a summer
— it would be possible." So Ruth had been arranged for — for those
weeks while he would be going up to the danger zones of London, to
certain marked towns in the dreary undersides of "neutral" countries,
and to a few unmarked cantons, from Basel to the Valais.

When the locals arrived, a modest brother-and-sister pair of gentry
from the nearest reigning big house, and the headmistress of a neighboring school, who clearly held both them and the district in her intellectual power, Madame stood up, a figure finial to the massive fireplace
behind her, as if its tumbled gray carvings, arriving headlong down the
centuries, were brought up short before this small, heraldic construction in bone. She still possessed the ballerina's cool, pulled smile, and
didn't clasp hands with anyone except herself, inclining forward so
from the ankle, elbows lifted, each palm after a moment placed on an
invisible pannier at her side. Except for this mannerism, and the scale
to which she had been embodied (one thought of it that way, as if
there'd been a choice), there was nothing to relate her to certain long-

gone miniatures, enamel and real, of his father's Paris. Yet this was the moment at which he himself had been arranged for.

They had tea from the Stukely silver, and after that the daily war news, handed round like a snuffbox from which each impassive face took its bitter pinch. The headmistress, as if to palliate this with art's quick perfume, then urged Madame to repeat for them some of her own history. From this they learned that, born on the Île St. Louis, daughter of a housekeeper, she'd had a perfect childhood, commodious, clean, and situated among servants as devoted to their group life as the members of a commune. Who liked Riviera sun, ate fish with the aristocratically simpler sauces and reserved radical opinions on the city, though rarely deserting it. The judge, keeping his own counsel on her nationality, thought she had somewhere known upper servants very well.

From her own moderate bed — not the one in Dorset but a couch in the white-painted studio, lined with mirrors and practice bars and theatre caricatures, which she kept on under blackout in a street of barristers' eating-houses not far from the Savoy, behind the Strand — he had learned more. Born of a size to command, if never to be material for a prima, she'd grown up to a nose sharp and pink as a carrot, large swallow-colored eyes, and an intricately tendoned body in which the calves were the size of the breasts, the buttocks round and rosy-muscled, the waist sunk like a wedding ring in the sloping tutu of the hips. Between, the mound was bare as the armpits and not shaven, but in what she said was an old habit of the profession, plucked. Above all this a practical, steel-wired brain lightly rode her shoulders, as if in the adagio.

They laughed at each other, hand to hand, in the mirrors; they were of such a neatly matched scale. Agile from sailing, at the bar he did knee bends, which she called pliés, and he made a stab at their alphabet, finding that some of it — arabesque, pas seul — had been given to literature and the world at large. But he couldn't really credit a universe whose whole center was the business of moving the body to music. She told him, with coolly anatomical jabs of the fist here, and here — that he could never have made a dancer; embedded within him were the stolid bones of men half again his size.

"But incest was never my pleasure," she said, smiling. The troupe was indeed her family, and he surmised, though neither pressed the other to talk of former loves, that her alliances had always been culled

from the outside. He realized that he himself had never before chosen
a woman, large or small, because of her size. But there was more to it
than this of course on closer acquaintance; physically she was like a
trinket, but with that procurer's mind proudly in evidence, royally in
the service of the exquisite. He couldn't now imagine any other woman
who could have as dryly led him back to the sexual. Her ego wasn't for
itself only, but for the troupe. Emotionally she was narrowed, the
springs of her energy coiled round the passion of grace, even if it
should be (as some said of her influence on the dance) the grace of
ugliness. Her own art, clenched as it was in the total body, could never
be as impalpable as with the athletes of song or instrument. But she
had the performer's certitude: that heaven was attainable in the performance — *here*.

The war had perhaps subtilized her a little, as war did all onlookers.
But she still had the pug-and-terrier politics of the street corner; to her,
accession to power in the world was a matter first of the proper patron
and then the lingo. It was this which made him place her, if not in Les
Halles, then in the back and vegetable end of Covent Garden. Remembering that plucked pubis and certain winning coarsenesses of the
bed, he would not have been surprised to hear that at the earliest she
had at times been on the streets. What she would never be able to
understand about the world of the intellect, his or any, was that it
wasn't fixed — that its own towers still strove with one another, Guelph
and Ghibelline. She had arrived like an arrow on its mark. She would
never be middle-class.

So it was wartime that had really characterized their affair, and their
parting too. In the undercover but informal way in which the military
had arranged his and Ruth's departure — "My own little gel is with a
very delightful femmily in Ko-nek-ti-cut — perhaps you and your
daughter would be kind enough to call upon her?" — he and Ninon
had accepted the unlikelihood of anything more.

"Does Ruth have the bones for it?" he asked.

They were once more in the vast practice room down in Dorset, with
its elegantly drear look of a ballroom gone permanently to hard work.
At the far end of the nut-brown floor, a few of the eternal nymphs here
were stretching at the bar, with centrally absent stares, hands clasped
to ankles, as if studying the metaphysics of splitting themselves in two.
One dreamer was stubbing her squared toe in the rosin box; it was

more probable that she wasn't dreaming at all. He thought that Degas had understood them best, that the romance was always forward of them and even of the footlights, in the burnt scarf-tones and slate shadows in the eye of the painter, or the burst of spangles within the stage door — and once in a while, at the heights, in the ethereal pyramids and rosy formulae they made of themselves. Three of them passed him and Ninon now, going down the floor in perfect trance, exfoliating like flowers under film.

Ruth, who had finally danced for him (in a sextette so trimly matched to the accompanist's modish valse and to each other's angles that he could scarcely distinguish her) had slipped off to change into her travel suit, and no doubt to be kissed all round; they lived their whole lives here in nosegay. Even this woman here, at their very center, did this. Now, by some alchemy she distilled at will — by gathering in the room with a proprietary glance, raising her head Titania — he was being conveniently told this, graciously being dropped from his brief ennoblement.

"Oh — she has the bones. She is not as tall as she looks. Which is correct. For these days."

"But —"

"And she has the need. One has to have that to be anything. I am not sure that otherwise she — But she has that. It is recognizable."

He waited for her verdict. To have information on his daughter be the issue of his own love affair was in itself a marvel of how life transmogrified itself — always planing off and away, never quite terminal, even at the end. Through the mist of assessments and interviews — from schoolmistresses, doctors and always the willing priests that one's friends were — he yearned toward what his mistress could tell him better about his daughter than any of them: what his girl was.

"But —" He heard himself. Did he fear to be told that she was good for anything except his protection?

Madame's tipped eyes glanced away. She reflected, on that group now at the far end of the floor. Though her voice was clear, he had the peculiar sense that he was lipreading.

"My girls aren't stupid. Never think. But Ruth . . . She could be — a good enough dancer. And she would work. But she has too much — Not *mind*. Not like you. Maybe — *control*." She smiled. "Like me."

She leaned forward. "She's been excellent, with the others. Almost their elder — you know they squabble like ducks. Very tender with people, she is. I know girls. Such a quiet charm, like a bell that's never struck. But one knows the sound of it." She herself laughed softly. "I find myself as intrigued with the daughter as with —" And let that drop forever.

"Has she ever — confided in you?"

"No." A business voice. "But sadness at this time is not unnatural." She rippled that out in the flat neutral of her directive to the accompanist — *un poco andantino, non vivace.* She sat very straight; "What a back Madame has!" was always said from behind her. "She can be very *fun-ny* in 'er little way." The intonation was pure Cockney, as she tipped her head at him. "Did you know?"

He could wonder forever now whether she'd meant *he* had no sense of humor. That being what was sometimes said behind *his* back. Just then Ruth did come out from the dressing-room and they could both see her, surrounded by good-byes. "Maybe I can come back," they heard her say. "After the war."

They watched her, in that international posy of girls not the center, though it was she who was being said good-bye to. Was it only the travel dress? Or because it had been hinted that he fancied it? That alongside the dramatically servile body-rhythms of the others, all pliant to some beat they demanded be demanded of them, she would not blend? Could not.

"She is an assoluta," said Ninon. "Of somewhere. But not of the ballet."

They watched her come toward them with the same little duck walk as the others. As a parting gift, the others had done her hair up in a chignon. Elbows out, she clasped her purse in front of her. When she reached Madame and her father, she would bend her neck in the proper little obeisance with which all classes ended here, one foot toed behind her, one arm extended. It was always impossible to believe that one's children might be more intensely at the task of life than oneself.

He felt Ninon's whisper warm his ear, the last unaudited word they exchanged. "She means to be happy," Ninon said.

In the train down, reading the official account of the troupe in the signed album of pictures which Ruth was given in farewell, he learned that Madame, its long-time directress, was aged fifty-five.

But now, in the immenser dialogue of the sitting-room, as it took place each day — a body-rhythm that beat outward and beyond him — he could forget his daughter and himself, in the act of suspending them both in the larger rhythms of the world. In this room which had once been a bedroom, the small questions of particular life, murderous or joyful, pleaded themselves from his wife's desk, were asked of the wardrobe, which had no permanent inhabitant, and were answered, answered and rebuffed, tossed up shining for what they were, and sunk again in the waves that shook the wardrobe from beyond and flowed unceasing even through houses, front to back. Sitting so, he could see how certain men, made monks by time, sat in the silver silence of their rooms and received, as if from the wainscoting, the Chinese secrets of age. The peacock's-tail of his own thought unfolded before him, in every frail inch of it a spreading eye. All his thoughts existed at once, in this fan. Behind it the waiting pulses of life were held in abeyance, as tarnish holds light.

For a time, his own memoir of his father, of him and half by him, lay on the desk. Only the title, "How War Never Comes," was much his own, and the seed of that taken from Olney. Often now, he felt without amaze — except at how long it had taken him to see this filial ultimate — that he was thinking his father's thoughts. Why that should be so strange for modern times, he couldn't say — only that it was now considered odder for a man to be doing this than it ever had been in "modern" times before. His father too had written his papers, on "world" law most of them, his own curious phrase for "international," really an inaccuracy which merely sounded modern. The fragments he had left behind were a gentleman's, that is unpublished, and when reread — all those faint, Edwardian approximations of the great non-questions which would shake that golden world — so courteously second-rate. The one long-lasting idea his father had bequeathed him — only an image really, or an excitement, and blended now with Chauncey's "families that breed behind the lines" — had come in conversation, handed over to him in a restaurant, flecked up from that bon vivant current of living which both he and his father would have had to call frivolous — if ever either had dared to speak openly from their joint kernel of Jahveh's law. One of the arguments for the existence of

God must be that some great hand reaching down was always needed, to pluck the nutmeat of a life.

They'd been standing in the hallway of a brownstone given over to an eating-club his father belonged to, the Felicity, one of the rough-and-ready, oatmeal-papered retreats men of the era frequented as counter-tonic to the champagne hours farther uptown. This place was older and more furnished than most of its kind; the hat rack facing them, humped pell-mell with a score of overcoats, might have been the one at home. Hats still scattered it too, bowler and soft, and billycock — no caps. A few canes hung, or crossed. The time must have been late 1916, just before their country's entry into the war, and the next to last year of his father's life; he himself had not yet volunteered, or been turned down.

They'd already hung up their own coats, and his father the grand-father's silver-topped stick. "The stallion in the hallway," said his father. "That's how I always think of it. War. The stallion in the hallway, nickering at the male coats on the hat rack. And nuzzling them. I saw a horse walk into a house once, you see. I could scarcely believe my eyes. One never does." His father had murmured this, wine-loosed; then they'd passed on in to the tables, down every length of which young head chatted with old head tonight, blond with white, dark with bare, and all on the same subject — all their coats carelessly hung together, outside.

He sat now, and thought about the failed life. Flotsam and jetsam of *un*failed lives, civilizations one after the other were groined in sand. Scratch under any Pompeii, find the same archaeological cry. "How did we fail?" He and his father and their like, Chauncey Olney too, could they maybe make their own kind of answering? And also the billycock in the hall?

The anatomy of failure, what was it in a *man*, and was its language — if he had language — always grandiose? Was a life like Chauncey's, which pulled up short of its own endowment, always an abdication? In the beginning of his own trials, no one had seen them more conven-tionally than he. He didn't have the courage, or wonderment at the universe, to be Job. Duty to Ruth kept him in life if not health, he would have said. As to his duty to David, so early tied up with de-formity and disappointment, grudgingly he could even see that help-less parental answer ahead of him — was a son ever *meant* to be a father's health? Thoughts on the generations never led anywhere, except to lyric poetry, and back. The ages stood — for men and man.

But at first hadn't Chauncey too found it cynically interesting that the big act of retiring could give such an indolent keenness to the minor sensations of life, that he'd then had not just time, but honest time — in which to test and stare? The class of men who accepted society at once, and always had, weren't necessarily confident men, not even those who most appeared zestful and thick-skinned. Sometimes at school — prep school years were the prime for seeing it — the very earliest accepters had been the bullied and the effeminate, or at least the humiliated. Afterwards if these went on from there with wits sharpened to the power of society, it was said of them that their failures had worked.

But were there others more confident, who out of their own ardency and daring became the open failures or the secret separatists? If, like Chauncey, these finally gave their confidence and daring to the position of onlooker, what came of it? Had Chauncey too seen that as the biggest act of his life? And seen (far sooner than himself) that whatever excuse he'd taken for retiring — duty to the unloved or to the personal safety of the beloved — he'd been given time, borrowed from his own old age, to question the act of judgeship itself?

For after a while, the sensation began to be just that, as if one were just back from the dead, or more accurately had become one of the old people of this society — who, honored or not, were its zombies no magic was needed for. One had the insights, good or bad — of the finished life. As for his own father, totally a weaker and gentler man than Olney, one who could never have seen his own promise as anything to give up, but had had a piece of the onlooker's temperament; hadn't even he felt in his heart of hearts at the end that the dogma of every life ought to count somewhere to the world, as well as to the rosary of faces round a bedside — and hadn't done? To finish a father's memoir, was it more than an act of piety? Was it only poetry, to wish the old men back?

He told himself that it was. He could take the long view only because as a "failure" he had no shorter one. Downstairs in the study, he sometimes had the arrogance to feel himself the middle class dying, even against his own witness, and the wardrobe's, that a middle class was born every minute (like the class of suckers, but in no other way connected with them) and was therefore immortal, since its death rate, though high, ran by the year.

Upstairs, he knew only that *he* was dying, at his own sequestered rate. He was outside the currency of his time, in talk and ideas; instead of living a life, he was living an idea of life. Everyone active in the world and the war would say so. Downstairs, the splotched news-world exploded slowly, day by day. Upstairs, in the heart of family life, a man saw, like a frieze in his wainscoting, that violence couldn't detonate forever without reaching along the arteries of a civilization, to all its hearts. The education of most men was a gradual giving-in to the ideas of others. For a while he dragged each idea up the stairs like a heavy body. Up from that study so impervious with other men's books, to this room which was only for sitting, and murderous with reflected life. In the end, when he had ranged them all here, he sat like a man peering into a mausoleum to which he might or mightn't be related, seeing the immortal spidership of its corners, cataracted with failing light. In the end, all the bodies here were his own.

"How wonderful your refugee work has been for you, Simon!" Rosa and Athalie had said to him in the spring. His dear sisters had no trouble seeing the sun as merely a captious blood-orange hung in their Floridas, or — in the black cold that now gripped Europe — a poultice to get their brother's circulation going. "Better than sailing," they said. And not so dangerous.

"And a man like you is too valuable not to be active. In temple, Dr. Hildesheimer was saying it only the other day," they nodded, ever mindful of their membership in an even larger sisterhood. Strange, then, that like a sophomore trying his orations on grounds-keepers, he spoke his inmost thoughts these days to them.

"Talk *is* action, nowadays, isn't it?" he said idly to his sisters. At once it rang true to him. For where his own father would have gone into "rescue work" as what one did naturally for history and posterity, he himself had done so almost as selfishly as his sisters saw it, as his only chance, crannied between wars to share right *in* action. Only to find that the old-fashioned blood-and-thunder vision of action as supreme over thought, those vast gallopings into the sunset, had changed for him and others. Or except in the dress rehearsals of historians, had never been there.

"The thundering of events has never been worse, has it?" he said to bewildered Athalie-Rosa. "Yet talk *is* the action, now." In the peculiar transparencies of that newer generation just beyond his own, where everybody's language was almost everybody's, ideas *were* life. The natural mist between private and public action was going, one day to be gone. Or was this only what all men saw when they'd aged beyond hope of action? — which only his retirement had made him see in time?

Dear heart, their wrinkles now signaled one another — what a brother we two have! Oh, he never underestimated their value, lumbering alongside him like a pair of family cart horses, reminding him protectively every other day that the admiration of the stupid was an element of all power, radical or conservative. But now and then he took a feint at it, like a boy with a chocolate knife.

"Like the story of Mirriam's cancer," he said. There was a pleasure in talking of her to them. To them only, he mentioned her without effort, for their whole concept of her was so far from the real. "I heard it repeated only the other day, from Walter. Young Walter Stern, David's sidekick. And I thought — well, why not, why not. He was fonder of Mirriam than of any of us. And he has enough hump to carry of his own."

"But — Simon —"

It wasn't possible. Yes, it was. They believed it, now in perfect duet. They were invaluable.

"My God," he said. "The *two* of you? Why — you're like *Hitler*."

And to Dr. Hildesheimer whom they afterwards, in tears, sent to check on him, he found himself saying, "Doctor, forget my sisters for a minute. Doctor — it ever strike you that what holds wisdom back is only that everything of value about the conduct of the world has to be relearned every twenty-five years? Isn't it all as simple as that? So that if we're to survive, it's not the *matter* of achievement we ought to focus on, but the *interval?*"

"We really must have you to talk to the men in the vestry, Simon," Dr. Hildesheimer said. "They would really appreciate it."

He supposed this was part of what had made him a judge — that he could never wholly dismiss the stupid, either from his house or his mind. That was what real competitiveness was. You're the champ.

"I really came to talk to you about Ruth," said the rabbi.

"Yes."

"Rosa and Athalie are really very worried."

"Yes. What?"

"Even if you could get clearance — you're not really thinking of taking her with you?"

He expelled the shallow breath. There was always the chance that his special care of her would be noted, and wondered at. "I'll get clearance."

"But why?"

"It's *our* wartime." But people like us never seem to grasp the fact of it, hard enough for the spikes to enter our palms. Or is that our talent?

"Surely not that child's wartime! Not really. Not yet."

"No." But would history ever get to the men in the vestry in time? He and the rabbi were sitting in the long downstairs salon. He saw Hildesheimer glance around the room to reassure himself on Mannix with a sight of Mannix's own possessions. Maybe he was right; one didn't change one's breeding like one's brand of tea.

"Friend Simon. You really mustn't let personal tragedy —"

"Become confused with the public one? I wish it would. I wish it had." And there it was — out at last.

"We can't all be as holy as those martyrs across the water," said the rabbi. And bowed his head.

Foolishly or cleverly, his own conscience had gone on talking, confessing this easy, secular madness which even the good rabbi could understand well enough to be horrified over, while all the time that other private confession he must never make was pressed swollen under the tongue — and was, grant it, a little relieved. Talk *was* action. Or only all *he* had?

"Dr. Hildesheimer — every martyr's always half self-made, don't you think. Even those." For he'd been terrified to find himself thinking this even while at the work of helping. Daring to apply it, even during the nightmare, to the victim. Until he reminded himself that ever since Eden, it had applied to men in general.

"Judge Mannix!" Hildesheimer stood up. "In these times — you can contribute to that *rishus* against us, against the Jews! You, of all people? That we ... they ... are to blame?"

"No, no. We all half choose to be victim — to be the chosen. The whole world."

But the rabbi had his craftiness. He pulled an ear lobe, in lieu of a side lock. "Ah-ha. Now I see. You want just to be a man. Whenever I hear a Jew say that, that he just wants to be a part of mankind — I know it's that he just doesn't want to be a Jew any more." He took up his hat, an only very slightly broad-brimmed one. "Friend — why don't you give up that grievous work for a while? Why go to Europe at all, just now?"

"Think I'll lose my faith?" A pertness straight from his youth, from that period of it when his newly discovered brain, still shaky with its own smartness, had found a nervous balance in the company of the stupid, among whom his mother had been the one he knew best.

"We leave that to the Catholics." From Hildesheimer's smirk, he'd made this joke before. "No, but I often speak of you with Guedalia the sexton; his brother had you in Hebrew class. A regular Isaiah they remember you." He settled the hat on his close-shaven head; to do that while yet in the house was still a religious privilege of those who no longer wore yarmulkes or side locks. One could only hope they did have the best of both worlds.

"And I personally *know*," said the rabbi, "that sorrow is extra hard on a good brain."

"You sound like my mother." He hesitated, but couldn't resist. "Though *she* never claimed personal knowledge of it."

But the rabbi only bowed at this other holy mention. "*My* mother, *selig*, would say of you, 'He is busy with the wisdom of sorrow. But it will leave soon.'" (And later, by the calendar of events left with him, the Judge saw that, the next Saturday of May being the one before Mother's Day, Hildesheimer was billed for "A Mother's Day Sermonette.")

But seeing the young rabbi out, he had delayed at the door. "Yes, I was always 'precocious.' At least that was the legend — partly my size. But I never thought I'd get my old age so young." He put a hand on the rabbi's shoulder two steps below. "Tell me, though. Didn't the Jews, all ancient peoples, used to listen to the elders? They were aware of — that dangerous interval?"

"'When Job's wisdom was ended' — one of the books says — 'then he was ready for God's.'"

"Really?"

"Really."

"Ah, I thought you were never going to mention him."

"Job?"

"No." It had been vicious of him — but hypocrite to hypocrite? "God."

But the young man had given him his hand anyway, even enthusiastic over his spirit. Hildesheimer wasn't being false; he might even believe in God; it was just that the priests were all social workers now. "I'm going to tell Miss Rosa and Miss Athalie that you're really all right!"

And he'd half run up the stairs, to tell someone: "Remember that young rabbi who buried Mamma, the one who says "really" all the time? I know why. He's not *really* sure he's a Jew any more, or what Jews are. The Germans came just in time."

For the only one who would have understood this, and laughed over it, was Mirriam. Two weeks later, he and Ruth had left. He thought that perhaps Mirriam would have approved of that too. Although one must be careful not to ascribe falsely to the dead — even more than with the living, since for the dead there was no recourse.

And now he and Ruth were home again. In the depths of his madness he'd become very good on other people's deceptions; he had solved the world. Now the world was once more confused to him; he was living it. One sentence-long note had meanwhile come from Ninon Fracca.

"So now you're on the wrong side of the Atlantic again!" — a twist from a music-hall ditty current there about Americans: "So now 'e's over 'ere again, gettin' 'is tea, dooty-free, but on the *right* side awv ther sea!" No doubt she'd never expressed herself outside of theatre parlance in her life, nor written a note any longer than needed to be left with the portress at a stage door. And in the nature of men and their Cytthereas, it was probably as true that she was used to receiving incomprehensible letters like his, sent along with the rosebuds, maybe by a man who respected that plucked mound of hers for reminding him of his own deceptions, or because she might be the last woman he would ever touch.

His wasn't too short a letter to have spent the afternoon on. Men had sent more peculiar tributes — and had sometimes kept certain women to receive them as the safest shrines. Where else — from scholars or prime ministers of the courts or retired champions — did such faded rosebuds belong?

"But am I on the right side of the century at last?" he wrote. "How can one ever tell? I'm ten years older than it, in age" — as she herself was, a bond he couldn't mention — "and on the question of war and wars, I'm only catching up with my father and grandfathers — who didn't catch up with me and mine. On certain questions, we never catch up with the young. Nobody gets to posterity in time. Now that my present job's over, and the war will soon be — for it will, you know — I've been doing a little staring in other directions" — at wainscotings — "and maybe a little of the present age has caught on my knee-buckles at last. I'm getting the feel of what I wasn't born to, myself. I'm lucky, you know. We're still legion, our kind, and most of us never will."

It had taken him a long while to go on from there, confused as he was — now that he was no longer in that mausoleum where all his thoughts had come to him at once. In the way of letters, the page showed no sign of this.

> For without being a saint, these days can one ever forget that half the earth still lives as it were beneath the crust of the earth, in the leftover sun — or starves in the sight of everybody? All this now goes on in the sight of everybody. And this is the great revolution. There's no tucking it away any more, on any end of the earth nowadays. And what perhaps hasn't been quite seen yet in the world is that this, the greatest revolution, is in man's mind — why, even the coarsest grabber feels an arrow of it in his backside somewhere, or when he puts out his paw will cut himself on it in the morning mail, or will see its root in his fine heir! And this is irreversible. One needn't be a saint to see it, one deserves no credit for seeing or expressing it either — not any more. Of course, one still doesn't refuse a mistress or not buy the house of one's dreams because of it. And this used to be enough to put us in everyday Lethe. But it isn't, any more.

He hadn't gone on from there. Other men had done it better — if he wished, he could begin to read up on it, as was the way between generations. There must be a whole glossary of such letters as well, from men who needed to talk. To certain women.

But now he bent and wrote again.

> The rich are always antiquarian; they want to save themselves. The middle class is luckily too cumbersome ever to be such an enclave. People are draining into it from both ends, fastest of course at the bottom. Is there a chance —

Staring at his old brown escutcheon with its thirty years of clothes ahead, he could see well enough its characteristic occupant, not really rich but always somehow inheriting a never quite collapsible opera hat. To see clearly, as he himself proposed to, was merely the sort of generalized love such gentlemen had time for. Although his own "refugees" couldn't make him more Jewishly devoted, they'd helped thrust him back at his old pursuit of judging the world and himself in tandem — which was perhaps Jewish enough. But would anyone see that Simon Mannix belonged with the cranks now — that, too late for power, he too wanted to save the world?

He could see Ninon Fracca's face when she got his letter — a moment's bewilderment as she read, then the quick explosion — to herself — of experience. "What's he saying to you, m'dear, with his any mores? — why, he's saying . . . good-bye."

But that wasn't the reason he wouldn't mail it.

On his wife's desk, here all around him, the letters he had been reading for days, and had stacks of yet unread, spilled everywhere from spidery pigeonholes, and all over the desk's watery inlay, once blond-green as an early apple, for some Marguerite. The desk had been bought at an auction gallery, by *her* — how cruelly some women knew their own taste! "Oh, what a lovely tart!" she'd said, when it was brought forward on the stand, its ormolu pale from two hundred years of such trials — and had bought it in ten minutes; if her correspondents had thereafter taken it upon themselves to fill it with her whole life, that was *their* business!

Their letters piled it, in all scripts and voices. He'd begun going through them, not voyeur after lovers, only intending the dutiful consecration before the fire or the scrap heap; he had performed this service for the dead before. To him, at twenty-seven, his father's leavings had been an ancestral experience — the business records willed to him as history, the memoir as heritage — and all of it enlarging the inheritor, even down to the long box, gold-leafed by donor with a calla lily one dared not laugh at, in which his father had kept for himself, by means of a few rent receipts and pictures, his Miss Lily Orpe of the Louvre, and kept unwittingly for his son (perhaps because the son had seen the woman herself as she aged, reminisced and died) the sharpest sense of those dusky Parisian hours: another man's violets and passions — real. His mother's effects were always pridefully tidy for just such a melancholy ritual as his, and once the neutral furs and jewels of status had been handed round, were only the corn plasters, rhinestoned combs and bridgework that any old stolid dray might leave behind her — plus the burial certificate, well forward in a drawer containing as in her lifetime no other papers, nothing made of words, whose force on him and his father she'd always been so suspicious of — as if at the last she was able still to say to them, accusatory to the final crumble of her dust, "Nobody wrote me; *I* had no crimes." And no bills.

But finished, finished all — until now that had always been the sense of it. As the legal guardian of the family he'd become used to seeing the contents of a desk or bureau curdled into the pitiful merely by the death of the owner; *this* had been thought random? — *this* saved? Was a violent death any different, or an early one, leaving its victim unresolved *except* by death. Or did the unresolved last the longest, project the farthest, irritant as in life? For all these letters to her, not from her, crowded in toward the same purpose, and clearly left unsated, were, whether the sender was dead or alive, still palpitating waters, lives streaked with her purple, changeable oil — like his own. So many people wrote her — he had never known. Clearly, as with him, as with everything, she'd never answered them at their own rate. But they'd gone on writing, and agonizedly fascinated, he'd gone on reading and arranging. Had his own letters to her, not found yet, held so much more of receiver than sender as these did? Over half these records of her were now ranged in the desk in packets, according to writer, and with a chronology for each. The test for life was after all — movement. And among this retinue of letters, she moved as in life.

Her correspondents had *always* created her beyond herself, as they themselves sometimes seemed aware and one had said to her, outright. By never fishing for souls, never fastening on, she had caught them. And so, trailing the clouds they made for her, kicking at those gaudy chiffons like a bride who didn't want a train — she would not be responsible for their silliness — she moved still. In all those tumbled voices, hers spoke clearest. Toward her movement, they cast their essence. They had never caught her.

One packet of letters signed "Arne" he was still reading with painful care. Surely he had that right himself as a second husband, left by her in the first month of their marriage for a week's return to the first one — on return, her explanation: "Yes, Denmark. I had to talk to Arne. Now it is over for good. And I'm *here!*" The rest of her correspondents, as in life, were of all ages and sexes, on onionskin, pad paper and rag, women called Billy, men called Buffy and Tinker, Carmens and Leslies who might be either, bluff Roberts and Millicents, an agile Raoul. Certain largest packets considered themselves special confidants — but hadn't they all? They were the crowd. And where, for the dead, did the demimonde begin?

Some, he remembered: Angela Decies, of the feather hats and mortician dresses, the lady rotter who had once been in Holloway prison and written a book about it, preserved for him now in the white face powder of the twenties as in marble dust, and in the bad odor of her checks; the Noel Ammon who'd drawn that wasp-stomachered caricature of Mirriam over there on the wall; Olivia, Mrs. Kitt, a remarkable old actress from the days when those in her profession called themselves Mrs., who had retired to the old Hotel Seville, on Twenty-eighth Street, that tawny old hutch — and had attributed her longevity to an extra bone in the coccyx. There was no enumerating them all, their parties and jigtimes, arts and artistics, and hangover lures. And as with all human correspondents, there emanated from the letters half as the reason they wrote her — that they had all considered themselves remarkable. If *she* was, it was intimated — this was because they wrote her. And maybe that was the truth of it.

Was there no one, no human soul she herself had angled for? Sometimes, going back over a letter, a phrase, putting his own essence to all of it, and suffocating for the lateness, hearing hearing her voice, he thought he caught sight of him. From whom, though letters had been written between them, none so far had been found.

Finally, he picked up and reread his own unfinished letter. Those others were more properly faded to the desk; though he might go back to them, they were yesterday. Late as his was, it was today's. What it seemed to him to say best was good-bye. As yet, it lacked a signature — and had no salutation. In a scrawl that ruined the letter for any other than its true recipient, he wrote her name across it, and left it for her with the others. *Mirriam.*

4 Mirriam Upstairs

Voices. Letters. Verdicts?: —

I am the daughter, rampant. Built for the sensual light. Seen in it, often by the unsensual. Some women document chapter-thick with home, from beginning to end. I, who began that way like any other, a child seated high at table, between bony father and grape-eyed mother, retreated as soon as my long legs would carry me, to the outside, and the oblique. Later, I told my two husbands all — or all I could. I was never willfully alone. The crowd was always with me. No one ever got from me — all. All my life, people sent what they knew of me back to me, in narrow letter-flights that fall back from me now like a boy's paper darts. And all my correspondents write alike.

Both my husbands fell in love with me alongside that granite friend, my father. The second didn't know this of the first, until now. Even there, and before in my childhood, so much grasped for myself, I was always the daughter; if one were to pick a Greek epithet for me — as for the cow-eyed or the rosy-fingered — that would be mine. Oh this correspondence — why doesn't one come into the world, and suffer it, unattended? Yet, in their cross-hatchings, my friends have caught me. And the shadow of a man ever stronger, like the white spaces in a black picture. If the letters could have spoken each to the other, would they have seen him, the shadow you glimpse, Si, as you read them all at once? I told them over and over about him, but they never believe what you tell them, especially when the man himself is there for all to observe. Not that crowd. Do you expect anyhow that a woman like me *can* speak, one to one? They could see that, why not you? I can *not* correspond.

I thought you saw it. Or married you because you would be strong enough to stand it, when you did see. Arne couldn't. You can tell by his letters he couldn't. "You'll daughter him, as you daughtered me," he wrote out of the blue, when he heard about us. "Have you widowed him yet?" And when I went back to him, that first month of our wedding trip, Si's and mine, "You make the perfect widow," he said. Or he said it after. Letters keep coming. Their letters kept coming after me always, to the end. Not yours though. You're the champ.

So Si, listen. Listen *for your life*, as people say. For your life, which I never had wholly — and thank God for it. Which was why you could have me. No, I never told you — I don't tell things. Daughters — of fathers — don't. Do fathers' sons? Arne was a mother's son — I mistook him. His letters say that too.

"I don't suppose there exists a child of both a father and a mother," he said, didn't he. And then unfortunately added, being a foreigner, "In America." Before that, la, la — a perfect remark. Sculpture soured him into intelligence at times; I said that once. "It seeps out of the stone." Or the stone and I, we did it together. As you see, he didn't like my laugh any better than you. But you could always take it, darling. Why, yes, we always called each other "darling" — the crowd. A theatrical habit. When I wanted to call you, or anyone, something special, I said — nothing. I thought you knew. It can't be helped. Or maybe it can, if you read my friends all very carefully; they're eccentric, but they gabble well, don't they. Listen to me very carefully now, Si, through them. Add your essence, that beautiful goddamn brain of yours — oh yes, I said that, but who didn't, who doesn't — add it to my voice. I don't ordinarily tell things. But they caught me when I wasn't looking — and sent me back to myself. Listen to me. Listen for your life: Daughters breed daughters.

Oh, I couldn't know my own end, could I? What more could I tell you of myself, of us, if I had? I tell you *now*. That's *death* for you, every time.

And that joke was Angela for you. Her life depended on the jokes she could see in it; so would yours if you'd had hers; yes, she's the one said you had no humor, that you would never forge a check. "Don't listen to Angie," Noel wrote me once. "She's a dirty dike who sleeps with men." He should talk — whom she called her "best girl friend." She died of getting funnier and funnier. The two of them went to the Bahamas with a female balloonist — they came down in the gondola and were picked up by the *Queen of Bermuda* on an off run — and Angie's heart stopped "zizz" — from seeing a shark smile through a glass-bottomed boat. "Oh Father, forgive us —" wrote Noel then; they were both Catholic converts — "she died waving like a fevver on the breeze, she was the most romantic one of us all." And cautioned me to heed what she told me, after all.

I see her as a kind of St. Sebastian, truth sticking out like stilettos all over her skinny back. No wonder she was always on the move, *she'd* say, if she heard me. But I've drawn her that way, in her hat. Her life was better art than any of us. I'm taking her ashes *straight* to Paris — the return fare she had will do for both of us. And Mimi love — the final *délice* — she said she wanted you to have "all her hats." The dear pook. When everyone knew she had only the one Man Ray photographed. But darling, I want it. I'm montage-ing it onto the picture. For her memorial. And a gallery there is very interested.

But they weren't of course, so I bought it — and gave it back to him — that's the way it should be in art, shouldn't it, a world of friends. Just before we married, Si, remember? Why, it was the night that summer I first took you to Daddy's house; we hung the drawing of me that Noel sent to thank me. I hung it; I was taller. Under it, against the same wall, you hung me on you. Short man's stand-up love, your head on my breasts, a perfect fit. I said so. Tall man would have had to hold heavy me high. You knew your powers. You said so. But you'll have to remember for both of us. I never dwelt backwards like other women; I always remembered what I wanted next. *May the night bloom.* When we tottered back to bed, you turned the great, ugly silver ring Arne made, and read that engraved there. "What's on the other one?" you said. On my other hand, a matching frog-buckle: *In the company of friends.* We both shouted with laughter. Then you shut up, remembering I was his widow. But later, when you knew the real circumstances (only presumed dead), you said, "Marry me and you can get rid of those damned epaulettes."

Sex was your only humor, I must have said to Angie, who answered: "Otherwise, you say, his principles get in his way?" To which Angie added, from whatever alcoholic balloon she was on at the moment, "Goody. How I wish mine got in the way of mine." And when told that your artistic taste was better than ours (for it seems that sometime thereabouts, on the question of you, I did answer letters, and even entreated them) she commented, "Of course it is, dumb bunny. He's a patron of the arts. Not of artists."

But Arne wrote, when he heard of us.

Diamonds now, I suppose. Maybe you are just a good little Jewish girl, after all? When I asked you what you wanted of life, you said,

"To go over Niagara Falls in a barrel, every night." How was I to know
this is just bourgeois tease-talk! I should have put that on a ring —
and on the other "To be every night in cottage with the same man."
And both are true. This is worse you know than that I am not a faithful person — for this I *know*. Let me tell you, Mirriam, it is not
enough to be brought up dutiful, if you do not know any longer what
to be dutiful to. Or to be so honest you do not know the truth until it
burn somebody else on your tongue. Your father bring you up with
these big Jewish hungers like a son almost, he should not have let you
marry a Christian.

And postscript:

> I never thought he believe me dead. I am always sure he know it
> for only a courtesy. How is the old Meyer? I hope well.

How quietly we divorced Arne again, together, for good, Si, you and
I, and how close it brought us! To document your wife into being a girl
again, into your being, before the marriage service, to drive her downtown to those quiet legal streets at the bottom of the island, to bring
her, shining and shy, great eyes forward, long cool summer legs flashing past the secretaries, into the grave office of your good friend —
who needs to ask me a few questions. I answered them all, in my voice
to match the legs: Aged twenty-nine (this was 1925), not living with
first husband six years, one year under the desertion limit in some
states, separated mutually as far as I could define. But how tell your
monk friend, with his Lobb shoes and speckled cravat, about the flotsam of the studios? — how one could lose a husband as easily as a
locket in those high-arched places so drunken cozy in the evenings, so
cavernous in the morning, how, if it was one's temperate family habit
to drink only eager gulps of the sodden, seductive air of art, to gorge
only on its heavy conversations (always loaded with bitter plums for
stuffing the wombs of girls like me, and serving us up like squabs on
the altars we yearned for), that a girl like me could drop virginity,
religion, a four-story house and my grandmother's dowry string of
Burmese pearls, lose them like a pair of panties, all in one evening, and
meet on the way out another girl like me, maybe one with high-church
giraffe neck and nostrils, slouching in to meet her Jew.

I answered his questions queenly, your member-of-the-firm with his
flavorful name stuck like a bud of garlic among the *goy* ones, stuck
there for us and our world, and I crossed my legs princessy, in the way
of women accustomed from childhood to visit the offices which sup-

ported and protected them. For though the silences here were more calfbound and quiet than in my father's music-broker's office, with its tea-break snatches of Mary Garden gossip, and Caruso himself once, swelling his throat like a thrush, over a matter of copyright — I knew my place and privileges as I always did, and could get Grandma's pearls back any day, in a secretary's eyes.

And maybe your friend did understand that part of me better than you did, then. Maybe he already had a monk's sister, or daughter, at home — some pre-Penelope, knuckle-trained to sail Larchmont's blue money-waters and lie in wait for Newport's, but already slouching off with her sweet little bat-boned, Galician face set on finding a husband easy as a locket, in the land of Minnetonka-no-money, Minnehaha-no-morals — some worrisome little girl already weaving her mythical two-man raft, man-and-woman one, made of all the thin excuses we girls assigned to art.

"Was he a *good* sculptor?" said your friend, his great hungry eyes thoughtful. And I spoke the truth to him, to eyes hooded as mine but grayer-skinned, as mine might have been if given time.

"Oh, that wasn't to have been the point of it," I said, as carelessly as I must have said it to Arne. "Second-raters are so comfortable to be with, in company. How was I to know that as husbands they gave themselves such hell over being it?" And we all laughed, and I looked at you, Si, with such pride — you're the champ, and if some day we're to find that those can give themselves hell too, over me and my menses-dark changes, they can bear it. And afterwards, I quoted Angie, saying to me, "Arne always minded that *you* didn't, you cluck." So, here we're round to Angie again, and why not; she introduced us.

Noel was there too; don't you know him now, he was the one you called "the parlor snake." How that dates us. You wouldn't go on to the river-club with us; you called Angie later and got my number. You knew her father, and once, to get her out of a scrape, you pulled strings for her, telling her very kindly that it was likely the last anyone could pull.

"You rat," I said, laughing to you, not much later, "do you always know fathers?", for you'd met mine in the echelons of our race somewhere, and you said into my breasts, "That's how I've remained a bachelor. Until now." Then we opened our noses warily to the odor of orange blossoms closing in on us like the pelmets of the family bed down the hall from us, and I whispered, "How safe," but in the same

minute you put your mouth where it ought to be and I split my long
legs for you — "Propose to me again."

And Angie says here in this letter — answering when I wrote them
all to Tunis that Arne was alive, and all the rest of it:

> Dear Little Jewish Girl — how we howled! But really, what insight
> on the part of our Arne! I'd never think of such a thing myself; I'm
> absolutely sans race prejudice, even against my own. But Arne, come
> to think of it, was rather beautiful in that Siegfried way, wasn't he —
> I never believed he was dead. And you do have rather an expectantly
> Sabine look about you in a roomful of us blonds. Has yer ever slept
> with a Jewboy, honey?

The answer was no. I'd never slept with anybody but Arne before
— and that went into my wife-personality too. You believed me.
"You're good with innocence, did you know?" I said. But I was more
used to not being believed. That comes through best of all now, doesn't
it — at last. "I made wild remarks by imitation; after a while it came
natural," I said. Oh, I could correspond at first, with someone new,
when it was still like dropping pennies down a well. "I can talk to *you*,"
I said. Like a child to its daddy. But daddy mustn't save the pennies
up, or dole them back. Otherwise, there's his gangle-gawk of two
weeks ago, a long-legged madonna hunching herself out on the dance
floor flamenco with somebody else — the same as she did at fifteen.

"Oh Daddy, why did you —" I wrote my father from Bad Kissingen,
that terrible, itching summer of my girlhood when he sent my mother
and me to circle safely round the spas, me to nauseate in the corners of
my mind at all the human grotesques, yet never to forget them and
their sad toiletries — what a bal masqué way to learn pity-in-the-
round, from the turpentined wrecks of the mudbath and the high-
colonic, coughing their caviar-breath into their laces and suedes. No
wonder I was a little nouveau riche with compassion, the rest of my
life....

No, I couldn't think of that by myself, Simon, that's yours. . . . And
neither could Meyer Mendes, to whom daughters were as of the old
days, a special property, of the heart maybe, but of the blood and the
purse certainly — like the wives. You're a little like him in some of your
old-fashioned moral hungers — I flashed that at you once! — but not
too much like; never think that. Why, families like ours threw psychology away with their chicken bones; we're older than any of it, Jew-

boy, you and I. You were modern enough for me, my smart thirty-
four-year-old bachelor boy, with your sleek face like a carved ivory
button at the top of the shabby clothes Meyer Mendes took for a sign
of your Chasidic learning, not your vanity — but that would have been
all right, with him too; you had us covered, both ways.

That night, in our house, I took you to see yourself in one of the
netsuke figures in the Nipponese corner of our bric-a-brac, but you
scorned all that as pawnbroker's junk which you said the best Israelite
families still somehow got stuck with; "At home we had the French
version," you said, and we laughed, kneeling there in front of the
cabinet — you had to take your under-five-foot advantage when you
could; that's when we kissed. I already knew about your monkey-ways
with the women, from Angie, who called me before you did, and I
challenged you with the names of your mistresses, some of whom I'd
seen at the theatre — "Angie says you arrange it the French way, one
by one" — which a father would have thought proper too, and maybe
already knew, from downtown. If I could have been your mistress!
— or in the theatre, too!

But we had mothers alike, didn't we, my Sarah to your Martha;
though mine was the prettier, to the end like a raisin-eyed, Raphael
puddinghead; both of them brought us and our fathers their money —
you and I stepped hand-in-hand out of the nineteenth century there.
And good duennas, both of them. In Bad Kissingen, I'd found a fly
Italian boy on his way to Cucciola with his papa, but she found us,
behind the fountain in the public baths, at dusk only, but holding
hands too in the amphitheatre of our loneliness, all of whose aged were
still sleeping, except she.

"Did he get to you?" she said to me. "Answer me, did that boy get to
your funnybone?" Aren't the names they had for it vile, I once said to
you, telling it, and you recalled your little-boy shame at your mother's
"tassel," and how your father saved you there from her shames, you
keeping mum. We had children by the time we were telling each other
this, in our own marital bed, in that second entente, after *she* was born.
"After my father died," you said, "my mother said to me, 'He was a
good man; he never bothered me more than once a week.'"

Oh, the decade of the twenties wasn't so free as some see, but
floating still with *luxuria*, the genitalia of our parents — on our wedding trip you took me to see the Bosch panel, pointed to a kneeling

nude figure looking backward between its legs at the sprig of flowers in its own behind, and said to me right there in the Prado, "Our mothers." Oh, you and I understood each other — in our parents' bed.

I said nothing to you of fathers — daughters are shy. There by the spa fountain, I held out my elbow to my mother, only one step more innocent than she, saying, "Here?" Then wrote to my father — "Oh Daddy, why did you ever marry anybody so *dumb*." But her letter and mine reached him together, and he sent mine back to me, where it still is, clipped to his others in the iron-blooded file of them — spoil the child as a father may, with a whole Versailles of toys and even a sweetmeat entente or two secret between him and his bright darling, a law comes out in the letter — and the rod. *Respect*. Respect her whose money-blood I have mixed with mine.

"I'll see any kissprint you get on you," she said at the fountain. "It comes out on the skin." Though I couldn't see any on hers, and said so, and got slapped for it, flat in the teeth. Ahhrr — daughters.

By Arne's time, she was too dead to see the brown bruises I'd maybe after all have kept from her — mothers are shy too.

But Mendes guessed at those or feared it, and was glad enough that out of those dubious caves of art I'd at least drawn Arne, whose major-general of a mother owned a string of hotels. And maybe Meyer himself, deep in the cosmopolitan all around him, had a little hunger to see Siegfrieds in the family. How history goes back and back, but never fear, we'll come to all the daughters.

So Mendes married me to him quick, but with style. "What a doge your father is, I must *do* him," said Arne, though the bust when it was done looked more like Shylock and still does; Arne got no money from mother as long as married to me, that's true. And mother's sons wander. Back. And get their insights later.

So there Meyer and I were, father and daughter again, and I tried running around for kissprints, but on my skin they never showed. And you when you came along did your best for me, the best of anyone, I told the crowd over and over in one way, and you in another — now believe it. Who the father is doesn't matter in the end, does it — whether old Meyer himself, whom when I slanged or cheered I called Mendes like a wife, or the winner husband, or even, if one lives long enough, the son. I never for one minute begrudge you what Mendes left you, Si. "He'll be a judge, Mirrie. They say it downtown." Why should I? We were a trinity at last. You slept with me, in my father's house.

And I could walk with you — the way you meant walk; none of the mistresses had ever done that; I asked and you said so; you had never let them in there.

Nor would they have wanted to, with their cancan breasts and lace-stocking lashes; I kept no part-time soul mates, no copyists at the Louvre.

Ah, Simon, that's you speaking, not me. Let me. Walk me back into that autumn when I'd stroll down from our house to your place, in brogues and pushing my hands into the pockets of some soft sweater, shaking out my black hair like a city dairy maid, and you took me to the Billings estate at one tip of the island, to the market squares at the other, and chop-chop to all the slum-fairs between, and brought me home at ten o'clock like a college virgin. Or I arrived in sequins and a coiffure like a pear, only to slip nude into your man-about-town bed (my phrase), like a snake into a bowl of milk (yours, and Théophile Gautier's — and your father's) — and then slid back into my glaze in order to walk midtown east as if we were between ballrooms, while you talked of the great social staircase of the city, and brought me home, skyscrapers still chattering in our heads like icicles, brought the widow, the were-wife to be, to her childhood house not too far from balustrades you knew from your own nine-year-old betting days — back here, at dawn. Oh, we divided the city between us, like cubs their first kill. Can you walk with a son like that, with a daughter? Oh, why must there be these den-jealousies, in my father's house? Give the children to Anna to deal with; they're healthy. There are some roles I won't play.

Ah, now we come to talk of the roles. Did you once think you began that in me, with your teasing "You dress for your roles — even more than most women."

It was the eve of our wedding and we were at the perfect reprise for it, the first ice-skating night of the season, skimming the violet rink where you broke the ice of your boyhood confidences for me, once again. I was wearing a red tam-o'-shanter, red as a flannel-mouth — ah, Si, you think you can imitate my talk, bring me back like that, well, you almost do, not quite. Like the letters.

"Do you dress me for a role too?" you said. "Each time? Or forever."

With the ice-light mauve in my brown eye, I didn't answer, but some-where in that iris universe did I hope you saw it — what the first husband saw too late — that I didn't *know?*

And if I answer more now in death than I ever would in life, isn't that something? For deepest in the ice-eyes are to be seen the two children to come, perfect in their roles of a cold Christmas morning, in the twin red tams found in their stockings and put there by a father, who now skates them alone on the reservoir in the lurid looking glass of a winter morning; see their figure eight, how perfect on it, that trinity.

Look to the letters for further advice on me. And to two visits. The one we made together, to Mrs. Kitt, the memory of whose room, fluid with cats and her tongue, is a scene better even than letters. And the one to Arne — more a flight than a visit? — from the Prado to Den-mark, from Paris to Belgium, from a wedding to a wedding is so far. Which journey, only a month out on our own twin voyage — do not all relationships mix? — I made alone. Look to your daughter also, Si, to when a man might come to her in her menses, as you used to come to me, or before that time, to when these come upon her now, twelve to the twelvemonth, in inexorable tattoo to remind her of the first one. During that year-long serenade, what does she dream of me? No, look away from that garden, that spa is not for fathers. It was mine — or would have been mine. "She means to be happy." What childless woman said that?

Look to *my* letter, the one you have just found, not stuffed away thoughtlessly, like the rest, in a pigeonhole. Was it really filed neatly away for you to find, a monkey-puzzle for you ever to wander in — would I do that? I was never evil enough, you see, for a final verdict to be made on me. Who is? Yes, I had *that* amorality against final ver-dicts; I preceded you into the twentieth century there. The letter was in the wall file between your old armoire and this desk, the happy no-man's-land where I kept the "pics" of me and anyone else I could find, from ballet school before I got too tall for it and drama academy before too bored with it, from Brearleys before college and river-clubs after — and not specializing in family though including them, as if they were whatever I could find too. How I loved cameras — how they finalize a person, telling one afterward who oneself and anyone else were! You yourself were never in need of this sort of information before; were you surprised to find this file neat as my bureau drawers, and chronological as well? There were no letters to bother me here. As a last resort you scanned them anyway for the packet that must be somewhere — of your own. Few as you wrote me — since normally we were never more than a house or a crowd apart — they had existed. Now there appear to be none. Why didn't I keep them? Was I pinned down there in too firm an old incarnation, or were you? Can you begin to believe in what you were to me, now?

And the letter you've just found, would Mirriam ever have been devious enough to leave it behind with that intention — when did she ever bother to be devious . . . ? How could I imagine, Si, that you would only choose to hunt me down *now!* Though there was a time — "You slang the world you belong to on all sides, your bunch, but you stay in it, *you* stay in it with me," you said to me once. "What need then had I of your letters?" — didn't I say *that* once to you? Persuade yourself of it.

I thought you were never bewildered about me — I said as much to the others, and though unbelieving, they repeated it back to me, nagging from all sides, always the same refrain, "How can Simon . . . how can you . . . What is there between you, that it lasts . . . Who is he to know most about you, when we . . . What shadow does he cast, that we cannot?" And underneath all of it, the persistent sub-chorus — that they knew. Take that nutmeat of me — it is yours. Betimes I bewildered them, betimes I had a mixed relationship with myself. But always I thought you knew me. And betimes left you because of it.

"Stop that hyena-laugh," said my mother early. Oh, the dumbest women; there are things they know. There are roles I was not built for; perhaps instead I should have been an actress only, and superficially taken them all. No, I was not sick in my mind. But in the yellow upstairs room behind my high forehead, could you not hear the long hyena-muzzle of my compassion for all of us open its maw and howl? Couldn't you see it, from behind my own bedroom eye, through that far telescope, peering at you all?

To that letter I've left, then — half finished, crumpled down between pics of Arne alone and with me, of me alone and with you, with David, of the three of us, of David alone. Compare such resemblances as you will — the combinations aren't infinite. But the chronology is endless. And the letter, like the one you've just written, is uninscribed — a letter written to the world maybe, or to one shadow:

I know damn well what I am, one of those rich girls who marry sculptors — but not the second time. I was safely in society and yearned for the outsiders. On the rebound — what fascinates me about Si is that he is so *in*, not insensitive or anything like that and very smart — but he hasn't a prayer of what it is to feel alienated, envious, cut off. Neither do I really except through the artists; the crowd feels this too. Maybe they don't have all the charnel houses of the world on their consciences. But they want to know. I want to know. Though sometimes my only excuse is ennui. Never to be bored — is that pride?

He believes D. is not our son. I could make life simpler by telling him the truth. But this is the core. Because he believes but won't ask — I will never say.

Uninscribed and unsigned. But who appears best there, Si? I?

Three months to the day, from the morning I slipped away from our hotel in Paris — and from a night of nights there — "What makes you so *good* in Paris, Si?" — leaving you the note: *I just heard Arne is alive. From Billy, in the bar. I telephoned him. He's in Belgium. But I want to tell him about us in person. Chick will fly me. Back Thursday. And it will be like yesterday always, then"* — three months from that day (and four months to the day from our wedding — though to modern legitimacies this means nothing) — we appear together in New York again, you and I, downstairs in the Hotel Seville in Twenty-eighth Street, where in a room above Mrs. Kitt lies dying.

"Of being ninetyish, of course," I whisper, as we weave our way through the tawny columns of the lobby, in whose purblind dusk a mushroom-ring of ladies sits, sentinel, each with her toad-throat pulsing. "But even at ninety, of having an extra funnybone." I am chuckling.

"Thought it was an extra coccyx," you murmured, but not smiling; since Paris you hadn't smiled much — but I wasn't seeing *you*.

"Victorian for it, maybe," I said. "Or maybe that's where she thinks it *is*."

A little bonsai tree of an old lady — ah Si, you do remember how I said things! — lets us in, with a soft-moustached headshake, and there is our rumpled Shakespearean darling, her limbs sucked by the waters below blankets to the size of elephant feet that gurgle as she moves them, but dying above sheets in her own chestnutfreckled skin — seventy years ago, what a marigold beauty — and her blue eye bonnie for the stalls and boxes still. The cats, two Siamese and two ginger, cross each other's paths in continuous bas relief; their haunches stitch a pattern to the room that is eternal but of the period too, like the purring wheelwork of Hispano-Suiza cars.

"No, we don't go to hospital," says Mrs. Kitt in answer to a bleat from the bonsai, and who the "we" is today, her guests may guess at, from all the repertory of Queens. The marmalade fish-stink in the room knocks us back, but once one's inside — "Into the breach," you murmur — isn't deadly enough to stifle death's odor, which rides stately in the room, like the patient's pentameter breath. Old ribbons frame her, steeped in hair. And she heard you, her ear not yet too far buried to hear the prompter's box. And chips us both with the blue eye. Of you, Simon, never met before, she says nothing at first, beyond the sudden gurgle of one leg. "Mirrie!" says Mrs. Kitt, in the accent like a glass prism with a light in it. "Mirrie, daughter of kings, who dressed you in that hat?"

And who shall I say dressed me in it, that great pancake, Rembrandt's beret in the harlequin of Michelangelo's Swiss guards? Was it you and the other, marrying me, my father and mother bearing me, the sons and daughters to come and do *what* to me, all of you tailoring me — all the hysteric roles of my history rising in one gorge of calico? "And Mirrie — " says the tragédienne voice, with just enough fustian to make reality squeak with envy of it — "that outrageous dress! On you."

Mirriam, whom you never call Mirrie, Si, doesn't answer her, but looks at you. I can see that you don't think the dress at all outrageous. A darkish blue, wrapped surplice around me, it would remind you of some of your mother's if my bones weren't so elegantly long; my breasts fill it quietly; perhaps a dress like that thickens the cheekbones too much, nearing thirty; but surely all the rancor you know to be mine is in that great, flaunting salver which holds my head on it, upside down? I put my hands on my cheeks, to hold myself firmly upon it, saying to myself as well as you: I'm *here*. But you are remembering, as you have been for a month back, what I said when I returned from Belgium: "I intended great explanations of us, all round. But how the specters come out, Si, it wasn't my triumph; it wasn't that way at all. I can't explain, can I? Even if you would let me. I can never explain." Never in life, you can see I meant, now. But not then. "Well, it's over," I said, afterward, still in Paris. "And I'm here."

"I had it made for balance," I said. "It's to balance the heaviness to come."

And that great, revolving voice, swinging like a searchlight on the spy for its own death-scene, says from behind me, to you and beyond you, and even to the little gnarled friend at the bedside, her fingers laced like the last twigs of audience: "O Rosalinds, O Antigones — damn me eyes, Mirrie — if you were my daughter, what we could have made of you! You hadn't told him yet, had you. Look at him, with his coal-eyes burning Iago; is he jealous of it already, will the babe be black for him, or white? — You should play L'Aiglon, sir; you have the carriage for it — Oh, I feel immortal longings — for champagne. There's a sawbuck on the dresser, Carrie, run round the corner. And see the cats, how they always feel a scene — you shall have your cream too, you knowing creatures. Ah Mirrie, what a daughterly thing you do for me. To choose my old carcass to tell him over. There wasn't time, dear heart, was there, for you to answer my letters. So you brought him here."

And how has Carrie come so ancient-quick, the bottle pushed at her from the wings by the prop man surely? — while you and I are still silent in the theatre of one another.

"Lean closer, children," says the voice of Mrs. Kitt. "For the blessing. Ah, champagne. My bed is roses." Hear her leg gurgle. "But soft — which one of my ribbons falls there? Blue? Blue it is! For a boy."

So, let me walk, Simon; let me walk my upstairs one last time, stalking the chambers of our house too, in the slippers of all the mur- dering houris who engage others to help them do away with them- selves. That man. He was to take *your* place there. You would never have helped me at it. Your principles were too strong. He was there, where you should have been. I never meant it to be her.

See me. I was hopelessly polylingual, with emotions I could never speak, except in crowds — and to your shadow. A rich man's daughter, only one prince could come for me, to be flouted and turned away with his casket of guesses, and sought forever after, in crowds. What did you have there? What does the prince treasure there anyway, just as the bourgeoise fondles her artists? Is it the lovely black villainies of these other desperate — of the poor?

Oh, I was never one to be remembered like some — in their com- monplaces, in their chits and meals. Shall you be, Simon? Do you want that safety, now that you see what comes of the other? Or is my destiny only for women, who want to throw down their royalty and have it too? Are you a judge now, Simon?

Oh, what a pastiche we make of ourselves! And Simon, is it I who speaks now, or you? Drop us in aconite pure, so that we may rise to our Elizabethan roles, one riding the hill plains of women, one stalking the clanking seas.

You were my rhetoric, Mirriam.

And you were — do you see his shadow now? Where are *his* letters, Simon?

Where are they; who was that other letter for?

There is no allegory, Simon, no allegory, except what we make for ourselves.

Who said that? Which of us?

I said it to you, hissing it through the teeth which gnawed the chains of motherhood: Stay away from me, Simon, with that brain-gun of yours. Or shoot me with it — close.

I say it. I say it with you, Mirriam.

So, together, the dual voices. There is no allegory, except as we make it ourselves.

So — I must rove. Give me my character, Simon. As I give you my letters — and my daughter. See how she stalks our history, our chamber — her upstairs. Ware the character you give her. Will you give her mine?

Oh Simon, my voice *was* velvet — will you kill me now?

So. This is death.

5   A Bridge – *Fall 1944*

AT four o'clock, a church bell distantly sounded the hour, a bell buoy deep in regions of city dirt and air, and he raised his head in gratitude; he was finished with his service for the dead. Toward winter, the farther bells did this, on a clearest day striking their whims from across the park. Once in a while in summer, the house heard from the south somewhere a muffled, dropped plume. No church was near enough to regulate its hours. But into many pockets of the city, these continental sounds often wandered, a reminder that the whole island, spired to the sea by bridges everywhere, was still built on country topography, hilltop to sea level, valley and dale.

The final packet of letters had been a cleansing one of the children's earliest, bird bells from kindergarten or from the weekend house where they still went sailing, notes and rhymes long since read together with old Mendes, handed round in the way of families who had few or no other collateral children. At the outposts of this one, flocks of cousins, three or four times removed, were never much more than recorded now. Every twenty years or so, with a war or a martyrdom, a few more dropped in from abroad. But in the direct lines of Mannix and Mendes — as often after a generation or so of only children or late marriages — his two chicks were the last of what had once been, in his own boyhood and at the building of this house, two noisy, vigorous clans.

As usual, any slightest family thought swung his compass needle towards its north. Past time for Ruth to come home, an hour past. He stanched that worry — that was the way it always felt, a far trickle, bleeding in the mind — and went to the window anyway. The three boys, intent on Austin's homecoming, he'd already heard some time back, clobbering the stairs to David's room, and then down.

It was a sweet, sad November afternoon of a street, outside. The car at the curb was his own. Very soon he might get rid of it, or give it to David; he wasn't going anywhere. Between him and it, the present incumbent curbside tree had spindled and must be replaced. He enjoyed the faintest percussion of the seasons on this street, and knew his privilege; if he had his way every man, woman and child in the city would own this home-sense of a life scene stretching ahead of them like a line of merging Utrillos, except for a shutter painted or a door wreath, unchallengedly the same.

Deepest in his chest, he felt the inertia of family life. In the unconscious life of men in cities, it flourished, an underground spring neither diseased nor healthy, merely silent water, coiling at the family root. Armies of men and women stood at windows, watched fires, swallowed their bread and felt its power, narcotic in mouth and limb. To escape its terrible, impalpable sinew, some got out and stumbled into bohemias, or lay down amnesiac in Boweries. To this order too belonged the silent disappearers, those strange, often eminent men who left behind them nests in no apparent way fouled — and were heard of years later or lost forever, in clerk jobs which kept them at the nadir of personal life. The mass of men stayed on, clenched in their days, almost but not quite aware of it, to die unprotesting and loudly shriven. Family inertia! Most who felt it wouldn't recognize his word for it. But any man at a window now and then shivered at its argument, assassin deep in the breast. I must move. I must murder. Where is Joy?

He ran back to the desk, hunted and found a letter, seized and crumpled it, painstakingly reopened it to check — " . . . I will never say," and took it to the toilet, where he tore it into small pieces with an animal's concentration — as if he expected the secret of what it was to appear as he dismembered it — and furtively watched it go down. To dispose of any record was hard for him, both by profession and temperament. The rest of the correspondence could be left to accrete, as family history was left everywhere in this house; no one reading it in years to come — either to see how things had been in the twenties, the thirties, the forties, or even for the secrets of his progenitors — would be able to add his own particular essence to it. But that one letter had had to be destroyed. This household no longer belonged among those whose lack of drama could be trusted in. That letter had been the very kind which inertia itself, half vengeful toward lives that escape from it, might be tempted to let lie, in wait. And did not children always seem poised for successful escape?

He posted himself at the window again. And after a while, down the block, he saw her coming back to him, his choice, his enigma, his dear loose end.

She was walking very like those nymphs of Dorset, his land girl of the city, toeing out as sturdily as they, the key to this house flopping innocently on her breast. A tailor's boy, it looked to be, walked beside her, carrying what father and brother, for once united, hadn't teased her out of, those uniforms which her mother, for once stirred to day-time allegiance, had arranged for, autumns back. She was chattering, and the boy — as he neared the step, what a scarecrow! — was rapt, chin dug in the pile of garments he was trundling. Maybe she oughtn't to wear that key in such nursery-school trust. He restrained an urge to wave. Now the two were on the stoop, just below him. The boy made as if to hand over the bundle. She didn't immediately take it — was she going to invite him in? Stray kittens — she was that kind of little girl, or had been, before her trouble. She still acted as if there were no trouble, like a skater who never went near a known hole in the ice, yet never gave evidence of seeing it. He must not think of the trouble as hers. She was asking in the boy, who was staring up at the house entrance, his estimate of it hidden under a Fiji-mop of hair, blond though, and behind a comic pince-nez of string. Below, the door then , closed.

He opened the door of the upstairs room, where, if they came up the front stairs, she must pass. What more natural — he wasn't waylaying her. Yet in the continual eddy of conscience, as she did come up the stairs, alone, and stopped just below the top, seeing him there over her pile of garments, he said, "I saw you from here."

She nodded, taking the last step up with her burden.

"Want me to take those in here?" He gestured behind him.

"Uh-uh. I'll take them to my room."

"How's — every little thing?"

"Copacetic."

The old prep school word he'd taught her touched him, along with a memory of her seven-year-old glee in finding that he didn't know what it meant.

"So many of them. Still." He touched the dresses.

She looked down at them. "Oh — I've outgrown them."

"I should think."

"Oh, not the dresses. We all have. No, I meant — the girls." And suddenly she gave him a wicked, radiant smile that floored him — a high smile so like her mother's, but from his own replica face — and went on up the stairs.

He called after her. He must not. "Who's — the boy?"

He heard her dump the dresses and come down again.

"The Halecsys' nephew." In the dimness at the far end, he could tell only by her voice.

"Oh? Didn't know they had one."

"Neither did they."

He put his distance glasses on. "They didn't?"

She saw him. "It was his birthday. So I . . ."

"He doesn't look like the Halecsys."

"He isn't. He . . ."

He waited. She cocked her head, not to him.

"Queer duck," he said.

"No. Not really. Just the way he's — been brought up."

"Oh?"

But dawdling at the head of the back stairs, she said, "I've got to go down. Austin's having a fest."

And he was after all used to this routine avoidance of parents, to the hide-and-seek, the lavatory passions, the confab giggles behind stairs.

"Have fun."

And she was gone. He never thought of joining them, or never had until now. And now he couldn't, to slide awkward in on their fest, on that foursquare, strangely solid team. Austin, for one, would know what he was after, appraising both him and the newcomer with cool, libertarian eyes. David would be at once on the defensive too. On Diddy's score—that painful nickname first coaxed from the boy's own lips — he knew well enough whose side they were always on. No criticism would ever come from Walter, that gay, humble soul who merely loved them all. But if ever a girl had some day to meet the seamy side of the picture — as today even the Ruths did — then he couldn't ask for a better guard than those three would instinctively form. He'd never thought of this as strange, before.

Some minutes later, downstairs in the study, he was glad when she tapped on his door.

"Come in."

"It's the boys. They want beer. Anna won't. Unless you —"

"Oh, for God's sake. Tell her it's OK." And had better be for good, with Austin at college, and the other two on their way. Here, and in other items like lipstick or the girl's dress, wherever a sure social sense was needed, of his own class but above all sure, Anna's terrified, lower-class strictures couldn't help, even hindered.

"But —" His girl hesitated.

"Yes?"

"She's made a cake. And ice cream. In a mold."

"Ah. I see." He yearned with pleasure. His girl had it for herself, her own sense of the right. And that would — must suffice. He'd have no genteel lady-companions here, dragged forth by Rosa-Athalie.

"Tell her to give them whisky, if they want it. Long as they eat her cake."

She grinned at him.

"And that boy — is he still here?"

"Oh, Daddy —" She came close to him. "He'd eat the whole table. I'm sure of it. He's starved. Like an animal."

"But — 'sweet,' eh?" He smiled at her. This was what had always been said, time out of mind, about the kittens and other strays. Of Walter, God only knows, it had been true. Where had they got their pity, his children?

But she was older now. Her mouth, on which there was now an approved orangey-pink coating, like wax on a raspberry, opened, then closed. "Smart."

"Odd-looking boy." Or slum man. That was it, that early look.

"It's only his clothes. They're going to make him a suit."

"I'd no idea the Halecsys were that poor. We must do something."

"Oh —*would* you. He wants to go into politics."

"*Pol* — ?"

She nodded, heedless. "They're not like the Halecsys. They come from — somewhere — worse. Where there's rats. His mother. She doesn't talk hardly at all. Like somebody you — tell what to do. The Halecsys are going to make her a coat. He works at some restaurant job. He always has. Worked." As each halted phrase came out of her, a change, a stare, an intentness came over her too, haunting her gaze past his own. "And he loves school," she said, in a rush. "Like I —" She stopped.

"Yes?"

"Love Ilonka's." This was the ballet school.

He was silent, confronted by what children knew of themselves. "And — how do you know — what he wants to do?"

"Because he told me." She hesitated, like all the young over their joint secrets. "He says, 'Politics is the best mob.'"

A coarse hoot of laughter burst from him. He couldn't help it, almost in allegiance with what that tough had said. And at the word "mob" on her milk-fed, fastidious tongue. "Maybe he should join your club."

Too late, he saw his mistake. How did they do it? — she hadn't changed expression in the slightest. Yet behind it, she had closed. "I beg your pardon," he said. He reached out and patted her. She allowed it. "Really I laughed — because he's so damn right." In fealty, he offered her the "damn."

"He's alone," she said. "He didn't even know how old he was. Until today." But her tone was cold, without sentiment. Were there no kittens, any more?

"Romulus?" he said.

She didn't answer. But she didn't haunt off this time; she was looking straight at something — as one looked at a perfectly formed thought.

He tried to do the right thing, this time. His tongue had to be so delicate. To push her thought toward him.

"And where's Remus?" he said.

Again she didn't answer. But there was a vibration. He'd hit it somewhere. He waited.

"He's like me —"

Like you, dear? — how could that boy be like you? He didn't say it.

In tune, in perfect tune, he waited.

"His mother was raped, he said. That's how he was born."

"Like *you*," he said in horror.

She contemplated it.

"What can you two — *possibly* —"

She nodded at him, but her head on one side, her mouth tremulous. For him. For him! He had seen judges give sentence like that, joining themselves to the accused, in the charge. And the prisoner, bowing his own head, saw it also. But which was he? Judge, that ye may be. Was it his turn? — but which was he? Prisoner or judge. He didn't know. This was his final hallucination.

"Yes, like me," she whispered, retreating to the door. "Everything's already happened to him." And then hung her head, like a bride.

6 What the Judge Said – *June 1951*

Edwin bounded up the steps of the house, feeling well prepared. The front door was open; someone entering before him hadn't pushed it closed. Anna would have a fit about it.

He let himself in, paused by the stair rail, avoiding the hall mirror, where there was an early vision of himself always embedded, and walked left into a long oblong known as the "big" room, to distinguish it from the righthand "library," though the latter held less books.

"Great room," their journalist friend Blount always said. "Great windows, that pier glass between 'em great, great curtains Belgium 1880, great."

Edwin sat down in a chair near the door where Anna in passing would see him — so relieving his sense that he might be thought to have entered illegally, in order to catch the inmates of the house in the unofficial state in which they lay suspended when out of his presence. For though what the Mannixes were wasn't simply said, he was always trying. In his black notebook, he sometimes put down their chronology as it came to him from their own mouths, as if he meant to be a Bulfinch annotator of their legend, or needed to keep it straight in his mind when he was among them. They were his gods then, if it were understood that he was highly critical of them, and that theirs was a group he never hoped to join. He wanted to know more precisely what their nature was, from the same wistfulness with which the poor read in their yellow journals about the rich.

He knew that through the Mannixes' daily papers (which were whatever of the world's they chose to read) they kept reasonably in touch with the mass movements of guns, hunger and thought — and even of peoples — and, even assisted practicably there, as the Judge had done with his refugees. Oh, they kept up their charities — even though nobody spoke so knowledgeably as they themselves of what an

eyedropperful-in the sea of want these were. They *continued* — that
was part of it — and he could see how it would be sometimes into
mere smugness or self-love — but he didn't think he much romanticized the best of them. For they themselves had the most powerful
sense that *their* self-dramas, their lives, personal and as a class, were an
ever-running commentary *on* the world. In this, he was somehow convinced, lay the true seriousness of their life. For they were released by
money, yet immediately bound themselves into responsibility. No
wonder their mode of life was ambiguous. For as the people in the
house had seemed to him on that first visit, so they did still. They
transacted life in beautiful visits, which never needed to get anywhere.

He glanced at his watch; he was now some minutes late for the
Judge but stubbornly sat on, waiting to be discovered. As if this gave
him leave, he stared squarely at the portrait over the mantel. In
tawnies and greens, mud-pinks, and against a background of black—
from which the sitter gazed into a beyond which must be somewhere
painted as limply — it was a token portrait done in that accessible style
which quickest flattened the subject into eternity, and might have been
commissioned by a bank. For hints as to what the woman herself had
been, he much preferred the yellow and black drawing of her in what
seemed to be costume but might be some dress vagary of the 1920's —
a tinted pen-and-ink, signed with a Parisian scrawl, in which the spirit
of the eyes propelled a large head stomachered on a small body,
tapered behind it like a wasp's; somehow nevertheless, the subject
appeared large. And the drawing was easier looked at, being hung in
the room, once her bedroom, now a kind of sitting-room, used by all
and sundry for anything. Considering its owner's end, he admired the
Mannixes for merely nullifying the room instead of preserving or ignoring it. Understandably, they'd more or less walled up the woman
herself from their conversation at least with outsiders, though from
their occasional necessary mention of her — as on his first walk with
Ruth — he had an insistent impression that when alone they didn't
speak much of her either. Yet they had done their best; there were
pictures of her everywhere in the house. Or almost everywhere. In the
Judge's sanctum, there was none.

The picture told him nothing. He saw now that the frame had a
small inscribed gold tag attached to its nether side as in museums; if he
went up to it he would learn her name, which he didn't know. In his

notebook, she was merely Mrs. M. He sat where he was; she concerned him only in what her end had done to the Judge. For it was absurd to think that a man's bad luck didn't attach to his character. Just as her suicide had crystallized hers, it had at once made of the Judge a man who could choose a woman capable of committing it. Cancer had been rumored the cause of it — at Harvard where Edwin had heard all this, meanwhile watching gossip's interplay, taking a ground lesson in the politics of men before they flew off into outright politics. For, just as the ill luck of cancer had forever attached itself to the body of her character, whatever the Judge had done after her death was at once attached to his. Ill luck had made his personal character common property. Now men could say thus and so of him. After her death, he had for years retired from public life. He was *that* kind of man.

Yet because of what the Judge was otherwise, it hadn't been the end of him.

"Look — it stands to reason," had said one professorial voice, host in his rooms to the group of frosh law students who were pleasantly conscious of being as "in" as the imported ale they were drinking. "Some men's reputations *swell* in retirement. That's our country for you. We confuse it with purity. Anything he writes — be it ever so —"

"Humble?" said another. There was a general snigger.

"Not *that*," said the first. "But he was always a contradictory figure. Look at his early practice, a lawyer's lawyer, almost a yearner after the poetry of the law you might say — not at all in the style of the man you meet. Yes, I've been to meet him. And I'd have been tempted to put him down as a top trial lawyer, if we'd met *outside*. Nothing radical — if there was a touch of that too in the early days, I'd bet he cultivated it, to conceal a conservatism not in the popular style. Anyway, a tricky little Napoleon, to look at him. And on second handshake, an old-fashioned niceness that cuts a clever modern fellow — like me — to the heart. Juries would have gone under to it. And the very size of the man! Where little Mannix sits is always the head of the table — you have to listen to him. It's like sex."

When he had finished, a student voice said "Outside?" And got a student's answer, from a generation suddenly reminded that it was gossiping about its own.

"Yes, people mostly go there to meet *him*, I guess. But you'll find that's true, Benjamin, of a lot of us old gents. Though Mannix is only sixty or so." The speaker was perhaps fifty.

And then Edwin, in spite of himself, had interposed. "That's right, sir. He's sixty-one. He was born in 1890."

They'd all turned to look at him except the first man, who went on riding his hobbyhorse. "See, then? And already a sage. Retirement's only made him a virtuoso."

"On what, sir?" said the persistent Benjamin. The masters looked at each other, shrugging.

A new voice spoke, an eminent visiting historian. "On honor, I guess. The public honor. Those discriminations which can only be made by men who live in private. Not that *he* makes them. He's never done a damn thing since, as far as I can see — except his refugees, and that one little early paper he revised. Just lets his reputation grow in interview — or in talk like this. Naturally anybody's incorruptible who doesn't do anything."

One of the home crowd agreed with him. "Though there was rumor that even before his wife — died — he was planning to desert judicial life for another sort entirely. I'm not inclined to believe it. Has to be some better explanation of why he dropped out, gave up what he had. The talk has always been that maybe, during the interlude after her death, an improbable ambition he had became an impossible one. And he's never been able to scramble up the energy for anything *less*." The speaker's drawl was scornful. On the subject of inaction, these university shut-ins often were.

"What ambition?"

"Oh, it was absurd — the way truth can be. It was rumored he wanted to —" Someone must just then have realized that they were talking in front of Mannix's protégé. In the silence that fell he had heard the speaker's finishing whisper and laugh anyway: " — to run for *President*."

He went up to the portrait now, and looked at its nameplate. Her name was Mirriam.

Anna was heard coming upstairs from her lower regions, not ponderous, but moving always with the responsibility of creatures who must announce themselves. No reason why he should feel as if he'd filched a part of the house's silence. Yet when she saw him, he said, "The door was open again."

Under her regard, flat as at their first entente over hall toilets, his neat chinos flopped again into tramp-folds. He couldn't have cared less. Maybe this puzzled her.

"Walter and David here?" he said.

"Dey left again day before yesterday."

There went his "major" visit. Perhaps they were all too grown now for it ever to occur again. "Abroad?"

"Yah." She always grudged informing him of any of them, preferring to hold him on the side of those strangers it was her job to keep away from such information. Was it also because she thought him the Judge's favorite? He'd never thought of the word, until seeing himself again in her eyes.

"Mr. Austin, he's home from Korea."

Edwin knew who her favorite was — and why. "Yes, I know. Ruth wrote me from London." Only a card, but no reason to say that. "She back yet?"

"The two boys, dey gone to meet her." Then she said quickly, "I knew you be late again — you better sneak in, wait for him."

If they'd gone to get Ruth, what could it mean except that, unpersuaded, she, who had never been away alone before, wouldn't come back? He stared at Anna, from hairnet to apron, understanding her function better. Anna smoothed away the family thunder by giving to all family information the appearance of its being nothing at all.

"Not down yet?" he said.

"He don't look good. He been to doctor. *Him.*" On the subject of the Judge's health she would inform or consult anybody — and no one she loved ever looked too good to her. "What you tink — ?" she said. Since they were all away she would ask anyone, even him. "He bought a cane."

"Ah, Anna — " He flattered himself he was all Harvard now, make what she could of it. "That's to beat me with."

Just then the phone rang. She let it ring, counting — the Judge and she had an arrangement — then answered it. Her bulk filled the little niche in the hallway, through which he must pass to the Judge's study in the rear. He turned once again to study the picture, proudly not listening.

But she — when she hung up he had never seen her in such a state — nor in any, of course. Her face had mottled; she wrung her hands. Yes, he thought — how visible our kind are.

"That woman, she's over here; she's coming to dinner," she finally said, smoothing her hair as if inner feelings had worked on it. "*I* didn't invite her. Pauli say to tell *him* she's coming. You tell him."

"Who shall I say?"

Too late she saw how close she had invited him to come. "You just say —" she hesitated — 'the ballet lady! You just say it like that."

"Well, you always have enough to feed a battalion, Anna. I've heard the Judge say it time and again."

Right there, he saw her smooth over her own character, tug it, like a skirt or a blouse ruff, back into line. "Yah!" she said in broad relief. "Tank God, I got the fricassee."

They were still standing together near the entrance of the long room. An impulse made him touch her arm, perhaps because he'd guessed the identity of the newcomer. *But the best thing was Daddy and Madame* — somebody or other. *When the war's over, maybe the Royal will take me.* But Ruth had never dared go back, until now. "I've been looking at that picture up there. Mrs. Mannix. She must have been very handsome."

"Yah." Though she must know he knew the circumstances, she said it so calmly, prepared for all visitors.

"More like David." He didn't know what he was digging for, scarcely that he was.

Again she nodded. She hadn't really opened her mouth at all.

"Not like Ruth."

She shook her head minimally. She must be in a rage to get away to her dinner preparations, the only hours she showed temperament; her refusal to have other help was known to all. Yet she stood there, lip twitched to a smile, in a stance that half horrified he smelled out at once — her cul-de-sac.

"You tell Judge I put dinner later haff, tree-quarter hour," she said — and left him.

He found himself near the telephone, and shook a musing no at it. Wherever her fear of him circled, it wasn't in connection with the Judge — though it now seemed to him that he knew the Judge better than anyone alive, even anyone here. He'd never thought long of the mother before. Now it struck him that perhaps Anna was afraid that suicide was hereditary. But then why should her fear be connected in any way with him?

He was halfway down the hall before her own secret, as seen in that last trapped smile of the eyes, came to him. Anna was intelligent.

On the way to the Judge's study, he passed the hall mirror again, and made himself look there, as was his custom at least once on each visit.

His careless dress pleased him, now that he could carry it better than some aristocrats. He was no Austin. But he too had a lineage almost as formal. He too was the bloom of circumstance, in the directest line.

When his first suit, made by his mother's sisters, had been fitted on him, he had discovered this about himself. The suit was unwearable — and couldn't be rescued. One side of the jacket had been cut fatally too narrow for anyone, from the shoulder down. "No one could wear it," he said to them proudly. "Not even a Chinee." When he put on the trousers, he laughed aloud. The crotch was inches out of line with his navel. For a year after, the aunts wouldn't speak to him because of what he'd said to them. "I can see for sure," he said, with a snarl straight from the streets they had left him to, "neither one of you has ever been raped."

He'd thrown away the suit himself, denying them even the solace of their remnant bag. The act had given him his first inkling of the sensation that could grow so imperial here — waste. He knew his hatred was lost on the aunts. One day, he found it had turned to pride. And so, he had found his lineage. Nothing of the emotions, early or late, ever really went to waste.

He walked into the study and was in his usual chair, laying out the black notebook, use of which the Judge if anything encouraged, eagerly drinking in the details of the beloved oracle-spot — from the stamp wall to all a great man's life incunabula of paper, brass, marble and eraser crumbs, and on to the window through which he had first climbed in here at that man's bidding — when another truth struck him. He'd had to go back to the district for it, to his reservoir. Whatever Anna had to hide, her fear of him was natural. He was unlike the innocents she was surrounded with. She was afraid of him because he could smell.

Then he forgot it all — the whole afternoon's self-coaching, all his years of 5x8's, the sipping of imported ale, the new suavity of mirrors — and hauling himself up out of his chair, he was fifteen again on his eighteenth birthday — for the Judge, leaning on a cane, was here.

Doorways in this house were of a height to belittle almost anyone, but the Judge always paused for a moment in any, and never appeared to mind the heraldic majesty of some of his father-in-law's Venetian chairs. Larger men went shaggy in the hide, but age had found little surface to work with in this neat, unviolent bantam, except to flick with white its black poll — and since the Judge's weight and hair seemed likely to be permanent, he always appeared much the same. He'd been heard to say this could make a man seem unserious to contemporaries. He was smiling at Edwin as if he might have just said this, in the dry voice which invited one to disbelieve. His dress had never gone sloppy with retirement, remaining the same bluish or grayish or brownish, with white shirt and dim tie. But the cane, a black one with a thumbprint of silver on the top, was an embellishment. He and Edwin continued their steady mutual assessment of each other, an honored half-yearly ritual, before he crossed past the deck chair to an uncustomary one opposite Edwin's and sat down, twirling the cane between his knees. He regarded it carefully, as if its revolutions had nothing to do with him, then folded his hands on it, clearing his throat. He always began — with what might or might not be the motif of their hour's conversation. And he had several voices.

"I'm thinking of getting a mortal disease," said the Judge. "Though it may be too late for it." He tossed the cane aside, as if he could do this at will with sticks and diseases both. Then he said what he always said. "For God's sake, Edwin, sit down. And for mine too."

He'd meant to give Anna's message now, but the Judge suddenly reached over, picked up the black leather notebook, from its place at Edwin's side, and laid it on the low table between them. "So this is where you keep us."

For answer, Edwin pushed the book toward him. The Judge reached into a cellarette for a bottle and two glasses and poured them each a small glass of white vermouth, to Edwin now a drink whose faint herbs tasted totally of reminiscence and the harmonics of intellect. In his room at school he kept a similar bottle, offering it in the same aristocratic way — without ice and without alternative.

"Dates." The Judge sipped. The moment at which he enunciated his real topic was always hard to say, and the topic too, though Edwin was sure he was learning many things circuitously — the way one would if one could be led through childhood again, but with a fully developed brain. Indeed, because of David, he couldn't help seeing that the Judge sometimes talked to him as if he were the superchild for whom blocked fathers longed.

"Far as I know, Edwin, we were all born in wedlock. Nothing incriminating there."

"Or anywhere!" said Edwin. "Except maybe about Anna. And I don't know what that is."

"Anna?"

"You ever think —" He wasn't sure of the ethics here — the ones to be exhibited, that is. An echo returned to him, without helping him — *Servants, Edwin? Whether their role in our lives gives us the creeps, or we accept it as farce — shows our own role in the social scale. Even now.* "You ever think that Anna might have another life? Separate from here?" Saying it, he felt almost an allegiance with her.

"You appall me. On my part. For no, I hadn't." The Judge shoved his glass away. "Why?"

"She acts afraid of me. As if — because of who I am — I might more easily find out."

"Because of who you are," the Judge said slowly. "Maybe we haven't spent enough time on that. You always keep me so busy answering what *we* are." He carefully reached out — as if from a prescribed radius — and rubbed the cane. "She was married once. My wife knew more about it than I."

Since the Judge had never before mentioned either his wife or his retirement, Edwin found nothing to say.

"Ruth may know," the Judge said indifferently. "What Anna does with her Thursdays and Sundays."

Edwin did have his own ethics on this. Neither of the Judge's children was to be discussed with him — and Ruth particularly not now.

"Or my sisters might." Both he and Edwin burst into smiles.

"I saw them yesterday," said Edwin. "At my aunts. They're just the same."

"If all civilization would only subject its nerve ends to as little of the new as my elder sisters!" The Judge looked at his fingertips. "I figured out once — since my attaining puberty, my sisters have given me almost a hundred pairs of gray suede gloves. At two a year — *there's* chronology for you. The essence of family strength is in it — and because one can disregard my sisters themselves — in them." He clapped his palms together, leaned back, and straightened again. "Enough. How're you finding the law?"

He'd expected to be asked of course, and in just this way. "I'm *finding* it," he said. It sometimes tickled the Judge to hear apt imitation of his own verbal artifice. Who wouldn't want to please this man so viciously saddened, so horrifying alive in terms of what his own satisfactions appeared to be, this man who — yes, this must be the category — whom one loved. Whom, like a father, one loved.

But today this was received as a man in hospital receives flattery on his looks — with a disowning smile. Edwin sneaked another glance at the cane.

"Well, you're only first-year. But there're only two more. And I've an itch to see some of the young under my aegis work out." He paused. "Go ahead and look at the cane, Edwin. It was my grandfather's. Anna thinks I bought it — but she doesn't know all the possessions of this house."

"Very handsome."

"Hmm." He was poured another drink. "You haven't it in your background as I did. The law, I mean."

"Sometimes it helps. Not to have a category."

"Oh, you don't have the self-pity we're educated to. Wear your bone outside, I've often thought, not inside, like the rest of us." The Judge reached into the cellarette and took out a bottle of bourbon. "Don't worry. It doesn't show. Nice jacket, incidentally. Get it in Cambridge?"

He nodded. "On clothes, I just follow the mob." With some surprise, he watched the Judge, a light drinker, down a shot of bourbon and pour himself another.

"That other stuff doesn't —" The Judge looked up from his own mutter. "Join me? No? Don't look so worried — Jews like us don't make drunks. Doctor's been giving me codeine for a slight ailment. But I find it intolerable. Turns the whole world an Oriental yellow." He rose, walked to the window, without the cane, and leaned there. He turned. "How sentimental of me. I can still see you out there. Peeing. Edwin ... d'you still feel — 'Politics is the best mob'?"

"So that's the way I said it, that day! Always knew Ruth must have reported something to make you see me!"

When there was no reply — he never knew how far to go in personal talk with the Judge — he said, "*Can* one go after it honestly — politics?" Back there in the barbershop — that's how they knew when a man wasn't honest. When it went after *him*. In his excitement, he stood up. "I've thought about it a lot — we all do, at school up there. If they want to go into the business end of the law, they know how close a shave they'll have, all the way along the line. Even if they plan to practice otherwise. It's not like the judiciary — where a man has to wait to be found." He had forgotten this would be personal. But even a retired man must expect references to his profession, if he still allows himself to be called Judge.

"That your idea of the judiciary?" said the Judge, turning. "A man stands around in his honesty until he's tapped for it?" He came and sat down again, looking up. In a man of his age, this was always winsome. "It was true of Cardozo. Oh, among the greats, there's always a long list of the hyper-innocent. But Edwin, most times in the world you see a man with an appointment he very much wanted, you'll very much more likely find he's put himself in the way of it." He reached for the cane again, using the ferrule to inscribe a minute circle on the floorboards, punctuating his remarks as with a pipe. "Same thing can be true if he removes himself from worldly appointment. Though that's generally considered a less positive action. Some day I must tell you about an old friend of mine." He looked up, smiling. "As my father used to say, 'Some fine evening of my decline, when you come to see me in a fur hat.' " He held the cane still. "But right now, I'm too young for it. Though he used to say that too."

The gentle silences which fell to such middle-aged evocations — the halls of learning were full of these. "Memory soup," a cold-voiced student neighbor had once said to him of a professor presiding unasked in the dinner hall. "That's all they live on."

"I can use it," Edwin had replied. But now he stared hostilely at whisky glass and cane, each as damning as false teeth or the jaw-dropped aphasia of aging sleep. Each time he returned from school, he dreaded to find that the Judge might seem to him to know less and less of the law — and perhaps of experience.

Just then the cane smacked down. The Judge looked at it with surprise, as if a dog had barked. "I'm learning its gestures faster than I like," he said. "Edwin, no more large talk. We'll spend more time on who you are and are to be. You've a career to be — chosen by." In deploring their loss of the grand manner, the Judge seemed almost to regain it. "You better haul out that black book again," he said softer. "I've inhibited *you*."

Outside the window it was that exact moment before dusk thickened to dark, baring those city crocuses, the first lights. The day furled round the house in draperies the color of disappointment, funeral to the obsessive, Byronic visits of young men. For the first time Edwin anticipated the terror-ennui of those who were cornered in houses, heard the refrain, "What are *you* doing *here?*" — and answered it manfully, "I will stay. But I will also *go*."

The Judge put out his small hand, touching the notebook with a finger which to Edwin's dilated eye and imagination grew until it pointed on the black leather like a cane. "When do you appear there?"

"Where?" He recognized the question as one he had been waiting for.

"In the record. With us."

"I thought I was." Really they had never invited him to be prince — only to prove that he wasn't a frog.

"You know better than that. You're more intelligent than anyone we let come to the house."

"Austin is intelligent."

In the eye-crinkles opposite, he saw how young he was.

"And has been coming to dinner longer than you." The Judge glanced at his right wrist.

"I forgot to tell you — Anna said to say dinner will be half to three-quarters of an hour later — "

"Good. Gives me even more time to incriminate *you*. Which is one way of being made to choose a vocation. I imagine they knew that at the barbershop." The Judge took up a paper knife, absently using the haft to stir his drink. There was a physical simplicity about him which he didn't appear to know he had. All the formality of his talk didn't cover how he scratched his crotch in company, with a gusto so large for his person, and with a luxury the Edwins couldn't spare. Such habits endeared him to his children, exciting their fantasies of that life of the privates, or of the animal, he too must once have had. According to Ruth, David had once come upon his father alone at breakfast, bending like a guilty boy to lick his plate. And their father had said to him — very carefully so he would hear all of it: "In my youth, David, I used to catch your great-grandmother — who wore her hair à la Madame Pompadour — blowing her nose through her fingers. Honesty has to come out somewhere — like snot."

He found the Judge staring at him.

"Well, Edwin, since you won't talk — yes, I want to make you a proposal." The Judge poked into his drink, faintly smiling. "Used to be a picture at the head of the stairs, house I was brought up in. A young wench on a ladder, picking from a tree. And a grenadier clasping the rungs, looking up her skirt. My father got it in Toulouse once, and put it there. Outside his study, where all the young men visitors could see it. 'A Shady Proposal,' the title was. Or so he said. My mother never got the joke, though he shouted it at her often enough. 'A proposition,

Martha. For the love of God.' Theirs was an arranged marriage. Which is why the sons of such couples often marry otherwise — for beauty, say. Or for intelligence." He drank to the bottom. "Will you marry — for intelligence, Edwin?"

"Don't suppose I'll marry for years."

"I thought not, somehow. Then you've no strings." The Judge let a pause lengthen. "Well, then. Here's my proposition. Will you come to New York?"

"Leave *school?*"

"Glad you said it that way. Implying interest. Not just Harvard. No, of course not. My idea would be — you could switch to Columbia. Not a university very great in forward spirit. But well abreast of the conventions. And in your own city. Which, believe me, Edwin, is what a man best answers to."

"Why?"

"I'll answer that presently."

"No, I mean why should I change?"

"I was going to answer that too." The Judge checked his watch again. He saw Edwin see it. "A habit of public life," he said. "You know — until yesterday, I hadn't worn a wristwatch in — years." He reached for the black stick, held it for a minute above his head in the fencer's alert, and tossed it behind the desk, where it rattled, rolled unseen, and lay still.

"I don't fence," he said. "Nor hunt, fish or ride. I can mirror-write, lipread, am ambidextrous, used to play a mean game of chess and a meaner game of points, can calculate compound interest at a pace would surprise you — and tup the ladies at one that wouldn't. And once — I wrote a few tolerable reports. More recently I've learned to sail a boat — which some say can take the place of all the rest. When that becomes necessary. And — oh yes. I can guard a house. For the past ten years I seem to have done — nothing much else."

He broke off sharply. "Edwin — has no one told you the first principle of social behavior is not to stand looming over a man seated talking to you!" Then he said, "Sorry." When Edwin had seated himself, frozen into the quiet of one who knew what such insult meant to the insulter, the Judge said in a shamed voice that matched it, "Edwin. I'm going back into public life."

Nothing further was added to this admission that all the Judge's philatelies — from the charting of stamps to the cross-Atlantic saving of lives — had been private ones.

"How?" Edwin finally said.

"Hired a chauffeur," said the Judge. "To drive more and quicker than I'm allowed — I don't yet know where. Been offered a little back room, somewhere to the rear of the Low library up there at Columbia, and I've accepted it. To do I don't know what. I assume — the work it's assumed I've *been* doing. And now I suppose I want what can't be hired — a man to help me with it."

"You going to — run for office?"

He'd never seen so many changes pass across that ordinarily even face — whose almond planes and curled lip an Oriental yellow would have suited. "Edwin. What office could I possibly run for?"

"At school . . . I've heard them say —"

"*Yes*, yes — *what* is it — *they* say?" The Judge, finding his own hand on Edwin's sleeve, pulled it away. It kneaded his empty glass into the palm of the other. "Well, well. I discover that — apparently — against my better knowledge it's been my whole ambition — to hear *what they say*." His voice had changed, to an uncommon tremor. "But — what do they — Edwin?"

If he wasn't to insult, he must make the statement in a tone of possibility — where for all he knew it truly lay. "That you wanted to — run for President."

The Judge's mouth opened, not to laugh. Across it passed a caricature of trying. "*No* . . ." He bent his head. "Now I know how dead Chauncey Olney is. That friend I spoke of. Too dead to share a joke." He seemed to commemorate. Then said in almost a whisper, "No, my paranoias were — rather . . . greater. So it'd be wise indeed for me, wouldn't it, to have the ear of a young man like you — of more practical . . . scope. Although my present ambition is so . . . modest." He raised his head. "Edwin. Know what I think I mean by — going back into public life?" He pointed out to the hall which led to the front of the house. "I think all I mean is — getting outside that door."

He felt youngest in not being able to believe that this one of his elders — in spite of liquors and codeines, canes and memories — wasn't still firmly holding on to his sharpest internal self. He drew a brave breath. "Don't talk down — to either of us."

There was a pause. "Histrionics aren't for me, are they, Edwin? That's perhaps — why I've liked women who — have them. But honor my proposal, boy, by thinking of it. Don't answer now." He was palming the glass. "Maybe I need a — confidential secretary. Who would see to it that I don't confide. What used to be called an amanuensis."

Edwin could scarcely see his face. But he heard the glass being filled again, set down.

"Maybe we two could write the work I'm supposed to. Law clerks have lots of leeway. The Encyclopedia wants an article or two from me. If it's any good, you can publish it as yours. In the old days, men used to go to war by proxy, did you know that?"

"Yes, the Civil." He got to his feet again and went to the window, fighting the room's lack of light and its owner's replacement of logic with dream. No man *returns* to life, he thought; how did I know? Or not this man somehow, to whom honesty is a pearl.

Outside the low, open window, at the far end of the narrow garden, a figure had entered the garden, from around the front of the house, moving unhurriedly, but not as if it knew the place. He leaned forward, half reluctant to call it to the Judge's attention. Another intruder? — from the openly shared dream-life of cities.

"Shall I turn on a lamp?" he said.

"There'll be light," said the Judge.

For a moment, the words behind Edwin sounded rabbinical, or mad. Then, yards away and up, the water tower was under-illumined by a slender beacon which cast a modest gleam on the garden below, reminding one that anciently this had been sufficient.

"Nightly, since 1876," said the Judge. "Except for the brownout. We help pay for it." Through the open chair-back, the light touched a profiled head as bullet-shaped and frail-necked as a boy's.

Across the garden, always kept to grass, a few stone seats and its bending tree, the woman's slow, angled progress recalled the pigeon that had paced the wall. Her back was to Edwin; she was facing the city beyond. Not Ruth. Except for her almost miniature size, and the hair slouched in a knot on her neck, she might have been — it was in the way she walked. As she moved again and stood chin in hand, the patching light revealed an arm and elbow, white-gloved.

"Shall I close the curtain?" He said it like a child, hoping not.

"No, I don't ever. It's my audience — I'd miss it. Or I'm its."

Behind and above her, the water tower's outline squatted on the sky like a kindly ogre. The air between her and it and the window was edged with what he supposed was imagination. Almost musical, but on the safe side of silence. He was beginning to think like them. Watching her leading his eye into another plane of perspective from *his* window, he saw the reasons for statues in gardens. To show the limitations of houses — while nymphs raged and men traveled.

In the room, the Judge spoke. Always so many — ruminations," the voice said. "What a father never says to a son."

He kept silent.

Earliest here he had learned that none of the young people around David — Austin, Walter, or Ruth his own sister, would ever collaborate with the Judge in any of his allusions to David. A calm rudeness deadened their hearing, a blankness their eye, though they did it tenderly, in a pact to keep the Judge from his worser self — a silent pact which Edwin, unasked, had joined.

"One needs to . . . talk," said the voice behind him. "Anna swears I don't talk to myself. Or that she never hears a word. Sometimes I wish she would." To Edwin, the voice was the Judge's best — not a wooing voice. A plain one, speaking from a pain in the breast that could be honesty, ash-dry as it could have been in court.

Outside, he saw that in that interval, the woman had gone. No dinner bell had rung. He half listened to the multiple interior of the house, a delicate ear that rang.

He turned from the window. Anna's other message, which for a second he'd meant to give, skimmed away.

"I accept your proposal," he said. He felt a pain in his own chest.

The man in the chair, so short under its latticed back that the beacon barely touched his poll with its manufactured moonlight, was rubbing and rubbing his face in his hands, and might never have heard. When the face was raised, a dreadful smile had been rubbed on it — the kind the owner of a face didn't know was there. He spoke in a hoarse voice his audience had never heard before.

"I — *need*," he said.

Edwin, grasping the sill behind him, held on tight. I shall live here.

A pause between members of the same household had a different silence.

"Thank you," the Judge said at last. "Later, put my words down or not, as you like. I've put some down here, in a little memoir. But don't canonize them. Your job in this house will be simple. When I talk to myself, you will hear."

Fathers, Edwin. We've never talked about them. Only cousins, sisters, aunts, all the side bubbles of the family vortex, as if we were making an assemblage for a new ark. Or we sit and murmur sociologies at each other, like idle flybaiters in a zoo. While outside the grape is drunk, and the women are laid. That was the province of fathers and sons in my generation, and what men talked about in private. Politics and justice were for the dinner table. Reverse it, as nowadays, and both conversations are ruined.

But we know about mothers, you and I, even if society hadn't already told us and told us. Mothers are the tigress, the defender, force-feeding us by day, tender with night's poultices. I'm not so sure about Oedipus, all that. My mother was an enjoyably useful nuisance — and we could be tender with that too; our feeling for her was something like what one has for the fools in Shakespeare, though she was nowhere near so entertaining. But it is doubtful that I ever wanted to sleep with her — any more than my father did.

What is a father? You never ask. There's a word for it . . . if you ever ask. From his first breeze over my cradle, my father's success was that almost to the end of his life I never saw him except emotionally. He had a great, dripping bundle of experience in his hands, and as we talked or walked together, he never failed to break off a piece and give it to me, sometimes a berry, sometimes a thorn. Either way, I had to grasp it. And behind him, he had a house invisible, but not made of cards or of glass or any of the other corruptibles, not even of biblical rust — see Ecclesiastes. We walked through its rooms without ever speaking of it; its contract was never mentioned, yet every day we paced its boundaries and defined. By the time he was an old man and I saw him with my intellect — the bundle bare and the house gone — it was too late; he had already given me them. Fathers are where the dreams are.

And the art of failure, what is it? For in terms of the men my father shared a courtroom morning with, or a brownish winter afternoon on "the Street," or even, as he used to say, "a flossy dinner at Mouquin's"

— to all those Carters and Choates he never chummed with or took by
the coattails either but had to see almost daily in the way of business
— he must have been merely one of those non-bankrupts who never
made either a legal or financial success. In their eyes, surely that was
failure. But I never could tell, with him. Perhaps that attitude's a
hereditary strain in us somewhere — though my father went on working till he died.

But inaction helps make a man a poet if he's able; he has to gather
together the loose ends of his sensibility — or the kernels — and dare
to say to the world, "Here! Value *this!*"

Yet even in men of action there were great storytellers in those
days — mainly because there were great listeners, used to hearing the
world make habitable by talk. My father was always in this second
group — in spite of all the young men who used our house as a hall.
And emulating him — though it wasn't my nature but only my age —
so was I. Now, being a father, I can tell you the story, and you may
brood on the word for us. Or words.

Before I was born, my father had already built up a part-time practice in Paris, at first as one of the many in attendance on the Bering Sea
arbitrations between Great Britain and us. Look it up, that late-century
tea party — almost the last of the great Anglo-American disputes. Did
Great Britain have the right to kill seals in water adjacent to their
breeding ground — islands held to be our domain under the Alaska
Purchase? We lost — but for international law it meant a new turn.
For my father — it brought him into the world, if not the society, of
James Carter, counsel for our government, of Lucius Choate, the "great
cross-examiner," who later wrote Carter's memoirs, and eventually
much more of the same company, where — quite possibly for lack of
talent alone — he didn't belong. It's not a familiar role, the Jew who
isn't smart enough for a particular milieu or group of Christians, and
it's certainly not a favorite one with our people, but it exists. Maybe it
broadened and gentled him, but somewhere it must have dampened
and muted him too — my father-in-law Mendes, that old Spanish hawk
among hawks, would never have understood him.

To me, my father was always smart enough. If the young clerks,
junior partners, and now and then even students who sought the house
did so mostly for their own inter-jangling charms, I wasn't too young
myself to observe that a word from him, however modest and hostly,

nevertheless fell hypnotic on their abstract struggles — and in silence I measured this. Under pact of said silence, I had been allowed up — from the time I was nine — to learn what I could, plus the habit of oral memory as well. By then the Bering Sea business was long over — settled in 1893, when I was three. But it was always recurring, of course; one of the great aspects of the law is that its conversations go down the ages at will — and of course I was learning that too. For to me, the very words *Bering Sea* and *the seals' breeding ground* — or that curt, sea captain's phrase *off the Pribilofs* — were also an entirely other kind of island music. Even later, when I was studying for the bar exams — which if done alone, as we often used to, is like learning the separate names of ten thousand matchsticks — even then I could still hear it, and for its sake go on. It taught me that no matter how far the law recedes into infinite holding companies of itself, at sea bottom, it takes in the natural world. From there I wasn't far to seeing, if I hadn't seen already, how from the meadow to its owner, from a man's riparian rights to the water-music he listens to — the law takes in the invisibles of men.

I wonder, do you get that at Harvard — or Columbia? In the nineties, we could still study for the bar on our own — or with an office-father. That's why I don't mind your notebook. To know people, you should know about houses. And a father knows — though he can't always tell you — what is a house.

By the time I was sixteen we were all in Paris together; my father's practice there had never diminished so far that he couldn't find something to take him there at least twice a year, though this was the first time we'd been there as a family, on my mother's insistence that the girls and I learn French. That little picture of all of us crammed into a dogcart, our heads as flat forward as if we had no rear dimension, is of that time, taken during the *vacances* — mine, from the school I loathed. At that time I'd already attained almost my full height. My father, a six-footer himself, never seemed to mind one whit that his only son took after the maternal side, my mother herself being an ordinary five-foot-two, but with a known strain of dwarfism in the family, which I'd just barely escaped. Otherwise, he was quite impersonally prepared to believe that my bad odor at school — and bad French — was all due to my being an American — since he'd been born in England himself. At the same time, he trusted me implicitly because I was *his* — and since I so admired him, even at that bloody

school I couldn't do less than act as if I was. What invaluable guide-
lines to conduct there used to be, from unpsychologized parents! For
meanwhile I knew that if anything really serious ever went unfairly
against me down there, he was capable of thrashing the offender,
student or master, in the event that I was right. I'd given him this
allegiance ever since, the winter before, he'd thrashed me because I
was wrong.

But that year abroad, because he knew I was unhappy at times, he
gave me a lot of his time — and because it was also a duty he enjoyed.
Since we were both "collectors," we were particularly pleased with
each other's company when making the rounds of the dealers and the
museums. For the first time for me, Paris seemed to have more sunny
days than gray ones; the shopkeepers' singsong became funny instead
of nasty. I bought a number of "classic" reproductions — I was reading
Keats and Macaulay as a mark of defiance against Bossuet and Racine
— but found no Daumiers. My father bought a drawing he persuaded
himself was a Boucher, and a sly little fan by Conder — the sum got
for it after his death never ceased to surprise my mother, who thought
no decent family ought even to have such goods to sell. She wasn't
entirely philistine; her own parents had bequeathed us some respectable Dutch works which today would bring infinitely more. But I often
think that, if sold today, my father's hodgepodge of airy nymphs with
powdered hair and errant bodices, or not-quite-abandoned fêtes
galantes in Barbizon greenery, or coy sub-Titian call girls with pink
behinds as large as suns, could be billed as an intact example of a
certain brand of taste of the nineties — of the well-to-do, French-ori-
ented gentleman whose pictures were as much a part of sensuous
indulgence as his wines, and who therefore would have nothing to do
with the taste of the Victorian squires on the other side of the Channel
— with what my father always called the "cow-colored" pictures of the
English. At least this saved him from the Burne-Joneses; I once heard
him mutter in front of one, "Can't anybody see from his women that
what the man really loves is *mares?*" For to him of course, art wasn't a
lovable pursuit except in a major phase of it that the world's almost
forgotten for the moment. Art to him was the adjunct of the boudoir.

The morning I speak of was sunny, and the last day of my *vacances*.
One of the few words I could say with a good accent, on this morning
it rang in my head like the sad shriek of myself drowned. Next morning
at dawn, I'd find myself bound for those comfortless, gray schoolyards,

on a train with my other high-collared colleagues, and wishing myself
at least as graphically miserable as they; my time there was never hell
but merely an itching limbo, owing to what always ended by getting
me in trouble — that I lacked the capacity to be bored. And perhaps
because it was the last day and because it was the gloriously lighted
kind which has no moral to it even in memory — my father was especially restless. At times during the past two weeks, he had been this
way in spite of all our fun, and now and then at dusk, if our excursion
hadn't taken us out of the city, he left me abruptly, to meet again later
at the home dinners for which he was always prompt these days,
altogether unlike his habit in the States. This couldn't be because of
any Parisian cookery at home, since my mother had found a *bonne*
passive enough to do as *she* wanted. She was happy in this, and in the
possession of a German crony to whom she could deplore the perver-
sions of the country—scent instead of scrubbing, rank butter, gamy
meat. I had never seen her so tranquil. The truth may have been that
my father was sleeping with her, out of a duty motive which will
become clear. I knew his moodiness wasn't due to me, unless it was the
regrets of an old age nostalgic at the sight of me — he was then forty-
nine. We don't think of our parents as present people. Mothers in a
way may not be — they have the race to think of. My father was surely
enjoying my presentness — to him I was a schoolboy, but also youth on
the verge. Like one old teacher I had later, he never talked down to
me, and for much the same reasons — he respected my soul. And if
he'd never yet talked of women with me, it was only because as yet I
likely had none worthy of the name; on sexual matters in general he
was thoroughly decent with me, rightly assuming that, at least in the
head, I knew everything.

It was eleven o'clock in the morning, dewy fresh outside. The shop
we were in, though in a fashionable street, with silhouettes of women
passing the window clear as colored goblets — here an anise, there a
rose, there an oyster-pale water — had the antiquarian's divine musti-
ness. "They keep it that way so you'll think you've discovered something," muttered my father, but the dealer was servile, my father was
flush, and the day had to be ratified somehow. At the moment, we were
looking at a cigarette case of superb enamel — from the workshop of
Falize, the dealer murmured, done by one of the men there who did
these pieces on the sly — "for relaxation" was the actual phrase — and
had a talent for them. He did. Whenever I see the thing in my drawer

now, that airy joke with its upflung blue and white skirts, I think of it as the epitome of his era's taste in such matters — never quite pornography, often far short of art, but usually in the end settling for life, if in the preferred tones of peach and amethyst. The case's lid was painted on both sides; on the outer one a girl, curtsying toward spectator and her own knees, flung up her skirts from behind. Reverse of course, one saw the buttocks, just as in any postcard, but it was the conception saved it, no pantalettes, only the naked body and legs, exquisitely and strongly drawn. Though the dealer, like almost all in that quarter, must have had his "special" pieces hidden away, this case was with the regular art objects. Gaiety had saved it, and workmanship; it was like a choice moment out of a love affair — only an affair of course; it had an affinity to those passing, dreaming silhouettes.

Just then a man my father knew quite well entered the shop, one we'd been encountering here and there in our tours — once in the Louvre and once in the Musée de Cluny, with both of which he had some honorary post — and a third time I couldn't recall precisely where, only remembering that at each recognition he and my father were more excessively polite. Their acquaintance dated from the old Bering Sea days, when this man had been on the staff of the French arbitrator, the Baron de Courcel; my father always referred to this man as "the baron," whether in fact or jest I never really knew. If he wasn't a nobleman, he certainly affected the rich airs of one, all the way from his art interests to the hunt; he was reputed to be master of a private one on his own lands. For he was one of those Frenchmen who perennially find it fashionable to imitate the style of the English, in tailoring, haircuts and epithets, all down the line. By contrast with my father — whose mottled-gray pompadour, lean suitings of striped caramel, buff shoes and silver cravat, all slightly qualified by the military carriage some modest men adopt, still looked as French a dandy as any — the baron's head was grizzled square, his shorter figure announced itself in checkers as loud as a country lord's, the blond-bearded cheekbones had gone hearty with veins, and his French was so full of English that even I could understand it.

"M'sieur Mannix. Ça va?" Without waiting for a reply, he nodded brusquely to the dealer, his grass-green eyes, obtuse with the habit of purchase, taking in our situation. From our last two encounters, I knew that although my father had offhandedly introduced me the first time — "This is Simon" — the baron wasn't likely to greet me, even affecting not to see me in my absurdly tight and braided schoolboy dress, of which my father had suggested I lay aside the ridiculous cap. But I already knew French ways with the young, grown accustomed to being ignored even more than was done at home in those days. My father had also explained to me certain other French distances not only with foreigners but among themselves, how a man might be very close to you in a business way, eat with you in restaurants, even fraternally share your after-midnight pleasures, yet never speak of his family, much less invite you home. Meanwhile, among my own schoolmates there, I'd observed that the young middle or upper class Frenchmen, even when they approved of their fathers, openly talked of supplanting them, with a fierceness which an American, even if he knew he felt it, would do everything to conceal. Of course this was 1906. But it was therefore no wonder to me that elder Frenchmen looked at boys my age with a certain enmity. The baron's entry merely cast a momentary, disapproving shadow over my father's intimacy with me — which to the baron would look so rawly American — and reminded me that tomorrow was school.

As I expected, his eye passed over me. "Allow me not to interrupt," he said stiffly. "M'sieur Duprès" — that was the dealer — "has a Houdon piece I interest myself in. Lovely weather." He spoke in English, with a yellow smile from teeth the same color as the curtains in our dormitory.

"No, no," said my father. He gave Monsieur Duprès the nod that we'd buy. "We've finished. The boy here and I are just buying a present." His smile went past both baron and me, to the day, the hourglass women going by continuously outside, and no doubt — much as he cherished our filial time together — to the afternoon's release from me. What a dear, blithe innocent he was.

"Ah, oui. We see you two much together, these days." The baron spoke from a rudely fixed stare which half seemed to be making up the addressed one's words for him. As for me, I was annoyed that those teeth hadn't the bad breath they deserved, or had sunk it in moustache pomade. I was about on their level — and how we hate elderly flesh, all our lives. Not sickness — most of us are brave. And not ugliness — even with the women, it's not just that. Incapacity — that's what shreds. At sixteen of course, I wouldn't see that, only sensing that the baron no doubt had a schoolboy son like me somewhere, waiting to take over his father's hunt.

"Here, have a look at it," said my father. "Enameled on gold, not silver. Makes it jolly expensive." He always fell in with anybody's brand of speech or thinking — part of his listening, I suppose. "But from Falize. So I suppose it's an investment." He grinned at me, over the phrase we'd clapped each other on the back with, after each buy.

The baron leaned over to see, in spite of himself. With his long nail he pried up the lid with telltale familiarity; clearly this type of object wasn't as rare to him as to us.

"A present," said my father again, as if he hadn't thought of this before, or said it. "That's what it is. Yes, of course."

"For — a *lady?*" said the baron. The cushion of his forefinger smoothed the rosy glaze of the girl's rear.

"Oh no," said my father. "For him."

My father's eyes, looking at me, appeared to be twinkling. I had never before seen this moist phenomenon. Though I was no prodigal, I had already given him quite some trouble, from time to time. And though I saw him always as described, how can a son ever tell for sure how a father sees him? For once, I saw it. The perfect exchange of love, any sort of love, is a phenomenon also. Over the baron's head — and the cigarette case — we performed it. We had no idea of course what the baron thought he saw. I suppose we were a queer, unresembling pair to be trotting around town, my father and I, unless one knew the relationship. And the baron, at the outset of my introduction, must not have made that connection.

One needle-sharp point of his moustache lifted. I didn't catch what he said in French, but it had the shape of a proverb. Then he said in English, "How encouraging." Next he said something which made the dealer retire to the back of the shop — as for me, I might as well have been underground, staring up. "An investment, M'sieur Mannix?" he said. "So then, we don't meet for dinner this trip, you and I. Now at last I can say to myself why."

My father guardedly returned his bow. "All the family's here this time. My wife — and my daughters too. Though the girls are already back at school."

"That is so wise," said the baron. "But your wife surely consoles herself. With the beauties of Paris."

Here my father began to look puzzled — wives must never have entered their conversations before. "As does yours, I should suppose."

"My wife does not come to Paris," the baron said quickly. "Unfortu-

nately. Otherwise we would be happy to receive your — daughters."
He was carrying a kind of whipstock with handle and loops, not a
riding crop but a sporting beau's city affectation of one, and now he
cracked this against his calves, as if he wore boots. "But I can perhaps
— give you lunch?" He looked down at me, and away again. "If this
little — gentleman — will excuse you."

I had no idea as yet, you see, that I was being shriveled. Nor had my
father. Meanwhile, on the baron's watch chain, a rabbit's foot, large as
a shaving brush, had caught my eye — always nearer to watch chains
than most.

"Thank you very much, but you see — it's our last day together, he
and I," said my father. "Why don't you join us?"

Under the abstractions of politeness going on above my head —
which exchange continued — I'm afraid I forgot myself. I *was* never
bored, you see — that was always my trouble. And I must have been
wondering whether the baron could use the foot to shave with. I'm
afraid I reached out and touched it.

The rabbit's foot recoiled. The shopkeeper came running. The roar
above my head was the baron's.

"*Simon!*" said my father.

The baron's shepherd's-checks had swelled with him — I've thought
ever since that this is why pompous men wear them. And some small
ones.

"Whatever has come over you?" My father, I could see, was struggling not to laugh, in spite of his exclamations. "Apologize to the
baron."

My hand, harmlessly whacked by the kid crop on its way down, was
at my own mouth. "I'm sorry, sir." I felt my head for the cap now in
my pocket, made my deep, schoolboy reparation without it. "I do beg
your pardon, Monsieur le Baron," I said in my execrable French, and
to my father, "Criminy, I don't know."

Above my hand, my glance met my father's, severe as he could make
it. He and I already shared a certain light agreement on people and
character — originating no doubt in our joint amusement or annoyance
over my mother's estimates of the same — and only a tender shoot up
to now. But now it seemed to me, pressing my hand against my mouth,
that if I didn't keep it firmly there, our warm complicity would flower
from it in a great laugh.

The baron saw us both, I'm sure, thought himself mocked by both, and plotted his revenge accordingly. But first he had the glare on his own face to deal with. He settled this on the shopkeeper. "Not today, Duprès. Another time." To my father he said curtly, but this time looking at me, "Oh, I see. He's not French."

"Not yet," said my father, thinking this the baron's joke.

To the baron of course, it made a slight difference that I wasn't — though not enough.

"I'm thinking of palming him off as a Rumanian, until he does better." My father's manner was once more a parent's. "Think that would help?"

The baron showed his teeth again. "I yam not sure what is of help — to you or him. And I find I cannot lunch with you after all. But I yam thinking —" He used the crop again, sharply cudgeling a leg of one of Monsieur Duprès's old chairs. "I yave to be on my way to make a purchase myself. Will you care to accompany me. I yam appreciating your advice on it. *Both* of you."

"Delighted."

It was the least we could do. My father paid Monsieur Duprès, and slipped the case in his own pocket — which the baron watched cannily. But if my father had said it would be mine, it would be. I breathed over this with some apprehension. Complicity is one thing. Out and out confrontation — with one's manhood, paternal love, or anything else — is another. *Isn't it, Edwin?* Meanwhile, we all set off, out of the shop and down the street.

The baron led us through various crooked byways and half-blind streets which invariably turned out to have the one exit he knew, always meanwhile raising his chin to look about him at the broader avenues, then diving in again; it was easy to imagine him with his hounds, or in some mournful corner of the Loire country, welcomed home from here by an ugly fox-wife kept captive either by lack of funds (for the baron had the same look of dedicated fatality as those at school whose families could support only one member in style) or maybe even more austerely — by her own lineage. We came out finally on a crumbly, ochre neighborhood obviously new to my father, who however had his antiquarian's face on, ready for little shops the color of ambergris and dulled copper, out of which might come the brightly nacred picture or precious square of pen-and-ink which only he could mine — but all we passed were a few café holes, one Arab pastry shop.

"Must confess I don't know this area" he said. "Near Duprès's as it is."

In spite of our walk, the baron still looked touchy. "Not your hunting ground."

Now we passed a few murky shops and bookstalls, too swiftly to examine them, but I, stopped by one window, lagged behind to stare. Its wares — women's shoes — were extraordinary enough to compel even me, made for vampires willing to stalk on steel needlepoints, or on bursts of toe-feathers shaped like arachnids; some of the leg models wore knee pompons with mirrors in them and anklets to match; one stockinged leg had a flight of red velvet lips up the length from its pointed Turk slipper, and on a stool in the center of all was a plain black leather pump, with a heel about fourteen inches tall. The baron raised an eyebrow. "And not quite mine."

I saw my father's ears shift on his head; the countryman sniffs climate and the disorders of the universe, but a city man has only the general human evil and gossip to alert him. "Baron —"

"Yes?" We were paused in front of one of the inward, retreated houses of which Paris, Arab or not, is always half composed.

"Just what is this place we're going to?"

The baron pointed to a sign at the door side — a neat rendering, in a few bold commercial strokes, of a woman's dress form, in the hourglass shape of the era. "*Une corsetière.*"

"*Vraiment?*"

"*Je vous en assure.*"

The fine sunlight purred at the door, and got nowhere. My father brooded, I now know, on how far a parent must be the agent or preventer of experience; our illusion that we can do either arrives with the slap and the birth cry. He bent on me a look peculiar to him at these times; I had seen it before. He never in his life showed any disappointment in my size; I suspect he actually enjoyed my cockiness the more. Yet saw how I must sometimes appear to myself, and weighed that. After a moment, the two of us followed the baron up the stairs.

On the first landing, the wall held a dim, taped square at which my father peered, clearly still hoping that the baron was after treasure of the kind we were used to — but it was merely a map of the Metro. On the second landing, the door was opened to us by a female figure, shadowy against the hard shop lights behind her, under which there at first appeared to be an army of like figures; as we entered, we saw that these were mannequins, standing about like women, or lined up in front of screens.

It was a shop all right, and it sold corsets. But even I could see — with no more to go on than my mother's and the maid's spaghetti-stringed cotton garments seen drying in the basement at home — that, as with the shoe shop, other intentions were at work here, and in the same satanic reds and blacks, bold pinks and shrill satins, used here to exaggerate an ankle or an arch, there to tickle round a breast or a thigh. The language of lewdness is really very limited. In short, it was a sex-shop to which old men or young lechers might come in order to enjoy watching their "little friends" being fitted with creations tailored toward any impulse except straight nudity.

As for me, nudity was what I was interested in; in any of my mute sniffings at bookstalls and art galleries all my own hot young imagery had centered on that. But a boy of not quite sixteen, staring at nipples sprigged with roses, fantails of coq feathers, silver net panties clasped by black lace hands at the navel — and down the room all sorts of other piebald suggestions — might well be excused for wondering whether he and art hadn't lagged behind. All I'd wanted, you see, was a *girl*.

Then my father's hand came down hard on my shoulder. But his icy words were for the baron. "I could see this sort of thing in Soho when I was twelve, Baron. We're not interested."

If he had — I couldn't help thinking — then he and America had diddled me. He of course was thinking that the baron owned a piece of the shop — and maybe had further procurements in mind.

"Ah, you interest yourself only in objets d'art these days? Then maybe the one I show you will cure you. And the boy too." The baron for once stared right at me.

"Soho!" The proprietress intervened, maybe seeing trouble. She was dressed in black from neck to wrists and to ankle — like a school-mistress, or a backdrop — and not old, but her mouth, though she had teeth, seemed a black hole to me, perfumed with Sen-Sen. They all have a black, empty effect of space, within and about the mouth and sometimes the nostrils too — those who have exhausted sex to a business. "D'yer know me sister's place off Greek Street? — she's the one set me up 'ere." She was English. "Me older sister." She was even eager.

My father was the sort couldn't be properly rude to women. "No, I haven't the honor." It even sounded as if he meant it.

And I suppose he couldn't stomp out of there just over a few feathers and ribbons. I suppose he said to himself — "He's sixteen almost, and it's a man's world, even if this one isn't quite ours." He even looked to me for guidance. It's one of the more pitiful looks. Fathers do it often.

"Stay and see, do," said the proprietress. "Even if it ain't quite your style."

"And since you like miniatures, Monsieur Mannix," said the baron, with another stare at me.

"Do, and it's 'armless, there's nothing naughty goes on 'ere, sir." The proprietress squirmed her own shock at such possibility. "Might give you other ideas to be sure, who knows?" She tittered, gave me a sidewise look, and decided for us, by clapping her hands. "Coo-ee, the marquis's little elf is read-ee." She had switched to singsong. "Your littul elf is read-ee," she sang, letting it hang on the air unresolved, like a barnyard cry. She bowed herself backwards, against a screen.

A very tiny young girl, her black hair cropped in an explosion of curls, came from behind the screen, wearing only one short garment and high-heeled shoes, and stood obediently. Her kohled eyelids dropped before the baron's like a curtsy, but one subtle corner of her mouth acknowledged us; hands at her sides, she might have been wearing her communion dress. The brief corset she wore was as yellow as lemon curd, pleated like party firecrackers, and altogether ingénue — except that both tiny muzzle-breasts, outlined only with ribbons crossed as in a Greek chiton, were totally exposed.

"Yellow!" said the proprietress in an announcing voice, her eyes squeezed closed and neck swanned, as if she were drowsing in the finest soup bowl of it. "The color of youth!"

It was also the color of the baron-marquis's teeth, and of the rabbit's foot he was unconsciously smoothing. At a sign from him, the girl pivoted.

"She doesn't speak a word of French or English, 'is little friend, she's a Cypriot," whispered the woman. " 'E's going to 'elp 'er get into the hopera."

"To sing, no doubt," said my father.

"Coo, no — for the bally," said the woman, seriously, and behind her eyes too I saw an empty black space, in which hung two seraphim, trussed like chickens for the larder — one for her faith in the ballet, one for the poetry of elves.

I fastened on the woman, not daring, under my father's eyes, to watch the girl. Maybe for the same reason, he was watching me. We both looked away. Looks between parent and child always travel like contraband chemicals anyway — while both listen, as if blind, for the word.

The girl meanwhile was slowly revolving, managing those heels very adroitly for a ballerina I should say now, and came to a stop with her little rear in profile to us, on it a horse's-tail train of floating net scattered with brilliants, through which we could see the bare cheeks, flat as a child's.

What I was seeing, of course, beyond lechery or innocence either, was that even in her high slippers and with the help of all that frizzled hair, the girl just barely reached the same height as me. With the aid of these, in height she was my twin.

"*Alors,* Mannix. Here is *my* miniature." The baron spoke in French, which words I understood as if I were born to it.

My father bowed. I saw the uses of formality. "By rights, Simon and I should give the young lady the one we've just bought — but we'll keep it as a souvenir." He bowed to the proprietress too.

Any human address makes these women spurt talk. They're not used to it. "Proper minitaur it was to make sir, too; yer needle meets itself coming and going," she said, with a sally to the baron, and then, in a hoarse aside to my father, "Do the same for yer little friend if yer like, though it ain't often we job for the gentlemen. But 'e's a proper little fay, yer fancy boy."

My father was a swarthy man. He went white. I understood none of it.

And the baron-marquis said in English, "M'sieur Mannix — we are old friends, no?" Sportsmen are great sentimentalists, and above all on friendship; nobody knows more fondly than a fox killer, or a rabbit cracksman, of the romantic duties between men. The baron spoke both tenderly and rough. "This is what kind of rot for you, *mon ami?* For the English when they are in the boarding school maybe — that kind of pony. But sport for a man of your age? And to show yourself everywhere with him, anywhere — the Cluny, the Palais de Justice! Chuck it, I beg you. Give to that little *cul* his money — he will like that better than the Falize — and let him go."

"Why . . . you — !" My father's grimace, only for an instant bewildered, went past the baron, round and round the room, from headless figure to figure, unable to deliver its horrified burden on any of these frilled nipples and pussies, or velvet-beauty-spotted tails. Total license, as everybody knows, stops the senses from performing in the end — and begins with the tongue. His sweet, light-opera style of riskiness had nothing to do with the insinuations he found here. " — You stinking *Christian*," he said.

That's it, you know, still there as strong as ever, down at *our* bottoms. For a man with a house like my father's, it's still the worst we can say.

If the baron was an aristocrat, he knew that — and answered in kind. "Catholic, m'sieur. And my wife's prayers, thank our Lord, intercede for me as well. Maybe your wife do that also. But I don't ask what it is you tell her, or to *le bon Dieu* either. I interest myself more in what it is you tell your mistress, that blond English miss" — he hissed it: "mees" — "with the hair like this, so *raffinèe* — How is she been, that charming lady, since we all dine together, last year?"

I once knew a German lady, Edwin, a countess from a provincial town near Koln, who claimed she'd run away from home and her Junker father all because at a musical which her noble finishing school attended, one of the other girls pointed to the soubrette and said, "See her? That's your father's latest mistress." What a pity she didn't get the news under some situation such as mine at that moment! How changed her life might have been — depending too of course on what her father replied!

Though technically I'd heard all of what was being said over my head, I hadn't really taken it in — for, across from me, moving nearer to the baron and thus to me, even close enough so that I got a dose of that chypre she was soaked in — the little . . . darling . . . now tipped me a wink. It was a communication. She had a foreign way of smiling; the upper lip didn't move, and the lower one curled down from the tiny teeth into a V, as if she were trying for my language. Corset or no, this was all I saw. In answer, my hand, unconsciously I swear, stole to my pocket — to the cap I kept stuffed there. It was the same luckless hand that had gotten me in trouble earlier, and what was it trying to do now, make tribute? Or reparations — and to whom? To my father— and that house of his?

What in God's name did I mean by it? For, standing back a pace, and staring with all my might, I took the cap out, and placed it on my head.

I laugh about it yet — in memory of him, and of the service we did one another. For my father's laugh broke overhead, enormous, the great ho-ho-ho's of a shy man, infinitely relieved. It blew us out of there — but not before my father, toppling the room to nonsense with a final wheeze of it, had given me a push, making me extend the offending hand to the baron.

"Guess I didn't introduce you two properly," he said. "Simon — this is the Baron Godefroye de la Unnnh et de la St.-Blah" — or so it sounded to me. "And allow me to introduce Simon Mannix, Baron. Miniature — but a Mannix. This is my *son.*"

We left without waiting for the apologies. My father led us out of the neighborhood without once asking for directions, buoyed up by a vital energy arrived out of nowhere, which bounced from fingertips vibrating on my arm and flashed from his skittery eyes. "Miniat —!" Chortling over his bon mot, he adoringly guarded me, the cause of it, across street after street, until we reached Duprès's shop again, and turned from there onward to our usual street of restaurants.

"Let's not go there," he said, turning me away from the one we most usually frequented, and sat me down instead in another outdoor café around the corner, though not far. There was no reason for this — except that everything had changed. We sat for some time, saying nothing after the order was given. He'd changed that too; instead of a ragout and a sweet after, we were to have an omelet, and cheese. Then, as if reminding himself, he called the waiter back, and consulted me on my choice. But it was quite all right with me, I said. Then we fell silent again.

With the apéritif, he remarked "Opera house! They always blame the theatre for these things, poor dears." This emboldened me to ask if *cul* meant — what I thought it did — also what he'd bent down and said to the girl just before we marched out. He told me both, repeating the last. "*La jeunesse a sa propre couleur,*" he said with a flourish. "And I'm glad that you asked. Youth *has* its own color, Simon." There was his florid taste again, though it was the first time I marked it, plus the fact, though I didn't say so, that *I* was modern — our sense of modernity arrives early, and never does change.

With the cheese, he discoursed a bit on the baron's eccentricities — the Anglophilia which had made him act untypically, un-French. "It

really was an act of friendship, you know. Ordinarily here, a man
wouldn't think of interfering. Tolerance covers all." And with the café
filtre, which I hadn't been allowed before, he asked whether I understood what the baron had taken me for, and I said in a low voice that
now I had. (My hated school had done that much for me.) Then I
burst into wild laughter myself. There was a heady exhilaration about
both of us in all of this, a recognition of something precious. Lack of
pretense — that's communication of itself. One doesn't have to gabble
anything in particular, or over any kind of instrument — that's what
this century doesn't yet understand. But when he offered me a second
coffee, I answered, from some imp that impelled me, in the voice of my
mother — "No, it would stunt my growth."

Across that impossibly hopeful, absurd statement, we grinned at
each other. Then my father snapped his fingers for a cognac, got it,
didn't offer me any — he'd regained his fatherhood — and spoke. "I
ordered light lunch on purpose. We're going to tea with a lady." In the
lengthening sun rays of the slanting afternoon, and with his brown skin
and striped suit so dark against the white napery, his handsomeness
deepened, but as if about to edge away forever, into his gray hair. It
must have been time for him to get the violet buttonhole he always
came home with. At last he sighed, "I guess I want to show you. The
other half of my house."

She was thin, pale, with hair snailed in braids at her ears just as the
baron had indicated, and not young — and this is not her story, except
to say that aside from these intervals in her lone, half-expunged days,
Paris was her only companion; she was a copyist at the Louvre. How
perfectly suitable even the undersides of lives are seen to be, once the
life has closed! After my father's death and until her own, I visited her
once or twice; it was also a great boon to him to be able to leave me
private instructions for her pension. But I'd been too much of a success
with her that afternoon ever to go there often; I might have become
the son she had missed. When we left that afternoon, she wanted to
give me a violet buttonhole also, but my father said she mustn't — how
romantic they were, compared to us! But it isn't the war which has
coarsened us but something else newer to the world — which if I let it
will destroy the symmetry of reminiscence forever — let's not talk
about the world now . . . And on the way home, instead, he gave me
the enameled case — should I have seen from his hesitance that he

couldn't quite bring himself to caution me to conceal it from my mother? Sons aren't clairvoyant about the future until they become fathers looking back. Later that year, my mother found it in my laundry drawer and there was hell to pay, but only on my account; to manage this pleased my devotion to him, but my vanity even more. For I told her that the case had been given me, in the deepest friendship, by an aristocratic schoolmate — the Marquis Godefroye de la Unnnh — et de la St.-Blah.

My father was never sure he did right by telling me — how can one say for sure until all lives concerned are closed? And that means never; the underside of a family goes on and on, with the toughest genes of all. After his death when I was about twenty-eight, my mother let it be known that she had found out, though she never told me when. Her deepest outrage was for his having told *me*. She seemed to think that he had hurt *her* by telling me — *her* image in my heart — while all the time I was thinking of him in Paris that year — guiltily trying to give himself in so many ways, to her in her bed back there, to me in my cap.

"That dirty cigarette case with the girl on it," she said suddenly, one day not long after. "*He* gave it to you, didn't he. What things for a father to give his son." She spoke with a stumpy satisfaction in her own legacy — all the way from our close resemblance to each other, in which his lean, drakish looks were shut out, to the thousand and one physical touches and admonitions which mothers can supply while fathers are away, or dreaming.

"He gave me his house."

"House?" she said, staring. "Why, we sold that for the creditors, before he died. Oh, he was honest enough in the pocket, I grant you."

He left no real creditors — only debts to him. She knew nothing of his business.

But I was going over all the other things, the thousand and one dreams which come while closer hands are touching: my habit of Daumiers, descendant in a way of his Conders, those knickerbocker evenings I still listened for, my whippings, the memory of a day with no moral to it.

"Still, I've got it," I said. I was pretty romantic myself.

"Where! Tell me! In Paris? Who keeps it for you, now!"

I thought of a way of telling her, yet keeping it for myself always —
as if we ever could, without passing it on. So — I pass it.

"The seals," I said. "Who breed in the Pribilofs."

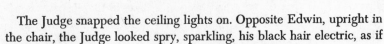

The Judge snapped the ceiling lights on. Opposite Edwin, upright in
the chair, the Judge looked spry, sparkling, his black hair electric, as if
memory had invigorated him the way action would.

His own tongue clove dryly to his mouth in the mournfulness which
came when one was waked away from erotic byways just then leading
to perfection. "Feel as if I'd been in another century."

"Maybe you have. Some of what my parents used to say came from
their grandparents — who lived in the eighteenth — and so it goes. I'll
trust the spirit of it — let the historians scrabble for the details. Whenever my mother said 'Steich mir am Buckel 'rauf!' I heard that cattle
dealer she denied we came from."

"Paris," said Edwin. "Suppose I'll remember from now on I haven't
been there?" He felt unfairly played with, cheated, as if the wires of his
emotions had been wrung, and not cheaply.

"Ought to get together and do it in clubs," said the Judge. "Remembering clubs. Reminiscence ought to be a respectable pastime — an
important one. What d'you think makes psychiatry so popular — our
anxieties alone? Nonsense. If you squeeze the air of the past out of a
man's head, it'll get out the back way from his guts — or in what he
whispers to his children when the world's not looking."

"At least I know I haven't been in the Pribilofs."

"And what has such a violet-scented story to do with you, you're
thinking?" Mannix got up and went to the window, grasping the sill,
which came just at his waist, with both hands. The arc light — which
Mannixes paid for — gleamed from his watch and from the even pallor
of his skin, picking out what was salient to this man, and maybe
hereditary too. In the houses of all Mannixes the inanimate had its paid-
for duties. Yet the man was trembling. "Or with me," he said. "Why do
you think I plucked you out of my garden — where you were 'answering a call of nature' as my father would have said? I didn't wholly
know why — but I'm learning. Along with you. The clock ticks between us; in some way we're joined, tick to tock. Or could be. Which is

it? Everything we say here I guide you in — did you think it was casual? — and yet I don't know why or where."

He beat the sill with his fist, but regally; the fist didn't forget that the sill was his. "You were a lone boy, peculiarly without family. 'Politics?' — what you said about it drew my attention to you, that's all — to your story — from where I was wool-gathering all those two years. 'He's like Romulus then,' I said to her when she came in and told me, but maybe she knew better, she wouldn't say. If you were really the savage at our gates that didn't interest her, as it might me. Wise girl. 'And where's Remus?' I asked her. What she answered — has nothing to do with you. But she saw too that you weren't simply lonely or underprivileged — merely a boy in one of those groves — you were *lone*. Family knowledge is the most important of all. I was brought up to believe that in one way — and *forced* to believe it later. And you had — not quite none. Such a strange, lone slice of it."

"So I was a specimen."

"Be fair. So was I to you. My own middle-classness never fails to interest me, does it. Nothing interests you as much about us — you think. And I thought all I wanted was to tell you about it. At our leisure." He shrugged, looking up past the arc light. Maybe we're both learning otherwise. *I* am. Living so much alone as I do. The city is all very well. But an audience is needed — in the house."

He raps the sill as if he could summon one, Edwin thought. "That why you told me about you and him? A sort of middle-class legend?"

"Anything about us'll have some of that in it. But — no."

"What other kind of audience then — than we've been!" He was furious, rent, shaking also. Their dialogue was falling to bits.

"You think maybe I want you to tell me about your sex life? Hmmm — no. Though those books over there, the risky little bits that bookseller sends — they're kind of a memorial to him too, a gentle little collection of nineteen-century erotica that some day I'll present to a university. The Simon Mannix Collection — Simon Senior. You didn't know I was a Junior, did you. Start thinking of me that way, Edwin — it may help us both. Tick . . . tock."

"I don't want to. Think of you that way. No younger man can."

"I know. And did I really say that about the seals, to my mother? I only remember that I wanted to. Family knowledge — you have to know us not only as we are, but as we think we are —" He was smoothing the sill now, over and over. "And were. Ruth was born in this house, did you know that? Not David. We weren't yet here then, but in an apartment; he was born in hospital. But even he and she were really too late for the other. Home birth stopped — for people like us — around 1912. And after the war, gradually for everyone. Even the rich couldn't afford it any more — only the deepest poor. And now even they can't."

He turned around and leaned his back against the sill, stretching either arm on it. "Know that a house with a child coming in it begins to smell of milk weeks before? Not just the body of the mother. And while the birth goes on, you find out what the air of a house like this is really made of. You lived in a slum — maybe you already know. But we don't — ordinarily we have to be told, or manufacture it in some other, abnormal way. On the day of birth, the air itself tells you that the house is made of blood and earth and amniotic fluid — water. And maybe a little claret — that the father, out in the hall at the bottom of the steps, is drinking. Or tea, or whisky — claret is what I had. After the birth, then it's all normal again; you can hear the death-beetle again in a room or two, of an evening — not because somebody died there, but because they lived. And you can see the scars on the newel-post. But not just then. Later." His voice trailed, began again. "Later you have all the time in the world to put the two halves together." He pressed a hand over his mouth. "As my father did."

In the silence they stared at one another. A clock struck. Edwin counted — eight. There was a rustle outside the window; it could be a leaf scraping the bench. "Why must you always — spoil it with the personal?" It was out. He felt relief. Opposite, as the hand dropped, the glow on the Judge's face surprised him.

"That's the first real thing you've said this evening. Edwin —" He walked over and put his hand on Edwin's shoulder; he had to raise his arm to do it. This brought the Judge's face within the downward range of Edwin's glasses, so that he could see the grain of the beard, how close-pored the skin was, even younger in close-up — though no one coming into the room would have doubted who was in command.

"Is personal emotion a filth to you, Edwin? Or only mine?"

He could hear the not quite vanished boy in the Judge saying: "There is a word for fathers. Thrash me, if I'm wrong." Then the Judge, taking his hand from Edwin's shoulder, thrust both in trouser pockets, shrugging. "Needn't answer my question. Shouldn't've asked."

"No, it's not filth. Just that it's — new." In each corner of the room he seemed to see all the members of his hoped-for major visit, one to a corner, hung there like subordinate saints each in its own oratory, humbly suppliant before this man. David — Walter. Austin — Ruth. Austin wasn't humble. But because of Ruth, he too was there. Ruth was the shadowiest.

The Judge had meanwhile leaned on the sill, looking out. "Someone in the garden, I thought," he said. "Went round toward the corner of the house — I couldn't see who." He turned away again, faintly smiling. "Maybe — some boy."

"You said a man whispers the past to his children," Edwin said harshly. "Why to me, then? Why don't you whisper it to *yours*?"

He saw the small figure wince at the breastbone as if struck, but rally. "Ah," said the Judge in a stifled voice. "You *talk*."

Horrified at himself, he said, "I apologize. I forgot."

"No, no, go on. It helps. And I know I'm — not always fair to him." He brought this out in the pinched agony of a man who hurried to name his disease before the doctor did.

"Ruth would listen." It made him almost see her there in the corner, a watercolor of a girl whose lineaments came out strongest in her absence, the head cocked to the speaker, her whole body and eyes receiving — but giving back only in the dance? "She's always listening. Though maybe nobody —" What judgment could come from her that those here were afraid of? Even Austin's devotion had that in it. Her brother's too, even with his stopped ears. Walter, with his saint's straightforwardness, was the only one oblivious.

"Nobody —?" said the Judge. "Nobody *what*?"

Edwin looked up. Is it because we've tried so hard here for honesty, that I — oh God, I am going to be able to tell when he lies? I *can* tell. Yet he hasn't said a word. "Nothing. Only that maybe fathers don't listen to girls. Though you did. When she brought me here."

"Yes."

Maybe in private she was listened to. She knows why *I* am here — she knows. "What did she say?"

"She — characterized you."

"How?"

"It was a confidence."

"About me?"

"Not entirely."

Then he and she did share something. And she had seen this too. "But it's not — what Anna sees," he said aloud, musing.

"What Anna sees?" the Judge said hurriedly. "What do you mean?"

"About me."

"Oh no." The Judge paid Anna the usual humorous smile. "No — we both know how Anna sees you." He looked relieved.

The hint of strain in the Judge's posture had gone. But Edwin could still remember Anna's. "Why did you say — that I was the most intelligent person you let come to the house?"

"Because you are."

"Why — *let*."

"Did I say that?" There wasn't the slightest pause, yet the Judge had assumed the courtside manner of a man who enjoyed all interrogations, unexpected though some were — and could answer truthfully. "One's habit of mind — " He shrugged. "Edwin, believe me, I live alone."

And will that be part of my job, to hear when he lies?

"What *you* are, Edwin," said the Judge. "We'll spend all our time on it."

"Sounds like a bribe."

"No, Edwin. Politics."

They were both smiling. But he knew he was being maneuvered away, though not from what.

"I had a background. Just that there was no name for it."

"Can you name it now? Now that we've educated you?"

He drew his shoulders square — to speak from it. He had no inherited cane, nothing but himself as he knew himself to be — in a suit that followed the mob. Yet it was as dignified a moment as the Judge's own entrance — this was the end of the boy bidden to climb in the study window, of the young man guilty at slipping inside an open door. "We are — legion," he said, as hushed as if he might be killed for it. "The kind you and yours never see."

When he saw the Judge's brows go up, he knew he wasn't even going to get his face slapped for it. Even before that, the minute he heard himself aloud, he knew with sinking heart that the statement he'd harbored so long, so long, wasn't even true, any longer *true*.

"Think you'll have time to humanize us — before you become one of us?"

"I told you I was losing it," said Edwin. It was his one anguish —

under all he always told himself on the way here. Sometimes he would look at his mother across the table in the lamplight, telling himself — *She* has it still, that old woman who never will know it. She has our old world.

"I listen to *you*, Edwin. And maybe you can save me from my own aphorisms — but not till you hear them all. Sure, you're losing it — that's the price of admission here, anywhere. Only youth keeps on seeing life in strict antitheses — black, white. When I found that out — all I did was give up chess. But for you boys . . . well . . . the youth of the world is over, too."

"I did think of — going for labor law." He brought it out half miserably. "But you'd say I was confusing poverty with integrity."

"Never to you. You know who I said that to."

To Walter and Diddy, when the two, following a step behind Austin's Quakerdom, went into social work.

"Never to Austin?"

"Austin confuses nothing. When that type goes in for self-sacrifice, there's no beating them. But they're born to be merchant princes of whatever they choose — don't go wasting your time in envy of it."

"I'm not jealous of it."

"No, your pride in what you are, regardless, is almost — Jewish. I've often admired it." The Judge came forward, and bent to scrabble for the stick. Edwin leaped to get it for him; they met over it. "Labor?" said the Judge, taking the cane from him. "Why not?" he said slowly. "There'll be labor judges on the Court before we can whistle. Listen, Edwin — what you need is a summer on the ward." He brought this out with no emphasis. But Edwin had a sense that it would have been ready all along. Whether he himself had plumped for counting angels with the schoolmen of the law, or had declared himself ready for oratory and the fine sack suits of a gangster's mouthpiece, the plan advanced would have been the same.

The night was now coming in the window, cool, dark and unhaunted as in the zesty days of the winter vacation times here when the Judge had worn no watch — and everything outside this sanctum had waited, for dinner and for them.

"The ward, David — that's the beginning of everything. I could send you to old August Manken's ward, the sixty-fourth — " The Judge's voice was dreamy, altogether different from the one in which he had been used to release all that stream of talk which only a strange boy (and chosen for that too?) wouldn't have recognized as already polished in solitary. He'd never called Edwin David before.

"August must be dead or retired," continued the Judge. "The older son's inherited the mantle. Putzi, the forger."

"The what?"

"Oh, he turned respectable; got a job selling advertising space for one of the dailies — I helped him to that lead, matter of fact. I don't boast the favor, understand — just want to enlighten you as to method. Anyway — he lives in Garden City now, keeps a voting residence in the ward here. And has modernized his father's, er, *mana*. That's anthropological lingo, David — for *pull*."

"Edwin, sir." He was filled with terror — was this what happened to one's personality when a parent cracked up or died — and was found?

"Sorry, it's the medicine. Took some after all — guess it doesn't mix with drink. Yes, a forger — 've you forgotten your barbershop, so quick? Thing a politician must remember — is that everyone in the world is searching — maybe venally — but for the fairer things in life. To quote a judge. Remember that — if you become one."

"*Garden* cities?"

"Oh, Putzi is a fart — never wanted to see him again. That doesn't mean you young ones mustn't be sent to learn from those people." The Judge held the cane like an artist's pencil before him, measuring a horizon. "And you already have what's invaluable; no *Auslander* is ever the same. Or ever more than a romantic doctrinaire on the subject. Listen to me, Edwin — David, *all* of you. It's no good living in the city unless it's transformed for you from *below* — and *that* you have to practice from a child. Where we lived, on the Drive, my father put in a revolving door to keep the wind out — the first anywhere, he said, in a private house. When he sent me out on a wild night for cigars, I used to think the rain-soaked park would never hold the river back. Eagles were still whizzing in my ears when I got to the stationery store."

Was this the talk Anna denied hearing?

The Judge fitted the cane's ferrule into a knothole in the old floorboards, fiddling the cane's silver cap intently as a crystal ball. "As for you, you had your grating you told me the bums walked on — a native son too. We do what we can with our nativity and get power from it — that's why I say — come home." The night wind blew in stronger, rustling papers on the desk. "Smell that," said the Judge. "I actually used to think the Jersey side of the river was Paradise Lost — some child's Milton I'd read. When the factories sent up their night odors I thought I could smell it, the burning, chocolate souls of the damned. In full view of the city, there's a pantheon for people like us, isn't there? We *must* understand it — to be able to live there. Or it isn't bearable. Why — when you think of what we must look like to a farmer still getting up in the old christly kine-dark of a farm morning! — thousands of souls in high buildings clenched away — and only their electric ease to comfort them. But even that horror is part of it — if you're born here. And part of what a father here gives his son — part of his house — if the son has ears to hear." He twirled the cane, scowling at it. "Walking. Walking. That's what I'd miss."

"Maybe he *was* Jewish," said Edwin, as dreamily as if he too had been taking potions, and thinking of his old fantasy of querying the nations of the earth one by one for his paternity.

"Who?"

"*My* father."

"Your — Ah yes. Well, why not." When the Judge thought he'd embarrassed someone, he flushed, a curious revelation on that opaque skin. "Or shall I deed you mine, à la that story? I scrabble on at that little memoir of him now and then — to go with the rest of the collection. 'How War Never Comes' is the title of it. From something a friend once said to me. But that's for another day." His voice trailed off.

"Oh, I'm used to him," said Edwin. "That raping stranger. Ruth told you that, didn't she? That first day, when she came in here to tell you about who she'd brought home."

"What you forget," said the Judge, almost irritably, "is that it was also my day. Which is why I remember it — and incidentally, you. I was upstairs, writing an important letter. And reading some equally important ones. That I'd never read before."

"When Ruth came down, all she said was, your door was open." He remembered how the word hit him — "Daddy's" — the idea that people had rooms just for themselves.

"No, this room is for — " The Judge glanced at his shelves. "Not for that. I always go up there — to the big sitting-room. If you really must know — I was writing to a woman. I still have the letter. When I saw it wasn't — really addressed to her — I never mailed it. Though it was to say good-bye." He made one of his half-boyish gestures. "And she never answered."

"Maybe Ruth didn't want to say. She never did like that upstairs room."

"Doesn't she? Nobody ever said." It was said so quietly, with almost a ventriloquist's removal. "We did the best we could."

No, it was a totally different voice, a natural one, a man's. If Edwin had dared, he would have put a hand on a shoulder. Ah, *you* talk. But the Judge immediately gave a practiced eye-slide at the watch he wore projecting just a minim from his right cuff. All that he had once been came back into the room with it. "We must wash, Anna'll be at us any moment with the gong."

"Jesus, I forgot to tell you. The reason dinner was delayed — Anna said to say someone else was coming. A lady. Just tell him 'the ballet lady,' she said." He couldn't help watching with interest, and felt a pang — would he do that from now on?

"The bal — oh." The Judge only laughed. "Pauli Chavez, you've met him, old friend of the family, of the Mendeses, before my time." He always referred to the Mendeses as if all knew who they were, an aristocratic unselfconsciousness he shared with the Fennos, who spoke of their distaff connections, indeed all others, in the same way. "Must've been the woman he lives with. Well, well — he's had a standard invitation to bring her, for years. Ought to be his wife. But she won't marry him. Blames us, somehow. Doesn't think she's good enough for him. Well, well — so he finally got her to come."

"Oh yes. Uncle Pauli. I met Ruth and him in the street once."

"Ruth's uncle entirely. As a kid once, she referred to him as her *female* uncle, to the embarrassment of no one. Pauli's a certain kind of European, that's all — he's simply been a special friend to women all his life." The Judge always spoke livelier when citing Ruth's bright sayings. "Leni, the mistress, is a ballerina of the old days." He hesitated. "Pauli knew my wife."

With these timid allusions to the wife who it was commonly agreed had half drawn him into retreat with her, was the Judge then really emerging again, into the society of couples as well? For of course he did literally go out the door from time to time — to committees, official dinners and the like — professional engagements, but must have made it known that he preferred not to dip into that other matrix. And no matter how importantly placed the people who came to dinner here were, they tended to be single, or even stamped with the classless aura of the stray. If family knowledge loomed for him, it must be always across the abstract vision of that absentee. And there was no picture of the wife here in the study — that was the omission — though sketches, portraits and photographs of her alone or among the Mendes clan were everywhere else; a large one stood on the desk in David's room; Edwin had never been in Ruth's. "I've met Mr. Chavez. Ruth characterizes well. From her own shadowy corner."

"Does she *seem* —?

"Shadowy? Not really. Or never when she's here. Only when she's away, and you think of it." She had no power in the house — that was it. They so rarely spoke of her in her absence. There was almost a conspiracy among them — not to speak of Ruth.

"I'm going to let her stay away, study over there, even go on tour, if she wants. Though she doesn't know it yet. I'm no dictator."

"She's never shadowy when you're here, sir. You two seem to complement one another."

"Oh?"

"Perhaps that's father-daughter — which I know nothing about." Wasn't he always maneuvered away from the younger ones here —if he had ever been near?

"I don't have my children's confidences any longer, Edwin. I merely keep theirs." The Judge turned to go — there was a small lavatory off the study. Suddenly he turned round. "Glad you'll come. Ought to have a conscience about asking you to. With you here, I may never get out after all. Or maybe you won't like the weather in houses."

"I'll chance it."

"We must take long walks if possible. Long, long walks." He hung the cane on the knob of the lavatory door. "I'll show you my city. Or what's left of it."

"And I you."

The Judge's tiredness came out in his smile. "City's only a single story. Only nobody can agree on the same one." He threw back his head in a characteristic, rejuvenating gesture, and saluted. "Ten minutes then. Here — don't forget your notebook."

"Won't need it any more." A wastebasket stood near. With a gesture of his own, he took up the small black leather book, weighed it under the Judge's gaze, and tossed it in, wishing he had the 5x8's too. It was past time.

"Well! What style!"

"Don't make me feel like two cents."

Neither wished to leave; did parents and children sometimes meet that way in household pauses, encounter newly, and stand looking hopelessly after each other, down hallways?

"Dinner'll taste good," said Edwin, stretching. "I'm hungry. For company too. It's a lovely evening, isn't it. A lovely house."

"I can't wait either," said the Judge. "For the open air."

They turned to go. But the Judge, perhaps more experienced in these moments, once more delayed. If a fly buzzed now into the room, Edwin thought, even it would be important. Everything in the room was as always, yet hyper-revealed. Here is Simon Mannix, of whom I know nothing.

"Aren't you afraid I'll read it?" said Mannix, pointing to the basket.

"No."

"Why not?"

"Because — you're rich."

"Rich?"

"Rich in — " His own glance was still powerfully enough his own to enumerate room, bookshelf, all a great man's impedimenta down to invisibles in corners; his own being here hadn't impoverished that. "In conscience."

"You don't know my guilts."

He had been flipped the standard social answer. But he saw the man in front of him, always walking the coastline of the intellect, examining its sands. Behind him — what?

Somewhere within the interior beyond the door, a gong rang, in this house customarily a sign to gather for the one drink before dinner.

Now it was Edwin who delayed, like one of those strange scholars, up from the rear of the class, who never could leave. "That story. Of you and your father."

"Call it a bedtime story. Told before dinner."

"I never had them."

"Not from your mother?"

"My mother's like the icons in church. You can talk to one. Or carry it with you. But it seldom talks back."

"And *your* father?"

"What do you mean?"

"You must have some image of him. Of your own."

"A mystery. In a doorway."

"So was mine. In the end."

"That's a filial mystery. It's not the same." When he stepped too quickly back into those other times, he had the sensation of clambering again through childhood's undifferentiated gel — and all to be defined over again, over and over defined.

"Mother, father, son," Mannix said, raising his head. "Screw that trinity, outside the church. It's too cheap a religion for — families. Freud was a Jew — he should have known better. There's more to it than that."

"Houses?"

"If you will."

"You said there was a word."

"For what?"

"Fathers."

"Fathers . . ." At the moment when word and pause became unbearable, like the silence between chess plays, the Judge moved. "A father — is an accomplice," he said.

"And a son?"

"A son?" It came too curt for thought. "A son is — *made*."

At the door, Edwin said "Thank you, sir," as he always did. A definition burst from him. "You're the richest man in conscience that I know."

Mannix made the queerest bow, stretching his neck as if toward a noose, then retracting it. "You must call me Simon," the Judge said.

Outside the study door, Edwin said it aloud, testing. *Simon*. No one heard it but himself. The hall as he crossed was empty, but he could hear murmurs in the big room. So, as always, as with kings and their audiences, he and the Judge hadn't been disturbed. In the same old washroom, he slicked back his hair, but with his own comb, though on the washstand that old couple, the comb and brush still clasped there, Abelard and Héloise. I could tell that to Ruth; She'd get it. But in the mirror, he shivered. I won't marry for ages. Mannix had told his story as a son, maybe. But when defining fathers, had spoken as one. Those double realms of the personal were ones to avoid.

He was vexed with this frippery of garden visions, conversations invested always with these double realms, yet always at stasis. Staring at his own eyes, he resolved to live the plainer life of the visual, saw fat pleb dinners, dockside cigars. Yet the shadows of this house beguiled him. By such slow-blooming family courtyards, interior from war shrieks and cavalry falling, a certain part of life went on being trans-acted, not divided from the rest, maybe, or even apart — harbored rather, like a bitterly fed, persistent glow. He felt the bones of his coccyx move to it, to the slow bloom of life here, as apes were moved to music, and men were led by snuff and spells up the ages, to the smell of ideas.

Coming out of the washroom, at the back of the hallway, he had a long view of the Judge, just pausing at the broad door of the big room on the right. He must have seen that the front door was open a crack again, though this time the fault couldn't have been his. Using the cane, he was tiptoeing to close it. That done, turning back to the room, he stopped again, looked down at the cane, half moved to discard it in the umbrella stand, then gripped it and stepped forward. Edwin, on the way down the hall toward him, heard the Judge, entering the room, say pleasantly, "Pauli. And Leni. How glad I am that you could come. Let me see, it's been years."

Over the Judge's shoulder, he saw Pauli Chavez, slender, silver-haired, and in his usual gray perfection of clothing European style — a man whose sweetness of nature and handsomeness were both instantly apparent even to men — along with the appraisal that Pauli had never taken or got full advantage of either. He was bearing on his arm a short, thickish woman, plaintively made up, whose greenish velvet only emphasized an all-over froggishness, in the pushed Slav face, and in the limbs too — a certain outward turn of the joints. Her hair was badly disposed. She looked triumphant, ready to be hostile.

"I bring *two* guests," said Pauli's voice, polished, accentless, yet European in its care. "We phoned Anna."

Then from the far end of the room, just below the picture of Mirriam Mannix, a laugh came from an unseen person sitting in the depths of an armchair beneath it — a pizzicato laugh, French as an arched glove.

"In this *fauteuil* you cannot see me, Simon, eh?"

The cane dropped, clattering.

"Ninon!" said its owner. "My God. *Ninon.*"

Behind him, Edwin picked up the cane, made a retainer's effort to hand it back to the Judge, and desisted. He would have had to follow a man who was traveling the thirty feet or so of rug with his arms stretched for balance, or in welcome. Whose gait had a faint halt in it, but whose face as he bent it to the chair hadn't the look of a lame man, but of one blind.

Halfway down the room, Austin Fenno, in uniform, also stood up from a chair to greet him, but the Judge's voice had already gone by him. Under the picture at the far end, a passage of sorts had already taken place, between the Judge and whoever was in the armchair. Only a sentence. But already an absent bird had been flushed from its shadowy brake to its corner, where it hovered over all, not asking to but accepting, on quiet wing.

"Ninon — how glad — " said the Judge. And then, "But why? Is Ruth all right?"

II
Families Behind the Lines

7   Accessory People – *June 1951*

Pauli Chavez had a loving submission to what clothes did to
him, and often put on a tattersall vest and walked in Central Park.
There, in the beautiful, spring morning haze, if people mistook his air
of the theatre, they went wrong only in putting him down for an actor,
oftener than not a star, of the European kind to whom middle age was
no handicap — none of which verdicts he had the vanity to see. As the
son (rather a long time ago now, for he was the same age as the
century) of a young maestro of the provincial European opera houses
of the eighties, and of an older ballerina whose dead, wreathed name
was still known to the devoted, Pauli was content to be one of the
theatre's countless circus children, those who never got to the real
trapezes, but to whom the tent and the snuffle from the cages was
home. From his father, earlier deceased, he had inherited a small con-
ducting talent, which he applied strictly to life. From his mother, forty
when she bore him between seasons, he had as her gift, rather than by
discipline, the golden-shallow Viennese temperament which, to the delight of her audiences, had been forever peeping from behind her triste
Russian nom-de-plume. He himself was born pleasedly into adulthood
every morning, often with a phrase of his mother's trembling on his lips
or sure to be cited over what some hour had either brought him or
must be spent toward: "Joy is in what is breathed away!" No wonder,
then, that he walked the park as if he came to it from the Plaza, and
could never be made to see any misfortune in having a mistress who
made any apartment they inhabited into a furnished room.

Their present rooms, like former ones off the Boulevard Raspail, the
Via Angela Masina and sundry other Avenidas and Tiergartens, were a
bargain got through the friendly network, and located also in a not
quite seedy once-residence, gone altogether to commerce on its lowest
floor. As with the French flats, a winding stair led into a good-sized
front room with ample fireplace, whose hearth, closed to all but curl-

papers, gave a lonely passage to the eye. As in the Italian flats, at certain hours the light over chimney pots gilded a dressing table strewn with stage-size tins of powder and rouge, candied violets, tweezers, court plasters, English pastilles for the throat, amber barettes for the hair, and among these, brought by a crony, one rainbow-catching flask of millionairess perfume. On the mantel here, a tree of red-paper bougainvillea vine from some *Cavalleria Rusticana* Pauli had stage-managered, grew dustier, like the huge gold fruit out of the Paris production of Offenbach's *La Belle Héléne*, or the bow and arrow affixed to the clotted Berlin wallpaper, after *Wilhelm Tell*. Ranged on whatever shelf had been designated the pantry, there were the usual bottles of Orgeat, Byrrh and Cassis which displaced each other with regularity, plus the one bottle of Scotch whisky, whose level was never disturbed except by a friend. In any of those flats, there might or might not be a hot plate. Here there was, not interfering with the orange odors of smoked salmon or rollmops in oiled paper, cardboard essences of pastry, or ripe marzipan, or the vanished chicken-scent of good dumpling soup sent up at any hour from the delicatessen below. The two closets were the same as always: one from whose storage of musty bronze stuffs, raging chiffons and melancholy furs no sensible woman could make costume, and one calm temple in which Pauli's few, exquisite needs hung clean as jewels, in a civet-leather atmosphere no moth would dare. Any programs or photos scattered about were either current ones or anciently permanent, never a matter of décor. The air suffered from a constriction of pillows. No wonder that more than one old friend come to a new country or in out of this one's sad barnstormings, sank down with a *"Vive-le, vive-le!"* or pulled out a handkerchief monogrammed with too many cities, and burst into tears.

If one happened on Pauli there at apéritif time, well before he had to be off to whatever small orchestra sinecure was supporting them, one found him major-domo among the afternoon papers, in his dressing gown. At these times Leni, in a coverall, her bulging curlpapers shrouded in linen, might be rousting out her closet. Or, with the hair wildly on view, and always to the same pattern of one spit-curl on forehead, one in reverse on a wide cheekbone, she might be on the other sofa — though they had clearly been expecting no one — in one of her chiffons. She had the snub cast of feature which in age went to frog or bulldog, but in youth had a thick sexiness of lip and round, glistening eye especially attractive to shy men; in the ballet her nickname had been The Pug. If out, she would be with others of her sort, to enter later with packages or to ring him from L'Éclair or another tearoom haunt; she and the home she made for him were always in character.

And like all the other places in which Pauli Chavez had lived with Leni Petersh, this had one eccentric luxury, here not as hard to obtain. Whenever the friends of this couple asked themselves, "Why won't such a woman agree to marry such a man?" the answer was agreed to rest somewhere between the two adjacent bathrooms. Though Leni was fiftyish at the least, more than one inquisitor had peered into Leni's medicine cabinet for the contraceptive apparatus, had marked the one double bed — and had still been dissatisfied. The two were still lovers certainly. She was difficult; he was romantic. But it would be in those two adjoining cubicles that the separatist psyches of these two lovers must lie.

For in the theatre, a single dressing-room wasn't only a convenience but a status. Leni, whose own tenure as a *prima* had been the briefest — could emerge from hers with a whole repertoire of complaint — and seduction if need be. Beyond that, their whole life, frail on the finances, strong on the conveniences, jogged along like a journal, in a continual conversation, to which both brought their anecdotes. His were tenderer, or gay. She had an enormous, instinctive tactlessness, which could go right to a point. And as was natural in a couple who made one room of three, they let nothing interrupt them. At times, often in those communicative intervals when dressing to go out together, they conversed as now, pot to pot.

"Hemorrhoids," said Leni. "They are the same as piles?"

"I think. Why? You have them?"

"Not since St. Petersburg. There, I think I had them. Or something." A silence. "There are things one get in Russia one never get anywhere else." When seized upon, for her impressions, by those who in these travel-censored times discovered that she had once been there, this was her invariable reply.

He heard water running, complementary to his own.

"But Pauli. There is a spot."

He came to look — back of one buttock, just inside the thigh. "Nothing. A prickle-heat. Put a little powder." Over and above love, at their age, they kept passionate check of each other's contusions, symptoms and surface changes. "What are you going to wear?" He spoke now from his own bath, the words elongated with shaving — and with the care of some days' discussion.

"The green. Your favorite."

Since several of her costumes — all of which had had to be at one time or another his favorite — were green, he said nothing. Years of invitation on the Mannix side, and fruitless pressure on his, hadn't got her to the house of the family she persisted in calling his "patrons" — though it was a Mannix contention that Pauli gave constantly of himself, and never let them make return. Beyond a few dinners, this was literally so. What they gave him just as constantly, he never attempted to describe. If he ever fell on really hard times, of course they would be there. But it was really their old-style formality of life — so cosmopolitan and at the same time so bourgeois-rooted! — which he deeply admired and liked to be part of, as rather more of a coffeehouse man, himself. And how he admired the Judge's "intellectuality," which for him — not the best estimator of such — was absolute. There was a forceful practicality about the Judge too, of which Pauli, had yet to see any venal side. Of Ruth, made almost his little foster-daughter by those fond intimacies her own august father couldn't somehow provide, Leni had the good sense not to be jealous. Indeed, why Leni, that spirit so generous to his every need, should stubbornly, even angrily refuse every chance to become as close to that household as he — he would never see. And now, some tangent had done the trick in a flash; he didn't yet know how or why. He had no fear she'd renege. Leni's petulance never exceeded her loyalty. But once at the Mannixes, it would be vibrant enough as it was. "And the hair?" he said. "High or low?"

"Low." She must be creaming her face, from the stretched sound of the word. "They would not appreciate the high."

"Oh, I don't know." Since the higher style was a señorita arrangement she wore to openings and other galas, he rather agreed. Best to give her the tone of the house, against his woeful awareness that he had been giving it, and she fighting its influence on him, for years. "That Blount is coming, the journalist. He has carte blanche there. Sometimes he brings a woman, never the same one, but always very chic. Or some native. It's a very cosmopolitan house."

And now she was rubbing the cream off, two applications, then lemon, then white-of-egg. The oatmeal masque had been last night.

After the egg was on, just when she shouldn't move a muscle — and just like when she had to have a candy, deep in its paper frill, the minute after the nail polish — she would speak.

"Pauli?"

"*Ja?*" They had no common language except the English they had learned here together.

"You know I wouldn't go there at all — except for Ninon." The words were tight, but not from mood. It was the egg.

"So you tell me, day and night for three days. Ever since she call up to say she's here. But you don't say why."

"She is here for some business between Covent Garden and the Met."

"Leni. *That* — I know." Sometimes it was best to wait until the rouge was safely on, past all the other successive stages. Or even to the mascara. But today, her giggle came early.

"You really want to know, Ha?"

"I *said*." He must show his impatience. It was ritual. And he enjoyed it. If he were a woman, he would giggle too. Instead, he slapped on cologne, and let her hear it. Slap, slap.

"A little too, she takes advantage to go *there* — because of Ruth, she says."

"I gather." *There* was Leni's word for that house; if ever he found an unlikely note saying "I am there" he would know right where to go. "If Ninon can't persuade him to let her stay on over there to study — who else?" he said carefully.

Equally, Leni knew who "him" was. So it had been pursued, for years. But this time, she was quiet for so long that he peered around his door into hers. With her back to him, she was putting on foundation masque, and might not have seen him, so he withdrew to his own side again, and sat down on the toilet seat to shine his shoes. When Leni was tender for disclosure, she was best left alone. Though one could never tell for sure; more than once she had led him straight up to a revelation and then finished off in Polish which she couldn't be persuaded to translate — and of which he knew not a word. At her worst, she would slam the door on his gaze like an empress — with a "What are you doing here, I'd like to know?" At her lovingest, she would beam at him, skirt spread languidly, from the pot.

"You can always bring the little Ruth here to visit, Pauli. I like the little Ruth. That you know."

"I know, darling. And how you are right. To like her." He sighed, with a stroke of the shoe-cloth. "Not so little any more. Almost twenty-one."

"But interesting. I find her *sehr interessant.*"

Though she couldn't really speak his German, she had caught onto some of it — why was there no hope of his ever convincing her that she was his superior all round? "She's just a normal, sweet girl, Leni."

"Mmm." She must be lipsticking. "And with so-so talent, says Ninon. On that subject, Ninon dassent hold back — not to Leni. We know each other too long ago, under too much hardship."

Was this why she would now go to the Mannixes — with the sharp Ninon protective at her side? He knew better than to push it. One black shoe was shined. "Ruth has talent enough."

"Oehrr." This was the lower lip being painted. "A sweet, normal girl. Just like any girl who the mother has been shot by a lover."

He dropped the shoe. "There is nothing to that story. I never even hear it from anybody except you."

"And who should you hear it from — there?"

He came round to her door again; she knew how to draw him. "You meet the husband and wife once for ten minutes at a restaurant — so naturally, you know everything. Or from the kaffeeklatsches at Éclair?" For in spite of himself, he wondered too.

She was seated at her second and real dressing table, looking at herself in the mirror with that special gaze, eyes squinted against the loss of beauty, lips parted for an angel to bring it back. "*Sehr elegant,* she was. No drink she took, no dope, not even a cigarette. But there she was, along with that crowd who took everything. And burning inside. What else such a woman is after, except —?" Shrugging at his image in the glass, she drew a significant finger across her throat. "From someone, she wants it. I know that kind." She shuddered. "I never tell you, Pauli. But, I think it was — from him."

"*Leni!*"

"I know, I know; you don't say it to me every day? A kinder man than your patron, never. Nine times a day people go up that stoop for a favor, nobody gets turned away. But I don't see your patron — that night at the party. I see the *husband.* So cool, so smart — there were handsome little Jews like that in Munich. They get the girls; often for nothing, for love they get them. But they never come to the stage door themselves."

She rested her chin on her plaited fingers and stared at him, a sybil to his image, or a Marschallin. "And such a father, you say afterwards — a double father to his child. But naturally. So — still I see the husband." She turned slowly, to face him. He noted — as if he needed any clue that the evening was important to her — that she'd applied the extra, single-hair lashes which took even longer than the beaded mascara, and that she saw and noted his approval. "So, naturally, if I ask myself how such a man would do it, I get the answer. He hires the lover to do it."

"*Aie.*" He struck his forehead, at the same time noting his watch. "*Now,* you tell me. For God's sake, Leni, if you are serious I had better not take you at all." They both knew she had no curb to her tongue — and were jointly proud.

"*Aie* yourself, *stupido.*" She knew endearments in every language, and he was happy with any of them not in her own. "I think that no longer. Not for ages." She stood up, brushing off nails squared down with the housework she could never be caught at, and tonight a shining, unmottled puce. How she must have kept herself from the candy! "Nyah — not once I know the lover."

"You *met* him?"

"I only need to once. Then — impossible. To hire him, the lover." She waited.

"Why?"

She gave him the grandest answer in her repertory. "Otterly impossible. I know *Poles.*"

And he could return now, if he wished, to the other shoe. In fact she saw him glance again at his *Gérard-Philippe.* But there was always plenty of time allotted to their toilette. This was why.

"You see?" she pouted. "You think I tell you everything — about me?"

He smiled. No, he did not think. Nor did she find it in the least odd that such an account should be referred to as "about her." As he turned, he saw that she was arching her head in a certain familiar way; one heavy shoulder, stiffened with the ailment of old dancers, gave an arthritic crack. She was preening. The hair? But they had already spoken of that. "The new corset!" he said, twirling her completely round, circling her himself, counter-clockwise. It was of white satin, thick in quality as the waist it enclosed, and nostalgically like the bodice of a tutu, as well it might be, its undoubted source being the "only" possible supplier of same. He touched its décolletage ribbon and then looked down at himself, he didn't quite know why — at his striped trouser leg, its perfect V on the lace of his shoe. From his vest, he took the extra handkerchief tucked there for fragrance — both of them had a French scorn of deodorants — and flourishing it to his nose, inhaled, cocking a beau's eyebrow over it. Both of them stared at each other in the mirror. "Beautiful!" he said.

"I got it at a price. Through Erminie."

There was never any other answer to his compliments than a murmured dossier of this sort. But in the mirror, she said, "I hear he's very attractive to women, your Judge. They say those *little* men often have — you know." Behind, where the mirror couldn't see, she tickled his curly silver nape. "Oh don't shock. Your precious Mannixes; you think he's all brain. But leave him to Ninon, I say. The one time I saw him —. I wouldn't want to be in the dock to him. He scared me blue."

"Leave him — to Ninon?"

"Didn't you want me to tell you, why I agree to go?"

He had forgotten. The mirror palled for now, under the force of this gossip. He considered. "Tcha!" he said then. "No."

"You think Madame would take so much trouble for an ordinary dancer — all right, the Ruth is sweet, she's got something about her, and you are her second father. But you can know Madame's standards when it comes to the ensemble — and still think that?"

"He pays for Ruth like for any student, that I know. And she is not yet in the ensemble. It is only a year she goes there."

"How many vacancies for students? And how long a student stays, if she does not make the ensemble?"

"She *told* you this, Ninon? That she is after him?"

"Over many years, I put two and two. And all of a sudden. When she ask you to ring Anna, about dinner. Then says, 'No, dahling, no need for you two to stop by for me, at my hotel — I arrive there at the house, by myself. Then I get it, all of a sudden — zrrt!"

"But he is what — sixty? And she —" He considered again. "Tcha."

"You have *seen* her sixty."

He caught the edge in her tone: You have seen mine. "It is true," he said. "She looks very well. And he of course never changes. And even so, such a distinguished man —"

"*She* is distinguished."

"Ah yes — yet, oh it is fantastic. For her to be after — *him*." But he began to smile. "I begin to remember though — our dear Ninon never — it is true, we never know her to pick one of us."

"I think . . . not *after*," she said delicately. She had taken up a pencil, and was feathering a brow to suit. "I think — *before*."

"What do you mean?"

Into one nostril, then the other, she touched a rouged fifth-fingertip, then rubbed the residue on the lobe of each ear. This allowed a shrug. "To see Ninon Fracca go after someone, even *him* — even for that I am not sure I would stoop myself, after all these years, to go *there*. That is of minor interest to me. But!" She clasped her hands and flapped her heavy-sooted lashes up at him. "I think it *already* happen. Years ago, it must be, when he and the child went over. In '44? Yes, I should not be surprised — I think your patron and our Ninon have already had their little *affaire*."

This of course made a difference — all. Here they were exactly of a mind. The present — that was for the younger ones. But the past, whose green leaves, flickering so with sun, could be turned like the fondest of diaries, whose winters shed their crystal now in the flutes of Rameau — that made the difference. He clasped his own hands, dreaming. The past was their affaire as well.

"So. That I *would* like to know," she said briskly. "But unless I see them together — well, there's your answer."

He chuckled. " 'Except for Ninon, you don't go.' "

She snapped her hands smartly together and bent over herself. Silk hose, panties — barring shoes, dress and jewels, which were always added in the other room, she was through here. "Oh here, hook me. I forgot."

Tender for her brilliant interpretations, he fastened the new satin, at the top back.

"I wear the velvet," she murmured. "Then I don't have to put over the head. And the Rhadames earrings." It was in these murmurings, never expectant of reply, that he felt her nearest to marrying him. "Oh, I forgot also," she said. "Madame has solved also a problem. What to do with his little Ruth."

He was about to go for his jacket, which with hat, stick and scarf, was all *he* needed. "Ah. She told you."

"So you know too, you foxy." But she liked this in him; she expected it.

"Ruth wrote me from London. But he will never allow it. Those tours that start in Canada, and end up in Australia. She could be away two years, out of his hands entirely. And he made her come home twice during this year already. He will never."

"And you say 'ordinary,' 'normal,' Pauli! You are more her father than he; who does she write to, about it? A girl not allowed even to go away to college."

"It came out that way, that's all. There was never a real — brouhaha."

"Tcha, with them is there ever?" She gave the theatre's shrug of contempt for its audience, then turned on heel. No, there was nothing more to be done here. At least — oh yes. She clattered over in her mules and sat down again, charily raising her café-au-lait, lace-encrusted slip from behind, modestly spreading a bath towel over her froufrou-gartered knees. Sound was permitted, but sight never. So ensconced, she put elbows on knees, staring ahead as if the future, like the sound in the toilet bowl, was only waiting for her, to form itself.

"Ha, that Ninon," she said. "I wouldn't like to be in the dock to her either. The two of them, they're a pair."

And from the pot, she gave him a smile at last, tender enough, but with the stinginess of a woman whose makeup was complete.

So, in some three-quarters of an hour — after two glasses had been sipped in toast to one another's appearance, they emerged from a door almost hidden by the double glass-and-chrome entry of the delicatessen which held up the old house from below.

Just inside the door, Leni paused, wondering aloud whether her pagoda earrings weren't "too much" for the imperceptible, pre-eight-o'clock, dusking wind. Pauli waited sleepily, aware that the earrings would be removed and replaced several times before their arrival, and that this uncertainty had nothing to do with the wind. He was always willing to pause here in the shabby hallway of a residence only a shade too expensive for his purse, happy in the thought of that room above, where all the necessary opalines of existence had somehow been preserved.

"I am glad we had the Chambéry on our own," said Leni. "I do not like to take hard liquor before wine, so now I can refuse. I suppose they will have wine?"

He nodded, not saying they would have been able to supply her with the Chambéry also, or that the wine would be beyond any criticism of hers. All of the household would be — a discovery unlikely to help either her feelings or her conversation. But they'd reached the curb now, at that corner where the bus could take them easily across the park and up, with only a few blocks to walk after, not too much for her high bronze heels. She still had the earrings on.

"Taxi?" he said. After all, their toilette had taken two hours, and almost twenty years.

"I don't see why. The bus always does for us. Just because *they* . . ." Because they — what? She didn't say.

Though he and she weren't late, the bus was a long time coming.

And he let it go by.

"It was ours!" she said, but she was already smiling.

"Your bronze shoes. They are so pretty." Cased in a hatbox the year round, their shine was as fresh as a pheasant's, the buckles like caramel. With a loving glance at them — and her — he snapped his fingers.

The cab drew near. She touched an earring. After twenty years, the cab will get them there so quick! But after all, what has that house done to her except share Pauli, for whose attractions they cannot be blamed? Never have they said anything against her; the invitations have always continued. She knows all about finger bowls. If the journalist has brought a fashionable woman, let the woman gaze at *her* shoes — and know them for what they are. She will leave the earrings on also. *Zut!* She has decided.

"It will be amusing to see," she said. "Him and her."

"And Anna," he said. "You will like Anna."

"Will I?"

He can hear she isn't certain. May all have been lost again?

"And maybe I shall find out as well — what makes Ruth so *interessant*."

He worried. "I hope — " That you . . . that they . . . What could he say to it all?

The cab was here.

He handed her in gallantly, got in after her rustle of perfume, and settled back, jingling the bus fare in his pocket.

"Joy — " said Pauli — "joy is in what is breathed away!"

8 Two on Their Way to the Host
June 1951

M EANWHILE, still some eight blocks south and east of the Mannix house, Blount and an observant companion were walking toward it. "Blount, the journalist," as he had been introduced, kept two unmemorable initials to his byline, but was known everywhere by that useful surname, which he had made wag in the mouth as easily as the name of a species. Accustomed to observation, he had the unremarkable flesh of many meals in Statler Hiltons, and the stilted walk of a man under whose feet the terrain might change at any moment, from delta to Himalaya, but via only the wheel, or air. A walk was his safari, as now. He never carried an umbrella, or wore hat, cap, topee or boots, or any shoes other than his present thin town ones, and was said not to own an overcoat. He could toy with all manner of banquet food but appear to be eating it, and however near he might be, glass in hand, to a host's shrubbery or plumbing, knew it had always been assumed that he drank what he drank — some colorless liquid. He was from Missouri. Had he a digestion? A religion? A weekly lay wherever he was? Nobody thought to ask any longer; Blount carried the questions, in tête-à-tête or crowd. He acquired people like answers, for an hour or an evening, jammed guest and host together at will, and never had to wait, any more than for saliva, for the pale newsprint to flow. By intent, Blount's company never compromised anybody — man, woman, hermaphrodite, two-bit Polynesian whore on his arm at the Eskimo Embassy, or Communist child. Nor much personified them. And nobody's reflection ever had enough time to settle on him.

At present walking, he had a companion just acquired at the Overseas Press Club, one Felix Krupong — six feet of twenty-eight-year-old African and a classical education, ebon as his suit, and by his six-inch laugh, happy to dine with unknown judges and stroll thirty blocks to do so. He and Krupong were going to be late. But they would get there on time. Blount was always late and always made it. He had made this one of his characteristics too.

"Fella in checked suit, met you with, Felix," said Blount. "He from your part of the dark continent?" He liked the clichés that made communication *easy*.

"Oh no, man, he's from East Africa."

"Where?"

"Tanganyika."

"Where?"

Mr. Krupong made a stand. He liked the interrogative himself — not that Blount had given him a chance at any — but was even fonder of the declarative, a mode of expression Blount seemed not to use at all. "Very depressed, that poor scubby, to find that people in this country know only Kilimanjaro about his country, and nothing else of consequence; yes, that is indeed a very depressed man." He sighed, with the pleasures of evacuation. And Blount, the person who had so offended, had already inquired the man's origin as well, from the man himself.

"Kilimanjaro?" said Blount, absent as a doctor with a stethoscope.

Was he aware of his reflex? Did he do it to give people the reflex habit of answering — and then slip in a ringer? Was he well aware that such a style could conceal the possession of knowledge as well as the lack of it?

Mr. Krupong blinked. "A mountain."

"Oh?" Blount swung his head from side to side as he walked, it was supposed in order not to miss anything, actually from a laudable effort to recall which system of traffic signals — left or righthand drive, zebra stripe, camel-train or laissez-faire — he was momentarily in. "He going to teach with you at Princeton?"

"Oh I shan't be teach*ing*, just visit*ing*, an American friend, a Rhodes scholar who visited at King's in my time, yes."

"Did you have a Rhodes?"

"That is *South* Africa, yes?" Mr. Krupong was learning. He waited.

"South Africa?" said Blount — and then — "Watch out! That car!"

Lucky that last hadn't been a question. It had been a near thing. "If I die here," Felix Krupong said to himself, "I should like to think that beforehand —" and then he leaped into the gap in the quizzing, as neatly as he had jumped back on the curb. Five years as a Latin and Greek scholar in Cambridge hadn't lost him his Accra agility. "No, that Tanganyikan now — he is living in Birmingham as a turf account*ant*

Poor scubby, there is a rumor" — a phrase seized from Blount — "he is in the Overseas Club to collect a bad debt."

"Bookie?"

"Oh, is that some of your American slang?"

"What does 'scubby' mean?" said Blount.

"I think," said Mr. Krupong, declarative with intent, and feeding it slow — "it must be what you are when you are a poor Tanganyikan turf accountant living in Birmingham and you are at the Overseas Press Club in America to collect a bad debt."

But "up against an educated native," as Blount sometimes phrased it, one had one's routines. "Tell me, Felix, what's the position of emancipated women in your country? At present date?"

"I hear a rumor," said Krupong, "that there are none from there as yet in Cambridge."

"You married?"

"At present date then, man, if I am not, should I not make haste?" said Krupong pleasantly, and rolled out his disarming laugh, and said quickly, "Are you?"

There were questions, of course, which even with a Blount were yes or no. Rare were those who got to them. "No," said Blount.

"You have children?"

The first thing people over here noticed about Krupong was that, even metaphysically, he didn't know what it was to touch his forelock. Claret in the common room had merely polished down a dignity which otherwise might have been too supernal, even there. The second was his gaiety, which Americans thought must have reasons beyond their ken.

Blount noticed, a rare sensation too, but rallied. "Have you?"

"Children need fathers everywhere," said Felix, smiling — "isn't it so?" He felt he had made an African cliché. But he liked to give good measure. "As we say, isn't it all the same, under the *tsetse* fly?"

Blount chortled. Once they started to kid, you were in. They loved a tease, and he knew how — why else were his return visits so acceptable round the world? "Like under —?" But whatever he'd been going to ask was lost, for just then they reached a curb again, and the other grabbed his arm and said, "Watch out! That car!"

On the opposite side of the road, and walking on, the other kept the firmest grasp of Blount's forearm, and Blount suddenly recalled a rumor, or rather a sports page — hadn't there been a West African, a few seasons back, top student in something or other, who'd also been a Cambridge Blue? And who had also —?

"You will answer the following questions, please, Mr. Blount — our host's name?"

Blount, still suffering the urge to ask, like an urge in the bladder, moved his arm, which was not released.

"In a moment, Mr. Blount."

"Judge Mannix," said Blount. In answer to a look, he spelled it.

"Judge *what* Mannix?"

"Simon."

"Of what court?"

"Retired."

"From *what* court, Mr. Blount?"

He might as well have been holding Blount by the ear, and they hadn't stopped walking.

"I — I believe it was the appellate."

"And that corresponds how — in British jurispru*dence?* — no, never mind. If you please — the names of his *family?*"

Blount gave them.

"Has he a party?"

"?" But Blount didn't voice it.

"*Poli*tical party, Mr. Blount."

"No."

"Rich?"

"C-comfortable."

"Distinguished, eh?"

"V-very."

"Old friend of yours, man?"

The word "man" somewhat relaxed him. "Yes."

"And you are privileged to bring a casual guest? It is o-kay?"

"Right."

Mr. Krupong, nodding like the tutor he may have been, gave him back his arm, plus a phrase of his own, appropriated. "I like to have a little back*ground*. And, oh yes, man — is there no wife?"

"Deceased." Blount felt like a beetle down off its pin. These affirmatives could be hypnotically relieving. He emitted — like a hiccup — a final one. "Shot."

Mr. Krupong did give him a glance. "Oh dear." For the first time, his accent lost its native lilt, in favor of its years on the Cam. "What a violent country! Was it an old lag he'd sentenced, did it? And did the Judge put the person properly in jail?"

What with all this trotting time, they had reached a curb again. Blount glanced right-left apprehensively, and kept at arm's length. "Well . . . as a matter of fact —" this was a phrase he hadn't used in years — "no." He coughed. "There was a ru —" The other moved nearer. "I have it on good authority . . ." But it was no use. "Hushed up as suicide," said Blount. "But everyone knew . . . she'd given him reason enough." He gave the squawk that plain statement induced in him. "No — a judge couldn't very well put himself . . . and everyone knew it must have been an accident."

Krupong's eyes really widened. "I have heard what Gorgons your woman can be. Self-*defense*. Dear oh dear."

And from then on they covered the intervening blocks without incident, on the stream of Krupong's grapeshot interest: "Nice block of houses, like St. John's Wood, would you say? . . . What is your opinion of the Korean conflict? . . . Is it your feeling that . . . ? Am I correct in assuming . . . ? How would you describe . . . ?" — and so on.

Until, a few doors down from the house indicated — one with charming curtains and that air of self-sufficiency which time and the exertions of tradition supply — Blount drew up short.

"Mr. Krupong . . . Felix . . . er, I may say 'Felix'?"

"You may."

Blount put on an expression, thin and wise. "Really a newspaperman, aren't you?"

Felix, examining the street at large, said absently, "Would you say Socrates was the first journalist?"

"Ah, come on —" Blount stopped himself, with an exaggerated gesture. "Say! The old steel trap is beginning to function. Aren't you that Nigerian whiz-kid sent a Latin poem to the *Times* on the subject of the pound crisis — and they found out he was attending *two* universities, London School of Economics in his spare time — told the press it was no trouble at all. I saw a Reuters bit on it. Ah-ha, Felix. Come clean."

"Clean?" Felix gradually swiveled from scrutiny of the street to the house just down there. According to which view of human nature one subscribed to — and Felix, with the advantage of divisible vitality and experience, had several — the house being approached either was the exact milieu for a *crime passionel* — or was exactly not. "I am *Christian*, oh yes."

"Aw, come . . . You are?" Blount's face was grateful. No crumb was too little for him — this was the secret of his success — and he would sweep until the end of time.

"Presbyterian — as a matter of fact." Krupong, who had walked them on to the house, and was now standing on its lowest step, nodded down on him. From his years among those who had a fetish for *not* asking the personal, it was his own pleasure to offer at times a plethora of naïvely confusing fact. It was a more ancient style of journalism than any Blount knew. "Now my friend back at the Club, he's still *Muslim.* But would you believe it, both we converts still suffer the same distress after meals, in the white countries! We discuss it the very moment you come up to us. Our poor stomachs are still used to only one meal a day. Biological persis*tence.* Remarkable. Comes of our regretta*bly* cannibal grandfa*thers.* Yes." He stared up at a window. "Mannix. I have never heard the name. Is it Christian? Like you and me?"

"Matter of fact, they're Jews," said Blount, blinking away his polite American aversion to saying what people were — they were so often, from terrain to terrain, something wrong. "I hope you're not — prejudiced."

Felix smiled his smile, every mahogany-bordered tooth a glistening echo. These fused. "No."

"Well, I expect you're hungry *now* at least," Blount said, gathering himself a large grin. "I am. Let's go in." But he lingered on the second step, though it was now after eight. It had struck his conscience, as never before, that he knew almost nothing about this gent he was bringing into a trusted friend's household. His own revelations on it had been already forgot. "I know lots of folks down at Cambridge," he said. "Down there long?"

"Up." When Krupong closed mouth and eyes, his very serious white linen took over. The effect was solemn. "Oh I stayed the course, yes."

An even worse thought occurred to Blount, along with the memory that the Mannixes had now and then cashed a Sunday check for him. Could Krupong himself be the Tanganyikan's bad debt? "Gamble much while you down there?" he said. "Excuse *me.* Up."

Krupong stroked his black cheek. "Every one of us Englishmen likes his little bet," he observed. Then he seemed to relent, and drew out his wallet, rather a large one — unless he was a bookie himself. The wallet, large enough indeed for a confidence man — or a renaissance one

— did in fact contain, along with his passport and other quite legal documents, that increasing burden of credentials and memberships which learned societies pressed on a man who'd taken honors in both classics and economics — and all the more insistently if the man were black. But in one section of the wallet there were some prized cards he dispensed seldom. Printed up at an Oxford stationer's (after a venerable joke common to both universities, and for the occasion only), they'd been given him in memory of his honorary induction — for one evening — into one of their drinking clubs. How well he recalled the bottle of port he'd had to drink down in toto! And the porter's kind, unprejudiced hand as he administered the emetic — "Think nothink of it, sir — they all 'as to 'ave it. Port's a fortified wine." It was true that his stomach nowadays was no longer strong, though for more graceful reasons than his grandfather's. But how he loved their humor, his English! Sometimes the whole net result of his double education seemed to him that now, instead of having only one humorous front to see the world under, he had two. And he wasn't averse to acquiring an American third.

He handed Blount the card, on which Blount read that Mohammed ben Ali Krupong, Panjandrum, latterly of King's College, Camb., Hon. Member of The Oakers and Philolexion, Oxon., was hereby recommended as a first-class courier, signed Edward, H.R.H. A sentence in Greek followed.

"What does that say?" said Blount.

"It says Honorable Candidate for a First in Greats. *Failed.*" And Krupong's laugh, an inch longer than usual, rolled down the stoop. After which he handed over to Blount a quite ordinary card of his own, listing his London and Accra University addresses.

In great amity, they went up the stoop.

At the door, while they waited, Felix said, "Human nature, sir" — he knew how the whites loved to talk about it — "you find it much the same in your travels?"

"Why, of course I do," said Blount, back on easy ground. As always when Missouri came upon him hard, his "I" had the sound of the "a" in "cat." "A do, A do, and thank God for it. How else could A tell the countries apart?"

Then, as the door opened, he held back a trifle, perplexedly aware that this had the sound of one of the profundities by which others were so often entertained.

The young man who opened it to them, Felix saw, wore a kind of uniform, not a domestic's, but not any military one he knew either.

"Why har you, Austin boy, har you!" said Blount. "Uncle Sam sent you back?" He turned to his companion. "L'me introduce Mohammed Ali" — and he quoted the card letter-perfect — "alias Mr. Felix Krupong, KCB, and future *OBE!* And this here scoundrel's Austin Fenno, one of our finest, Quaker Plenipotentiary!" His introductions always resounded, beguiling the listener to possible half-truths, and committing Blount to nothing. He liked to enter a room as an old-fashioned foreign correspondent should, talking fatter than he was; it inspired confidence. Afterwards people could forget him better. Men of the press didn't have to be these thin, modern-style sneaks with no style at all. Sometimes he *dreamed* he was the celebrity he *was* — and woke up perplexedly too.

"Why, *Simon* — here you *are!*" said Blount. As he circled the world — yesterday Alaska, tomorrow the Aleutians, Tokyo, Melbourne, Tierra del Fuego, with intermittent stops between Statlers, the Algonquin and the Hotel Inghelterra — it did seem clever of people to be right there in their homes to receive him. "May I introduce —?"

This time, he gave each man his proper names very quietly. Under the Judge's eye, he knew just who he was — Dan Blount. As for the companion he'd brought here, one last look and he left him to be on his own, he'd been eviscerated and had given up all the answers D. V. Blount had time for, barring one reference, like a souvenir bought at one railway terminal and discarded at the next. "Why, Judge," said Blount, pausing like a chamberlain at the long room's entry, "what a fine lot of human nature you have here today."

Felix, looking down it to the large picture at the mantel end, saw only a pair of women, one rather splayed and thickish, one very tiny and pointed, who looked up at them. The young Mr. Fenno who had opened the door stood near a snub-faced bespectacled young man of about the same age, but they weren't talking; Felix had one of those early, to be trusted impressions that they were not at ease with one another.

But the Judge was the shock. In size, features, eyes as young in that head as if only lent to it, the Judge — barring skin color, and a few ninetyish wrinkles he would surely live to acquire — might be Felix's own grandfather. Above all, it was in the head and the posture, and the size — though this man was by birth what his grandfather had shrunk to. On state occasions, his grandfather had worn an out-of-style jacket, with much the same comfortable breadth at the lapels. This man's hand, small but not shrunken, pouted on the head of his cane, in the same way rejecting it. But he, Felix Krupong, couldn't believe Blount's gossip about him. Not after knowing his own grandfather. For the very same reason, he would believe almost anything else.

At his elbow, he heard Blount say, "Don't see the children, Simon. But I suppose these days, they're anywhere. All the same these days, isn't it all the same — under the tsetse fly!"

9 Dinners with God and Man
June 1951

Austin Fenno's paternal grandfather, until recently still
surviving on in a house in Wiscasset, Maine, where he broke the ice on
the pitcher half the mornings of the year, had been a minister-reformer
and formidable diner-out for his own causes, to the end of his life still
fond of haranguing any family gathering which had steeled itself to
"having Father Fenno," on the text "The meal is the parable of
society." This most famous of his many sermons had exhaustively
probed all the variations of breaking bread, from the more intimate
breakfast trays and peasant gobblings to the banquets of kings and
episcopals — and all with the usual wealth of classical allusion, inter-
spersed as the years and dinners went by, with really rather sharp
homily from what increasingly appeared to be a worrisomely modern
mind. Since Father Fenno's own father, the great-grandfather, had
been missionary to China and other places then far, the discourse was
chock-full too of those foreign details which had been the romance of
pre-airplane generations; indeed, Austin's father had told him that the
sermon's sub rosa name among the minister's own children had been
"Food in Many Lands." Delivered in full, like an extended carminative
grace, of a Sunday morning in the old days, *Dinners with God and
Man* must have sent home the old man's parishioners roaring hungry
for a roast without any moral significance whatsoever. Over the years,
as the number of courses in a family meal had declined from the
Victorian to the dietetic, the most senior Fenno had become resigned
to spooning out the sermon to his progeny in as many small sections of
it as he could get down them — like a nurse feeding children whose
mouths were otherwise open — before their attention got back to what
he was doing and the meal in any case ended. On his more recent
visits to Fennos in Manhattan, Glen Cove, Guilford, Williamstown, or
any of the other places where Fennos typically scattered, the old cam-

paigner had even been caught adding so-called anthropological details to titillate them; certainly the sexual significance of suckling, or the pre-mastication of love offerings between Hindu newlyweds, could never have been in the original version. For by then, no living Fenno had ever heard it all.

But to the clan's surprise, *Dinners with God and Man; or, Meals As Parable,* when its author's one precious steel-penned manuscript of some forty-nine pages was borrowed for an honorary publication on his ninetieth birthday, had been found to contain all these allusions too and more; its author, in addition to other causes espoused, had been a just barely not too scandalously early follower of Darwin — and more. Privately printed, the pamphlet might yet become an item for cogno-scenti, in the same way that Austin's music-buff friends collected a concert recording by a rich amateur soprano of parts — some missing. As with Mrs. Jenkins's colossal swoopings (where one heard the sub-lime in the very notes avoided), there was something remarkable in hearing in the language of Emerson, Macaulay and two lady poets named Hemans and Ingelow — but always under the aegis of God himself and his disciple Fenno — an entirely verifiable account of tapeworm travel.

Otherwise, disclosure had been a miscalculated blow to the balance of the old man's dinners, throughout which, until he died — and against all daughter-in-law effort to exploit him for visitors: "Do, Fa-ther Fenno, give us the part on Table Talk, Tête-à-Tête and The Divine Monologue — the old man had remained glum. He was too intelligent to allow his share of the clan's power to be made into mere vaudeville. No Fenno of the blood — the pamphlet had been a project of wives — would ever have asked.

"It all ought to have been kept private," the old man said pitifully, but ministerially strong on his future past imperfects or whatever they were, even now. "In January, it'll have been a year that I sh'll've wished I mought never've let it out," he said to Austin, whose favorite elder he was, on one of their last icy mornings. "Should have been kept to the family. There was nothing to it any more, without me."

For a true Fenno intelligence prided itself most on its self-awareness — more of a clan instinct than a personal insight — of what it *wasn't*. Austin himself, the old man's direct descendant, knew for instance that by and large Fennos hadn't the nervous tissue to be artists, or the emotional intensity of their Jewish friends; when a Fenno had money, he tended to become an enlightened patron of both; when he hadn't, he and his sons went to be ministers, doctors or other servants of the populace. Often, like Austin's own father, Warren, they were in the highest sense mercantiles of the moral good. And of the median. In the performance of this, they often married sidewise into sterner dedications or odder clans; Austin's own Quakerism came to him via his mother. Back in the eighteenth century there'd been an authenticated Indian — and an unproven Jewess, of whom they should've liked to've been proud. Physically, in the matter of ships and seas and good Hudson Bay furs, they had been pioneering enough. The family fortunes had often been high, and never fell to creature-comfort poor — in this they honestly preferred temperance too. Otherwise, they were downright ascetic, stuffy or sensible, as you cared to look at it — but they were almost never too intelligent for their own good. And as with Austin, "by and large," for Fennos usually included the Fenno who observed it.

Many a Fenno, if he was tempted to exceed his tissues (Austin had observed) — why, his own instinct held him back! When it didn't, the clan did, even if this took till the member was ninety. As Austin regarded his grandfather, he could wonder whether this hadn't happened to him even earlier — there had been other remarkable things in that pamphlet, none of them to do with sex or worms.

"James," said Austin that Maine morning, "those last parts of *Dinner with God* — whyn't you ever give them to the family before, until now?"

The old man's neck cords were what held the gaze now, extraordinary flying buttresses which held up the chin and the great flapping ears, lobed slightly to windward, of the long-lived. One of the cords flickered now, at this young man who could address him, the nonagenarian, as a coeval, and without insult. Austin had always had that faculty with his elders; the best Fennos did; it came of manners all round.

"Warn't old enough," said James. If his small face, long gone impassive, gave a sense of oracle to anything he said, *he* couldn't help it.

"You or us?" said Austin. He had a delightful casualness with other people's enigmas — a better part of his averageness, too.

"Both." James let this sink in, unexpressively. But his honesty wouldn't let him take oracular advantage of it. "Go on," he said. "Go on and ask me. What I can see *clarifiedly* enough you'll've been wanting

to ask." His English trembled a little these days on the sublimer edge
of wrong, or of antiquity. "You're the only one I could see give it a
thought. And I mought not be here, if you get back." He gave a
swallow, defiantly honest also.

On Austin's almost naked head, already shaven for Korea, the old
man's "if" settled like a late fly. "OK, then. In those days when you
wrote it. When you had the St. Margaret's parish. You ever deliver it in
full — to them?"

The answer had been no, of course not; James had had the sense
never to deliver the thing in full anywhere. As for the clan's suspecting
this, Austin's own father, Warren, had put the question in his mind.
And when the late James's long-gone action was reported to him — in
a midnight father-and-son whisky-soda after the funeral — Warren had
thoroughly approved, without any doubt in his mind that Austin did
also. Toasting the departed, they'd not even needed to reassure themselves that James's eight young children at the time, and lack of other
competence than the property in Wiscasset, had had nothing to do
with his caution; the family had never lacked the courage of its views.
Austin, though as a pacifist Quaker exempt from direct military service,
was on the eve of going straight into the carnage, not to kill, never, but
in service to other people's ill-got, unpacific wounds. If he died, the
family wouldn't see him as a martyr — not that they couldn't see that
martyrdom had had its point down the ages! — but out of a real humil-
ity which saw that it was inappropriate to them.

"Deliver the speech in full? It would not really have been useful,"
Warren said.

So there'd been no harm, in the end, in James the maverick; at
ninety it was even pridefully allowed — and surely at ninety-three and
dead. "Quite a vogue for those pamphlets," said Warren; "family's had
all kinds of requests. Not sure I approve of the spirit of the demand.
Best we send the balance of them to the Historical Society up there.
Let them take any profit in it."

What the Fennos knew they weren't, excellently preserved what
they were. And certainly it was typically Fenno of Austin, that one's
thoughts approached him first through other Fennos — since his own
were likely to do the same.

Now returned from Korea to the luxury of dinners, Austin, going
north on a Madison Avenue bus, was thinking of the pamphlet and

these other matters also. Private thought hadn't been much allowed him this past year, even though he had been in Asia, once the hub of it. He was aware that others in the bus were obviously perplexed by his minimal uniform — the blue-black serge and silver insignia which gave such specialists as he just enough identity — above an enemy's and below a padre's — not to be killed by their friends for it. His "civilian" clothes were now sizes too small for him. Even in this uniform, to the world and its buses he supposed he was in civvies still — which bothered him not at all.

As for James's pamphlet, and James's life also, by now it must be a harmless part of the family mortise, moldering up there on the Historical Society's shelf. In his own two days at home, James had been mentioned only once, in entirely another connection. Gone to family mortise — there was so much of it! But now, once again on the way to a civilized dinner party — and to the Mannixes — he could hear James's voice, taking clan privilege, the night Austin, en route to ski, had brought brother and sister both and Walter too to stay overnight at the grandfather's house. "Like the girl, don't you, boy? Oh, I know you're just friends. But you like her. Now, that could be — ponderful."

He knew now what the Mannixes were to him. During his year out of their world and his, the whole public artillery of the world's misery had been turned on for his benefit. So that he'd remember, when he got home to Murray Hill and turned on a light bulb or a faucet, that somewhere on other sides of the world children's flesh still exploded in fireworks, water puddles were lakes of brain — and around him and them were still the incommunicable nets of star. He'd remember. Some sermons last. More especially, when one has been taught them beforehand. But what he'd brought home for himself — like a vial of teardrops held aloft in the sea of charitableness — was a sense of what *personal* suffering might be, to those whose nerves were more naturally kin and heir to it. Such a sense went against his grain — and was the more precious to it. For he knew that he was constructed to an emotional largeness which trained with difficulty on problems beneath the skin.

Why, even on that august field of international relief where his father served so well, there was always some little tribal pebble which resisted the good plow — grind me down ye shall not! He remembered evenings when his father, thumbs locked behind him, gloomed moodily in front of the fireplace, unable to see why such a pebble, after one so dutifully washed and tended it, should still bleed. He himself didn't yet understand that other world of feeling, unsure whether he ever would. But he was able to imagine it now. Long ago, a quality in the Mannixes had drawn him to them; now, home from the wars, he could begin to identify it.

Practically, he was still hardheaded enough to suspect that this came of his being among those Protestants who very probably romanticized Jews, particularly the ones they knew. In his own family there was already a tradition of it. His mother liked to recount — often to the friends in question — how his little imp of a sister, home from a party where all were large-eyed and red-lipped and boisterously changeable, none like herself flatly blond, open and serviceable — and where family life was played more fife-and-drum than harmonium, and more solo — had wailed, "Why can't I be Jewish too!" He didn't want that. Certainly their complication attracted him, all the more because it too, like his own so different character, took its place within a clan. Watching David Mannix, he saw that David wanted to save the world not merely because deafness might have taught him that others suffer, not like Austin because first and foremost it was right, but because otherwise, it wasn't bearable — to bleed too. In this, David was more selfish than himself. And watching the Judge (as much as any young boy-to-man flying in and out of that house had had chance to), any Fenno could see, the way a practiced banker saw the man at his desk in some recognizable shape of credit, that the Judge, for all his language, stuttered over action. Fennos bounced on, never straining at gnats. Yet the Judge, a boy could see, could go beyond them. Never stirring from his seat, he would swallow a camel, and manage it. By being — Austin now suspected — more personal about it than any Fenno would ever dare.

That must have been what he had been watching them for all these years — the way some of his own cousins watched artists, not to be them but to *have* them, for how they worked — like those awesome Swiss timepieces, signed by the master himself, whose dials opened like lips, on all their innards exposed. Whether the Mannixes were as they were entirely on their own, or the quality he saw was really part of their Jewishness, he couldn't say; they were not only the Jews he knew best, but aside from his own people, the family he knew best. And if he romanticized them, he was scarcely to be blamed for it. He hadn't chosen to. As artists of the consciousness, they — or the Jews — had chosen themselves. And conscience — quite another thing, it seemed to him — was only part of it.

Two girls in blue school uniforms opposite were clearly talking about him, almost but not quite vulgarly giggling. They looked like his sisters. No doubt they found his looks reassuring. He looked like them. Their mothers needn't worry that they'd think too much. He'd never seen his looks so clearly as in the two days he'd been back in the family house — almost as if he himself could see the median outline of the mold he and they'd been made in, running from high forehead, between level eyes, down the straight nose, chiseled lips and squared chin.

"I beg your pardon," said the more forward of the girls — "your uniform — what is it?" Her well-bred speech said how all right this sort of thing was between them. She'd guessed right, of course — his accent was exactly like her own.

"Mainly a kind of Quaker unit." Small, recently organized, for medical service modestly called *extra*-hospital, limitedly open to other nationals who would do anything on a battlefield except fight on it — and as hard to stay alive in as a team of brigands. Though he didn't say any of this, he thought she got it, already used to this sort of clue.

"But not the Field Service, the Ambulance?" said the other girl.

"No, not organized by the Americans, though we can belong."

"I thought it wasn't," said this shyer, second girl. "My brother . . . is . . . in the Field Service." Her eyes filled with tears.

"Taken prisoner," said the first girl quickly. "We're sure of it."

"They don't —" He checked almost as quickly. "I'm sure of it too," he said, and smiled. The pair of them, especially the one with the brother, were a lot like his first girl at that age, and both of them, when they got to college, would be like the girls he had then. His only girl they didn't resemble at all was the Korean one — and he wouldn't get into that again. Sex for him shouldn't be that much connected with one's other pities. Or with a hopelessly foreign, stick-like devotion — of such tenacity without hope that it had quietly taken itself off before he knew he wanted it to. He couldn't say he hadn't enjoyed what he would never in this world call "going native." But it was why he had requested leave. It was possible to say that he'd been drawn into the affair all the easier because of wanting something else — Ruth and he had gone on exchanging letters of a sort all the twelve years of his friendship with her brother.

"What's your brother's name?" he said.

"John Carter Tolliver."

"Johnny Tolliver? From Atlanta? Why, I —"

"I thought you were —" said the second girl.

"We *thought* you were —" said the first.

He finished third: "— was at school with him. We used to —"

"I remembered you," said his sister. "From his graduation." She blushed.

"What's his outfit?"

She told him. No prisoners would have been taken, where Tolliver was. Not now.

"Let's see," he said. "He got married. To some town girl, up there at school?" And went into the navy, I thought. No, that was Yortchley.

"Oh no, that blew over," said Tolliver's sister, in her soft Southern. "Papa said chickapenny-boo to *that*. And Jon-nuh went off to Princeton like a lamb. But then he did get engaged."

"To my older sister," said the first girl.

"To her sister.' Tolliver's sister's eyes filled again.

It was some blocks from his stop, but he pulled the cord anyway. All too much of a capsule, Tolliver's life. Whom he'd been mistaken for, now and then. Though there had been at least ten others who had looked just as like. "Good-bye — what's your name? Jane." And the sister, with her sweetly curved, sorrowful lips? "Susan. Good-bye. My best to you both. *Best*." She'd known him at once. All the way from his prep school graduation, when she couldn't have been more than a kid. Maybe that was the answer — and the danger —to other possibilities he'd been thinking of. The clan — knew the clan.

Eight o'clock, but since Anna had put dinner ahead, he wouldn't be late; he still had time for a walk at a clip. Warren, his father, and many of *his* colleagues — the executives — walked to the office for health; it was the hoi polloi, heavy on starch — and on distances of course — who rode. Fenno Juniors walked because their fathers did, and if away at school, because the stauncher prep schools forbade cars or even bikes, except for day boys. The mothers took more taxis than the men, but often came in saying, "God, it was lovely — and I had so many errands — I must have walked forty blocks — in these heels!" The men took taxis when they were with the women, or with business outside the firm. And none of this had anything to do with having the fare.

As he walked, Austin began to laugh; he had forgotten so much of this; his clan had its subtleties after all — or niceties. And he would bet that this girl, not the Southern girl (hers would be another style, which he knew equally well) but the New York girl, had a family that did just the same. Others in that same uniform, of course, might be anything from chauffeured Cadillac down, even — in other accents or these days in other colors, in a case or two — poor. But not that girl, he could tell; she came of that indefinable line, so exact to themselves, where comfort crossed wealth but didn't quite reach it, seesawing sometimes up or even far down as in the 1930's, but almost never taking a complete fall. So did the Mannixes. But Jane Whatshername already had the recognizable "line" of her sort, in which, from bus stop to cotillion, she would be able to talk to all and any men of any age — who could talk it back.

Ruth Mannix's line was — personal. In his pocket he had her London card, picked up from the mail tray when he left. Mailed three days ago, it was typical. "Come to dinner. We'll all be home, it seems. The boys are here, and bringing me back. I've been offered a year's tour, incidentally" — here cities were listed — "and hope to accept. We'll see. Welcome home anyway. Love. Ruth." Nothing indiscreet, ever. "The boys" more than anything made him feel far off; it had used to mean himself as well. He could still smell that crayony, nursery-tea atmosphere, hear that gym-sweat noise and lesson-cackling, outside of which, tactfully off center, surprisingly welcomed intermediary — to what? — Ruth had used to wait. Or preside. Possessor of a face quietly left vulnerable to memory, she was still a little hard to see. Was she as alive, quivering too, as over the many months and a few letters he had come to think? "Lovely little girl," James had said when further queried. "Yes. I can see you and she are — friends." Long before that it had come to seem to Austin that Ruth, like a prisoner whose form was defined by the bars, was limned in the loving forces which silently intersected and held her — fixed? They loved her. A friend saw the spaces between.

Warren, his father, chancing to pick up Anna's call when it came in, had handed it over to him; since the age of sixteen, Austin's affairs had been considered private to him — and expectantly blameless of course.

All the more surprising then, when he put down the phone, to see his father still hovering near.

"How is old Mannix these days?" said his father.

"Well — I hardly —" It was only his third night home. He hadn't yet been anywhere else. "— I suppose he might be old, by this time."

His father's long, clean mouth moved at a corner. "When I came home, in '19, it felt as if the century'd already changed again, before it even had a chance to get started. Expect it had." Silent at the fireside, his father locked thumbs behind himself. "Moling said only the other day, the Law School'd given Mannix an office up there." Moling was the figurehead at the foundation where his father was the working associate, and Moling was a trustee of that law school. "If Mannix would make *half* a move, Moling said. They still expect him to do something more."

"Like what?"

"Oh, he was mentioned for the presidency one time, I think, but it was quashed. By himself, I shouldn't be surprised."

"Of the country?"

"Good God no. The university. And I wouldn't blame him, if he did. They need a money-getter, not a — *senator*." His father gave it the Latin pronunciation, and the Roman meaning. His father had had Dr. Brace too. "No, I don't think — government — somehow. I don't think they know what they expect of him. His only political or public life's been in the courts."

" 'The thing a politician must remember,' " said Austin, in the pontifical voice of quotation, though the Judge hadn't used that tone, " 'is that every citizen is searching. Maybe venally. But for the fairer things in life.' "

"Eh?"

" 'To quote a judge.' "

"Him?"

"He always says 'to quote' et cetera. I think it's him."

"The foundation dinner! We had him for honorary speaker — and there were things he said . . . You're right. I remember several of us said later, 'Which judge do you suppose he was quoting there — Holmes?' Nobody knew exactly, or wanted to ask. Certainly none of the legal men there." His father coughed, his only form of criticism. An absurdly sweet-tempered man, almost as addicted to plain living — within the urban frame his lifework necessitated — as James, he had one helpful luxury, his "more in sorrow than in anger" attitude toward those who worked only for themselves. One couldn't call it contempt, it was so benign.

"Well, maybe if he spreads those quotes around long enough, they'll think of him for the courts again." He saw all the dinners-at-the-Mannixes in his life, as in that game where one sat in front of a small mirror with a larger mirror behind one — to catch destiny. One's own, but why not somebody else's? What things a year away did for one — even on battlefields not one's own. "For *the* Court," he said. "Yes that would be in his mind, if anything."

"Aussie!" His father's mouth turned up at both ends. "Maybe *you* ought to go into politics." But his father had no fears; they both knew that public service of another sort was in his blood — and in his reach. The foundation's London office had been spoken of for him, when he came back for good. This wasn't nepotism. At a very early age his father had begun talking to him like this — as if to a degree he must be taught the workings of power, but only to use it in the service of public pity. Other people hadn't much wanted jobs like that until now — at least not in their world. The ones down under hadn't known about them. Or if on the way up, would stay a mile away, as too recently charity's recipient. He couldn't see Edwin Halecsy wanting such a job, even now.

"Well, well," said his father. "Wonder what Moling will think of that. Must make a mention of it."

The fire on the hearth might have been burning, instead of dank with house-enclosed June air behind its pleated black paper fan; they were so silent in front of it.

"I suppose the London job —" said Austin. "These days, I may have to run for it."

"Every Tom, Dick and Harry who's had a course in 'public administration.' That's what they're calling it. Never thought I'd see the day where my humble efforts to lighten the misery in the world would come so in style. Got a tweedy young social worker in my office right now, put there to tell me what my principles ought to be on it."

"Well, I suppose that's what we've always wanted," said Austin. "To have the whole world concerned. To have our work spread. Haven't we?"

What he wanted as well was a London flat for a London marriage, a flat hard by Covent Garden, or wherever that ballet outfit hung out.

Jane Whatshername would have understood it perfectly, that although marriages were no longer for convenience, the ability to make them conveniently often had much to do with their being made at all.

His father had given him a typically careful Fenno answer. "Oh, you needn't worry, Aussie. It'll come out all right."

Then he'd teetered on his toes, giving the old library — with its porridge paper, greenish bookshelves, bleary vases, and rugs that still smelled of 1870 wedding-trip camel and had never been Bokhara — a smile of inherited love. "Notice any change about the old place?"

At first he hadn't. The bookshelves, like the rest of the house, looked faintly dirty, but on testing with a finger would be found to be quite clean — which came of having one inherited domestic and half another. The books were good, in a narrow range which did not favor the present. Nothing in the room was at all valuable; anything precious in it had been made so by dead tastes. The fan in the fireplace, made by the imp, his youngest sister, was new. Upstairs there were two more floors much the same, and one below. It was a hard-worn place, but in spite of its lost colors, almost always one of good cheer, made up of innocent toastings in corners, bedrooms always being redecorated in cheap chintz by a sister with Christmas money, or being formed into cells of baseball lore by a grade-school boy. It had never had much time for nostalgia; his five younger brothers and sisters had seen to that.

"Not much," he said. "No — wait." Faucets. "You've fixed over the hall bath!"

"Well —" said his father, looking ashamed, as was proper, but squirely too. "It was a violation of the building laws, you know. Those lavatories without air shafts."

So it was. And had been, ever since before he was born.

"And there's a new icebox, I'm afraid. Lutie insisted. And Lutie's got her granddaughter to help her — your mother insisted on that."

There were doubtless further mild innovations which would be broken to him little by little by the others, who were always harboring ideas for just such waves of affluence; he had done it himself. Whatever it had been, he had never got it — almost no one ever did. And a good thing too. They'd benefited from all the thriftier instructions of the imagination, yet when they grew up, had this house to come back to. In which the top floor had not been made into either a puppet theatre or a basketball court.

"I saw her." There'd been a Fenno family dinner. "But I thought she was just for the night."

His father was peering sidewise at him, in the guilty style of such times.

"Papa," said Austin. "*Who* died?"

His father shook his head at him. Nobody new had died then, in the family, while he'd been away; at the dinner he'd have heard of it anyway. Then his father burst out laughing, delighted at Austin's recall of an old family joke.

"Incredible," said Warren Fenno, more suitably solemn. "*In*credible."

So it had been James, then. As everyone had expected. And from James's style of living — which could never otherwise have been quite so Spartan yet hospitable — had had every right to expect.

"Absolutely incredible. We had no idea."

They never did. Weren't supposed to, when an inheritance was so obviously near. When it was a good way off, properties might be talked about — in terms of interests and mortgages — because of the need for the young to be trained in the responsibilities of how real property had to be gone about if they ever had any. And sometimes, though more rarely and vaguely, money to come might be spoken of, for a crasser knowledge of this was needed these days too. But, like mourning crepe prematurely worn, they all assumed a black ignorance of anything on its way to them, the nearer it fell due.

"Fifty thousand," said his father. "After the fund to take care of the museum and so forth."

"In toto?" Somehow, he would have thought it would be more. James had been so canny.

"Good God, no," said Warren, truly shocked. "To you."

"To — me? But what about the others?" He thought of them before himself; this was one of the things of which he hadn't need to be aware.

His father was smiling. "Your share of the residue. As the oldest. The others each get a little less. In time."

"And you and Mother?"

His father hung his head. "I'm *afraid* – it's going to mean pret' near three-quarters of a million." And he meant exactly what he said.

Austin stood still. Money made one smile. He was no hypocrite.

"Poor Mother," he said after a moment. "She's going to have to stop her Woman's Exchange way she says, 'Well, of course *they're* rich.' "

His father grinned. "Oh no, she won't. She'll say what three-quarters of a million says of one million or more, 'Well, of course they're *rich.*'"

"Will it make a hash at your job?"

"Not any more. When you were a boy, it might've — they used to think a man with a competence wouldn't work hard enough. Or ought to work for nothing. Now they like it if you can afford to be what they call 'disinterested.'"

"Mmm."

"Mmm. You know, Austin — might make just the difference for you on London too. Though we'd have to make thoroughly clear to them here that you'd want to know they felt you were the best man anyway — as you are. They'd have to reassure us of that."

It was conversation any member of the family could interpret. No inheritance Austin knew of had ever been of this size, but they would face it like any. They had their standards.

"Means your mother and I won't have to alter the house," said his father. "Must confess we were thinking of it. Top-floor apartments. Even had a builder in."

"Oh *no,*" said Austin. It had never come as far as that.

"Being done, you know. As the children scatter. Even where there's money. It's chic." Warren squared his shoulders, relieved from that. "Now we won't, of course. So we felt the bathroom — wasn't out of line."

Austin reached forward on the hearth and took up his sister's paper fan — she'd done a good job of it. It was she who had naïvely asked — when his mother wore a state jewel they'd none of them known existed — who had died. Now that the children had dispersed to schools, many such jokes, once as numerous as the family pets, were on the wane. They were a humorous family — or a large one, preservative of its own sayings. Now that he was older, he could see that perhaps they'd never made the distinction clear.

"Oh well. It's all *relatives* — whom've I heard say?" he said, absently pleating the fan.

His father smiled benevolently, but minimally. They had loved old James. Not that James himself would have been anything but happy to chime in on this conversation.

"Thought there was no point in telling you out there," said his father, rather heavily for him. "Thought it could keep."

Had his father heard about the Korean nurse? In the network of friends' sons out there, it was perfectly possible. And if, from a continent away, his son had made noises about marrying this girl? Though there'd been no child, and Austin would have done it only out of the strangest remorse for being so authentically loved and still chill to it. He'd been aware that none of the others in his own outfit, good fellows all, would even have considered doing it. But if he had, would Warren have accepted it? And at once silently begun her induction into their midst here — not just Kim Yong Mai, Tokyo-trained daughter of village schoolmaster, bird-boned but not beautiful, three teeth missing in token of Japanese bullies, and a liking for rice wine in their stead — but also the Fenno's latter-day Pocahontas? It was perfectly possible. But Austin hadn't made noises. And Warren, knowing what strange independences sudden money can cast on the young, even on the wary sons of the wary, had held off — this was the most probable of all.

"Well, Father. Guess I better go shave."

"Late dinners, they have."

"Somebody coming last-minute from abroad. And they only have Anna."

"Ah?" said his father. The implication was clear. Like our Lutie. Like *us.* "I didn't know." It was assumed that Jews made more show of their money. From the looks of the two houses, Austin would have had to agree. Though the Mannixes might spend no more money than here, even on art objects, their racial warmths and comforts betrayed them — they knew how.

"And Ruth and David may get there too," he said. "They're coming in from London with her. David and Walter, the boys." He liked saying it, still.

"Young Stern, isn't it. The hunchback boy, whose parents were killed. Years ago. Father had a brokerage house."

His father had many linking acquaintances; though the Mannixes didn't come here they well might have, if his parents, who stuck year in, year out to the same round of intimates, had ever done what they called "entertain."

"Yes."

And still his father delayed. "They have an interesting crowd there?"

"Oh, more a collection of the faithful," said Austin absently.

"Jewish, you mean," said his father, absent too. "Those good old families stick to it."

"Oh, not necessarily. No, it's cosmopolitan enough. Just that one gets to know the regulars. Mostly, that's what there are."

"Guess he likes it that way. Those independent characters often do." Warren's profession, dealing so often with rich eccentrics, or international ones, gave him a special psychology of which he was rather proud.

"I guess." He'd bent the fan's folds out of line, and was trying to restore them. "Father . . . What would you have had to say if I married out of — well, what we shouldn't say, but do." He looked up. "Out of the — race."

"We-ell, Austin." His father gave no evidence of surprise. Indeed, he seemed to be spreading to the question — one that the committee knows the argument of beforehand, but is committed to go through. His thumbs came unlocked. "You know how we've brought you up. On your own." And expectantly blameless? "And the world is coming closer to our point of view." He spoke in the tone of foundation meetings — as if the world were present at the board of directors' table, a new member delicately being referred to, shortly to be urged to join *in*. "What with the war after all, and what it was fought for. Why, some of the flower of that race is here — look at Einstein." This was from an address.

Austin looked up, to stare at his father. But Warren was oblivious, or seemed so.

"Won't say there mightn't be problems." Warren's thumbs crept forward, to hook on his vest. "But you're a Friend, and luckily your mother's sect has always easily —" How Warren had always enjoyed his wife's Quakerism, on the grounds of which so many family avenues were left open, all the while his own mild Fenno churchship was excused from blame! "But it isn't as if the girl were an unknown."

Austin felt his hands drop to his sides, almost military. At the same time, though he was rooted motionless, he had the sensation of rising to his toes.

"After all, you two have known each other, what is it the British say — 'from the schoolroom.' " His father chuckled. "Why, your mother and I often said — the Mannixes fed you more often than we did." His hands slipped into pockets. "And 'tisn't as if we hadn't — your mother saw her dance at a benefit, years ago. 'The little Mannix girl is lovely,' your mother said, way back then. And I met *him* once or twice of course in the war work, over there. Why, even your sister Alice — she and the girl went to the same dancing school." His father coughed. "Alice not for as long, of course — I understand the little — your friend wants to be professional. But all the girls do these days, don't they? And give it up just the same, when the family comes along. Your own mother."

Alice was his middle sister. And until his own birth, his mother had indeed worked as a volunteer among the respectable poor of Philadelphia.

"Well, Austin? Hope that answers your question." Warren fiddled a fingernail on the mantel, producing a dull, cricket-summoning sound. The rhythm became clearer. Tyumpity tump, tump tump. Tyumpity *tump*, tump tump. Warren had been with the Fighting 49th. And had returned with it, straight up Fifth Avenue, from Washington Square. And France, of course. "As I say — you know how you've been brought up."

Now and then before the eyes of one or the other of one's progeny, usually caught when alone, and on the brink of something which either family intelligences, or even progeny itself, eager and trustful of advice, had revealed — the whole Fenno fan of mutual funds and ideas *freely* expended was unfurled. All without obligation.

"It isn't our war," said his father, as if suddenly. "But it's wartime. Not the worst time to marry. Not the worst time to marry — somebody we know."

So there it was. And there was always this informative little coda too. Which led up — and back — to why his father, after the phone call, had lingered on. He felt ten years old, fifteen — or eighteen, when he had come in dead drunk for the first time in his life — and twenty-four.

Suddenly, without meaning to, his father looked into his eyes, and Austin saw in his father's, large and yet humiliated or humble, what always got to him at these moments — his father's terror of not being as good as he had set out to be, not as good as one said one was. A small terror, Austin suspected, compared to what those sufferers, the Mannixes, were capable of. But one he shared.

"Your mother and I would take it as a great compliment," said Warren, "if you cared to bring the young lady to tea."

There was no explanation he could give at this moment; it would take a recounting of all his other life in that household, of all that hadn't been said yet, even to himself. "Thank you, I — can't. I never have before, you know. Brought her here." He gave it up. "We haven't ever spoken, you see. I haven't. We haven't even seen each other, for over a year." That quick trip to London — for the job as well of course — before going overseas; he saw now that it was no wonder if his father had thought on other matters. "I couldn't — unless it was *after*," he said. So it was practically a promise, never to be exacted, of course, unless from himself.

"Dear me," said his father, "Have *I* spoken too soon?" But it was mildly clear that he thought he hadn't, at all.

"Father —" said Austin, trembling. He had imagined this — out there. "In Korea. Out there. I —"

His father's eyes closed like shutters. "Austin. Do me a favor. Don't talk to me about the *war*. Some time or other later. But not now. We had a pair of those little Hiroshima girls in the office yesterday — the ones brought here for rehabilitation. They kept bowing — in their bandages. They bowed themselves out the door." He rested a hand on his son's shoulder, that mock uniform. He would not have gone to war again himself; he always said so. "I know what you've been through. One of the reasons why we thought — But not today, Austin. Not today."

Austin had been trained to recover his emotional manners very quickly. In a family of eight, who, jolly and unrepressed as they were on occasion, lived without "scenes," it couldn't be otherwise.

"Sure." He was rather proud of a father more complicated than he had thought. There was so much of home — the overtones and inflections which even this household had — that he'd forgotten. Perhaps Fennos tended to oversimplify themselves. Or perhaps he was not the maverick he had begun to think.

He'd even been tactfully able to end their talk without awkwardness. "Too bad about that tweedy nursemaid down at the office. Male or female?"

His father winked, before going off to patronize the new bath. "That is still to be decided."

Left behind, Austin kicked at the fan on the floor, now a ruin. He must remember to tell someone that Caesar, the one remaining dog, was not responsible. His kid sister would have to make a new one — the way she made jokes. Luckily, she was still young enough to know how.

As he was going out, encountering his mother, ready in her gray satin and handsomely blued hair to go out with his father to a theatre party, he told her. If she knew, by this or other means, that he and his father had had a little talk, she gave no sign of it. "Poor dear Caesar," she said.

They had a drink together. He had already told her where he was due for dinner, but she made no mention of this either. As he went out the door, she told him — as she told any and all of her children when they set out for the toils and lures of society — that he looked wonderful.

And there, down the long block, almost at the corner of the avenue, was the Mannix house. He liked walking to the houses of friends who had houses like these in common with him, liked arriving, light and easy on his own good shoe leather — at least his home shoes still fitted him — to be let in, not by the flunky-of-the-week sent by the Elevator Operators Union, but by some ample Anna or Lutie, opening an old-fashioned, civilized door. Otherwise, the city itself, for itself, meant nothing much to him; it was the sum of the mechanics, sometimes efficient but getting dirtier and dirtier, in which by day the office and its good works were maintained, and by night "society" carried on by electric light those seasons which had so little to do with the weather. The city was his home of course, but he would never think of walking there for pleasure, even with a girl. The real homes for that use were the Wiscassets, even if these days they hung in the mind like the coal dealers' Christmas calendars — hooked on the pantry wall last December 31st, and scarcely since ever turned. Up there, and in the "camp" his parents kept by the sea, he could still have counted out every railroad tie down the other and wrong side of its tracks; from boyhood he had known every inch of those rural slums. Here — though he hoped to dedicate his whole life to charitable workings commanded from this city — there were neighborhoods, blank to him, that he saw no need to enter and probably never would, even in the way of business. His business wouldn't be that personal — and would command the better for it. Because of what the city was, and Fennos clear-sightedly knew always had been, even its wayside meditation ought not to be too trusted in.

Actually, he felt great. The very rhythms of his flesh felt biblical; he wondered whether this wasn't the case with all "soldiers" who had been saved. Out of the bowel of the bloodletting — temporarily — suffer them to come unto me, to clean underwear and bathrooms without violation, for a home leave.

Just short of the house, he halted. For a moment, the house after a year was his again, alone.

It was where his nostalgias were kept. Before tonight, he hadn't been sure of this. That lamp over the stoop hadn't been stolen by Bedouins; the inner lamps were lit too. Anna's window boxes were in full flair, their ceaseless ivy letting down like hair from the lattices of this summer night. On the curbside, thin as a bugle, was the eternally young tree. They had a deal in common with him and his kind, this family. They had their houses in common. Why did he always feel so grateful coming here — was it that?

There was a schoolroom as his father had said — though being an atmosphere, not a room, it had wandered all over the house, in those long afternoons smelling of games and mustard sandwiches, during which friends' sisters became sisters, and sisters became wives. And friendship took care of all the spaces in between.

Behind him, a continent back, the war crept like feelers on his skin. Beneath the skin — that wasn't ordinarily his way. But didn't he have to have her, for her own good? He was so good with other people's enigmas — having none of his own.

He knew what they were to him, these people, these sufferers cached here so quietly, ticking on in their own silence. They were not his tragedy. They were his charity.

Once a century or a war, or a young man's lifetime or a summer evening — the maverick bloomed, intelligent beyond its sphere. The tenses of the evening gathered from their spherical sources, fatal to whom?

He knew what they were to him. He went up their· steps, to their lamps, their daughters, saying it to himself — and felt the city gather him to itself like dirt does a man, like imagination.

I know what you are to me, you're my charity, that I must have — to be me. I know you. I know what's here, in this house.

"Oh, God help me," he said, as he went up their steps and in. "I've always known there was something wrong."

10   The Young Three – *June 1951*

Whenever any of the three eerily attractive young people crammed into the airliner row of seats spoke into the quiet zoom of mid-Atlantic flight, an intimate secondary atmosphere, like a chrysalis the three shared, was apparent to the stranger in the row with them. He listened humbly, intent on whether to disturb their line of three one more time, by getting up from his window seat to go to the toilet for a nip from a second pint bottle still in his pocket, or whether he dared haul it out and offer it around. Every year he set out for his two-month leave in Europe or Asia, resolved not to drink away his fear of flight, on the way over, not to waste his trip in the lonely professionalism of the libraries, or in hotel after hotel, staring over an address book of introductions he could never bring himself to use. During the other ten months of the year, he never got even as mildly stumble-drunk as the whole plane knew he was now, coming back. Knew his name. Knew his story, boozed out from aisle to seatmate, until the captain had settled him here.

Almost from birth, he, Casper Friend, had understood that he was a peripheral person. His mother, after equipping him, sixth child of eight, with whatever the others had, might as well have slipped a blueprint of his orbit-to-be in his own crinkled red fist. The bland channels of Midwest town and school — maple-leafed all the way, like a dull, hesitant but safely continuous Sunday — had been perfect for his position in life. By now, at thirty-five a sort of city-clerk-of-the-mind to the young — actually an assistant professor at an enormous city college, teaching Shakespeare (which there, like the Bible at home, was one of the ecstasies to which one could openly rock) — he knew that most of the young had the same exclusive, excluding way with them as these three. Something the young couldn't help. Actually he felt more comfortable with them because of it, since all their other elders in the faculty of life were excluded too.

He'd been listening for some time, with the mulling, poetic intentness liquor gave him. On the sidelines, one could always listen without guilt.

"I'd have come back anyway," said the girl of the three. "You had only to phone. *That* only costs twelve dollars. Four guineas." But her small-featured face had a faint glimmer, at her age lovely as an almond on whose curve a Chinese artist had brushed downcast eye fringes and a tipped smile.

She was all in a fuzzy pale green, even to her beanie, a twig of wool in its center, as if she'd dropped into the plane straight from a tree. He'd bet she hadn't yet dropped from the sexual tree, though under a daringly short skirt the leg she'd managed to cross bunched at the calf muscle every time she twisted the hidden foot, a mannerism persisted in like an exercise. He wouldn't have been able to see her at all, centered like beauty between two young guardian beasts, if her right-hand neighbor, the small hunchbacked young man with the curly, oversize Raphael head, hadn't been in the next-but-one seat from the window, at Casper's left. On her other side the tall boy with the black box on his ear had his very long legs in the aisle. As it was, Casper had an excellent view of them all. The one break life seemed always disposed to give him was — a good view.

"My fault," said the hunchback, with a winning smile. "My uncle. He's had another try at his obituary. Left us all the same careful little lumps of dough he did last time. 'Bequest to nephew Walter Stern' — and various servants and cousins et cetera — 'fifteen hundred dollars.' After all, you can't gamble your whole estate, arranging your own fake death." When the young man shrugged, his hump remained unmoved, like a basket hung on him, or a slipped hat. "And who can spend money like that on anything real? So I thought, well, neither Diddy or I'd flown before; we always boat. And Diddy thought it a good chance to see what it did to his box."

"Noisier for me than for you," said the boy on the aisle proudly. "More vibration." He was leaning back, his Roman profile and high forehead cocked to the ceiling, like an early drawing of what would some day be a very distinguished-looking old man. He sat up again almost at once. When Casper had chanced to move his lips a moment ago, the traveling eyes had focused there. The eyes consumed sight like headlights a road. No one could note their special glances.

"He make it dead?" The question fell as ordinary from the girl's lips as asking the time of day. This was always the way with them too. They had no balance yet — or maybe all of it, alive in a world without periphery, free-swung of the character they'd end by imposing on themselves. How he longed to be back there with them — where he had never been!

"Don't know yet. At least this time, he's working it from a small town. Somewhere in Utah, where he has a mine. How he ever expected to make a hoax like that work last time — from Mt. Sinai Hospital . . . ! But that's my *uncle!*"

"He's the swimming pool one too, isn't he," she said.

"Yop. Though that was two wives back. She took that house with her, when she went. Lasted long enough to get Diddy onto crew, though." The hunchback reached over to touch the deaf one's arm. " 'Member the day the butler fell in, running to answer the phone?"

The three burst into laughter, enjoying it hard, like a sweetmeat munched.

"He *cried*," said the girl in green. "I remember. You two told me. No, Walter."

"Who did?" said the one called Diddy.

"The butler. You told me, Walter. Yes, you did; I particularly remember. You found him in the basement with the ruined jacket. And I wormed out of you that you'd given him your whole next allowance —"

"Never mind," the hunchback said quickly. His skin had an apricot tinge, suggesting a constant low fever.

"You never told *me*," said Diddy. "Was it the famous day Austin came down from school? And we had the fest. The day you learned to swim?"

"No, not that day; Christ, what a day for me. No, it was — some time before. Never mind."

"I remember particularly. Because I couldn't," she said matter-of-factly. Now and then in his classes there were dove-colored ones like this, who wouldn't preen for the light that brought out their under-feathers in rainbow. He felt of the bottle in his pocket, a lump of bottled feeling to help him with knowledge never projected — past the rim.

"Couldn't what?" asked Walter. He had the pure, innocent face which often grew from humps.

The deaf one shook his head just perceptibly at Walter. One didn't expect these faint conversational clues from the deaf.

"Cry," said the girl.

"Dr. Joel said it was your tear glands," said Diddy. "Had nothing to do with — how you felt. And you can — now. I saw you." He smiled down at her, if a guardian beast, a loving one. Why such a defense? Swain? "Yesterday. Not when you left Ninon. When you said good-bye to the girls. The troupe." He grinned over her head, at Walter. "How I hated to leave that clutch of girls. I could cry myself."

The girl looked down her short nose at him. She had the look of certain Jewish girls Casper had grown used to identifying — the ones who looked like Christians. "Oh that," she said. "Only a brother would think . . . That's just the troupe. That's just *tears*."

"Do you have to learn that too, like for the stage?" asked Walter. "Only I thought, onstage they use glycerine. Or that's the movies, I guess."

The girl looked at him fondly, then gave him a light hug. Another brother? "No, we don't have to learn. It's just the troupe themselves — boohoo every time. Glycerine. You're always about forty years back."

No wonder if the boy was that way, under that Toulouse-Lautrec vest. That compressed, eagle effect of the breastbone — who could expect modernity from it? Shakespeare's eagle of pity, in a checked vest — or was the phrase Casper's own? He felt of the bottle again, but was now too compelled by the three to leave. Clearly they had all known each other forever. No one knew him like that. Boohoo. *Merde.* The flask in his pocket — Italian or French? He couldn't recall. If he had a hump, or a little black box, would that make him brave enough to take the bottle out and drink it down? Or offer it.

"Ninon's superb," said Walter. "Like a hummingbird."

The other two broke out laughing again.

"With a very long, sharp beak," said the brother. "Pity she couldn't ride along with us. I'd like to know her better." He looked down at his sister. "Your — what is she? Boss? Is that what one calls a ballet mistress?"

So. That would account for the girl's air of confidence, short of a prima donna's but, in a certain prescribed orbit, a star's.

"She had to go on ahead," the girl said lightly. "Ballet biz. With the Met. But you wouldn't have got to know her any better. She's all there already. In what you see." She turned to each of them eagerly. "That's what I like. For a person to be all there already. At least . . . I think." She looked down at her hands, tightly clasped. "Oh, she lies a bit, now and then. But that's only — theatre. Only pretending. And she lets you see that too."

Both looked at her.

"And she wants to talk to Father," said Diddy. "About you."

All three were silent.

"Really, you were awful," the girl said again. "The phone would have only cost —"

"Four guineas," said her brother. "The British have at least made you begin to count costs."

"The troupe again," his sister said, grinning. "Buh-lieve me. Bed-sitting-room values, they said. If I expected to go on tour with *them*. Marks and Sparks for lingerie. And mince."

"Pie?" said Walter.

"A sort of hamburger."

A silence fell again.

"Your uncle," said Diddy. "Always wondered . . . if he simply had to see his obituary, then . . . Well, not only 'if,' of course. *Why*."

"Has eighteen movie theatres, four wives, couple of racehorses. Old masters. But only one obit. Seems the natural thing. He ought to have that too. While he can. Which is his motto." Walter hesitated. "Has a bum heart. Nice guy really."

The girl chuckled. "I know what Anna would say about him. She'd say he was a bit *fast*."

Laughter again.

"If he really wants his obit so bad," said Diddy, "can't he bribe it out of the *Times*. They keep 'em canned and ready, I understand."

"The *Times* — you can't bribe the *Times!* That would be like bribing —" She searched for a comparison.

"Father," said Diddy.

Rhythms of others came clearer when the mind was liquored. The rhythm of these silences was plain.

"I won't bribe Father," said the girl. "He'd take it."

"Trouble is, my uncle did try," said Walter quickly. "Trouble was, there wasn't anything on him, it turned out. All those racehorses and wives, and he didn't even rate an obit set up ahead of time. 'Tween you and me, all he wants now is to spur them on."

"From Utah?" said Diddy. He was fiddling with the black box, his long fingers delicate as calipers.

"Why not?" The hunchback's great, clarified eyes went from one to the other happily. Yet he had a certain solicitude for them. Who was guarding who?

"Oh, those Mormons don't mind multiple wives. But multiple deaths?" The deaf one had removed the box from his head altogether. And now he was tinkering with it, cocked intent on it in his lap, like a surgeon repairing his own stomach, or a scientist examining a spare, detachable head.

How cruelly scientific the young were, no matter what marshfires of emotion already surrounded them. No picture slot of death-for-them had as yet opened in their breasts. Their breasts were like armor, not to death itself, but to the idea.

Casper was about to get up. No, he wouldn't offer the bottle. On the rim, one learned to be stingy. Finish it himself, and the great strophes would swing right through him. He would *be* Shakespeare.

Just then, the girl impulsively touched her brother's arm. "David." She waited until he raised his eyes to her lips. "Does the vibration seriously bother you?"

He understood perfectly. And answered joyously. But no sound came from the words his mouth shaped. Was that what the box did, then — helped him voice? He was swift to catch on that he hadn't. "Oh no," he said more carefully. "No, it's wonderful. The *noise*. I float in it. Like being massaged — by elephants." He leaned back again and closed his eyes.

Left alone, the other two were silent at first, as if it wasn't fair to talk until their companion once more opened his eyes.

"I like those flashes out there on the wing," the girl said then. She looked briefly past Casper, through the window. "Comforting. I suppose too that's how they see us, down below." As she leaned back again, her eyes met Casper's. She smiled tentatively. Well-bred virginal fires; he had no trouble with them, nor with those Bronxy student wenches whose lips hung like vulva over their teeth. His short, mushroom-brown looks were said to be attractive to them, and his haircut and hornrims were a concession to that professorial image, never taken advantage of. Shrugged at the window, he hugged himself. I'd rather buy it. From the endlessly receptive whores, who were toothless down below. Then what was so familiar, crossing to him from this girl? Had she been listening — to his listening? Nobody ever noticed it.

"Walter," he heard the girl say softly, as if their companion in the aisle was sleeping, though the deaf boy's eyes, staring straight up, were open. "Watch out, I'm going to shift legs." Carefully she did so, turning one foot from the ankle, round and round.

That bunch of muscle at the calf, only ugly thing about her. Whisky in him made him letch, for more whisky. Must be England he had embarked from. Or Japan.

"You do that for exercise, don't you," said Walter. "All the troupe."

"Mmm. There's a better one. Shake the leg all over. From the hip." She giggled. "Two of us were doing that once, on the railway platform at Euston. Narsty-minded Englishman brushed past us, one of those city men with hard hats. 'You Americans!' he said, and pointed to the washrooms. 'In *there!*'"

David, the deaf one, turned his head at their vibration. He looked past both her and Casper. "I like those flashes." He was just putting the black thing on again. Had he somehow heard his sister's remark, through the back of his magnificently long head? No, hold them all up by the legs, out would tumble all the same sentiments, like loaded dice.

Meanwhile, the liquor was dying in him. I am dying, England, dying. Fading like verse. After dying, going to be sick. Multiple obits, in any washroom.

"Know what the Halecsy sisters have over their beds?" said the girl. "An electrically pulsating bleeding heart. I saw it." She made a face.

"In the kibbutz, they *worship* electricity. Don't they, Walter." Her brother fingered the material of the seat in front. "Plastic? They told me some of the new plastics are stronger than metal. They want to be as modern out there! — and not in the service of the golden calf, either. When I go back, it won't be Tel Aviv, but the Negev." He smiled. "Oh well, the Halecsys, poor things. Not the brightest."

"Poor things?" said the girl. "The Halecsys? I was glad not to have to give them dresses any more — to outgrow *them.* They *left* Edwin and his mother. I know it. Though he's never said."

The two young men relapsed into a conventional male pause easily identifiable by any other male. Whoever Edwin was, they didn't like him.

"Zoom," said David, his eyes closing again. "My head's in the clouds, and I'm following it. At the safest actuarial rate. What a healing vibration! Next best thing to my old dream of being inside a piano."

"What dream?" said Walter.

"Guess I never told you," said the deaf boy, with no sign of having heard. They would all know each other's questions, though. And answers. "Wouldn't have told you for worlds, once. But I don't have it any more. Not for years." When he wasn't looking straight at you, it was a little hard to catch his own words. "I'm inside this big concert grand, and I begin to feel the sound. First the thumps of the bass — like they did teach me, you know, hand on the sounding board, up the scale. In real life, there's a point where I can't feel the vibrations any more. But not inside that — dream. I go up, up. The treble is like a stair. But the last note at the top; that's like a finger. That reaches out and touches me. Where I am, at the center core of all those tickling strings. It reaches out . . . and touches me, all by itself. And then — I can hear." He opened his eyes, the dream still on his face, and saw their faces. His solicitude was immediate, for them. He went into a clown-flurry of gesture, slapping the seat, stamping his big feet in the aisle.

A stewardess went down it slowly, smiling side to side with that pretty, mandarin doll nod they all adopted, or didn't know they had. "Boy," said David, grinning after her. "What a piano."

"Zoom," said Walter agreeably. Casper now doubted they were related — except by handicap. But the girl, so much more than sister — where was she in this? She had a nagging familiarity. Like a telephone number — did that make sense?

Most unfortunately, for the past few minutes his head had been clearing. The secret bottle at his side warmed him, like Sterno. Not much left in the other one anyway, when the pilot himself, called by a stewardess, had come down the aisle. To speak severely (but like a gold-braided angel too, fair-headed past president of the Demolay junior Masons, and not blushing, like Casper, for having belonged to it) to this drunk in the back seat who'd kept falling asleep with his head on an old hen turkey's shoulder. (Lord God, who would choose her to do that on; nobody, no doubt why she complained.) "Mr. Friend. Mr. *Friend*," said Prince Hal, consort of all the stewardesses of the Western world, toss in the Low Countries too. The tone, as always, made Casper pay for his name. They'd have gotten it from the reservation, personal touch. "Afraid I'll have to ask you for that bottle, Mr. Friend." And the voice, a steel lever performing the task of a nutpick, had lifted Casper from the back seat and placed him in the vacant window seat here. "You three be all right?" the captain said, leaning over the seat with a Zeus smile. After which he'd moved forward to the cabin again, to consider the stars.

"Oh, planes can be anything," the girl said. "The one Daddy and I took back during the war was dark as a stable. Full of wounded soldiers, but going home, so they were gay. 'Is this a bomber?' I said. And the whole caboodle, must have been eighty of them, heard it and laughed. And took turns holding my hand every time we veered. To evade. Though they said there was nobody out there. Like being on a roller coaster. And we had spiked tea. I loved it."

"You said that on purpose, I bet," said Walter. "About the bomber. To make them feel better — I know you. Why, you'd already made all those model kits, baby. With us."

She didn't answer this. "Fly, fly," she said to the air at large, fluttering her fingers. Her shoulders narrowed. "Why dance?"

On either side of her, the two guardians sat up. And spoke together, yet alternate — like the paired Dromios in the plays, or the gentlemen from Verona — or one Laertes, cut down the middle. "You *have* to talk about it sometime, Ruth! What are you going to tell him?"

The girl halted exactly as she was, one hand lifted at the wrist, in an artifice she seemed unconscious of. "He *wants* to let me go, really. Didn't you know?" She bent both hands, making them relax and arch in what must be another exercise — or entreaty to private magic. "And I'm afraid I want to stay with him, really. That's why I was glad you came over to get me."

"So it'll be the same as always," said the hunchback, and the listener at his elbow could hear the yearning stuck like a bone in that chicken-bone chest. "You'll stay."

"No, Walter. I'm just coming to tell him. I'm going. With the troupe."

The two made no comment. The brother's eyes never left her.

"Oh, I know I'm not going to make a dancer, for long. Ninon knows I know that."

"Then why would she —?" said her brother.

"Oh, I don't know what *she*'ll say to *him*," said the girl. Turning away brusquely, she looked straight into Casper's eyes, denying it.

He was still drunk enough to look back. Do I know your telephone number? He was the first to look away. Outside the window, the flashes were still at it. Glow, little glowworm.

"But I know who *is* going to be bribed," he heard the girl say.

"Who?" they said.

"Edwin."

"*Edwin?*"

"Yes, Edwin. I don't know exactly for what."

"If anything," said the deaf one, in his cleanest articulation, "it would be that young bimbo —"

"You don't understand Edwin at all. Neither of you. You never have."

"He's remarkable. And Father helped to make him so." Her brother slurred the words roughly. "What more is there to understand?"

"Bribe him for what?" said Walter. "*Who?*"

Silence. O perfect caesura, O dangerous.

"Why, your father's the most honorable man in the world!"

That might be. But the young hunchback's will to innocence was as touching as his sternum, exposed forward and plain to all. "He took me in too . . . and he never . . . He could ask for anything . . . I could give. Why, that afternoon, day after my parents were killed . . . when David brought me home from school with him . . . I've never spoken about it, but —"

"Never mind, Walt," said David.

"Sorry," said his friend. "Trouble with air travel, takes your feet off the ground."

"But you did speak!" The girl's voice burred through the seat like electricity. "Don't you remember? It was what my *mother* said to you that day that made you — stay. You told me, Walter. I've never forgotten it."

Mothers were awarded silences too, in this crowd. But shorter.

"Oh, I did?" said the hunchback, with such unease that Casper turned to look at him. Neither young man was looking at the girl. And she? She sat with peculiar stiffness. As if she wasn't looking at herself.

"Will we get there for dinner?" said Walter. What distress, from cheekbones that didn't look as if he bothered with one dinner out of three!

And the deaf one said, "Oh look. Here comes God again." Several seats around tittered, as the pilot began his royal way. The young passenger had miscalculated his own loudness, as the deaf do. Or had he?

Casper got up. "Sorry," he said to the girl, as he worked his way past her. He knew what it was like out there, where she was. "I go to meet my captain." Who doesn't know that I have a second bottle.

"Wonder who's he coming for now?" said the deaf one, oblivious. Casper felt, rather than heard, the girl's tense *Shhhh* behind him.

Casper reached down and tapped her brother's black box. "Washrooms lead lives of quiet desperation," he said. "Does it know?"

He stayed there until somebody knocked. When he came out, the strophes were riding, riding, and the corridor too, in great humps of mul-ultitudinous . . . carpet. This was the way to get over the rim — if you had no swimming pool. He paused at the head of the aisle. Royally.

Beautiful nihilists, those three down there, those plastic-lovers with their own cheeks still fleshly shining, hot and organic as peaches on the dead sideboard of the world. But young and kind before everything. They were disposed to be friendly. He could see that. Also their faces, if he gave them his card. My name is Friend — story of my life. No, too neat for the tear glands. Besides, the plane was too near New York now. *Had he told them everything?* But he had her telephone number, if he ever needed it. She would listen without guilt. Like me.

He nodded from side to side, mandarin. Last trip out, he'd crossed in a double seat, next to a man reading from a book printed in some unknown Oriental script. The man had had a large nose inhabited by a tic. At intervals, nose and upper lip screwed toward the heavens in revulsion, but though all across the Pacific the man spoke steadily of his own life, Casper could never find the connection between tic and what was said. That time, Casper had shared the man's bottle, a large one of Very Old Sun Tory Japanese whisky, brought out at once. He never learned the name of book or man. But he remembered the man's life as if it were his own. The ocean, seen from above, must be scored with these trajectories, every wave peopled with character explaining itself, preparing for the silent vise of home.

The important thing was — not to mumble. One doesn't mumble Shakespeare. Had he been sure to speak loudly enough to those three in the seat — life companions forevermore? Had they got what he said to the black box? Or had he been mumbling all along?

He stopped in the aisle, just ahead of their seats. They had changed things round. The girl was now in the windowseat, then her brother, then their friend. The aisled seat on the end was ready for him. Had they done it for the girl, or against him? "I'm sorry," he made his gaze say to her. "If I leaned on *your* shoulder, I would do it from choice."

She smiled up at him, this observer whose handicap he recognized. She was an ordinary girl, plunged in the Shakespearean ocean of life like any other. What had taken from her the power *not* to understand?

A passing stewardess, no older than this girl, frowned at him to sit down and fasten his seat belt, but he wasn't going to have this moment taken from him — in which his trip united with his life. This was the real trip.

He leaned across the seat and spoke, this time he knew for sure aloud. They and he would remember each other forever. The plane lifted, surging on his strophes, borne upward by garlands of glowworm into the ever-expanding dark — forward into port, into the time when he too would be young.

But somehow, one didn't speak to a person like her directly.

"She does even better than me," he said clearly, and held out his bleeding wrists to her. "She listens without guilt for *any* of us. Does she know?"

11   The Honest Room – *June 1951*

Eₙₜₑᵣ the dining-place of a house and the family story begins, pastorale or head-horror, but out of the dogshit of the streets. Home as sinecure didn't end with the revolution — which revolution? Only a family at table can ask that; here gather all the secret conservatives of life. I, Simon, know this.

You Edwin, of no family table, you Leni, naiad of the bathroom, know it. Blount, meet yourself coming and going, but you know of a kitchen table where all your safari began. Austin, this oval table here, eaten at so often, is only the reverse of a long medal, isn't it, the Jewish side of the communion wafer, close as a lion to its victim — this, your other home. Mr. Krupong you are black, and first of your generation to be named Felix, but your grandfather is here, isn't he, under those broad lapels the same cannibal flesh! Dear Ninon, Venus Callipygian of the small, steel buttocks, where was your table really, the one that was never on the Île St. Louis? . . . The room knows this.

Grace is always spoken by someone in these places, by an elder who may never say a live word:

. . . *In the eye of the whirlwind, eat home broth once a day.* That was Meyer Mendes, builder of this house.

. . . *Use your first name at this table, Dan Blount, respect answers, not questions.*

. . . *Go to England, grandson; one pod of cocoa was enough for Tettah Quashie; one pod and a blacksmith brought our farms to us, from Fernando Po.*

. . . *The meal is the parable; no living member has ever heard it all.*

. . . *Fathers wave the palm of opinion here, Simon, mother cutting with her manicure scissors at his broad leaf. Mine was Hungarian. He knew my mother, according to the oldest testament. She kept our tools safe from roaches, in a tin box. The rats are always outside — even with us.*

. . . Childhoods collect here, Edwin. In farina and short sentences, we teach you nothing wrong here; outside is the dogshit, don't bring in any on your shoe. Oh my children of the airplane, fly home safe — and drop like Icarus, on this collection plate.

"Everybody's family here," said the Judge. "Leni, at last you're with us, you sit here on my right. Ninon, my dear Ninon, on my other side. How long since you two have seen each other? Next to Ninon, of course Pauli — you three have so much to catch up on. Next to Leni . . . why — Austin. How good to have you here again, Austin. Welcome home, boy. . . . Mr. Krupong, will you take the chair next to Austin . . . you'll find his father has been in your country many times. And our mutual friend opposite you . . . Dan, on Pauli's left please; Pauli, tell him about that palace in Vienna where the architect forgot the bathrooms — if he doesn't already know. . . . And Edwin, I've been saving you for . . . Anna, since we're not going to wait dinner for those three, perhaps remove their plates — yes, that's better. . . . Here we are then. Ninon, Pauli, Blount. Leni, Austin, Krupong . . . And Edwin . . . at the other end. It's not the foot. Opposite me."

And unbidden guests arrive without warning at any time between gong and coffee, drawn out of their graves to the plate that is never set for them, never lifted away.

(*I shan't do over the dining-room, Simon. Black holland covers on the Jacobean, gravy-brown wood and vanilla white. It's been that way from the beginning; they'd turn over in their graves. So I'll leave it as is; I know when I'm beat. It's an honest room; I'll say that for it.*)

"We've never changed this room," said the Judge, sitting down.

(*Seating and setting, Anna*, said Mirriam, *that's all I'll ever do about dinners here. Hire a flock of helpers, if you want. Or have caterers in. But the people and the flowers are all I'll do. I'll expect you to take care of the rest.*)

Mirriam, how you neutered people. The flowers were your allies, swarming in corners, offering bowers for the animal in us to lift a leg at, splitting the house safety with a liana of green, transfusing our minds to the yellow, jaundiced rain of autumn, outside. Yet you were such an urban woman. *Stay upstairs!* Anna does the flowers now.

"Why, it's an English-basement house, Simon, isn't it, with the dining-room below street. Like mine."

"You have a house, Ninon?" said Leni. . . . She has everything she wants, one can see. And she *wants* it; she's no American fool; she's like Pauli and me. "Ah, what happiness." And maybe, visits from us.

"Half belongs to the ballet, really. You know how it is, Leni. The choreographer always has a garret. To be sick in, and nursed. You don't know Rupert — but they're all the same. Then there's always some stray girl down with something — usually love. Second floor's for meetings, all projectors and files. We're very modern, now that we're nationalized."

"No room — for husbands?"

"Now girls, girls." Pauli rubbed his elegant hands, delighted. "I'll have to be stage manager again; I see it."

"Ah, Leni, you were a prima before me." Madame's décolletage sparkled, but lacy as it was, her toilette had the solidity of their profession; that hair ornament would ride every tour-jeté of the evening. "You do everything ahead of me."

"You were never a prima, my dear."

"But Leni, she is going to be a Dame."

Leni's eyelashes cast themselves up, two sets of them. "What titles, the English."

Nearest Pauli, Ninon's left glove had its fingers tucked back into its opera opening, for eating, but wisely covered elbow and upper arm where he knew she had those veins; she would still be no bigger than a mosquito in bed. Now she fluttered the hand at Leni. As of old, her double ring joined second and middle finger, but the fourth was beautifully bare.

And would remain so. "What a glorious acid-green you're wearing, Leni *chérie*." . . . And how exquisitely I can still lie — I ought to do it more often, such fun. But she does have a good corset on. Anyway, I've made them all recall now — that I am French. . . .

"You don't have the little studio any more, Ninon, behind the Strand?" . . . Her perfume was the same, or to the same purpose, the only cloudiness about her. . . . Let those two hear him, he didn't care.

"Oh, that was just for the war. A tiny house now, Simon." She made it sound like an assignation. "On Clipstone Street."

People's houses so often sounded like them. When Edwin himself first came here, his confusion was all visual. Now the room, long since settled as to its objects, resounded with echoes; maybe a family never heard its own. They weren't as musical here as he'd thought; they'd merely inherited musical interests, along with the money on which he supposed this house lived. . . . If I am offered a salary — must I take it? They'll make me a sensitive hero, yet. But I always have my reservoir. . . .

The foot of the table had no women to tuck in. Austin had gotten the old vampire-bag under the table with all her skirts as simply as if she came greased for it. Women would, with Austin, down to the slit. . . . In the bar, the spoiled priest speaks from painted nose, while Edwin and his mother scrub the taps. "Keeps the rats down and blessed, boy, does the alcohol; even priests use it. But if woman-slut is your trouble, I know naught else that will do." . . .

"Never thought of this room as a basement before," said Edwin. His military stance had attracted the eyes of the others for a moment. He had been the last to sit down.

"Nothing for the table like white damask, is there, Ninon," said the old bag in green eye shadow.

"Nothing," said Madame. Leni's dress, slashed here and there for the gold lining to show through like tarnished skin, made her laugh; it was so much an old-style Viennese dressmaker's concept of sex — plenty of handwork, to draw the eye *in*. But she agreed on the damask. Damask was what would have been had in servants' quarters on the Île St. Louis, of a Sunday. Upstairs, seen from belowstairs in a certain rectory in Islington, it was what they had had.

The two old girls down there at the host's end were nodding like two peddler-wives on Grand Street. The lacy one looked down the table at him. Queen Mab on wires she was, even at sixty or so, pink all over as that nose, he'd bet — on every pointed end of her, a dancing sex.

"Nothing like a white table," Madame repeated, staring down the length of it. That young man with a suspicion of snout in the face, what possessed Simon to have him here? She could smell the slum ragout he'd been nourished on a mile away. Something non-aristocratic too in the hairline at the back of the neck, where it always told. Nobody could tell breeding better than she, learning it at the start as she had, in the place where it bred.

She smiled across-table at the other young man, in official blue, dowdy, but still a uniform. His extreme good looks were racially impersonal, with the same handed-down air which kept the right sort of clothes from ever looking new. She was surprised to find the type in America. In bed he would be adequate, even hot, but to topple over the last edge of excess was unlikely for these guardians of the seed; in bed he would be a heavy-flanked breeder, the slightest bit too considerate. . . . Thank God, at sixty-two, but with all organs intact, I can still think of bed. I never really was a dancer. Whores make the best executives. . . .

"How very charm*ing*," said the black man to his half-grapefruit. "Like a clown with a red nose."

At every place, a sawtoothed half-grapefruit, mounded with sugar and a maraschino cherry, sat on its concentric pedestal of plate and service plate, making a consciously festive ring around the table, outside an inner circle of huge, coned napkins, starched stiffly enough to stand.

"These napkins!" said Pauli. "One gets them nowhere else."

"How does she ever starch them?" said Blount. "Would that she could give the secret to the laundresses of the world!" . . . Starched to stand, yet silky to the lips; my mother used to do it. . . .

"She?" said Leni. "Your servant?"

The Judge made a face at his spoon. "Maraschino. My wife used to say, 'Sherry, not cherry, Anna.' But now she puts both. The menu is hers, I might say. And we're not to notice her, until dessert. Till then, she thinks of herself as invisible. And won't have help. After that point, when her *crise* is over, it's permitted. She may even notice *us*." As she does all along of course. Anna knows her place. . . . But why don't *you*, why won't you stay upstairs, why must I mention you? Because of Ninon. I'm so seldom taken by surprise. It would be good — to take . . .

"Anna's our housekeeper. In the family since the children were young." The Judge noticed that his spoon was ahead of his napkin, and shook out the cone's folds. "My father-in-law required them big. To tie round the neck. These came with the house. And that way of folding them. The children used to call them Everest."

"And I used to make napkin mice for them — see," said Pauli, whipping one out in front of Leni. Worriedly, he could see she hadn't yet chosen her style.

"She sounds more like a concubine, Simon," said Madame Whatshername, *Fracca*, with a laugh, her smile lingering on Austin's uniform. Taffy-haired, amazing of skin, she didn't fascinate Austin for herself, though he'd been to dinners abroad where there were women like her, the least malicious of what was said about them being that they "kept themselves up." He preferred women her age to be like his mother, behind her armorial satin a body fashioned only for his father in long-ago moments one didn't think of — a woman now modern enough to dye her hair to a shade just blue enough to advise all men it was really gray. But this Madame the Mistress Royal might know how it was, how it really was — with her charge. He wouldn't say his "beloved," even to himself. The word smacked of Bibles given to dutiful sons by fathers; this Fenno might maverick yet. And would be the first Fenno to choose the dark city. He looked at his neighbors — in this room consecrated to middleness, bland with it as the chicken which was by the smell on the way — and wondered why he thought that.

. . . *Used to, used to*. The air here was anaesthetized with its own legend, beautiful visits that don't go anywhere any more, having got all that was wanted, long ago. Or what was not wanted? Surprised at itself, the foot of the table stared at the host. But the whole world already knew merely that about him. Yet *I am more intelligent than anyone he lets come to the house*. . . .

"A concubine?" said the Judge. "Mine?" Glancing up, he saw in the younger men's faces the barometric halt that came when any older person, hoping to be contradicted, referred to his age. . . . *Edwin's embarrassed, as one's children are, by one's sex. Is personal emotion a filth to you, Edwin? Against all Harvards, is that where you'll always be — second-class? Or I'm a father to you, is that it? Are you dear to* me — as a son? . . . "No, not mine," he said aloud. "Maybe someone else's. Edwin thinks she has a secret life."

Austin's embarrassment at that, the Judge saw, was different — social. . . . Yes, I know one doesn't discuss the servants. Women make us vulgar, Austin — haven't you yet found that out? . . .

The Judge's smile at Austin made no effort to win him, and never would. . . . You're not a son to me. . . . At the boy's glassy coolness, he himself felt a certain withdrawal, recognizing the slight chill that came upon meeting an equal. . . . Is it because you've been to the wars and this house has never been, even in your uniform? No, we were equal even before, you and I. Don't worry me, boy, don't let me guess it. . . . Austin, Austin, what do we share? . . .

Edwin turned from watching Krupong, up the table at his left, who was penciling on a memo pad some kind of diagram too sidewise for him to see it clearly. "Oh, Anna has secrets, all right," he said, in imitation of the careless style here. "Don't know whose." Had he done it badly? No, the Judge's cold stare seemed to be for Austin. Who had done nothing, in a casualness not to be imitated. . . . Simon — a god shouldn't be frightened. Simon — don't be Simon, to *me*. What have you let into the house, Judge Mannix? Who? . . .

"Oh, this house has depths," said Blount. "I never ask too many questions here." He looked up, startled. "Why — it's *true*. That's why I come here. Isn't it?"

Felix chuckled. Austin smiled at him.

"And it has a *bidet!*" said Leni. "Upstairs, in one of the baths. I saw."

Chuckles flickered round the table — tentative. Were things going to warm up? Will we be friends here — for a summer evening? Will the floes melt a little closer, merge for a night in the same life-direction — and move on? Down the table, grapefruit halves were withered, gutted, sprung or untouched pearly, according to each person's habit. It had better happen now.

"*Fin-de-siècle* depths," said the host — and in laughter, the ice broke. Leni bridled like a wit. Pauli clapped his hands.

"Oh, Dan gets the credit for that remark," said the Judge. "Long ago. See here, let's have the wine." He began serving up an entrée from a tea-wagon at his side. "A little salmon with water chestnut. That's *my* choice." Two decanters stood ready on the long oaken sideboard,

whose heavy ox-yoke handles clinked when a drawer was pushed in —
a sound unique to the house. "Austin . . . will you? — that's right, the
white. And Edwin, the red. Thank you." He patted Leni's hand.
"There, I've got the younger ones working . . . May I tell you your
earrings are very handsome?"

"*Aida*. Munich. Long ago . . . Oh look, Pauli, two kinds of wine!"

Long ago. Memory soup. Edwin, getting up for the decanter, caught
the black man watching him, and said quickly, "Taking notes on us?"
Sounding nastier than he meant.

"See what you have been missing, darling," said Pauli.

Krupong wrote a word, then closed the notebook. "Not exactly. I
make book." He grinned at Blount. "What's that in American?"

Blount grinned back. "Take bets. What odds you give us?"

"We?" Krupong was watching the wine go round. Decantering
might mean either that the host wished to mask an indifferent wine, or
knew how to treat a good one. His bet was on the latter.

The two young men had gone round the table in opposite directions,
and now approached him. Both were blond, and in knee breeches
would have made a passable pair of footmen, though the nonmilitary
one was too short for it, and the other too much at his ease. The short
one, who had just now addressed him, the one with the decanter of
red, was covertly watching the young man with the white, copying his
general style of pouring well enough. But Red hadn't yet noticed that
White was filling his glasses, very properly, only halfway. Krupong
watched with interest. Wine protocol was effete only to fools; at home
he'd seen similar subtleties served up with the fresh blue entrails of
beasts just fallen. "Ah," he said, as the two drew up on either side of
him. "What service. I am the last, eh. I warn you, I like wine." Red
poured first, stanching the drop at the bottle's lip with a napkin. "Well
done." The glass was filled to the brim. Krupong stole a look at White.

Austin filled the glass slowly to the halfway mark, a very little more,
then stopped. About to return his decanter to the sideboard, he saw
Edwin staring at the two circles of glasses down the table, all the red
ones full, and Krupong's eyes on himself. Austin moved to fill Krupong's glass of white to the brim, thought better of it, and stood fast.
Then both young men went to the sideboard to leave the decanters,
and resumed their places at table. Like chess, it was. But it was White
who flushed.

"You did well," Krupong whispered, as his neighbor White sat down.

"And you did right, by our laws at home too; you were compassionate. But you blushed for the *other* one — Mr. Red — who won't like that." Lifting a glass, he stole a look at the foot of the table. No, "Ah," said Krupong, inhaling but not tasting, "I've won my bet."

"About us?" said the host, who'd seen all this byplay. "Ninon — your glove." He rescued the glove from her glass. Earrings and a glove, and a dinner, long ago. *Stay upstairs.* "That thing on your hair, why it's got a sort of crown on it — just there." He touched it.

"To be presented in. Just in case." When she moved her nose, she knew it pulled her upper lip, in youth too rich a Cockney pulp for some, but now shrunken only to adequate — poor Leni's was cross-hatched like a bad darn. . . . Simon always did notice cat-close. There, he's scratching his crotch just as if he wasn't born to a sort of crown himself — a Jew, but on the Disraeli side. He could have been a prime minister — with us. And the daughter — an assoluta — but of *what?* That state picture of the mother, in the drawing-room. I don't believe it — there must be a better, somewhere. Though I don't want to know what happened to him. Nothing gets farther away from the truth than the truth. I should know. I *want.* Must be because I still have all my organs, or never gave birth. Where would we go? I shall drink and eat all I crave; tonight my waist will get its own exercise. Where *will* we go? . . .

For God's sake sip, mine host, Felix Krupong silently intoned — taste your wine. . . . He twirled his glass, politely waiting. Was this an uncommon household in America? . . . Or shall I find it at Princeton too — only one servant but the air so swaddled in *safety.* "There's a war on," as is said here, but the air everywhere seems so dry of swords. In England, the houses were thick with other hypocrisies, but war's a penny-dreadful they don't hide. Always some old assegai of a relative hanging about, or the colonial ghost of a limb left on the battlefield. That little War of the Roses we had a minute ago was interesting. And up there, at the head of the table, is my grandfather, I would swear it, under those lapels. Drink for the love of me, Grandfather. Ah. There. . . .

He sipped. After a moment he said a sharp, pleased word in his own Efik dialect.

"What?" Edwin leaned toward Krupong, across the memo pad set carelessly in one extra service plate Anna hadn't after all removed.

. . . Ah, a researcher; those so often came from the foot of the table. This chap, Mr. Red, bore that with some dignity, or maybe was used to it. But I, Krupong, must keep in mind that there's no need for me to understand social power here. It's all *white*. "And I am black but oh my soul is white"? Nonsense, it's my *tongue* that's white. Like the wine. . . .

Felix's laugh at himself, often so pleasantly disconnected with what it saw that it could be taken for innocent, drew all the table. "Montrachet, yes?" he said.

On Austin's left, Leni, fixedly attentive to the Judge and Ninon, said suddenly, in a loud confidential whisper to them, "Imagine, he knows wine. We had one of them like that at the theatre in Vienna, black too as the ace of spades, a woman, a dresser, she could find out anything, for the girls. Any man who came to the stage door, if he was young, she could tell a girl next day how much his inheritance would be, if he was old, the state of his health. Whether he was *clean,* you know. She could always tell. And she could make a juju — a charm, to help him marry you." She saw the Judge was listening, and leaned toward him. She had had three *framboises,* before the wine. "Mmm, those days. But I imagine *you* never had to wait at the stage door."

Pauli clasped his long, silvery hands and shook them nervously. Madame stretched her long neck and lowered her eyes.

"I am sure, Madame Leni, that you never had to use juju to make any man fall in love with you," said the Judge.

"Juju," said the black man gaily. "Who is talking juju?" And Dan Blount said, "Are you an expert at it?" and Leni, shaking her head, smiling into the creak of her corset, said, "When they are black like that, they are of the blood of kings."

Down at the foot, Edwin, fiddling with one of the small table ornaments that stood at each place — a minute porcelain rose-in-basket, found it come apart in his fist. "Oh hell. I'm sorry."

"Oh, *those,*" said the Judge, lifting his chin to see. "Whatever possessed Anna; I haven't seen them in years." He took up the one at his place. "They're made to come apart — the children used to know how." Very carefully he probed, and drew the rose out of the basket on its green china stem. "There. Horrible Nuremberg-style gaiety. They were

my mother's. She used to bring them out at family weddings. Well."
He lifted his glass. "Austin. You haven't said a word. Not a word. But
that's understandable. Austin's just returned from the wars. To —" He
stood up, pushing back his chair, and took up his glass again. "To . . .
this." He twiddled the rose. "We drink to you, my dear boy."

"How lovely old-fashioned it all is," whispered Leni to Ninon. "Like
home." . . . Like the Rue de Bellechasse, the Via Angela Masina. Home
is always *was*. Yes, Pauli, why didn't I come here before? . . .

They drank.

Austin, bowing gravely to the Judge, picked up his rose and raised it
in acknowledgment. "To family weddings," he said, and inserted the
rose in his buttonhole.

"Charming!" said Ninon.

Pauli stared at Leni, who returned the stare.

"What hour do the children get home?" asked Blount.

"Any moment." The Judge sat down.

The Nigerian turned to the young man at the foot. "Ah," he said low.
"But you have really broken yours now though, haven't you." He regarded the ornament under Edwin's fist. "Look. I will show you my
juju." He showed Edwin his note pad. On it was a diagram of eight
crude circles in an oval roughly corresponding to the positions of those
at table, some inscribed within. "I used to do it in England. Here, they
said the society would be simpler." Edwin naturally looked first at his
own circle — which said RED, just as Austin's said WHITE. "I think you
show everybody his own juju," said Edwin. "Isn't that it?"

"How quick you are, yes. But no, not everybody." Over Edwin's
shoulder, Felix pointed, left of the Judge's circle to Madame Fracca's,
above which was inscribed: "She is only as French as her kiss." To
Edwin, he added in a whisper, "And would kiss me."

When Edwin laughed, showing strong square teeth, his somewhat
morose face brightened, more in line with its fair complexion, but
above the pug nose, the Slavic crease of his eyes lengthened.

"You have better teeth here than the English," said Krupong.

"Not as good as yours."

"Oh, we have lion's teeth, yes."

"From diet?"

"Of *Christians?*" Felix extended the old joke out of courtesy. "No, no,
those are the Yoraghum, the *real* cannibals. My tribe is Efik." Privately

he felt that most Westerners had teeth like baby crocodiles. From eating *us*. "And you, sir — are you perhaps Mongolian?"

"*Hungarian.*"

Almost frightened, Felix snapped shut the memo pad. He was careful not to see the thin red trickle beginning to come from Edwin's fist, bearing down on the china bits on the cloth. Had the Judge been confused — surely this must be the young man who had been to the wars?

The young man spoke. "I'm interested in what you have on the graph, about the Judge."

"Ah, yes, Mr. — excuse me?"

"Halecsy. Just what is — 'A member of the Egbo'?"

"The Egbo are a great secret society," said Felix in an undertone. "Were. In my grandfather's time." Yes, this young man's dissociation from himself, from his own flesh, was fearsome. Primitive. He could not bear it. "Mr. Halecsy, excuse me, sir. But you have cut your hand."

Luckily the cloth wasn't too badly stained. And the young man was full of manners about it, very Harvard after all. Anna would have his head off, he said.

Austin, disengaging himself from the bathrooms of Vienna on his left, was amused to hear the tail-end of Edwin's remark — "unless you're a *witch* doctor, too?" and the Nigerian's response, "Oh no, sir, I could not help put a head back on. I am only an *economist.*"

And Anna came, bearing the soup on a second tea-wagon which she set at the Judge's side, the dishes on the shelf beneath, and on top a huge casserole and ladle. All heads turned toward her and obediently away again. She wore a dark brown but silky dress with a deep lace collar, above a token apron which any housewife might wear on maid's-night-out, but her hair was netted, as a good servant's should be. She removed the first- and second-course dishes to the original tea-wagon and wheeled that away, without a glance at anything above table level.

"*Sehr elegant,*" said Leni airily, adding some even more foreign syllables in an aside to Pauli.

"Now, what language was the end of *that?*" said Blount.

"Polish," said Pauli meekly. "Leni has never taught me it."

"Two tea-wagons, is what I said. What a useful system, I have never seen. Did she think of it?" Like women immemorially, Leni, who had never had a servant of her own in her life, when nodding toward the kitchen lowered her voice.

"No, my wife did, as a matter of fact. She had quite a hand for such things, people used to say. The tables were already here."

"Very like what Ruth would do," said Madame. "Do you know, Simon, she is beginning to be a very good little ensemble choreographer, in a small way."

The Judge was ladling out the soup, a steaming yellow in which dumplings bobbed. "Very like Ruth?" He steadied with his left hand and poured slowly. "It is?" he added, and gave Madame the first soup.

"Ah-ha, you two know each other well," said Leni.

"Of course they do, have you forgotten — over Ruth." Pauli was consulting his exquisite watch. "They should be calling us from the airport. She said they would."

"*You* don't forget her." Leni turned to the table at large. "They write each other like — father and child."

Simon handed her plate. "Yes, we know each other, Ninon and I. Very well."

He'd given Leni three dumplings, a reward over which she exclaimed, and saw Pauli put a restraining hand on her tendoned arm, which could have used a glove. . . . It's all right, Pauli. I don't mind who knows, even the children. You be their father, tonight. *Stay upstairs*, Mirriam. I don't mind, even if *you* know. . . .

Madame was looking at the ladle, as it slowly served, Edwin stretched forward, carelessly. He'd put a butter plate over the stain on the cloth, and the scratches on his hand had dried immediately, as all cuts did with him; whatever chemical in the blood did that, his was in good supply. The wine had elated him also, giving him sway over both his reservoirs, the one above the salt, and the one below. "Was it you in the garden, Madame, before dinner?"

"Ah-ha, you caught me there, young man. Simon was talking; *you* didn't see me, Simon." . . . I heard him. When he talks, a Disraeli. No man like that stays here, like a widowed banker, he and his Anna, unless he's in hiding. . . .

She watched the Judge rise and this time go round with the wine himself. No one would mistake him for a *sommelier.*

"No, I didn't see you. But I'd have taken you for a vision anyway." He refilled Edwin's glass. "Who let you in, Ninon?".

"The door was open."

Both Blount and Pauli laughed. "That door."

"Wasn't me," said the Judge, filling Krupong's dry glass. "I haven't been out since —" The doctor that morning. "Must have been Edwin."

"Anna will have *your* head, yes?" Felix whispered to the Judge, smiling at his surprise. . . . No grandfather, only a deduction. I have not your juju. Who does? . . .

"Or a ghost maybe," said Leni. "In the garden, eh? What solos we dream of there. Eh, Ninon?"

"We have lots of ghosts," said the Judge, smiling at Ninon over Austin's glass. . . . Let them *all* watch. . . . At a sign from Pauli he passed over Leni's glass, then found Blount's still almost full, and sat down again.

"Why is good Jewish soup always so wonderfully the same?" said Blount. "All over the world."

"*Is* it the same, Dan? Heard you say you were just in Germany." For the moment, only the busy soup spoons answered the Judge, clinking from bowl to mouth, like petitioners satisfied. "No, don't answer, Dan. Let's not get into that. Though I live to hear you make a statement. And I suppose these *are* matzoh balls. Hasn't been kosher cooking on either side of the family for a hundred years, but I still know that, somehow. Curious, isn't it. And though Anna herself is Christian."

"*They* are all the same to me, yes?" said the Nigerian. Everybody laughed except Leni, who was busy stealing Pauli's fresh glass across the table, and now sipped from it defiantly.

"Are Jews all alike basically, Judge Mannix?" said Austin, almost harshly. In an allegiance which even his Jewish friends didn't always sustain, he hated to hear them say so.

"Maybe Krupong can tell you more. He's our sociologist."

"Oh no, sir, classicist."

"Really? Better still. Much better."

"Thought you were an economist," said Edwin.

"That is for America, yes," said Felix, again to laughter. "The other was for England."

"So you *are* that guy," Blount said, softly for him.

"Yes I am that poor scubby, yes." . . . And home, Grandfather —
what will I be for home? . . .

"Edwin. You've known other Jews. What do you say?"

"They were pushcart Jews. But they all have the same pride in what
they are. Even those who paid me in rotten fruit."

Austin turned to look at him. "Sounds pretty sociological to me."

"What's wrong with sociology?" said Blount.

"Sociology has no principles, that's why." The Judge held out his
hand for the empty soup plates, which were passed to him to be
slipped on the lower tray of the tea-wagon, Leni watching admiringly.
"It merely records. That's why it's always so easily and dangerously for
hire."

"Jesus," said Blount. "And I been doing it all the time!"

"Hurray!" said Mannix, chuckling. "A statement, boys, at last." He
touched a little bell he used instead of the electric buzzer Mirriam had
had installed under the carpet, too far for his foot to reach. At the same
time, he checked his watch, then softly lifted Madame's wrist, pushed
back the glove with a proprietary finger, and checked hers. The whole
table saw, as well as the way the pink-pearled wrist was held for a
moment before released.

Madame looked down at it herself. Then she touched her pointed
fingernail to his wrist. Everyone heard the intimacy, though not all
understood. "Your short cuff."

Everybody took a sip of wine, or water.

Krupong touched Austin's arm, speaking softly too, as was becoming
the mode. "But it's very simple about Jews. Every Jew is a *Jesus*, yes?
Why does everybody forget?"

But Leni, leaning into her wine-dream, spoke up loud, in her Seventy-second Street patois of salt fish, liqueurs and transatlantic perfume. "No, we Poles kill for love only, Judge. We are not for hire, are
we — *we Poles*."

Anna, by now invisible, because the inner clockwork of his house
was perfectly absorbing her in her role, brought in the meat.

"Fricassee," said the Judge, giving it a heavy German accent. "Till I
was grown I didn't realize the word was French. To me the dish is
always and above all — Sunday. If it appeared in Hades, I would
know the day." . . . And the mixed parental voices of a made marriage,
in all the terminal attractions of need. Those jointed chickens of hell,

which we somehow manage to enjoy. A family is *made*. . . . Is this why I married a woman who had no Sundays? — and am drawn always to those? . . .

As a host without hostess, even he could feel what a woman of the other sort must feel at a time like this — the perfect synchronization of her house with its own meaning. Every dinner party was an impressionistic performance, an obligatory dream entered into by both host and guest, to help keep themselves in the practicable world. Menus, from offal to ambrosia, only set the tone; he could imagine that young Nigerian, at home in Lagos or Ibadan or on the shores of a diamond-fire Lake Chad night, gathered with his own relatives and friends around a roast gazelle of meanings just as significant to them, and as hereditarily prepared. . . . One entered a dinner party as one did a chartered bus; destination: the world — that's why I never go. . . . "We must eat," he said grumpily. "So we embroider upon it. And that's society." Sending down the last plate, he smiled in apology, unnecessary, seeing no one at this point believed him except maybe Edwin, the foundling — who wouldn't know.

He didn't know whether he believed it himself, and in an extraordinary, uncalled-for happiness jolted by the wine, got up from his chair to pour more wine on this vision of gardens, of burdens lifting, after ten years' labor, from his house.

"May I —?" said Austin. Bowing, the Judge let him have the decanter of red. Standing at his place, he watched Austin go round the oval of the table. A perfect son-in-law. At once he could see it, amazed he'd never seen before what every man craved for his daisy girl — no stallion, no faun, no satyr, but a good sound horseman, both in the head and in the hands. No yes-man either — not in that stubbornly dowdy uniform. In the flesh — fine for any girl. . . . I swear I don't think of the bank side of it — any more than fathers must. Bed — can I see them there? I can prefer not to — which is all a father can do. And can admit I don't think of *Austin* at all. This room *is* honest. Mirriam, you were right. . . .

"A toast —" said the Judge, then remembered he'd already toasted Austin. . . . We're always toasting the stallion in the hallway, we who have never been to the wars. . . . In his mind's eye, Austin's white-blond head, scarcely muddied with experience, blended with those young heads mixed among dark ones or old, at that long table in the eating-club of 1916, on the eve of war. Austin had returned. Yet one saw them now everywhere on the streets in wartime, these young heads with the astral look of the already fallen. In the candleglow of aged wine-tears, the young and brave of forty years ago kept their precarious health. "No, Austin, you'll have a chance later. To make a toast. It's Pauli's turn, as the next senior member." As father-confidant pro tem — what would *he* fancy for the daisy girl? An uncle who knows the past, but never played an important role there; that's what Ruth loves him for. "Pauli — a toast!"

Pauli rose, in all his silver grace. "If Leni here wouldn't never forgive me for it, I would tell who is senior here, you or me. Look at him, Ninon! Not a wrinkle, not a change. Since the war, can you see any?"

"Only in his walk," said Ninon. "But to notice that is my business."

Down at the foot, the faithful protégé raised his bent head. There at the side of the Judge's chair was the cane which he had followed the Judge with out of the drawing-room, and not knowing what to do with, had placed there.

Leni pointed a red fingernail at the Judge. Even her nail polish didn't chip in this house; she should have come long ago and enjoyed herself, Pauli was right. "Even the suits, they must be the same too."

The black man's laugh was ahead of the rest, the first time he had sounded like a native. Leni took it all like applause, the Judge's especially.

Pauli, standing tall, looked down at her with pride — frog-princess daring to be so much more squatly natural than he. He tossed back his head, loving the house which fitted him in where he belonged. Often and often he'd told Leni how lucky they were in being accessory people, in the cast, but not at the top. In exchange, though they suffered the neuralgias of memory like everybody, the tragedy of life itself would let them escape its central core. And here in this house, they were accessory to the best. He raised his glass. "*Vive-la, vive-la.* To society!"

Usually he would have let it stop there. But he'd never before dared to let himself look ahead, past the hope of Leni's liking it here.

Now that moment was here, melting like a praeludium. She was in the circle now; she had chosen a style for herself and saw it relished; she might marry him. He grasped the wineglass between palm and thumb, the stem dangling, his pearly cuff shining like a concertmeister's, and passed it back and forth across the table between them, drawing her alto music to him. In freemasonry, he hailed host and Madame too. "To weddings!"

Around the table, he saw the three young men smile; this came out of the past somewhere, wasn't their *affaire*. At home in Seventy-second Street hung a framed notice of which he was proud: "Young Herr Chavez — who as his fellow duelists at the university have reason to know can rattle the saber like a maestro — wielded the baton like an officer." A gust of Heidelberg blew from these young men here toward him, cutting his cheek as in the old days, though theirs remained round. "*Gaudeamus!*" he said, and sat down.

Under cover of the toast, Felix whispered to Austin, "What a fine figure, yes. One would think him an emperor, if it weren't for his clothes."

Edwin saw he hadn't been chosen for confidant. Austin, the settlement house boy, took that as his dower. And maybe it was. The foot of the table has to stand alone.

"Edwin, you're drinking nothing," said the Judge. "Come, come."

"A flaw in my character." By effort, when in company he now ate so slowly he sometimes came in last. Beer he liked, and liqueurs in memory of the kümmel that had helped give him a name. Whisky he could manage, among men, though he never took it when alone. But wine was too subtle; it filched his own flesh from him and in an hour made carrion of it. Or brought out gamy flavors in it he never otherwise knew. . . . I'm the sort that *ought* to starve. Lean and hungry, that should have been my beat. . . . He lifted his glass of red — filled to the brim, what was wrong with that? — and drank it down.

"*Gaudeamus*," said the black.

Austin was humming. "Our housemaster used to make us sing for our supper with that. Dr. Brace. It's the only Latin I know."

"Shall we sing it?" said Pauli. "*Ach*, Austin, I am truly glad to see you home."

"I've no voice. But thank you, sir."

"I have," said Krupong.

Pauli knocked his knife against a glass and lifted it, up, *down*. They sang charmingly together: "*post iucundum, senectutem*," Felix's dark bass vibrating low at the close, drawing out the long *nos habebit hu-u-mus*, the older man's precise reed coming out clear and young. *Let us rejoice, for we shall soon be underground.*

"Hola!" said Leni. "But the end means something nasty, that I know."

"Oh, I am not sure it must, yes," said Felix. "Translated freely — 'we shall inherit the earth.'" He smiled at Blount. "We meek."

"You going back to Africa?" said Blount.

"Next year, it has been offered me to stay in Cambridge. A post there. Or in London. But my whole schooling has been government-sponsored, you know, by my home country. So I owe it to them, yes, to return there?" Deferentially, he made it a question, but let everyone see the proud tendon in the neck, the glare of the eye.

"I envy you," said Edwin. "Going back where you belong."

There was a pause — the forks at rest, the song, the wine-dream pierced. At the bottom of civilization always this cannibal debris. Austin turned in his chair, full to Edwin. Under his focus, Edwin, at the foot, seemed more isolated than before. "I find that an unnecessary remark."

"Oh no, Austin." The Judge sighed. "You Harvard boys, always misunderstanding one another. He means *he* can't go back. Didn't you Edwin."

. . . So, you humiliate me. By being personal. Not for *me* the courtesy of being left unexplained. . . . "Some people are more comfortable in their skins than others." Edwin's bow to Krupong made clear who he meant. "Maybe to see that requires having had early discomfort in one's own."

"Very graceful," said the Judge, with a quizzical look. . . . Wonder if Austin recognizes the origin of my protégé's style. . . . "And now allow me to give everybody some more. Though I warn you, there'll be a kind of savory — an English custom my father-in-law's family brought when they came. My wife kept it on."

"Just a little of that oyster plant with the nutmeg. Oh God, that is good," said Leni. "And to be greedy."

"You *cook?*" said Ninon.

"Of course not." Leni drew herself up. "That's for the married."

The Judge burst out laughing. They all did — any pretext. "There should be more women at this table," he said.

Now the salad, a great bowl, was wheeled in, to Austin's shamed relief. He'd never before lost social control here — or, anywhere. It's the war, they would think. . . . I wish it were. This table is too small for private silences to go unnoticed for long. . . . According to his grandfather's pamphlet, silence was a loud contributor in the parable. *Table Talk, Tête-à-Tête, Inner Monologue.* But for a moment the talk did disperse. Through the gloom of shame — was he a prig? — he heard only bits of it. Trouble with Fennos, they didn't know how to question themselves.

"*Salade panachée,*" said Madame. . . . And a mixed bag, this table. What's more, a table still with a wife. How sharp would one have to be, Simon, to gnaw you free? . . .

"How glittery your accent is," said the Judge.

"Don't you have to be English, to be a Dame?" said Blount.

"You are — journalist?" Madame, waiting for his answer, drew the feather boa from the back of her chair, posed it round her neck, and when answered, spoke over it, raising her eyes as one would for a flashbulb. "I am — English enough."

"But that is true of everybody in England, yes," said Felix. "Here, I am told, each man is a social phenomenon, all by himself."

"Oh, we're not a young country any more," said the Judge. "My private opinion is, Felix, that except for the few huntsmen at the very beginning — we never were." This was part of an after-dinner speech. In a lifetime, a man found himself only a few strong opinions and insights. If these in turn found the same words every time he voiced them, it was too late to feel insincere.

Under the table, Ninon's ankle warmed him, delicately but unmistakably, as from some *ancien régime* of love.

"Ow, Simon, you were never an émigré." No one was fonder of his adopted country than Pauli — who would have been happy anywhere.

"Tchah!" said Madame. "People at the top are the same everywhere."

"Tchah," said the Judge agreeably. "What a politician's wife *you* would make!" Nothing made one feel more foolish than footie under the table. But it was years since he had felt so political, that old Jack-Horner-pie feel of the table, with all the strings held.

Across the table, Leni smiled at Madame. And Madame smiled back.

"But *I* would be a stock character here surely, yes," Felix said quietly.

"Oh in this country now aren't we all?" said the Judge. "It's mass culture, the news services tell us — those old individualists. Edwin here says that for younger people the whole notion of a person with a fixed character is obsolete. Isn't it, Edwin?"

No answer.

"The current of the times," said Blount. "Isn't that what I always said?"

"Is it, Dan?" said the host. "*Answer* yourself."

"Well then . . . yes." Blount grinned. "Simon, you like to hand *me* my character, all right, all right. May I have some more of that salad? Field lettuce — how nice of Anna to remember."

"Are you too warm, ladies?" Pauli said anxiously. "Would you like a cigarette?" He never liked to see either courtesy, weather, food, or any other basic of life neglected for ideas.

"Beware a man whose life has been very contemporary," said the Judge. "Nobody's dead quicker when he dies." Edwin was smiled at. "To quote a judge."

To Blount, his host looked flushed, as a judge who'd had to quit his way well might. Shooting a wife was contemporary enough, in its time, Blount thought — down where he kept his private thinking, in the tiniest print. "But when a man's lively enough at it, won't he become history? Look at Pepys for that matter. I carry a Pepys with me everywhere." He lowered his eyes modestly. "Not many people know that about me." Only those he didn't tell, or who didn't read.

The Judge groaned. "History. The eternal excuse of the journalist. Here's your salad."

"Yet it is true, isn't it, Mr. Blount?" Felix said mischievously. "One wouldn't read Juvenal for the same reasons one reads Lucretius."

"Let those guys read me," said Blount. "I'm a contemporary."

"I read you," said Edwin.

"Y'do. Wudga read me on?"

" 'Hot Pursuit on the Yalu.' Only yesterday. In the *Trib*."

"Oh, you did, eh?" Well, if they didn't go to war, they at least read about it. "Ask me about the Koreans, I'll be declarative enough. If they have a character, sure isn't flowing *our* way. Just like the Japs were. A monkey puzzle inside."

Austin looked up from his reverie.

"See," Krupong whispered very low, only for him. "I would be an *idea* here too." Aloud, he said, "I am too *white* for this country, yes."

The pause was general. "How so?" said the host.

"To this noble household — I am noble too. Everything savage and good." He shook his head. His smile had too much gleam. "Too white for me. But to the rest of the country, what am I likely to be? Black *ivory!* Too white, too."

All the men laughed. Into that Leni whispered clearly, "Pauli says it's bad taste to talk a person's color here." The laughter doubled. As Anna brought in the next course, everybody was pleased. Between simple personal wit and the spice of foreign dangers, the room was filling with clouds of pseudo family feeling — the safest kind. And the waistband of the evening spread, could be relaxed. Through curtains down here parted over window boxes, a glancing light came and the city shuffle of feet.

"Grouse!" said Blount. "My God, what's her source of supply? The Black Forest?"

"I'm afraid, me," said Pauli. "And the Maryland Market. But only domestic game hen. I brought them for Ruth, who loves them. And Diddy too." Or at least they once had, in the time of dollhouses. "But too much, with the chicken. Anna changed menus, because of two extra. I told her not to cook my birds, but she did anyway. I am sorry to think we made a *crise* in the kitchen."

In the immemorial way, the two women looked pleased, as Simon saw. Another's household should never be perfect. . . . I'm subtle enough with women who are game-tame enough to allow it. Mirriam, you may *remain*. To watch. . . . "We'll never know," said the Judge, toying with the little brown bird. "We must never. You know Anna." At the same time, he disengaged his foot, for the moment. Though the muscle doctor might be glad to hear of certain therapies. "Pauli — just go round again with the wine, would you?"

"Are we going to get drunk?" said Blount. "I thought Jews never did."

The Judge saw Austin raise his head again. . . . Ah, our young protector, shall *I* speak to *you?* So that daughters may be understood between us? . . . "Oh — for you Christians, we Jews are always such repositories of moral force, aren't we? While you have the weaknesses we crave. To sin fashionably. Alcohol. Sex. But we're always too serious in the end to be chic, aren't we? Just, as in fashion, our ladies are too lavish."

Blount was attacking his bird, the only person to do so. "May I quote that?"

"Not in Germany. They already know." The Judge smiled at Madame — for the loss of his foot. "Not here either, in case I should ever go back into politics. I was never Jewishly safe there." He tossed his head, tired of being safe. Thank God. "But don't make Jesuses of us again, as I saw — heard — Mr. Krupong suggest," he said slyly. "I'm afraid we do that best ourselves." Wine made him possessive. Even his lipreading powers seemed to increase. . . . I become as hungry after young minds as old homos are for young cherubs. Am I so sure Austin as son-in-law would share a dialogue, as young Fenno, David's friend, never would? What is it we'd share? . . . He stole a look at his watch — where were those young three? "A penny for your thoughts, Austin?"

"Yes, they're overdue," said Austin. "I mean — the flight." He saw Pauli twitch a collusive smile at him. . . . What does *he* know, this "uncle" who knows Ruth? Not a man here I could tell about Kim Yong Mai — except Blount, to whom one tells merely everything. Back there in the coarseness of war, everyone knew. How tiring civilization is to us, on our return. "Now that could be ponderful." . . . "Sir? — I guess I was thinking of my grandfather." . . . Who has left me the wherewithal for a flat in Covent Garden — for my reasonable sins. . . .

"Oh yes, I saw the death notice, some months ago." . . . And the probate, later. "Not a contemporary man, I gather." The host smiled.

"He left you some money, I saw," said Dan, pushing back the bones of his bird. "Modern enough, in the end."

Everyone looked with distaste — at the bird.

"He was the one who was in my country, yes?" said Felix.

"No, that was my father."

"As a missionary?"

Austin considered. The panorama of the Fennos spread before him, a pleated fan. A family for jokes. Comfort overwhelmed him; *Aussie, everything will turn out all right.* "Only in a large way," Austin said.

Dinner had shrunk Felix's laugh, but it was still loud. "Capital, oh capital!" He clapped Austin on the shoulder. The two grinned at each other like equals, and shook hands.

"Excuse me, Simon," said Pauli, "but I am always foolish nervous about flying. Leni here always says it is because I was only in the cavalry." He was kneading his conductor's knuckles around a note he made them all hear. "I go and phone the airport, hah?" He was shivering. Ruth was unlucky. He'd always been convinced of it.

"Of course," said her father. "Telephone on the landing." He turned back to the company, spreading his hands. "Who has the children, here?"

Madame's voice was soft. "Only you, Simon."

Why should Leni, who had none, look daggers at her?

"Cavalry?" said the Judge, as Pauli left the room. "I never knew."

"*Leutnant*, Owstrian Army, 1918," said Leni. "He would get a pension, if we was not here." . . . Of *course* he never said. We fought against *you*. . . .

"Year I was turned down," said the Judge enviously. "Shameful. How we never get over not having gone. Against all conviction." The weather and the city came back for a moment in the clatter of heels on the level above their heads; this was a basement after all. He found he was praying to the air, to be careful of his children. . . . Oh air, lanes of air, where will I take this woman — with your kind permission — tonight? The air, heavy with wine too, held them all fast. . . . Mirriam, *stand by*. . . . He was just about to say anything — to Dan, to whom one could — when Austin spoke.

Austin's hands were clasped between his knees, his chair pushed away from the table; both were unlike him. He had a somber little smile on his face, a contradiction also brought into being since the Mannix household had last seen him. "I have a little sister who wants to be Jewish," he said.

Leni gave a parrot cry.

In silence already spelled by the phone on the landing, everyone waited to hear what the Judge would say.

"Does she now." His voice shook with tenderness. Could he say it? He dared. " 'We have a little sister, and she hath no breasts.' " Only a Jew could say it that way. "The Song of Solomon." He leaned forward carefully. "Maybe she'll marry into it. Some of you are lucky for us. You yourself have the look of a man who brings luck with him everywhere." . . . *Mirriam, attend these banns.* . . . "Even here. And some of us, maybe, are good for you."

Pauli was back, beaming. "They have docked, I mean, what is it — parked. *Ach Gott,* I mean — landed. They had a delay, somebody sick on the plane. No, none of ours. I asked."

"What name?" Blount.

"Name. *Aie,* yes. Freund. Friend."

Blount shook his head.

"None of ours," said Felix pertly, like the prep school boy he some-times knew he was.

Elation was all right now — safe. The Judge stole a look at Ninon, who had come to help him give up his daughter at last. Did she know? She was staring at Austin. He'd never seen her bemused before. It parted her lips and widened her eyes, making her younger, though the shadow-cleft between them deepened like a shaft from her hair-jewel. "You . . . are positively — " She reached out and flicked the young man on the back of his hand. Her finger released a blush that aureoled him, all blond and red in his battle-cheap indigo. " — a type!" she said.

"Well, Austin, well." Not for this house, did she mean? The host's color was high also, two dark spots under the linenfold upper lids, on the cheekbones. "This is an honest room, eh. And Ruth is home."

The two of them eyed each other.

"Anything *bad* —" said Leni, the slits in her dress quivering like gills — "one would have heard."

The Judge touched the bell in front of him. "We'll have coffee in the — ingle." He leaned sardonically on a word inherited with the house, though he liked the large, sofa-enclosed bay. "They'll be a while yet." He made no effort to move. Hopefully no one noticed that for the duration of these spasms, he couldn't. The tall-backed Mendes chair, so much too big for him, now supported him. "One more glass of wine, everybody? Mr. Krupong, will you do the honors? Glad to see you like wine."

"Good as this, yes sir. People are very wrong about this country, yes."

"Well, you're always welcome here, in this house — may I say 'Felix'?" It was over. Release from any setback (which was what pain *was*) always made him mischievous afterwards, arrogant in the face of the force behind things. This was when he had been in best command of his wife. When he had been "Si." "Incidentally, Felix — you don't have to worry about being 'an idea' here. We Jews feel guilty to *people,* not to ideas."

"Why . . . yes sir, thank you sir." The young man's long, powerful jaw came forward; the brows knitted. How foreign he was, *yes.* "B-but — how did you hear me say that?"

"How?" The Judge's eyes were half closed. "Maybe I belong to the same secret society as your grandfather."

"The same," said the Nigerian. "The *very* same." He half rose from his chair, smiling, but in the sheepish way he looked down at himself — suit bought on King's Parade, long white cuffs on his marble-dark wrists — the struggle going on between cloth and skin was apparent as a child's. "I said it to myself when I first walked in, yes. *Woo-oo yes,* I know him." He sat down again, twitching on and off the smile.

"Just a trick, Felix. You'll understand it, if you meet my son."

"Oh —!" said Austin. . . . All these years, and I didn't know. Mannix can lipread. But how unfair! Would one of *us* do that? . . .

"Do you belong to that society yourself, Felix?" said Simon.

Felix had regained himself. "Grandfather sent me to Cambridge instead."

"Ha. Well, you must call *me* Simon. To avoid confusion." The Judge took a long draught of wine and set down his glass with the firmness of a man who says to himself, to the company, "The last." Hope you do come, often. We like intelligent young men here. But mind — *we're* not noble, eh? We're very middle-class, here."

. . . Simon, Simon. Not with me at the foot. . . .

"Aren't we — Austin?" said the Judge.

Once before at this table Austin had been chivied like this, long ago. They could use a bit of Fenno hard-mindedness, now and then, his pet Jews. "The middle class avoids definition, Judge Mannix," he said. "That's what a middle class *is.*"

Felix said very softly, "Hear *this.*"

"The *hell* you say," Edwin said, standing up, staggering back against his chair.

And it was true; he saw it in their aghast faces — they'd forgotten him as if he were the ghost at this table. Though his flesh was solid with what he had learned here. The flesh of the disciple is solid with what it has learned — or else it is carrion. All down the table, the tops of the wineglasses gazed at him unwinking, monocles screwed into the red eye of anti-Christ — though he had never seen a monocle in his life. . . . I swim *toward* these people — up, up from the dirt floor to the wicked debris of dinner, up through the wine — to the top. Father Dialogue is who you find there — at the top of the wine, his locked, Mongolian face.

The face confronted him. "Edwin."

Down in the cunning depths of his own reservoir, he saw — with a savagery reared by icons who wept when carried into warmer rooms — that he was still honesty, to them here.

"I" Felix started to rise. When the Westerns quarreled among themselves, he felt infinitely more aged than his grandfather, and with the wrong education. "If you will excuse me. I feel your beautiful wine after all. I will go for a walk around the square, yes." Often in Cambridge he'd done the same.

"Of course, we all need some air. Austin, would you open another window in the bay. We'll all move over there in a minute." The host stood up. Everybody rose in the sweet, tranced lull that came with these social directions. . . . Politics is quickness before anything, Edwin; act in the rush of *other* peoples' blood. And give the men you know least the auxiliary jobs. . . . "But first I've an announcement to make. And a toast of my own."

Leni leaned out from under Pauli's restraining wing. "A wedding! I knew it. I have heart."

"Yours, Leni?" said Madame.

The old one in green drew back as if two pieces of ice had been dropped in those icebags, her breasts; cool the head, those would. "Fill my glass, Austin," Edwin said. "Aus-s-tin, fill my glass." All was wine-mist and glide up there at the far head of the table, but he could stand up to it. The arm he pushed forward extended like a cue at pool. " 'Member the day I ate the ice cream from the serving bowl?"

"The day you came?" said the Judge. "*Edwin.* No. No, you can't drink to this one. My toast is to *you.*"

Turning heads, they all saw him. The table was small enough, big enough — middle-sized. He saw it contract, expand, a heart, a bladder, or a surface plant seen from the water bottoms below. . . . Will I be a filth to you? . . . "I am being *personal*," he said.

The Judge lifted his own glass high. "A fine maiden speech. . . . To anarchy, then! . . . And a summer on the ward!"

"On the ward . . . ? You are sick, Simon?"

Anna had come in, just as Pauli spoke.

"No, it's a phrase, Mr. Chavez," said Edwin. "Used by us politicians."

"Never felt better in my life." Over his glass, the Judge glanced at Ninon. That's the way declarations should be, at our age. In cliché. And the rest of it — under the table. All down his festive board he could see life beating, for the old ones at least, being passed back and forth like money under the table. . . . Pauli, you're too aboveboard — never get Leni to marry you that way. Sweep them off their feet vulgarly, downstairs, in front of a curio cabinet belonging to their father. Or upstairs, and let who will watch. Yes, nod at me, Ninon, I see that brooch of yours already sparkling, in the bedclothes. "So . . . you've made your decision, boy. A toast, then . . . To Edwin Halecsy. A learner. . . . And now — an announcement." Picking up reactions round the circle of faces, he thought he saw Austin's stiffen. So the boy was human enough to be jealous of Edwin's place in his own affections. . . . Never mind, boy — I'll have you both in the house yet. . . . "To Edwin. Who's kindly promised to come and be my — political secretary. Who will be one of us truly now. Who has promised to come and live here."

Had he? He had only time enough to think it.

From behind them all a dish crashed to the floor. All faces turned. Luckily, the dish had been a clean one. Anna faced them quietly for a moment, as if she was being introduced; then she bent to pick up the white spears of china. They saw Edwin spring forward to help. The two heads almost met — blond snub-face, heavy blond-gray. Then they all saw the snarl from the lace-collared head, the boy's recoil — that shocking slum kinship, two animals over a garbage pail. The boy, standing up slowly, nodded at her, as if to say — our kind of friendship. Bending over had made him sway. He flaunted a weak smile at all — yes, I'm that drunk — and turned back to Anna. "Will I be a filth to *you?*"

Crouched, she picked up a last shard, arose heavily, and turned her back on him. No, she was turning again — one mute look at her master. Her heavy face struggled to communicate what it had trained itself not to — and lost. She left the room, wheeling out the tea-wagon.

"Edwin, you need air. Mr. Krupong — Felix. Take him with you. Go straight out that way, the basement door. . . . And now, let's leave the table."

Awkwardly, chairs were pushed away, the guests straying against one another with the regretful feel of parts of a pattern which, in spite of all, had pleased. They disposed themselves in other chairs, looking round the new niche warily — would this pattern be as good? — in the thought that the evening wasn't over yet; there would be more.

Outside the dining-room door, Edwin stopped, looking back, though he couldn't see those in the ingle. Now the high-backed chairs in their flowered black covers were empty again, as he preferred them to be, holding immanent the absent family that owned them — out somewhere on its beautiful visits, powerful in its absence, sure to return. A cane leaned against the head chair. He turned his back on it.

At the basement door, which as in all these houses led out into the areaway below the front stoop, Krupong said, "Is there a toilet down here?" Edwin pointed down the lower hall and waited, but shook his head when the black man, returning, offered to wait for him.

"No." He shook himself again, like a swimmer. "That's Anna's bathroom." He steadied himself. "Let's go." At the door, he leaned a finger on Felix's lapel. "Krupong —?"

"Yes?" The face above seemed very patient. Brotherly.

"What's my juju?"

When Krupong's teeth showed, the effect was lost.

"Anna knows," Edwin said.

"Does she, now." Krupong couldn't place this secretary — what a fascinating house!

"She knows how I'm going to pay him," said Edwin suddenly.

"How?"

Oh nigger, how smart you are! To say *How?* at once. Not — *Who?* . . .

"In rotten fruit."

"Watch it," said Krupong, opening the door for him. "When you hit the open air."

Back in the ingle, over coffee, the others heard the door slam. "Funny," said the Judge. "Only wine does it to him."

"A matter of breeding." Even in the squashy seats, sighing with inches of down, which Mirriam had placed here, Ninon sat straight as in her box at rehearsals.

"Well now, Ninon, be careful. All he has, he got here."

"You think so?" She shrugged. "What marvelous chairs." She let herself sigh, and before their eyes made her own outlines melt and soften. . . . Watch, Pauli. Yes, admire. Leni, poor jointed Leni who can't any more, remember how this is done. . . . "Wherever did you get them, Simon? I shall fall asleep." She already knew the answer. Why he wanted her to ask these things wasn't her concern. Men were always wanting one to pull at the thorns other women left in them, and one did it, a whore's job too.

"We used to sit here a great deal, in Mirriam's time. She got them. Mirriam. My wife."

They all had a moment's general silence in which to recall, as happened at such dinners, that they were not really a very close company.

"Austin, do me a favor. Get me that bottle from the sideboard."

Austin carried it over reverently. "I've never had it, sir."

. . . Bit of a prig, sirring, aren't you. But you'll call me Simon in the end. . . . "In praise of several occasions," said the Judge, and checked his watch. He settled back. Now that those other two had left, the rest had the relaxed look of nationals left to themselves — all except Austin, too young a Fenno yet to admit that a black man or a slum-born one were different from him. Even a black man whose grandfather heard everything.

"Well now, Austin," said the Judge. "Tell us about the war."

On the instant, he knew his mistake. In their faces, he caught it. He wasn't of their breed, or wouldn't have asked that spectator's question. They'd all been to the wars in one way or another, even Leni. He was the foreigner here.

Blount came to his rescue. "No, I will." His job excused it. "Bet none of you know the term 'hot pursuit' isn't just a newspaper head." He culled a murmur of assent from the Judge, blank looks from the two women, the proper silence from Austin.

But Pauli stood up, fondling the glass of yellow liqueur against his cheek, over the saber cut his mother had always been so proud of. "I do, why, of course." Journalists who hung around opera houses in hope of "notices" to write were his whole experience of Blount's trade. He had the European indifference to it, vaguely connecting it with Paris and women like Nana — whom he thought real. "In the academy, we learned it. When we studied that old von . . . who was it, the adviser of Bismarck? 'Jawohl, meine Herr'n,' the teacher used to say. 'Kindly remember "hot pursuit" has nothing to do with the study of love.'" The cuff around the dandy wrist he pointed at Blount shone like all the linen one couldn't get any more. "Your State Department, it keeps asking the allies for permission to go across the river, but it won't get it, am I right?" He sipped from his glass without emphasis; such wines were his due. "Excuse me." His smile was deferent. "My State Department too."

"Von . . . was it a von . . . who was that man . . . ?" said Blount. "No — they won't. I was with the Eighth in North Korea in January, when it was driven out of there."

"Ahh . . . you were *with*." Paul interpolated a sip. "Pyongyang. Once I was near there."

"With the *army?*"

"*Ach,* no, no. After my home service. Long before we came here, eh, Leni?" The women, in adjacent chairs, were deep in their own talk. "With an opera troupe. We got stranded." God knows we did, I and the woman. She was worth following out there, a whole troupe in herself.

"But you've *been* there." Blount turned to them all. "Yanggu, I want to go. The Communist capital. A Peiping broadcast to solicit guns for them came through yesterday. Through Reuters, Hongkong. Everything's open enough." He turned back to Pauli. "You've *been* there. Tell me now . . ."

Under cover of an exchange in which Blount, once again happily moving the world about in question ("North bank of the Hwachon reservoir . . . ? Hyon-Inye road cut . . . ?"), was in return being given a tour of the Chinese provinces via *L'Elisir d'Amore*, Austin — who'd been near enough the main defense triangle three weeks ago — heard himself addressed by the Judge.

" 'Scratch any Austrian,' my father used to say, 'and underneath the waltzes, you'll find war.'"

"Scratch any refugee, too."

He'd never seen the Judge flinch, before.

"Ah yes, the ultimate medal. To have been — with."

"I only meant — my father. His line of work."

He weighed that, scanning Austin's face as if it couldn't see him do it. What children those two might have. . . . "You'll follow your father's line, when the war's over?"

"I hope." The face bent over its uniform, raised eyes very slightly widened — allowing itself to be scanned. "In London, I hope. I have a — promise."

"Ah. London. . . . Austin — would you do me a favor?"

"Sir?"

"When Ruth and that crew come, take care of her for the evening?

Air travel excites. I know them — they'll never want to go to bed. Ruth and I — we'll talk tomorrow." He allowed himself a glance in Ninon's direction. "I want to talk to Madame first." . . . Was there scorn in the boy's face? No, this boy wouldn't allow himself . . . bright . . .

"I may have — competition."

"Eh?"

"Everyone's fond of Ruth."

"But the boys have just seen her, eh? David, Walter."

Austin said nothing. He was good at it, the family always said.

The Judge's lips opened . . . but closed in time. . . . No. He's like a son to me. Edwin. *No.* He'll never — dare. He comes here for *me.* And I . . . why . . . I'm *leaving.*

Judge Mannix's face hardened. "We may all meet in London yet, Austin. All of us. Say nothing yet. But I may be leaving this house of mine."

"Do my best." Opposite Austin, for one second the eyes seemed to be pleading, an intenser variation of his father's. . . . I'm old; I may be evil. Get to me in time, Austin. I wouldn't wish to disappoint you. Get to me in time. . . .

When they turned back to the others, Leni was saying, "Hot pursuit — and not love?" She shrugged happily. "What could that be? You never told us."

Austin spoke ahead of Blount. "Military term. Von Clausewitz." He bowed at Leni, smiling at a point above her head. "The brief pursuit of an enemy, to finish him off."

"War." Leni gave it the proper, chapfallen stare, then tossed her head. "Half the time, I never know who the enemy is."

"I *al*ways know," said Madame.

Unlike as the two women were, and in spite of their words, they smiled a rare smile at each other. Like women always, like cats bringing prey in to master, they had frivolously brought in the aspect of eternity, useless anywhere to daily living, and now left it there, on the hearth.

There came upon the dinner party a longer silence. Leaning forward, they communed with themselves — and took their rising warmth for intellect.

Leni, in that heaven of possibility which was her present, felt her lingerie, silken on her haunches. Beauty was her topic. She no longer felt awed here. Each one of her gaucheries had been successes; she was dimly conscious of arranging them — the nigger, the bidet — like a girl her baubles. One of her sets of eyelashes dragged on the cheekbone like a bird-wing. Sitting there, she saw deeply into her own perfume, a woman who was loved.

Austin's rivalry was engaging all his mind. As a Fenno, he was thinking practically, not of his feelings but of his rivals. In Edwin, he saw a fellow who could never take on more antagonists than two, himself and another. Edwin had to have an answer to his status here. A low answer was what the Edwins would expect. Yet, in Austin's own line of work, oughtn't he to know how it felt — to *feel* status? As for the Judge — since a boy, Austin had viewed the Judge with question; now he could let irony fall for sure, like a headsman the black cloth. The Judge, a man who bled toward holy things perhaps more than Fennos could, was not yet by any means eating with God. . . . He himself could sit stock-still in his chair now, clasping his good glass with a look almost of middle age, as if he had text already sewn on him: Waiting for Ruth. He waited for her like a rival.

Pauli, proud of Leni, proud of the Judge, "breathing away" in so far as life had let him teach it to, offered Blount a cigar.

Blount took it "for later." Clearheadedly was the only way for the wasp to buzz, politically continuous round the world. Dinner tonight is *here*. He made a digestive sound, fondling questions-to-come like lances. Even a buffoon knew his effect was to remind each person of what the person was privately in pursuit of. Sufficient unto the day, the news. *That* was his answer.

The Judge was telling himself what he always did whenever talk of war entered his house seditious as gun smoke, further clouding the citizen-guilt of houses. Civilization is *here*.

Ninon was hardest for the silence to crack. Finally she got up and walked about, stiletto heels held back in tribute, as an animal retracts its claws. Though the dress she wore was a clinging one, her waist dipped with each step as if it peacocked a crinoline. But her head bore its own rhythm like any other woman, Victorianly away from the cigars. . . . I've never been *home* with a lover. Never known love-terror, nor the terror-lack of love. Follow no love; love follows. Dip to the cigars, but avoid the smoke. Always know the enemy in time.

And Leni, the specialist, leaning forward into her own heliotrope, said with dreamy, sure emphasis: "I remember very well your wife, Judge Mannix. Much more beauty than all these pictures. Even at a restaurant party — such presence. We all met once together. Remember. Before she . . . was killed."

A lesion opened, not in their quiet — in the silence of the house.

. . . That's the feel of it, at that word, like something you see, marsh gas or summer lightning, but think you hear. The house, opening its years like a wound, gives to each the echo he is prepared to hear. . . .

So she was *killed*. So *he* killed her. *Who?* The husband? The lover? A hireling?

Who? . . . Yes, which was I? . . .

Which? All the same under the tsetse fly — accidents are all the same. . . .

Where? . . . So this is you at home, Disraeli. . . .

What . . . did you see, my dollhouse doll? Breathe it away! . . .

How . . . may I serve you, my sister, my rival in suffering? . . .

Why? . . . So that you might kill yourself, Mirriam — and still stand by. . . .

Sometimes the years of a house opened to no listener but a passerby or the wind, or a mercury-blot of light gilding an attic window shade. Or to that great legatee of houses, the inheriting dust. Or some houses were left wisely early. But this house, in the old-fashioned way, was dining with its retinue.

Before pictures could fall from walls, or echoes cease, Austin Fenno, in the cold, cordial voice of a son-in-law who learns too quickly what is expected of him, began to tell them about the war.

"Down there is the Cen-tral Park, yes? Let us walk there."

"I never go there. OK."

Strangers here, they listened to the ring of their own steps and said nothing, the city an intermediary which didn't need to move to stay with them. Now that it was summer, the streets were wetted and softer, the exudate of some long, listless dragon who lay just beyond.

Edwin's head was clearing, but he let Krupong lead the way. Few were on the streets. At those who were Krupong nodded approvingly. Under his breath he was chanting or humming, in a nasal language that might be any. When they reached the Fifth Avenue corner, he stopped. "Has a constant shimmer, this city."

Across the way, the line of young or stunted trees was abloom with mist, as if with apple or oleander. Nothing was on their branches. Edwin knew his city, full of other evasive seasons, any time of year. Tonight had fallen from first expectation, but this was the fault of his monologue, not the city's. He had always kept them separate. "Don't they all?"

"The ones by the sea. Naples. Constantinople."

Behind them as they crossed, the great, protected avenue looked as usual, glittering idly on in its own repose. He'd never thought of this city as a living organism before. That idea belonged to *them*. The city was an arena to be coped with, and not to starve in. That other was the romance of the rich. Deep behind the sternum an examining army doctor had identified as the barrel chest of early hunger, he let out a laugh.

"Eh?"

"I was thinking that the *poor* never say what *they* are." Down there he'd never once heard the word itself. They spoke of it between the wishes. "I'd like to cover this dirt floor, some day. With linoleum." Those dumb wishes, which sometimes couldn't *let* themselves be satisfied — his mother, unless commanded, still wore her old coat. He hadn't yet dared dispose of it, as the aunts had advised.

"So . . . but the rich hide their condition too. Look there." Krupong pointed back at the eastern side of the avenue, at a set of shrouded windows, hoarding their inner light. "He's not letting you see what paintings he's got, man."

"Right. It's only the middle who're always telling you what they are." His head was clearer, but the wine was still in his shoulders.

Krupong laughed. "That young warrior. Clever, what he said."

"Austin? Pacifist." One had to be fair, even if classified for home by a healed TB spot one never'd known one had.

"Fight like the devil, some of those do."

"Quaker family."

"Woo-oo, yes? I rowed with an English one of those. Curious people. Very objective about Africa." Krupong faced the park. "I would like to go in — it is permitted?"

"Supposed to be full of knives. But in New York, you'll find the sinister street is always just beyond the one where you are." Or the golden one. It took a foreigner to make one feel ownership here. He followed Krupong in.

After a twisting of byways he hoped his companion would know

how to return through, they stood facing the great south wall of buildings that bordered the park. Above that pride of light, the sky was
smeared to white, as if foghorns had just left off sounding. The buildings shifted continuously, as stars did in the tear of the eye. "But it is
humming too!" Felix said.

It was, the whole spectacle. It always had. "In winter, the lights
snap — like twigs." He looked about him mazedly. He felt his ambition inside him, a cautious song.

Once, after a street fight, Felix had seen a man raise his head and
speak like that, enlightened from within, "Dark people, you are." His
chuckle faded. What an empty place, really; among these millions,
this sad forest — of twigs. "People . . ." He raised a hand, as if to
decree them.

"You don't like us?"

This Halecsy was a plug-ugly when in wine. Or when emerging from
it. The brain, clearing, shadowboxed its own violence; Felix had seen it
many a time; he was not afraid. "Cities . . ." he said falsely; leaving
London had been a wrench. But no, he didn't like this New York —
producing its own phenomenon higher and higher, while the classics
tumbled their warnings. A city so young should have more ambiguity,
so that men might be heartened as to what they could still become. A
city of any age should at least go veiled, under knowledge of its own
sores. The snapping of souls was what this young man was hearing
maybe. *Et mentem mortalia.* There was nothing like a bit of Vergil to
light up the modern sky. "You are feeling better," he said.

"Tell me what you think, though."

"What a catechism! You study to be a priest?" He could see him, a
papal secretary — to that judge.

"The law."

"Ah, to be a judge. Well — in that case — " Felix paused, turning to
go. "Well then — does *everybody* here have the city on his back?"

They stayed on, silent for some minutes, then turned to go.

Edwin trotted after him. "You've such an excellent sense of direction,
one would think you'd been here forever. Is it from —"

"Africa? No. London."

"What's that you were singing? On the way."

" 'Now it was the custom,' " Felix began buoyantly, meanwhile continuing their pace, " 'of the sul*tan* Harun-al-Ra*shid* to go sometimes
during the night with his vi*zier*, through the *city* in dis*guise*, in order to

discover whether everything was quiet' — you remember? From *The Arabian Nights*." Felix's chanting died away. It had been English after all.

They had reached the park entrance. Ahead up the long blocks was the house they were bound for — veiled.

And Fifth Avenue had waited for them. Its traffic tranced by, and would forever, waiting for new observers to be born to it, against all the rural poets of the mind. "Look up there, man." Felix pointed to a line of second-story windows. Diaphanous curtains fell with the closed radiance of waterfalls. Behind these, shadows moved sublimely, with the confidence that shadows always had. Felix scooped a handful of gravel from the path. "There, that window! Shall I? And when he opens up, I'll halloo at him. 'Ahoy, there! What paintings do you have?' "

"You would, wouldn't you. You'd even knock at the front door."

Eheu, how nasty! And how explain himself to this weird collegiate with his white canvas shoes, and those spectacles, and bung-all kind of drunk behind them? What Harvard words would there be, to tell him? That when one's been made to travel fast enough cross-world, with the iron key of Latin around the neck, proud as any Jew, on the snowshoes of poets, over the camel humps of time — such an émigré isn't to be dazzled by a little savagery that stops short at the skin. . . . We have racks and pyres still in our psyche — just behind my granddad's hut, Mr. Halecsy — that could extricate you red as a mullet, dripping at all pulses, from your silvery skin. *Language is my juju!* The English, a colonial people, understand that, and gave it me at once. . . .

"Ah, Mr. Halecsy, remember Harun?" His tongue began of itself in the Arabic, then changed gait. "Remember? They knock at the door of a house*hold*, he and his *vizier*, and are admitted, by *Zobeide*. And *she* says to them —' "

"Does she." Under a streetlamp, strange as a moon in its own cloud, Edwin's glasses were still raised to those windows. Mist condensed on one lens and ran down it like a crack. The eye didn't blink. Suddenly Felix's companion relaxed, fell into a mock crouch, shuffled his feet and sparred at him, with a mock fist. "OK, Harun. I'm not drunk any more."

"Good, Mr. Halecsy." He felt the social pleasure he often had had, escorting home safe some companion whose rickety Norman frame couldn't hold the Merrydown cider like his own. Look at him now, smooth as a clerk, wiping his glasses. "Maybe by now, Mr. Halecsy, the three will be home."

A bus groaned by before he was answered. "Call me Edwin, chappie. Your vizier was a doorkey child."

The traffic signal changed. They stepped off the curb. Felix often asked what a phrase meant, even if he knew. At times one ceded that to them, like a handicap. But not now. Under the signal light he saw the pink sow-glare of the face, for one second intent.

"Righto," he said carefully, as they reached the other curb. He cast a look over his shoulder, whistled. Every man here carried the city on his back. But this man, how dangerous it was for him! How dangerous a man *is*, grandson, who lacks pride.

Going down the side street, he gave a humble, conciliating laugh. "Edwin."

"Hmmm." Grunted. Hands in pockets.

"I know too many languages now. Going home in August, I'll be bloody scared. We always are."

"Don't give me that stuff. We're always the same. As we started."

They covered the next block in double time.

"You rowed, Krupong, Blount said."

"Yes."

"David Mannix — at college he rowed."

"Ah, the son."

"He's deaf." A pause. "But he can lipread up a storm."

"Beg pardon?"

"Lipreading. He's a whiz at it. And so is his father."

"*Ah*." After a moment, Felix said, "A joke on *me* it was, then. How very friendly of you. To tell me." . . . And a hyena to who else, comrade? . . .

At the last corner he said, "Interesting, those houses here. Rather British."

"The old Ralston houses. Are they."

"Well — here we are." . . . And I'm not sorry. . . .

"Here we are." Edwin hesitated. "Wait here a minute, will you?" He gave Felix another buffet with his fist, coaxing, almost shy. . . . Why, how charming he was when elated, or sober! The face good-featured again, conventional as dozens here, the snub nose only merry, the eyes extra laughing because of their slant. When he was brash it flickered all over him, like his intelligence.

"Be my juju," Edwin said, walking backward while smiling at him. "Don't go till I come." He waved, and disappeared around the back of the house.

Mr. Krupong gazed up at the entrance, so warmly lit for welcome. A long window box, carefully crammed with green, had been set out on the stoop. This house must give many the feeling that only they were specially bound for it. Yet when its owner said, "Come again," he'd felt trapped. Nothing happened there except in those granular scenes one was taught to call society — in which each and everybody merely grew the heavier in what he already was. Yet he felt drawn to it, as animals sometimes were drawn to cages. It was such a civilized house, fatally attractive to so recent a citizen of the open air.

Krupong gave a short laugh, and stepped farther back to regard it. A temple of the hidden? He could scarcely believe what Blount had told him. Like so many temples, it might have nothing within except what one saw — a tinkle of cymbals, or the brass prayers of the English. Yet he couldn't help himself — who could, with temples? He would come again — back.

He looked to the right and left, down the street. Such an open city. And this house — veiled? *And Zobeide said, "You are welcome. But while you have eyes, have no tongues; you must not ask the reason of anything you may see, nor speak of anything that does not concern you, lest you hear and see what will by no means please you."*

Looking up at that façade, he declaimed the succeeding passages, as if the house were waiting for him to inscribe them there.

In the garden behind the house, Edwin checked the rear windows, dark all the way up from the study, then urinated. The water tower's light had gone out at twelve. He was where he belonged. Now and then in his swift little pilgrimages here, some late pigeon walked the wall, and he always watched it, savoring the breeze naked on his cold boyhood; he would never be fifteen again.

He tiptoed round to the front. "Talking to yourself? What language d'ya use?"

Krupong wheeled, saw him. "Arguing . . . No, I really do not believe it. Not even on the best authority."

"Believe what?" He saw Felix hesitate.

"Blount said it was common knowledge."

"If *he* said it, then it is. About what?"

"Your patron."

"My —" Well, it was what would be said. And true enough. And I'm sober now. . . . "You should hear what they say about him at Harvard." He said it proudly. "He's made himself a national character, just by retiring."

"That is how it would be — yes." Felix's head bobbed and shone effervescently. No gesture could rob it of dignity.

The night was clearing after all, for a major visit, with everybody home. Pity he hadn't seen earlier that a spade like this, of whom there were certainly none in *his* Cambridge, could be a natural friend. "One guy said — he'd become a virtuoso of the public honor." Edwin underwrote this with a laugh.

"Ha. I know it well. That kind."

"From England?"

"No."

Edwin moved slightly nearer, hands in pockets, head bent. Felix remained in the same attitude. The same spot on the pavement engaged them both.

"Is your grandfather . . . really like him?"

"Profoundly."

Both faces raised at the same time. On each was the same wistful expression.

"Why do you think we are scared *not* to go home!" Felix let roll his laugh. His long dark hand, gleaming at the cuff, advanced oratorically, but his voice lowered. "That's why I could never believe . . . there must be some other . . ." He looked up again at the façade of the house. "My grandfather would kill his wife too, yes. If it became necessary. Just as that foolish Blount said . . . Then he would retire and mourn her. Publicly. Yes . . . But he would never let *her* take the blame."

He took a look at his companion. The "Yes?" ever on his lips froze there. That yellow color the Westerns lapsed to when the bile hit them, how could it be preferred to decent ash-gray? "It is the air," he said hopefully. "When it hits you, warm like this. And the bile. Makes one drunk all over again."

Often it had been the same in England too. Drag one of this kind home to vomit, get him past landlady or porter, show him what black respect to wine and wine-friendship could be — and maybe even as you held his head you would see it in the sudden tension in the cat-bones, the ice pit in the eye — that down in the marrow of him he was still master of it, if not of you, that he couldn't get drunk at all.

He wasn't sure of this one, though, until the curses came, in a dialect which though it must be English, Felix could scarcely follow, the words steady on, in matched pairs as in Beowulf, repeated and reversed, as if the man was filing his teeth on them.

Then he was inordinately pleased — at the hand extended.

"Oh, Felix. Shake. Grandfathers or not — you're my friend."

"And you are *not* drunk?"

His strange secretary-friend walked ahead of him, stiff-legged, down the steps to the basement door. At the door, Edwin spread his fist on it like a man who was going to live there. "No, I've swum through the wine. To the top."

The door was opened from within. The girl who stood there had the light behind her, giving her the vague, graceful outline of any young figure in the soft white stuff of a summer night, and an aureole of hair in which the face remained dark.

"Ruth."

In the light cast from the lamp on the stoop above, their faces must be clear to her.

"Excuse me." How polite Halecsy's voice was. "This is my friend Felix — er —"

"Krupong," said Felix, disliking his own clarified voice. Play with his name was so often a put-down, whether or not the Westerns understood so.

"Alias Harun. He and I've been out taking a look."

No, this was only a young man trying it on with a girl, in that light, undergraduate way in which this kind could snap back.

"Welcome." Her voice was matter-of-fact. She stepped forward politely to let him inspect her, rather than the reverse. Gravely, she allowed it. He got the shock he always did, meeting what so few were capable of here. Sensitivized in spite of himself, he could tell it before these rare ones opened their mouths. Not always good people, or gentle. A navvy could have it; it came of how people saw themselves. She didn't see him as black. What she saw him as, he couldn't say.

"Welcome to the Mannix house," the girl said.

Letting him precede her in, she wavered back against Edwin. "Wait . . ." She turned back to Krupong. "Tell my father . . ." She hesitated, her head hung like a culprit's; she offered herself for inspection. "Tell him — not to wait up."

She and Edwin were off, before he had time to answer. Either an assignation, or she'd maneuvered them both. Krupong hesitated a moment to look up at the sky, which was clearing, drawing back toward the zenith cool. In it the stars shivered at him, the last friends here as everywhere. He waited until they'd murmured their Latin to him. Then he went into the house, carefully closing the door.

Austin, by no fault of his own, had been telling the others what they wanted to hear. Short as home leave had been, he'd learned that the civilian had far truer instinct for war's horrors than the men who were engaged in them — his own conclusions had only come to him once he was home. "War is hell" was a soldier's generalization. The home front required more specific for the bad dreams it already had. When it wasn't forgetting altogether, its conscience was far busier, more objective than anyone under fire had time for, asking after the worst details like any sheltered wife at eventide — for connection's sake. Home could take horror, if adventure came with it. What it had no time for was the dullness of life under siege.

". . . but I shouldn't. Dinner party, after all." He'd been brought up to a reserve which declined to speak of these realities at dinner. He could have bawled now, at all the passion and wretchedness a man could experience, only to find himself stuck again like a sprig of ego, in the old society, back here. Had his father gone through that, a maverick too? Outside, at intervals, a car motor inhaled, exhaled, then sped off with an expiatory sigh. "Hospitals. They're the happiest. Even the wounded children's. Those above all. Everybody's trying of course — that's why. Every hospital out there — beautiful. In spirit. In spite of all the ghastly. . . leftovers. Or because." He smiled at them. "Every damn hospital's a pantheon of peace, of the ideal of it. Maybe because it's the only place *where*." His voice cut, but he could still hear that fatherly one. . . . Aussie, you were born to it, to be with us. If only the London branch could see you now. You were born to tell others what they want to hear. . . .

"Dinner parties. Through all that. Maybe we shouldn't be having them."

"Oh Simon, what soppiness." Madame, stretching with a dancer's extension, was no longer a small woman. Her tiny bodice, a moment ago lace and brilliants, now proffered real breasts. "Or is it this class thing, always worrying you because you're not supposed to have them — you're all so self-conscious here. True, you've never been bombed." Her arms paused on the air, like wings. "During *our* war — that was the only class thing going — were you there, with the bombs? Those were the aristocrats." Surely they could all hear it in her laugh, as Simon did — that Cockney *eow*. She grinned. "Except for the children. We sent those away — so we could give dinner pa-owties. And what ones we gave. Remember, Simon? You were at one of them."

"I remember. In that basement theatre near the Underground. We all brought gifts."

"Of food." A faint, wicked crinkle of her mouthlines, long droop of lids, reminded him of their first night together — and made sure the others saw. "You brought a lemon, remember. The only one in London."

"Left over from our luggage. On the boat." He was embarrassed, as then, at the eternal role of the American, scatheless, bearing gifts.

Madame Fracca got up from the chair into which moments ago she had melted so demonstratively, strode halfway to the dining-table they had left, turned her back to it, and confronted them. She was still a dinner guest somewhere, but by the thinnest line — an aura around her own attitude, perhaps only muscular — she had put distance between them and her. She was onstage. He'd seen her do this in the studio, explaining a movement to a group of girls. "After the performance. Couldn't use the green room, there'd been a direct hit the week before. Some of the music hall people who owned the place trooped us down to a cellar it has, next door to Waterloo, deep down." She drew the ingle down with her. "Basement light." She said it like a command. "Brown. One always knows it. Twelve by fourteen room, and there were thirty of us. Stacked high with song sheets the place was, too. Somebody said it was against the fire laws, all that paper; he'd have to bring a complaint, he was a warden; that broke everybody up." Over the stage she dispersed them, her ring finger imperious. "Rupert was doing an adagio, with a ham his mother'd sent him." Walking steadily nearer them, she decreed it, and a laden table too. "And whoever had folk in the country. There was even Devonshire cream. Best food any of us had had since Dorset. And we were all from the theatre. No audience, except him." She pointed to Simon. "He'd gone back to the hotel, when he saw what we had. On foot, because Jerry was at it again overhead. He had to take his chances, just like us." She made a wreath of one arm and drew it inward. "Rupert'd put a tutu on the ham, and he was just holding it up in one hand, arabesque, finale." Her tiara sparkled as her arm rose, bearing a weight. "And in walks Simon, like an Erl-king from abovestairs — with his lemon."

"Had a bottle of bourbon, that's why."

She gave him the white glance for interruptions — in all his attendance at rehearsals he'd only seen it needed once, on a governmental visitor — meanwhile holding the illusion, choreographing it steadily in the core of her hand. "But it was the lemon we couldn't take our eyes from. Everybody gathered round it — like that old ensemble in your *Cavalleria*, Pauli — and everybody had a touch of it." Stepping softly, or seeming to, she circled it round them, and they saw it, doubtful only of whether they too ought to reach out and touch. "And remember what Rupert said? 'Saw an onion not a month ago, down at me mother's. But a *lemon*. It's Spain, girls, Tangier. Shall we all 'ave a suck, since we can't 'ave a pudding?' And one of the girls said —" the hush wasn't in Madame's voice but in her limbs — " 'If it were an onion,' she said, 'we could cut it up and all 'ave a good cry!' "

Smiling now, the ballerina's correct smile, Madame again passed the lemon around for all to see, hot, gold and oval under the brown, ruined light of war. Using an intricately weaving combination he ought to know — pas seul? — she made each of them see it, and supremity of art, that it was an illusion. She deposited it in Pauli's lap, where it lay for a moment. Then, with a flourish of the hand, all was over — Madame's "demonstration." Clasping her hands, she raised her eyes to a curtain she made sweep behind her, pressed her hands back against its billowing — and bowed.

Simon was the first to clap, then everybody at once, even Leni, who cried, heavily moving a foot, "That — from *Giselle!*"

"*Wunderbar.* Fracca, you could dance even now. I am ready to believe it."

"You were always ready, Pauli. To believe."

How dared she whisper that, forward from the waist, arrogant as a diva, with Leni looking on? If Madame didn't take lovers from the theatre, Pauli must have been an exception. Or to her mind, an amateur. "Ninon's a directress," said the Judge to Leni. "She can make us believe anything."

"Oh yes, Simon? Even that I am *not* Madame?"

"*I'm* audience."

Leni made a sepulchral sound. "We are all audience now — at our age." Didn't she know best of any of them what theatre was? "Now it's time to go home."

Pauli whispered to her, looking at his watch.

"Oh, you were never just audience to us, Simon." Ninon stood in front of him. "You brought your daughter to our war, which made all the difference. We never asked why. But once — she told us."

"Told you. What could she have told you." Stiff-lipped, he couldn't make it a question. Women were the daring ones. While their men went to work or to war, they rose, like slaves freed of all except themselves, and lit the revolutionary fuse in the drawing-room. Waiting for Ninon's answer, he heard another, long ago. (*It's the honorarium you men let us have, Si. For being what we are.*)

"She said . . . 'My father couldn't come without me.'" Ninon shrugged. "She didn't say why. But our Ruth always speaks the truth, have you noticed?" She sat herself down between Austin and the half-dozing Blount, and cupped the younger man's chin in her palm. "*Here's* an audience. What year were *you* born in?"

He couldn't laugh. Her touch penetrated, agelessly a woman's. "Nineteen twenty-seven . . . Tell us more. About Ruth."

She turned away from him to Simon. "Later."

He might be going to hear, maybe years too late, the inner tale of his daughter; would Ninon be bearing it to him? But he should never have brought them *all* here together. People carried revelation with them for years, like germs; it only needed a presence, and a cough.

"Of *course* she speaks truly, our Ruth," said Pauli. "Look who her father is!"

Blount, the observer, was now asleep. The rest gave each other little smiles at the sight, drawn closer by it as people are.

"No," said the Judge, "that was her mother's bent. Mine cannot — compare." His eyes watered — like some murderer's, returning after years of useless safety to place a late rose, so that all might know.

"So often you speak of her tonight, your dear wife. Is it a special occasion?" said Madame.

The Judge's hand gave a small jerk; it wanted its stick. There, at the table's edge, so far — who had placed it there? "One of a sort. Pauli . . . I'm going to let Ruth go. On tour."

"There," said Pauli. He took Leni's hand like a pledge. "Did I not *tell* you how things are managed in this house?"

Leni gave him an enigmatic shrug — she was not to be managed — and leaned over Blount as if he were the last recoverable man. "Shall I wake him?"

"No." From Pauli's gleam of teeth, he'd understood more of Blount's yearning for Pyongyang than thought. "As my mother used to say at the end of a season, 'He has been too many places at once.'"

"On tour with you, Madame?" Austin, as always even under the influence of emotion, was determined to bring something concrete from it.

"I don't go on tour, Mr. Austin. Only the young ones." She took up the boa lying on a chair and drew it across his knees, to her own. "The *second* company."

"Yes, that's what we are, of course," he said.

"On the way to being the first, Austin, I assure you," said Simon. "As for the tour, I haven't told Ruth yet, Ninon, so let's not —"

"I never talk about the young behind their backs."

"Hoping we won't talk about you?" said Austin.

"My God." Madame gave a stare for the manner which could carry this off so politely. "He gives us lessons, eh."

"*In vino veritas.*" Austin nodded at Pauli. "That's the other Latin I know."

"What does that mean, Pauli?"

"In wine, truth — Leni. Best at weddings."

She snorted. "*That* language."

Austin got up and stood by the window, in which the curtains were moving slowly back and forth over the window boxes.

The Judge's eyes followed him. "Yes, Austin?"

"Diddy speaks the truth also. David."

After a minute, the Judge said, "I'm glad you're my son's friend. So you still call him by his childhood name for himself — came out of his deafness, you know. Does he speak of me?"

Austin turned round, confronting him. He drew a long breath, "No." Just then he thought he heard the shuffle of feet in the areaway and made a quick move to look out over Anna's window boxes, but instead stumbled from the countering pain in his hip, of which not even his family had been allowed to make mention. He forced his hand back from it, to hang at his side.

"Austin. *Austin.* No wonder you knew so much about — *You've been wounded.*"

Even Blount woke at the Judge's cry. It was almost a cry of joy, of annexing joy.

Austin gave the classic answer, smiling it up at Pauli, the military expert, by the light of whose toe-caps troops could have been deployed. "It was nothing."

"Wounded? Where?" said Blount.

"On the map? Or on me?"

This time no one could laugh. The women's nostrils opened to the scent. The poppy of war was nearer — near.

"Nothing serious." Exactly what he'd told his family, in the reverent hush round his return. They'd finally sicked his little sister on him, to use her direct angel-honesty to find out. She hadn't. He would *not* have his body made public; that was what it amounted to. He'd seen men do that, letting it be dragged out of them by the nearest civilian. Oh, he'd learned so much that might forever devil him — about men and feeling.

"Ah, here's Anna. Wonderful dinner, Anna."

Everybody made an assenting murmur. Anna, apron removed now to show the long string of huge amber ovals given her by the Judge's sisters in their disposition of his wife's effects, took the plaudits gravely, standing in front of the swing-door to the pantry. "Leni, Ninon, this is our Anna. Anna, this is Miss Petersh and Madame Fracca." Anna's netted head, nodding to Ninon's coronet and Leni's earrings, had a queen's dowdiness. She handed the Judge a slip of paper. "For Misser Stern, a call to call this number. I go off now, so I give you."

"Oh, Walter. We'll give it to him. And good night Anna, don't you stay up now. Sleep well."

A strange adjunct to a housekeeper's good night, as the two women were perhaps thinking. The male habitués of the house were used to it, Austin taking it as part of the Mannix warmth, along with the way Anna was looking at him — like any friend of his mother's, who had watched him grow and had always favored him. He gave her his hand. "Anna. Good to be home."

"Misser Owstin! Oh, Misser Owstin."

"Mr. Austin's been in hospital, Anna," said the Judge. "But he says he's all right now."

"Yah, I know."

"You know?" said the Judge. "How?"

"Your Lutie," she said shyly to Austin. "We go same meat market."

Her face assumed the same holiness Lutie gave to her shibboleths of health. "Drink lots water. So near the kidney, you got to take care."

Mannix gave a choked guffaw. "The gulls have their lanes." He couldn't seem to stop laughing until he blanked his face with a handkerchief. Above the white folds, his eyes were merry, or derisive, or only very sane. "See, Austin? We even eat the very same meat."

"I guess." Another bond, that he might sometime tell his father. Lutie must have come upon the leather brace he'd been told he might begin to discard. He could still keep to himself the pin in his hip. "If we'd had you and Lutie out there, Anna, things would have gone faster."

Nobody believed this, least of all Anna. "Yah? And what would your mother do without her?"

Everybody smiled speciously at this terrible clarity — especially the two women, long accustomed to hear men patronize their own feminisms in the same way. Anna picked up a vase from its pedestal and turned to go.

"Indeed!" her master called after her as she departed. "And what about *me*."

"Graz!" Leni got up from her chair to walk about. She halted, center stage. Forty years late, her figure, nullified to grace, held all the middle-aged negatives which made for power. The neck strengthened by a rear hump, could move forward only. The skeleton, once tortured to suppleness, now had the strong pout of permanence. Under that authoritatively ugly dress her body suggested a new, heavier nymph in stone, monument to all the more important reveries of flesh. Beside her, Fracca, reclining with pointed chin on palm, lissom arm still gloved, was an annihilated girl, grace too sharply preserved. "We know about military hospitals, la, la, Pauli and I. Didn't we meet in one?" She inserted herself between Pauli and Austin. "Our troupe came to entertain the officers, in the hospital at Graz. We were — what you might say — quarantined there."

"I was not wounded." Pauli might have been snapping to attention. "Only by her."

Blount, with a large stretch, began picking all his own pockets — ready to make off. Leni, with a night-owl shrug, grasped Pauli's arm, then Austin's. "La, la, what we didn't do with you, the nurses did!" Dividing her smile between the two of them, she slid her hand down

Austin's niggardly uniform, over the bare, unmedaled pocket flap, to his waist. "A man can do all right, eh, when only wounded in back." She squeezed him to her. Memory exuded from her like sweat, like sex. "No ballerinas, a nurse will do very well, eh. Legs like sticks, those Chinese girls. Pauli has pictures of the opera one . . . he wanted to bring her back with him but she turn him down . . ."

"Leni! I better take her —" Pauli was ready to give up even his worry, his Ruth.

Austin had been congratulating himself on the discovery that life at the root was never vulgar. Now Leni's heavy arm pinioned him under another: No one was really vulgar who *knew* that this was so.

"In the echelons of *our* race, Austin—" I met *my* father-in-law, Meyer Mendes; is that what I really want to say? . . . "I've sometimes met *your* father. At a dinner only recently. We talked. He understands a good deal." About *us*, the Judge was about to say, meaning to set forth how hopefully well Warren Fenno understood the conventional usages of the Jews. The quizzical smile on his face was for what Fenno wouldn't understand (which perhaps Warren's bright son one day would tell him). How a Jew could become competitive even about failure. And could blame his race in the bargain, just like any Quaker or communicant of St. Thomas's, for whatever he himself was.

"About me?" said Austin.

"We always speak of you."

"Oh?" About Korea, then. He could imagine his father worriedly seeking a Jew's opinion about *race*. Austin rallied against that knowing smile — among Dr. Brace's boys he'd been the best broken runner of his year. "In the hospital, I met someone who knew *you*, Judge Mannix. Said he'd met me here as a boy. I didn't remember, myself. Afterwards, he didn't want to talk about it."

"Oh?" The Judge's mind was still on the elder Fenno, one of those fascinatingly dull do-gooders whose perceptions had been enlarged not through thought but by their own acts. "Your father understands about other races in the oddest way. Out of politeness, I think. For which he would die, of course. Not for the other — combatant."

"Other? Father's never been much in Asia." Austin, finally released from under Leni's arm, wanted to make amends for her, to Pauli's silver discomfort. And through her, old unstoppered vial that she was, to Kim Yong Mai. "Come to think of it, most of my mother's friends have legs like sticks." Then he blushed. . . . *I* sound vulgar, when I only meant to be fair. . . .

"What race *is* a Jew usually talking about? Especially when he's talking to a Christian. But your father brought up a very subtle fact about us — that we're not really an urban people but a desert one. Even warlike, only that circumstances. . . . Excuse me, did you say military hospital? Where you met this boy?"

"While I was an aide," Austin said. "Not a patient. I was the medical aide at his — operation. Somebody addressed me by name, when he was just coming to. He said it over and over, the way they sometimes do. Later, over the dressings, he asked about you."

"Dressings," said Pauli. "Ah, God, I remember the smell." He glanced all down his own perfumed tailoring, as if he understood it better. "I used to know all the boys who came to this house. What was his name?"

"No smell," said Austin. "Aren't given time. The antibiotics." He scanned the dimple from the saber-cut in Pauli's left cheek. "Did see his name on the register — he never gave it to me." He rubbed his temple. "But he wasn't a boy, Mr. Chavez. He was a middle-aged man. An officer. Regular army, I'm pretty sure."

"Tom Somers?" said the Judge. "He was at the Point when he was young. But no, I got stamps from Manila from him yesterday."

"Don't think this guy was ever at the Point."

"Some old politico on the lam, maybe. War's often providential, for some of them. He didn't want to be known?"

"Got the impression, from something he said, that he knew — Anna."

"Anna?" When the foot trod thin ice, the foot knew first. In the same way the sensation of drowning was known to the lifelong inhabitants of dry land. "Why Anna?" And why should Austin duck his head in the prep school nod of years ago, of all David's friends met on the stairs — that half-flinch, half-ogle which said with green-blazer irony, "Is *this* the great man?"

"He'd had a bad time. Almost the worst a man can have. I attended him for a week, when he was coming out of it. Every morning, until he did, he'd say it. 'Is Mannix the champ she always said?' "

. . . So for that man too, far out there on his raft of war, *her* eyes had never really closed. . . .

He didn't feel tired any more, that was the sensation of it. . . . I should have had them here all together before, but how was I to know? . . . "Not — Anna," said the Judge.

He couldn't say more, going from face to face. Ninon, if she guessed, wouldn't say. Blount had clicked his tongue, but by principle could not declare.

"Who could it be?" said Pauli. "She had so *many* friends. Mirriam."

"But her letters —" said the Judge — "they were all to me."

Austin had already turned to Leni. "I thought he was Czech. Anna's Czech, isn't she? Now I remember. It was a name more like yours."

"Like mine?" Leni, warmly forward, drank this like compliment. "Like Petersh?"

"Something like. With a P. Not a month ago. How could I have forgotten it?" Austin rapped his chin with a clenched fist.

"He didn't want you to remember it," said the Judge.

"He was a big, blondish-gray man with good features, blue eyes, a good nose. At least he gave the impression he'd been a big man . . . before. The face wasn't touched . . . Surely you must remember him. Someone must. He used to come here."

"Yes," the Judge said. "I remember him."

"Like mine?" said Leni. "*Pauli . . .*"

"I knew you would." Austin gave him that junior nod again.

"Did you. And what did you tell him?"

"He *had* asked me that question about you." His own severity surprised him, the same irritable paternity with which Warren had sometimes spoken to *his* father — James. "And naturally, I —"

"You said I still was." The compression of the Judge's lips was both mean and proud — the sort a man adopted to say he could be modest, but wouldn't. "The champ."

He was rewarded. In Austin's eyes a flicker he'd never before been able to make rise there. But there it was and for the future they both knew it. *You Jew.*

He turned to Ninon. "*She* always said that . . . Yes, I knew the man. Though I never really knew his name." Now surely — barring what Ninon might tell him of Ruth — he had told everything.

Just then, there was a noise from outside in the areaway. Over the window boxes, the filmy curtains were flung aside. Two heads ap-

peared there, golliwog, over the ruff of foliage. David, his lean body
jackknifed, shoulder to shoulder with Walter, whose hump wasn't visible. Without it, under a Raphael-thatch even touched with gray, his
face was still a boy's, too heavily lined with kindness. David had his
ear-box off and was smiling, as in those snapshots which showed him
between oars at the boathouse on the Charles — an irregular-faced tall
Apollo, surely from a long line of the same.

"My God, what an entrance," said Ninon. "Only the young!"

Now that she'd pointed it out, yes, this was youth's way of dealing
with the borders between the gypsy and the tented. This way of looking in a window, like a young old-clothes-crier, new to the trade, not
really wanting what would be sold inside.

David Meyer Mendes Mannix smiled straight in at his little father.
Electric-green in the blend of streetlamp and house, the plants in the
window box between them bobbed artificial, rubberized by the light.

The Judge stood up, bringing himself eye level with his son. . . .
Over the balustrade of night, who looks at me from the bush of long
ago — a rose of Sharon bush, and a home-walking boy betting with
the dime in his pocket? Is this one from the boy-bush of myself. Is he?
He is so near. . . .

"Give up!" David said, in the voice that was "placed," but never
deafly loud. "I heard every single word you all said."

This was from the family humor-book, one of the first jokes in it,
derived from their earliest morning lessons, where sometimes the
happy, deaf child had repeated conversations (sight-read from a father
unaware of it) of the night before.

"We did." Walter's voice always astounded, rich marvel from that
cave of papier-mâché, his chest. David lending him a hand, they
stepped up on the outer sill, legged it over the window boxes, and
stood there smiling, inside. If compensations like this — length of leg
against hump, voices for ears — had crossed their friendship as boys,
now as men, even the emotions roused in the spectator by the incongruous pair were by habit forgotten by the two themselves. Only, like
any such devoted pre-manhood relationship between men now grown,
unsuspect as it was otherwise, it had kept them boys.

"Hallo, Diddy, Walter," said Blount, whom youth always awakened.
"You're late."

"Came in one of your grand pianos, Dan," said David. "That's why.
How can you stand them? Too much opera for me." But his face was

serious. "Hallo, Dad." He nodded at his father. They hadn't shaken hands since David — aged ten and already taller — had dropped the custom. Traveling the circle of known people, his eyes blinked shyly by Ninon, paused at Leni — "I don't think we've met —" and stopped. "Austin. Dear God. *Austin.*"

"David." "The Judge's accusing voice was the same he always mustered for his son. "Where is —" He couldn't finish.

Pauli could, darting forward, the buffer. "Ruth, where is she — my God, they said an accident but that everything —"

"Yes." David couldn't know that his stiff, ever-patient speech, giving every word the same weight, made the anxiety intolerable. "She left separately. Why? Isn't she here?"

"Separately?" In Pauli's clasped hands foreboding was already being hoarded. "In another plane? From London?"

"She's left then." The Judge had turned to Ninon. Another woman, this was all it took. "For good. I always knew she would."

Walter stepped forward, between David and his father — and took the Judge's hand. He could do that; he was of a properly hunched size. "No, everything's all right. She just left the airport here, separately." His great eyes were happy, in that sight of love demonstrated which he always found here. "There was an accident, just before we landed. To a guy who'd been sitting with us. She went to the hospital in the ambulance with him. Diddy and I followed, but our cab got tangled in traffic. And when we got there, the hospital wouldn't let us all see him. Poor guy, he'd seemed to — take to her." He smiled, for how reasonable this was. "But any moment, she should be here."

"Take to her?" Her father's voice was coarse. "What was his trouble?"

"Simon. You know that with her, everybody —" In relief, Pauli spread his nervous hands, took out a cigarette. David lit it for him with a lighter, though David himself didn't smoke.

Austin, stepping back to allow the members of the family all precedence, recalled how David, as a boy ever being taught to tame his excessive gesturing down to the normal, had as a man become a picker-up of hats and coats left behind, a caretaker of packages, an offerer of pencils, an opener of doors. Whereas Ruth, without any effort to be the explicitly quiet one — He drew in his breath. No reason to think of her as having had to make effort to appear other than she was. She had no flaw.

"Guy'd been sitting next to her. Drunk, was all we thought. Meek little drunk. Anyway, when he went to the men's room, Walter and I made her shift to the window. When he came back —"

"It was a mess," said Walter. "We thought he was just going to vomit. He was holding himself." He reddened.

"At the crotch," said David. "In a muffler. I was ready to hit him. I got up to."

"Pushing me out of the way, as usual," said Walter.

"Then he simply — said something to her. And fell forward."

"Putting out his wrists." Walter stared at his own, hairy and large as a true-grown man's. His hump sat on him. "Which he had cut."

"Ah, God, the poor darling." Pauli couldn't avoid a downward look along his pure tailoring.

"Poor *man*," said the Judge.

"Yes, of course, Simon of course," said Pauli.

"He bled all over my sister," David said. Queer to say it that way, to her father, but the deaf's choice of words sometimes was. "She didn't turn a hair."

Austin stepped forward. Coming home was a continuous stepping forward and back a dozen times a day, across the enormous ditch — of difference. Though he wouldn't mention hospitals again. "Women. Often they don't."

At his voice, wistful with that distance, the two young men were upon him, in flurry of shoulders pounded, hands clasped, which the two old men smiled on uncertainly.

"Watch out for him, boys, he has a wound of honor," said Pauli.

"Nothing," said Austin, on a cold note which his friends seemed to recognize. And at once fell in with. "Nothing, Austin," said their faces. "If *you* say."

Pauli coughed uneasily. "Maybe she stopped by at Augusta's. In the old days at Ilonka's — you know that school, Ninon? — she kept a change of clothes there. Because it was so near."

"Augusta's?" said the Judge. "At going on one in the morning? Why would she ever want to go there?"

David, watching everyone with a ceaseless annotation of the head, spoke up gently. At times the box on his ear communicated voice before meaning. Always it had a special voice for Simon, its first teacher, tonight even gentler than before. "For *Augusta*," his son said.

"What children you have," said Madame, engaging Diddy to come talk to her.

Walter was meanwhile smiling up at Austin with the surety of a seraph whose values, useless in this world, might be all-powerful in the next. "You've changed. But you're still the same."

"Meaning?"

"The war."

"I've come back."

"But you've — been."

"In the end —" Austin watched Blount draw the Judge aside, make a swift adieu with a sign not to disturb the others, and slip out into the hallway with him. " — I think of *my* father. Who went. In the end does it make any difference?"

"You're the same, or will be," said Walter. "But maybe, not for a while. Not just now."

"I've been feeling — maybe I'm going to be the maverick Fenno."

They both laughed.

"Or do you mean . . . I'm not one of you any longer?"

"Yes and no."

"Oracle."

They were both watching the door.

"*Where can she be, can she be?*" The whisper — blind, fierce, Austin's — surprised them both.

Walter sighed. "You're getting to be as bad as David. Always worrying about her, never any reason why. 'Sisters,' is all he'll say. And of course I have no sisters, so how I am to —" He glanced up sharply. "But you —"

"Three." As light broke on Walter's face, Austin couldn't help letting it creep sheepishly over his. His father no longer seemed to him precipitate.

"Austin. Austin. Of course. *Of course.* You and she. Forgive me — if I never thought of it before. You know me, I'm not geared —" Walter's grasp of his limits was firm. "One of us, indeed." His tone was holy.

"Of *them*, you mean. You'll be one of them."

"Hush, Walter." As of old, he spoke as to a child. And listened for the wisdom not of this world. "Haven't even seen her for more than a year."

Walter, to his dismay, didn't dispute him, or reassure. Often, by the way that heavily beautiful head hung toward its sage little vest,

Walter's friends kept track of the simple clouds which could pass over his sunniness. In their boyhoods, that head, dropping so tiredly under spectator pressure, had often seemed to yearn altogether for the body's smaller scale. Now, bent as it was, quizzically regarding very much the same vested body — it belonged more to its hump. "We've grown up," said Walter to his vest. "I've got gray in my hair." He grinned up at Austin with the glee of one years ago warned that he wouldn't survive his youth.

"So you have."

"You'll do what's right, Austin. Whatever you do."

"Ha. Aren't you confusing me with David?"

"Oh — I can hero-worship you all. And with reason." Walter's very frankness laid his love lightly on them. "I should have known. You're usually ahead of us, Harvard on in. But this time . . . Lean down closer."

Austin did so.

"David's not far behind you. He's got a girl."

"Who?"

"Alice Cooperman."

"I — don't know her."

"No. Since you left. And — you wouldn't. He'll tell you. There's a difficulty."

"With the girl?"

"Not — exactly. Not yet. But she's proud."

"Is there *always* a difficulty? I'm beginning to feel . . ."

From Walter's face, *he*, Austin, should not be asking that. "Not always."

"What, then?"

"She's lovely, brother. A glass fairy. Spun glass, delicate. Brave, too."

"But doesn't love Diddy."

"But does."

"Not — religion. Cooperman."

"No. And neither too rich nor too poor. Nor from the dime store. Nothing in the world is *wrong* with her, except —" Walter couldn't be fierce but he could be sad. "Except what Ruth says — that it was bound to happen. And some people can't take *that*, she said."

"I don't get you."

"She's deaf. Alice. Talks beautifully, almost as well as Diddy. But far worse off, once. She was a mute."

They saw the Judge re-enter and come toward them.

"Hush," said Walter.

"Ah," Austin said.

The Judge handed Walter a slip of paper. "Anna took the call, a while back . . . What's the matter, boy?"

"My uncle. He — excuse me. I've got to phone."

"On the landing." Austin said it as if he had been here yesterday. "Remember."

"His Uncle Samstag?" said the Judge. "I suppose."

On the way out, Walter was halted at the stairs by Leni, who must have been sitting all this time in posed meditation. Now she half rose, arms outstretched with a peculiar cajoling, a stage beggar, asking alms. As the Judge and Austin watched, she reached out and tugged the hem of Walter's jacket.

"What's the matter with the woman?" the Judge said, sotto voce. Pauli, engaged with Diddy in the ingle, hadn't seen. "She a little mad?"

"I've seen it happen to him before," said Austin. "With — a certain class of people."

As they watched, fascinated, Walter bowed his head, allowed her to rub his hump, then went up the stairs.

"Perfect Balkan logic, Simon," said Madame at their elbows. "It's done for luck."

Leni was bearing toward them, carrying her fist holily. "What a house, eh, Ninon? Pauli was right. I should have let him bring me years ago." She turned to their host. "You wait," she said, in reciprocation. "I'll remember everything yet. But first, I go upstairs."

"If you want a — retiring-room, Madame Petersh," said the Judge, "there's one down here. Anna's. Perfectly clean. Down the hall. Through there."

"Not Madame." Leni cast a sly look at Ninon. "Miss." She went off, still carrying her luck.

"Didn't want her up there after him," said the Judge.

"Pity," said Ninon. "All she wanted was another go at the bidet . . . And now hadn't I better get on back to the hotel, Simon . . ."

"No." He was kneading her hands between his. "This is an *eve-*

ning . . . This house used to stay up till dawn, many a time. And we're all so bright; look at us!" He let go her hands. "Soon as Walter — I'm going to phone Augusta. Or the place where they took that confounded man . . . Austin? What's the name of that hospital?"

Austin, seated to rest the wound which tired so quickly out of its brace, was watching them dreamily. "U.S. Military Base Hospital Number One, Area —"

"No, I mean where they took that man from the airport. Excuse me, Austin. Still think of all you young ones as together." The Judge took this chance to rest a hand on Austin's shoulder. "No, don't get up."

Walter came down the stairs and went at once to his friend. "Diddy . . . My uncle. I have to go."

The box on David's ear *brred* like a stammer. "*Utah?*"

"He never made it there. Happened here."

"I'll go with you."

"Thanks. Please."

Without a word of death spoken, death's timbre traveled the room, a soft noose slipknotting all of them closer around Walter.

"Your Uncle Samstag, Walter?" said the Judge. "I'm sorry."

"Let me to get the cab," said Pauli.

"Thank you . . . Uncle Pauli. They're sending the car."

"To be the uncle here in this house —" Pauli bowed deeply.

"He was — the last link," said Walter, who looked about to cry.

"Anything we can do, Walter — anything."

"You've already done it for me, you Mannixes, years ago."

What more natural anywhere! Yet Austin couldn't help feeling that over the Judge's and Walter's sudden, almost ritual exchange, the shadow of another emotion hovered — Hebraic, prayer-shawled.

"You're not orphaned now, Walter," said the Judge. "Always remember that."

"I know, I know."

The two men, by chance almost of a size, were even rhythmically swaying; hunchback to miniature, they were perilously near that chorally stunted misconception of their race to which even certain Fennos clung. Pauli, probably a non-Jew, stood with head bowed, come as far as even a willing adjunct could. David, like so many of the young today, was tall. Locked for the moment in the reticence of friendship, and for life in unrhythmic deafness, he could be taken for anything. But he was almost surely one of those of whom Austin's unprejudiced father sometimes too fairly noted that "like the noses," *it* seemed to come out in them with age. Like David's own father maybe. In whose preoccupations the Mannix family, Jews — and maybe even the middle classes — sometimes were messianically one.

Alongside of which Austin stood Orientally fascinated, envious — and uncomfortable. Wishing that the car *would* come.

"It goes without saying, Walter, what *you've* done for us. David might never have . . . without such a . . . brother. In fact, I could wish . . ."

Except for David, Austin said to himself, this man can wish for anyone to be his son. Even me . . . Why, that's not fair! Like evil, like ozone, a thought breathed to him — *That's* what he'll teach me — not to be fair.

"I'd never have finished school without him," said Walter. "Or seen the Negev. Or learned to swim. Without any of you. You, Ruth, even Anna, even —"

"You're family." The Judge broke the rhythm, or righted it. "Let's leave it at that."

But Walter was on tiptoe, pink at the cheekbones with the enthusiasm which must be the reverse fever of saints, or their stamina. "Then I can say it. We mustn't worry so, about Ruth. You and David. I myself." At self-mention, he could stop short. "I don't mean only tonight. Though if that poor guy wanted her to hold his hand, who could blame him? . . . I don't know anybody I'd rather . . . at such a time. Ruth doesn't say much, but she's —" His smile shied briefly up at Austin. "She's . . . everything we all *think*," he said. He alone could go up to the Judge as he did now, close enough to be personal, to put a hand on the other's shoulder, eye to eye. The Judge's were sardonic, as if he knew this too. "She or any of us," said Walter. "Wherever we are, this house goes with us. We don't really leave."

"Ah Walter." The Judge said it with infinite fondness. "That why you can speak to me — as one orphan to another?"

But Walter's innocence couldn't hear him, went on voicing it itself, baritone from that bird-body, and from some optimum heaven where all shoulders were straight. Often it was listened to not for its meaning but in reverence that it should exist at all. Which was why so many saints came to nothing, Austin said to himself. . . . Yes, I am home from the wars. : . .

"That day you took me in," said Walter. "So long ago. *She* held my hand too . . . sick as we all know she must have been then. And talked to me, about — the family. Not about herself — though she must have had the cancer even then. Nor about Ruth, who was just a kid of eight or nine. *About David. And about you.* And the way she listened to me, for *me!* Though I hardly said anything at all; hardly even knew I was miserable . . . When you lose parents you scarcely've had a chance to love, sometimes you don't know . . . But *she* heard." Walter steadied his voice. "Tonight, when the poor guy on the plane said so much the same thing about Ruth — all I could think of was how much I wanted to tell *her.* Death or not, I'd always thought — some day I can tell them. That Ruth, just a kid then, not even spoken of — is now just like *her.* I see it more and more. How I wish I could tell *her:* 'Ruth's everything you and her father could wish. Mrs. Mannix,' I'd like to say to her. 'She's just like *you.*' "

Even his innocence felt the silence. He looked at his friends. The father's eyes were on the son. David's were closed — as in the days of the lessons, when he could bear no more.

"Forgive me," Walter said. "I just wanted to say — not to worry. There's no need." On these fading words his hands crept to clasp at the peak where vest covered sternum. The vest's brave checks, the bright secular gold of the watch chain, gave him the semblance of a saint too thinly disguised by his tailor, praying despite himself, in that pietà from which his friends would never let him escape. His head now cached itself between the shoulderblades — which occurred only when spirit finally tired as much as muscle. He was feeling the weight of his hump.

"*Attendez!*" said Madame. "Isn't that a car?"

She'd say this, Austin thought, whether or not she knew anything about this family, out of to her the supreme propriety — that such a scene needed ending.

With the others he strained to listen, hearing only the nadir of the night exchanging into the marvel of how late it was, feeling round his neck, as they must, the single cat-bell of the human condition — how extraordinary, that we have come this far! . . . It so happened then that they had moved closer together.

A single, light tread was heard coming down into the areaway, passing the window whose curtains a film of wind had closed, pausing at the door. Impressions so often came from a person's tread — reluctance, assurance — but this step might be any woman's, except that it was light. Then the door was tried.

"Open the door for your sister, David." The Judge leaned, clasping one thigh. "I must have locked up by mistake."

David, still reading Walter's face devotedly, didn't hear. Before Austin could get forward, Walter ran briskly as a page, his deformity bobbing faithfully with him as he opened the door.

These downstairs doors, designed for tradesmen, were out of sight of anyone in the dining-room. But here Austin and the rest were standing to receive her at the dining-room door. If they hadn't been impelled by tangential death into that close half-circle, would he have seen what must always have been here? If he hadn't been to war of course, that too. Otherwise, he'd been away from this household many times before, always to find it on return only what all outsiders cherished it for — much the same.

Only the war could have made him, in his few days home, sensitive to so minor a tremor of human behavior — those shrinkings into oneself which one employed if one meant not to be a hero. Or a heroine.

That impression — of what otherwise might take months, or a marriage, to name or discover — was instantaneous.

"Oh . . ." She didn't hold even the naturally delayed pose of greeting, as anyone might have done, much less take a pretty girl's sweeping advantage of the page's services. She slipped in quietly, the green beanie in her left hand swinging a little; though there were things she mightn't do she wasn't doleful, she was young. There they all were though, the circle of those who intensely loved or knew her, wasn't that daunting? "Hi — everyone."

She'd come maybe from a deathbed — and of a stranger who had insisted on his mysterious need of her — to a father she was planning to leave. She had the bright, over-stimulated gaze of the plane traveler who has watched time-space stream by. And a little of the scuffed weariness of city walkers who haven't found cabs. She said this last neatly, at once. "No cabs." Then gave Pauli the kind of kiss due him. Accepted from her father the affectionate grip of her face between his hands — she bent for it — that all had seen exchanged for years. "Madame — welcome," she said. And gave the genuflection, one foot behind, which must be a ballet mistress's due.

She gave them all their due; only Austin was back from the wars to

see how it was done, that it was done without art or craft but like a
walking on wires which had become normal. And that on this night,
intersection of so many crises implied or accidental, there should have
been more of — herself. That was it!

"Grouse," said Pauli, doting, as she kissed him. "I brought you
some."

"Oh, I'm starved. Nothing since the plane. I must just go up and
change my . . . Grouse!"

"Everything will be all right," said her father. "Ninon and I'll . . . talk
. . . on our way home. Are you all right?"

"All right," she said. But did not look at Ninon.

"What an extraordinary stole," said Madame. "Or is it a bedspread?"
Austin saw that draped as she held it, it covered her, a thick, tan
mantle, wildly embroidered.

"Augusta's. It always hangs in the lobby. She wasn't there."

"How is he . . . you stayed on?" said David. "That guy."

"He . . . made it dead," she said.

There was a flash of feeling here whose terms were unclear; it belonged to those three. Walter took her hands in his, through the
stole.

"His *uncle* too," said her brother. "Walter's."

"Not to Utah," Walter said.

"I'll —?" She could start a statement like a question.

"No, Diddy's going with me."

" — stay here." And finish the other way round.

And finally, to Austin at the end of the line, she said, "Austin, Austin,
I saw you the minute I came in." She put her arms up and around him.
"Welcome home. Oh Austin, I'm so glad. You're home."

Because it was the same hug she'd given him on graduation — and
because he couldn't bear to be public — he made no more of it. But
when he didn't move to kiss her cheek, she kissed his. The long en-
veloping stole fell back slightly. Even before that, he felt the unnatural
stiffness of the dress underneath. Or smelled it. War had done that for
him too.

On the pale ground of her dress, almost the same green as much-
washed army fatigues, the soaked-in stains had dried to the color,
not black, not red, found on the chests of the ambushed — men he'd
brought in six or seven hours after, too late.

"You're . . . covered with . . . !" Even if he hadn't heard the circumstances, he thought he would have recognized the spots, the great artery-drops cast on live men or dead. She was covered with it, covered with it. But it wasn't her own.

She nodded swiftly. He'd never seen her secretive before. Following her glance, he saw that the others had made an effort to ignore these two exchanging endearments.

"Only on the front," she whispered oddly. "Nothing on the back."

Time out of mind he'd seen his own sisters cry; he'd never before seen tears in this girl's, his friend's sister's eyes. The dark blood-smell sickened him, yet joined together the two parts of his recent life, war and home. This girl just turning away, still half against his chest, was the first civilian here who hadn't that distance in her, between the two.

"Well . . . I can *cry*," she said.

She was looking past him. "Where's Edwin?"

In the slowness of the others, Madame obliged. "The secretary? He's with the African. Walking off the wine."

"Secretary?" To her father.

"Edwin's — coming to live in the house. Since you won't."

She smiled back at him, gently; she wouldn't have a scene. "Since I won't be." Perhaps she did look at her brother, to see if he'd read this. Then, decently caped for death or dinner parties, not for one moment a heroine in the face of any of this, she went quietly out and up the stairs.

"There they are!" said Madame at the window. The wind, deeper into night, blew the curtains straight in against her ruffled bodice. One arm raised, she looked prepared to evoke any spells needed here.

The car at the curb, flanking the ingle window, looked to Austin large enough to carry the uncle in state to his nephew. Maybe it had. A chauffeur entered without ringing, and with a touch of his cap drew Walter outside; the other men followed, in a rallying which could spare him. It seemed to him that the whole evening bore toward what had been instantaneous, yet now had to be named.

"She was covered with it," he said, in his horror. "Did you see? Blood."

"Oh yes," said Madame, in the voice women could put on anything. "Everybody saw."

But not like him. He leaned forward. "We none of us know one word about her. Not one word of her own. I've just realized it . . . I've just come back."

"Sit *down*," she said. She forced him to. Doubtless she did this every day in the studio; her wrists were as strong as a handler's. Then she stood off to regard him.

"What Walter said — she's what *everybody* thinks." he said. "Never a clue from Ruth herself, is there."

"What would you expect there to be, in a young girl? I've had dozens of them under my care."

"And are they all like that? Your ballerinas."

"She is not a ballerina. Not the type. The company is . . . good for her. And she craves — the discipline."

He stared. "She can't dance?"

"Oh, well enough."

"And you let her stay, Madame? *You?*"

She shrugged. The two older men were heard re-entering the hallway. "Maybe — for an old friendship, eh?" She preened, smoothing the pearls at a wrist.

She saw that he got it. His face was burning. "Tours are helpful," she said slyly. "And weddings. Maybe she will marry."

She measured him, columnar neck to flank, and maybe relented at what she found. "You're right," she whispered. "I do it for her. Because she is what *I* think."

"What?"

In the face of the oncoming gentlemen, she murmured a foreign word in his ear — of which he caught only the ending -ta — but when he pressed her would mutter only, "Ask him" — meaning which of the men he wasn't sure.

And Ruth, in a white sweater and skirt, came out of the swinging door from the kitchen, eating grouse from a plate.

"You look like a Backfisch, fourteen years old," said Pauli. "Only if you had not cut the hair." He sighed. "Now we go home. I call you tomorrow; there's a concert." He looked at his beautiful Gérard-Phi-lippe. "*Ach, der lieber Gott.* I think Leni fell asleep upstairs — so much good wine."

"Leni is *here?*" said Ruth.

He smiled at her, tremulous. Between the hairline stripes of his treasured suit, in the crease between sideburn and ear where massage didn't reach, in the very crest of surviving hair, one saw the age of this hopeful bridegroom.

"Ah, Pauli, how wonderful." She smiled at her father and Austin. "Everybody's here. Plus an African. Who's he?"

"Dan Blount brought him. But had to leave." Father and daughter exchanged grins. "Maybe we'll have to put the boy up. Or maybe Edwin has."

Ruth shook her head. Nibbling her bird, she did look to Austin as she had at fourteen. Or twelve. "They only have a room and a half."

"You've seen it?" said the Judge.

"The Halecsys have. The sisters. His mother won't let them in; they won't say why. But they got in once, through the super."

Austin stirred uneasily; that she should know such dodges, such people, gave him a distaste. Until at least he knew. What he thought about her. "Maybe we could — put him up. Half the kids aren't at home."

"Oh?" She resented his offer, he could see that. On Edwin's part? "How's Alice?"

"Alice?" he said absently, watching her turn over the little skeleton on her plate, to the breastbone side.

"Alice *who?*" said the Judge.

At once she was at Austin's side; how had she moved there so unnoticeably? It was their old basement connivance, silently taken up among the four of them, against the authority upstairs. Once, too, during a game he had hidden in a closet with her. There had been nothing, but he had never forgotten it.

"Austin's sister," Ruth said.

Pauli was calling to Leni.

"The concubine, you'll wake her," said Ninon.

"The con — *Anna?*" Ruth's laugh was new, Anglicized or merely grown up, very slightly on scale. She sobered. "No, it's Thursday, isn't it? She's gone off to her — She's gone. I looked."

"Friday, it is now," Pauli said. He called upstairs again. "Leni, for God's sake. Come along. *Ach*, Simon, it's been a beautiful evening, like old times. Or new — maybe. Wonderful."

"She must be making up her face, to go home in," said Ninon. "Or thinking of that man's name."

"Both," said Pauli. "That's when she thinks best. There, I think I hear her." He left the room to go after her.

Austin put his finger on the carcass of the bird, its flat little breast-bone. "Grouse?"

"Shh. In June? And here?" She put her finger to her lips. "Don't let on. I guess it's squab."

"Walter —" he said, leaning close over her — "he said he'd like you to hold *his* hand, if he were dying. . . . And no wonder."

"Don't. He's got to have an operation some day. That thing on him — presses in."

"Why did you say — you *could* cry now?"

"Once I couldn't. For a while."

He could feel her patience — with whoever pressed in.

"You like us *all*. Don't you."

She twiddled at the bird. "Yes. All."

Again he felt that distaste — as if she might have meant not only all of them — but the world. "Tell me. What are the classifications for ballerinas? How does it go — prima, secunda, something like that?"

"Oh, not secunda!" Again she laughed.

In the ingle with Madame, the Judge put on his glasses, to see his daughter. "Night owl. But take it easy with Austin. He's — just got home."

"But you're all right, Austin, aren't you?" she said on her way to the sideboard. "You're *always* all right."

His turn to laugh. "That my classification?"

"The whole country's," said Madame.

"Come now, Ninon," said the Judge, "you haven't crossed the water just to give us that old bromide? That we've never been touched."

Madame, walking toward the center of the room with the first abstraction the younger man had seen in her, was observing Ruth, who had just begun to dance, holding the bird on its plate in front of her. "To *be* touched, Simon, it had to come to us." She spoke as if she had pins in her mouth, or had just said to a stagehand, "The light should be there!"

An idea came to Austin that if he wanted to leave this house for good, Madame could release him from its mystery, by somehow telling him what she mightn't know herself — the way men might go to whores, to be released from the domination of love.

Ruth, balancing her plate like a salver, was executing steps minimal but defined; on the plate, the carcass, traveling axial to her, controlled her, delicate as a pet bird which itself never moved.

"Entre*chat*, yes, yes, and *then*, and *then*, yes, yes, and very *nice*," said Madame, nodding as if counting beads. "That recovery — very good. What is it from, not *Salome* . . . From Rupert's — that passage with the vase at the fountain? Or that old, old *habanera*, *not* from *Carmen* —?"

From the hallway came a short, triumphant cry — Leni.

"She's remembered," said Madame in aside, still fixed on her dancer. "Or the eyelashes are bung on again . . . But *my* memory's gone blotto. What's that from, girl? I'd swear I'd never seen it in me life."

"That man in the hospital, Austin," said the ingle. "You never said what his injury was."

Austin refused to move over to where Mannix sat huddled up like a heart-sufferer judging himself. Back in the base hospital, the rugged head of the unknown man, pale with drugs, once again lifted visor-eyelids, electrically demanding, and closed them. "They haven't told me yet, Fenno," the mouth said. "What's gone . . . I'm a judge of character, Fenno," it said through its closed smile. "You'll tell me, Fenno. Which part of the pain is real."

"He's an amputee," said Austin.

"They've flown him back? He's here?"

"That was six months ago. I dunno. You lose track."

"What kind of amputee?"

Back there, that man had still been the electric center of himself. "Never let them dwell on what parts they're missing," said the therapists in the prosthetic room, calm as compasses among the metal claws and pulley wires, and the smell new rubber had in the sun. "Emphasize what they *have*. Or will get. We have no basket cases in this war." All patients were put upright as soon as possible, for the circulation. "Blue sky," the man said when they raised him. "Nice, but I'm sick of it." Though this raising wasn't done on the veranda, but indoors, where the mirrors were. It was done as soon as possible too. In the quiet, all the other men waited for what this newest recruit to their ranks would say when he saw himself. When it had been said, Austin, loser of nothing, present only because he was well enough to help as medic, was the only one who didn't laugh. "Like a totem pole," the man said. "But with balls." He was new to the room of course. The patient who'd lost what there was no prothesis for had laughed hardest, that was all.

"Triple," Austin said. "He's a triple."

After a long minute the voice in the ingle — Austin had his back to it — came again. "Yes, one loses track. It can be managed. You never hear."

In a war, civilian, one is meant to lose track. "New York?" said the man that once, turning him off. "Ah, forget it, Fenno. I never hear from it. It'll never hear from me."

"Of course you haven't, Madame!" Farther in the room, threading between table and sideboard, Ruth was dancing; her voice was breathy but triumphant. "It's not a passage that's been anywhere before. It's *mine*." In a twinkling series of turns done as if she were on pointe, she circled the table, executed a run which brought her past her father, to end before Austin and Madame. "I'm doing Rupert's part. It'll be adagio. He'll be holding the girl. Dressed like a bird." Slowly she lowered the plate, cocking one toe behind her. "What shall I call it? The Ballet of the Grouse?" At a noise behind she turned, the toe still at tripod angle, still on stage.

In the doorway, Leni was triumphant too. Her maquillage renewed shone white on the cheeks, black at brows and eyes. There had never been such a stage-green as her dress. Pauli, behind her, was almost effaced. Her head lifted. Beauty was behind her; the past was her topic, sweating memory like sex. She had remembered.

"His name was Posliuty. Stanislaus? — was it Stan *she* called him? . . . No. *Nick*. Nick Posliuty." Others might be dancing, but now she, Leni, was entering, the prima. Nearing Austin, she flicked his lapel, her hand pausing there, fan-shaped. "Posliuty. Like Petersh. You were right." Stub-a-stub, her bronze feet stammered toward the Judge in his ingle. She was dancing now, the ballet of how beauty, settling for the past, became harridan. "*Sehr elegant,* your wife was, hmmm? How she sat there, so dark in that restaurant, all the other woman décolleté." She turned sideways to Ninon a shoulder heavy as a bolster, but the arm floated, correct. "The ensemble black, with silver at the sleeves, marvelous raglan sleeves. I remember it like it was yesterday. Two nights before she was killed. Burning inside, she was. And not even a cigarette."

Behind her, Pauli made an abortive, trailing sound, but he was merely the conductor, he could do nothing.

"Yes, I remember." Leni's reddish hair dropped backward over the neck which no longer could bend back of itself. On the hand spread across her puce mouth, one nail had chipped. " 'Is he a policeman, your friend?' I said to her. When he went to the men's room. So big he was, when he got up the table almost went over. She didn't answer me. Not a word, remember, Pauli? Not a word. Until he came back." The palm pressed for a moment on the Judge's shoulder left a powder mark. "*You'd* gone by then; you had to leave. 'Soldier of fortune,' your wife said then, 'that's what Nick Posliuty is. Who doesn't go to war.' And I said, 'Posliuty?' And he looked up quick and said, 'Polski?' And I said in our language, '*Glos* —' " The palm rose in smart salute. " '*Glos wolny wolnosc ubezpieczajacy!*' An old proverb. And she laughed. How did she know what I said to him? 'A free voice guaranteeing freedom.' Remember, Pauli, later when you ask what it mean, what I say to you? 'Ask her.' "

The Judge sat as people did when old times were recalled to them, looking past the narrator at the still, small voice of the scene itself.

Pauli advanced, putting his arms around Leni from behind. With an almost lithe pull she took advantage of it, spreading skater-like back against him, his hands gripped in hers. She had involved him now, he must stand and support her — the prima, gone from the rib cage down, but the face possible to imagine swooping forward, suspended at the breastbone, riding aloft a man's hand, with swan-lengthened eyes. "He saluted me back," it said. " 'Not me, *I'm* not the champ,' he said to her. Your wife's friend, Judge. The Pole."

Ruth was moving, taking the minimal steps to carry the plate, which she was still holding, arrested there in her little spotlight of her own making, over to the sideboard. She wasn't the prima, this slightest passage of the limbs demonstrated, merely a member of the chorus entrusted with the safety of a prop. She put the plate down carefully, a tranced but good child moving to an invisible beat. For a moment her hands, freed now, hung at her sides. Austin had never seen hands look emptier. Was she still dancing? — then she was a marvel at pantomime. But one of her hands crept behind then, to touch her dress at the seat, to wipe off blood which wasn't there, then recalled in time that there was no blood on it, that she had changed.

To Austin, from a family of sisters and girl cousins, this was a known gesture from the decently guarded monthly trials of women, which a brother wasn't to notice, sitting rigid at fourteen for instance, eyes straight ahead, while his mother whispered to Alice, "Take little Di upstairs, tell her she's come through." He sat like a brother again, uneasy, marveling, eyes straight ahead, once again bereft forever of that straight-legged sprout in jeans, his cousin Di. But this girl has never been seen before for what she is; isn't that what lovers always say? What she is, what she feels — never by anyone, except me. Bright chains of love-friendship interchanged themselves in his breast — reaching out for all their family pain, hers, so needlessly dabbled with blood. And it appeared to him that all this pain in him was instantaneous.

Pauli had already spoken, a stifled blurt of outrage at Leni, who leaned against him now like a statue which had begun to fall. At Austin's side, Madame placed a hand on his shoulder, pressing like a signal. She was watching the Judge. How could a man who limped like that get so quickly to his daughter's side?

"That business on the plane . . . why should you . . . why should it have to be you?" Who was Mannix angry with, his face so white? "You want to go upstairs, my darling. Tuck yourself under, hmmm. Go and do that."

"I'm not tired. I'm never tired."

It was such a standardly bold young disclaimer. Austin himself had made it often, before the war. But surely there was a bit of the girl herself in the way she leaned to pat her father's cheek, being taller.

"Who's to carry me," she said, "now?" Then she flushed, dark and deep. "No, I'm all right."

A knock came at the door.

"Edwin, it must be Edwin!" She cried it as if rescued. "I'll go. Let me." But first she ran to Ninon. "You'll want to talk to Father." Then to her father, "You'll want to — talk to her."

A second knock came.

As she passed Austin she whispered to him, "Edwin. You still don't like him, do you."

"Should I?"

She sighed, went on past him to the outer door. That sigh chilled him, so near, so far. Why do I think of her as "the girl"? Her name is Ruth.

They heard her step outside the door, leaving it ajar. The city drifted in to them. They raised their heads to it, all but Madame, who was a foreigner — did they own it, or were they owned? Intently listening, all of them, after a murmuring out there they heard the door close.

Krupong came in uncertainly, clearly surprised to see them all still there, quickly debonair. "Your stars are out." A whiff of these came in with him. He saw that his quiet, poetic tone was welcome — young Fenno for one looked as if he could have used a more elegiac end to the evening than seemed likely. But it was not in himself to maintain it. "But Blount is gone," Felix said. As usual, everybody had to laugh; the sequence of his thought was so fresh — or different from theirs.

Austin stepped forward. "Have you a place to stay? If not — we can put you up. At my house."

"Thank you, I am stopping at a club. But what I would like — there is an all-night bar I have been told of. Will you come?"

"Did Edwin come back with you?" said the Judge. "Are those two going along with you?"

"Alas, they did not say. She said not to wait up."

Everybody suddenly said it had been a wonderful evening.

"I should have had you all together long since," replied the Judge.

"Can we give you a lift, Ninon?" said Leni. "We *always* take a cab."

"Thank you, I shall stay on a bit."

"Remember now, Felix," said the host, "come again."

"Thank you. May I just —? He was directed to the hall. Madame, following after, turned and went up the stairs.

"Good night, Uncle Pauli. *Gaudeamus.*"

"Good night, Owstin." Pauli leaned closer. The dinner party was over; already a part of the calendar to be pieced over at will. It belonged to the ages, maybe some day even to Rameau. Outside was life, fanged and waiting. Important things must be said hurriedly between the two states of being, at the door. "Such a darling," murmured Pauli distractedly. "Will she be all right with him, Austin, that Edwin? She has such bad luck!"

"*Sehr interessant!*" Leni was still at such a height — or now felt the Judge and his house to be — that only another language could convey her compliments. "*Sehr interessant,*" she repeated, until dragged away.

"What a handshake that woman has," said the Judge, after her. "Once a European gets the idea of them —" He saw that he and Austin were momentarily alone. "Austin —"

Was Mannix going to ask him to go after those two? If so, he was prepared to counter — "When is *he* coming to live here, in the house?"

"Triple amputee," said the Judge. "God, that . . . conjures up — The man was *all* physical. Anyone could see that."

Austin supposed a man would prefer to think that about his wife's lover. Until now he'd assumed a man wouldn't talk about it.

"Think me a shit if I asked you — which?" The Judge drew his palms down his cheeks. "I can get rid of the image maybe. Once I know."

"I can do better. I'll tell you what he said when he saw himself. In the mirror." He told him. In the older man's stricken look he saw he'd have done better to call him a shit. "He's got a leg," he said. "The left."

They heard the outer door being tried. Neither man went to help. If I see her come in that door again, Austin asked himself, standing his ground — what will I know?"

The door was pushed in jauntily. A breeze came with it. Edwin came in, riding the breeze. Not drunk any more, he looked as Austin had used to glimpse him in their coinciding years at Harvard, when he'd already had a reputation, as much for circumstance as mind. In physique nothing much, his face and manner had already had a duality; it was never quite possible to tell from either what Edwin *was*. This made for a secret power most sensed but few knew, like Austin, the source of — that Edwin himself hadn't been brought up to know.

Austin squared his shoulders. No holds barred — will *our* kind of training be up to that? He saw that his rival was elated.

Edwin walked straight up to the Judge in his chair in the bay. "Just came back to be sure Krupong told you. Not to wait up."

Strange advice, from a secretary! But the old man ignored his presence. In spite of black hair and eyes, Mannix could look old when he needed to. He was examining his own hands like a palmist. "I could mirror-write once, both at a time. But the one thing — they wouldn't do for me." He looked up, at Austin. "*He* — did — what he wanted to. A leg. A leg . . . You tell him — I would know him anywhere."

"I don't ever expect to see him." Or tell him if I do.

But the Judge was ignoring Austin now. "Edwin — where's Ruth?"

"Down the block."

A child's phrase, and a city one; used past childhood it belonged to those who lived their life in the streets.

"We're going on the town. Her idea of it."

"Where?"

"Not to a settlement house, Fenno. You wouldn't enjoy it."

"*Where?*"

"My old neighborhood."

"Is it safe there?"

"Safe, Aussie? You'll have to ask her."

Not just a street insult. What it said was, "*She's* your rival, Aussie, isn't she? And *I* know."

Krupong and Madame leaned in from the hall, arm in arm. "We're going into the garden," he said. "To see your stars." She waved.

The Judge smiled at both young men. "Wait up? No. Tell her I won't." He made as if to get up then, but his wife's soft chair held him. He stretched a leg, reflectively. "Not for a girl who's old enough — to go on tour."

"Then she's going?"

"Why, yes, Edwin. You'll be the only young one in the house. Or maybe we'll all decide to leave . . . or meet in London." He was struggling to get up. It became clear to the two young men that he couldn't. Each reacted in his own way: Red; White. Austin, relic of James, remained quietly waiting. Edwin, relic of nothing beyond his dialogues with the Judge, walked forward to the head chair at the table and picked up the cane beside it.

"Just a civilian wound," said the Judge. "Nothing to yours, Austin, or to — Edwin, did you know Austin'd been wounded?"

Edwin was weighing the cane. "No, Sorry to hear that." He said it with wooden sincerity, his thoughts elsewhere. "I'll tell Ruth."

"Never mind that," said Austin, in utter fury.

Edwin didn't, toying with the cane. "She wants us to go to see a night court session.

"Night court?" said her father. "She say why?"

Edwin brought the cane forward. He was carrying it like an equerry, or a street boy acting one, guying a cop — or yesterday's friend. He presented it. "Good night —" An ancestry came out upon his face then surely. What else was it when a man's brow narrowed like that, feral but innocent? "Good night, *Simon.*" Quick-fading as a street runner, he was gone.

"Who's in charge here, I wonder." After a minute Mannix shrugged. "When you say that, I suppose you no longer are."

"Shall I go after them?" said Austin.

"Why?"

"No holds barred, with him. With *them*. I can understand that. But with him it's more than that. With him, you don't know what holds there are. *He* doesn't. And that's dangerous."

"Ruth knows. Ever since she brought him here." Mannix peered up at him cautiously. "She even says — he and she are alike. In a way."

"*Like!* — why, she's known what she is, every day of her life."

"Yes." The Judge fingered the cane's silver crook. "Night court. Her mother used to do that in the thirties; it was chic then. But they're in for a surprise; I don't think that kind of city court is held any more . . . What you young remember, eh? Enormous, isn't it, Austin? But I can't deal with it any more." With the aid of the cane, he stood up. Then he tossed it away.

"You in pain?"

The Judge looked down at his leg. "Just something for the doctors to settle. Otherwise, if you ask me . . . may I say 'Aussie'!"

"My family calls me that."

"Know that drawing feeling in a wound? That's what I'm in. I'm in *healing*. The two sides of my life, the two halves — are drawing together. It's the most extraordinary sensation."

"Halves?"

"Everybody."

They heard the two others come in from the garden and go upstairs.

"We better go up to them." At the dining-room door, the Judge turned to look back at the chairs ranged round a table shining now and cleared, a court ever in session, waiting for the family to come. "Sorry, what I mentioned to Edwin, about you. Shouldn't've."

"It's all right. Realized that when you told him. Doesn't help any, not to. Won't help what I feel."

"What's that" — the Judge drew breath — "my dear boy?"

They avoided looking at one another. A woman peering in wouldn't have known that they were both moved.

"I don't feel private any more." It struck him — a mere pebble — that he had come to the end of his youth. "Everything's in question," Austin Fenno said. "Every*one*. I never knew."

The cane had fallen across the entrance. The Judge bent with amazingly convalescent lightness to pick it up. "My grandfather's. And my father's too." He stood it carefully in a corner. "Will *he* be able to . . . get about? The Pole?"

"They'll — think of something."

"I can see I shouldn't have asked that either. Why do we have to . . . keep track?"

"That's easy. Because you're a civilian."

"That's honest of you . . . Aussie. Look at that dining-table. Know what I think to myself, every time I see it like that?" The chairs waited, regal, ugly, comfortable. "Families behind the lines," said the Judge. "*Families behind the lines.* I often wonder. Is it only — with *us*?"

"Of course not. My own father did fight, but he wouldn't again; he's said so. And he wouldn't. The world *is* changing. As for mother's side — " He grinned. "*We* go to war. But we don't fight."

"That's honest of you," the Judge said again. "But as you Quakers say, you're 'concerned.' Publicly. What men do or don't do privately is harder to —" It was a word he didn't like to say. But there was no other. "To judge."

On the landing at the turn of the stairs up above, the tall clock struck the only hour it was ever known to, the half — known in the family as "the pawnbroker's hour," though none of them could tell a guest why. It wasn't clocks he needed here anyway, but compasses. "I —" said Austin. "We —" It seemed to him that war was contained, or violence was, like a seed in the vitals, which only some men had a chance to drop. And that such thoughts free-floated eternally, waiting. It wouldn't take intellect to catch them, but chance again and a catalyst.

For it seemed to him that here in this house, the change of guard was actually occurring; the gap between generations, which moved so slowly in ordinary day, tonight in performance could be seen. At the same time, he knew that these were visions — or that he was haunted by visions which were too much for him, for which he was not the proper vessel. Life as energy and will he could handle, but life as insight, intuition beyond his lights, wasn't for him. It would have to move on.

But he would manage to marry her before that, because she, with her clan, gave him the power to think beyond himself. And because there was something wrong.

"No," he said. "You people mean to be honest. We only mean to be fair."

Together, they went up the stairs.

At the top of the stairs, they separated. Krupong and Madame were waiting for them. Krupong took Austin's arm without a word. The Judge ranged himself beside Madame. After a moment, he climbed one more step of the flight which led to the story above, which put him higher than she, though this didn't seem his intent. In height he and she were a remarkable pair. Madame herself was standing under a prism-hung light which made a thousand repetitions of itself in a dress thickly sifted with sequins the color of nacre, out of which her shoulders bloomed, fleshly present as a woman's should be, with the beauty that is for a time. No man could keep his eyes from her, or would want to. She tapped Austin's arm lightly. "Legs are only the *Ameri*can part of a woman." This was her good-bye. But as he closed the outer door behind him, he saw that slowly, gazing into nowhere as women did it, with a rhythm for somewhere — she was drawing off her gloves.

12   Red Rooms – *June 1951*

"Coromandel, brocatelle." Had he really said aloud that old musical direction, less faded than the furnishings it stood for? He'd pushed her in here, naked already from one bout of love in his own bed, through the dressing-room, past that table, neatly laid with silver-backed brushes not guns, to the room where in spite of all a servant could do, his wife waited up for him . . .

Had she said it after him with stage obedience, taking in at a glance the old drowned French-de-chine of a room whose nacre must once have outshimmered the dress she had already dropped for him, adagio, in the other, sucking in her cheeks for what that pale vinaigrette of a desk must hold, going up to that wasp-stomachered, foreshortened drawing, plainly not all caricature, of the wife he so clearly wanted *her* to mention. Staring into its eyes, which must have been as oversize as the artist had made them, shaking her head over a yearning in them she couldn't speak for, in just the way her own lively little ballerinas shook theirs over some dead, pictured arabesque of absolute line, *"This is no coryphée!"* Meanwhile lightly fingering herself where hair had been let stay — being dun not white, and all the time saying to herself, not to any other person ever, "Well, Ninon — you have once more taken off your gloves." . . .

Old musical directions, I know that, you don't have to tell me; on this couch, set where once a bed or chaise must have been, were they murmuring only this to each other, tongues meanwhile lodged like ruby sparks in each other's mouths? Or much more, that even at their age was yet to be said?

The upstairs room was glowing with sexual light, hot as those rooms always were which existed behind the foreheads of bodies still joined at the Venus-point, the eyes still closed. On their opening them, its red light might be real dawn, or the mosque of a lamp. They were still in that valleyland of the flesh whose images waited ready between the thighs, as the retina waits for light, were satisfied by love as the eye is by opening, but went on breeding afterward. They held on, as sorry to leave as any pair. After forty years of the satisfaction itself, in this valleyland they were virgins still.

He opened his eyes. Below him, hers were closed, but he wondered if she hadn't really been first; she rendered the smaller services and tacts with the grace of a woman who never doubted her own lone path — and would never call these obediences. He arched himself, in animal listening. To the rear of this room, in the usual extension, windowless at the sides, of most brownstones, his own room, the smaller and altogether windowless, gave on the backstairs landing, otherwise exactly like the center rooms of the old railroad flats of the tenements of the same era; even the mansions had had these cells. He liked that innerness, but this front room had the weather. The air now had that dead cool just before the night took its first bluish step away. He'd heard nothing downstairs. Breathing an emperor's forgotten air, he cared nothing. Houses livened to a birth, were publicized in deaths that would not die. His body, swan-smooth, without malaise, reminded him that only copulation made them private. Below him, the woman's eyes opened, became Ninon's, still candid; no, she hadn't preceded him. Slowly, her half of the central red they had made between them retreated behind her forehead as his had done behind his own. They were separate.

Beneath him, the bird-bones of a true miniature made his weight a delight to him. Raising himself with arms powered as much by this as by sailing, he stood up, lifted her against him and carried her back into the rear room. A brown and white one, all his, down to the memory tufting Moroccan under his toes as he held her, on the spot where the obsessive valleys of the invisible had assailed him, octopal arms and owl-septumed faces advancing to clothe the nakedness he had desired to hold against their ranks. If honesty was nakedness, then this was a better way. Behind, in the room they'd left, the sewing-room sofa he'd brought her to as to a chaise became a chaise, the draperies regained their roses in the international yellow of a summer morning that would not fade. The woman in the wasp-drawing on the wall hadn't yet begun to wait. Halves of a life could be forced together, not kept in a lily-shaped box like his father's. One half must be made to violate the other if necessary. Even at sixty not all the *luxuria* in a life needed to be of the past.

On his reawakened bed, her undergarments, flung there, lay precise as a game of colored dominoes; she never wore black — too thin for it, she said once (or because black was a whore's choice, or mauve or scarlet) — but seeing this pale orange frilled with peacock, he remembered hennas, Francophile mists of nude or navy, other erotic in-betweens of a taste that like her accent was still too original. On the floor at the bed's opposite side, her dress lay stiltedly, its encrusted bodice returning the bedlamp's fire; like its owner upon the bed it could make tasteful the crudest contortions asked of it, by being too poised for love. A second time, she had led him back to the sexual, but she was perfect for a purpose beyond that. He congratulated himself on his choice.

The owner of the dress returned his gaze. Estimation of what time had done to each other's bodies had been taken care of in the first lightning glance. Satisfaction was a fact. Other nuances were now lulled forward into the present again. Years past the age for a young man's biography to be lisped against a breast, or a young girl's to be clenched behind the teeth or coolly manufactured — they still had to define. Out of the valleyland again, any couple, any encounter found themselves asking it. What's new in this? For me. For us.

She put a prettily shrunken figleaf of a hand on him, in the proper place for it; he shook his head. She shook hers. Sitting up in the embrace of gossips, they drew each other onto the pillows, silent over these last charioteering moments of the flesh.

On her belly, once muscled strong enough to stand on, there was now a scapular-shaped dimple, just above the hair. He touched it.

"Not what you think."

"What do I think?"

"I *have* all my organs."

So the years had done at least that to her self-confidence — God knows, not much. But like a sultan who had slept only with virgins, he saw those years in her, a whole era of women he had missed.

"A hernia op. So — I don't teach any more. I won't let others demonstrate for me."

"An immortal."

"No, Simon. Only as old as you."

Plus one. He smiled at her, wishing he could say how much he preferred a woman who could lie, instead put a hand on her loins. "You let it grow again."

"I haven't been — *dancing*." Her upper lip twitched for him. Liar or not, she had a whore's sense of the proprieties, or a flirt's.

"I prefer it this way. More — unprofessional. Tell me something . . . were you and Pauli *before* he knew Leni, or after?"

She laughed herself straight up against the pillows, legs squarely in front of her as a doll's — the *poupeé valsante,* with a small-of-the-back of steel. "So that either way I answer . . . are judges barristers too?"

"Matter of fact I was, almost. Cardozo was an early god of mine." (*Barrister law, rare in America, Simon. Do you really admire that man so much? Altogether too refined, for us Olneys.*) He began to laugh — with Chauncey, that ever-present audient. Who would have been an interested onlooker. But to bring poor Benjamin to bed here!

"Who?"

"Supreme Court Justice. Second Jew."

Even a younger woman might have drawn the covers over herself, but her honesty was here, or a vanity not crossing its arms over its breasts. Small, they hadn't much dropped; the nipples were like her lips, not yet shrunken brown with permanent cold. Only the quality of all the flesh had changed, dead-sugary where it had been taut, hard gloss at the shins, certain nuances of the underarm, navel and knee lost forever to a millimeter of slack. And everywhere, under the once subtle, tender powder of pores that had concealed it, now rising ever more intricately green, this organism's map of the world. He was surprised, pressing in his hand, that none of this damaged lust, which as of old multiplied in him with use.

"A Disraeli, you might have been. With us."

Lazily, he remembered her politics — all patronage. "Royalists, all you women. Even in bed. Most of all, in bed." His hand probed. "Does that mean, if I come over, you'll have me about?"

Her glance swept over and past them both, to the wings. With a choreographer's sense of her own body in space-time, she'd once told him her vision of her own inner anatomy during the love-ballet of the thighs — the clitoris, a fleshy sea anemone waving in its grotto, ready to receive. Like so much in the ballet — from the misalliances of princes and birds to that wildly misconceived stage set of herself (the flower was apparently at the *bottom* of the grotto) — what was anatomically wrong was somehow made lyrically possible. He'd never told her of her error. By whatever grand jeté, Nijinsky had always arrived.

Now she was giving his body the stare; out in the open, so to speak, she was clinically accurate. But in the matter of preservation he too had done as well as Pauli had said.

"Good show." Her feet, pampered cripples of art, were crossed fastidiously at the ankle, as he was sure they would be if a whirlwind sucked her up to heaven — to a full house of balletomanes. Or found herself escorted downward — by a sextet of Don Juans on pointe. Without moving the feet a minim, she expelled his hand. "But now I must be off. Afternoons I should be free about six. Why not call me then?"

"So businesslike, so soon?"

"Not me. No theatre business gets done here until past noon. And *I* have no rehearsals. All rosebuds this time, and money talk." She stretched, harmoniously. "The nicest kind. Not *ours*." She gripped both ankles, bending in the legs until the soles of the feet touched, in that cult of the body which never stopped. To a man, it was still inattention. "No, not me. But it's getting light."

"This is my house." He sat up, magisterial: let her eyes rove him. Then he remembered that just as he read lips, she read limbs; she thought in posture, and spoke in it.

"Why did you take me into the other room?" she said.

"Part of a ballet," he said. "The oldest vengeance in the world." To say, Mirriam, you voyeur, don't wait up any more. "Don't tell me you've never seen it."

"Yes," said Madame — that was her tone. "You talked about her all evening."

"Who?"

"You — who never talk."

"Some say I never stop." It was a relief to be with those whose prime language wasn't words, an honesty, like copulation. "You can't want to talk about her. My wife."

"*You* do." She shrugged. "So then . . . I."

She reached for a cigarette pack on the night-table and took one.

"Never knew you smoked." It was forbidden the troupe.

"An early habit. Comes back — at times."

Taking the matches from her, to strike one for her, he saw she was trembling. The slope of the shoulders was familiar — complaisant, distant. In the other room, the blind flapped at a front window, always kept open in these houses for the cross-current. Even back here, the milky diffusion of night by dawn had begun. He could have sworn he smelled the feathers-and-pork of a charcuterie getting its early takeouts ready; no, it was all the hotels of convenience, from the Rue de Bellechasse to the East Seventies. All the *jolies laides* in them, pretty uglies pushing back the breakfast tray, lighting a fag, to talk — you all want to talk.

"You were once in the business," he said on impulse. "I always knew."

She reached over her knees almost awkwardly, picked his shirt from the bottom of the bed, and slung it kimono around her. Hunched there comfortably, she smoked; that was her answer. Above the man's collar, the salon-curled hair — that was familiar too.

He had the wit not to apologize, not to touch.

She turned bright eyes on him. Tears? Mirth. "What a relief. In almost fifty years . . . nobody's ever brought it up."

"You were — *twelve?*" An age that peculiarly horrified him. At which everything happened to them.

"See you've seen the documents. Oh, I don't mind, I lie about it for the fun of it. And because it's the thing for us to do, you know."

"You have the body of a woman of forty."

"Forty-five or so," said Madame, measuring herself. "Except for the veins — I always had them too prominent. I saw Pauli looking at them, tonight. The gloves, I mean. He gave me forty pair of long white ones once. From Trefousse." She cast him a glance. "*Before* Leni, of course; you don't fancy she'd speak to me without scratching, otherwise. And who else but him would have got me into the bally?"

She passed him the butt to puff on. He puffed it obediently.

"Twelve to fourteen," she said. "They'd turned me out, you see. Then for a while I'd no need to — schools in the profession are like convents. Then later sometimes, when I was down on me luck."

"You have a child?" He said it unsentimentally, as they did.

"I'm barren, shouldn't wonder. Dancers often are — or until they give it up." She took back the cigarette — held it, staring. Her sudden puff of laughter sent sparks all over the bed. After they'd spatted them out, she, still on her energetic hands and knees in the bedclothes, shook her head at him. "Good God — you meant a child by the first one?"

"You did say — they threw you out." At twelve.

"An old balls of a boy — he was seventy." She carefully brushed her hands together over the ashtray, leaned across him to set it back on the table. "Next question — don't I *mind?* Or it used to be." When she smiled, her nose, not quite as pink as in her native air, still moved with the lip. "After him any man was young. And a man."

"Oh?"

"Not you, you clot." She passed a light hand over his outline six inches above, as he had seen it down in the rehearsal room, correcting a muscle, a position — with the dancer's surety that it was also correcting a soul. "The silhouette, that's what one sees. Your body's very little older than mine, to look at. Broad at the pectoral, long at the waist. Actually, two or three years younger, I should think."

"Ah, you've seen the documents."

"Aged — I should say — about forty-eight."

"Says Madame. You should tell fortunes, Ninon."

"You think ensembles are put together by lot? S'truth, though, we smaller blokes have better economy. We live longer — a long middle age. Tall ones have got too much to carry about — for the long pull. Like that young man tonight — the one in uniform."

"You looked greedy, never mind. I saw you."

"Going to get heavy in the hams, he is." But she grinned.

"You mix the generations all together." He sighed. "I'm not able."

She shook her head. "Besides — he's not for me."

A pause. "You do tell fortunes. You're a lot like Anna, all that ham and kidney talk."

"Your concubine? Yes, she sees things." Twisting a foot, she regarded it like a vis-à-vis. "The kitchen sees a lot."

"Woman stuff." Idly he smoothed her inner elbow, where there was a tender patch left over from a girl. "Like that recipe for the skin, you once told me."

"To pee in your own bath? *Very* good for it. Go on, laugh. But it is. Asses' milk — what else did the old saws mean by it. Go on, laugh."

"Heredity, more likely. Good Channel air." He cupped her chin. "Calais side, of course."

"We're a pair, Simon. Aren't we. You still scratch your crotch in public. I saw."

He did laugh.

"Go on, go on. I've cheered you up now. Say it." She arched

pleasedly above him, near enough for him to put a mouth to, if he slid an inch or so down. He saw the two of them in London — not married, for she would never, nor perhaps he — but in the state he had carefully phrased; they would "have each other about." Even women with histories came to say it: "We're a pair."

"I've not been dancing," he said. "Either . . . Oh, yes, you have. Immeasurably . . . Oh, go on then. *You* laugh."

"Just that you're so much the same. How wild we'd have sent each other, when I was — "

"Twelve? Don't be so elegiac."

"Eh?" she said. "Smarty went to a party." She saw his face change. "Ah, I see. You would rather. That I'd lied."

"Not for what you think."

"What, then."

"My wife always told the truth. For the fun of it . . . No — that's not fair. Not *true*."

"Still sorting her out, aren't you." Back to him, she gathered up her underwear, slowly making a hen's nest of it around her. "After the garden, I had a look-see in the house. Wasn't sorting *her* out, I can tell you. But there she was, in every room I saw. And I didn't believe a one of them, not even the cabinet photo on the piano. Not till I saw the one in there." She pointed.

"Tell me about — Ruth."

She tossed that aside. "Must have been very tall, wasn't she? Your son's so tall."

"Yes. My son is tall."

"So you'd rather not talk, after all. . . . *Or* — " In the odd way her unconscious — what there was of it — made use of her, the *r* had a Parisian roll to it. "Or-r, you wish *me* — " She scattered the lingerie and ran off into the other room, buttocks and toed-out feet at their exquisitely broken-jointed angle.

"Caricatures are best," she said, returning. He saw that if her hands appeared to clasp at her loins more than ordinarily, it was because the arms had been trained to their eternal wreath, and the arms were long. She was holding the drawing by a corner — it weighed only the few ounces of the cheapest mail rate, Paris –New York, 1924. She came and crouched over him. He rose to receive her.

"Wait." She put a finger across her mouth, withdrew it. "Why did I do that, eh? But listen." She cradled the picture in her lap and bent over it, eye to eye.

"Done by a friend," he said.

She turned the thing over, then put it aside, casually. That pleased him. "Listen. This woman here . . . No matter what Leni says. She killed herself."

"You are supposed to lie," he said.

She turned away and began to draw on a chemise. In the depths of the house they heard the street door open and close.

"The concubine?" She drew on a stocking, picked up the dress.

"No, she goes for the night. The children, one or the other." He lay watching her. "Don't go."

Shoe in hand, she swung round, to stare. She would do what he wanted, without protest. She wouldn't whip a man; a less perverse woman he had never known. But for what he wanted of her she was perfect, not in danger herself, long since safely attitudinized. He leaned forward, softly took the shoe from her hand and dropped it.

"What do you want of me?" Her voice didn't hush. With Mirriam, daring had always been amateur.

"Family . . . life," he said. "How can I explain to you?" More than love or hate — this rhythm implanted in him, never to be dispossessed, called a house-rhythm because he knew no better name for it, had enraged the other against him, against herself because she was the same. "Once — " On another long night. " — once I was going to say to my wife on the telephone . . . 'Bring him here . . .' I was at a friend's, an old man who'd have understood it well . . . And I had an impulse I didn't obey . . . To say that. 'Come on over. Bring your lover here.'" Scenes without intellect, without reflection, those were the ones that were at the heart of family; everything else was afterthought. Scenes that the rhythm made, or halted before aghast — mindless in an old marriage bed, or on the cuckold telephone.

He reached over and took hold of one of her feet, scrutinizing that carefully maimed foot as if it could explain itself. "I mean to make you public."

She lay back on elbow; no, she wasn't ordinary. "For whom?"

He didn't answer at once.

"It's getting light," she said after a while. "In there."

"For myself," he said, as if he had just thought of it.

"Not — for her."

He looked down at the drawing. "We hung it together," he said.

When she spoke next, her voice was businesslike; she understood these things, as a matter of business. "What did you think, then? Did you think I could gnaw you free?"

"You can tell me — about Ruth."

She sat up, threw up her hands. "Look. This is what I tell them all. The parents." She drew up her foot, the same one, took it between her thumbs. "For us there are three kinds of feet. First the strongly knit one, little or no arch, short or medium toes. Here you have it, *mesdames et messieurs* — many in the corps de ballet have the same. Or they may even have type two — a foot with what appears to be a high arch but is really a loose ankle joint with long forefoot and toes. Quick in action, delicate in makeup." She was singsonging. "Lightly built dancers have it — "

Forward, in his wife's room, night was lifting away in an ebbing whiteness which barely fogged the central reaches of these houses, but from the façades was like a great window blind raising on a nameless city, here two centuries of forever, yet each dawn cast on an emptied plain, in new hexahedrons of web and roof-glitter and black-dotted humans, the total name of all of which by nightfall must be relearned. Meanwhile he and this woman, crouched absurdly in bed, were revealed in their own quattrocento cone of light extending backward through the flattened perspectives of themselves, through the foot bent upon by both as over a holy child, on and back through another window rear, giving out on the precise olive of the beyond; the world would not be held in abeyance to be returned to; they were enmeshed in the world. Behind her foot was the Place de L'Opéra, whether or not she'd ever seen it, in a line of coryphées jigging down the cadres of history until they met hers. Behind him was that plane he tried so hard to define as middle — in a latitude somewhere between the Metropolitan Club, an armoire and a water tower, the stamps with which he tried to sail the world — and the Pribilofs of a memoir not his own. On a desk there was the paper he'd begun in tremor and hope only two days ago, meanwhile staring at his unplumed pen as if it came from a sarcophagus, at the ink bottle which held the arrogance of those who dared to add to a Bible, and at the page itself, on it a first and only sentence which he might bend to as if it were holy: "Almost every political question in these United States sooner or later becomes a judicial one."

"— the third type of foot," said the voice beside him. "Which gives the real trouble."

"Yes?" he said, returning. "The foot that gives the real trouble. Yes?" All expertise was holy, a holy kaleidoscope.

"In which the bones of the tarsus are piled into a high arch *loosely* knit, *long* ligaments — and weak foot muscles." Her face told him nothing, blankly courteous as a magician's, intent on elsewhere. "A foot requiring more work than either of the other types . . . and alas —"

"Yes?" he said on the instant. "*Alas* . . . Ruth?"

She sat back on her haunches, with one quick move dispersing it all, as she had the lemon. "Never have to tell the parents — what kind of bones they think they have given their daughters. They always tell me."

"Alas *what?*" he said, crouched beside her.

"So beautiful."

"That I know," he said.

She leaned back on the pillows, once more only a woman in bed.

"Are they right, the parents?" he said. "Are they always right?"

"Watch out."

He'd almost knelt on the glass of the picture tumbled there in the bedclothes. She freed it, handling it to him. Neither gave it a look. "Who're you trying to sort out?" she said. "Can't be done. *She's* alive."

Because the drawing belonged to the dead, and to the dead when still young in a life then scarcely crept into his own, he got up, took it back into the other dulled room and hung it on its faded square, doing for it what he had done for his mother's stout dressing-table secrets, his father's slender artifacts. The truly dead had a right to linger, for healed old men to eulogize. *My wife was a remarkable woman, Simon. The dead should be sat up with in company, boy — the women too.*

And only for one night. Through the half-blue of the front window, he saw many cars now, anonymous at the curb. That other night had been in a winter city. This was going to be a dead-hot morning, the color of harbor water. It was a truism of cities, or of humans, that one season couldn't be vitally remembered in another. And of the healed, that all seasons took on the same demi-vierge light. Why he should think of it that way, he couldn't say. He went quickly out of the room.

The insoluble rhythm went on. He walked with it, limping not quite ahead of it.

Still on her pillow, she watched him dreamily. "Got to have a bath."

"In there." He came and sat on the edge of the bed. She made no move to get up.

"And I'm to breakfast here? In that?" The dress on the floor gleamed fastidiously at them, doll-empty, its bodice bent. "Public is all very well, Simon. Whatever it means to you — I don't mind." She wasn't perverse, merely obedient — Will you be whipped before, sir, or afterward? She stretched. "But one should never make oneself uncomfortable, really now, should one?"

"Right." Again he congratulated himself.

"Get me a cab then, do. Soon as I dress."

"I could go with you to the hotel, have breakfast there. No, it doesn't matter, really. Just so long as I never again have to think —" Of what others may think. "Much more comfortable. And it doesn't matter when we leave." He rubbed his face on her thigh, smelling himself there. Home births.

"Times three?" she murmured back. "Afraid I can't."

"Just being nostalgic." He raised his head, smiling. "Coo, the bally. I'm thinking of joining it."

"Are you now. What about your third leg?"

"My — ?"

"Cane."

"So you noticed. You would of course. No one else did, much, did they? Except Edwin."

"Who?"

"The *other* young man."

"Your protégé." A nostril wrinkled.

"You and Anna — "

"Yes. The kitchen knows."

"Kitchen?" he said. "Ah. I see. Where else could you have been thrown out of? At twelve."

He waited. But she didn't tell him he was clever.

"Does *he* know what's wrong with you?"

"No one does. Nerve ends maybe, the doctor said. Or nerves." He grinned, shifting up until he was even with her on the pillow. "Edwin I'm sure thinks it's age."

"He's had no experience — *here*." She said it professionally, giving the bed a smart rap.

"None? I — guess. I'm not surprised. He's from unique beginnings."

"Protégés always are," said Madame. "I never have them." She had coarsened her accent, always a hint he was to heed. "I should take care, I were you. Is *he* to help you at it too?"

"Too?"

"To be public again." She rubbed his beard. "Poor Disraeli, I have hit it, eh? D'ya know, Simon — you must be a terribly *good* man, in some ways. Because in so many others, you're not very sharp."

"Bless you." He circled her in his arms. "May the night bloom."

"It's day," she said. "And afternoon in London, that elderly nation. Ours is to be a limited engagement, yours and mine." Her tongue tripped quickly over this. "I don't make any others, not any more." She sat up. "Christ in the cornerhouse — what's that!"

From below they heard sounds unidentifiable except as rackety — thumps, shuffles, a scramble.

"Your son?" said Ninon. "He moves large."

"David? No, he was to stay with Walter." But downstairs, a sudden silence gave him time to remember his son's one violence, that one night's smashing rampage through which he had slept. Noises came again now, mysterious, methodical — would it have been like that? "I'm going down."

"No, don't." She was cocking her head like a telegrapher. "Listen. Two bodies, there are. Heels — a girl. And a man." She turned to smile at him. "No, you mustn't go."

He didn't know what his overwhelming rage was most for. "Maybe you can also tell me *who*."

Through heavy oak double floors, fourteen-foot ceilings and the draperies due civilization, they couldn't tell whether the sounds they heard, voices now, were muffled or strangulated, vicious or soft.

"Not the breeder," she said. "The other one."

He'd never felt such a vise as she held him with, not male or female — a snake's steel. "She's *alive*," she said through her hold. "Be still. Let them be. She's alive."

Or did he want to be held? He bent his chin into his neck — and broke free.

As he was at the door, she said, from the bed, "Will you go naked to her?"

"There's damage down there. I feel it."

"There may be." She lay where he had broken from her. "Shall I tell you about your daughter?"

He came to her, as on a reel she was winding.

"She's got a father," she said, "who brings her to bed with him."

As his hands went to her throat, she brought her lips to meet them. "When another woman's there."

Fists in his eyes, he put his head on her breasts.

"They're not much," she said. "I never had a child."

"You'd gnaw me free," he said. "If you could."

"Hush."

"I'll tell you about my daughter," he said. "That'll stop both our ears. What I know — and what I don't."

"It's quiet down there now. Listen."

It was. It seemed to him that for a moment there was no rhythm at all.

"It's natural." She smoothed his face, whose indecent yawp he had turned away. "Their sex oughtn't to be real to us. Or ours to them. It's more comfortable."

He raised himself, remembering a waitress in Brixton who'd said to him, *We can't have another war, it's not comfortable.* "It's morning."

"Your beard, it's black. Even if it was gray, your skin's that olive —" For the first time, she sounded exhausted. "It's when the gray shows through on a red skin that I can't abide . . . Little drops of sweat, like. Color of a pearlie's buttons."

"Calais?" he said.

"You know better," she said. "A rectory, in Islington." She raised herself suddenly on elbow. "By God, I'll tell them so. When they Dame me." She beat her fists on his chest, in glee. "We're a pair. Aren't we."

Already, before she lowered herself beside him, she could see that they weren't quite. "But it's good to be where we are," she whispered. "Not yet at the end. And in a minute — a bath."

He yearned to pay her a compliment nearest her life and comforts, and to what she called "Where we are." Nothing fell so far short of that as talk of youth, or love.

"No, you're *French*," he said. "You're French."

She was hidden from him by his own embrace.

"She's very like you," she said. "Didn't you know?"

They lay side by side, lightly almost not touching, in the valleyland of the hour and the season — of the minute before baths, the interval before age — in the musky bedclothes of what wasn't birth any more, but wasn't yet death.

The steps that came up the stairs were heavier. Heel of a shoe, one foot unshodden; one foot unshodden, heel of a girl. That was the rhythm. Alas, so beautiful. The lone steps stopped at the landing, dragged at the door. Listening? Or fallen. Didn't go on.

"Open it," said Ninon. "Oh Simon, open up to her. There's been damage done."

13   Hunting a Judge – *June 1951*

The secret of cities is a simple one. Everyone believes himself to be
the lone inhabitant. And is subjected to the sight of the others twenty-
four hours a day. Between these two poles — of our natural meditation and its rebuttal — breed fantasies with which every police
sergeant is familiar, every doctor. The law does only sharply remind
us of this, our inalienable — fact. The question of civil law is not
justice, but equilibrium.

> — JUDGE SIMON MANNIX
> *Address to the Bar Association
> of New York*

"To QUOTE A MURDERER," the two personalities of Edwin
Halecsy said to themselves, and took the Judge's daughter by the hand.
He had no idea as yet that he meant to make her pay for it.

The twin lamps of the police stations were the same all over the city,
in wealthy precinct or slum. Downtown in his old neighborhood — in
those richly endowed blocks where the worn stone of the stoops was
soft enough to sit on, on those hot nights when people boiled out of the
burning anthills, or hung at the windows like a chorus of those too
tired to be saved — there was always twenty feet or so of luxurious
silence in front of the stationhouse, slunk past by moustached youths
on their way to felony, given a wide berth by the baseball voices. Down
there the twin globes gave a light that was known to all, testimony to
the underhand machinery of life.

Up here, in this poor environs that scarcely knew it was also a
"precinct" — where the undernourished garbage cans held lobster
husks, plus all the steak juice which could be brewed from stock certifi-
cates, but never the rich purple of a human fetus, rarely a rat — the
two lamps were weaker, almost anonymous. Foot traffic ignored them,
lonely lamps of some all-night post office, kept open for messages
between the two worlds.

"I came here once. To look at the list of missing persons."

"Here?"

"Downtown."

"Who were you looking for?"

He didn't answer.

"Oh, of course — you told me once. How you went looking." She slipped the hand he had let go into his again. "And here you are." But he didn't appear to hear.

Inside, this place was the same as the stationhouse where he'd seen his first typewriter. The identical seamy-sallow air, half a locker-room's but not so sweaty. More the color of the backs of stamps and the fronts of workmen's compensation notices. With only a little more officialdom than hung anywhere there was a clock, a desk and a man. Still, a place where matters were glued together, stitched with the dark streak of the telephone, not quite jailed.

He wished to tremble again. But he knew the names of all the objects in the room now.

"Gwan," said the man at the desk. "You college kids. Not since the thirties, that real all-night public show. Been cleaned up. What do you want that for?"

"My idea," said the girl. "I was taken once. When I was little."

"For a lesson in responsibility," the boy said.

The man ignored him. "Little, hmm. And when was that?"

"Before — I was twelve."

"And how old are you now, Grandma?"

"Twenty-one."

On the desk there was a heavy-paper accordion file. The man fingered it. "Sorry, kiddies. Not in the 64th." His eyes frisked the boy. "Maybe in the Bowery. They still have the old line-up there."

"Sixty-fourth," said the boy. "This is the 64th?"

"Where else."

"Is Putzi still around?"

"Who?"

"Putzi the forger."

"Look," said the man. "Whyn't you two go have scrambled eggs at Child's?"

"*That* was the forties, officer," said the girl. "Wasn't it? People went there then, I've heard."

He took off his cap, ran his finger around the band, put the cap on again, smiled. "Right. That was me."

"*He's* a law student," said the girl.

Her companion bowed. "Her father is a judge."

"Is he. Could have saved you two a wild-goose chase then, couldn't he. What court?"

"Retired," she said.

"But he keeps busy," said the boy.

"Look at the time!" she said. "Is that right?"

"Very right, sister."

"I just got off a plane. And is that . . . all the time it is? Three?"

"Enough for most people, kid."

"Not — when you see somebody die."

"Around *here?*" said the officer.

"You saw *what?*" the boy said.

"You kids pick each other *up?*" said the officer. "You know this boy?"

"She picked me up," said the boy.

"He knows me, better than anyone else," said the girl.

"Where was the accident?" the officer said. "Airport?"

"On the plane. To a seatmate. I went along, in the ambulance."

"Better take her home."

"Oh, I'm all right. Just — not sleepy. Not . . . sleepy."

"Comes as a shock, kid. First time you see somebody go?"

She hesitated for a minute, then put out a hand, almost socially. "We mustn't — take you from your work."

"Phones do ring." In the few moments they'd been there, none had. The officer sat there immobile, arms folded. He might have been cautioning them to listen for one. They could hear each other breathe. They moved to the door.

"Had two years college myself," said the man at the desk. "Nights. At Brooklyn Cee . . ."

At the door, the boy turned back. "Knew you weren't a Mick. Even though you put on the 'gwan' stuff. Why?"

"In the force, you're Irish. No, I'm Hunky. From the edge of old Yorkville itself. Born in the precinct."

The girl started to speak, but the boy got in ahead of her. "Which one do I come from, would you say?" Eyes narrowed, cheekbones high, he could have been asking this of the nations of the earth. Or telling them.

"Why?"

"Might want to join the force."

"Don't have to be a Hunky to do that." The officer squinted. "Not a Jew, I'll say that for you."

The girl smiled.

The phone rang.

Over the ringing, the boy called, "Edge of Chinatown. The Third."

The phone was already being talked into. The man covered the mouthpiece; it couldn't be said for sure that he had heard. "Better go scramble those eggs."

Outside, Edwin said, in his best imitation of his student self, "Well, that was informative."

The street had lightened, but it was still technically night.

"That you aren't a Jew?" She pointed a toe, swept it around and behind her.

"*Do* I know you best?" he said. "Or is it only that the others don't bother to hear."

When her profile didn't move, he said, "*Was* it the first time?"

It moved at once. "Oh, I'm all right. I'm always all right."

The lamps confirmed her fresh dress, swinging purse, all of her so quietly ready to go on tour.

"Shall I? Take you back home?"

A finger touched his spectacles, ran itself lightly around one rim. She grasped his shoulder where it pressed hers, rubbing the cloth of his suit like a girl who knew cloth. "No. Keep me out."

"I wondered. Whether you saw them."

"Madame and my father?" She was carrying a pair of white gloves, and now drew one on. "Years ago, Pauli and I — used to have hopes."

"Not any more."

"You must ask — Father's secretary." She had on both gloves now. "Where shall we go?"

The secretary had his head averted. "I could show you — our place." He said it without smirk. He would never be that collegiate. "I thought of it, earlier."

"Your — mother won't mind?"

"I meant the old place. The basement. I still check on it, sometimes." He took up her gloved hand, examined the palm. "Like to go? Down to the Third?"

"Corner of Pitt and *Gooverneer?*"

"That was the school. That was only the school."

"Yes, let's go there," she said. "Can we walk?"

"Mother of God," he said. "No."

"I know how far it is. I just meant — *let's* walk."

He was already trotting her at a pace. "We'll take the subway. Like anybody who doesn't *have* to walk." The kiosk was four blocks away. He felt a harsh, self-cleansing elation. "You and your family *talk* walking. Walking the *city*. *Taking* a walk. A walk is to get somewhere, when you have no other way. And a key hung around a child's neck — is to let him in."

"We let him in," she said. "Shouldn't we have?"

"What I don't know," he said slowly . . . "is how much you know." They'd reached the kiosk.

"I know nothing," she said. "About the Third."

Downstairs, they had the luck to catch a train for which a group had already collected on the platform, old women made baby-faced by babushkas, all wearing strong black coats.

"The cleaners' train. Some of them get on here. My mother and I once used to catch it from a job further down. We're lucky. Last one down until six."

In the train, he sat her across the aisle from them. The same crowd, it could have been, rocking with the car like the pros they were, full of the same sturdy, unionized talk.

"What did you and she clean?"

"Bars."

She looked across the aisle, at the line of black oilcloth bags. "Didn't know there were that many bars to clean."

"There aren't. This is the aristocracy you're looking at. But we had a bag like theirs. Maybe we still do. She doesn't like to throw away."

"What do they clean?"

"Offices."

Across the aisle, one of the women sat apart, intent, in her hands the power of the rosary.

"Clean is my mother's God."

"I only met her that once."

"She's all there," he said. "The aunts'll tell you no. People as stupid as my aunts never can believe there's anybody stupider."

"I could never stand the Halecsys."

"Because she didn't tell them, you know. When it happened to her."

"When what?"

He turned. She *had* remembered Pitt and Gouverneur. "Me."

"Oh yes," she said at once. " 'Dead, divorced' — what was the other?"

" 'Disappeared.' "

The train rocked.

"Used to be tribes," he said. "That didn't understand the connection."

"The —?"

"Between having kids and — you-know." It had slipped from him without thought, that earliest euphemism of the schoolhouse stairs, dropping like a penny into the well of his older intelligence, starting up bright, concentric ripples between that world and this. She'd taken off the gloves again, in one of the fake subtleties they swallowed in place of living; her hands were bare. He didn't touch them. "Fornication," he said.

Her face didn't change. "Where were they, those tribes?"

"Some archipelago."

He watched the sisterhood across the aisle get up and file out as the train stopped, in the rear the one who had prayed. "My mother's all there. It's just that what you see — that's all there is."

"Just like —" The train was roaring on again. He'd never seen her face like that. Surely she'd said it. " — like mine!"

They were drawing through one of the longest station approaches, a no-man's-land in which pole after pole crept by.

"We wait here. It always waits here, doesn't it?" she said.

"You've been before." He had meant to show it to her first — the monstrous death's-head of *his* city. But the city was open to all. "With Austin? That settlement house? You don't have to tell me."

She didn't. Her expression was the one they all knew. She hid behind it. None had ever realized that except himself.

The train drew into the halt, fans whirring. As minutes went by, the few passengers exchanged rigid stares in the non-language which was the proper code for the bowels of the earth. Nobody got up and beat at panes or broke tongue; this was the city too.

"Lots of intelligent people too" — her eyes were half closed — "never can believe how many others are stupider than them."

"Not Austin." He gave his rival careful justice, half wishing Austin could hear. "Austin knows the scale. He was born to it. That's half his intelligence. Or — did you mean me?"

She bent her head, a sudden noncommittal curve of the body professional. "No."

Who then? The train began moving. "*Anna* is intelligent," he said. "Why is she afraid?"

The train shadows took up her profile, enlarging it.

"Oh, not just of me," he said. "I know why that."

"Servants are always afraid."

"Not of you. *For* you. Like a — bodyguard."

The flickering light passed over her face and over.

As they stepped from the train, he found his hand under her elbow, and felt a spasm of pride. Manners were instinctive with him now.

Under the steadier lamps of the deserted station, he held her still, and studied her.

"*I'm* intelligent," he said. "He's always telling me. I kept a little notebook, telling myself. I only threw it away today. That picture. The big one, in the big room — Anna caught me studying it. There's one of her in almost every room, isn't there. Kept there. Because none of them really look too much like her, do they."

"Almost every. She was a difficult subject. Everybody said." She didn't whisper.

He passed a hand over her face. They stood there on the platform's edge, oblivious, courting danger, or each other.

"*You* do. You look like her," he said. "That's why Anna's afraid, isn't it."

She moved her head from side to side. Into a yoke, out of it. As long as she kept moving — the motion itself seemed to say — she looked like no one in her family, only herself. Her mouth closed, opened again. "I mean to live. I mean to *live*."

A rush of the unknown welled up in him. He felt it — the unknown. Or it was hot in here — and he had his mother's eyes. "Let me show you my place." The personal wasn't filth, down here. He eased himself into it; down here nothing was personal. Tenderly, wielding her like a trophy, he went up the familiar stairs.

Nothing had changed in these slumped barrows along which he had toiled with his ikon, the hours growing on their joined backs like a spine always testing upward for the scope of that day's food. Orchards of night-bruised fruit; he could smell its dark mauve. Nothing had changed in these grand banks of his beginnings. He could always depend on it.

He wasn't surprised that it was all still here. In the nameless merge of its seasons, nothing much was separate except the light from the dark, the empty bowl from the not quite filled, chill cellarholes of time when the bugs were silent, bustles of heat when the rats were brave. How beautiful it had been. There were no visits here. In the small center of their round, he had carried his ikon, she had carried him.

"Nothing," he said aloud. "Here's the school." They passed it, in a golden shower of 5x8's.

"But it's not there," she said.

Only a scoop in the earth, with a crane hung on the sky behind it like a huge, idle spoon. "No, it isn't. But nothing's lost."

The church was still here. And the spoiled priest who wouldn't leave the all-night bar until the first bell for Mass had rung. " 'Puts a little religion into the morning,' he used to say . . . There's the door where they used to give out the shoes." He didn't turn his head as they passed it.

" 'Keeps the rats down and blessed,' " she said. "I never forgot."

When the twin lamps came in sight again, solemn here and dangerous, she put her hand in his and made him keep it. The cellar door, familiar to him as their holly-wreathed knockers to them, was just around the corner. He stopped her before it. "Here's our stoop."

"So near? To the police?"

"The less wanted."

"Edwin." She dared a laugh. "Even then, you were political."

They always dared to laugh. That was their style. He could have it in time. In exchange for a rat.

He lifted the cellar door; it was always open. "I was here last year. Checking my property." He dared to laugh. "Nothing surprises you, does it — not even down here. Is that you yourself? — or in all of you? You're never surprised."

"We used to walk near here. I tried to tell you."

He held the door for her, leaving it propped open behind them. But he already knew, as they went down the steps of the correct number, into the pissy, wood-and-rag quiet and the crockery murmur of the pipes, all correct — now in subtraction we add back and verify — that no one should have been brought here.

"Some old bum's been sleeping here. Always are. Smell." In the corner, there was still a table. Scarcely more than boards, it could be anything. "Could be ours." There was no tin box. Opposite was the newspaper pile. While they sat on them, he refurnished the place for her. "He burns candles too," he said. "See there."

"What was in the box?"

"Scissors. Couple of spoons. Knife I bought." Plus some scavenged items, including the tube he'd been sure was a thermometer until he'd learned it came with contraceptive cream — and an eggbeater they never got to use.

"Hall toilet's that way. . . . Listen." Intent, he held her close. "You hear a rat?"

"Maybe there is." She got to her feet. "But I have to go."

"Take a candle."

She had to climb a flight, but she'd find it. She was gone quite a time, but he didn't worry about her, sitting here, seeing this place first through her eyes then through his own, with the shutter effect of those card movies in the oldest penny machines. The dark was moving, arranging itself as it had used to do — but nothing any more was nameless. He had his legend now, if he wanted it. It had been here all the time.

"You all right?" he said.

"I had something in my bag. Kleenex." She crept back close to him. She hadn't got up, then, in order to get away.

"Guess I'm the cleanest here," he said. "At that."

"How do you know the — the *person* who lives here — is a man?"

He marveled. They were formal with people to the end; not even a bum huddling in a corner to scratch and push at himself was one of a legion to them; they personified to the end. As they had done with himself.

"Because of the smell," he said harshly. "That fishy smell." Let her figure it out for herself.

On their two pallets, he and his mother had turned their backs to each other, in dumb continence. Since babyhood, he had tended himself in all fleshly things; she liked the touch only of the soap, the water and pail. From their memory rose a manger smell, ammoniac and straw. He could smell it now, the hard metal scent that sweat became after days of cold. But like all innocents, those two had never smelled themselves. In the dark, without fathers, a son was made.

"I never met any woman bums. Mostly they have a doss somewhere." Old hags, with a den to scream at the kids from. Or — you-knows. "You all have a doss-down somewhere," said the spoiled priest to his mother. "Even you."

He got to his feet. "Come on, let's get out. How do you stand it here."

"We can't go back yet," she said. "You have to keep me out."

"We can sit upstairs. We used to do that."

On the middle step he turned, waiting as he had so often done, bracing the metal trapdoor on his bent neck.

"Aren't we going to blow it out?" she said. "His candle?"

"Let it burn."

She went back and did it anyway.

"The old john will never know we've been here," he said. "We have no scent."

"Haven't we?" She stopped beside him. "How can you *do* that. On your *neck*."

Holding it, a proud Atlas-weight grinding his shoulders, he let himself be kissed. Then she went up, before him. Outside, just above pavement level there was a ledge broad enough to sit on. He let the trapdoor fall, looking down on the clang. "We did nothing wrong," he said.

In the sky, roughly northwest from where they sat, a line evidenced itself, scarcely light, more a wearing through of the dark. "The market line, we always called it. That's how we told time." When working at the stalls, it had been the time he rose. An ozone always came with it — chlorophyll. His mother still got up to it, in the electric-veined dark.

"So your father toured the city with you," he said. "I can imagine, those 'Here's Fraunce's Tavern, and here I was born' walks. Now you're going on tour by yourself, he intends to take me." But his voice was almost tolerant. She had already paid for that.

Going to be a lot of traffic before long — the cursing trucks that would take the wrong turn into these narrows, against foot traffic of the earliest trade-hours, the chicken-slaughterers on their way to the synagogue first, and others en route to the more Christian rituals of the river — chandlers with shaved heads and leather jerkins, bums who still thought they were longshoremen, helpers with the wide, cutpurse mouth that often signified the handlers of fish. But for a half-hour yet, it was still all roach-shadows, scuttlers passing anonymous.

"Not him," she said. "Her. She walked me everywhere. Talking, always talking. From the time I was little. He never knew."

"Speak up," he said.

"You think we're all talk."

"Not when you speak of her." He was watching her face. "Don't hide. When you don't speak of her . . . how you hide."

She opened her purse. The gloves, crumpled, were in it. "He sometimes took us to the park when we were little. For the park. She never bothered with that."

A rusted garbage can lay on its side near him. Using the toe of a sneaker, he began dislodging it from the refuse pile behind. "Where did you and she go?"

"Anywhere — she didn't care where. She only lived when she was moving, acting — she said it herself. Action, she meant. She couldn't *pretend*, not at all. She always had to speak out. Diddy and I overheard them once, quarreling about it."

"Can you?" he said. "Pretend?"

"I dance." She gave a sudden, tender laugh. "So did she a little, once, whatever they did in those days — flamenco, Isadora Duncan Greek. She taught in a settlement house once, the old Meinhard, uptown — Grandfather Mendes knew old man Meinhard. First time she went — she was sixteen — she gave the kids a talk first, about ancient Greece. When she got through, one of them said, 'Ain't any Greeks around here, miss. Can yer do the split?' So she stood up and did it. After that, she had them in the palm of her hand."

"Palm of her hand." He kicked the garbage pail upright. "My mother told me about a pig-sticking once."

"I was just — telling."

"So she told you all about life," he said. "What else?"

She looked at him steadily. "Life." Even in this light, on this ledge, her face was no different from the way he and they always saw it. "Fornication."

The market line was widening. He could smell it now.

"She told me everything," said the girl beside him. "Her side of it. But it's never enough."

Two people passed; it must be close to four. He let another pair go by and dwindle before he answered. "Is that what we share?"

"You feel it too," she said.

"How we keep them on!" he said. "Your mother in the house, my father — in the hallway."

"Yes. Oh yes." She said it passionately, into the distance. Then she buried her face in her lap.

"But you can't pretend either," he said. "Not like him. Do you and he ever — quarrel about it?"

She lifted her head, in one arched curve like an exercise. Her upper lip was white, or the morning had crept to it. "I used not to be able to. Pretend. But I have got control of it."

The market line had widened now beyond repair.

"That unknown, in the hallway," he said. "Sometimes, I almost — know him."

The girl leaned her cheek against his. "She comforts me. She tells me the truth."

"How you speak out. When you speak of her. Is that why they don't listen to you, at home?"

"How can you say that?" she said. "They listen for me all day long."

She was answering him plain, as he thought she always had answered anyone — but from a frame of reference so far back or deep that all she said or did came from it; if he had the frame, he would have everything.

"Because you know? About him?"

"I always knew about him. She never stopped talking about him. What I wanted was — to know about *her*."

The twin lamps behind them shone weaker.

"Tell me. What she said about him."

She shrugged. He shook her. Her head bobbed in the light of the lamps. "It's only that you already know." He could feel her body feel his. "That he was too good," she said. "With the innocent."

In the refuse pile, there was a movement, a tinkle, of glass somewhere dislodged.

"She used to say that over and over . . . Now, of course, I see for myself. 'It's the Jew in us, Ruthie,' she used to say. 'We give an eye for an eye, a tooth for a tooth, just as the Bible says. But not always only for vengeance. Nobody notices that we do it for pity too. *He* thinks he does it because he never went to war.'"

"But that's *him* talking!"

"It was her too."

He was watching the pile. "*Take* an eye," he said.

"She said 'give.' "

She leaned forward, not to him. " 'Simon has a genius for private life; he'll be a great man there,' she said once. 'Chauncey Olney told me so; he asked me to come and see him, Ruthie, and I went. "So many of your race have that, Mirriam," he said to me. "But public life, so many of your men fuddle there. Give him ten years, Mirriam." And darling Ruthie, I said I'd try. But I'm so afraid one of us'll be the one to do him in. It doesn't matter if I tell *you* . . . It won't be David. Your father doesn't feel toward David — but that's another story. And it can't be you — not in that short time. So it'll be me. I can't convince your father, you see. That I'm bad enough.' "

She hadn't mimicked, except in the pace of a woman walking, bearing down on the child, with a voice that maybe was to be the child's. "And she couldn't, you see, she couldn't convince him. She couldn't convince *me*."

"She was mad, then?" he said in awe. "Or that would be his excuse."

In the pile, there was a rustle. Always moving, moving; the test for life is movement. To quote a judge. He could see how it would be in a family. In some alliance in which all four Mannixes stole from and gave full pity to each other — the Judge had been quoting *her.* Did the dead still move?

"No, she wasn't. That was her trouble . . . Excuse for what?"

"Her death," he said — and listened for the echo of that.

She didn't falter. "Often I can't tell any more, whether she said everything to me. Or whether I — After." Her voice changed. "She doesn't really . . . come to me. But she *comes* to me." Her voice was happy. "I even know . . . a little something about her that no one else did. Or almost no one. I was never sure she knew it herself."

"Would it concern — David?"

"In a way."

"Well, sons are *made*," he said. "I've no pity there."

"You're a Christian." She rubbed her face on his shoulder.

"So everybody says."

"But you see? How one can get to know — about both?"

"I'm not likely to hear voices."

She turned his face to hers. "Phew, I'm tired, Edwin. I never knew I could be so tired. And you?"

"Not me. I was only fifteen yesterday."

"That would help in the theatre, not to know one's age. Know something? Your face hasn't changed since. Not an iota. And I don't think you have, either."

"Don't go to sleep." His voice wasn't gentle. It went with the face he could see as well as she. His own.

She leaned against him, her voice drowsy. "Helps though, she always said. To talk to someone. Even if you can't tell them everything."

"So you *are* alike then. You and she."

She sat up. "I was once. But I got control of it. You can be like *both*. You can. I finally remembered that." She followed his glance. "What's that?"

"It's a rat." Sometimes in the lone bed-dark when he couldn't be continent, he felt this same satisfaction — halfway between gain and loss. "Two of them."

In the refuse pile, first one head poked out, then the other whole animal — the peculiarly glistening haunches which slimmed to a cord, had without warning a head. Some said the human hand was what confounded artists — but if you could draw a rat, you had drawn everything. "I been bit by a Mexican chicken," the children sent to the school nurse said with aloof smiles. Men coming into the barbershop after a bought night, to have a scratch dressed, an eye leeched, said the same, with the same smile. The two animals prowling here, tough between the discs of tin marked Coca, Kraft, brave with summer, might have been nibbling a pile of goods as high as the resurrection. The girl beside him hadn't moved; she was cool. With what she must once have been witness to, why wouldn't she be? He stood up. "They don't eat for nothing. Somebody pays for it."

"Where did they *go?*" she said.

It was never possible to tell the exact rat-tip when they had gone. Once they had, you always knew. The cellar door didn't have to be open for them; she could see that. The lore of his city was simple. "Where do you think?"

She stood up and kissed him — not for himself but for what they all treasured him for, for his *life*, before he had met them.

"Want those eggs?"

"No. Take me *home*."

"I'm not sleepy either," he said.

At the end of the alley, they both turned to look back.

"Know what it looks like to me now?" he said . . . "Just a habitat, that's all. Like it says in the nature books: 'Mexican chicken, habitat all hemispheres, low ground.'" He smiled at her, the way he had at Krupong. "I won't go back."

She took his hand and swung it. "Yes, we're alike. The way I've always thought of it."

"How?"

"Everything's already happened to us."

He had the wit to walk on, not to ask details. He was at the beginning of everything now. He had the clearest sense now of how young he was. Of the blatant power given him by circumstance. Of how protean it was in his will to become. Could Putzi the forger walk both sides of the street any better? Any lipreader have a finer sense of what others missed? Or any dinner guest make a more knowledgeable payment — for what he was about to receive. In return for having been the most intelligent who had ever been let in the house.

"Don't know that we can get a cab here." He had a concern — like a dater's — that this tender means to an end should not be jarred.

"I use the subway a lot."

"No," he said, "we're not so different."

In the city habit, they waited in total silence for the train back. In the train they said nothing, saw what they saw with the train's rhythm, side by side.

Outside it was morning.

At the head of the Mannix street, she took the key out of her purse.

"Not around your neck any more."

She walked on without reply.

"Still have your club?"

Fair enough if she wouldn't answer; with these little hostilities he was warning her of what was to come, and she was taking it in. "Used to be a stone bust in the window of that house across the way, and a silver pitcher. Real thief-bait."

"They're gone. It's apartments now."

"Seven years."

"And seven maids, and seven mops," she said.

And seven visits. He lingered at the bottom of the steps. No one sat on a stoop here; it merely provided a natural pause for reflection for all classes, as to whether the caller was going down in the world or up. No apartment house ever did this as well.

She was looking up and down her street. Its pale, private trees were new ones. She was looking at her habitat the way all her class did — as if they had made it themselves, and knew the price to be paid for it. They were not to be surprised.

"What's the matter, don't you want to go in?" he said. "It's still a very quiet street. No revolutions here. No murders."

Twin lamps over her head shed safety only, from her own house. He climbed two steps above her and looked down at her, laughing. A red commune, rolling heads down society's staircase — as her father was so fond of calling it — was the last thing he wanted. What he wanted was to get to society in time, before it exploded into new proletariats — to get *his* fill of it.

"We're the revolution," he said. "We're what the world's going to be."

For his answer, she handed him the key.

They went up the steps, stood in front of that door — there were doors that didn't need to be braced with the neck, or didn't let on. "Maybe it's open," he whispered. But on this night the Judge had closed it well. And she wouldn't help him with the unfamiliar key. Fair enough. He'd warned her.

Where had she learned to twist into him now like a finger into a buttonhole, holding him there, under the lintel of her own house? "What's he bribing you for? Why?"

In any court of night or morning, such a question was its own answer. At last, with trembling lip, she herself gave it. "For me?"

Again he had that same sensation of gain-loss as after his nightly trials in the dormitory bed linen. Now it was over, in the lonely court of himself. And he had done nothing yet. Nothing personal.

Entering the house ahead of her, he turned around to face her. "Welcome to the Mannix house," he said, then drew her in and closed the door.

As in all his visits, the hall mirror waited, holding in its gaunt pool all the elusive dynasties that had gone before. He could see himself perfectly there. Edwin the learner — who dealt with it as it came. The power of a person shouldn't be diminished just when he understood everything. But it was. Hunt down a judge and this is still all he can tell you, from the moment he catches you buttoning your fly.

He took off his jacket and hung it on the newel-post. She was still standing just inside. "Can't *you* get past that mirror? I could break it for you."

She shivered in his arms. "I'd still be there."

"Funny, I can see myself there perfectly. But not you." He touched the glass. "Edwin Halecsy — and who?"

"Friend. *Friend.*"

"I take all bribes," he said.

He began mothkissing his questions over her cheeks, scarcely caring whether she heard. "You saw somebody die tonight. *Was* it the first time?" His lips murmured over her eyelids. "Is there a picture of her, in *your* room?" In her mouth, his tongue prodded, and withdrawing itself, said, "You're the perfect witness. The daughter of the house." His stretched mouth breathed heat into her ear, the tongue circling it. The tongue inserted itself and said, "He killed her. You saw."

All this time, against him from breast to knee, she didn't move, even to the swelling of the rod against her own mound. She wasn't going to resist. He hung on her in a sawtoothed pit of regret for that, motionless.

She spoke, hard-voiced, from a cold distance he hadn't touched. "I'm not bad either. No one will ever convince me of it."

He held her, a fist in her shortened hair. "You want my dirt. When you have so much of your own — why do you want mine?"

When he began to take her, pushing aside the bloody-wet contraption between her legs, which couldn't save her, she hung on him, arms and head drooping at a thieves' angle — as if he was the cross. For that he would beat her, but afterwards. He held her wrists behind her — limp, but in the attitude that was correct. Over her shoulder, through her hair, in all the cups for light that a personal outline could make, he saw the hallway. His jacket on the post, immobile. In the niche behind it, a woman's boa, on a chair. Pitiless, the pointed light hung above, through all the convulsions of his loins. If he could only let go of her wrists, he had a strange emotion toward what she could do for him; she would reach up gently and take his glasses off; then she would sink her teeth in him. If she hadn't refused to be saved — he could have let her go.

He had to take his glasses off to beat her, which his own fists did for him efficiently, as if he had never left the district, quietly reddening the skin, not breaking a bone. At last she resisted him, and he could stop. He had a little of her blood on him, but that was natural.

They couldn't immediately release one another. Sprawled at the bottom of the stairs, they might have been hanging there in a colloquy of love. Then, slowly, each began to move. A blind hand groped along the floor. The eyeglasses, flung against the mirror like a marriage-cup, were within its reach, but it could not seem to find them. A hand not its mate found them for it, gave these into it. Miracles happen, gently, but too late. The hand that owned the glasses felt over them. One lens should have been cracked, but was whole.

The unknown form that was himself stood up with him. His arms hung heavy, Neanderthal, but tiny fingers at their far ends buttoned him intelligently. Below him, she was moving, repairing herself, in the attitude that was correct. Surely he had convinced her now.

"Poor rat," he said. "You found me."

Closing the outer door behind him, he had a moment's confusion as to why, for he lived here now. Then he walked rapidly to his other house. Entering, he mounted the stairs as noiselessly as he could, for the hugeness of his outline was still with him, and people in fifty-dollar-a-month houses often slept until eight. When he came downstairs again, he was carrying a coat. Napless now, scarcely black any more, it was one coat of a legion made to last. The only wonder of it was how it had been kept so clean.

He had to go out in the backyard behind the tenement to burn it. Yards were his habitat; he scavenged well. Here or there at this hour, a solitary super was often to be seen over his small pyre, getting the world well ready, before six-o'clock Mass. The church next door had no bell, seldom a sacristan; he wasn't even sure that it was consecrated any more.

The coat was hard burning. A sleeve protruded arm-length with a gust inside, the old shawl collar billowed up the gray of winters, one lapel trembled over the other to keep out the elements; the coat would not give up its shape. A terrible stench came from it, clearing his eyes.

Some men would hide from that other house now, or go on their knees to it. He would go back there this very evening, with a fresh batch of clothes. They were always explaining themselves there, and calling that civilization. Let them explain to him their yearning to make him one of themselves — when all the time they'd known they were no Lourdes for the curing of men's souls. All they could tell him in the end was what he already knew and had long since paid for. That the ward was the beginning of everything.

He could imagine himself a politician now. The best mob was a mob of one. He saw himself in the Mannix house, writing the Judge's essays, a power behind a throne he would gain his own power to desert. A man who didn't know the difference between right and wrong had more moral suasion at his command than anyone — and had to watch out only for others like himself. He could do anything now.

On the fire-pile, the cloth coat rose, full of red, hung for a tattered moment whole, and fell, giving up all its element. Poor rat, you had me. He began to tremble then, just when he had nothing more to fear.

There was nobody in the church next door, except the Heavenly Father. He ran there, to deal with his mortal one.

He got behind the confession box only to see if he was small enough. It was large enough. They could come from all the nations of the earth, to meet him here. Devise realty, bequeath personalty. Now he was trembling, shrinking between the sheets of himself, which was what prayer must be. It was large enough in here for all the nations to present themselves and fall back again, one by one — leaving only one. After a while, that one separated from the others and came toward him, his father — a man like himself. *I appear in the record.* The box where he was kneeling couldn't prevent it. In its old yellow panels he saw the pinholes where the wood louse made its entry, every pitiless detail.

His father touched him on the loins, leaving there his mother's blood. Crouched over it, Edwin spat up the communion between them. One word, in night court — only one. *"Rapped."*

14 Finding a Girl – *June 1951*

"There's been damage done."

It hung in the air of the stairwell, in the pure morning nimbus falling through the skylight above. A white dress was lying at the top of the stairs, crumpled enough for anything.

Naked from their own bed, they ran toward it, still with all their organs, the semen not yet dry. He stood over his daughter again, sex hanging, an old balls of a boy. Behind him, his bedmate, leaving herself bare, silently held out to him the garment she had seized on the way, and he took the frilled peacock and covered himself. But it was she who bent to examine, peering over the reddened skin, the bruised eyes — a pitying whore, executive. "The dirty — she wouldn't let him do. So he's pummeled her, good as any nark."

Below them, the eyes opened. The woman's hand, thrust under the girl's skirt, was intent on other business. "Hah. I see. Some men are like that. She was that way, and he savaged her for it."

But he saw the eyes. The flimsy dropped from his loins. He knelt over her. "Alive. She's alive."

"Alive enough, the more mess to it. Get off of her, Simon. Fetch hot towels, cold. Anything. And take your time."

When he went, she leaned over the girl. "There, there, my duck. More things happen to one. You'll be happy yet." With a practiced lift, she raised the girl's body, saw the muddled skirt behind, and laid her quickly down again. Her head bent, nostrils dilated, then she spoke. "The ponce. He did it anyway. Then beat you for it. Is that it?" Now she knelt, whispering, her naked haunches skinny up. "Get us to your room, girl. I'll tell you what to do for it, if you don't know. You poor silly little mark, it was the first, wasn't it."

Then the father was back, a eunuch bearing towels and a basin, babbling of the hot mound of them in one arm, the cold in the other — and saw the bloodied skirt. Robed as he was now, he got down to her again, the tassel of his sash dabbling. In the yawped face he turned up to Ninon's, the lids were almost shut. "Her poor blood. I'll kill him for it." He bent over the girl again. "Was it —?" And thought better of it. "Who?"

At his side, the woman swabbing with towels, cold for the eyes, hot for between the thighs, stopped her work, caught even now in an attitude so predestined a man could hit her for it. "Don't tell him, Ruth."

He turned on her. "What have you to — Hold your tongue."

"Don't, Ruth," said the woman, ignoring. "Don't do."

"Leave off, you bloody —" His mouth stuttered, working.

"Whore," said the woman, and went on swabbing, her breasts swinging, small as they were.

In the cleansed face below, the swollen lips parted, speaking without sound. The father caught it; he was expert on such mime. Maybe the woman serving the girl did too. "My blood," the lips were saying. "It's only mine."

"Oh, Disraeli!" said the woman. "Had a daughter." Working with towel and basin, wiping soft, cozening the matted hair of the girl, her own nakedness looked motherly. "Better tell him then, Ruth. About us whores." She dried the girl's mouth. "Then nobody will be killed."

The eyes closed again.

"She's fainted," he said, agonized. "I'll *carry* her up."

The woman dropped her work, stood up. "I've got to have some *clothes*. That where her room is?" She stared down at the girl. "No, it's just she doesn't want me here. She'll be all right. Let her be for a minute; it's an exhausting —" Her own mouth worked — "experience." She turned to go, turned back, foot one step up, hand on balustrade, nakedness forgotten, or proud. The lines of her face joined with those of her body. "Maybe I better do the telling, though — she'll never. Because you have such an effect on us, Simon, on all of us, that we *can't* always tell you — what we want to. For your sake. Not because we lie." She came up to him stunned there, twisted her finger into his lapel as women did when charming a man, or loving him, laid her head for a minute inside his robe, on his chest, then stood back. "She let him," she said, and left him.

As she went up the stairs, the sun rose upon the skylight and halted there. The virtue of these houses was that dark as they were at center, bound windowless to each other at the sides and not well cross-cur-rented, once a day the sun sent its long shaft down their spiral, often to the very bottom, and all their gildings, any gold or crystal they had, were caught in this illumination. She walked steadily up and through it, a mote rising in the beam of a rose window, and lost herself in the shadows above.

Below, the girl tried to rise, lay back.

"I'll help you upstairs," he said. "I won't carry you. I can't."

The girl struggled up on elbow slowly, towels falling from her. He stood beside her, not hindering. Her lips parted. "*I* am the missing person. I can't pretend, any more."

His face went down on his clenched fist. She stayed as she was, to watch him.

Now that she'd told him what he wanted to know — that she knew what she was — she was old enough to watch a man cry.

There was a heaving, no salt wet. He spoke. "Make it the night before. Oh Ruth, Ruth . . . make it the night before."

Above, the woman watching them come up the stairs together to her wept as women did, scarcely knowing why.

Scenes without intellect.

III
Beautiful Visits

15   A Buzzing Man – *Spring 1954*

SOME people were elated by the ancient-culture sections of museums, striding the Egyptian wing, the Iranian, the Hittite, with their chins high, in the supreme command of being modernly alive. He often forgot the exhibits, in watching them. Others went down the aisles in a slight, persistent dusk of depression over so much beauty and inventiveness, all much the same under the superficial glazes, and all eventually congealed. Outside on the steps, ready to go down into the city again, most of any kind managed a romantic sigh, and could be done with it.

But to David Mannix, since the age of thirteen or so when he'd first begun coming here alone instead of with a school group or a chum, these friendly palaces of quiet, where the furnishment changed now and then but was always ultimately familiar, had become the haunt where he could best be at ease with an emotion he couldn't have named then, and at twenty-eight had only begun to define. Somehow these spaciously dedicated halls supported it in him. Only they were comfortably big enough for his strong, constant, pressured pity for human beings busy at life, in the world.

Out in the streets, the busyness never quite obscured that. It had been the same in the college dormitory, the embryo political clubs and even the first ballrooms of his youth — in wherever men congregated to buzz over what was being done in the world, or could be. Outside, one at once had to do something oneself about that vast "it" of human suffering. From grade-school days on — when he'd brought home anything from a wounded pup to a Walter — he had been practical about it. He now belonged to as many relief committees, in every cause, as if he were a Quaker, besides being a contributing foster-father to as many Indian children on reservations, war orphans of any side, as he could afford on the income from the trust fund Meyer Mendes had left him.

"It'll come to you in 1948," his grandfather had begun saying to him from his teens, maybe when they were watching a couple of comers in the prelims at the Garden, or two Greek imports massively wrestling over who should throw the next match, rehearsing it for the syndicate in some dead-end of the Bronx. Or once, after a regatta in which David himself had been a participant — an activity which his grandfather, a privileged in-bettor in rougher circles, may well have thought effete. "In 1948, when you're twenty-two. Don't rest on that money, David. It'll only be your leather, and your jock."

On receipt of it, Meyer long since dead, he'd quit Harvard midyear, plunging at once into the charitable works which were the only solution he knew of for his kind — or the kind he'd been brought up to be. But the mildly dispensing side of the science of human rescue — on which Austin had been very helpful — wasn't what Meyer had meant or he himself could rest with, whether the money was his own or other peoples'. Against purely political solutions, his own father, with the Chinese water torture of his conversation, had made his children sophisticate. Another element in the family texture his son never phrased to himself, hating to think of his own pity as in any way personal — allied in any way to a guardianship — of a sister, of a mother before her, or of a father who never dreamed of it. Born in some way he couldn't help, he had to guard them all, the human race included. And couldn't act upon this from a distance — he had to anoint. Alongside that, his deafness was nothing; it even made him gay. Its real inconvenience was that it gave an arena all his own — scarcely communicable even in a crowd of two — to the suppliant cries of the world.

Here in the museum, everything had already been done, Sumerian to now. Even to his deaf ears the quiet was a special one, the ultimate after such noise. Here the buzzing demand could stop. Staring at the left-behind bowls and spoons, the sarcophagi, he found relief, even a kind of joy. It would go on, the suffering, but it could stop. What he should have been, of course, was a rabbi.

So, at least, they'd said to him in the kibbutz — where action was daily, and anointment even of their "own" barely rabbinical — and the ills of the world beyond frankly a Gentile matter, scarcely at the moment even the province of God. But those men back there were the businessmen of retribution. They saw "rabbi" in him because they unwittingly agreed with his own father's low estimate of his brains (as he did himself) — and rabbis who were not too intelligent were the preference of businessmen everywhere.

But there was another kind of man out there again in the desert now, more modern even than the chemists. On his way home, he'd stopped off in London, to talk that over with Austin.

"But that's the military, isn't it," said Austin, leaning back in the spartan rocker he'd had set in his very formal office — of the sort, he had just remarked, with which the wiser foundations concealed the revolutionary nature of their benefices even from themselves.

"You're not surprised?"

"At you — and that? Should I be?"

In two years abroad himself, Austin hadn't changed a whit; all his attributes could merely now be seen foreshortened, in the way of any man who rightfully becomes what he had promised to be. Still, David chided himself as stupid for not having seen this before. "I am. Surprised at myself."

Austin looked out across the square, at what he had pointed out as the only building more purely Adam than this one — the Chase Bank. "What'll you be doing for them — if you go?"

"Radio communications. And allied — arts."

"For how long?"

"As I please. But I must take on citizenship. And a kind of . . . contract. For some years."

"Will you be home long?"

"Just to tell *him.* I never can write him. And to see how he is."

"Hear he's in a wheelchair. But going out more than he has in years. Warren wrote me."

"He can still walk. But he conserves it, for the evenings. When he writes, Ruth says. Ruth's home."

"She came through here on her way," said Austin. "To stay?"

"She did a ballet, down under. *On the Wallabies,* she called it. Says that's Australian slang for an uncertain path."

Both laughed.

"She's the clearest of any of us," Austin said. "I'm not sure why."

"Cheeriest?" said David, hand on his box — though he thought he had heard right.

"That too," said Austin. "Out there in the Negev — what about your tin ear?"

He had smiled; it was so characteristic of Austin, to give him only *one.* "They'll take me." He had got up to poke the fire in the grate. "Think Simon will be pleased?"

"How like him you are, Diddy. Must be your sizes, that we never saw it."

"Am I?" The box squawked, which it did sometimes, when David swallowed. "I think I admire him more — than anyone does. More than — Walter." He dug playfully at Austin. "More even than you."

"So things are better there," said Austin quickly. "You call him Simon, now."

"My ambition is even greater," he'd said. "To call him Si."

"Has anyone, ever?"

"My — foolish mother."

"I never thought her — that."

"The dead — are foolish." He bent over the coal grate. "Nothing to be done *with* this fire."

"Why, that's the equivalent of a Second Secretary's fire! You should see a Prime Minister's. Barely any at all."

Each leaned back, testing the overtones of the other.

"But that's an American rocker," David said. "You can't be going to stay on forever in this green drool. And how do you feel about Israel, by the way? From here."

"From the land of old White Papers, d'you mean? Well, I'll tell you. First you see — well, there's yaws. Still a lot of yaws in the world, and the Foundation has always been very concerned with it. 'Yaws, Mr. Fenno,' the old head here told me when I first came. 'Yaws has always been our pigeon here. We're also rather proud of getting the Iranian Muslims to stop using arsenic depilatory. Poisons the wells. Ah yes, we've always been *very* international.'" Austin rocked. "So we gave him a larger office and a smaller fire, and he's scarcely noticed yet that our sights have shifted. To diseases of the atom, you might say. Preventive medicine is what we're after. We're not as interested in cures, any more. But we're still very international." He stopped rocking. "So you'll forgive me if the glories of Israel scarcely engage me at all."

"Goddammit, Aussie. Don't scold."

Here in the museum, waiting for the person who, from countless assignations here, he almost identified with the place's cool, post-Vesuvian repose, David leaned forward to peer at a card in front of a small ewer from the Euphrates — and gave the fire in Berkeley Square another poke. "OK, Aussie. But what about — the *six million?*" His box always gave it a sibilance, almost a trill, as if they were in there, trying to get out. "Do we just leave them, to their museums?"

"The dead aren't foolish," Austin had said sharply. "Not unless we make them so."

But Aussie had never been sharp in his life, except when he wasn't sure.

"God. I congratulate you, Aussie. As the first of us to achieve the long view. You Christian." He had smiled, to soften it.

"You — muscular Jew." Austin smiled too. "I can see what the desert does. You never used to swear. You never even used to mention God."

A clerk had come in then with the tea and gone out again, a long English girl, in dun worsted.

"Do all the women here dress in those darks? Like the Sunday night soup we had at school."

"Other wools are still for export. It's called 'utility.' "

"She looks useful. Just don't marry one of 'em."

"No — I — No," said Austin.

"Oh," said David, "I see. Anyone I know?"

Even if the girl was from home it wasn't likely, and he'd had his own reasons for not pursuing that line.

"We're not the only ones interested," Aussie was saying, "in disarmament through world law. Guess who sent me a paper he's just published on the subject. Edwin. Edwin Halecsy."

"Well, he's a lawyer. Still wants to be buddies, I suppose."

"You know — I think he never did. Oh I know why he sent it to *me* — something personal." Suddenly Austin got up to stare out at the morning gloom. "It's a remarkable paper. I wonder now. Did he even want me to see in it — what I saw."

"Bright guy. Far brighter than me. Maybe even than thee. What's so strange?"

"Nothing about the article itself. It's superb. Unless one happens to think, as I do — that your father wrote it."

The clerk tiptoed in for the tray. "Be sure you have your own elevenses, Miss Fry," said Austin, and watched her close the door. "Do you think Edwin could possibly have any . . . have you ever thought he might have something . . . *on* . . . your father?"

David's first concern was for his box. In the hazards of assisted speech, it sometimes spoke aloud for him what he hadn't known he breathed. Nothing, Austin, that I can tell even you.

Here in the museum, a week later, he breathed easier. Even if one day he were to speak aloud, unaware, what he'd so long kept to himself, in that presence he was waiting for he needn't worry. Behind her back, should he conceivably ever need to — he could shout it aloud.

Back there in London, he'd said merely, "Judges — all have secretaries. Or maybe retirement's made him — quix-ot-ic." The box had a bad time with that one. "You probably heard though — that Edwin never got to live in the house."

"I didn't . . . I mean — yes, of course. But — why?"

"Anna. She said if he did, she'd leave."

Austin had turned from the window. The green fug they lived in over there had lowered even his gilded looks to pallor. "Aussie, you look off-color. How's your wound?"

"*That* war? I never think of it." He slapped David on the back. "Come on. Time for a quick one, before your plane."

In the pub, he downed a whisky, then a pint whose mug he clicked against David's. "To Anna. To Anna my hosh."

At the plane — for he couldn't seem to let David go — he said, "Maybe I need a touch of your desert. I can't seem to help people *except* from a distance. Whereas you people — you all *have* to be there."

"Should I've been a rabbi, you think?"

Austin put down David's bag he was carrying up the ramp. "Now I *am* surprised."

"Not — at the other? You never did say."

"I always thought — it would have to come out in you, some way. Ever since — that day I barged in."

It had never been mentioned between them — that Austin had inadvertently seen the house the morning after his own rampage, and had guessed it to be his.

"In envy, believe me," said Austin. "I can only — whatever it is we Fennos do. I can't rage."

The plane was delayed.

"I've got to tell Walter too," said David.

"He's not well enough to go with you?"

"Well enough to do anything he really wants to. But he won't. He thinks as you do, Austin."

"How?"

"That it's the deafness coming out in me. At last."

The plane was ready.

"I'll be home tonight."

"Write me once in a while," said Austin. "Not like you do Walter. But — write."

"I'm accumulating so many people — to leave," said David.

"Give them all my love," said Austin. "Especially Anna."

"Too many, maybe," said David.

"Can't have too many, sometimes," said Austin. "Nest of Fennos, even here."

"You're not wanting to — leave the clan?"

"Not joining it," said Austin. "I might manage that."

They shook hands.

"You're OK, bo? Sure?"

"Oh, I'm all right," said Austin. "I'm always all right."

Two days home, and his own decision had been settled, if he had ever doubted it. Out in the desert, all his former clownish gesture must have melted away without his noticing, under the noble attrition of life in those winds. His huge frame, sweating western rivers, had energy left only for the classic services to his own body. The days and nights, no matter how modern of intent, cut their way between sand and the oasis of a cup, from midnight's planetary cold to noon's high, solar scarecrow, and always suggesting a truth muffled by the impedimenta of cities — that life was classic everywhere.

Whereas one night in that cat's cradle of balances, the family house, and all his awkward clapping and stomping had returned to him, doors to be opened, matches to be struck, geehaw up from the chair, down, and all more wildly than in other men, the whole repertoire of acts of obligation by which civilized men placated the other, a whole vocabulary of nonviolence against what Austin had rightly called it — rage. In the desert, not to waste one dog's life was almost enough. Here he would explode again one day, with the violence of keeping still. It was his bad luck to have found that out about himself, just in time to tell this girl.

She was Sumerian, in her silences. He watched her coming down the long aisle to meet him here, a woman of that ancient stillness, made for him now. In silhouette she was Egyptian, but taller and not black or swarthy, a slender girl with a scarab's clarity, dressed in pale fresco colors that suited the ages, but made bisque and blond by being alive.

Actually she'd been made for him, and for herself, by the most mundane potters, necromancers and slaves that fortune could assemble to rouse a mute beauty. Twenty doctors had worked in vain to unstop those ears and at any slightest advance in otology were pressed by her family to work on; twenty others had unlocked the tongue. The subtly retracted profile came from the father, one of those equivocally red-gold Jews who so often came from the borderlines of overlapping frontiers — Alsace, or the edges of the Ukraine or of Friesland, or the *alpes maritimes;* when she turned front-face, she revealed the Polish blades of cheekbones got from a mother whose ancestors claimed South Germany for five generations. She was no more of a mixture than anyone, but early muteness and its treatment had made of her a kind of ornament which could be turned more than other people, from side to side. Her residual quietness allowed it. Mind — which she had (and stubbornness) was a surprise, and on the instant forgotten again. Under that astral voice, people said of her, how could one remember it? He had no real knowledge of that voice, only of the stillness of which even when speaking she was never quite dredged — that flaw which to others made her too fairy tale, too much the doll reawakened. Which to him made her his. She could hear nothing at all. Against that his own deafness was an oaf's, braw and mechanical.

She had flown in from the family's country place; ordinarily, by their wish, she never flew, even from there. In the city, she lived almost across from here in her own apartment at the Stanhope, in one of those exquisitely pale, neutral decors which decorators managed for rich Jews who weren't quite past being ashamed of their feelings. Her family had had it done for her, a display box by which they might show themselves and the world that they were proud of her as she was. No doubt they were as much against her marrying him — for the social defeat of her having to marry her like — as his own father would be, for deeper reasons. He had already slept there across the street, ridiculously but peacefully, in a round bed with silvered headboard, shaped like a nut. He thought that in his long absence, no one else had.

Tonight, whatever they decided, he knew he would sleep there again. None of this made the difference.

The real fairy tale, which would be so for him forever, was in the concrete circle they made between them past anything the normal could do, in the quick of their own persons. Talking with never a voice or even a parting of lips, and the box at his side silent. Conversing with eyes and hands only, in the language he'd been forbidden in his childhood and she had taught him — the manual alphabet of the deaf and dumb. They'd met first on the bench in front of the color organ at the Modern Museum, in the darkly curtained alcove where everybody sat in front of those visions as silent as she. She enjoyed that equality, she said later. He couldn't claim to have suspected she was deaf, during the minutes after he became aware of her. She'd known it of him at once, by his box. She had been the first to speak, with a hand-pattern on the air — to which he had shaken his head. But he'd known at once, by that vibration of nerve messages and tension clues which were the data of the deaf, that she wasn't to be pitied. At the end of his first lesson in her alphabet, he had signaled this to her, his big hands painfully slow. "You remind me of my sister, Ruth."

She saw him now, down a long aisle between glass cases of amphora, and he strode to her. They embraced, mouth and arms, but the real kiss was in the hands, like other people's tongues. Then they had to part, so that they could *speak* . . .

"So you flew," he said. "Was it like a piano?"

She didn't answer at once. Even when they were only lipreading, as now, he had a larger, freer economy of words. Words to her were spells, or pearls excreted out of the inner nacre of being. His little share of outer hearing made all the difference; he could waste.

"You *wrote*," she said.

He knew what she meant — that he'd never before written as fully or as well as in these last months. Yet he had told her none of his intentions, recounting only the daily. "Walter said the same."

They were voicing, waiting to work their way back to privacy like any long-parted lovers, and spoke no further in any mode until they had traveled through several galleries, to a favorite bench. Few came here, except a curator passing on to the better eighteenth-century rooms, or perhaps some connoisseur who had noticed that the large window, which framed rear lawns declining softly to the western barrier, did it in exquisite lithograph, as if outside there was the antiquarian future, and in this room the real present, thudding with quiet, in which one could *hear* an old century speaking, now.

The air outside there was mezzotint, the lawns carefully printed and bordered under the rare jonquil light of that future spring. She sat down in front of it, in the room's four-o'clock shadow, of say 1754. Her silence became either age. How could he begin to explain to her what was her rival now?

They had once had a little ceremony on meeting here, in memory of that other bench on which she had first explained to him the other alphabet. When she didn't begin as usual, he felt that fear of change, fear of no change, which was the dread of all homecomings, and began the ritual himself, taking her role. "Do you not know it?" he said, his lips moving slowly and carefully, the way she had first said it to him. "Dac tyl ol o gy?"

She was trembling, at his ash-burnt skin maybe, or the white nudity of his lower face. Just before coming he'd shaved off the flowing beard and moustache of a land where a man could newly choose to be one of the chosen, biblical *and* military, young and a patriarch too. But she wouldn't have been able to read his mouth.

" 'There's a one handed sys tem,' you said." He took her hands in his. " 'But most people use both. Like from the Dal gar no alpha bet. I could teach it to you. And all our signs.' " He took one of her hands, molding it into the *In hoc signo* sign — second and third fingers up, fourth and fifth bent under the thumb. " 'There. It's the sign the saints make, but to us it is the let ter U.' " She'd taught him all the little academic jokes and devices of the science. " 'And the sign for the word *and* is the quick est like a rab bit nibbling.' " He made four extended fingers vibrate muzzle-fashion, against a thumb. " 'There.' "

Quick as a flash, back there in that first museum, he'd made the U sign after her, then the *and*, then pointed to himself: *You and me.* "No," she'd said, in her literal way, in the voice whose faint vibration his box had never been able to bring to him. " 'Those are the signs. But to spell it the M is like this and this is the E.' " He wondered now why he should be trying like mad to convince her that all was the same — when he had come home to confess the opposite. "Of course," he said, casually aloud. "It's my box. I forgot." He always took it off when they met — to make things equal. He blushed now — to have said that to a woman: I have forgotten how you are.

"No." She sat so tall. Had she voiced it? "Keep it on." She touched the box, even with interest. "I'm teaching now, you know. In a hospital."

"You wrote," he said. "The larnygotomies."

"How well you say it," she said. "I never knew."

He had barely understood her, she mimed so fast, or her lips moved so slightly. "I must go and watch. How you teach them."

Again she didn't reply. He felt like an amnesiac returning. Surely there was something that teased. What had he forgotten about this girl, or never known?

"I met your father," she said suddenly. With her lips. "He was there just the other day to see a friend."

"Repeat," he said. "You speak so fast. Or the desert . . . has made me slow." And when she had done so — "He — knew you then?" How should his father not know her! How many deaf girls of that name, that description, would there be, other than the one with whom the son-of-the-name was rumored to be in love!

Again no answer — like a signal from a farther area of deafness at her very recesses, never discovered before.

"He's terrifying," she said then. "You never told me. He's so small."

"What did he say . . . to scare you?" he said aloud, starting up.

"Nothing. Relax, David. I thought you said the desert had changed you."

"I have relapses. But what has changed you?"

Again no reply. Maybe to remind him that he had the explaining to do.

"He used to . . . terrify me," he said with his lips. "Inaction does that — to people like me. We think such people have a secret. Of how to live . . . by thinking only. Because . . . we can't. So I used to just — act happy instead . . . or helpful." It was a long speech. She had listened to every word of it.

A guard looked in on them.

"We're stealing nothing!" David said to him gaily, in flashing sign language, and turned to the girl. "See!" he said aloud. "My Dalgarno. I had no one to keep it up with. So I spoke to the heavens."

The guard came forward.

"Nothing!" said David aloud. "Go away."

"Go on," she said. "About him."

"Even you . . . say that," he said. "After only one meeting. 'Him.'"

There was a pause. "But . . . don't let's talk like this. Let's —" He took up both her hands, gently forcing them into the air.

"Not yet," she said. "Not . . . yet."

"Or — not here," he said humbly, and turned his head quickly away to the window behind them, so as not to be sure of her answer. The city itself had no creeping moral poetry for him; he left that to his father. His own ears and box kept a single locale for him anywhere. He felt her hands seize his, and closed his eyes. The girl's eyes calmly stared down the guard.

At her side, David opened his eyes. "I never feel childish with you." Lifted like that, his long, handsome head with its broad forehead and chin, hair crimped like a Grecian bull's, curled mouth and jutting nose, had a dignity he himself never saw. "He and I talked last night. Half an hour. Long . . . for us. 'We're not . . . a serious family,' I said to him. 'We don't do enough in the world.' "

". . . I take it you don't mean just me," his father had said from his chair, with a forbearance which could have made those still on their two legs feel guilty for it, but comically scratching that way at his own crotch. He could charm the bees.

" 'We'd as soon spend action outside our own circle —' " said David slowly to the girl — " 'as spend capital,' I told him. 'If that's your middle class, I'm done with it.' "

(And his father said to him, "There speaks your mother's son." Never forbearing there, his father. "Action never helped her, David." And I said to him, "I'm *your* son, too." I'd never shown him before that I knew he didn't think so. He wheeled his chair up close to the mirror beside where I was standing — the big pier glass in the downstairs hall where we were waiting for Charlie, the new chauffeur I'd never met, to carry him up — and said nothing. Sometimes, my father looks to me like those men (you can see it in the hawk of the eye, the quiet of the hand) who in some way have succeeded, though in no great walks of life. At other times, often during the same evening, he reminds me profoundly of certain others encountered only in those prominent walks. Those famous men — distinguished at once by the breath of bitter almond in what they say, the gelid bird-flesh of the eye — who have failed.

If I could disavow *him*, I thought — would I? "Walter had a letter from her once," I said to him. "About you and me. He's never opened it. She said it was to be for me." I stared at him in the mirror. For me, in the event — of an event. But I refused it. I was afraid to lose you for a father — can you see? As afraid to lose you, as you are me? "And you wouldn't ask to see it?" he said. "No, I won't ever ask." He gave me the queerest . . . no, the most direct look he'd given me since I was grown — like the looks he used never to know I saw, in our lessons. "So you wouldn't ask her either," he said. And when the chauffeur came in, my father refused him. "My son, Charlie," he said — "my son will carry me upstairs.")

The girl had been listening to him; she listened like the heavens, giving him all the time in the world for what he'd never been able to say to anyone, by any method known . . .

(To the heavens out there, I cried it all, with my fingers. It amused my father's son, to do that. The tea out there smells of ram; the air smells of our gunpowder prayers. No house out there, no door, no stairs. The stars cram close, interested. I flash it to them, Dalgarno. A system made only a moment ago, in the sixteen-hundreds, and in Aberdeen, but the stars understand it, they are very intelligent. "He's never really thought I was illegitimate," I said to them. My mother had it all wrong; maybe he doesn't know it himself. What he really can't face is that I'm here. He can face that better in Ruth; he has so much worse there to bear that I would carry him on my back for it forever. And her . . .)

"And . . . what did you say then?" said the girl beside him.

"Oh, I said it all to the desert," he said, head cast down in profile. "One day, if I've nerve enough, I'll say it to you."

(Hand to hand. In the black desert air, I practiced them for you, the sentences ingrained in me like those old conundrums in which "your father's daughter" and "my father's son" all turn out to be thee and me. My father's wife — meant to shoot a lover. My mother's husband — walked in on them. In the melee, who knows who shot her? My father's daughter. Saw our mother die. Our father's wife.)

"Say it to me," said the girl, and he turned to her amazed, almost thinking he heard her voice.

"By night," he said, aloud. "I'll learn the *one-handed* alphabet, and say it to you. The one you said an abbé invented." He thought he'd gone too fast, and repeated all this. "That's all . . . the dactylology . . . it takes."

"The Abbé de l'Épée," she said. Softly. Or so it seemed to him.

(And at breakfast only this morning, after hearing of his intentions, his father had said to him, on their being alone, "Families *disappear* at the front, David. That's how you and I come to be here — our fathers didn't go. No excuse, either way. I wanted to go once, myself. To war."

And when I denied nothing, not even that war would come out there, he said to me, "David, David. That's not *Zion* out there . . . now." As I stood there, risen from my chair, I found my answer. He, my own father, had given it me. "Then *I* shall disappear," I said.)

"That means sword — épée — doesn't it?" he said. "What we aren't supposed to perish by." He mouthed it for her carefully. "Sword. A one-hand alphabet."

"You wrote . . . like that," she said. "From Israel."

"So he met you. So he got to you ahead of me," he said, slurring. She had always been even quicker at lipreading than he, smarter, from need, at all of it. "He'd charm the bees. He's always ahead of us. But it doesn't matter. What it really means is, you charmed him."

"He never knew it was me," said the girl.

"You mean . . . he never heard your name? That you were Alice Cooperman?"

"Repeat," she said. "Repeat." He must have spoken so fast that he was unintelligible; often when the box was on he did that; but why should that make *her* look ready to cry?

He repeated, watching her answer him in careful mime.

"His friend — Mr. Somers — simply said . . . 'This is . . . my Miss Cooperman.' I might have been . . . anyone."

"Might you," he said. "Might you. *How?*"

He'd never said anything so cruel, to anyone. Here was the heavy underbottom of that pale ice floe, his pity. He felt it rise in him as it had in the desert — the black basalt cliff of his rage. In the Sinai, in the Arabian black Harra, one understood God better, that two-faced

Adonai. Eagles pick the stars clean, and *that* is pity. Ice melted astrally — and disappeared. Elohenu. Blessing is double-faced too.

"My father." The box squawked, he spoke so large. "The smartest man on earth. The champ. And he didn't recognize you? A *deaf* Miss Cooperman, who teaches mutes to whistle, like herself?" He raised his head, the high, hewn profile given to prophets, as the possessors of such heads should — in full knowledge of it. Under his hands, at her wrist, he felt the bracelet made of the triangular forehead-piece of a fourteenth-century bride, identical with the one he had sent his sister, from Jerusalem. He peered closer at the face above it. "You — don't remind me of her, any more."

The face was answering his whisper, with tears. It had never stooped to tears before — that last resort, beyond even hands. Under the running wet, the face looked almost — ordinary. Cameo out of the matrix, it came forward, discovered of its own pity and rage. It bent forward, hiding in its own lap how cruel it felt, to be real.

What should he say to it, out of the fear in him now? He could test her, in the way he tested his own box. "Laryngotomy," he said aloud. He wasn't touching her. She couldn't see him. But in the electronic center of her, unreachable by alphabets, he saw her quiver — who couldn't see him.

He felt his mouth's lassitude. It wanted its beard. Oh beard of change, cover me! "Marry me," his mouth said, to that hidden face. "Then I won't — disappear."

The head rose from its lap. Yes. It had heard, it had heard. "Won't you?" Her lips said it, full voice. Her voice, heavy enough to carry, entered his box, and was carried to him. In the ordinary way — for him — he heard her voice.

Then her two hands, clasped against that but powerless, broke into their true language, telling him, telling him, scattering their frail ideograph everywhere, so that it seemed to him the gallery walls must be stamped floor to ceiling with the pale track of these waste butterflies. She raised the hair from one ear, to show him the shaved place where new bandages must have been, and in a coronal of fresh little head-scars, the perfect ear. She spoke to him in mime, then, touching his box, in voice, and when she saw he couldn't or wouldn't understand, at last once again with her hands in the true communication. She said the same thing over and over again. She was showing him how she could waste words. He sat dumb.

In the window, the city was real, but one could turn from that. He lifted his own hands to answer from their lost inner circle. He tried to answer her, from his desert of one. He couldn't shape it, one-hand method or two, or say it. Maybe in time he could breathe it to himself, to be lost in his box. *You disappeared first. But I shall manage it.*

The guard checked in and out again. How was it the guard himself didn't see her last true communication, not in sign language but painfully spelled out in their alphabet, black-tracked on the walls, engraved on the dusk coming of age here down the ages — her ideograph fluttering everywhere — in the raised fifth finger and clenched four of the sign for I, in the open tiger-cry of the C (four above and the thumb-jaw below), and the long, pointing, parallel forefinger and second, of the H.

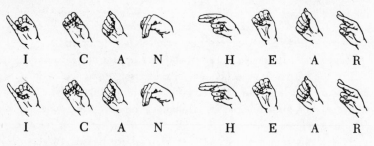

I   C   A   N   H   E   A   R

I   C   A   N   H   E   A   R

16 The Servants – *Spring 1954*

HORSES were gelded there, for the trade.

Often the Mannix children heard Anna's stories of her early life there. And of how she had come to work for *them*. Though she couldn't tell them everything.

The gentleman advocate, retired to the farm estate outside Prague for which household Anna's father had been majordomo, had had both a Montenegrin wife, on whom he had fathered two elegantly lineaged children, and a German mistress, very little younger than the wife, who lived on the estate as part of the family, along with her child by the advocate. This girl — a long, stringy, lime-colored child, dressed by the mother in the stripes and mauves of a court harlequin, with thin, fair hair allowed to dawdle below the waist like a beauty's — had been just Anna's age, and Anna's imperious, spiteful friend. There were eighteen people on the estate, among whom the German, a foolish, gone Rubens of a woman, fadedly resembling the copy of a Venus by that artist which the master kept in the gun-room, was easily passed off as a cousin, for the gentry's sake. The advocate's domestics, from garden to chamber, had a prouder sense of drama, however, and among themselves never let drop the special sense of sin of their household.

No one kept them all in their places better than the parvenue's sprig — or thought she did. Anna's friend, the skinny bastard girl, got sugar-holes in her teeth from the extra tea-sweetening required to assure her that no wormwood had been placed in it, berated the laundress over any imperfection in the German's laces — and was the one child of the family whom the advocate took on his knee. To Anna in her corner, a humble, plump girl whose only distinction was a father who could swallow hot peppers whole, this girl would then send a covert smile — afterwards coming down to the kitchen to seek her out like an *agent provocateur* for the sexual, to whisper of her own mother's arts, and on one rainy night after the other servants were in

bed, to show her the advocate and the German through an industri-
ously widened knothole. Anna, already informed of what she was to
see, had seen it. Madeleine, as the master called her, or Big Tits, as the
kitchen did, could tie bells on them, and twitch them to a rhythm, if
not a tune. Through the hole, the daughter breathing down her neck
in back, Anna saw the brown teat long as an udder, heard the bell.
Neither had waited to see the whole performance, if there was any; the
daughter had been so eager to get away and talk about it. In the
kitchen, over the pan of yogurt to which the girl had access, and for
which dainty, when sprinkled from a bag of chocolate shot always in
the friend's pocket, Anna had a sick weakness, she was asked to bear
witness to having seen two bells. But Anna, whose father had that day
gone off to the lung sanatorium, had replied in a rare outburst, "I saw
only one."

That had had little to do anyway with the spaniels which were
always being kicked for sucking themselves bright red, in the kitchen,
or the master's rage when a farmhand was caught with an animal — or
the gardener's wink that had convulsed the staff: "Bred stock, too!" —
or with the cow's lowing, clover breath, on her way to the bull. The
kitchen was what mattered to Anna, the white air of its fall mornings
nourished by the blood oranges on the dresser, all the safe, slow fruit
of its seasons, the tickling pot of its afternoons. The whole while she
was saving for America, she was scarcely frightened; she was on her
way to some kitchen there.

Once in New York City, shut up alone as cook-general to a four-
teenth-floor box kitchen in which after a week the refrigerator was a
scorn, the four-burner never a friend, the one grocery cabinet a
parched amazement — and the middle-aged, dollar-colored brother
and sister who owned all this scarcely an afterthought — she began dreaming, night after night. And of all things (with all the rest
of the estate to think about, animals, land, privies and women, all
smelling high as its blessed cheeses, prickly to strangers as its own
hedges, there on the opposite realm of the world), of one thing only,
the Montenegrin. A tall, monkish woman, the order of *her* laces was
never in question, nor her beauty challenged by the growth of down on
lip and jaw. When she dined downstairs, rigidly fair to all at the
tureens, the harlequin was for once quiet. When she had a migraine,
her own children spent hours with her in the suite from which their
peals of laughter were never censored; afterwards, during her angelic

recoveries, the maids fought one another for the chance of a charmed remark from those pillows, for the privilege of taking it its tisane.

In New York, Anna, waiting for the grocery order which was telephoned for her, or walking the dog, the only time she was expected to go outdoors except Sunday, thought of her — the Montenegrin — as the gentry had always been heard to call her. The Montenegrin had never gone out, though she could have come and gone as she pleased, and had never had a dog, though in other ways she had been herself round the clock; the male servants' other name for her had been "the angel without legs." Anna remembered her, as through a knothole.

At the employment agency, the harassed woman who spoke Czech said to Anna, "I can't understand you girls, that's Park Avenue, Mr. and Miss Forbes, and the pay as good as you'll get, even from the Jews," but Anna came every week now as to a clinic, walking the dog. She was watching. Once, twice, in the line of armchairs where sat waiting clients, she saw Mirriam Mannix, who required an "experienced." The third time — she had been praying all week and had dared to come out without the dog — she had gone down on her knees to the dark young woman with the arched nose, sitting there in her riding boots, all in plain black except for the horsewoman's jabot of a lace any decent girl from Prague would recognize, above it the wild migraine, bold and remote, of those eyes. Anna, having no English as yet, had dared to touch the starched jabot, shaking her head over it; she could do better, she made that clear. Then she spoke the one word which surely she and this woman would have between them. "Madame."

They were her aristocrats. At first, her young feeling for "the fine ones" — and for these four of them who were her portion — expressed itself as promised, in a severe care of their personal effects, not for their adornment alone, also for a mutual honor's sake; the thirty pairs of curtains inherited with the brownstone house were part of an escutcheon reassuring her of the quality of those she served. In time she came to scorn certain gifts, or even a family purchase, as not good enough for the house. The butcher knew her arrogance. In her middle age, she began to express her very sense of time passing, in the solid, impregnable cuisine with which she bound herself — to "them." By then, the mutual psychology was fixed. Both sides knew.

They "loved" her remotely enough so that she could be sure it would last, and would require of her that "best" which she had been taught she must give but might need help in holding to — obligation was the real emotion in her life. In turn, she expected "them" to be above certain things — and with the secret, deep *Hola!* of the stable and the keyhole, felt them capable of anything. For they were the only wild- ness she had. And like babies, must be protected from the conse- quences of it. Having had no mother, she became, in a stately way, the more motherly herself: "As peasants of good temper invariably do, Si; the hysteria of us women who from that same history are incapable of it, is reserved for the *haute bourgeoise.*"

When the crime came, she was ready to be part of the concealing circle of family. As they knew. She felt confirmed by the deed, in a course that was familiar — there was now a special sin in the house- hold. As the children puzzledly made note, it was only afterwards that she became at times satirical. This was necessary, for balance. She knew. All. And in the smallness of the staff here, had no one to tell it to. From room to room, she grew used to her mistress's pictured eyes saying to her, "Anna, you know all about it. My accident." As those eyes followed her, in the housecleaning which was her meditation, she wondered hungrily if they knew that their accident had deprived her, Anna, of her only confidant. For any servant has to have a hutch of her own, according to her nature. And a day off, in which to do there what she will surely rue. To exert her own appetites and shames. And those Montenegrin eyes had been told of it.

On a day some twenty years later, and two weeks after the first cable came to Judge Mannix about his son, Anna walked over — as in recent years she could do most afternoons — to her own habitat. In the way of neighborhoods in this city, it was only a few blocks in one direction, then another. No one, outside the Mannix household or in it, now knew of this place. If she died in it, under that other name, "they" would be safe; she thought of it that way still.

Once, in the earliest years, on her way back to the Mannixes from her first place of her own, only a furnished hole, she'd passed their dressmaker and her sister, the Halecsys, and had had presence of mind enough to duck into a cheese store, midway between the neighbor- hoods, where she was known only in her capacity as servant. In the store, she had stood bemused. That night she had gone to the mistress.

"Since when! Anna! Two years! Why — we would have given you a wedding!"

She felt the heat pinken even her arms, and fixed her glance on them, clasping tight the afternoon's swollen, aroused glands in her breasts, knitting close her thighs.

After that the mistress said only, "You *are* . . . though? And since when did you know you want to keep it — dark?"

But she had never been able to say since when, even to herself, and finally said, "Since the cheese store."

The mistress asked only once more, "But you're not — there's no child?" and receiving Anna's mum headshake had intruded no further.

But in time, she came to know everything, which wasn't much, and didn't change. On Thursdays, Mrs. Mannix often came and stood in the pantry, clasping her own breasts, said in a low voice, "Do you need anything?" and left again. Once the two of them, coming in late at night alone, met at the door (Anna just out of the taxi she took back on certain nights only), and the mistress said like a conspirator, "Are *you* all right?", flashed a naked smile at her, and went on by. Bonus afternoons became regular, and sudden sums for nothing done extra — "For the flower arrangements," the mistress said once. Nothing more was said. But *she* knew. Had known.

Two corners from her own place, Anna stopped at a bistro named Auf dem Schwarzen Adler to pick up an order of sauerbraten, purple cabbage, and a pint of beer. In all the years, she'd never cooked a morsel over here; there was a stove in the place but nausea locked it; she couldn't mix food with what else was over here, nor make a kitchen of it.

"Tomorrow's order?" said the waitress, leaning on a zinc table.

Anna grasped the table edge also, holding the tray in the other arm. Days at the Mannix household passed lovingly between the tasks, like between the hedges at Praha. In steady imitation, she had created here also a routine that squeezed, but let her by. At moments like this one, she came out into a wilderness, of no fences. And this time there was no one to tell, except the portraits. Over the wires of the past came the voice of the mistress at telephone, a practiced glide, refusing anything from a dinner to a person; God knows what posts *she* had squeezed through, until the last.

"Nothing," said Anna. "Nothing for tomorrow. I'll let you know."

The builder of the house she entered, a tenement with "inside" water, had had the ghost of a brownstone in his memory, even to tin ceilings pressed in a fleur-de-lys that took the place of the Mannix plaster roses; it was natural, just as the fiber trunk Anna had brought across the water had been patterned after the family's great leathern steamers, with a paper lining, to their cretonne. Going up the stoop, she felt herself note with stealth, that Popich's Upholstery, whose owner lived in the first-floor back and went weekends to the brother on the shore, was already closed. From the neat hallway beyond the mail-boxes, stairs led up five flights, each floor divided in half.

At the third-floor back, she stopped, wishing as always that the door didn't open direct into the bedroom. But it was the bigger room, had the fire escape and window. Beyond it, joined by a hall sink, washtub and toilet, was a windowless backroom of a sort other tenants in the line used for sleeping. An armchair was kept there and a radio, a bottle of schnapps for any faintness after the clinic, a real leather shaker for dice, never used, and usually some old raffle stubs from the Turn-verein. She weighed the tray in an arm, feeling for her key in her purse, where the cablegram also lay. Two weeks ago the master had called her in to tell her that David's plane had been lost. But the strangeness had only begun today, when she had picked up the yellow paper dropped in their travel haste in front of the wardrobe in the master's bedroom — and had stolen it. For herself — in imitation of what, she couldn't say.

The man on the bed was sitting up, propped on his many tobacco-yellowed pillows, stained at their centers with his hours of catarrhal sleep; if ever any blood came — from the nose only, she was sure of it — he left that too. Two minutes ago, he might have been at the radio. She had a cart horse's foot, he always said — and she was sure he always heard it in time, on the stairs. How he kept himself — clean as a razor strop, the sideburns pincering evenly the hollow cheeks, the moustache trimmed and pomaded, even the back hair done with clip-pers — took up the shuffle of his day, all on display for her. Nostrils cleaned with a spill, ears oiled against wax, he had climbed into the malicious funk of the bed linen, pajama top buttoned for warmth over the sunken, scarred rib cage, but the pants half the time open on that sprouting animal pink, those urea-colored bags in the hair — and was sitting up for her. She almost never failed to come.

"Popich's boy brought it yesterday," he said at once, watching her set his dinner for him. "I knocked with the stick." It was feigned between them that the stick could be heard three flights down, just as it was kept up that he never went out, except to the clinic or the barber. On the bureau was the clinic visit book, prominently displayed — but she never asked any more what the doctor said — along with the cards with which he played solitaire, and the buffer for his mooned, sharp nails. Sometimes she imagined that he even still waitered as an extra at the hofbrau where she had first met him; the union card and book were on the dresser scarf too. She could have reached for it, or for the thick leather folder he said was his "accounts." What he really gambled with or on, she never knew or asked, only that it was not with those soiled cards, those unused dice. She thought of the gambling as a sinkhole, swelling with the weather or his illness, toward days when he would say, "They're going to collapse the lung again," or "I must have extra, the doctor said"; then she would give him the money, to vanish into the sinkhole. Maybe he won, too. She still paid the rent and expenses here, but wouldn't have a phone of their own. His operations had all been years ago, but the rest was long since routine. Sometimes he gave her leave — or command — not to come, saying he was well enough. When he said he wasn't well — as for more than a year now — she came with the dinner, every night.

For the other half of the day, eat or not, he must fend for himself; she never inquired how. The dinners only were her obligation. What happened between the two of them afterwards took place without regard for illness or health. When she had to serve late at the Mannixes, she brought him his dinner at midnight, or extra the night before. She had missed only once. Once, ten years ago — no, eleven — at the mistress's death, she'd had to telephone to Popich that she wouldn't be there. Yesterday, and all the day before, she hadn't phoned.

On the dresser, she saw now, as if out of a new corner of her eye, that there was nothing of hers. Bankbooks, burial insurance, wardrobe, everything was in her room in the other house; for seventeen years she'd come here in the clothes she stood in, never carrying even an umbrella between the two. She shivered now, remembering who the insurance was in benefit of, something she had known she must never tell the master.

As her husband ate, daintily as ever, his moustache lifted finicky over the beer, he seemed to her unchanged from that assistant headwaiter at Jaeger's, whose coquettish toilette had come from his native Vienna, where he'd been a house servant too; who on trips with his master had been to a kavarna in Prague, and had quoted her the national dishes, national buildings, one by one. He'd been a thirty who looked forty to her then; he was a fifty who looked forty now; they were the same age, but maybe she had known from the first that of all his features, his hollows — in the cheek, in the conscience — were the most durable. "Where do you work?" he'd asked, and already two years at the Mannixes, she'd heard herself say, like an animal hiding its haven, "A brother and a sister, by the name Forbes." All her reactions to him were animal; every time she went with him she had the impulse to scratch earth over this place, and walk away.

Over the years, she'd cannily enlarged for him her own gray memory of the Forbeses, telling him that they wouldn't stand for a live-out maid or a hang-about husband, and that because of a claim adjuster who had long plagued her for a bill fraudulently put upon her in her greenhorn days, would say no one of her name worked for them, to any man who called. Each year she had someone check in the telephone book for her that they were still there. Somehow she didn't despise him for not taking a stand; he was her obligation. A sick taint, that she could never trust at the Mannixes — a man who would live like that in the bed linen, in the must of what she and he did there! But in some way he eluded her despising him. As for the money she spent — he considered that his due, he'd say, with a mocking lift of the waxed lip, though what she gave him would be repaid by the death benefit he had maintained against all odds, even before he knew her. He never had asked her about hers.

"You're an *honest* criminal!" had once burst from her, one of the phrases, caught from the Mannix children, that she couldn't always resist. He could understand these; he was a man of culture; unlike herself, he could read. "What fine talk!" he'd said. "You get that at the Forbeses?" After that, to the saga of the Forbeses' kidneys and their pale menus, she'd added a niece and a nephew of just the ages of the Mannix children, plus a few other flourishes, airholes through which she could breathe here — of them.

He had finished. His hands — resting there on the tray with maybe the card dealer's delicacy, but a servitor's too — were the part of him she could look at. She recalled with a start that she'd brought him no mohnkuchen, the bakery cake he savored with a child's regard for treats from the store. That leaden yellow wad in her purse had made her forget. In spite of his manners, today he'd eaten quicker than she'd ever seen him.

It crossed her motherliness — or would have in her other world, where she kept count of all the anxieties which ran between health and food — for once to ask him how he managed during the day. But for years now, because of the pure acid hopelessness of him here, she could be more truly domesticated to the Mannixes. And it wasn't possible that he was starving.

"Only once before you do not come like that," he said. "But that time, you phone." He waited.

"Do I?" He never probed as to why she couldn't bear mention of that time, of the mistress's death — give him his due.

"Three days you were away then. No, four. Popich's wife manage for me; it was just after the pleurisy. She was alive then." In the last year, he was always onto her about dates, until it had reached her — in the dim painful way things did reach her from him — that he had so few of them.

"Nineteen forty-three," he said. "Winter. When you came back, you took the suede shoes to Moroni's for me — remember? He said it would be the last time he could do anything for them. It was. And for dinner you brought me —" He wasn't looking at her but at the fire escape, through which the southern light declined on the one plant on the sill, a cactus, withered almost to cork between its gray spines. Sometimes she couldn't resist, and tended it. In the faded light, he could still pass for the one description of him she had given the mistress. "Give me the folder," he said. "The leather one." He'd never let her touch it. She handed it to him. The calf was butter-soft, of the finest.

"January," he said, in the deep voice he kept for this. "Nineteen forty-three." Inside its fine cover, the paper was bulged and dirty, with penciled droppings the same color as the bed linen. He shut it, but kept a finger on that page. "For dinner that time . . . *Spaetzle. Und Knockerl*. Not from the Adler. All the way from Alt Heidelberg. *Linzertorte*, too. And afterwards, you tell me about the children. That the Forbeses have a nephew, I know already this. But that they have a niece too, I did not know. And how is she, the little Forbes niece?"

"You keep what I say — in there?" She chafed her head sideways, like a child who couldn't help prattling of what obsessed her, wearing to the elders though she saw it to be.

"Only the dinners," he said. "But they go back, all the way." He seemed to bestir himself. "And how is that no-good no-relation, the Edwin? Does he still come there?"

"He comes. But not for her."

"Twenty years, yes. They would be grown."

She wanted to take the tray from him, but sat on.

He closed the book. "Other people's business? Why should I keep their business here!" He flung open his pajama top, wide. "Behind my scars!" As he sat back, the pillow behind him fell from bed to floor. As she bent to pick it up, he could not meet her eyes. She slipped it quickly behind him, took up the tray, went into the hall where the sink was, and stood there, blindly running the water over the dishes, which she could never let herself return unwashed, as a true restaurant patron would. Noiselessly, she dried the Adler's dishes, folding them in a plastic she kept here for that purpose and leaned forward, clasping her breasts, to the vista of him, profiled in bed, two dark steps down the hall. He had changed the pillowcase. Was he dying, to do this? Now she remembered, he had done the same that other time she had stayed away.

She took the two steps that brought her to the bedroom. He still would not look at her. They hadn't done anything in the bed together for a year. She could go now — without a word. But there on the chair on the other side of the bed was her purse, with its lead weight. And at home — no one. To the house already half draped for summer, a knock at the door had come, a yellow paper, and master and young mistress had picked up and gone at once on their proud business, leaving her no way to ache for the boy she had once wrestled with, no one to tell it to except the dead. She went back in, to her purse, and sat in the chair.

"Only this time," he said, "you don't phone." Yes, he was thinner, or shrunken; her father, before he went off, had looked like that. Not really sick, not even frightened, only humble, like the nags that were picked up once a season in the knacker's cart.

She cradled the purse, waiting for the question that surely he would ask. Then she could tell him. He always asked her questions that would let her tell him whatever she had to tell. Then, like that other time, she would get down on the bed. He had never forced her, give him his due.

But he said, "My accounts. Why you don't take a look at them?"

She took up the folder and studied its pages, recognizing the calendar divisions; numbers she knew, and the days of the week, the months. Only a step more to the words her tongue knew well enough; sometime, without thinking, she said to herself what later proved to be right. Poring over pages, she saw the menus, and like a map, the gaps of her absences. There was another pattern too, little stars now and then on some of the days she had come, but not always. "What are these stars?"

When he didn't answer, the interval told her. Her face burned. *This* was reading.

"Only menus," he said. "Ja. I had *them*." He watched her put the book on the bureau. "And you," he said to her back bent over it. "You know how to read chust for their grocery labels. And their envelopes. We're two of a kind. A pair. Intelli*gent*." He gave the word the German pronunciation, but the word was a Mannix word too. A whip they kept for themselves, not for her. He should not be using it.

"Popich's boy can read," he said. "He's gone to college. Gone."

She shrugged — then at this last word, lifted her head to ask something, and bent it without asking.

The man on the bed spread his pajama top again — she saw it had been pressed, by God knows who. He might have taken it and the case to a laundry. "*Our* business, we should keep here." Below his breastbone, crisscrossed at the sides, scar over scar had purpled with his thinness. He beat on that cage. "Ours." The word caught in his throat, but he coughed, and swallowed it. He sat upright against his pillows, the breastbone swelling and swelling. Underneath, the rib cage held by its seams, a bag reduced by the mending of it.

He closed his mouth hard, as to a reminder, and began taking breaths of a size suitable. "Why do you hold your purse?" he said then in a whisper. His lips attempted a smile. "Is the mohnkuchen in there?"

He had left himself open, naked. She held on to the purse.

"All right," he said at last. "What are you going to tell me this time?"

She had been waiting for it; it was like the toilet once you were trained to it; until you got to it, you could hold the worst. She let go, in a scald of tears. As the tears roused, her head reared back on lengthened neck, the jaw elongated also. After that expulsion, her lips closed, on a sob. He watched. The mouth had barely come together, not yet to the line it held when she entered with his dinners. Her eyes reddened at him, from some inner, ennobling light.

"What are you yammering over," he said. "Popich's boy?"

He studied her face, as he sometimes studied the kings and the queens in solitaire, royal as anyone, trapped on the card.

The light had dwindled, mournful anywhere to a room's dark occupants, a day taking leave of a pillowcase.

In her purse, the cablegram had tangled with their household keys. She smoothed it free. How these things were sent was still a mystery to her; beloved hands must have touched it somehow; they wouldn't send by strangers such a message from the grave. Carefully, she laid it on the counterpane. There's blood for you.

The posture of people reading was what she could read. He never liked to read to her. "They would let you go to night school," he used to say — "Ask." In the dining-room, they said of her, "Dear Anna. We can't get her to *go*." They liked her better that way. She knew.

"So?" he said. "Where did you get this?"

"After they leave. It's mine."

"You don't know what's in it?"

"I know from two weeks ago — a plane crash." She pointed at the yellow form, to letters she knew weren't English. "In that country."

"Hebrew," he said. "The country of the Bible."

"He would go there." She nodded, tears beginning again. "Such a boy. He would go there."

"She told you? The mistress?"

She sat up. He had a glimpse of the power she would be in that other household, white-bosomed, hair a tame crown. "The — little Ruth." She drew breath through her teeth, as people did for the holiness of their own pain. "Her brother's body. They do not find it yet, she said."

"The country of the Jews," he said.

"Read," she said. "I know how long it *take*. To read. They find him? It says — they find him?"

"They leave," he said. "And they do not tell you?" His slender fingertip traced the words. "No, it is not yours. But I tell you."

"Do not tell me. Read."

He held it out to her. She knew what he wanted — that she come to him. She came and sat in the foul bedclothes, unable to keep her glance from the pillow. Side by side they sat. She stared at the cable, penetrating the design with her eyes. Four, five lines, and a name.

MY DEAR ONES NOTHING FROM HERE BUT WHAT YOU KNOW STOP THEY SAY AIR PHOTOS OF WRECK SHOW NO LIFE BUT THEY WILL SEARCH ON STOP BETTER FOR US TO MEET IN LONDON STOP THEY VERY KIND BUT

WILL NOT SHOW PHOTOS STOP PLANE WAS MILITARY STOP IF FOUND ALL
HONOR WILL BE DONE

LOVE

WALTER

She listened.

When he had finished, he said, "Who is Walter?"

"A friend. His friend." She touched his hand, and in answer he read it again.

"My boy," she said. "My boy."

"Anna," he said. "*He is not your boy.*"

She snatched at the paper in his hand. It tore slowly in half.

"*Nothing* is yours," he said. "Nothing. Will you never see it?"

"You don't want them to be mine." She shrank from him. "You do not know them. And you will never."

"Your Forbeses? With a Ruth and a David? And the chicken soup. And —" He broke off. "No, I do not know such — Forbeses." He fluttered the half of the paper in his hand. "But I know *them*."

She grabbed for the paper. It came away in her hand, on his loins.

"From *there*, I know them," he said. "Not from the paper. From there." He stood up to face her, fallen back on the bed, her hand on her mouth. "No, it's not on that paper, the name and address; you don't think I see where you cut it away? You want me to tell you — the names. The house?" He began telling her, the name she never thought to hear from him, the street number, other identifications. His voice went on, opening up the walls here to them where they could see in on her, dozens of knotholes on her and him.

"You follow me," she whispered. "All that time."

"No, I don't follow you. Not like you think."

His pants had dropped from him. He stood reflective, in his skeleton. He wasn't showing it off to her. Even she could see that. "Poor Anna. How you think you can keep such a thing. For such years." His voice fell sad on her there on the bed. "Poor Anna. I follow you in the head. And here. And *here*." One hand on his chest, one at his loins, he wavered at her. "Poor Anna. I can *read*."

How could she never see his skeleton before, how could she come down all those years side by side with it, star by penciled star, and not see! He was hers, in imitation of nothing she could say.

"Get out!" she said from the bedclothes. "Go."

He grasped the dresser edge. It was clear he couldn't stand for long, without. By chance, maybe, he had touched the folder. He inched it into his palm and leaned there, not frightened, already looking back at her. He knew what was going to happen to him. For such occasions, one finds a clean pillowcase.

She took up her purse. She could leave in the clothes she stood in. For such occasions one prepared, not knowing it until the day comes. She got up, from that dirty linen. The door to the outside was handy, right here.

No sense of millennium came to them. They had the pure triumph of utter involvement only in themselves.

"Take the tray," he said.

Downstairs on the stoop, she peered closer into Popich's. The store wasn't closed as she had thought, but emptied altogether. Wife and son gone, Popich must have moved away. For a moment she faltered, then bent her head and plodded on. She was carrying the tray.

Outside the Adler, empty-armed again, she half hailed a taxi, her habit always after the bed, and brought her arm down again; now there was no longer any need. She walked farther and farther from that other hole, not to return. That would be the safest — for them. A skeleton must take care of itself.

She had dates of her own, confided to no one, following her down all the rooms of her years like a mistress's eyes. There was the time the mistress asked what he looked like, and she answered, "Like the king on the stamps on the letters you get from over there. Paris?" For she wanted to know. For both their sakes. "Ah," said the mistress. "Ah, Anna." The mistress had a laugh at these times that Anna waited for. "There's no king in Paris, Anna." Anna had shown her the envelope saved from the wastebasket; like a pair of girls almost they were, over it; maybe the master knew the mistress still got those letters, maybe not. "Belgium, Anna. That's Alfred of the Belgians!" the mistress said. And there was the night years after, when Anna came in the taxi, home, and the mistress, going out, not alone, leaned close to her and had said it to her, with the laugh that was like the shiver of a single bell. "Ah, Anna. The stamp king."

When she got to the house, she went up the stoop with a heavy varicose love. "Good masters find good servants," the advocate said. For her it had been the other way round. To come here, she had knelt.

But the mistress had never told anyone. "Ah, Anna. *Hate* us a little!" the mistress said once. But that she could not do, not for herself alone. "To squeeze sexual sin from the household of the world takes both servants and masters!" said the Montenegrin, taking her tisane.

Inside, in room after room, were eyes which had paid for their own days off, very dearly. Now that hers were over, she couldn't wait to get to them. They were her royalty; ah yes, all here in this house were that, dead and alive. After her own death, when she was beyond protest, her money would go back to the house. Not to the master. To his child — whom all one winter Anna had watched the mistress steal back from him. To the daughter of a mother who could make anybody do anything for her — and knew that Anna would never tell. To the girl herself — who'd known for years where Anna went, and never told. To Ruth, who had her mother's eyes.

She closed the door of the Mannix house fast behind her. In front of the large picture in the salon, she stood for a while, hands clasped, before going downstairs for her own supper. Tonight the house was all hers. Or she had no other. Now she was all theirs.

The eyes — large, bold and dead — stared back at her with their old, kitchen answer. Horses are gelded for the trade, Anna — and in their own way, the mares.

17 The Great Blues – *October 1954*

W<small>ALTER</small> Stern was in hospital, to have a modern experience. His congenital hump was pressing in on him in a number of medically disapproved ways, all degenerative. If left to its clutching company, probability was that his body would die — of that long association. Some fervor of spirit in that body had kept the two companions going for much longer than any childhood prognosis had been willing to stretch. Clinically speaking, the doctors couldn't really say how that delicate *body* had done it. Thirty years before, when religious phrases were still possible, or evolutionary ones, they'd spoken of the "will to live." Now that cost-methods engineering had given them so many phrases better geared to the labor movements of modern lives in general, they spoke to him of "incentive." Walter's was little different from anybody else's; he wanted to see what would happen, for the longest possible time. What he'd come up against was the doctors' own incentive; they too wanted to see what would happen, indeed felt obliged to — and by one of those strange involutions in which the Hippocratic oath was reconciled with impersonal inquiry, had no objections to finding out on somebody else's time.

Even doctors who met Walter for the first time often had an impulse to stroke his hump for luck. For an ordinarily good-looking face to be crouched under that hump and still remain pleasant must have been achieved at the cost of some equally severe recognition down below — but this too appeared to be only the most general avowal, like that of any man who knew himself to be of a certain height, weight and hair color, whose more arguable personality then began from there.

As a child, his closeness to his parents had early been muted by the swathed emotions of a friendly divorce, and much passing back and forth in an interrupted circle of relatives who were nice enough, concerned enough and rich enough, but whose main constant to him was this interruption. So it was that the car crash which had killed his parents had caught them coming to see him in the most civilized way, in the same car — and the relative most accessible and able to make the special trip to Walter's boarding school to inform him had been one of so many who had been at intervals almost anonymously kind to him. It was possible of course that he was a psychological marvel; with so much to weigh him, he had by chance never been given the emotional space in which to break down — and so had achieved control. His emotions gravitated, rather than swelled or snapped — not to say that they weren't deep. He saw the great blues, the great greens, and admired them for what they were — trees and sky. But by the time he came to know the Mannixes, he was like a boy who walked a wood that was lonely but known, only to meet one day upon the path one of those mythical palaces of blandishment, the air floating with colored birds, its tables set with the finest viands, the whole of it built out of the loveliest filigree of affection — and all real.

"Walter? One of the blessed," the Judge said of him. "It hasn't been given to him to question the significance of his life."

He was used to doctors being both tender and irritable with him. What they couldn't bear to sustain was their own reasonably accurate knowledge of how long he had to live as was, against the chance that they could "do something for the boy." It was at this point that syllogism took over. Ten years before, or even five, when "the end" hadn't been so visible, they'd never have suggested anything so radical as separating the two companions. In the interval, nothing in medical science had occurred whch strictly said it could be successfully done. But there was still no certainty, they told him, that it couldn't. If it was tried, there was an outsize probability that the "body," which as much as anything *was* Walter, wouldn't take it, in other words would die much sooner than by natural processes, more than likely "on the table." But that was *chance*. The other, though two or three years in the future, was *certain*. "Well, I got into bad company at the beginning," said Walter ruefully. "Couldn't I *stay?*" But in the end, of course, the matter had been put to that old incentive of his — which the doctors had somehow managed to turn into a version of theirs.

So here was Walter, ten days before the date in question, entering the hospital bright as a dollar, to be "built up" for it, giving up his outdoor clothes to a nurse who made him enumerate them on a form for that purpose, but in consideration of the ten days, allowed him "for the time being" to keep his watch. During that period of course he would still be ambulatory and have the run of Lenox Hill Hospital (particularly the brace shop, whose handicapped aide was a friend, and the children's orthopedic, where he himself had once been a patron); he was pressed to have all the extra wine and food he cared to pay for, and allowed visitors and phone calls at almost any hour, since the man in the other bed of the "semi-private" room was only in traction for a ski-twisted leg — who knew but that the kind hospital had arranged this too? Every one of the many on staff who knew Walter was bright and cheery with him; he was accustomed to bringing that out in people, but now this was especially so. He himself was by all odds the cheeriest. Though at certain times it did cross his mind that in spite of the warning asthmas, syncopes, and outright harsh pain he still suffered (no slighter than before but scarcely worse yet either), he was still marvelously well for a man who could sensibly apprehend that he was going to die of his "illness" next Tuesday.

At other times, particularly when he opened or closed the door of the tin locker where his changes of invalid wear were kept, and he saw on a rear peg the necktie he'd neglected to give up on admission or to list against possible loss to himself or his heirs, he stood for a moment under the most surreal feeling of self-imprisonment. It was now October, to him the most beautiful month of the year. If he demanded his outer clothes and left, he would almost certainly see Christmas in his own flat, Whitsun, Easter and a number of other holidays round the world by easy stages, if he still chose — and even another October. No one could stop him; he could imagine himself ten minutes from now, bulling past all their red tape, their religious disappointment in *him,* walking down the hospital steps, shutting its door forever on all that cheer, and standing in the broad autumn velvet of Park-Lexington, a gold lake of air, streaked with the early charcoals of winter, in which he could still swim, his excited pulse fibrillating too fast to die. His own necktie had played hooky. Why not he?

In the end of course, he hadn't. Mornings, when this willfulness was strongest, he was sure to be interrupted by one of the details of the building-up process — a pathologist to test whether his blood was worthy yet, an orderly with his euphoric milkshake. The one was too stupid to understand Walter's feelings if told, the other too enlightened. At night, the hospital, as if it understood the psychology of this all too well, gave him a sleeping pill — and trusted him to take it.

Some grim synonyms for this clever little Totentanz the community and he were now sharing did in fact occur to him. But after eight days of the soothing ritual (and in spite of a fair education as a citizen of the very century of analogy) he could still have laughed if anyone had suggested any parallel in the hara-kiris, euthanasias or even death battalions by which men anciently — and to the public honor — had cut themselves out of experience. He was doing only what men had done immemorially — dealing with life in the modern way. And it was now the ninth day.

Life meanwhile continued as was, relentlessly experiential. He could have afforded a single room, or a suite if one existed, but knew his own stubborn conviviality too well.

"If I'm not to have my hump, I must have someone," he said to the doctor. "For company, afterwards." To himself he said, "For before." Nurses wouldn't do for it. They had a nanny sympathy, or a sister of mercy's, but kept their little locked store of the secrets of your condition always in reserve, and like the most devoted visitors, got free of you into that other culture, at least once a day. Their own lives, all long since written up by Abou Ben Adhem, were useless for exchange. What was needed, he remembered (now that once again he had it), was a sharer of one's own situation. And this, to all except the sequestered rich, a hospital lavishly provides.

In his many trips here, he'd had roommates of all classes; once, in a shortage of beds, even a woman, all Cockney scrawniness, anthracite hair and hemisphere earrings, who got herself up every morning to the bravos of the nurses, afternoons to the visit of a lover, evenings to the weak husband and harsh children who corroborated her tales of life over an Amsterdam Avenue bar. And under the night-light, lay back like a sharp-nosed girl, hugging to herself the short ward gown or her own blue nylon ruffles (neither of which hid the osteomyelitic erosions of her spine) while she set before Walter all the clandestine delights she still intended for that waiflike remainder of bone. Walter recalled these persons only when he himself came back here. Addresses were almost never exchanged between these confidants; indeed, their ill-matchedness was a very part of these honesties of the crutch and the catheter — severable in an hour by a "getting out," or a "going up" from which there was no return. What he was having was a "semi-private" experience.

This time he was in luck, with this literate, pleasant man, youngish at forty-odd, already head of an organization whose publishings included legal ones — Goodman had even heard of the Judge. His open blond looks, and the intelligence which came from them like a surprise, reminded Walter of Austin Fenno, though Austin's accent and background, authentic as jewels, were more easily defined. Nothing was so diagnostic as this listening, in the haunts of the night and under battle conditions, to a voice without a face to confront you, the voice of the stranger on the adjacent bedpan, telling over its life for the privilege of listening — to its own life. This was the first time Walter could recall telling so much about himself. But then he had never before been the more "serious" of the two beds.

"So you've been in the Negev," Goodman said. "Twice." Below his tractioned leg, his arms were free, one hand holding the slender olive-gray book he'd been reading, Stern's privately printed edition of his friend Mannix's letters.

"Once *with* him," said Walter. "Once — to search for him."

"He didn't go down in Germany?"

"Took off from there. Düsseldorf. He'd already left the Friends outfit. Came to say good-bye. To me. I saw the plane take off."

"Oh?"

"Actually, that plane landed safely in Beirut. The plane was a commercial transport; they can be . . . pretty blithe . . . about passenger lists. And there'd been several stops in between. After Düsseldorf. No reason to suppose that David wasn't still on it, though. The German reports, all very thorough, showed that he was, far as their borders. But the plane he was bound for, to pick up in Beirut, was the one that crashed. Inside the Israeli border, several hundred miles in."

"Out there, they were — thorough?"

"They were very kind," Walter said. He was leaning forward, sitting on the edge of his bed, in his dressing gown. All day he'd been hopping about; now that the place was oozing toward its evening quiet, he couldn't quite forget that by tomorrow, in any case, he wouldn't be able to move at all. "Though no bodies were recovered . . . May as well tell you. The Judge for a long time kept insisting to himself that David was still alive, somewhere. He couldn't go see for himself. And maybe he felt . . . that he'd never . . . unbent enough, when his son was alive. You know how families are."

"Any reason?"

"Not on David's side." Walter got up and peered out through the pane, cocking his head up, through the city's angles, at the sky. "He was . . . a perfect son."

"He comes out very clear here." His semi-bedmate — what other word was there for a man subject to the same sheets and regimes? — laid the book down, closed. "Very plain and simple, and nice."

"No more?" Walter turned from the sky. In pajamas, without the affectations of his dress, he looked scarcely deformed, merely a man excessively bent from stretching his small allotment of flesh over such a large solicitude. "Lots I couldn't put in of course. About the work he was going to do out there. Or personal things. About *them*." He hesitated. "So the letters don't strike you as — anything extra?"

"*They* do. His family. They appear there, amazingly. And in what you've been saying — of them." Goodman smiled. By day, his blue eyes had a clarity that didn't seem to reflect, but at night, shadowed, he deepened, like a well giving back what was told him, in a profound listening. Or maybe that too was the hospital situation. "You know how families are."

"Only one," said Walter. "Only this one."

"Any chance — he's still alive?"

"None. Amnesiac? — He was somehow the last person in the world — No. If there were an ounce of him alive anywhere — I'd know." Even when Walter looked unhappy, the rings around his eyes dissociated him from it, like spectacles. "The Judge didn't feel I looked hard enough out there. At the time. But if David were alive — it would be like not having my hump — and not knowing it." He raised his chin. "Glass of fresh water? *Want* anything?"

"Nothing, thanks."

Walter came over and got the book, fussed with the other's Kleenex box, put it nearer, hopped around his own bed to his own night table, ran a brisk hand through the pile of mail, his stamp catalogues in particular, gave them all a long look, and left them spread, like talismans. Then he got into bed, and lay back. In the semi-private experience, when the twin, turned-up toes of the inmates were quiet, a room looked into was a line drawing hopelessly unvaried — but Goodman's traction pulley, Walter's cricket motion, made this room livelier. Still, the pair were silent awhile, now that Walter too was in bed — for the night.

After a while, Goodman said, "What was it like? In the Negev?"

The other bed took a long time answering. The beauty of the semi-private experience was that it was as good for talk as a journey with whose mechanism one had nothing to do, though all the while one was going somewhere — in this case either "up" or "out."

"Military," said Walter. "And biblical. Like him."

"He was — both?"

Again Walter took a while to answer. Back-rubs were over; they could hear the nurses trotting the halls with the evening pills. "He had armies in him." The violence in his voice was unnatural to his own ears. It came from the brute heat of being alive. "Armies. He never knew."

Nurse came in with the pills and laid one down for him, in its little frilled candypaper cup. "Tonight, you must take yours, you know," she said softly. Sometimes he didn't. Other nights he'd had that option. But she left it for him. He was to be trusted. "Good night, gentlemen."

Goodman had the option. They both let the pills lie.

"Armies," Goodman said slowly. "Doesn't sound much like — *him*." From which usage, Walter could see how well he listened.

"*She* said that. Mrs. Mannix. She and I talked once, about David. When I guess she knew she was going to die."

"David got it from her, then," said Goodman. "From what you say of her."

"They're a family of — both sides," said Walter. "That's what's so wonderful."

Goodman was moving in his limited orbit, and from the random sound, only for the sake of it, kicking out his free leg, opening and shutting a drawer. "Do they know, he and — Miss Ruth — that you're here?"

"He does," said Walter. "Not her." Echoes came to him, from that dinner party the night of his uncle's death. He and the Judge had never been closer than then. "She's like the mother too — but different."

There was the pause of men talking in hospital.

"How?" Goodman never lost sight of a question waiting to be asked.

"She can — do injury to no one."

Again there was a restful pause.

"*Damn*," said Goodman.

"Bedpan?" said Walter. They'd become as alert to each other's bodies as the married.

"I — Yes," said Goodman.

He got the pan, and stood at the bedside, his hair tufted, like a competent child. "My uncle left me a Cézanne," he said. "I've left it to her."

"A Cézanne!" Goodman said. "Landscape?"

"Green and blue. I don't know painting, but I was always fond of it."

" 'Je continue donc mes études,' " said Goodman. "His last letter."

"Cézanne? Ah, you know then. About painting."

"Got a friend."

"My uncle always said it diminished a man, not to care about the arts."

"Some it might," said Goodman. "Not you."

Walter put the pan underneath the table, on the shelf. "Anything else? Can't I — get you anything else?"

"Not just now." Goodman watched him climb back in bed and sit there against the pillows. The hump was himself. Walter knew. "If I think of something, I'll ask," said Goodman.

After a while, the man in the next bed to Goodman said musingly, "You listen well." In bed, with his malformation in back of him like an extra pillow, he looked more fully a man. "Never talked so much before. About *myself*."

To this Goodman said nothing.

"If I —" said Walter. "I mean to make a friend of you."

"You have me," said Goodman.

This was the last quick response that either made. After that their remarks floated the room, not in strict sequence, like the breath of some apparatus that not even the hospital knew the name of, left for them to share.

"Consciousness. *He* made a remark about it once. I can't remember it."

Goodman took awhile, long enough not to make it seem a suggestion, before he carefully said, "London. Never really believe it's on the other end of a phone. Even when it is. Guess I'm not modern enough."

"The desert's not timeless. One dies there just the *same*," said Walter. "Leaving as much behind — as anyone . . . Oh, I'm modern enough . . . Used to get called out of class, in school . . . And my uncle's voice would say — from his yacht on the other side of the world . . . 'Guess

where we are *now.*'" For a while Walter could be heard padding
among the papers on his night table without comment — Goodman
wasn't much interested in stamps. "No, we had words . . . I suppose,"
he said then, a note of surprise in his voice, as if he'd found the stamp
he'd been looking for and it after all wasn't much. "The Judge and I.
He wouldn't accept a letter I'd been — entrusted with. Not for him, it's
true."

In contrast to Walter, the other occupant of the room, his leg high in
traction, looked like a man permanently frozen in the act of a huge
running start. Sometimes he reached forward, as now, to touch the leg
as if to press it forward, on. He saw that the rustle in Walter's hand
wasn't a letter, but the paper cup with the pill in it, like his own. He
lay back. "I'm not good with other people's secrets," Goodman said.

"Something that *fails*," said Walter. "Wish I could remember."

The wind blew in a swathe of night.

"Consciousness? You said."

"Secrets . . . I suppose one doesn't think of others as having them,"
said Walter. "If one has none."

Again there was a rustle of paper on Walter's side, but Goodman
couldn't tell what it was.

"I suppose he meant *me* to keep the letter . . . *forever*." The voice on
that penultimate was stronger than Goodman had ever heard it — the
voice of the hospital itself. Something fell into the basket at Walter's
side.

The man next him raised up. "Walter —"

"Just the pill," said Walter. His knees were drawn cozily to his chin.
After days on a pulley a man couldn't help but envy him. "I shan't take
it. Just for tonight." He looked across at Goodman. "Don't tell."

"Walter," said his roommate, "do something for me. Close that window." He watched the other spring up at the word *do* — if Goodman
willed it, he could keep that small figure all night in his service; would
that be the kinder? Or to leave him. Goodman put his head in his
hands.

The window was high; Walter, after a struggle to reach it, agilely
climbed a chair, and brought it down smartly by a push from the top.
Behind him, Goodman swiftly took his own pill. He had that option.

"Blowing cold," said Walter, back in bed.

"October." It was the last word Goodman said.

Walter sat, embracing his knees. "I've remembered." He wasn't surprised when there was no reply.

When the nurse came in for the ten-o'clock check, she said, "Shame on you. Look at *him!*"

Walter did so.

"Want another?" said the nurse. "I'll leave it for you. Just in case." She brought it, a smaller one. "There. You can take it in a half-hour or so. So you won't bother us. Gotta real emergency down the floor, and we're shorthanded; Carter phoned in sick tonight, gotta cold. Gotta boyfriend from home, more like." She smoothed his bed for him. "There. That'll hold you. Sleep tight." She hovered. To the initiate in their ways, they let drop what they knew, without knowing. "I'll still be here to give you your injection at six." She nodded brightly; it was her way of letting him hold her hand. "You won't feel a thing."

Walter nodded.

"Tell him good night for me, in the morning," he said.

He sat bolt upright for a while. The time passed for when the extra pill was permitted, but he didn't take it. "I must feel," he said to himself. "I *can* feel. I — feel."

"You've a lucky hump," Mirriam Mannix had said to him, the day after his parents' accident, when David brought him home to her, from school. She reached out and smoothed the hump almost avidly — not for a moment's luck but for a lifetime. "Come to us. You'll be lucky for us." No one had ever wanted him for that before. That afternoon, it seemed to him that she scattered truth like beads; if the heavy amber necklace on her breast were to break and he to garner them, each long bead would contain a hard, flat truth. She'd seen at once what was bothering him. The tie between him and his parents had been so distant, for what he should be feeling in the hour of their death.

"You don't need to dwell on it," said Mirriam Mannix. "Let no one convince you. Of what you ought to feel. Like they convinced me."

Much later, when just before her death she brought him the letter for David, he still remembered it. She knew how not to dwell — even though she herself couldn't manage it.

"I ought to burn all my correspondence," she said, in her high, handsome way, her dark cheeks kindled with the winter frost that set his marrow aching — and with the fire she had lit for him. "But some of the people who write me have nobody but me. You know how it is."

He sat on the sofa beside her, enthralled under the wreath of her arm, her hand nursing their luck.

"It would be like burning *them,* poor things," she said. How marvelous she was in her intensity — how she could feel! "I've burnt Simon's," she said of a sudden, and saw his face.

"Oh no, my dear." Her laugh went *link, link, link,* in a chain that drew. "When you live with a person, it's the other way. You don't want bits of the progression that brought you together; you even hate seeing those. You want it all in the present, whole."

Though he knew he would never live with a person, he was thrilled to his core. She made him a candidate for it, like any other.

"Besides — Simon doesn't need them. He won't need letters," she said. At her age, so much nearer death than his eighteen, it hadn't seemed to him strange of her to think of it.

How hotly she'd breathed of death, though — almost in love with it! Later of course, he knew why. "Except this one," she said, handing him the letter.

"But — it's for David, you said, isn't it?" He only wanted to be sure, for the envelope was unmarked.

She nodded, narrowing her eyes at the photograph of herself on the piano. "I'm giving it to you because I can do you no injury by it," she said. The crook of her mouth bewildered him, but that was his ignorance — of the charm of mothers, or their mystery.

He reached into a portfolio of the latest issues of commemorative stamps. The letter lay there, brought with him just in case — in spite of the silent phone — he should wake to find them standing here. If they should come — and for a while he imagined it in spite of all — it would be both.

"No, it's David's letter," the Judge had said harshly, after the plane crash, when Walter first offered it. "It belongs to my son. Keep it for him."

A month ago, Walter had tried again, on hearing that the Judge and Ruth were once again going to London. In spite of illness, the Judge took every chance to go there.

"I'm going in for that op," said Walter. "I could have mailed it to you." Somehow, remembering Mrs. Mannix, he hadn't. It would have been — like a burning. "It oughtn't to be found in my papers perhaps. Just in case."

This time the Judge had said, "Come here, Walter. Closer to my chair. Walter — why do you think I go to London?"

He'd reflected, then said what honestly came to him, considering it all. "For Austin."

The Judge's eyes widened; since being chairbound, he was less impenetrable of face. "Walter, you're a prize. Most people still help me to think I go there for a woman." The Judge put out a small compact hand, and for a second Walter put in it his own long fingers. "The agencies are there. For lost people. I worked with them before." The hand was the iron kind, musclebound with weight-lifting, which the chairbound often had. "Don't think I accuse you, Walter. Not after my first — grief. We each believe as we have to believe. If he's dead, then he has you to believe in him, of those who loved him. And Ruth, I think — too. But if he's alive somewhere — he has only me."

What the Judge had said was so like *her!* Walter almost spoke of it. But he was older now to the wonders here, and could let the house rest on this — that it was a house of both sides. So when he turned the study doorknob, to leave, he still had her letter.

"Wait." The Judge stood up. Terrifying to watch him. It was done without visible struggle — that was why. "When you going in, Walter? The fifteenth . . . I'll tell Ruth?"

"No, don't," he found himself saying. "Promise me you won't. She's had enough." (Of what, he didn't know, except from the silences of his friend's box, the loudness of his protectiveness. Too much had been put upon her once.) "Enough!" This was merely the expression of all he felt about her, coming out, as things did when one was tidying one's affairs. In so far as he'd ever thought of what could have happened to her, he'd place it as among the horrors that in alleyways did assail young girls, had hoped it was more imagined than real — and hadn't dwelt upon it. He'd forgotten that a father would.

Worse than seeing the Judge rise — to see him draw back, and sit again in the chair. "So you know," he said. "Well, I'm glad. That it's you. It's just that I always thought you were — the most innocent."

"I don't know what happened to her, sir, I only know that you all have always . . . David too —"

The cry came sharp. *"Did her brother know?"* And quick on its heels, "Don't answer! That's his!"

This Walter could answer — "I wouldn't know" — dully hoping that in all this tidying, the house which even into his manhood had remained the same, wouldn't disappear.

"I see well why Mirriam gave you the letter," said the Judge. "As well as something else, about myself. For if you *had* known about Ruth — I see I'd have welcomed it. Not just because it would be safe with you. Because I'd have — welcomed it. And I can't afford to feel that." He looked wan, failed — if a man assessing himself so grimly could be said to. Or it was the mystery of fathers. "Walter. There *are* some things I'd rather not know. So oblige me. We ask those we love to oblige us. Read that letter — and destroy."

"I can't promise," he'd answered. "Not yet." Though why that he couldn't quite say. The dead do not consult. On the night table, beside the phone for which he had all privileges any hour, the smaller pill gave him its candy smile, full of possible companionship. For the phone wasn't going to ring. He hadn't made a promise. But the Judge had kept his.

He sat like a man at a desk, meditating business to be done. . . . What must I feel *next?* . . . Suddenly he got up, inserted his feet carefully in the warm slippers given him by Anna last Christmas, scooped up the pill, trotted to the toilet and cast it in. About to draw water in a glass, he recalled just in time that he wasn't to drink any more liquid before the anaesthesia. But he still had water in him. "Futz," he said, and urinated upon the pill. Then he climbed into bed and read the letter. Though in memory now Mrs. Mannix seemed a woman who was always speaking, he could recall quite clearly that she had never said much at one time. Inside the blank envelope, whose freshness made him shiver, even the page had no salutation.

> Take care of your father. He is your father, you know. And give him my love. I hope — if you get to read this — that I have done him and you no injury.
>
>   MIRRIAM

He'd never known his friend to call his mother Mirriam. The scrap of paper warmed his hand, amber from a breast. To the father, through

the son. His friend, refusing it, had said simply, "No, you keep it" —
being the man his friend had been. But the father, a judge, was used to
harsher solutions. "Read it" — for it ought to be read by someone —
"then destroy." Safest that way. For the dead do not consult, Walter.
And you are going to die.

Until now, he hadn't been so sure. He'd left himself the human
margin. And day after day, in his talk of them, what had he been doing
but imagining them here? But where his daughter was concerned, the
Judge was like rock. So would any man be who was her father. That
was her quality; who could say why? "We obligate those we love," said
the Judge. "So I do *you* injury, as to any humpless man."

Six feet from him, the man Goodman rolled over in his sleep — not a
bad man to die near. He could send some message by Goodman,
maybe that he, Walter, had done as asked. No, what a burden to leave
them, his own weakness reaching out for a last touch. No message was
best. He had talked enough.

The letter, torn into a heap of the minutest pieces, lay before him
now, like the rainy-day work of a daydreaming child.

Behind him, his true companion pressed harder into the pillow, and
into him. Life, private life, is never that artificial — cheery as they are,
here. It will provide you the last feelings. You needn't choose. I am
your dear hump. With me on your shoulders, they could love you
purely. For who could bear to do you more injury than you already
had? I am your dear hump — and that is our luck.

Toward morning, he began to feel immortal. The emergency down
the hall sifted unmistakably into death; the sure nun-feet of the nurses
wavered at these times, and their voices also; more than once he'd seen
the cart that came. Whereas he, Walter Stern, could feel with magnificent certainty — in the center of a hospital that would strive with all its
might for him if he had a syncope — that he would be alive until eight
o'clock.

He could use the pan; they wouldn't mind now, if he rang for it. He
refused to get up for it, any more. In his mind's eye, he did get up,
strode to the wardrobe, called for his checked vest and his watch chain,
shrieked to them all, "I will not have your comforts!" and strode down
the stairs. He sat on, hard against the pillow. Far away, across the
stretches of vanished swimming pool, across Utahs, his foolish uncle
beckoned to him, waving him a last bequest — and he saw what he

had done. Where his uncle had failed, he was succeeding. An amazed whimper broke from him. Had his roommate heard it? No, Goodman was dead asleep. He could let escape his message to them all.

"I still feel — so *good.*"

In the bed, his head sank further on his chest; his hands crept up either side of his neck to grasp his shoulders, the long fingers pointing backward, in the attitude that best gave him rest. Trembling in his diminishment, he fell asleep.

When he woke, to the hypodermic, the man in the other bed woke too, and began talking to him, Walter answering for as long as the drug allowed. Both of them knew the obligations here. But Goodman was more delicate than most. For he was talking of the Mannixes. A good listener, he now offered the fruits of it, and kept Walter in their company, bringing them as best he could to the other's bedside.

Orderlies displaced them, transferring Walter to a wheeled stretcher. Light as a feather, Walter gave them all his help. His stealing hands pulled the long sheet to cover him, as far as the chin. From the door, he saw his bed receding. He felt a terrible concern over its being empty; this was the moment when he knew to the full that he would die. He had succeeded — in arranging his own fake death. But he was already in the ritual — where no one could do the subject any injury that he could feel, or could hold his hand.

He saw the bed as it would be tomorrow or even tonight, stripped down to the harsh, striped ticking, the curtains being drawn around it, while tossed from inside there accumulated at the foot the stained sheets, drawsheets and pillowcase, in a small pile. Two nurses always did this together. In the most modern hospitals, the bed itself, already the "table" as well, could be wheeled straight up — and sometimes down again. His would have to wait.

"Graciously, my spittle," he said to it, and saintly or not, these were the last words he spoke.

Upstairs, the actions of others, gathering around him, made a chancel which hid him from life, from the Host which was no more his own. They took his hump, leaving him two scapulae clapping in the soundlessness of the world. Consciousness is the experiment which always fails. And begins again, in another bed. The whole hospital hushed it to him, semi-privately. The great blues moved toward him, and those great greens the nature of whose paint he would never understand. Hosannas of flies bore him upward and into them, ever upward, never down.

And so Walter Stern at the last did question the significance of his life.

18 Getting There in Time
October 1954

"Why was I *not* to be told? *Why?*"

Minutes passed. His daughter kept her back to him, staring down into the hotel yard.

The view from Dukes was deceptive, as was this small establishment itself. Up the hill of St. James's, giant traffic streamed almost into the heart of Piccadilly, yet these side passages were remarkably sedate, here a stationer's, there a turf accountant or other modest commercial flashes, along rows of those blind buildings of which so much of trading London was still composed. At night even the hill was quiet, almost deserted of foot traffic. Dukes's cul-de-sac had almost no light at all. Cabmen knew it of course — a small hotel with one elderly factotum at the telephone who doubled at night as porter, and a lift which stretched to three, put in for women and Americans. Or you might healthily walk the wide, red-carpeted stair, meeting there the walrus-moustached half of the couple who shared your bath. Rest assured, he wouldn't greet you, not a blink; the county had a talent for not encountering those it shared a bath with at such places; if you couldn't manage it, your fault, for being American.

Dukes since the Judge's father's day had been much the same. The housemaids were British sub-Annas; he heard a pair in the hall now, at whose end he had engaged a room for his chauffeur, Charlie. No meals here, past the "Continental" roll in the morning, but just a walk away, to Bentley's discreet door, and the truth about this city overtook one — that all its true tavern flare, and the chandelier lunettes of its greater conversations — were on the inside. He and Ruth had eaten there ever since the old days, at the buffet where one had Colchesters and Stilton in the company of those from the Temple or the City or Whitehall whose long legs were equal to the high barstools, not a head

turning as the Judge climbed to his — more unblinkingness of the kind
he loved this city for. Nowadays, his wheelchair was allotted one of the
coveted tables at the entry; he and she should be meeting Ninon there
a couple of hours from now.

And he hadn't yet answered his daughter, hunched there with her
back to him and the room, in a rejection so powerful that he too was
mute. The room, smaller of their two, was the dullest, cleanest hotel-
Victorian; up to now soothingly just that. Wasn't the room to which
Walter had come, fresh from his hunt for David in the Negev; that one
had had a view only of chimneypots. The ones during the blitz had
been lower down. "Will you require the same rooms?" the hotel always
asked. He always said no. But the porter, faithfully of the same quality
through a number of factotum faces, was sure of finding him anyhow
— with the hospital's cable in answer to his own. Allowing for the five-
hour difference, it had been morning there when it happened — for the
Judge a brilliant afternoon among the booksellers on Hayhill, in an
October beautiful across oceans. But by any reckoning, when the
cable came Walter Stern had been dead a day.

He'd just told her, not five minutes ago. He was always stumbling
nowadays, with his daughter. In the days of his mystification, he'd had
a blind love-surety with her — in those tender "copacetic" years after
her crime. But once persons identified themselves as "the missing," they
truly were. They escaped.

"Why?" he repeated after her. If he could tell her why, wouldn't he
have explained what people thought of (in agony or the silveriest retrospect) as "everything"? "If —"

"Oh please — no *language*."

It hit him that she was humped in a dancer's mime of the man who
had died — striving to bring him into the room, in her way out, from
language.

"You knew he was going in? And let us leave anyway?"

He'd never understood her dancing. He should have gone to see her
perform. But had left her this one sure way out. A pain shrouded him,
from the leg that kept him in the chair.

"He made me promise," he said.

She wheeled to face him. "Are you sure you didn't make him?"

"No, I'm not sure," he said.

She gave him the queerest look; over her ruff he saw their resemblance. She was judging *him*. She was striving to bring him into the room: aspects of you, are they aspects of me? In all the one-way violence of his protection, he'd never really thought of that.

She came closer to him. She was scrutinizing. Or recognizing. "Why did we really come here? Father?"

He spread his hands. In a wheelchair, gestures are few. Hard not to acquire the papal air of a man who knows, and blesses. Helpless to assure her he wasn't cultivating it.

"David was my brother. If he wasn't — dead — wouldn't I know? But if it comforted you to . . . hunt. That's why I came, I thought. Up to now."

A flash of hope illumined his face. "Families disappear at the front. I said that to him. And he —"

"He disappeared from *you* long ago," she said. She looked around the room — recognizing it? — and inhaled deeply. At the same time she took a step away from him. "With her."

He recognized this place too now. Home. That's why we came away, but it has followed us. After so long, never before in all those years — he heard his daughter mention her.

"Maybe I did too," she said.

"Children always live downstairs. In the houses of their parents." He gave her the smile for quotes. Old Meyer.

She nodded, looking around again almost wildly.

"Not that I —" If he weren't in the chair, he would take a step toward her, to her side, as if by accident. "It's all yours. The house," he said. And gave a shamefaced smile. Givers do that, he thought.

"Father —"

Of a sudden, he wheeled himself close to her. "Ruth. Speak — of her."

In his twelve-year image of just this — though she would speak, she always at first recoiled. Here was his daughter receiving it as if she spoke of her every day. Or staring past him, across the home-yards of London — to her.

"I spoke of her. To Edwin. Once."

He wheeled himself at once — away.

"Not far enough," she said bitterly after him — was this his daughter? "Yes, that's why we came, how simple. To leave home." She strode toward him and put a hand on the arm of his wheelchair; he couldn't recoil. "Why Walter? Who did no one in the world any harm, even by loving us. Why him." She put her young hand hard on the arm of his chair. "Oh yes, I see why. Why you could be jealous of him. *She* brought him in!" She gave the chair a push, sending him backward, against a wall. It wasn't far. The wall held. The room contained it, what was happening here.

She raised her head, on a column of neck that was no Mannix's. "So I speak of her!"

"How angry you are." He could only whisper it. "I never realized."

"Oh no," she said. "Not angry. Not until *now*. None of you know what you want, what you are. But I have always had to know."

It reverberated. But the walls held that too. He huddled there. In her blast. How familiar that was. "You're like her. Walter was right."

On the other side of the room she bent her head, backed against her wall in her brownish velvet, of the same cut, like a pageboy's or a poet's, which seemed to come out for the girls every year. "So he's dead. That's the way people speak of them, when they are." She was coming back to him. She even smiled. "We always knew that. In the basement."

"The way we take advantage of the dead, you mean. But I felt that too, at your age! I still do. So you see! You see!" He held out his hands to her, his arms.

She was unmoved. "Did you know what she was like? Did you?"

He clasped his hands, brought them up to his teeth — and in the instant knew who he was mimicking, bringing in here.

"No language?" his daughter said. "But I had to think about it — what she was like. Afterwards. For strength. She knew what *you* wanted. She knew — what we are."

And then she glided toward him again. "Walter had a letter."

"For David."

"To him."

"Your brother told you?"

"No." She was gliding nearer.

"Walter, then." He couldn't move. But it was a dance.

"Walter? Never. He never did a soul harm. That was his **triumph**. That people thought so much of him in spite of it."

And he had thought this girl without intellect.

"Then, who?" It seemed to him that she had already said it.

"She told me. She did." She leaned forward; she might have had him between her fingers like a bird on a plate, and now be dancing with it. He had seen her perform after all, his mind elsewhere. "We took walks," she said. "She told me — everything she could. I was only twelve. How often I've heard you say that. 'When Ruth was thirteen, or ten, or six, or two,' you'd always say, harking back. But whenever you came to twelve, you said 'only twelve.' Marking it." Her fists clenched over one another, like her tutor's once. But there was no lemon in them. She smiled at him, the ballerina's cool smile. "Like a shot."

He sat heavy in his chair. No, he couldn't carry her any more. But he felt her weight, as men of the audience, in their chairs, he thought, feel that adagio, flying weight on their shoulders, and the assoluta, turning one wrist from her pinnacle, carries them.

"Oh yes, we had walks," she said. "We Mannixes walk and we talk, don't we. How old did you think twelve was!"

"Old enough — for her to tell you what she wrote? In the letter?" But he didn't put his face in his hands. He could bear it, from her.

"No. No." He saw her falter. A ballerina shouldn't speak, he thought. "Father — you've read it?" she said — and she was only his daughter.

"Why should I? It was for him. David."

She was silent.

"Would it have had — anything about me in it?" he said.

"About her." She stood clumsily now. "It was only to be opened if she died. Or maybe — about all of us. Didn't you know what she was like?"

They looked at each other like colleagues.

"We're the experts," he said. "On her. Oh Ruth. Language's my way maybe. But you and she talked too."

She gripped her hands in her hair. "She was making me into a woman, she always said. But whatever she told me, it was always about all of us. Never herself alone. Or just enough to make me wonder more."

"Us ... *Make* us ... That was her charm."

Reverie had entered the room so quickly, like the balm of a night plant, nicotiana, kept outside the window to feed sadness away.

"Strike you this place isn't so comfortable any more?" he muttered.

But she'd already said it. The deaths of two had been received here. It was home. "She used to call the boys your three musketeers. Remember?"

She came close again, but only not to spring at him. He saw the real face of this animal, young and itself. "No, I won't have it. Memory. People are living now. And I could have held his hand."

He took hers. "Who leaves letters for the family these days? But so much of her life was letters. All she wanted was to insure that we speak of her. That's what she was like. And that's memory! Now!"

"She always had to act. To her — it was an act."

"In our day — letters still could be."

"Then I'm old-fashioned," she said. "You made me."

"To hear you say it. That helps — close the gap."

On that long neck, the head that had just been gnawing its red, pristine lip leaned back and laughed — the kind of laugh that stood on the air like a motif, ugly only because of this — perfectly on scale.

"The inter . . . penetrations of things," he said, staring. His daughter shouldn't dance, but sing. "One can't talk about it. But I try. Hence — my language."

"How you talk to me!" she said. "As if I were intelligent."

Over her shoulder he saw her brother, her mother too. "I apologize. I apologize to you all."

Again came the laugh — as if she were practicing. "What life's like? Let me tell *you*. A day after his death, and yes I think of him — but of the message he might have left me too." She put her hand to that long throat. "I feel . . . he would. That part's all right. But then . . . I keep thinking, right here, *now* — maybe he's left *me* the letter. Like people who wait for the will, for their money . . . You let us leave. Knowing. I'll never forgive you for it. But the other, that's part of it too. *Right now*. That's how mercenary I am. Life is."

Her cheeks were dry. If she'd buried them in her hands, it would be only a speech. Instead he saw her advancing, with measured laugh, with unsure step, to the fulcrum, to him.

"But it was destroyed," he said hoarsely. "I asked him to."

Her mouth opened, and closed.

"David wouldn't take it," he said. "How should I? If it had anything in it, wouldn't it have been about Arne? Your mother's first husband. You've heard about him — if you and she talked. She used to keep up with him. After he went back to Belgium, Switzerland, I don't know where. By letter . . . And once in Paris. Once — she went to see him from there. And I used to think . . . All David's lifetime I did think . . . Oh, never mind — he knew. But wouldn't deign to read the letter from her. So I apologize to him now."

"That's why you hunt for him to — be alive! For yourself."

He scored at the hard-rubber tire of his chair with his thumbnail, deepening a groove already there. "Leaving letters. How absurd. They're finding more instant ways — of memory. Or my generation may be the last to value it at all."

When he raised his head, he saw she had taken up her overnight bag, a kind of duffel that always hung about somewhere, and was looking around the room for anything of hers left in it, as one did when one left home.

"Ours," she said with a shrug, sliding the strap over her shoulder. "They say ours will be the last. For anything."

"Where are you going?"

She gazed back at him. "So it's all to go unrecognized, then? Wasted. He'll have left some — message. I know Walter. But not the letter. Not if you asked him to get rid of it."

"I asked him to read it before."

The bag slid to the floor, slowly. She covered her mouth.

"What is it, Ruth? For God's sake."

"You used him. As a . . . as a —" again she tried. "Mercenary. To do your own job."

"Language," he said.

"We learned from you." At the mantel, she picked up the heavy bracelet her brother had sent her, and snapped it on her arm. "Oh, we mimic you. Because we admire you. Why do you think David went to war? The way you used Walter. The way you used —"

"David didn't go to be a — mercenary. He went to be a soldier of — God."

"Can one be that? I suppose. From a grave." She hoisted the bag again. "But I didn't mean him."

On that brown velvet, the heavy sporting bag looked so — absurd. "Ruth. Where are you going?"

She shrugged. "Maybe you — came to London for that too."

An incredulous twinge vibrated over him, from those depths where he was unable to forget how to play chess.

As she opened the door he said, "But why then — did you want the letter so much?"

She was kneading her breast with the heel of her hand. In spite of the breasts it was a child's action. "I thought — she might tell me once again, from her own mouth. That I — would do her no injury. Did her — none."

Then he remembered who he was talking to. With *whom*. It was like coming out of a madness — of murder, or a bed — of love, to realize the other person. Who had now made him drop every term of the silent entente under which the two of them had lived.

Don't you know yet, Father? How you used me?

She rubbed her cheek. "I can't cry. Again. Apologize to Walter for me. For that."

After the door closed, the Judge, finding himself staring at the olive-yellow army blanket that covered his legs and now went with him everywhere, quickly wheeled himself to the window, in time to see his daughter emerge from the porte-cochère below, walk across the courtyard, the red bag bobbing in the dusk, and turn left up the hill. She wouldn't have waited for the lift for just one floor down; she wouldn't hail a cab. Mannixes walked, where it was possible; even in the century they lived in, they flaunted it. Of her two probable destinations, one — the theatre — must be about the same distance as the other. Both were possible. They escape. After she had gone he stayed as he was. The blind listened in order to see, the chairbound waited — but in the mind's eye they were moving, walking the streets that came toward them. "No more memory!" What a young remark!

He caught himself glancing at his legs the way an addicted smoker took out a cigarette — to celebrate his helplessness. And to take heart. In what century now were the old "neurasthenias" of Goethe's spa-Europe and of his own parents' — surely fizzing away like modestly bad sulphur water, somewhere still? Hypochondria, which once drowned its hyenas in holy waters, now took them on leash to some confessional: "What have I *got?*" A man still couldn't quite choose his disease, but he could choose the century that named it — and sometimes compounded it. His own disorder was some mortar-and-pestle mythic of nerve, soma, and bone — a couple of vertebrae once cracked while sailing, a degenerative thinness of the discs between — and the cortisone which could cure at intervals, by killing him for good. Plus a

will of his own which, like the masks of Janus, looked both ways. No
wonder the orthopedists had no name to give him to pass on to his
well-wishers; there was always the possibility that such conditions as
his were the product of a life! He himself was holding back before he
either gave his disease a name, or his life a century. A man of intellect,
and some money, could to a degree determine both. And men of intellect, even without money, always had.

He was going to have to give up London. Now that his daughter had
been empowered to leave him — and not just for the ballet, her mime-
life. She'd even hinted that he himself might have provoked the loss of
her for her own gain — and his own relief. Once, he'd heard an older
colleague and his wife, good people with a great cornucopia of family
in which surely nothing was criminally hidden — sigh to themselves at
the wedding of their youngest, in the champagne wisdom that his
abnormal parenthood had kept him from, "Well, there's the last one off
our hands!" Within the lordlier rise and fall of the civic generations,
the personal seesaw of parent and child was so little; wasn't it *all* a
getting there in time, or a giving up? What Mirriam, no one, could
accept in him was that he lived his life in these rhetorical questionings.
Sometimes he hated the habit in himself, but he had to accept the
questioning. He couldn't see life as others did, as merely the color of
events. A barrister to *life* was what he'd wanted to be, from even
before his thrashing for that moneylending episode. "I swear to God,
Simon," his father had said, much later. "I know I hurt you; you yelled.
But you received each lash as if it were enlightenment."

His father was right. "And each *yell*," he had replied. His father had
whipped him the way a good poet used reason; he'd been listening to
that pendulum. For this same talent, his colleagues had later murmured him upstairs to a judgeship. But the courtroom was a drama
which expected answers, plus the arrogance to believe them; he would
always be a cabinet-judge. And be disliked for it. As were all those who
live by the mixed breath.

The phone rang, at his side.

"Mannix here." He admired the Anglicism, so economical.

Factotum had rung through to the restaurant, for his 8:30 reservation. "Will you have your own car, sir?"

"No, Charlie's at Blackpool for the day." He could see a downstairs
screw of distaste for all this democracy, but couldn't resist adding to

it. "Visiting his old mother." True enough; she was a character actress there.

But the class below still retained the privilege of putting one in one's place. "Indeed, sir. Kindly order the cab in good time. I'm alone, sir. I'll ask the cabman to come up."

He was alone here now. Factotum knew that too. As well as that he never allowed his daughter to touch his wheelchair. Nor any family; family wasn't for that. Rosa and Athalie never dreamed of "taking him for walks," although for the last two Christmases knitted Afghans for his knees had supplanted the gray mocha gloves. The army blanket had been acquired when he thought he was going in, in 1917; there was continuity for you! Maybe his sisters, that formal stupidity of theirs, might all along have better instructed him how to be with his daughter — if he could ever have told them why. How had he used her? How did one mourn the young?

He hung up the phone as quickly as decent. "A vulgar instrument," his father had said laughingly, after being on it to his mistress — "no gentleman wants to be any closer to an absent woman than the *pneumatique.*" There was continuity for you. And the gap as well. For where his father's era had found the thing foreign to its manners, he resented it because of its empathy — and Mirriam had clapped it to her heart like an artificial — heart. And his children played tricks with it early, and more serious games later — dispensing emotion everywhere. Even David (though his box heard better than normal over it) in the days of his last home visit had refused call after call from a woman, saying to him once in passing, "Can't stand the phone somehow, after the desert. It's too close. Know what the phone is to some people? It's fucking, by ear."

Oh my son . . . in the privacies of life anything may burst through a door.

In half an hour or so, his daughter should be at the destination he was betting on, allowing for that peculiar ballerina gait which had to acknowledge the ground in the act of covering it. The other probable one, the theatre, might be a few squares nearer. If she'd had any intention of going as far as Ninon's house in Clipstone Street, she would have taken a cab. "We had walks," said his daughter after twelve years, and burst down the door. Dukes fell in ruins, his wife rose again from her grave, and his son lay down in his like a soldier — and Walter, so recently dead, was the liveliest. And I, what do I do?

I rise from the chair.

He couldn't do it all at once of course. Nightly practice of the past two years had helped. Once a day the chair whizzed this way within a room's limits, like a friendly amah, trundling its charge — who was preparing to get off. Now to the cupboard for the aspirin; he'd given up the codeine as too Oriental for him, and all the other Pantopons, Luminals, Nembutals, morphine derivatives of the soft, lethe-like names. Aspirin — like the pain of standing — was only cumulative. If taken at intervals, the two kept pace. Most spinal pain had some posture of remission. His was to sit; he and Charlie often joked of it. He himself had been the one to break down Charlie's English stage-servant manners to a comfortable exchange of obscenity, most of it about the Judge's ills, when they were alone. "Eh well, in a household of women 'tis needed," Charlie said. "Eh well," the Judge said to himself — for it couldn't be said to Charlie — "In a way too it's like having the wife in the house again, for this Jew."

Shirts and suits were hung low enough for him to reach. He stripped his upper body, splashed it with cologne and powder in lieu of washing — Europe again — and began taking off his pants, an involved snail-inching in which every muscle reprinted its image on his brain. At a time when exercise had still been suggested (and before a spinal fusion had been tried and found wanting) a therapist trained to polio cases had taught him the names. "Merry Christmas," Miss O'Neill had said last year, off on her holiday, "and remember to keep your hamstrings loose!" Mirriam, who was never even in this city with me, laugh anyway; that's what she said.

Muscle by muscle, thong by thong of meditation, he dressed, missing Charlie's Mersey-stream of backtalk. Jews in their own households often never swore even to other men, keeping to manners Chasidic or soft. Often, even in the middle classes, it was the woman who kept obscenity fresh, with a midwife's coarse righteousness. Until Charlie came, he hadn't realized how much he had missed Mirriam's command of it. She'd had the affectations of her period. Where his own mother had dared only a domestic "*Scheiss*" or "*futz*" — like a peasant when a pot fell — Mirriam, like the artists she knew did when they cut their fingers, said "fuck." At a dinner party, she could pass the psychological penises around gravely as anybody, a scholarly artifact. In bed, she said anything that came into her head, from wherever she found it. "Women don't say 'cunt' though, do they?" he'd once said, and had in reply her high, señorita shrug: "Why should *we!*" Adding, "I got the rest from friends; Father would have died."

But Meyer, to him, had said with a twinkle, "Oh, the Old Testament keeps us Jews healthy and sex open, not separated from life. Milk and meat is what shouldn't be joined — when we go to the whorehouse what we should be careful of is not to eat shrimp. Diet is what is sin! So instead of repression, we older Jews have flatulence. The Jew doesn't use orgasm to bow to the life force with; he farts." And had added, "Thank God for it, Simon. I see some of our younger men drinking up the Christian sense of sin like alcohol. You mayn't have stomach trouble yet, but you're one of the old sort, like your father. You're still *ours.*"

Naked in the chair, he felt the aspirin give him a hitch toward blandness and took two more; in ten minutes, pain retreated to cortex, he would be able to stand for forty, without more than he could bear. At the age of seventy-six, old Meyer, after living with them in his own house for four years, had left for the Fifth Avenue Hotel, where until he died he'd kept the management on the qui vive with his late poker and visiting cauliflower ears. "I've begun to fart, Simon. And my tongue's begun to like to letch. It's time." Up to then, he'd still had women. "Sex in the afternoon, Simon; reminds you of younger love affairs, but you send them an orchid in the evening, and get your sleep. Very practical. Leaves the young woman *her* evenings." In London here, Meyer's birthplace, he came alive again, in his sporty suits and Limey speech. In a moment he'd enter the door his granddaughter had gone out of, up from the glassy dusk of Dukes courtyard, in his spotted tie and Yankee snap-brim, bringing with him a farther London's itching cries. To him, his son-in-law's neat nakedness, the chest hair barely grizzled, would show up plenty live. "Get up, man, legs like a five-day biker's, and look at those arms. Old Testament kept you young in the proper places, but don't pick the wrong book. Judges *sit*, and you've sat, that it? Get up, I know a young singer at the Palladium. With those Japanesy looks of yours . . . I never was much for spas."

The phone rang. From his daughter? Or her destination, calling to say — how would it be said? — *Just to let you know she's here.*

Ninon's secretary. "Madame will be kept at the theatre and will come straight on to meet you."

"At eight," he said. "Bentley's in Swallow Street. I may be a few minutes late." She much preferred Boulestin or Rule's, but they were too far for what he had in mind; the other place was all he could dare. He'd no idea how much time he would need. But the ten minutes was up. Now came the part he always hated, even in the lone sessions he forced himself to at night at home — when all he did was to pace the floor of the room to whatever he had set himself on the pedometer, or ghosted it down the long hall to the open door of his son's room. To stand there breathing, and pace back.

The dry corset was hanging on a rod over the washstand — he had three, and he supposed the chambermaids understood what for because of the chair. At the Lenox Hill brace shop it was called a brace, but to any man brought up in a basement of just such strings and eyelets, it was a corset, unsavory on him now as in his boyhood the rumored secret appliance of a bladdery-lipped old aunt who'd wetted each newspaper page with a large flat thumb he'd somehow connected with her truss. He pulled the strings tight now and knotted them; he was a man who couldn't tie a bow. Some, luckier than he, got by with a sacroiliac bellyband, with hooks. This thing gave him a waistline he couldn't bear; he now realized that Pauli must wear stays. With it on, he wheeled the chair to the mirror. "Your — undergarment, sir," said Charlie the first time he saw it, never a valet before and wanting to be sure of his terms. "My phylactery," said the Judge grimly. "I'm thinking of having it done up in black lace." And Charlie, serving him from the tender distance of a brother widower — "Wife killed in the blitz, sir, and a daughter in the convent when she isn't running off to the old girl in Blackpool" — always thereafter called it his "prophylactery." Funny, but no one to hear. Every time he put the thing on, he thought of a man he and Mirriam'd known, whose wife had found him hanging — dressed in *her* clothes, down to the high-heeled shoes. In the months he had been wearing it, he'd begun to surmise what the really old looked for and missed in the dead. "Look, Mirriam!" he'd say, "Travis McCardell!" Just as she began to laugh — for she would laugh; she'd had a thousand letters, he saw now, which had sought that laugh or answered it — he would top it. " '*Gott sei dank!*' " he would say, in the very voice of his mother and hers: " '— that *such* a man was no Jew!' "

On the night of her death, in that second after the shot when he saw the deathblood running slow, he had felt the loss first in his genitals, where there was a place to feel. Cubs, after the mother-kill, must wander analogous, thinking teat. Men when hung, erect — how that

must have looked, in the short skirts of 1928. Mirriam! Laugh! There
was no time to mourn you, until now; I had to mourn her. That's how I
used her, surely? She herself said. Or didn't say. Now she's gone — and
I think, provided for — I can mourn you. The laugh I hated, the
"lady's" laugh! Now that all the letters are dead, send me it. Let my
mind not letch.

Along his spine he felt the gradual lapse of pain. Or that tired truce
which was still sensation. But like the flush of a late climacteric, must
suffice. He remembered that first social ease of her being dead. Age
wasn't merely in the muscle, but in the closing of the ranks when it was
too late for it, Meyer coming into this room, Mirriam into his mourning,
and who next, all bearing the same message? He found he could lift his
legs now to put on his pants, knowing that all the ridiculousness would
have to be borne alone.

In the wardrobe, a hotel try at what the county and he had at home,
there were two new suits; he'd had to give up his thirty after all, to
accommodate a brace ridged with whalebone. Hung within his jacket,
he found the pedometer and put it aside as one did a toy soldier.
Tonight its tidy spring, set to hall distances, might get a shock. Shoes
next, the sweat stealing down his arm. Propped in a corner was his
third leg, near it another cane almost its silver-ebony twin, sent him by
Ninon for Christmas, to the hospital. "Oooh, whoo sent you that?" said
the nurses, Floradora round his bed that morning. Yoo-whoo did not
die in hospital. The witness sat up with his harness on. Nothing was
effete in hospital. Sex was angry elsewhere. "My mistress," the foolish
witness said, sitting up on his rubber ass and fondling his urinal. Let
me not letch in the mind alone.

Ninon knew of his chair, but had never seen him in it. She never
wrote, had never missed letters begun to her and never sent. Sometimes, when Ruth was in London, he rang up Clipstone Street from
New York and he and Ninon chatted of her, like good foster-parents.
Ninon never rang him. He wasn't to feel — that he had to feel. This
was how she released her lovers, from limited engagements often re-
deemable. Since becoming a Dame, she'd acquired certain dying British elegances which in her hands became Gallic again, like some
French convert to citizenship. He doubted she'd told about the rectory.
She was dancing again. After middle age — just as after a pulled
tendon or a love affair — the body "got better again." She had this

same answer (or no other) to any of it. Or to him. And none of this was ever discussed.

Thursdays, though not at the theatre, she couldn't see him, being in the habit of attending the directors' meetings of Hoare's Bank. "Very mind-sharpening, Simon." He assumed that one of the directors — some red-faced securities-drinker thatched with gray finance — was being shaped up too. When her gift stick made holes in the hall floor which Anna nagged over — for in his night walks up there he used both canes — examining it together, they'd discovered it to be a shooting stick, opening under her knowing pressure — "I know these from the farm!" — into a seat no bigger than her palm. How they had laughed together! In the absence of "the mistress" — and the mistress — he and the concubine were left to laugh.

Three months after his operation, he'd said to Charlie, handing him an address, "Drive by and case this joint. See if it has an elevator. Understand there's no question about the quality of the girls. But you can't *carry* me in." The place had been listed for years as Cheval Merde, thanks to the innocence of the telephone company, and was found to have an elevator. There was also no question about the quality of the girls.

Three months after that, he was being wheeled along in front of the Plaza on the first summer evening of spring, as his father used to say of New York's weather. "It's called Grand Army Plaza here, Charlie, but that's pedestrian." As they moved in and out of the pattern of a throng circling where the moist flower patch raised its mystery to the horse cabs, crossing the avenue in wild ownership, streaming past the portico of the hotel under its high lamps, none daring the gloom of the great bordering park — he and Charlie stopped to watch the pattern of the sauntering girl, perfect under the lamps in her white cartwheel hat with its band of black, white suit severe as a debutante's, black stockings his own daughter wore, black gloves, and a little cool smile perfect on her pearly face. Only the pattern questionable, back and forth and across and around — like a model for whom there was no photographer. Just past the lamps, she took or gave the telephone number (more than once to men of his age) with a social pause suited to a dance card signed — and moved on again. By himself, he'd have watched, for the pleasure of the evening, of how Parisian New York could be in this one embattled place. But would never have approached her, not on two legs.

"Car's just yonder," he said to Charlie. But servitors as formally devoted as Charlie — or because of it — expected the pleasures of their masters. 'We're pedestrians," Charlie said, and wheeled him into the light. "Guess you can come right along, Daddy," said the girl lightly, in the accent with the cheap sweetness of street cries, and slipping him the room number in a hotel around the square. "Be my guest. Chair'll get you past the badge." But on that evening, he had risen from the chair first, to take his short regime of paces on the sidewalk, outside. Afterwards, he was in his chair again, and had hoisted himself into the rear seat of the car, Charlie up front giving him the back of the head like a good robot, while his master waited for the "Where to?" that Charlie hadn't yet said. The plaza, empty now at two in the morning, was like the stable yard of a château in some inaccurate, fifty-year-old memory; the General's statue smelled of horse. His own hat lay on the seat in back of the folding chair — a fedora he never wore. The hat was for check girls and the cloakrooms of formal dinners, where excuses to linger were almost political; since the thirties, as coxswain of the younger style to his coevals, he hadn't worn a hat. He put it on his head; now anyone who wanted to could see him for what he was. Dr. Hildesheimer would approve. "Charlie?" he said. "Yes sir?" But still Charlie hadn't asked where to; he had his lapses. Even knew when he ought to have them. "She was nice, she wasn't even too young —" said the Judge, and at his voice, Charlie's "Where to?" came quick, not quick enough. "— but I like it standing *up*. Let's go eat, Charlie. Let's go have some shrimp."

Thinking nodded in a chair, grew diffuse, wheeling itself over and across the same territory, with a hand that wore a glove against dirt and calluses, an old mocha suede one, of which it had a lifetime supply. At the sink in the corner, he now removed it, washed his hands. Leaned them hard on the marble. Then he stood up. Whalebone upheld him, angling him forward. Men in mail must have been cuirassed into more than just courage, gently pitched forward into the fray as well, by this duenna from behind. Grasping the sink, his shoulders crabbed from hoisting himself, biceps as bulging as a samurai's, he could have gone with his peers to any of their wars; his size had their majesty now. Wasn't done to pee in the sink here, but he couldn't waste steps to the bath. Then, breathing deeply, he stood alone, and the spire of pain — in a marvelous column of identity up from the heel to the sartorius muscle of the leg, to the gluteus of the buttock and the trapezius of the back — upheld him too.

He checked breast pocket for aspirin and an arsenal never used: capsule of codeine, one of Demerol, and for emergency one final capsule, slipped to him by his doctor as something new, sworn to give anybody any time some hours of peace. Then he took up both sticks, Ninon's for the right hand, his grandfather's for the left, and plotted his simple itinerary: out of the courtyard, up St. James's Street, past three short streets (and all uphill which might be harder, he wouldn't know yet), then Piccadilly, which he had only to cross. Or he might turn right at Jermyn, and come out at Duke Street a little farther on past Old Bond. Turning right on Piccadilly in any case, he'd pass Burlington House, then Sackville, then Swallow — down whose crook he would enter, and be there. He always rehearsed this way for London, as a walk this one was unusual only in its limits. He was only doing now what other men did earlier or as a prodigy he had done too early. He was trying to see how far he could go. And being goddam pompous about it — as men in armor were. As he went out the door, very softly for such a man, the aspirin really took over, and he began to laugh.

He came face to face with his sharer of the bath. Unblinkingness held, or would have for those of normal height. But a man of five feet at a stretch saw the mouth, and if much given to sitting, the irresolute stop of the leg — being interested in legs. Bathmate had been observing him all along — and knew he ought to have been in his chair.

"Howja do," said the Judge, standing aside to let the man take the stairs if he preferred. With a shy, walrus snuffle, the man did so. Quick military thinker. But no general, for at the third step he couldn't resist a look back.

"We're all *more* American —" said the Judge grinning inside — "when we're away from home." Paralyzed, the man nodded back, turned and went down; one could hear him saying to his country wife later, "Fellow *spoke* to me. Didn't hear what he said."

Standing! In a dream of envy, he reminded himself, as the lift came, that this was he. The imp who'd spoken was himself too. How smart *I* was, at twelve. Daring. I'd have done anything. Dangerous at any time, this elation — without the means then, without the muscle now. Did I know then, what I was like? I didn't have to know. Or people told me. But we never told her.

Downstairs, the slow lift deposited him at the desk. Factotum blinked, even came forward and stopped at the sight. Out of sheer pleasure at the sight of *him* the Judge slipped him a two-shilling piece. For the silvery retrospect, for what people thought of as "everything." "Walking's what I miss," said the Judge.

Now. I stand in the doorway. The Judge stands in the doorway? No. This is the secret self, deep under the category, never inadmissible. Here I am. The Judge is upstairs, or even farther. To this walker, the Judge is in that house in full view of *his* city, a man sitting in a chair, at home. *He* thinks that the *I* part of us is a snuggery. Walkers know better. Action is the best rhetoric of all. How long is it since I've been this daring trapeze artist outside the walls, this schoolboy without a hat, smart young fifty-year-old going home from his Chauncey, all of us effortlessly swinging the distance from I to thou, and with nine lives a minute to do it in — how long is it since I the Judge have also been I?

He looked down at his legs. Now I have four, almost a machine. My son had a box — David, are you anywhere? Came here for you, didn't I — for a hint of you behind some beard in the front line's desert light? No, she was right. On my two legs, between a shooting stick and a hereditary walking stick, I know better. We came here for her. To-night's for her sake. And for *hers*. Neither is the woman I go to meet. And Chauncey is nearer than he ever was; what era is ever only itself?

The Judge back there had always considered himself an analytic traveler, for whom London, for instance, was a refreshing bath in what remained of the class system, among a people who studied the body politic harder than others and so seemed to have more of it — all conversing in a language like a cathedral in which only tailors were talking. Or, unofficially, it was Ninon's studio of sex.

The man standing here at the corner of Little St. James's Street and St. James's was different. Travel for him was still a sexual excitement in which the love object was unknown. Often, in youth especially — before either physical or spiritual home was formed, any new Illyria, where ever it was, honed a man to a focal point of aloneness in which he knew himself biblically, and saw everything in its unique character. The man here could remember French loneliness — a clarity in which one sinned. The English version was grander and more diffused — a royalty ruined, more to the middle-class taste. Though the I has no audience, it's audience to the world. But London is still the place where a judge can disappear.

He began. At the head of the street, after about as many paces as it took to walk down a hall, he changed his itinerary. He decided to turn right, down Marlborough Road to the Mall, making the grander circle a man should if he had women on his arm, dead or alive. The soldiers of God lie in the grave, but women, foot soldiers of memory, are stalking everywhere. The I outwardly accepts the calendars men give it, but remains implacable. "Ours is the last, they tell us," she said. And could still smile. So, Mirriam, I must rove.

But at the bottom of the street he remembered the steps to climb up from the Mall to Carlton House Terrace, and turned into Pall Mall instead, a man's street too. He walked slowly; his Judgeship might be at home, but the witness walked to tell the tale. And who, with a cane in each hand and a memory on either arm, is champion? As he walked, to help ease that cloudless ache in him where for the space of about four inches there seemed to be no vertebrae at all, he began naming to himself certain sights not on his way, one to a vertebra: that's for the cream colonnades of the Haymarket! — one to a step: that's for the National Gallery, dung-whitened like some penguined coppice of the sea. As I was walking — *step* — down St. James's, not the Infirmaree of my homeland, but past the Army-Navy to Boodles and through the back door of Mr. Trollope — with my American club foot. And I wear corsets — oh pornography not of Paris, but of the little bookseller in Cecil Court, what century is this, am I? Ladies on my arms, what are you dancing to — the Esmeralda Waltz? Not the right period for either of you. Take your ease in any case. We have made it — to St. James's Square.

He rested on his two canes. Now he had only to go half around the square, past Apple Tree Yard to Jermyn Street and the cut to Piccadilly, crossing which he would be right at Swallow. And in back of the phones in the Piccadilly Hotel. He had a bet on, burning like bus fare in a boy's pocket. No fixed character in the world any more, Edwin? That's the remark of a man without one. That's the character of the age. But I've forgotten I don't speak this way to Edwin any more.

Suddenly he opened the shooting stick that the past few minutes he'd been yearning for, stuck it in a bit of lawn and carefully sat on it, a trick he'd practiced too. From this post, under a night sky opening like a Turner, he could see across the gardens, or thought he could.

Down there in the mist was the Duke of York's monument. *He* had a
century without a doubt, and one with character, too. Duke, may I ask
you something? — since I don't speak to Edwin except in the way of
business, which he considers his bit of blackmail, but traps him, poor
barbarian, far more than I. And since the young man I hope shortly to
speak to on the phone may be otherwise occupied. Duke — will my
age be the last to see life as a consecutive story? . . . Ladies, listen to
the Duke's answer — aspirin can have as many visions as alcohol. Listen . . . *Dear* fellow. Dear Mr. Justice. That was *mine*.

So the Judge is here after all. Sitting, *I* disappear. We must both of
us remember it. Duke — I was taken early to see the monuments.
Cities of the plain, that is what the generations are, each mall magnificent with its dead. Now we're told not to honor the I of any one man
alone on a cenotaph. The young say — honor only the people thronging the stair. But I was taught to take even the mob one by one. So, in
the end, will they?

He stood up. Now I am *I* again. And not thinking clearly, or thinking
of everything at once. Only the dead are so privileged. Dukes are
privileged not to answer, as well. *Ave, Ave,* Walter, David. One always
communes with the nearest dead. And the certainty is that every dead
man is a duke. Women are different; they never cease to commune.

He turned to go, his itinerary running in his head. The streets of
one's native city one doesn't need to name. I see it even clearer from
here. Traveling, I see everything. Back there, over that city, the slow
ogives of the century are closing, more than halfway. A city names
itself constantly into the century it thinks it is, its bridges zooming
bizarre into the night of never-really-ending, an endless sunshine of
machines stopping the psychic rain of the minutes, enormously roaring
straight into the tender cockles of the heart. Under it, in it, in the house
that confounds him — what date is a man who lives in a house not
built that morning? — the Judge is choosing a century, shuffling up and
down his hall. Chaired by day, he chooses his story too, that single
story in which he believes. Somewhere nearby him, the soul wheels
itself out of a corner and watches, small as Hadrian's. It has another
name now, is not the soul, and is not Hadrian's ever again, but no
matter. It watches as I watch now. For the enormous hush of the
century when it shall be over, for the enormous answer: O my native
city, the universe.

Pain returned, prompt as his watch. He fingered the pills in his pocket, by shape. The sale of aspirin in the dark continents runs into the millions, though neither they nor we know how it works; good as religion you are, but I shall have to desert you now. Codeine brings that Jungian feeling I can't bear, and with Demerol one can't have a drink. I'll have the pax vobiscum.

But he hated to give up his autonomy before the pain took it from him, and when he crossed Jermyn Street still had the unknown pill in his hand. "You've a high threshold of pain, Mr. Mannix," said the orthopedist. "You can take a good deal. Too bad. You should have come to us before."

Mirriam was the last one to "mister" me. I have you two ladies, mother and daughter, one on either arm now, like any paterfamilias. Curious, in all the years since, I've never imagined you together, never thought of it. We are a family who take walks.

Down there's the Ritz, Ruth, where my father stayed when he was flush; Quaglino's, over on Bury, was where Meyer and your mother used to go. How we can talk now! — why? Mirriam, you were just back from here when we first met. Remember that party? — all your letters were there, larger than life. All the men, epicene or not, were stallions; the women had waists as narrow as the decade. (You have a waist like theirs, Ruth; daughters are a little smaller than life. Or we have kept you so.) Mirriam, as usual, you hid nothing. Nostrils dark as stencil edges, in the yellow fire of a half-photographic evening your laugh leans back on old batik divan covers, bringing the gruff-voiced parties back like an evening disc on the gramophone. Ruth, you hide everything. In the perfect reprise of such parties — your mother and I barely met — all three of us are there. Both of you laugh. How did we use you, Ruth, she and I? Mirriam, how did we use you — she and I? How we use.

And now *I* am here. At Piccadilly he realized he'd left the shooting stick in the turf back there. "I call you to witness," he said to the porter at the hotel, "I have only *one* woman on my arm."

In the phone booth, he took the pill. Now he knew his disease, any pill would do. In the midst of his pain, it began to help hold him upright, a separate backbone. For once, he felt no repugnance to the telephone. Had they closed bets so differently after all in the old days at Epsom? Meyer's tout, and his own, had been from their own London offices — a crook-eyed little score-copier, with a sure thing in every musical sneeze. Important thing was, you yourself never had to appear.

Covent Garden. A decent flat there must have been hard to find.

"Hello?"

"Simon Mannix here." He pushed the button, so that the other could hear.

"Hello." A voice that found what it wanted. Could be bet upon. And in its downbeat, acknowledged this, after three years.

"Only want to ask you one thing — " Either way, I'll be answered.

"She's here. She's going to stay. And you may ask *me* anything."

Once I saw a horse walk into a house, his own father said again. *One doesn't believe the eyes.*

"Has she — any message for me?"

"She's not — saying anything, just now." The voice was literal, and soothing, half turned away from the phone. "But she is going to tell me everything."

And I won't be there. But I could come. I could come on over. And listen in a corner, like Hadrian's soul. "Could I — "

The voice cut across his. "I'll give her your message."

He paused; was this peace from the pill? I don't have to appear. "Tell her — I know how she was used."

"I think she knows." The voice had no enmity toward him. It was on its own flight — toward her. "She knows everything."

"Tell her that I — "

But the voice went on in its own highest emotion. Eleemosynary, would have been his father's word for it, but the word meant charity. With a width one must hope wouldn't prove too wide. "She's always known what's wrong," said Austin Fenno. "She's going to tell us. Me."

How to tell him? How to warn him? Let her bear the brunt. As herself. For once. Bank on his intelligence. As I should have, on hers. Get to him in time.

"Can she cry?" said the Judge.

On the other side of the phone, he could almost hear the Fennos gathering.

"I mean to make her comfortable," Austin said.

As he went down Swallow Street, his pace dragged, though the pill was a fine one, though he was a walker who won his bets. Once he sat

down again, he'd be the Judge for good, a man at home everywhere, in a city where he could still disappear. Daughters die when
they marry. He could already begin to feel the social ease of her being
dead that way. The loose end is tied. Their bed — he must not imagine
it. Austin's would be — charitable. What would she tell there; what
would she hide? After the wedding, the old parents, who are never old
enough, join hands and whisper-wonder, "What is *her* 'everything?'
Don't mourn *her*. Join hands. How did we get her *off* them? How did
we do it. How dared we do it! Whisper it." Mirriam, you can speak the
truth; you threw psychology away with your chicken-bones. Oh no, Si,
you're the champion.

What a quiet street, where the true tavern flare awaits. I'll be able to
sit down again, and lose you. But first — once more. Mirriam, Mirriam.
Retire not that talent of yours, which was death to hide.

In front of the restaurant, in all his armor, he waited, and it did seem
to him that he felt his wife's voice knock the truths into place one by
one, each a vertebra. He trembled with the distance covered, and was
proud with it, wishing for his pedometer. The fertility of the soul is in
question at least once in every man's life. That night was yours, Mirriam. Will this be mine? What can we do for her now, in hers? The
poem of the soul waits for every man, and is implacable. Austin, whatever they're calling the soul in *your* century, you're the man to know it,
and be charitable.

When she tells you, tell her this:

Your mother courted death everywhere. Your father couldn't strangle her.

Mirriam, you courted death everywhere. I could not strangle you.

Suicide! — how I murdered you! . . . We were not opposites.

How we used her.

How I mourned her. The substitute.

Inside the restaurant he was met, had his father's stick taken from
him, and was led up to where Ninon sat waiting. She was always
prompt. He was only a few minutes late, by his shorter cuff. He
watched her face light in amaze, wanting to tell her how he'd left her
gift, rooted under the starlight like a small monument, but could say
nothing.

"Simon. Haven't I told you? The muscles can do everything!"

He nodded and sat down, himself again, lost in his own estimate of her after so long. Very little shrunken with the years, still so much herself. Not monster, not narrow — merely like those pretty seahorses which resembled our smaller, baroque dreams. She was all the gallantly frivolous part of woman without family — made to perform. She could have all his evenings — or this might be the last.

"Yes — I'm out in public," he said.

19 The Assoluta – *October 1954*

Oh please, please, *please* . . . I understand everything.

Once I had done it, I had to become the most intelligent person in the house.

Make it the night before. But first, make it all the days of that year. I was twelve, not an odd age. Breasts like twin almonds, ears silky with wax, bicycle-knees running purple as the pictures of the Sacred Heart, and a stomach like a slum. Figures of laughter, a club of our own giggles, we stood on our hands like thralled fays, peering at the upside-down nerve ends of the world, our hair falling toward gravity, perpendicular. When we vaulted to our feet, harpsichords shaking like throstles in the old gym piano, our heels felt the kettledrum in the thighs. Going to the bathroom at night, looking for the blood, my toes tested the floor gently, parts of a vine nuzzling out its earth. My teeth ached with music in every wind — nothing I could tell the dentist, who knocked them severely for collecting the world's tartar, tapping with a little hammer — the world's, I supposed — which I bit and broke.

"Wish it had been his finger," I said to her, snapping my teeth again; all the club nervously home-studied its own gestures, to get used to them. "He leans too hard on my chest. And too long."

She walked me away from the waiting-room, with the laugh that always made me proud and warmed me, velvet-safe against the cold. A little of the harpsichord in it, much more of the drum. Some day it would be mine. Meanwhile — I was hers. She was walking me almost every day now, seizing every chance in the afternoon schedule that the winters of girls like me were provided with. Older girls, wanting to talk of lovers, sometimes walked us like that; I thought of it. She surely knew everything about me already, I thought. What she didn't, I told her. Being in love too.

"Say *breasts*," she said now. "That's what they are." She was wearing the coat we called "the Windermere," tweed from those hills, and the band of beaver at the bottom swung delicious against my knees. I looked down at their bare chap. "My knees are *plaid*," I said.

She stared, then hugged me. "Oh, women!" she said, and tucked her arm in mine. "But you're not cold?"

"No, I'm never cold."

"I remember." Sighed, then lifted her chin; she was forty-six; I shan't be able to queen it like her, at that or any age, but I'll remember. She had her right arm in my left, and both our hands were in her muff. "I'm walking you the way they walk pregnant women, just before the birth. That's all that's wrong with you, you know. You're waiting for the blood."

I nodded. I had the pins and the belt and the pads in my drawer, but I was to come to her at once anyway; at any time of night, I was to come. "We all are. Except Lavalette, who's already got it. She got it early."

"Catholics!"

"But her mother never told her."

"Heaven is their destination," my mother said. "I mean to tell you everything."

And in the days to come, she tried. Those fall-to-winter days with her, they blend altogether. Afterwards, in my night thoughts, I tried for years to separate them — my hand in hers. Heredity is a haunting. They blend in me. With her real lover. She talked to me of *him* as if I had never met him, never would. Nor have I. When she said merely "Your father" to me, he stood aside. But now and then, when she said his name — with the blue spurt of a match as she lit up, in front of a certain bookshop once their meeting place, or drawing me into a café she said had been there forever — I heard him as clearly as any of the letter-people she sometimes made live for me, a razzle-dazzle chorus of them, one after the other, out of her handbag. Was he known to her, for what he was? Is the sibyl conscious of her cries? His name was Si.

"After women give birth, they sometimes go loony for a bit with it — it's so weird. Let no one tell you it isn't, why should you? — you'll want it for that, the way you'll want everything they call weird — if you're like me." She had that smile which sat on her lips like a circumflex. Her face was like a sculpture of a girl in a corner, resisting the lines that shadow and skin put on it. "I was for a few hours myself, the first time; I woke up dreaming love-dreams of the gynecologist. Imagine — that Irishman with a eunuch's prolapsed stomach and a bottom-of-the-sea fish-eye from looking too much into women's insides!" She squeezed my hand. "But the second time — that was *you* — I knew who I was in love with. And when you came out, I loved what I saw, too."

"Didn't you — the first time?"

"Yes, of course. But it was different. Because of something else." She was always casual over what I shouldn't know, intense on what I should; any child knows from that where the real secrets are. "After I gave birth to you, I flew away from the bed for a while and sat like a raven on the housetop, chattering of it. But then they brought you in — and I flew back." The smile bent to me. "What?"

"Did you stay?" I wanted to ask her, "Don't you still fly away?" But I knew better. I always knew how wild to let her be. He didn't. Or something in me stopped her.

"You're a pre-partem bacchante just now, that's all."

"I sure hope it comes," I said.

"It'll come. That's why I want you to know everything. Because my mother didn't tell me."

"Nothing?"

"She slapped my face for it," she said.

We walked on; we were approaching Second or Third Avenue, one of the streets with the old elevated trains; she always liked those. "Your father never walks these streets," she often said.

We walked in triumph, for the street, and for the slap. "Oh, it's one way," she said. "I'll never do it to you." How she wooed me: "Oh — we forgive them. Your grandmother was just a puddinghead, married for her money — which you'll get — and for her puddinghead. That's the kind of ancestry the old Jews loved — where the father is to be the intelligence in the family. Si had the same background, that's something. We used to laugh about our mothers, in bed. In her old age, his mother took to saying, 'I'm essentially a simple person.' And he said behind her back once, 'When you hear somebody say that, run! They *are*.'"

"I won't laugh at you," I said.

"I hope you laugh with me," she said. "Know any jokes?" And we stood right there in the street, like two members of the club, and laughed until we cried.

"Oh Ruth, Ruth, Ruth," she said. "It'll all come."

But that must have been early, when I was only eleven, which was when she'd first taken it into her head to talk to herself, through me. "Up to now you've been your father's girl." Oh, I knew I could never hope to be Si's. "Now you're to be a woman, we can talk." But after a while, she strode and I listened, hopping alongside to catch up.

. . . People who aren't a mystery to themselves, Austin, aren't that to others really, have you noticed? Father knew all about himself from the beginning; all he does is go over it. My mother knew almost nothing — she was still finding — and she knew it was hopeless. She was the most wonderful companion in the world. He knew that too. They were married for life. She looked at me once, that last night, and said, "Help me escape." Sometimes she talked about the cosmos. "Imagine *me*," she said. "Talking about that." But she always knew that those were the people who really could.

. . . Remember, Aussie, how we laughed down in the basement, over his aphorisms? "That's a Simon!" we used to say — and then we'd reverse them as he sometimes does himself — only we'd do the ones he hadn't got to yet. *The law* — remember that one? *The law is experience*. That was the first time you joined in, Austin — you were shy. But it was then I realized about you — that you had his kind of intelligence. "Why —" you said, with a look of pleased surprise that you were down there with us at all — "Why, *experience* — is the law of the world." I could tell you didn't believe it, though. Because I'm like her. I did.

. . . Austin, are you a mystery to yourself? . . .

"Essentially, your father's a very complicated person," she said to me with her smile, as we turned down that street another day — which? I didn't ask her whether one ought to run from those. She never ran; she fed us all just enough of her mystery. It didn't occur to me that she might be hopping alongside of him, to catch up — I thought he was there in her handbag with the others, like me. For by then, I would have written her a letter at any time. I did, in a way. What I said to her then. That was the turning point.

"Is — *Si?*" I said.

The look she gave me! Like no other — except one. "That was a weird thing to say. Maybe I shouldn't — am I making you weird?"

I'd scared myself, that was so private. "Maybe I've . . . got it," I said, standing with my knees together all of a sudden. I was always "getting it"; all of us were; there's almost as much moisture to becoming a woman as to being one. We girls were always going off to the bathroom "to see."

"Go see," she said, nodding me toward a store that sold health juices, where we often stopped. "Ask them to let you use it. I'll wait."

I remember that store, kept by a Turkish family, as if it were a Turkoman's-land prepared just for me by women — the essence of the harem. They looked at me moist-eyed, letting me pass in as if they knew; behind the partition, I heard the two nearest my age giggling; when I came out there must have been all ages of female eyes on me and her — as I shook my head at her: "No." Under their eyes we drank the tomato juice they pressed from the real fruit, not red as in cans but pale and straw-colored like serum, the real juice of the love apple, never quite tasted since, lost with them and their store.

She and I said nothing when we left it. But after that day, she sometimes looked at me as if I were her rival. It never occurred to her that like the rest of the people in her pocket, I was his. She spared me nothing from that day on, mixing it all up like a paste, a lure — her special agonies, reflections — and joys. "Oh, you won't do him in," she said to me now and then out of her fears, and almost a jealousy. "That's why I can talk to you." And from that time on — I would have done anything, for her. But I have fooled her in the end. In the end, what I remember most are the joys.

"I'm taking you in," she'd say. "To my confidence. What I've got of it. As one does take — the child one bears. Against *all* husbands." And drew the man Arne, for instance, like a letter Belgian and real, out of the deep brown cave of her bag. "It won't be my fault," she said, "if you don't understand everything."

Pale, alum-colored afternoons of fall those first walks were, along that upper part of Second Avenue where the verdigrised El stanchions made an almost pleasant Rialto of shops, hopefully near enough to supply people like us, whose pavements were scrubbed. Later on of course, she took me on the desperate lower avenue where the drabs hung from the railroad hotels, calling out the names of the cars below to each other over the ooga-ooga of the horns — later she took me everywhere. Yet even early, when the girls asked, "Where you keeping yourself?" I pleaded study or dancing school; I knew I had a secret

twice precious because there was something piteously wrong with it —
that my mother was taking me . . . *following* me . . . everywhere.

The dancing school, Ilonka's, was the one place she wouldn't wait for
me, or ever enter. "No, it's to be yours," she'd said, when she made
Pauli choose it. "I'm not to be trusted around any art." And later, it was
to be the place I could feel safest; it was all mine. But just then I
wanted her; all the other mothers were there. Just as in Sunday school,
where though I despised them in their fat fur and diamond knuckles,
I'd felt all the more lone, I now wanted her to flash among these —
long, subtle and opal. One day I asked her.

"These are only stage-mothers," I said. "But the kind who'll never
make it."

She stared at me. Ordinarily, she had too much style to recognize her
own — but this was unmistakable. "Did — Pauli — say that?"

I could never lie to her. "No."

We couldn't look at each other. I'd mimicked her to perfection —
why should that make us both feel miserable?

. . . Austin . . . if I say that I report the growth of an understanding
between two people, *not* a relationship — will that clear it? Everything
I make her say here — she said. My understanding should have tagged
behind. When one person wants to *be* the other, then it's dangerous . . .
I couldn't help it; already, without any Ilonka or Ninon to name it for
me, I felt what I was watching.

"Onstage as a mother?" she said, raising those huge eyes. "No, I'll
never be that." Ninon said it for us so many times later, but I already
sensed the path of her I was watching. The progress of the assoluta is
always alone. Everything strummed in me, a rising convergence of
events beyond me, which we were only giving the name of my blood
to. "I'll understand," I said. "Or it won't be your fault." I remember it
because in our rounds again we were just passing that same store, or
where it ought to have been.

"Look," I said. "The Turkish store is gone."

She was just leaning down to cup a match — one of the kitchen kind
she'd taken to carrying, in a man's leather pouch with an emery striker
on it. The blue phosphor, before it went, kindled the crushed blue of
her wide belt and of her hat; the rest of her was black. If I noted her

dress narrowly enough, I caught her mood; one thing sure, she was always dressed too well to be walking a daughter. The smoking was new; I never saw her do it anywhere except on these tours.

Following my pointing finger, she nodded at the blank glass there between a little fish store wet and gray as a bivalve, and the hot beads of the Italian fruitstand. "The little stores that sweat family," she said, in her new, smoking-voice. "Oh, there'll be another. Always some new family of innocents. It's the city replenishment." She threw the match in the gutter.

"It went with your hat," I said.

"Too much," she said somberly. "Or else my *nails* should be blue too."

I was right not to laugh. She had meant it. She saw through me anyway. " 'Oh, sweet patootie —' " she sang out suddenly — "with all yo' beauty — You'll nev-ah make it, nev-ah *shake* it, at the *Co* — Coq d'Or!' "

"What's that from?" I said, proud that I knew it was *from* something.

"*Tiger Woman Rag*, I think it was called.Two performances, private, at the Mad Hatter. Noel and Angie had a hand in it. Never got put on." Often her chatter with me now had these little rough edges of old song in it, and maybe always had had, but by then I had seen her files, once the family's, that went back beyond her father's company's *Aida* days, everything from gold-colored menus to signed pictures — always by the same pen it seemed to me, whether Calvé or Tagliavini — to programs that rattled out those years like music boxes: *Chu Chin Chow*. The crowd had known the casts of everything that played, she said — and I had begun to know the crowd.

Taking my elbow — she'd begun to appropriate me with touch too, as not before — she peered into the store that had been so full of women. One counter left, and a roll of paper on the floor. "Blue-hoo with cold," she said.

And I knew the rhymes of their old songs. We often made a rapid-fire game of parrying them; "blue" went with "true," or "you." "Maybe," she'd say, in a voice gone barrelhouse. "Oh God yes. That was 'baby.' " She might have been tuning me, like an instrument. What for?

"What'll I do-oo?" I sang. "When I'm *old*."

She didn't smile. Then she did, like an older girl. "Darling, you break me up." She straightened, turned from the window, and threw the cigarette far, with perfect aim, into the gutter. She stood for a moment, looking down the street as if we might be being followed, putting on her gloves. Actually her nails were high and buffed, with a deep collar of white, a kind one didn't see around any more, even then. "Put on your gloves," she said with a cool change, like a mother playing mother.

We waited at the corner for the flower cart to go by with its nag; January was far too late for him but he had somewhere found a hundred aster pots. "I love those carts," I said.

. . . One was outside your house, Austin, the day you took me to tea there. I liked your house for that. After a week at home, it was like still being on tour . . .

"You're right to love," she said. "I'd never tell you otherwise. Even my parents never did. But what to love — oughtn't I be able to tell you that?"

Down the block ahead was a dirtyish café — dark inside and nothing like the awninged famous one she'd once taken me to — into which she always glanced when we passed. As we approached it, she looked back at the cart. "Bright with war, the flower-war. Did you ever see a street that looked less like a war?" The café seemed to rivet her attention. "They'd all go, like a shot." Then she leaned down to me. "But we mustn't stand and gape, must we. Have to stiffen our backs. Your father wants to be a judge."

No wonder I was frightened. It was the first time she'd said anything irrational to me — why, at age six, I'd made a Sunday dinner-table howl, saying to him, "Aren't you ever going to be a mister?" He'd been a judge all my conscious life.

. . . And so easily explained away later, wasn't it? Years later, at tea. "The Court," your father said to me, Austin. "At one time, *your* father was very much mentioned for it. Not so long ago, at that." . . . And I didn't ask when.

But at the moment, I give only her portrait, by her own hand. Like her death, later. "Even when the coryphées are ablaze," Ninon is always telling us, "the assoluta remains sane. She is not the Queen Bee — no, no, my dears, leave that to the premiers danseurs." No laughter, in the rehearsal room; no one dares. And Ninon goes on. "She is not of herself only — and fights being that. But gives in only to that. Those poor mad Lucias — leave those to the coloraturas, my dears. We do not sing, here. The role of the assoluta is to keep the balance — to which all eyes must now and then return. It's the wildness, with the truth in it. . . . But none of you is one. Else you would know." . . .

At the next corner, I knew by my mother's pace that we had a destination. "Not to the dancing school, no. You're going with *me,* somewhere. How's your French?"

"Bad," I said. My tone carried its conviction.

"Like *his,*" she said with a grin. "And how like him! You. Come on." She led me block after block away from the East River, past our own avenue, on to Fifth, then for blocks down. I forgot my fright. One accepts things, walking; it's a parade of acceptance, in oneself, or between two . . . You and I haven't walked that way yet, Austin; I suppose we will. . . .

In front of a house on Fifth Avenue, second from the corner, she stopped. "One on the corner's already an institution. That huge one. This one's just barely escaped."

"Our house has an institution. On the other side."

"Quick, aren't you," she said.

But I wasn't sure why. "What is this place?" I'd come to ask this often, as we walked the battered streets or the luxurious. She always told me.

"This place?" She spread her lips in the way that meant she wasn't talking to *me,* and said it too quickly for me to get. Her French was always perfect. She said it again, through her nose, as she pressed the bell. "I often visit it."

The manservant who opened the door was so perfect in manner, woodcut spectacles and a string tie, that though I'd never seen one like him, I recognized him at once. Behind me, I heard her ask in an offhand voice to use the phone, then the total change in it as, leading me into a long room on the right, she called out to a person there whom I couldn't yet see. "Enter!" she said, not to me. The voice was the one in which the crowd must have spoken to one another; any record buff knows it, from some rough old disc cut by black singers in the Paris of 1925. It pushed me forward like a ticket stub and left me. "Entah — the *demimonde!*"

He was in a chair by the window. Yes, he was handsome, even though old, with that Jack Hero face from which women will tolerate even virtue — anything. . . . And I was wrong in what I said, back

THE ASSOLUTA 475

there in the room at Dukes, to Father. What is so live as memory?
There must be many who are as glad as I when this old man steps
forward for them as he does into mine. . . . But I looked over my
shoulder to be sure she had left us, before I fell in love with him. He
stood up from his chair at once, old as he was, to meet me. It's not very
common, to women aged twelve.

We made friends there on the spot, in a number of musical pro-
posals; he had the kind of whimsy children could bear, and the room
too had the expectedness of bygone illustrations — the cut of its ogives
and its teapot had been under my pillow many a time. He caught me
watching Proctor, and drew from me, "He's so much the way he's
supposed!"

"Ah well, after all, we've been supposing him for so long!" Chauncey
Olney said — and caught me catching it.

Children like to see the centuries before, but unguided — remember,
Aussie — like sage young sprouts of the time machine, by themselves. I
had just time to begin, when she came back, and I was banished to a
sitting-room next door, given an album of views, and as an afterthought of Proctor's, a queer stylus game whose antique lever when
pressed made marvelous geometrical patterns, the only part of this I
sometimes think of as dreamed. Proctor was agog with me — or with
her. "I'll bring something delicious, miss. It's called a milkshake, I
believe."

"Thank you," I said. "And close the door after you, please."

He gave me an admiring look, and did so. My mother's genie-laugh
came through the painted transom. He must have known that perfectly
well. What a servant he was. In my mind sometimes, I marry him to
Anna.

"Posterity can hear us," said my mother. "I can hear her."

"From next door. As is proper. We always kept the amenities
here."

Proctor was giving them tea first. Then he left them, I hoped — to
get mine. Closing the door.

"So I heard," said my mother. "So I once heard."

I heard the old man's chuckle. "Nothing before the servants. Whatever else you do, Mirriam, I see you still keep to that."

"Some things you're given, you can't throw down. No matter how
hard you try. Oh — I keep everything."

"Don't much care which side of the world you put *us* on," said old Mr. Olney. "Demi or not. Long as you give us *some*. Though I like my window."

"Oh, it's the side Simon says I'm on," said my mother. "Without any real reason to be. If I stole, I suppose he thinks, or painted. Or lied. He may be right — what's dancing at a supper club? This way, I'm not much of anywhere. And not with him."

"Oh the demimonde is not what it was," said Mr. Olney. "Like the *Social Register,* these days. Simply anybody can get in."

She burst out laughing. "Oh, Chauncey. I like your window too. That's why I come."

"Same view as his. Only you're not married to it."

"Same? Not by half." She sounded like my grandfather Meyer, his London twang. Out of the room, I heard things I'd never heard before. "You've got a fuller view of the city. I don't know how you do it. Miles away from your money though you are."

He chuckled again. "Who told you that story, Meyer? Or . . . did I?"

A hesitation. I knew it well. Whenever my mother did stop to pause, she was sad. "You did, Chauncey." She couldn't help it. She always spoke the truth.

"Thought I must've. You're a tonic, Mirriam."

"Don't flirt with me, Chauncey. I don't come for that."

"You flirt with life. Who can resist that?"

They must have heard Proctor coming up the stairs. I did.

"No one," said our host, in the familiar, wrapped voice which elders suddenly assumed. "Man, woman nor child."

"I've been taking her everywhere," my mother said nervously. "Maybe I shouldn't. As one does take in — the child one bears — I find." She sounded surprised. "Or maybe to show her how miles away we all are. From everything."

"She'll be safe *here,*" Mr. Olney said. "Thank you, Proctor, we've enough hot water. Been having trouble finding wicks for that old urn, Mirriam, but Proctor has found just the thing. What did you say it was, Proctor?"

"In Woolworth's, sir. Wicks is gone out altogether; I've done with pipecleaners for years. Can't get them because of the wire in them — the war. But there's these toy animals still made of them. I believe they're called a *shmo.*"

Proctor came in to my side, carrying a tray with a long yellow drink capped with cream and a dish of biscuits with lemon curd and mauve fillings. Downstairs taste, and children's. I crooked my finger at him. He bent to my whisper.

"It's called a *shmoo*. I have one. But mine is shells."

He nodded. Gave a flip to the transom — I would swear he slanted it more — and went out. Servants like the double life.

Against the teacup clink, the old man said, "*Simon* can't resist. Do you have to flirt with him, just now?"

"So you've heard," my mother said. "About — Nick."

"Not by name," he said. "I've no interest in that. So — it's true."

"*This* time — it's true."

I had drunk all the tall glass and begun on the biscuits. Very slowly, I began to draw with the stylus, which made a scratching noise.

"What's that?" said my mother.

"An old game. It fascinates them. My — adopted daughter had it."

The stylus made pushpulls and penmanship circles almost without help from me. I delved deeper into its geometric heart, full of so many tangents and talents I didn't have.

"I won't ruin *him*," I heard my mother say. "Not that one. Anything of value I have to say — he already knows. He belongs to the world a-comin'. Besides, he's getting out. To the war."

"There's always a world a-comin'. Though mebbe that doesn't sound too well from a nonagenarian," said Olney. "And you can't keep everything."

"Double or nothing!" said my mother. It had the loud, defiant sound that always came when she tried to lie to herself. She never got control of it.

"D'you know — ?" said Chauncey. "My wife once felt the same. Whereas I'd have settled for one woman or tother. Meyer ever tell you that?"

"Not he. You men stick together. But I heard. Of a — ménage."

"My secretary — a Mrs. Nevin. Proctor reminds me of her. She was so much — as we supposed. Quite willing to retire. To her native heath — France. And bring up the baby girl there. It was my wife who explained to her — that she couldn't have everything. And to me."

There was a stifled sound from my mother, but no words. The stylus made a small blot in the red ink it was using, then continued its rich tangle.

"Oh, my wife suffered too. Good hard businessmen often breed daughters like that — with robber-baron consciences."

"No one ever accused me of that before." My mother sounded soft, almost childish. How good he was for her! The biscuit I took melted slowly in my mouth.

"Maybe only a Christian would see it."

"I never usually can talk — to one of them. But to sleep with them — that's . . . now I've shocked you."

"You hope," said Chauncey Olney. "And it's really quite pleasurable for a man of my years."

"But you are a Christian. We're brought up to think they don't really shock."

"That so, Mirrie?" he said politely. It was hard to hear that the old man had any voice but the polite one, but I heard. "You shock Simon. Not sexually. You get to him somewhere. I don't know how. But isn't that enough for you?"

The drink had made me sleepy. I put the stylus down. In the silence next door, I trifled with the ink bottles ranged in slots at its side; it had viridian and prussian blue. And a number of designs I could learn to copy too.

"He's like a son to you, isn't he," said my mother.

"Yes," said the old man. "A bastard son." How queer that he should sound as if he were smiling. I'd known what "bastard" meant for years. She told me everything.

"Simon's father was a romantic failure, they say. I never knew at what."

"Give him time," said the old man. "That's what I — didn't have."

" 'They say he's going to be a judge, Mirrie.' I remember my father saying it. And later on too, when he told me he was going to leave him the house. I didn't mind that. That's the way it should be." Was she smiling too? "But do you know how I had to learn of Simon's larger ambitions?"

"I can guess."

"Yes. Nick has his connections too."

"Simon would never mention the Court. Even to himself."

"Then it's true."

"I have a bet on it I may not live to see," Chauncey said. "Give me time too, Mirriam."

But he had so much already! — I thought — and listened for my mother; the silence was so long. How sad she must be, almost sad enough to cry. I had never seen her. Maybe here is where she came to do it, I thought.

Then I heard her speak, very low. "I've been taking instruction — that's why I haven't been here. . . . Oh no, Chauncey, don't look so St. Thomasy. Not Catholic . . . but I've a dear, silly friend in Paris, Noel Ammon, he's a convert, and every time I get a letter, he presses that. Chauncey . . . it might sound funny that what he says weighs with me." My mother still sounded sad, but she was talking. "He's a convert all right. Changed his sex, and married his gallery owner. Or maybe she changed hers." When she waited for others to shock, my mother's long eyes elongated even more, her mouth corners subtled, and one shoulder held still — that's how I always knew she meant *them* to be. Never me. There were other times, terrible ones, when I was shocked, and she was past knowing it.

"We had the classics in Virginia, Mirriam." He sounded as if he had his chin in his hand. "Go on."

"But when he write to me, he changes back. 'Darling. Take instruction. *Do.*' And the tone carries *me* back. That was my decade. They were my crowd. Their wants . . . and sufferings . . . were the ones I knew. If somebody's sick in the spirit, or brave in it — what does it matter if the only way he knows to say it is 'I have *such* a *yen*'? . . . They said '*darling.*' All the time."

I looked at the transom, so high, and the keyhole beneath it, so low, but had no real need for either. She'd be sitting straight now, looking straight out, and I knew that voice — the one which cut across the slang, or used it like a whip. Children at home don't need keyholes; the voices and silences of those above ride the pipes with the bathwater, plugging ears, nose and throat against the morning cereal. The children of those who love are in the greatest peril too. Sitting at table with them, children hear the true voices, in the basement of their souls. The deaf hear that piano. She was talking the way she sometimes talked to Father. The one she was really talking to was Si.

" — But I couldn't take religious instruction, Chauncey. We *are* it, Jews like us. It's in the family inflection even if we don't obey one of the laws. Know what my father used to say? '*God* could be converted maybe. But not one of *us.*' "

"St. Thomasy indeed!" said Chauncey. "But, go on."

"So I went where you'd expect. Where so many like us do go, espe-

cially the women, in times like these — when the men still have their
— busyness. 'OK, Noel,' I wrote, 'I'll try looking at life through a glass-
bottomed boat. And when I see a shark smile, I'll try not to let on I
know it's me.' " A silence. "I swore I'd never go, Chauncey. But I did. I
guess you know where."

"To Paris?" the old man said. "Hope you had the grace to go over
there, for Simon's sake. Though they still have them here, I suppose."

"Dozens," my mother said slowly. "Chauncey. Mind telling me just
what you thought I meant?"

"Why — a brothel. Male brothels, as a matter of fact." I heard his
hands clap together. "Praise be. My century's shocked yours."

After a silence, my mother said, "I wish I'd had you at the doctor's . . . Do you think that girl's asleep?"

"Proctor's eggnogs have a good deal of sherry in them . . . Ah —
doctors . . . Well, each fifty years to its own. My father-in-law's was the
century of steam. You young people are more interested in your own
self-combustion."

"Young, Chauncey? . . . And what's yours?"

"A man never really knows the watermark of his own age."

Century, century — it was a word to put anyone to sleep. I thought I
was.

"But that's why I went to the doctor," said my mother. "God forgive
me, I don't know why it should be me to see it . . . but I'm afraid I do.
That's what I told him when he asked what I was there for. 'I'm a
woman the wind blows through,' I said. 'Tell me if it speaks the truth.' "

I was asleep. For a minute, or a century, which has taken me all the
years since to reconstruct. For when I woke, or seemed to, she was
talking in the way I dreaded, that no one could stop, nor she. How
terrible it is, Austin, when that wind blows through the one one
loves. Chauncey wasn't in love as I was. He loved my *father*. That was
the difference.

"The doctor couldn't help me," said my mother. " 'The open secrets,'
I said to him — 'those are the ones I am doomed to keep.' Oh, at first it
was easy . . . 'I should warn you,' I said. 'I'm used to telling people
everything; this is nothing new to me. I give you all little shocks —
because the bigger ones you would never believe. Not from me, anyway. Especially not from me . . . Oh, when I see the shark smile, you
see, I always know it's me.' 'Shark?' he said, and began to write. But
after a while, he began to get used to me. And to dismiss my language.

Which is all I've got. 'Tell me who you think you are,' he said, 'in the plainest language you can.' 'My language is always plain,' I said. 'Some think it's too sharp altogether. What you want, Doctor — is obscurity to me. But I'll try.' . . . His office is on a Park Avenue corner. 'I'm one of the women upstairs,' I said. 'I'm a woman upstairs.' '*Upstairs?*' . . . 'Yes, Doctor, you must have dozens, in this apartment house.' (They have, Chauncey. The sibyls of society whom nobody will believe. Who have the vote.) 'Driving their husbands mad with closet-building, Doctor. Do you tell them how to live — or how to build closets more happily?' . . . I could tell from his smile that the charm had begun. 'They tell *me!*' . . . So I told him. 'So when you were young you wanted to paint, draw, dance, be an artist, Mrs. Mannix?' 'Never,' I said. 'I was never one of those.' 'Why not?' 'Because I was brought up a connoisseur!' 'So you collected artists,' he said. 'Why?' Oh, he was sharp — those are the ones I charm best. And he helped me of course, like any audience. Those long-ago studio days, why had I hung about to reverence anyone with clay under his nails? 'Because when the wind blows through *them*,' I said, 'it stops. For a short moment — it stops.'

"And it was that second I chose to want to burst out crying, Chauncey, isn't that strange? I never cry, not since I was fifteen. 'Why are you shivering?' he said. 'At the truth,' I said. 'A silver flash between the tongue and the ear. Even when they're only mine.' . . . They don't cry either — catch them weeping for the world! . . . 'So you're hollow,' he said keenly. 'Yes,' I said. 'Like a harp.' And because they love to talk about money, it obsesses them, I leaned my glove on the desk, with the dollar for the cab already in it. 'My family made its money out of music, Doctor. So I suppose it's natural.'"

I was asleep in the deep of the chair, of this house. I was safe here. Out of the wind.

"And the next time, for there were only three —" said my mother — "when he leaned forward — he always sat opposite, I'll say that for him — I gave him his money's worth. Not sex, Chauncey; that's only *their* language . . . 'Tell me more about the women upstairs,' he said. 'Women?' I said. 'The hysterics of society. Whom nobody believes. And they've reason. We never stop. Your own mother was probably one, Doctor. Men like you always have them.' 'Not mine,' he said. 'We weren't from your — echelon. She had to work.' . . . 'No exemption. We Cassandras are from all classes. My husband's mother's family nickname was Xantippe — a lower order. But sterner. She never wanted to get out of the cosmos, that one. She stayed and stayed.' He burst out laughing. 'That good old Jewish mother-tongue. Yes, I recognize it. And then he said, '*Out*?'"

In my dream of sleep, or of terror accompanied, I heard the old man get up from his chair. He had a walk like a pendulum. "Mirriam." He must be standing by her chair. Virginians give a little flip to one diphthong. I hear it yet as he said it. "Out?" And then — "Mirriam. You're not flirting — with *that*?"

You'll have seen clocks that don't have arc pendulums, Austin, but a little cage that turns this way, then that. My mother's changes were like that, not an about-face or an arc — a turning, this way, that, of the cage itself. A role that doesn't stop — won't. Can't. "Oh, I couldn't have been an actress after all, Ruth," she said once. "I won't bow."

"No, not with that," said my mother. "I told him so. 'I've got nerve enough to talk, even to act. But I can't bow to the cosmos, Doctor. Not that far. You'd have done better, you men, by sending women like me to war. Not just giving us the vote.' 'You envy us men?' It was the first satisfaction I'd given him. 'Oh, not your physique,' I said. Poor dry man, he believed in talk even more than I did. I couldn't say cock to him. 'No, Doctor. But men can pretend to die for the world when they're really only dying for themselves. You're Christers all.' 'When there's a war on,' he said, 'a lot of private neuroses shoulder arms. And call themselves the world's.' 'Or the whole world's got mine,' I said. 'Have you thought of that?' 'You aren't called upon to carry the world,' he said. 'Aren't I, though. You don't know the women upstairs. But you don't have to worry, Doctor, there's no war on here.' . . . I can always shock them in the end. 'Not for us,' I added. 'Not for anybody who's not *there*.' I saw that he'd certify me as sane after all. Though I hadn't asked. 'Isn't there, Mrs. Mannix?' he said. 'Then where's my son?' I felt sorry for him then. He had the look of all the men who come to Delphi despite themselves. '*He's* there,' I said. 'But not you.' 'I give what I can,' he said. 'We owe this country a lot. We're not people like you. We were immigrants.' 'People like us?' I said to him. 'We're the first to know. The first.' . . . Chauncey, I used to hear my father say it to every boy who came to the house: 'Well, sir — on what argent fields have you played today? Or are you bound for?' To me, a girl, of course he never said it. That's how we come to see it. Nobody's at a war, unless he's there . . . 'Nobody, nobody, *nobody*,' I screamed at him. And stamped my feet. That's why we're not listened to, but can't help. 'No, Doctor,' I said. 'You sent a substitute.'"

In the silence, the old man made a sound, just a memory sound.

"I told you, Chauncey," said my mother. "I keep everything . . . All the doctor said to me was, 'You're not a harp. You may be a weather-vane.' Poor man, he was trying to talk *my* language. 'May it be of use to you,' I said. 'I fancy you've got a wife something like me, at home.' It was the only remark of mine he didn't answer. So when I got up to leave for good, I said, 'Don't bother to pay me now, Doctor. I'll send you a bill.'"

Now my mother's voice was gentler, like to me or David at bedtime, years back. "He was such a thin, nervous little man. Like a Jew butchering pork."

"You people. Why are you Jews so hard on one another."

Her voice was almost inaudible. "Love." If it hadn't been for that word I wouldn't have heard her. This must be the way she put herself to sleep. Instead of with tears for all she *couldn't* say — like me. "That's why we only go to ourselves . . . for instruction. Otherwise . . . it might take."

"Do you talk to Simon like this?" The old man's voice was sharp.

"Never aloud," said my mother. "He hears every word."

"That why you married him?"

"Part of it . . . And because he resists . . . *resists*."

"Change," said the old man, not as if he were asking.

"*Me*."

Her high heels, in which she could walk me for a whole afternoon, clicked across the floor. "He tells me not to let people use me as they do. But that's *his* mother in him, her stinginess. He's generous. I found that out by trying it endlessly. What he really means is — I'm a waste. And arrogant about it. But life *is* movement, Chauncey, isn't it? And that's what he doesn't see. He looks at our world as if — it still was."

"Ah? And isn't it?"

I heard another sound I knew well, from home — the spit-spit of the nails which weren't blue, against a windowpane. "Your view. Your beautiful view. It's two-way. In full view of the city. Like Grant's tomb. Like us. People like us."

"Like us?"

"Ahrr, the life in this house is over, Chauncey. But *you* know. I wouldn't put it past you to know."

But *our* house was alive. Dark sometimes, and — even I knew it — desperate. But alive. With the imperial right to be unhappy if it chose. Like her.

"Personally, *I* may've been dead for some forty years," said Mr. Olney. "But I never confuse the class structure with myself. Or the class *struggle* as they're calling it nowadays. Same thing of course. Though it's not polite to say . . . There'll always be a middle and an upper, Mirrie. Though it mayn't be *us*."

"You talk to me as if I were intelligent." That's when she was tenderest with David. When she felt like that — against *him*.

"Women sense certain changes quicker. But that's fashion. Don't elevate it to prophecy."

"Ahh-hr, I can't blame you," she said. "Why should it be someone like me? Why should *I* be the one to harbor it? Sometimes I feel the world-to-come, the world right ouside our door, like an egg inside me — that I must bring to him . . . *Me,* who never could stand a mother's role. Maybe women like me are a new, non-sex to come, nothing so simple as fags or dikes. Hummph. Nothing so mystic, either . . . But I tell you, our world is over." I heard her walk back to him. "Chauncey . . . Oh, it's not just a question of bongo-bongo, or whatever twelve-tone city lights they split this year in Jimmy Ryan's, to some hot-pash dance tune. The *polite* world is over . . . Funny, some of the very rich are getting cozy bedded down with the new one — but not us. Never us. I don't mind — for me. I just want him to see it. He's the one wants to be a judge." She came so close to the panel between us that I could hear the stuff of her dress against it. "So I have to slap him back for it, every time."

"Is this other man — political?"

She moved off. It was her slip made the noise, really. Taffeta. "Criminal . . . You're not surprised."

Now the old man got up from his chair. I heard his cane, like a shrug. "My father-in law was that . . . Oh, it dies every ten years, the polite world. . . . Maybe your twenties was a weathervane of the century. But that was *twenty years ago.* Shall I tell you why you see — what you see? You've slept with a member of the lower classes. And that's your enlightenment."

"Ah-ha," she said. "If that isn't like you all. Or to the nunneries with us. When Simon and I were on our honeymoon . . . no, we were still on it, but it was over . . . I'd come back to Paris and we'd left it, but we were still in France, in the Loire. We motored past a convent wall, of the Carmelites.

'Custodians of the Unregarded,' the stone gate said — I've never forgotten it. 'How wonderful!' I said. 'To be that.' How beautiful. You see — I thought it meant the nuns themselves — that they did that for the world. But Simon only laughed, and said it meant the order itself — that kept *them*. The extra women. 'Some of the best names in France,' he said. 'My father knew a baron once, who it turned out kept his wife there.'"

"Unregarded!" I heard the cane again, and in my half-doze protested it, for Anna's floor. "Meyer spoiled you."

"He gave me everything," said my mother. "But never told me what to *want*. That's for the sons."

"Nor what not to want, apparently."

"My mother told me that," she said. "So, sometimes, when he was impatient with her, he called me his 'little mother.' That's all she got for it. Oh, it's a simple, biblical family line."

"And Simon?"

"Simon slept with me, in my father's house. . . . Sleeps."

"Ah-ha," said the old man. "Ah-ha."

"Ah-ha what?"

"It's very simple, what you're suffering from."

"Is it now," said my mother. I could have warned him, hadn't I been fast in the chair, my drowsy arms pinned.

"Two men at once," said the old man. "Somehow, women over here aren't — brought up to be fit for it."

"I ought to laugh," said my mother. "I ought to laugh. Or ask — what about the men."

He chuckled. "Y'all can say that all your lovely lives. But it ain't synonymous. Simon have a mistress?"

"Not that I know of. And I'd know."

"Too bad. What would you do — if he had?"

"Not bring her to live with us."

His laugh had a cackle, the first old age I'd heard from him. "So you see, how times've changed. But women — let me tell you . . . When my father-in-law heard about our ménage, he had me in and roared at me . . . The criminal classes're often sexually stricter than us, Mirriam — have you noticed?"

She got up from a chair she must have sat in, and prowled, but didn't answer.

"When he found out it was my wife who'd insisted, he was knocked off his pins. 'That do-gooder, my daughter' — my wife was an active suffragette. 'She must be insane.' I knew how to talk to him by then. 'Oh no, sir, she's suffering from a female disease.' . . . '*Is* she now,' he whispered — after roaring at me again for not taking her to better doctors. '*What is it?*' But when I told him, after reminding him of a business deal or two of his own — he began to smile. . . . It's what you're suffering from, Mirriam. And not only over your — Nick."

Or her Si, I said to myself. Or her Si.

"Well?"

He cleared his throat. "Woman can't bear the difference between legal and ethical experience."

My mother began to laugh. "*Vive la différence*. We can understand it though! — And did she ruin you for it. Because you *could!*"

"Public life is harder for men than you think."

Oh stop her laughing stop her.

With a great effort that I could almost see, my mother stopped herself, and I awoke.

"Simon won't meet him," she said, low. "I tried. Will you do me a favor, Chauncey? . . . Have him here."

"Who?" A pause. "*Who?*"

"Both."

A long, long pause. "You'd shoot a man, wouldn't you. Only to get him to look at you hard enough."

"Not Simon." My mother said it so softly. "Not him." It was my mother, only my mother; why should I be terrified? "Maybe the other. He's going off anyway. But not him . . . No . . . to get Simon's full attention —" She broke off with a short laugh. I could imagine her shrug. " — I'd have to get him . . . to shoot me."

After which Chauncey Olney said, "Get out of here, Mirriam."

I heard my mother pick up her bag, click across the floor. I shut my eyes fast; kettledrum, harps, I heard them all — and my own blood.

"All your talk about two worlds," said the old man. "You want to ruin him, don't you. God knows why. Or just to see the two of them in the same room."

"Didn't you. Want to."

"No! And *vive la différence*."

"And David too," she said bitterly. "We might have him."

"I apologize," said the old man. "I forgot how he is, about the boy."

"Oh — if someone's going to be ruined, it had better be me," said my mother. "I'm glad you think I'm bad enough."

"I forgot," he said. "But I'll give you a bit of truth to put between your teeth if you want it. Mirriam . . . *is* it out you want? Or in."

I could tell how it would be when she was shivering. She must have put out her hand. "Well, thank you, Chauncey. For your instruction."

He must have taken it. "Mirriam . . . you will take care?"

"You're on his side, aren't you. That's why you let me come here."

"A man would be," he said. "I thought you knew."

Her voice was farther away when it came next; was she going to leave without me? I couldn't wake.

"She did ruin you, didn't she," she said.

She was hysteric of course, from seeing the truth, unable to act on it. That's what the truth *is*. If you want to know, Austin, how I know — she told me so herself. How else would I remember all this, if she hadn't said it in one way or the other over and over all our lives, to Simon-Si, to me then, in bits and pieces to everyone. Later, what Chauncey said was the only part I had trouble with. Finally, that too came back — like those cued parts they give actors, I had only to remember her.

But now as he came toward me in my chair, I kept myself in dreams of sleep. Century. I was a child in another century, any that would be secretly gardened, tunneled with love — any cave out of time. I meant to be happy — or for a moment, floated free.

I felt him lean over me, slip the stylus from my hand, and look down on me. "On what argent fields . . ." I heard him murmur it. I let him pat my shoulder. "All right, posterity," he said. "You can come out now."

I opened my eyes, letting him see they were clear and bright.

"What lovely designs you made," he said courteously.

I nodded. "I mean her to be happy," I said.

But outside, where she hailed a cab with a boy's whistle — two fingers hooked between the teeth, right there on Fifth Avenue, and a girl's tremulous smile down at me afterward, from under her matron's hat with its Diana-wing of blue — I wasn't sure whether it was her I meant to be happy, or me. Nothing was separate.

"What did you whisper to Chauncey?" she said. "At the door?" She leaned over me. The cape she wore, lined with monkey fur, dated from her wedding trip and had charmed her by coming in again; I hated its dead-black gypsy forelocks — for suiting her too well. But she'd made it smell of my favorite scent on her dressing-table, Guerlain's *Vol de Nuit*, whose label she'd once translated for me with a smile — adding with a scratch of her nail on the zebra-striped box: "A *lady's* bestiary. A *lady's* night out."

The cab hadn't started yet. They always waited for her. I whispered it to her. "I said to him . . . that maybe *I* could come back."

"You heard," she said low. "Everything."

"I was dreaming," I said. "P-part of the time."

She raised a brow.

"And — I won't understand the parts that are bad for me." It was what I had said to *him*, when he caught me with his edition of the Decameron. Maybe she knew.

"Won't?" she said absently, glanced at her watch, drew a bill from her bag, slid open the glass panel between us and the cabby, said, "Drive round the park; I'll tell you where later" — they would do that then — and had us off, settled and yet afloat. She was always so quick at that. She'd left the panel open. "I'll feed you your instructions as we go, driver." She nestled back with me. "That's what a mother's for." She nestled down. "Oh, I can see how late it is by your face, you truant. Let Anna wait, for once."

"She doesn't know I'm with you," I said doubtfully.

"Doesn't she though," my mother said. "And your father's not coming home. He has some dinner on. Every night this week. Tonight's the one for him."

"You could go." I knew just which one of her dresses I would wear.

"You can go with him," she said. "When you're old enough." I saw her eyes elongate. "I'll *save* the bronze dress for you." The scent of her was strong. It wasn't her only one, but the one I knew. "Wouldn't you rather have me here though?" She cradled me. "Who do I love?" she said low. Meaning me.

Everyone? Too many? Not enough. Or how was it too much? . . .

How could I answer her, even now? . . . I did my best. "Even that doctor?" I said.

She fell back in the seat, away from me. Smiled then, half shamed, as boys in a street fight do, when struck the first blow — when they already know the secret of what they will do. "Ruth." She said it as if she'd never heard it before. The lights of the avenue were sliding across her face. The driver was taking us to the park's northernmost border. "Ruth. You know what that doctor said to me? That we get to the unborn before they're born. That then they just have to live *us* out." She sat up straight, the fur edging her like extra shadow. " 'Ha-ha,' I said to him. 'What a dull man you are. I wouldn't tell my children that if it was the last thing I did.' . . . 'What would you tell them?' he asked me. 'Oh, I wouldn't,' I said. 'I don't know what it is yet, you see. But I'd *show* them.' " She leaned forward. "Ruth. I guess I'm telling you — everything I don't know. I have to, you see. Your father knows so much."

The lights were sliding across my face too — they made a screen. "Do you tell David?"

She took a long time to answer. "No. He's just like him. He's your father's son. Remember that. Always remember that. He's your father's son." She bent her head after this gravity; I heard her breathing, then her lighter tone, almost gay: "And your father's not like us — he can't face the world as we do. It's not allowed him. He has to dream. He's a man."

She sat silent after that. We'd begun to move southward through the park at a stately pace; we might almost have been proceeding by horse. My parents both had a special way of talking in moving vehicles, and a special, important face for it — like land people on ship board, not used to the third presence of the sea. Or as if things not ordinarily said could come out now. Some of us are still like that — when airborne. My mother, though silent, kept the face and the posture, a royalty, reviewing the army of her life.

. . . You and I don't see the park as our parents did, Austin. Or the city. It comes to me that you may scarcely see it at all — or not like me. Are we really as they say, children of the city, as you people aren't? I never remember the park as green. For me it's all rough, porous slabs of city memory, those sweating arcades with the yellow smell where the words are; it's a city vegetation of people, magenta-voiced plantings from Puerto Rico, the platinum voices of the tall shines moving cheek-ily bamboo along the paths. A rising peonage I half-wished I was at school with — streaming through bushes public as a urinary, fresh as the new bread they never ate, old as any grass. My parents saw the park as they thought their ancestors had — a Winterhalter drawing without the woman in it and so nothing until supplied one, perhaps from a stock of her own satin ball nights, seen through a bead curtain of snow. Or sometimes as he did, through parades rewound like toys whenever the bunting was brought out again — the little botanies of war. Come spring, they saw it in a stage set of perfectly matched lights marching upward — like the notes of the same Maggie Teyte *Plaisir d'Amour* they all remembered — toward the giant cubist glories of a skyline they'd begun to confuse with themselves. Summers — when the park defecated like a child — they never entered it. Though our house stayed open, my parents when there seemed to breathe incognito, from a snobbery that wasn't social, only habitual — to the gills of the kind of fish we were. Meanwhile, we younger ones used everything — but never thought of the city as being *ourselves*.

But that night, as the wheels galloped like horses, and my mother passed bill after bill to the driver, destination after destination, she was more modern than any of us; she used everything. And I began to see her winter Barbizons. When the cab left the park's borders, she squeezed me under her long, sheltering arm. "Little mother," she said.

We'd come out at the park's south end. My mother leaned to look at the meter — a lot of love and silence, six dollars' worth. "Out of the park now," she said. "We can't be protected forever." She pointed to a tall building on the opposite corner. "Driver — in front of there." He U-turned, and eased us to the curb. A doorman put his hand on the knob, hesitating when he saw us two, and said, "The New York Athletic Club, miss?" She slipped him a tip. "I — we only want to look." But the explanation she gave the driver was for me, for my possible embarrassment. Even she didn't know all of me. I never thought *she* was strange — not for herself. When awkward or ugly people happen to carry the strangeness of the world about with them, one can clearer see that they *themselves* aren't strange. Lucky or not, she was beautiful. "My daughter's new to the town — to these parts of it."

The driver spoke, not turning. "Men. It's a place fuh men." He sniggered for some reason. "Fuh dere healt'."

We gazed in, unable to see much but a decent marble gleam; the men sauntered out when in couples, strode purposefully down the steps when alone. If she tensed at each arrival, I only recalled it later when there was time enough, or never time enough. Bear with me, Austin, and with her — she won't be with us long.

When she told the driver to move on, "Anywhere, tell you in a minute," the doorman was still watching us. As we left the Athletic Club, I looked back at him. He had that seedy-soft look a man gets from carrying around prejudices that don't belong to him, when, six feet or not, the flesh isn't up to it. Maybe she'd given him the quarter for that. "He doesn't look too healthy," I said.

She didn't answer until we were well away. " 'You're a hysteric,' the doctor said to me. 'If you can't *stop*.' There's only one answer to that. 'And the ones who *have* stopped, Doctor,' I said, 'what are they?' "

I used to remember what she said by the destinations. Over the years they've blurred — was it the settlement house came next? Or that Hotel Seville we only slowed past, en route by accident, or that corner hotel on the west riverfront, with the workmen's clothing store stuck in its side, where we'd certainly never been before, but sat outside of, for five minutes by her watch. The driver said nothing more, though she'd left the panel open. Maybe she wanted him to hear. Or to have an audience larger than one.

Some of the places I already knew. At the settlement house, way over east, she leaned out the window into the fruit-smells; I thought she was looking back at that part of her dancing girlhood. But when she spoke, she said, "Life is movement. Tell me how to stop." I thought she was asking me. Until she leaned back in, and said, "I asked him that."

We went back uptown after that, by slow stations, and more bills. At the little hardware store in those El blocks not far from us, she leaned forward again. We'd often passed it on foot, Posliuty's Hardware, glanced in it, but never gone in. The same old woman sat there, huge flab breasts resting on her navel, the kind of fat that, until I knew more of diet and brassieres, I thought exclusive to the poor. Tonight, no one else was in the store; sometimes we'd glimpsed a man. "Yorkville has everything," said my mother in a dry voice. "Just like any neighborhood." Nobody was needing hardware tonight. I sat thinking, at her side. What do we ever know of what a parent or anyone means by "everything"? But another idea was growing in me. While I squirmed with it, peering out, her voice continued its musing. "We're miles away from our money. Many times as I've heard your father tell that tale, you'll never hear him say that. None of us, our kind, ever sees the real city. I only meant to try. That's all I ever meant to do." Then she looked up from her watch, and saw me, my face. "Hungry?"

I wasn't. But I nudged her, at the driver. "Maybe him."

"He'll tell us." Then she squinted at me. "Have to go?" she said, and before I could answer — "Or —?"

I could never be sure of that these days without looking, but I shook my head. And finally I blurted out what was preying on me, which until this ride all our walks hadn't made me realize. "Are we being *followed?*"

. . . It's possible isn't it, Austin, that I'd got it right. And have it wrong now. For when someone follows an idea that way, or a person — in a haunting of places that person isn't, might have been ten minutes ago, or will be an hour later, but at the precise moment never is — all of which is meanwhile known to the pursuer, who maybe wishes the timetable to go wrong, to catch her, the seeker, unaware — isn't that being followed, in a way? . . . I followed Edwin that way for a while, for what he *was* and what it meant to me, not for himself. I hope it's not the way I'm following you . . .

My mother said nothing at first. She passed a slow finger over my mouth, as if in marvel at the words that could come from it. "Like a cliff-hanger movie?" she said then. At my nod, she nodded, faster and faster, suddenly tapped at the pane, gave an address unfamiliar to me, and said, "Driver, all speed!" just like in the movie installments. We sat tense, clasping each other, fists against fists. I had a feeling this address would be the last. There was an ozone of action in the cab now, like the smell of a metal thought to have none, or like the air that comes through a real window opened high above in a theatre — when the people in the loges stir against its current on their necks and bury themselves in the play. When we stopped in front of a café, one I'd never seen, even the driver knew that this time we were going to get out.

When she asked him to wait for us, he wouldn't, even though she offered him a sandwich inside. Maybe that was why. She'd spoken to him half as to a man — for his hunger — and half as to a chauffeur — when he was only a cabbie. Women aren't ever as libertarian as they think. My father, who never faltered over his position in life, would have managed it.

"Naw," said the driver, getting out to look up at the café, then at the whitewalls of the two long cars he had drawn alongside of. He had his cap down. Neither of us ever really saw his face. In those days the city was still full of these faceless — friends. He kept it down when he refused the last bill she held out — one too much. We already had our backs to him when he spoke from the curb, from inside the cab, just before he drove off, and we didn't turn in time to see him. "Naw," he said. "You two can get your ashes hauled inside."

We hadn't turned in time. I hadn't got what the words meant but that was the feel of it. She held on to me as if we were hearing a tocsin between her two worlds. Or maybe because he had included me. I found that to my liking, even then. Clasped together, we stared at the café. From those narrow pavements we could have seen in if the windows hadn't been blind, very decently painted in dark green, above it a frosted design. There was no name such as I'd seen in our recent travels — Blarney, or McDonagh, or the Ould Sod — but it had an Irish look to it, by the smell of it sold food, and had an air of being better than it should be for these streets. Two neighboring Tudor-roofed houses of the old New York sort also did. One, a lawyer-real-estate combination, was dark. The other had the floors above well lit, and a brass sign saying it was a club. The Conestoga? I've forgotten. Something Indian. She ignored it, her glance on the two cars, one a roadster, one a limousine with leather top, both black, and better than they should be, here. She stood there in that street, while an El train clangored above us, and checked her watch. What schedule did she have inside her? Mine was a raven's. By the smell there would be those hot roast-beef sandwiches sopped in gravy brown as shellac on the dead-white bread, and more filling than good food. I couldn't ask, though a small sign on the plate glass reassured me. I could feel how far away she was from me now. But we stood so long. "Are we going in?" I said softly at last, but she didn't hear me. That often happened too, these days.

"Oh yes, we're being followed," she said suddenly, and the voice was the loud, strident one I feared, the smile too. "He's even followed us here!"

And precise to whatever her watch said, the gleaming, brassbound door opened — not a swinging half-door like the ones in my father's plates of Old New York — and two men stepped outside, one large in the light behind him, the other small and rotund, made penguin-shaped by the same black and white in which my father went to dine. I saw the second one melt, into a car. He took the roadster. That left the limousine, my mother and me, and this man.

Austin . . . you remind me of him. That face hadn't been made in ten minutes either. Older in lineage than ours even, maybe, not a Phoenician curve in it. But to us, and forever, the fair barbarian. Otherwise — he was himself, neck and shoulders looming with a crudeness from wherever he immediately came. His flesh had such direction in it. He hadn't an extra word in him.

He motioned us in.

She circled me with an arm. How pitiful she was when she tried to lie — this tall, older girl. Only the truth came out, inverted. "Oh no!" she said. "I don't walk her for that!"

When he did speak, clefts above and below his lips scarcely moved. "New-style customer on my beat, I hear from Posliuty's. Never goes in."

A dark blush bloomed upward from my ankles. For her.

He glanced at a striped cuff twice the circumference of most, under it a quiet watch that made a schoolboy's of my father's. "You know my beat. Sent him on to take care of it. For an hour or so."

She drew back, head bent, but only to open her bag. For a bill? A letter?

A match. The spurt of blue was already there in front of her, in his hand. I smelled the phosphor. She faltered out a cigarette to meet it. The cuff fitted his wrist.

"Drive you home, if you want."

"He took the roadster." She said it like conversation.

I knew these exchanges; younger girls get these duennaships early. Or apprenticeships. And I knew what a beat was. Places — one walked.

His shoes were a no-color — not sharpy. A gentleman's. Above me I heard him toss her what he had for her, his hand on the door. "Home? Or in? Say the word, Mirrie." She looked sideways at me. I'd never helped her before. This was the moment it began.

I pointed at the gold lettering of the small sign on the plate glass. I'm not funny, really. Quick, rather, often from shame. Or an understanding my parents must take credit for. "Ladies invited," I said.

Inside it was all elegant yet easy the way men can do it, mahogany and spittoons, and a long bonfire of a bar. The whisky breeze was familiar to me from my grandfathers, and the fine blue smoke from the Upmann's she'd taught me to buy for their birthdays. She and I entered together behind him, two old-fashioned girls who knew cigars, she looking neither to the right nor left. She was the one who had been here before. The men sitting at the bar had behinds too big for the stools but moved within a peculiar narrowness, turning from the neck and tapering away from us again, like seals.

He bore us to the dark port of a table. "What'll you have, girls?"

"Nothing."

She said it for both of us. But sometimes a duenna wants to be a child. And speak as a child. "Mustard sandwiches," I said.

Why should her eyes fill just then? I saw them. She turned away. "Yes, I know your beat," she said to him. "Which one of them gave you the white feather?"

The stuff of the banquette we were sitting on was leather, the same color as the jodhpurs she wore when she rode. Girls rode sidesaddle once, for fear of breaking the hymen; she'd told me that. I squirmed, thinking of it. Or waiting for his answer.

"You," he said.

Bear with her. She won't be with us long.

She saw my squirm, thought it the ever-present riddle between my legs. Or it was convenient. I was convenient. She pointed. "Over there."

I went. A yard away, a man's urinal. Before I closed the door, I heard what he said after me. "Little Napoleon. Or his daughter." Then I shut the door.

My pants were always damp those days, the black dance leotards smeared at the crotch with white. I sniffed like an animal at this inner saliva of myself, though I already knew its polypy, seaweed smell. But it came from outside too, something from outer space kissing me there.

When I went back, words had been said. My sandwiches were on the table. As I ate, a man from the bar called out my mother's name. "— Mrs. Mannix!" She didn't answer. Terror over what to do flooded me. Our companion had noticed that she didn't, at once. It wasn't new to him, either. I thanked him with my eyes for his gentle touch on her arm. "Jim Mandel, Mirrie. Used to be Judge Mandel. Better speak to him."

I could tell she didn't want to leave me with him. Duennas are all alike. But she went.

When she'd gone, he looked at me in that certain way elders did at times like these, even he. As if he were going to hire me. For a confidence. "I see you know. It's come on your mother so gradually. Think she knows?"

"She knows everything." I spoke from the heart. And another kind of knowledge. For this that was happening to her was only the smallest part of all of it. She would never have wanted out of the cosmos only because of it.

"They talk more," he said, watching her. "Even when they don't quite let themselves know yet. To cover up."

"Not my brother." I shouldn't have said that, not to him; that was family. I sat tall. "My father can lipread. So that will take care of everything."

"Got it screwed around, haven't you, kid? Oh — you mean he'll teach her how." He folded his arms. The men in that place never folded their arms, not one of them. I had watched.

He didn't raise his brows at me, or shake a sad head. He knew he had my confidence. But an expression changed his face — the only time — as she came back to us.

"Congratulations on your commission," she said. "I didn't know . . . And now we'll go. Come on, hon." Suddenly she grinned at me. That "hon" had come out of the atmosphere here. We never used it. But I liked it. What a pair she and I could have made down here, if we'd been the same age!

"Yes . . . that will take care of everything," he said — to me. But I couldn't tell whether he was speaking to me as to a duenna, or as to a child.

"And now you'll be making the rounds," she said. "To say good-bye." She was staring at his lapel. He didn't nod. Would she laugh? No, it was like with the match. One could feel what they were to each other. My breath crept with it, maybe my blood too. "Call me a cab." She said it as soft as I ever heard her speak. Never to us in the basement. Sometimes, to Si.

"No cabs here. Except on order. You know no cabs come here. I'll drive you and her home. Then go on."

"Home. And then go on." Close in, she heard everything.

The two of us walked behind her, to the curb. She bent, peering into the enormous car, an English one with a righthand drive. There was no chauffeur. "He took the roadster." She said it exactly as before. Then she whirled on us — I was at his side. "Which wouldn't have done for three. You planned it all from the window, didn't you. The minute we were seen. To get me back home without a fuss — and in the safest company. Hers. The way you plan everything. Quickly. I've always admired that. And now you're due at — where is it next? — Donofrio's, and so on and so on, but not for business tonight. To say good-bye." She caught her breath, or speaking at such a rate, it caught up with her — and she stopped. When my mother did stop, her gestures were strange for common life, but beautiful, calculated from far within, to an audience beyond us. Anyone in the ballet would recognize them.

"To say good-bye," she said softly, bemused with it, drawing off her winged hat, and all her hair, tumbling from the tortoise pins that held it, fell behind her, neck to waist, and hung there in the windless cold. There's a picture of her like that at fifteen, before her features were formed — at Montecatini, with her mother. The daughter. I used to think that if she'd only worn a ribbon behind her ears, it could have been mine. She bent at me now as if I were new to her — even a child of hers never felt itself stale to her, totally known. "Grave novice," she said. And before he or I could think, opened the rear door of the car, clapped me into it and was in front behind the wheel, her hand at the dangling keys, the motor purring like a tom. People admire themselves in others. She could think quickly too. She rolled down her window an inch or two. He could have stuck a gun in it, if he'd wanted to. "Your car will be at the door. Mine. And the keys — upstairs. I'll be — the last on your beat."

He folded his arms. . . . Austin, I'm not enough like her — for you to remind me so, of him. He was so much better than he ought to have been. I rolled my window down all the way. "Thank you for the sandwiches," I said, and extended my hand. He'd noticed me, at least enough to call me what he had. I wanted him to see I'd noticed him. To see his expression change. I whispered what I thought would do it. Instead, he tipped my chin, and kissed. "The kiss is for you," he said. But I never saw him smile.

If I'd been in the front seat, would she have slapped me for it? There was nothing wrong with her eyes. The car roared, bucked like a boat, and left him behind with the lamppost. That was our getaway. I looked back.

She drove like fury, through traffic signals when she could. No sirens charged us. People like her get caught when they're ready. At the first impasse, she put up her hair. "What did he say to you?" She spoke without turning.

My intelligence began then, silent as an antler growing upward in the hair. "He said — the kiss was for you."

And in the paneled backseat of that car, lonely as a drawing-room, I folded my lips in my teeth, locked my thumbs at my nape and tightened my diaphragm against the sob, but the tears ran anyway, for the wretchedness of my joy. Everything was converging; nothing was separate. We'd given it the name of my blood, but it was for both of us. The car lurched to a stop, and we were home. We had come to the end of our beat.

The two of us sat on for a minute — she in the front seat, I in the back — and looked out at our house. Down below sidewalk level, the dining-room was dark, but Anna's kitchen-glow shone from the rear, and above it, glossy behind the curtains of the parlor floor, spectral from the hall, all the various pulse-lights that were never turned off. My father's study, over the garden at the back and behind the water tower, couldn't be seen. Bedroom floors were dimmer, personal. For her, it was the house she had inherited — for him. For me, it was the house I always knew I was meant to leave. We women "keep house," as the saying goes, Austin, but what you don't know about us is that we will keep *any* house, most of us — and make it ours. It's the men who want — theirs. While I looked at it, my face dried.

She spoke suddenly, still without turning her head. "So the kiss was for me, eh. And what had you said to him, to make him do that?"

This was the hidden side of her — and still is — the part that she could always manage to keep opaque. Maybe that's what this man was to her. When she was with my father, I knew her down to the ground. I even knew her with Si. I hesitated. I couldn't hold back yet; later I got control of it. "I said —" Again the big man looked down at me, the fair barbarian, the lamplight glistening on a bit of blond stubble in the deep-shaven cleft of his upper lip. Again I held out a cool, social hand. How had I known the words to make him bend? "I said — 'You must be Nick.'"

"So you were dreaming," she said, in the hard voice I knew quite as well as the velvet. "Back there at Chauncey's. And you 'won't understand what's bad for you.'" Her mimic was cruel. "Don't you think I was a daughter, once?" She turned slowly. Was she going to slap me for it, now?

And saw my face. Her own mouth stretched in pity, unhinged, awry. She put out her fingers, touched my face, left them against it, so soft that I scarcely knew when they drew away. "Ah, Ruth." In that darkness of many nights afterward, she said it. "Ah, Ruth. They *wait* for us to cry."

There's a lamppost near our door also, sometimes deplored. You know it, Austin. It shone into the car, onto her hair. I could see the high arch of her eyeball, the long line from nose to mouth, behind which the face was cornered. She hadn't put her hat on. Her voice had retreated, the farthest back I was ever to hear it. "I dream too. That doctor asked me to bring him my dream, but I never brought it." She turned to me, full face. "I dream the same voice every night. The same words it says to me. And every morning I wake up and recognize it. My own voice."

When did I begin to feel what she wanted of me? Of us. Not of me in particular, Austin, you see; I now see that. I think it was just then, outside our house. Poor thing, she'd got it all twisted. It wasn't my father she wanted ruined, or even that man. But at what she wanted, how could I help!

How could I help ask her? She'd half turned away again. "Mother? . . . Mother! . . . What does the voice say?"

That voice, round, rich and strong, almost sexless, has never faded. It's a cadence, not a dream. "Oh fix my fancy!" it said; it says — "am I possible?"

Then we looked vaguely about us, and got out, remembering the car wasn't ours. Neither was the house in a way, but we went up its steps.

She hadn't brought the hat: she must have left it in the car. I sometimes think of what his thoughts were, later that night, after he left our house, when he saw it there, on the front seat. But she did take the car keys. After all, she took the keys.

At the top of our steps, the door was closed. Open, it might have meant that my father, always careless with it, was still in. "So he's gone," she said. "Not to be ruined." She delved vaguely in her bag for the house key . . . Always we delve vaguely in our bags, Austin, that's our gesture, and no matter what trivia we find — a puff, a lipstick — we bring it out as if we left behind something else of importance, there in the bag, that walks with us, as I walk to you across London, with mine . . .

She put the hand with the two sets of keys in it hard on my shoulder — this same shoulder here, where the bag strap crosses it. It was lower then, by a little, but bore the weight. "What shall I say to myself at the end of my life?" said my mother, low. "I can't think of a thing." Then we went in.

But our walk wasn't finished yet, or I didn't want it to be. Once inside the house, I felt myself losing this woman who walked me, wooed me. Into being a woman. And over onto her side. The two go together, Austin, always. Between a mother and a daughter. Inside our house, I felt only her wretchedness and forgot her joy. I spoke my fear, almost as Chauncey had. It's a standard voice even at twelve — in which people speak that fear. "The — end?" I said.

She bent her head to me. It was the next year I grew, though never to her height. Her eyes curvetted from side to side. From those eyes, to the draped purse with its weight of letters, to her finger rings, all of her couldn't help glittering at me with the decade she loved. Or forward and past me, past him. With all her messages. For the eyes did fix on me at last, her mouth shaped its endearment. She never mumbled, but the words came out soft. "Grave novice." Her finger touched the tip of my nose, and retracted. "Maybe I should have told you nothing. Like Lavalette."

I shook my head. No, no. No. No.

She dropped to her knees. Crouched there, she put her arms round my waist, reached up and drew my arms onto her shoulder. Clutched so, we breathed. "Little mother," she said.

So I'm here, Austin, I'm here. Sit me down, I can't speak yet. My flesh still has another direction. You take the bag from my shoulder as if it were a wreath; maybe it is. Heavy enough, yes, though it has no letters in it. *Walter.* There. I've spoken. So I'm not mute. I thought maybe I was. Soon I'll tell you all of it. But I have to remember everything, before I can speak. So sit me down . . . How like you your flat is. As like you as that Hitchcock rocker in your office, as your parents' house. I'm less like my house than you are. Or such is my — fancy. You look so grave — like a man about to hear *his* destiny. Should you have married the Korean girl? We heard about her. I can see her in your house almost better than I see myself. Don't inherit, Austin. My mother was right; it's no longer the world for it. Not for houses. Don't inherit only your house. Though maybe the men can't help it. My mother's second given name was Sheba; she inherited everything else. Though my father try to hold me back from it with all his might, so will I. I will inherit her, Austin. I will inherit my mother if I choose.

Now comes the shortest part of the story. So short. What is shorter than a gun? Hold my hand. It has to remember everything. So we plight our troth, over the gun. It will speak, soon.

It's the night. I'm in bed, after throwing up the mustard sandwiches — and all the woe I could. My breath is sweet again, my bowel clean. Anna has been serviceable but no longer nanny-close, not since the walks, which she won't speak about. What have I outgrown? I fall asleep in the sense of it. My bed is no longer an extension of the elders', a half-cradle still only a trundled yard or so from their night care. It is about to be my own.

At a time of night I have never met before, I awake. Twenty times a day I've sneaked a look between my legs and found nothing; now I don't need to look. But I do. Yes. How small a spot of blood, at first! Yet all the perfumes of Arabia cannot contend with it. The strings between the stars, slightly loosened, absurdly weakened, reknot themselves in the curled small of a female back. Grandiose, unimportant, she is tied to the tide — and takes care of the universe with a cotton pad. One weeps beforehand, about nothing. I had wept about something; maybe that was the difference. And I was to go to her when it came on me, at any time. I brushed my hair and put a new ribbon on it before going down the stairs. Who does that in the middle of the night, except a woman? I hadn't seen David since morning, and never thought of him. My father was out in public. Tonight this was a woman's house.

So I entered her room without knocking — as never before. Her bed, in the alcove that faced the door, was empty, but I already had it fixed in my mind that she would be as I had so often found her — prowling, or at her desk in one of the greenish wrappers that matched it. She always dressed for the room, maybe to remind us all that she had been born in it.

They were on that chaise, grappled in the hump and muddle that coupling is. When you're outside it. Her head hung over the edge, upside-down under that double-rocking, the mouth turned the wrong way, the eye-discs closed. His backside reared over his head. Which raised like a turtle's, and saw me. And his face never changed. Battered, half-strong against us, it would not change. For a premature minute I saw through the charged clouds behind the hymen to what men were—only the other hagridden part of life. "That's a universal tenderness" — she'd say — "which shouldn't be felt until life's end." If my father had been the one there at her, maybe a simpler jealousy would have kept me from feeling it. It didn't last long. I was already out the door again, even careful to not quite close it, when the pain seized.

It's only the body pushing against civilization. She'd told me that too, while she prowled. "Men when they have that cramp want the wilds, or war. We have to creep about on the subway once a month, daft with it, wanting the real pangs. When you have a baby, for once they'll let you walk it as it should be, letting the watery animal drip down." Oh, she'd told me everything — except how to walk that pain up the one flight to my room and into it, when at my back she'd begun to whimper with that other real wild which she hadn't told me of. And when, two flights above us, Anna had come out to the stairwell and was listening.

Houses like yours and ours, Austin, are built for listening. There's a quiet to them in which the family can work upon a person, no privacy closed to that inner ear. It's a comfort, that you know. You and I are closer in that heritage than many a Jew with Jew. And in knowing how people in such houses breed a reserve as thick as the palate of a mute. David could never hear any of that listening. Into it, *against* it, my father constantly spoke. And my mother — slapped its family face. I could hear Anna's listening now and the quality of it, like a creak upon the stair.

There's a closet under the stairwell where I crouched. . . . You and I hid in it once, later; I could feel you feel me there, and not touch. . . . I hid in it now. Against the shame of Anna's coming down, against my pains — and against the listening. I belong in my mother's line.

I heard Anna come halfway down the stairs and stand there. For a moment, with her there, my mother giving tongue in her bed, and me clutched over my new swollen belly with its moil of eels, the house was all women. Then my mother stopped. Then the man uttered. Then Anna crept back. And I was left to give birth, under the stairs.

In the slums, girls do it that way. And if it's a lucky miss, throw it in the can. Sometimes even if not. I had heard of it. I had nothing like that to give birth to, yet I was filled. Crouched there, hearing her rail at her lover, not at me — did he know it was for the world? — all my body-images mixed — with hers. Eyes oozing upside-down color, ears expletive in the dark, my brain was damp on my forehead with the sweat of it. In biscuspid darts of pain, my tongue tore at my hymen, which would not break. Then an animal spoke, piteous — she — and her throat swallowed my heart. I broke from the closet, carrying my belly, and ran to her. I thought she was crying. I had to see.

She was trying to get him to murder her. But he wouldn't. His gun was out of *his* reach, not hers. "Get the gun!" She said that to *him*. Her wish was so clear to me. At the end, she saw that. She saw me. What she had done to me. And what I would do — for her. She tried to say it all, so quickly. The words came out in that utter truth of hers — double. Somebody had to ruin us. But she never meant, always meant it to be me. "Help me!" she said — "escape." Other nights I might not have been her daughter so dutifully, but that one night I was. Life is movement. The little gun, clean and gray, was on her dressing-table, beauty's toy, often in her handbag. We're all of a piece here, nothing comes out of the wings. Hysteric with life's messages, I picked up the toy and saw her approve. In monstrous love and tenderness, I gave her the hate she could get from no one else.

"It's come, Mirrie," I said. "The blood." I could call her Mirrie now. She was only an older girl who had given birth to me. Or I had. To her. I remember the moment of death is guiltless. I saw.

As my father ran in and to her, she met him with her answer. She had stopped. As he turned to me, to pick me up, the real thrust of my blood gave me mine. I could have walked my pains, but it was too early for it. The gun dropped from my hand. *Vol de nuit.*

Austin, Austin, *do* I understand everything? You hold the catatonic's hand as if she does, and is about to tell you it. I try to imagine that I already have. From Dukes to Covent Garden is a fair way by foot, but the mind's path is quickest, getting even behind death. Its light-years steadily reach their star. All the way over here, it shone its story into your waiting face. You sat just as you sit now. Your face, now that I've reached it, is the same. Grave, a man's face which has kept the promise of the boy's — eager to be haunted by me. Yet I am still mute. All I could say when you opened the door to me was *Walter*. Even his death seemed to me still so far in the future that it had scarcely a voice. It takes time. To come forward to you. Yes, Austin, I know you'll wait.

Bear with me. I have just shot the gun again. I have been mute like this before . . .

When my father came to my bedside with the doctor, I'd already heard that great clear cry of his stumble through the house. I hear it yet. *There's nobody young enough to mourn her.* Why? *I* was young enough. If I'd opened my mouth, I'd have said that to him. Of my father the Judge I had never been afraid. But I had robbed him forever of being Si to her. I felt that Si in him already reach out to me. And was afraid. So I said nothing. Once I answered a question from the doctor, but that was nothing.

When I woke from the drug, David was lying across the bottom of my bed. I woke straight into his eyes. *We are left,* his eyes said to me — *we two are left,* to deal with it ourselves. They had left us together, or bowed to it. And after a while he could speak. He had had to learn how to, once before. He expected little more of speech than that. Or not as much as we. "You saw?" What should I answer? *"Did she — do it?"* Yes, no; yes, no. The double message. Now I harbored it. So I said nothing. Even when my brother said, "We will protect him." Straight into my eyes.

When Anna came into my room again, at the sound of my brother smashing his way through the rooms below — we clung. What control it took from her, against her lifetime care of our objects, not to go down and stop him! I felt it shiver her, like a prayer. And guessed it wasn't me she asked and got her guidance from. *Let him, Anna,* the voice said. *It's me, in him!* So we listened together this time, and clung. I had no fear of her from then on — it is good to have one like that. But I had already spoken to her that once — too much. "Sleep!" she said, straight into the face of the morning. She cradled me. *"Here* it is night." So I had to shrink a distance from her too. In her huge, faithful dreams she'd have made a daughter of me. Or a mother. That "night before" when nothing had happened yet, how could I make it come again, except as I did, from then on? Except in a lifetime, who could remember it?

So I became intelligent. And mute. The brightest animal in the wild is the one who manages to live on. Every breath against his skin changes the direction of his cells. Sensation — a brilliant tic-tac-toe always at work in the vitals — is his *thought*. I was that creature now. At school, they were always setting us projects, teaching us to live ourselves into living. Cowering in the cloakroom of their sympathies, the day I returned there, I conceived my own — and was grateful. I was to pretend I had words, and knew how to sup with human spoons. I had to pretend I was not in the wilderness. Oh, that's already human — yes I know that now. Everything is human that we do against the wild.

But then — I was grateful for anything the concrete could give me. Consciousness, when first frightened into being, wants all the more to live by the fencepost and the stone. The human part is in speaking of it at all. Where I might have to lie. But I could have told anyone at once, like a shot, what I was afraid of. Anything in the bestiary describes its fears — *as it moves*.

Remember that rainy day we were all down in the basement telling our worst dreams — or elaborating them? My brother said, "I dream I've lost another sense — like touch. Awful." Walter, ever agreeable, answered. "Then I dream that the rest of you are crooked. And poor Suzy Stern is out of step again — he's *straight*." "Oh Walter, you'll *die* agreeable," you said. Austin, how did you know — so early? Isn't that why I've come to you? Like I almost told Augusta, once. We tell the ones who almost know. Because I feared these explorations of the quick, I said, "Suzy, Walter? Do you dream you're a woman?" "Oh, no, half-chick," he said. "That must be *you*." How I loved you all, always, for laughing at me. At *me*. "Your turn, Austin," I said. You were always bad at these metaphorical games we injured ones loved. "Oh, I don't know," you said. "Dreaming old Latin tests maybe." We didn't laugh at your normality; we were too much in awe of it. You are romantic to us.

Then it was my turn. How grateful I was to the ballet — for providing me with stage fright. "I'm on — in a solo I never heard of, which the audience knows by heart. I can see them, a thousand dolls, all alike —" But I was never good at it, either lying too little, or too much. "And two, first row front, whose faces aren't blank," I said. "Those are the worst of all." The rest of you were silent. Then you said, "What's that in your hand?" Nothing. Thumb over three fingers clenched, the trigger one pointing — but nothing. Only my fear — that the fire of thinking might explode like smoke — in my hand.

The ballet was my place to hide. No real dancer does that. It's their speaking. The wind blows through them — she was right. They quiver with it. I can't do that — not in the dance. Maybe there's still some other way, I used to think, that would be mine. But I always know when they are speaking that way — without vanity, not for themselves. That's why, later, Madame let me stay.

That first month after, Ilonka's was where my muteness went unnoticed, and I could heal. She allowed mere babies on pointe too early and too much, but I had just come to it, late. To pack the box of my shoe with lamb's wool was a poultice, to dip it in the rosin, a ritual. Sewing at our ankle elastics, poring over old prints of Camargo in *la cachuca,* Fanny Elssler, Karsavina, Pavlova, we were novices imitating our saints, some of whom were still alive. Old custodians of the order came to sit on the gold-chaired sidelines, nodding their coifs from ruffles that smelled of maraschino and chocolate, pinching our unformed muscles with their eyes. When for three days running the assistant mistress, whose much-argued custom was to put a spot of glue between the heel of her tights and her shoe, had a broad raveling rise up her rear while she was at the bar — was when I found I could smile. I carried the smile like a bonbon, home to my father. Who was saying good-bye to Augusta in the hall.

She cupped my face. "You still look seedy," she said, and traced the purple under my eyes.

"We're learning the single pirouette from the fourth position," I said, measuring the distance to go past them. *Un petit changement de pieds* — and I could make it. "It's hard." For in the dry marionette words of the ballet, those light, eighteenth-century improvisations for the clockwork of the limbs, I had found my way back to speech again. What better way to learn the terrain of one's tongue, and how to walk backward, forward, from an event? They were both watching me.

"I saw Nijinsky once," said Augusta. Great poor dear, with those shoes of hers from some improbable *bottier* of the past, she belongs to that long line of spinsters who have had tickets to many halls — once. I stared at her feet; ballerinas do. If anything could make me cry, it would be those Watteau boots — on her.

"Your —" My father, moving suddenly in the shadows by the newelpost, squaring his shoulders, only making himself smaller. He's never realized how many times he mentions her — by default. Under Augusta's inexorable family eyes, he went on; we all knew the story. My

mother had met Nijinsky at fifteen, when she and *her* mother were
going round the spas. "— your mother met him once."

In my mind, I did a quick *petit échappé, pas de bourrée,* and got
past them. You'll understand I named the steps only in my mind, often
jumbled and incorrect, while my feet moved almost normally. But it
was the way I was managing. These exact orbits took the terror out of
space. Under stress, they still do. And it hadn't been a month yet. "So
did Ilonka," I said coolly, and was past them and up the stairs before
what I had felt in Augusta became clear to me. We were both a little
afraid of him. But after that, he and I could speak . . . Austin . . . it's
when he mourns that I am most afraid of him. Until today, I never
knew why. I thought it was because of *her* . . .

And then — the month was up. Until then, I'd never dared visualize
my secret. Or had no words for it, in any pattern. In the depths where
such things rested, its image steadfastly withdrew and yet remained, a
hot, glowing cave, arched like a red Moorish window and blank, what
one saw when a human finger was held against an electric bulb —
mine. Now, each month of the menstrual round, my mother came into
that cave and stood there — in all her — *attitudes.* She had more of
them, in every combination and alternation than we'd ever been given
at Ilonka's, in any mode we had ever struck there, in all the dimension
there was. *Croisé, effacé, en avant et à la seconde, en l'air, en diago-
nale,* she knew them all, although the vocabulary — come down
through the long *chaînés* of those winged daughters of the dance passing it along to me with their wreathed arms — was mine. *Port de bras.*
So, each month, we began to put each other through our paces. She
and I. So I showed off to her what I knew, as we did to the older girls,
as I do now to you. So, finally, one month, we were dancing together.
Grand jeté en tournant entrelacé. Sometimes her hair was down,
sometimes up; my head was often bowed, hers flung back, mouth
ashriek. But always we were silent. Then she transcended that too, and
began to speak. And I began to listen to her. In all the words she had
ever said.

So, month by month, I gave birth to her again, but gently. We give
birth to our parents, through the past. I only did it a little early, before
my time. She stood still now as she spoke, neither awake nor asleep but
gently dreaming. Of me.

Until Madame. What Ninon knows of it all, I can't tell. She has her
own allegory, literal as an ant's. But *Madame's* power was to make

each of us see ours. I can hear her at the novices, that summer of the war — at a student newer even than me — a pink chalice of a girl, still swollen with the air of Wales. "You're a pewter candlestick, my girl. But you shall still shine." So a girl would be told — that she never would be silver. "Woman-lump!" she'd say. "Add a few slivers of gristle, you boys. That's all a troupe is made of. After some pre-selection in the provinces, frequently wrong." After a while, we began to see it all for ourselves. "But born perfection doesn't interest me. What I like to do is polish the flaw."

She'd lift her chin at us — an ugly Pierrette who had done it well. She only looked ugly when she chose. We were never to forget — that sometimes she chose. I never did. At the back wall of the practice hall, Rupert, the perennial assistant — lamed, it was said, in her service — slouched on his shoulderblades, with an "'Ear, 'ear. Spirit of Dunkirk itself!" One of the third-year boys hushed him — we all knew she wasn't really French. Her lies were as transparent as the glaze the cook put on the Sunday buns, through which we could see, just in time not to break tooth on it, the hard wartime truth of Saturday's dough. Rupert, upper-class we suspected, had become Cockney in sheer imitation. Or that was the part *she* had given *him*. To be her interpreter, full of just such lèse majesté.

"Her's an obsessive," he said one day, adding a dollop of the broad Dorsetshire that surrounded us. "'Ow, Rupert," said a girl, in craven imitation. "Y'r sow original."

He was going down the line of us at the bar. "Got bad feet, gives you time to think anything up . . . God's sake, Mavis, crack that elbow. Is it Isadora you think you are?" Mavis snickered, but sobered. Madame often sent off the failures here into that other dance world, as to the tumbril — with some tender remark — "You'll love it there — they'll teach you to hiccough from the *waist*." And Rupert went on musing, slapping in a girl's hip with the side of his hand, twisting out another's kneecap, down the bar. She'd chewed him out that morning. "Not a romantic, mind, that's what's so bracing about our Ninon. Her'd murder her mother, her would. If it would give us a better *Swan Lake*." "Here, Ruth — hold on to the bar." He always dropped his fooling for the new ones, the untalented — and for me. "Hold on to the bar if you still must. But turn that ankle *out*."

I held on — Austin, it's much better when it comes that way, natural — and knew that I never wanted to go back to our house. "'Swat's wrong with 'Itler," said Rupert, going on to the next in line. " 'Swy 'e's so original. Thinks too much. Got bad feet."

So, under the domain of total ballet, I began to see the world as it is. Often the balletomane himself doesn't know that this is what he's really watching. My mother, girl-haunter of other studios, had known it best at the end. All the way from Covent Garden, — linked with Places des Opéras and solid Ilonkas round the globe — I began to see our walks for what they were. But it was Madame — who gave us all her confidences publicly, and never asked for ours — from whom I took instruction. And it was Ninon who relieved my mother and me of our dance.

As for my father, who likes to quote his old preceptors — how I yearned to quote him mine. Through her, I still thought I might be able to tell him everything. Those years, that's how I managed to live with him, my part of it. She was only teaching me to go forward again. Some day, I thought, I would know how to let him take my confession from me, so I could take his burden from him. I could let him see that what I had given birth to was my own. It would happen, I thought, where Madame had given me my rank in the company, my true role.

Once Madame had awarded a person his or her rank, it was held sacred by all, never protested, least of all by the recipient, who was helped by all to act it out — that's what a company is. We craved that discipline. We wanted to be ranked. Oh there were furies and catcalls, and jealousies about roles in the repertoire — "Take any four women, and it's a jungle," said Rupert. "Especially when some of them are boys."

But the rank itself was always sacred — the guild. Once we flew across the Channel, the whole troupe on a gala weekend, then by bus to Chartres down the new highroad he said the French wouldn't admit was a copy of the Autobahn. When we stood in the nave, in that rotunda where all the stone people are in their ranks of noble and grotesque, a mixed guild of the ages, here a Grisi or a *Marie pleine de grâce* — Taglioni, and there in that dark corner an Eglevsky, Rupert raised his putty nose *di mezzo-carattere* against one of their stone ones, swept an arm against that whole medieval circle of them, and said what we were all thinking; "Why — it's only *us!*"

And afterwards, they made a game of it. "There's Danilova as the queen; no, it's Gollner." Others stood in front of their counterparts, waiting to be noted. And someone whispered, "There *she* is, in *Sylphides.*" She, that one of us who was already great, or about to be, stood aside. As did I. I couldn't find myself anywhere in that round. I stood where I knew I must be — altogether out of the ranks. And Rupert, the ever-noticing, fussing us back into the bus, stuck next to mine his true gargoyle face that belonged anywhere, any time, the backbone of any company. "Bide your time, bunny." Ninon hadn't come along. "Why does she keep me on?" I said. He was embarrassed. They thought I didn't know my father had been her lover. I looked back with Rupert, at that pile of spires. "I didn't see myself. In there."

A male dancer at his best has a cruelty which extends from him like perfume. He must think only with his body. Kindness is out of his sphere. Rupert knew which lack had lamed him. "In there with *us?*" he said, mugging. "How can the girl expect it!" He gave me a push on the buttock, onto the high step. "Into the bus with you. *American.*"

That was the place I came to have for most of them. Sometimes, Ninon may have been seeing my father in me, but I knew I puzzled her in myself. I would have told her the plain facts. "But what were they?" said my mother, striking a match. And in what words would I tell them, I wondered — like Rupert's that day at the bar? But the body was Ninon's direction. She would never answer me in any other terms. When we asked for direction, she never answered us otherwise. Demonstration was required — of our own secrets most of all. She would take up the chalk. I could see her mark the large X on the floor. For my mother. Maybe a circle round it. "Or does she move?" Madame would say over a shoulder, as she knelt. "Speak up, girl. In your dream, does she move?" I would know better than to answer, "She speaks!" — hearing the reply, "We have no recitative, here." But I could come forward, to stand on the X. "*If* she moves, Ruth, *you're* to make us see it. Or partner will, at your command." Then Madame would hand me the gun, according to what she thought me capable of — a toy got from the prop-room, or a black soft shoe with its uppers gone. Or a four-inch block of air. "All right, now. You're going to tell us. How it was." Madame never said "show." "Ready, Ruth?" Then a clap of the hands. "Dance!"

And as I dance it out endlessly, I hear the sibyl-voices, hers and hers, my mother's and Madame's, both of them dancing on the practice floor of my mind. Men inherit the houses, and the wars. We inherit the sibyl-voices. Unidentified or known, they wash over us — which of them the mother-by-choice, which not? "The moment of conception!" says a voice — "There's a magnificent ballet, for you! The motile sperm, more

instant than thought. And the ovum, arrived slower than an infinite line
of tortoises — already there!" Is that voice my mother, moving my
hand over the stylus of sexual knowledge prescribed — or Madame
loftily guiding our feet to some early notations of Laban? "The ballet is
virtuoso calm, demoiselles, in the center of feats of strength. Action is
ceaselessly resolved." That's Ninon for sure, quoting from some old
master whose name she'll never give us — who we believe to be herself. "We're *always* trying to get out of the cosmos!" says that other
sure one, ceaselessly resolved.

The chronology is endless. I used to try. One day, I was dancing by
myself in a corner, half watching myself in the great mirror which had
migrated from Dorset to London, war to peace, effortlessly as a sky —
when Madame came up behind me and stood. The technique is to go
on dancing; I was good enough to do that now. Madame made a sign,
and I continued backward from the glass, until our images stood beside each other. I was a head taller than she now, though I was not on
pointe. She spoke to the mirror, not turning her head. Was she going to
assign me a rank in the company? Often she let a girl know she was
going to be kept on by a casual, "Take one of the blue lockers. From
today on." Her voice wasn't like that; it gave me no rank. It was like
the atelier-master's downward sweep of the pen, correcting the apprentice's drawing of himself. "You always dance backward, away
from. Never *toward.*" She kept her eyes on mine in the mirror. And
never asked me what it was I was still moving away from — in a
revulsion so deep that it was calm.

Sometimes there would come a day when Madame was deep in one
of the grand invocations she made almost to herself, beginning low with
the low: *pas de chat, de Basque, sauté de;* on from *glissade* to *en-
trechat six de volée, sissonne tombé* to *failli* — ever on to even wilder
astrologies in her quest for the impossible. She would turn suddenly
even on some prima who was slacking off. "When did they practice to
the left in your school — in their bath?" Then I used to think that
surely she would notice me also. To say, "Ruth, Ruth — walk *toward.*"
Or that she would notice — toward the end of a session, when the
body carves itself almost free of its own sweat — that I was doing it.
But she never further instructed me. So, the years went on, and I came
to have my place. I was the dancer without rank.

Once a year, usually at end of term, when she was having to
send the younger ones off before their characters were formed safe

against the solider fantasies of Surbiton, or the seniors to grand performances they might fail to recognize, Madame had a speech she gave us. "Oh God, here it comes," Rupert would breathe, perfectly audible. " 'Virtuous calm, girls! Virtuous calm.' " While she gave it, that chant to the impossible she required of us — or hoped — I watched her feet, clothed now in plain pumps. No leather could hide that great squared-off metatarsal. "The arch that has soared never sits well again in the shoe!" said Rupert in my ear. Around us, heads hung embarrassed — hadn't Madame herself always said it — a ballerina should *not* speak? The word "assoluta" is rarely heard among them. Nymph in the cave of all their thoughts, she moves with the most silent, unrosined footfall. Madame, in these moments, is only Ninon, pink-ringed and raucous-voiced, pimping for her own vision.

"Why does she always look at *you?*" says Rupert, and his tone, kind but puzzled, carries all my rank. Yes, she is looking at me as the speech ends, always on the same syllables, "— impossible." She too must have received her answers early. How else could she describe such Snow Queens, such nymphs that the wind blows through — so well? How better describe that silent partner of mine, my mother, than by staring at the ones without rank, like me? I turn to answer Rupert, grizzled boy, lamed in a service too. "She knows what she can't be," I said. Like you, Rupert. Like me.

. . . There's your telephone, Austin. Yes, go answer it. No smell of girls here, is there? I know you. You'd hunt the red Indian in Soho — but never bring her home, unless she was from home. But point of honor — if all the women you've ever had chose to call just now — you wouldn't lower your voice. Why must I know us all down to the root? Will it be good for you and me, that I know you so well? As I know who you're speaking to. Voices that speak to *him* are always the same. Mine was, until today. When we talk to him we deceive ourselves, but find out, later. What's a judge for, if not that? It's me he was mourning all that time, wasn't it. As a man does mourn, against all bloodstains, all wives — the child born to him. Poor man, he never knows in time what's vital to him. I can love him now. If I don't have to talk to him . . .

The bathroom is as good a place as any, to get away. And I always need to go, at the important time. There are some girls the months follow. A fact giggled over at junior proms, and not unknown at some weddings. Poor Lavalette. Maybe it's the months trying to warn us what are *not* the important times. We often wondered what call girls did about these calls from nature, and actresses — and shrugged ourselves the answer. The couture is always the same — and close the bathroom door. So here's my satchel, full of months.

. . . And one I shan't tell Austin of. Because he knows. Edwin's a user. That's the kind to use. A girl with my parents should know. But Ninon cleansed me of it. Later that night, when she came into my bedroom — and swabbed me clean. I was lying down when she came. She was no Anna. And I had different wounds now. Of which women easily speak.

"Get up!" she said. "This is no time to lie back." She had a douche bag in her hand. Where she got it, I never thought; she was capable of dispatching my father to find an all-night drugstore. On one of those errands — for medicine, cigars, pastrami, medicine — that he often said were the hallmarks of a city — though he never sent David or me. Or she's capable of carrying one of those things in her bag until the end of her life; she has such a cat's-claw sense of her own femininity — and ours. She put me in the bathtub now, and showed me how to use what I'd often seen hanging in the matter-of-fact English bathrooms, though the troupe itself didn't have too much time for sex — and the dancing bleeds it out of you. Sweats, I should say. *This* is blood. Better than some kinds. My mother used to say that bathrooms were the surgeries of the soul — against all those bright razors, what chance has a wrist? Why haven't I ever felt that? Here is where it most wells up in me, that I mean to live. How hard it is for women not to be normal — or casual — about blood. . . .

"What a deal of junk women have to carry around with them," she said, leaning over the tub. "Jockstraps are nothing to it. Or rubbers. I suppose he didn't wear one. Your rapester boyfriend."

We were through. I got up weakly; my outer bruises were worse than the other, though equally invisible. She helped me back into bed. How tenderly she could tuck a person in, this hellcat who at dress rehearsals I'd seen drag offstage a girl who'd forgotten to shave under her arms, with the cold whisper, ladylike enough for the back balcony to hear, "*Three* is too many, my dear."

"It wasn't rape," I said.

She smoothed my hair. She'd never touched me like a person, before. "It rarely is." She shrugged, straightened up, folded her hands. "Good.

You understand that. You'll live." She'd half turned to go when she reversed, with that telltale poise of the neck. When young, she would have been a dainty dancer, never in a dream, reliable. "Why did you let him?"

I was too tired to say it fully. "Here."

"Here?" Those huge eyes of hers paused in their scrutiny of the room. She knew my father. I went with Edwin. In my father's house. Daughters do it all the time. Your sisters may, Austin, even though they haven't my father. Or the same heavenly one — in which neither of us believes. "Ah. Simon."

But that was all she ever said of him to me at any time. And not because he was he. Women reveal reluctantly what they learn of a man by sleeping with him; it's a pact they don't like to break. Whatever comes of us, Austin, I shan't reveal you.

"What a queer picture!" she said, taking it up.

He gave it to my mother for a joke. During their engagement. But she always kept it. *Behold Now Behemoth.* And I stole it afterwards. "Just a Blake litho."

"No picture of your mother?" said Ninon, putting down the litho. "So many, of course, everywhere else."

Not in Father's study. I gave mine to Anna. There aren't enough pictures of her anywhere, to challenge mine.

"No, Madame," I said from my bed. "But I always feel . . . you know her. Knew."

"I? How should I —?" I saw it cross her face that my father had somehow lied to me of their affair. All of us knew Madame's face as well as she knew our bodies. So, when in a few minutes or so, she gave me my rank — I knew it for that.

"Your end of season speech," I said — "when you send us home." I raised myself on elbow to meet the personage entering my room now to stand there with us, body-connected with us through my father — and through women, and life. "She was like that — in the way she was. The way she died. Everything."

"The way she died?" Madame said softly. "By her own hand."

I shivered. My hand lay on the coverlet. If I looked at it, Ninon saw it, who saw every muscle in flesh. "Not by his."

"End of season." Madame's face was sunk in her hand. Not her habit. There was no figure at Chartres exactly like her — in that posture. "And what do I — did I say?"

The word is so rarely said among us. I couldn't say it, to Madame who was never it, who was never more than the Queen Bee in miniature, steady on her own flight. Ninon has no wildness; she's like me.

"You know. How everything is arranged around her. Like when you explain to the boys how it should be in the adagio, if ever they find themselves dancing with the real article — and meanwhile with us. How she is the visitor from the impossible." But when Madame used to explain how she must be touched — impersonal, there I was sad and did not wish to follow her.

" 'She does not communicate,' " I said. Why was it this next part always made the tears come? I was only quoting Madame. " 'Though she tries, she carries too much.' " Tears were all right among women. I let them fall, like that time in Nick's car. " 'The impossible,' " I said. Madame, watching from the wings, must once have seen such a one, to make her speak like that — maybe early, when she herself was still a tidy butterfly with the glassy wings of the divertissement stuck to her shoulders, crowding with the others to watch that marvel, maybe in Prague. That was why she always looked at me when she said it — another watcher from the wings. " 'She carries the impossible,' " I said. " 'That is her freight.' "

Madame stood up. She does this, after performances. Saying nothing until ready. "So. No wonder no one can compete with you."

"Compete?" *I?*

"In his eyes."

She looked at me for so long that I shivered again. There was a figure at Chartres exactly like hers — in that posture. Then she reached forward, flicked a finger under my eye, and looked down at the pearl of wet on its tip. "At a time like this — cry for *yourself!*"

But that pearl of wet on her fingertip! It was mine. "I have to walk backward," I said, looking at it. "From that."

"When you can cry for yourself," she said, "you'll understand everything."

Did you? I didn't say it aloud. She heard. She looked down at herself, still in the towel she had knotted around herself, from my father's bed. "Got something for me to put on?"

"Of course." I went and got a sweater and skirt from a drawer. Over the exchange, between our two man-tired nakednesses, a tenderness, all motherhoods mixed, brought our heads close. "Get back to bed," she said. Her hands hung veined in my sweater, like girls whom the

weather has wizened. I lay back on the bed, all my pangs outwalked.
She gathered up the towel.

"Leave it."

"And the douche. I'll leave that." She smiled slightly. "Take it on
tour."

"So I'm to go?"

"You can have Rupert's place."

Not to dance. Not ever to dance. To watch everything from the
wings. I turned my head on the pillow. Self-pity. I felt it. At last.

She came toward the bed. When Madame is herself again, and most
serious, she has the lightest hand. It grazed my forehead. "You'll carry
your weight. Your own weight and more."

I turned my eyes toward her. She stood fast, hands clasped, not
recoiling from me. There's one like her at Chartres.

"That's it, that's it, my girl," she whispered. "I could never quite see
what it was, before." Her head shook it out at me — custodian. "You're
— to understand. You're to be *that* one." Then she shrugged, just as
she had over the girl assigned the blue locker, and left me to take it
from there. On her way out, she gave the Blake a scrape of the nail
that's still on it. "What an old balls of a boy!". . .

. . . We give birth to ourselves, but slowly. As our parents came to
give birth to us, they died a little. We die a little, giving birth to them.
I lay there thinking of them both. Equally. Tonight — we three are
equals. Neither of them with the power to come to me, to guard me, to
use me any more.

My crime was my pearl. It was given me. But something in me had
given me it as well.

I chose her.

I took sides. I chose *her*.

I had all my slow life to forgive them for it. Mine own slow life. To
understand from the beginning. To have had to understand then, instead of at the end — that's the pearl I carry. Walking backwards, until
now. To love someone, will that be to turn round and walk toward?
Toward them? Mother! Bathsheba for whom I wasn't named! — I
mean to live. And suffer, Father — if I choose. Father! Judge me. I
mean to suffer if I choose.

My pearl of wet. I am young enough to mourn you. You are mine.

We give birth to ourselves. And close the bathroom door behind us . . . Austin, you have the look of all the men who come to Delphi in spite of themselves. Hold me — I'm beginning to speak. I won't be the mystery any more. Take the mystery from me. You're to be my past, from now on. You're to understand everything now.

Father, I'm going to speak now. David, Walter, strain from your graves; help me to speak well. Austin, you'll help me to speak. How am I to begin it all? Oh Austin, everything is in question. I always knew.

"Oh please, please, please —"

I speak. I *speak.*

Oh fix my fancy. I am possible.

20   In Full View of the City
Winter 1955

Between potted palms set at diamond-shaped intervals along all ninety feet of the ballroom at the top of the Ralston houses, three men were running power-waxers along the intricate parquet. At times they got down on their knees to do the borders by hand, talking meanwhile of the weather — a brilliant February snap whose snow had mounded like gravestones all the air-conditioners in the new apartment house across the way — and of the owner here, in whose other houses they had also worked.

"Give them knee breeches, they could be footmen!" said the Judge, from the central grove of green where his wheelchair had been placed. "My God, did you ever see such a room? In this sun!"

Warren Fenno, sitting perched on a small ladder, only because he didn't want to emphasize his own physical well-being by standing, nodded absently, leaning forward to listen to the men. Ever since the foundation had put some money in a survey of city migrations — and in property, though that was an accident — ethnic groups here had begun to interest him. He heard that the two Irishmen had each come through the snow by car, from "double frames" in Queens. "My grandfather, he lived in a tenement in Hell's Kitchen owned by Ralstons, once." The fourth man, the German foreman, was engaged in a last touch of the brush to the exquisitely pseudo marble-painting on the walls. "I live now by York Avenue. First when I come — Washington Heights, they tell me to go." He shrugged. By which Warren deduced that though by his age he might have been fleeing Hitler, he wasn't a Jew.

"Looks like the Frick," Warren said.

"The Frick?" How anyone could compare that heavy tycoonery with this delicate, Byzantine-etched room! — unless Fenno meant that both were fakes. There wasn't an ounce of plush, gilt or carpet here; even the swags at the windows had been penciled in, and the two chaste fireplaces had no mantels other than faint pickings of blue and bronze, aged to a Renaissance tint just yesterday, by two Italians who had then left to clean the acreage of Ralston terrazzo in Palm Beach. To think all this restoration here had been going on next door to him, for two years! "I suppose you mean the palms in Frick's garden, around the fountains."

"Matter of fact, they're all palmettos, aren't they?" said Warren, toward one of the Irishmen though not actually addressing him — he never felt really comfortable with labor, except in Maine.

"Dunno, he never takes us Micks down there. We go to the Bay — Oyster, Bolton Landing — though that ain't been open three years running, Tuxedo — before he sold it, and now here. Down on the Chesapeake, he uses colored. Fisher's Island, he don't have nobody at all."

"Where does the man *live?*" said the Judge irritably. "When he's working for you, Fenno. If he works."

'Two rooms at the top of a house in Henderson Place," Warren chuckled. "Oh he works. So hard, the office began to think he was put there to spy on us. Hardly a social worker type *we'd* ever seen before. But we never suspected any of this. Until the papers carried the engagement announcement. And your address."

"Henderson Place. Do I know it?" The gulls surely had their lanes, otherwise. For the present Ralston heir to offer this place for the wedding! To him of course the Mannixs were merely the people who had always lived next door to a house of his — one house. Two years ago, he'd bought it back from the intervening owner. Restoration was a hobby with him. He'd pleaded with the Fennos most gracefully, to let him "warm the room" with their son's wedding. He always warmed a new place at least once.

"Henderson? Oh, it's a little corner," said Warren. Ten blocks or so away. He didn't like to think of it as restricted any more. Still, the Judge — who acted as if the gold keys of the city had been stuck in his mouth at birth, didn't know it. "What was the Ralston money, originally?" said Warren. "That cereal?"

"No, always been property. Their sense of it hasn't skipped even the collateral line. This is the grandnephew of course. Our Ralston never married."

The two gentlemen laughed. "So many things skip," said Fenno. Though the Fenno guest list was large enough to make these quarters convenient, he and Margaret hadn't thought it quite the thing, not to marry off one's daughters from home if one could — and next-door certainly could have managed it. What they liked least was the Judge's morbid enthusiasm for property that wasn't his own. And Mannix had told them the tale of Meyer's own purchase of course, the punch-line distinction between Jews and god-damned Jews sitting rather peculiarly on his smile. "Well, I don't find that too jolly," said Margaret Fenno, afterwards. "Will he tell all the cousins it?" Warren had answered, "No, I don't think so." And surprised himself by adding, "*We're* jolly. They're *not*, somehow. They've got *wit*. I think it would be valuable if thee and I could both remember that." She had laughed and said she would take the thought with her, to Meeting.

One of the Irishmen, working the border to the left of the Judge's chair, spoke suddenly across it to the third workman, a silent Puerto Rican who was coming up on the other side. "Where *you* livin', Manuel? You never say." Whether or not all had taken in this property talk above their heads, the Judge couldn't tell, from the faces. All workmen had faces now, as his children had heard him say. Blaming him, of course, for daring to be born before this was the case.

"One Hundred Forty Street," Manuel said proudly. "West."

"You don't say! My aunt used to live there once. How long you live there?"

"Ten years, I move uptown."

"You don't say. That neighborhood used to be all white."

Manuel, white as anybody who was white, nodded politely, scrubbing away. "Nineteen-thirty-two, I come from Ponce. To the Tee Ee Are AY." He brought it forth like an ancestor.

" 'N hell is that?"

Warren stepped forward eagerly. Onto the border, unfortunately. He stepped back. "Transient Emergency Relief Authority. For destitute nationals without state residence at the time."

"Thatta right." When Manuel beamed, he had more face than any of the four.

Twelve o'clock struck. "Lunch," said one of the Irish. "Now what church would be that? Could that be St. Stephen's of Hungary? I was married there."

"Too far," said the Judge. "Except on a wet day. No, that's Ignatius Loyola." Another bell struck. "And that's St. Catherine of Siena." He waited, grinning, for the third. "Our Lady of Perpetual Help."

Warren burst out laughing. "How do you do it? And not even one for *us*."

"Oh, I married into the music business. Had to do something." Not that the Mendeses had ever been performers, or even listeners. "Pity for Ralston's sake, Ruth won't have his string trio." But she hadn't wanted any of this elaboration. Only Austin had persuaded her, for the clan's sake. And because it was not to be in her own house.

"Well, must go and dress," said Warren. He hadn't been needed here. Margaret, like all women, thought widowers needed help. Or wanted news she wouldn't come for herself. "Thanks to the arrangements, there's plenty of time." He couldn't help his expression. Married by a judge in chambers — it was known to happen. Even if the chambers were a flat over on Central Park West — and said jurist had got his start in a dubious kind of law. But for none of them to be there! Nobody except Judge Borkan would see the young couple until the reception. Austin, saying only, "We want it private" — but maybe silently imploring? — had persuaded the Fennos to that. Oh, it was going to be a peculiar affair all round — though he was sure that the Fennos would carry it off by sheer numbers. Plus the powerful presence of the Broughams, Margaret's people, who were too plain to speak of their family, but on the frivolous occasions of others seemed often innerly guided to stand silently, thinking about it. "Better — than no wedding," Margaret had said. "Warren — you don't think that girl has a look — of a girl who mightn't go through with it?" The assurance he'd given himself, he couldn't give her: They've already had an affair. And this time, Austin will go through with it.

The Judge looked down at himself, once again in the ancient morning coat which would do him until he died. He wore a smaller brace now. And could dress himself, once a day. "You know where they are now, I'm told? Together. At the park, I believe. That's the way it's done, these days."

"Well, I'm off."

The foreman stepped forward. "But now the fountain," he said. They'd forgotten it, the fountain which both sides in agreement had hoped to keep hidden away. Ralston at their sole joint meeting with him had promised it. In a last access of restoration — and in a hysteria of delight at his own. "So good to be out in the *open!*" said Ralston, clad in a suit made for him in Hong Kong, thick as a secondary pelt. The Judge hadn't dared meet his daughter's eye. "So glad," Ralston was singing, pumping Warren's shy, dry hand. "It's been such tough titty, being underground!" But when Warren turned round, Ruth — whose tact went all to that side these days — was gone.

They watched the German unwrap the fountainhead, oddly small, disappointingly chrome. "From Hammacher's," said the Judge. "Well, maybe the water improves it."

"*Nein,*" the foreman said. "It works only the champagne."

Upon which both gentlemen shouted a "No!" It was really their best moment together, to date.

"Maybe Ralston won't come," said Fenno.

"He comes today, *ja,*" said the foreman. "From the house in Lago di Lago." Still protesting, he went to lunch.

"It uses the same wine over and over," said the Judge, reading the directions. "That's how the rich get rich."

"Disgusting, either way."

"And I'll get blamed for *my* ostentation," said the Judge. "By three hundred Fennos."

"We did rather pad that list."

"You did, rather."

They were both smiling.

"For a boy like that —" said the Judge.

"Austin's head over heels," said Warren. "Naturally. But I think you might like to hear what Margaret said, years ago. When she saw Ruth at dancing school. And again when he brought her to tea with us, last fall. 'The little Mannix girl is lovely,' Margaret said."

"Last fall?"

"September, I think."

Before Walter died. "My daughter's a mystery to me." He spun the pamphlet with the vicious aim of the legbound, straight into the box. "As for that thing — I'm beginning to think old Ralston himself was part Jew."

"You people," said Warren. "Always that chip on your shoulder."

"Sorry, does it show?"

"Yes. But I admire it. Came across the figures for the people you yourself brought over, the other day. During the war." He'd gone out of his way to get them.

"Oh, that." He'd kept them out of his consciousness, ever since. To do otherwise would have seemed like buying himself from God — with souls.

"Weren't all Jews you saved, Simon, were they. Didn't I hear you had trouble with some of your co-religionists, because of that?"

"A little." The judge felt the light, almost palpable breath of air when one seemed about to make a friend. "That was *my* war."

"Quite a war. Four hundred and some people."

"I hear that blasted foreman on his way up. Maybe *he* was one of 'em."

Warren knelt to examine the contraption. "Wonder if this thing couldn't stand a little adjustment," he said suddenly. "My boys've taught me to be pretty mechanical."

"Sailing used to be my speed." He wheeled himself closer, watching as Warren disassembled the pieces very handily. "You and Austin've both been at the front. My son David when he met his death was on his way to war." Saying his death aloud didn't make him believe it, even yet. " 'Nobody's really at war,' he said to me. 'Unless he's there.' "

"There!" Warren said, standing up. "Let them try make that gadget go without this."

"What is it?"

"A sort of gasket. Water or Veuve Cliquot — no runnee without it."

"You like wine?"

"No, 's matter of fact. Margaret's people do, Quaker though they be. Though I make her the excuse lots of ways, I guess, for not being luxurious. Wives're convenient." He said it deliberately, pocketing the piece of rubber meanwhile. Naturally, marrying into a family, they were curious about the mother. In the name of their future grandchildren even had a right to know. But Austin, on their mentioning it, had been furious — a new thing for Austin.

"Yes indeed." The Judge looked so small and forlorn, sitting there under his army blanket, that Warren put a hand on his shoulder. "Women are funny at these times," he said. "Girl ought to have her wedding the way she wants it."

"Wives *are* convenient," said the Judge dryly. "Particularly at weddings. I'd even thought of acquiring one myself." Yes, he'd even done that, when he got back. By a letter. Which, this time, he had mailed. "Didn't work out."

Warren removed the hand. They did go too far. One could depend upon it. "Austin told us, by the way. That she'd told him everything. Family history, all that. Nothing mental, I gather. He didn't tell *us*, of course. Got our own skeletons. Told him so. 'Austin,' I said, 'tell them about Aunt Elsie.'" Warren gave a short laugh. "'How she left her money — away.' So it all ended in laughing. Our family — usually does." He got off that — not to sound superior. "But how Austin does love that girl, Mannix! All he's thinking of is how to take care of her. Protect her. All day long. Says he's going to spend his life at it." His son had struck him as rather intense, and he'd told him so. Maybe too sharply. "Company one keeps," he'd said.

"Oh?" That scary quality which was somehow in the Judge's very size — Molly, the youngest girl, had said so — had now returned to him. "He'd better do more than *that*."

So they parted. Maybe it was Mannix's joke — a rather nasty wedding one. He couldn't tell. Or whether it was only him he felt uncomfortable with, or all of them. The family all meant to do their best with the girl. As Warren went off, he felt the piece of gadget in his pocket, and revived. "A tisket a tasket, a green and yaller gasket" — It was the kind of joke the family loved.

"Until four." Mannix nodded good-bye. He could feel it himself. The delicate breath of friendship hadn't lasted too long.

When Charlie brought him over home, they found Anna in a state because the bride hadn't yet returned from the park—and hadn't promised to. Anna's anxiety was clear to him, if not to herself. Somehow, it was harder to imagine childhood friends married to one another than it would be to accept a stranger. Or maybe neither Anna nor he could believe that their guardianship was over, all, all ended now. "Well, she can't run away, Anna. She'll turn up. After all — she's with him."

Meanwhile Austin, on his way to his own wedding, strode through the park without seeing it. He'd meant what he had said to his father, in the nearest to release he had permitted himself to come. Though he'd keep the London job, it would never be his main job again. In one stroke he had become one of those men with lives divided by women. One saw or smelled them out everywhere, men who were openly hobbled or resigned — bled away by invalid wives or extravagant mistresses, or those others, grayly present at a board meeting or a family council, all the time secret abstraction suckled them. Fenno men weren't exempt. Indeed, were more vulnerable, as men who coped, and weren't destroyed by their demons (or angels) but merely — divided.

He'd no more dreamed he might become one of these than he'd aspired to be one of their opposites, those men of total vocation — to art, religion or ideas — through whose grating he'd always peered with respect, tinged with the slight distaste of the moderate. Knighthood to anything, much less a woman, made his whole generation squirm; for him at best manners were enough, and not to be a pig at any trough.

But that night, as she spoke and spoke, and as the great ravine of pity and horror had opened up in him — to be sealed and never spoken of after — he'd already resolved. In a yawn almost of relaxation from jaw to loin, he knew what men felt who had a vow, or had a job for life. Or had had an abbé with a Rupert-nose say to them, "This is *your* role."

At the beginning of her recital, she was like a child leading him through the forest of her life, in which only he was lost. She already knowing that when they got to witch territory he would find two of them, the old and the young. "To see the shark smile, and know it for oneself!" He had to remember — all the while his hatred for the mother grew — who had taught this girl that! Later, as the girl grew out of her own childish womb in that midnight closet under the stairs, he wept at her accouchement like a father — of the child. Still later, when in her grown self she at last faced him and wept, she was like a medium, piteously strong, whose ghosts, when the lights went up, couldn't fade. Men married women for their intensity, kept them or left them for their tragedy. She brought him certainty like a pearl saying, "Take this treasure, now. Be keeper of it." "Men are only the other hagridden part of life" — she could say that to him! Oh, he knew now what she meant to him! If he could have said all this to his father, presenting it to him like the patents, land grants for a new country, it would have been said easiest: "So one becomes a maverick."

Last — when she had finished — she scanned his face, for his forgiveness. Didn't find it. And was satisfied he knew it wasn't his or any man's to give.

"I hope to understand," he said. "As well as you." She'd given him her everything. And this was his.

Like any woman she became his, came to live with him in the flat, cooked her first awkward meals for him, lay for him — not so greenly, he thought — and never became to him like every woman. Her jokes wrenched him, when he thought where they came from. Sometimes he thought of the children of such jokes. "You *are* funny," he said to her, in his arms.

"Oh, you *like* black women," she said, rolling over on him — did any difference she could find in him excite her? "Or — your mother's Indian. I'm that. Maybe not quite red enough." From which he gathered his mother had taken her through their collection of rewarding ancestors just missed. *Ruth the Red*. But his intelligence refused to play at what was dangerous — and so much was.

"You're the most honest man," she said. "We're not marrying, are we, *because* you know?"

But stupid he was not. Had she given him all her mystery? Could a person? "Because of what I don't know," he said.

Their days before coming back to New York were a continuing conversation. Their elders might have thought they drifted. On one wild wet night, their last before coming over, he went to the theatre for her. Though he'd never said he'd disliked coming, when she saw him hanging about in the stage line among the other Johnnies, the only American among those romance-filled bowlers and baby cynics from Harrow, she gave a little laugh. "Next time we'll meet out front."

Home in his flat, peeling off her clothes, she'd said what still chilled him. He could see the bunched calf come gleaming out of the tights so thick in the hand, so gauzy onstage. Would there be a next time? How often he'd seen her hands grasp the square toes to exercise them, not to hide — and hadn't asked whether she meant to go on with it. Were her words — out of the blue — an answer to that? "I must have mystery," she'd said, and for a while couldn't look at him. He hadn't asked her to explain.

Next night on the boat — for they were lovers, they had time — riding the black jointure of sea and sky in a single deck chair, they'd exchanged their views on the possibility of God. Their elders might have heard it as the proper prelude to a mixed marriage. "Universe is such a well-run clock, must be a clockmaker, the age of Newton used to say — but I'm not so sure," he said. While in another sky, fragments of mortars and children glinted, like fireballs of slow magnitude, and fell. Those who had seen that — it was his one small claim to be with her, in her universe. "Oh no," she said into the clouds, like a child, "it's much simpler. If there's a God, it's because there's nobody else old enough. To mourn." Though there was no one on deck, they went below. Before love, he buried his face in her, so as not to ask, and asked it. His first question in all those weeks. "Am I mysterious enough?" In love, gripping him, she answered him. *"You're* to be my past. From now on."

As he neared the ice-skating rink where they were to meet now, he couldn't see her on it. Leaning over the rail, he checked his watch, nervously early; after all they were to be married at four. Awkward with this lack of ceremony to which they'd set themselves — to scold their progenitors for what lacks he couldn't quite say — he was already formally dressed for the ranks of Fenno cousinship one somehow oughtn't to annoy; he would not skate. Girls' social rebellions were thin-skinned; even if they'd lived openly with a man before the wedding — as none of his cousins had done — in the end they often proved ro-mantical. Romance — in the end they were its custodians. He hoped she was, so that for the conventional period — of at least a day — he might be part of it.

Here his outsidership was a help to him. He was sure he now under-stood the Mannix history better than they ever could themselves. Old Miss Augusta was an observer of a sort known to him; old maids of her type transcended clans. Taken to tea just yesterday in the clean, mag-pie maidliness of her hotel room — "Ah Ruth, here's your great friend" — he saw at once that without hostility to him, she still didn't wish the marriage to occur, and wondered whether this came of anything she knew. If Augusta half hoped (as he thought Anna and the Judge didn't know they did) that Ruth would back out at the last, they didn't know her. Waiting now, he drew his muffler up against the bleaching cold, not flinching at why *he* had no doubt of her. The kindest woman might leave a lover at the altar. But would keep her word to one who was only — a great friend.

For a man who was to be married at four, when it was now three — and received into society at five — he had considerable phlegm, stand-ing quiet enough for the pigeons to pick their way round him, paying his formal dress no more heed than the other frozen watchers. He was not the man to care for comments either way, or for the graffiti of the crowd anywhere. The park, he saw, had kept its snow. Once, as chil-dren, he and Ruth and the others had skated on the natural lake way uptown, among a few dozen more. Here, on a rink man-made in a bowl of timid park dells, the circling skaters, much dotted with red,

moved in a heavy drove bound by the sad, jouncing music — a civic
Currier & Ives. Ruth often skated here, disdaining Rockefeller Center
— "They put out too many flags for it."

Perhaps in reverse of what wives were expected to do for their
husbands — to bring the gentler things — she would teach him how to
bear with the crowd-life. For unlike the Judge, he could see that for his
own times this was going to be necessary to bear. Already, in the
enigmatic reversal of the ages, he and his young kind were only *self-*
made men.

He checked his watch, scanning the entrances. If she didn't come,
he'd go straight on to Borkan's; she wouldn't fail him there. Oh, she
saw everything, except a resemblance in herself he hoped she didn't
see — and meant to save her from.

Across the arena, Miss Augusta, who was farsighted, saw him,
framed between two mothers whose heads were following their children with doting arc. Though she too was here for a purpose, opposite
to his and to her as strong, she watched the crowd like an old cam-
paigner, enjoying it. The city interlude *was* her life. For excuse and
escort, though not today, she had Dog, her long line of Chummies, plus
the absolute confidence of her parents' era — that the city *could* be
circumscribed. Out of it she had almost consciously made a psyche, her
life passing in a strong visual state which only the restricted lingo of
the new era would dare to call loneliness. From her window in a four-
story relic of the early 1900's called the Jackson, she could see hard as a
cactus opposite, the Diamond Exchange of New York. If she wanted
fountains, a new skyscraper bank had just built her some — Louis XIV
could have done it for her no quicker. Her own block had three famous
theatres — including the one her father had lost his money in. According with that purer era of matinee idols, the theatre to her was sexual
excitement, always seedy even at its brilliantined best, the tiaras always
royal paste, the furs rented. There was a race of inhabitants here who
didn't disabuse her of this — homburged men with canes of malacca,
Worumbo overcoats covering the last twenty years, and home haircuts.
A breed of crones in once-important turbans came out of the corner
holes here, in furs the exact color of the pats of horse manure across
which, fifty years ago, she had walked to school. It seemed to her that
the physical constituents of life repeated themselves well enough. Hot
chestnuts came regularly to her corner, on the first of November. If she
wanted a sight of wealth, or other crops, the delicatessens had their

netted melons and rows of marrons. Theatre crowds, glowing food shops full of neon and fluorescence, nursed her to coziness. Back at the hotel, such was her personal strength that she did not even become a "character." They could do nothing with her personality there, not even with her rich connections, which were obvious, but of which she made nothing. Truest of city-dwellers, whatever passed before her eyes was already expected, and the thought of enumerating it never crossed her mind.

Her two rooms were big enough — "London bed-sitters remind me of your place, Aunt Augusta" — in the second a daybed on which Ruth had sometimes slept, and could again. "Bed's made up," Augusta had managed to say to her in a moment managed away from Austin. "You can always come. *No matter when.*" And faltering — for she had defied the family only once — "Simon wouldn't have to know." She was proudest of the fact that the family scarcely knew Ruth came there. They never walked, but sat in Augusta's rooms and talked. It was her inside life.

Twelve years ago, after that first sight of girl and father in the hallway, and even before any sign of trust from the girl, she'd gone home to educate herself for just such a moment as now. Or for when the full confidence would come. It never had. That expectation had been like her own childish yearning for Simon — which dream it had for a while replaced. If she knew better now on both scores, it was because of this girl. Who by her presence alone had done to her old cousin what she did to everybody — educated them.

Scanning the crowd, Augusta's head didn't move with it like the mothers'. . . . Through her I've had as much inner life as I'm able, and thank God for it. I shot my own one bolt in the family forty-two years ago, when I left Mrs. Delano's boardinghouse for the Jackson. If she comes to me now, it won't be for long. . . .

Not that her own preparation had been worthless — from direct mail courses in electronics to sex magazines, both of which she gave neatly packaged to the night clerk after she had done with them. She'd been readying herself not for the new era — which women like herself could handle with one wrist — but for what youth, in the embodiment of this girl, might tell her. And so that she might cushion the Judge and them all against the downfall of what he believed to be "his" house.

For it was Simon she'd first fixed on as the guilty one. . . . But I'm not to be fooled on Simon or on any of his blood — ours. Young man across the pavilion, I've nothing against you for yourself — nothing at all. Except that you're not the one for her. Not to marry. Oh poor, glorious young man, I know what you are — who should know better than me? You're — the right one to have told. And to pass on from. For she'll have told you by now, what she would never let me hear. What I've never once let myself — say to myself. Why couldn't I let myself be fooled? Why can't I, still?

Scanning the entrances, Austin said to himself: I'm not bedazzled by her. I love her — and see her clear. I see all of them, clear. She'll come.

Scanning him, Augusta said to herself: Oh, why do I fool myself? She'll go to him. For a time.

Then they both saw her. She ran prettily out on her skates with short chopping steps, gave herself to the gliding wave of the crowd — a white beret and jacket in the dotted sea of mufflered faces riding intent on the music's wire — and was lost there. It was always surprising to both watchers — that there wasn't more of her.

She emerged first on Augusta's side, and the old woman, squinting in the dying sun, against the mass of capering boys and toddlers, made out that like any girl she had dressed for her possible role — or so that she might go anywhere. Her mother had used to do the same. In that fur tam and jacket she could come to the Jackson like any rosy niece, or to the wedding gala which would know the fur was real. Head bent as in meditation, she glided past, holding tight as a prayer book the round muff that the old woman herself had given her — Augusta's mother's ermine, tissue-papered against yellow all this time. Anna would recognize it. And must be wild, with waiting. She knew all, of course, in that way servants did. And served Ruth mistakenly — acting as *our* nurse and duenna. It's Simon we all really serve.

As the skater neared Austin, the mass was going so swiftly that he caught only the rear whip of her skirt against the steel-bunched calf he knew so well, ugly and real — then farther on, the whole angle of her, chin up, leaning into the wind. She could still be in hiding; he wasn't fooled — though all consulted dictionaries of the classic ballet had been no help. The Mannixes themselves had educated him beyond his sphere — like Edwin in a way! For knowledge of her he ought at once to have gone back to his depth of years with them. His heart ached again for his first friend there . . . David. Who even when they were boys couldn't bear to see anyone suffer . . . Ergo Walter, and later, Alice

Cooperman. But that was minor. His own father David could never
hope to please; trying to atone for his deafness by physical prowess, he
never saw that the Judge was jealous of it . . . As for your mother,
David, the dead like her are never only foolish — that was your mistake. But it was through you I first sensed your sister . . . David's life
with her was spent in those constant acts of sympathy, unphrased, terrified, but not direct — because he wasn't sure of her circumstance. She
never told . . . It was harder now to see the real skater, in this orange
light spreading the afternoon before it fell. But she too was never
taught to trust in other people's suffering, to let it be. That form of
Christian trust. She can't bear it yet, either. Ergo, David — she'll come
to me.

Augusta, straining, could no longer distinguish that white in the
whirl of the others, but she could see the tall young man, next to a
couple who just then pounced on a boy and dragged him from the ice,
struggling. . . . I never was fooled. Simon never believed David was his
son. It was never the deafness. And it was worse after her death than
before. That way he could revile Mirriam's memory, and justify Ruth
in his heart — she did what he wanted to . . . Oh, never justified to *me*,
Mirriam — whom the two of you laughed over, don't I know! . . . But
in his poor, enlarged Job-heart. Half the Jewish fathers in the world
are Jobs to something. Like that little money-Job they laughed at too
— *my* father. The rest are like Meyer . . . Simon's favoring of Ruth was
always multiple. Beneath the need to protect and conceal, which was
paramount, were all these other motives — for in a way, Ruth is himself. *Isn't she, Mirriam?* And in a way, she is you to him now, because
she has a great flaw. But not an obvious flaw like David's. And he is
certain she is his child. So the natural parent can love his child — and
pounce on him . . . Now I'm an old woman, I can see I too was an
unnatural daughter. Like us all. If she comes to me — shall I tell her
that?

The skater came around and around again, to them both, for they
were now opposite each other. On the swelling light of the music, she
rose and fell, a white jacket among other whites. No red on me anywhere now, Austin. Somewhere beneath a skating skirt long enough for
a wedding, a bride's spot of blue, Augusta. Maybe I'm coming to you
both. It was the moment when the afternoon fell, the woods parted in
farther and farther dusk, and the snow became the music. Once more
she passed them, skating the thin, silver line of her own thoughts,

their choral behind her — for the young man had seen Augusta now. "Yes, here I am, the groom." And she had acknowledged him. . . . "We're on opposite sides. She can't come to us both."

She saw them! But she wasn't alone; neither of them had ever really thought it; the assoluta never really dances alone. Madame, if she were here, would say it too, Austin thought. Who it is that still dances with her in the whiteness of white — in that samite in which *we* clothe all the dead that still live.

Augusta, watching him, thought, "Yes, she has a great flaw, and that attracts all of us, young man, you too." The girl was skating slower now . . . Her parents had always told how they skated together the night before their wedding — which was all that era would allow — to be told. It's a family story . . . But only she knows that I watched them there. And walked home reconciled — at the sight of such a beginning — saying, "Chummie, the city is beautiful." So I've no doubt who's dancing at her side now. Oh, Cousin Simon, so controlled, so calculating since our cradles, ever only cousin to me — how you fear the hysteric in her, as you did in her mother — and admire it! What are they not capable of! Oh, what a catch you dance to, Simon, your syntax and your coattails flying! You're in a wheelchair just to rest from it — don't I know.

Across the rink, the young man's eyes said to her: She's mine.

Across it, Augusta shook her head at him: To my cousin, if to anyone — she's been the perpetration of all his controls.

But in the end it was simple. On the next round, the girl waved to Austin, but respectful as always, veered toward the old woman. Augusta, military in her tweed, fair-dealing as a duelist, stumped around to the entrance side — and there they three were.

In her whimsical way, she looked up at them, one to the other, while she sat and took off her skates. They had only to understand her. And tell her themselves what they wanted of her. When she was quite sure they wouldn't, she stood up and flicked a small box Austin was carrying. "What's that?"

"You're entering a family that hallmarks its sentiments." His own father had given his mother the *Nonesuch Weekend Book* of June 1924 — another relished but tender joke.

"You think we don't?" But she took the package, like a lure.

He had his daring, Augusta thought. Plays his allegiances well. A habit we share.

"Found it in the Charing Cross Road."

It was a Florentine-printed volume of excerpts from the *Encyclopedia Spettacolo*, giving the classifications of the ballet. Over Ruth's shoulder, Augusta, who knew Italian from a coral-beaded year at a Miss Beard's-style pensione in Perugia, read a passage aloud. *"A cominciare del 1766 troviamo nei programmi le prime distinzioni: quella dei generi (ballerini 'seri', 'di mezzo-carattere' e grotteschi') e quella della gerachie: 'primi ballerini seri assoluta' . . ."*

Augusta was to be a functionary here and knew it, already hearing it in her own voice. "There's a glossary at the back. But that's French." She caught a glimpse of it. *"Demi-plié; fouetté."*

"A vocabulary of life," said the girl. "Particularly if you don't know much life. Or much French." But she was smiling. He could take it that she wasn't going to go on with it.

"Come to a wedding." He spoke to them equally.

For a moment, he and the old woman were a twosome, watching the long line of her neck as she leaned away from them in the projection that this kind could make of their bodies — toward the rink of people and past them to the high, fractured walls of the middle city, only the knot of hair, which she had let grow, holding her back. He had an impulse to grasp it. She turned to him before he had to.

Augusta, missing Chummie, looked down at her boots. Or come to me, at the Jackson — am I a fool, not to say it?

"Augusta —?" said the girl.

A violet steam rose from the snow. Out on the rink, the few skates left made a sound of thawing. Otherwise how could they have stood here so heedless, so warm?

"It's natural," Augusta said gruffly.

"Your boots," said her young cousin in a choking voice, her eyes bright and sad. "Your beautiful boots."

The lights sprang up as Austin led them out of the park. They all looked properly dressed.

The marriage took place on time — in what Judge Borkan called his "front" room, although all fourteen, through most of which they were conducted, banded "the most comprehensive view of the park you're likely to find" — at this hour duly magical. "Front room" in Borkan's heavy consonants was scarcely the term for this forty-foot expanse, whose stilted *bergères* and "Louie" mirrors aggrievedly faced east, to the side of the park they should have been on. Borkan led the couple to a positive altar of photographs, flanked with flowers. Farsighted as Augusta was, the large, vacuous script in which a vanished society had signed them was clear. "Your late wife was a DeKalb?"

Borkan assured her of it. "A street in the Bronx is named for them."

"Brooklyn," Austin said automatically. And suddenly he and Ruth burst out laughing. "Not bad for a Maine boy," Austin said. Borkan, squinting critically at their group, like a photographer, pinned a flower on each of the women — a florist doing it for free. "I'm nervous," he said, laughing. A line of warts along one cheek extended his smile. "Never married anyone before. After all, I was a lawyer to the theatre trade. Never dealt with real *criminals* before."

The wedding party stood up straighter — all except Ruth, who was looking out the window, past the passionate flow of the drapes. Noting that, Borkan faced the three that way, his back to it. They all had a view of the park. Though the air was dusking, they all stared into it as if they were seeing it — while Borkan began to address the couple in a short, neatly phrased homily on life, life in common, and their participation in common life. The *bergères* attended it well. And *cum grano salis*, the photographs.

These mixed marriages were always awkward affairs, Austin was thinking, secretly relieved his parents weren't here. In recent years as guest or even attendant he had seen quite a few. The place was rarely right, nor the minister; a spiritual uncertainty hovered, always coming out somewhere, in the wrong hues between flowers and bridesmaids, or between the two sides of anecdote. He shifted his eyes to Borkan. His grandfather had had a line of warts like those. "Like the girl, don't you, boy. Oh, I know you're just friends." An old gaffer at the rink had skated like James, too. Austin glanced toward where the rink should be in the twilight window. But James would never have let us go on seeing him dead; he was a practical man. This was an idea so much in his bride's style that he looked down at her — had they already begun to exchange?

Augusta saw how the girl's eyes went from one to the other, not wandering, just as if in some ballet of entrances all on the right, she'd come in on the left, and was watching her turn. She still held the book, like a clutch of prayer. She's human. She's not to be fooled as we are, any more, but in some other way. She has no self-center yet, or not enough. But she'll — educate herself. Who would come for her, to meet her then — with his own tragedy spread like a bird across his shoulders?

"And now," said Borkan, "by the authority vested in me by the State of New York —"

They were pronounced man and wife.

As they kissed, she saw in his eyes what had made her come here and drew her still — his terror of not being as good as he had set out to be.

"What are you looking at?" he said to her afterwards, at the window. She pointed across the park, to an approximate spot. "Our house."

"Common life," said Augusta, grasping the brandy Borkan had brought her. "There's too much of it."

By the time Judge Borkan's Cadillac, cutting around the park via the Plaza, brought them to the Ralston house, it was glowing abovestairs, the reception in full swing. Judge Mannix's chair (as he'd been explaining to several) was set in the only new patch of floor, where the central staircase had been — now closed over because of the fire laws for a multiple dwelling. What a weight of scorn he put on the word "multiple." Warren and Margaret Fenno, though near him, had formed no reception line, her Quaker simplicity rising oddly to the fore even to her husband — until he saw that by this device each family was able to greet its own. Fennos were overwhelmingly — Fenno, and had brought the young of Guilford to meet the young of Williamstown. Broughams stood about with luminous looks (as if inwardly painting their own portraits in the manner of Eakins) and were greetable.

Judge Mannix's list, culled in part from public dinners, was impressive in that style. Judges were present of a rank which thought little of Borkan, and several deans of law who could nod across at Moling, the head of Warren's foundation, with the "Ah-ha, so you're here" of men accustomed to meet in narrower categories than were here today. He had wanted a few criminals too — as he had said to Edwin, to whom on certain bases he was talking again — "Respectable, of course." A few of the more politically responsible had responded. Mulling the choice of a judge to marry the couple, he'd thought of Borkan, as veteran of a mixed marriage, but from his own sentiment too. For, now that by virtue of his column he was out in public — "Print in a London monthly, Moling for dignity; syndicate in the States for money, and give the money to charity" — he'd at last made the great middle-aged jump from feeling to sentiment. It was the house he was really giving this gala for.

Not all the old faithfuls were here, though Blount, stopping at Port Harcourt en route from the vast holdings Krupong had acceded to, had sent one of those garbled, globe-circling telegrams without which no present-day ceremony was complete. Charlie was behind the buffet with Anna, who was watching Ralston's caterer with a home cook's eye. Austin's Harvard roommates were here, and some of Ruth's troupe; otherwise this was scarcely a young wedding, at least on the Mannix-Mendes side. Most surprising of their arrivals was Leni. At last admitting herself to be at that age when women open shops, and finding herself to be one of the happy ones who lost all ill-ease when they could meet the public on a cost-plus basis, she now called herself Gaby, after her line of corsets, and wore black. Ninon, unable to leave the theatre, sending both Ruth and him notes, had as usual gone to the heart of things. His said, "Thanks, my dear, I don't approve of first marriages." To Ruth she had been equally brief. "I'm willing you the house in Clipstone Street."

All others were accountably absent.

"Nothing happens on these occasions," the Judge said to Borkan at his elbow. "Certainly not the marriage."

"Oh, they all hop into bed now right away," said Borkan.

"Didn't we."

"And *say* they did," said Borkan. "My God — who owns this place?"

"My sisters found all these spidery chairs," the Judge said to Margaret Fenno. "Didn't they do well? Ralston's enchanted." And so had he been. "Originally, the place was furnished by Cottier, dealer my father knew well. Rosa and Athalie did quite a research job. It's given them a terrible mistrust of their own mahogany."

"We're not rich enough for antiques," said Mrs. Fenno.

Did Quakers still tremble with emotion, in Meeting? In society, his new in-laws gave no sign of it. How neatly they walked between the two bazaars of ethic, Christian and Oriental, settling for no consciences but the best! "Do sit on one anyway!" he said.

"What a fascinating crowd," said Mrs. Fenno. "So various."

"The small size of the soul, when it goes out in society! One of the most frightening things in life, isn't it?" Turning, he saw she didn't know how to answer him; she must always have thought her own decently large. "And the recurrence of types! I mean — surely you and

I've seen all these characters before." He waved at their line of vision — hands with champagne glasses, declined waists, expanded bellies, striped serge crotches with a shrunk hint of "prostate" in them. And one towheaded Fenno chick, and two pliant boys shifting past, sweater dress and corduroy, faultlessly young. "Spoke at Harvard not long ago. Going across the Yard, caught myself saying, 'Why, there's young Hayes, and there's Steinmets!' — till I remembered they'd been upperclassmen even in my day. And at Columbia."

"Young for your class, weren't you?" said Warren.

"I've never seen *him* before," Mrs. Fenno said.

It was Ralston. He was wearing a suit of black horsehair apparently, with pipestem legs. Like so many rich who could indulge themselves, physically he was almost entirely the creature of his own imagination; even his sideburns didn't cling as convincingly to his cheeks as did Rupert's, who was near. He wore blue glasses, which he now removed to show bright eyes distraught with intelligences of all the other worlds he wouldn't have time to join. Plainly his social-worker seriousness had saved him from *some*thing sexual, though precisely from what would probably never be clear to anyone, including him. He had each of the bridal couple by a hand. "How you've warmed me!" he said.

He professed himself delighted with the ferny bower the foreman had made of the fountain — "A six-sided star!" but went off to see if it couldn't be made to work. At Warren's side, his youngest girl exploded into giggles. "A tisket a tasket!" she said.

"He's hooked on arenas now," Warren said to Mannix. "Says this is his last house. Says a hundred years from now, everything's going to be in public performance areas; real estate might as well get ready for it. Hordes of us, just milling around outside. Private homes will be a thing of the past."

"Everything?" said Mrs. Fenno, faintly.

"With fountains of course," said the Judge. "One could hide behind them. Well, the rich are always on the side of anarchy, in the end."

Dr. Hildesheimer came up, in Rosa's tow.

"Very good of you to come, Doctor," said the Judge, introducing him.

"Especially since he couldn't officiate." From behind Rosa, Athalie waggled a finger at the Fennos. The sisters had agreed to take the jocular approach. And not get *too* close.

"Modern life!" said the rabbi, spreading hands of amity wide. "Modern times." It was his newest blessing. He bent confidentially to Mannix's ear. "Frankly — I was glad to be of use about the picture. Mirriam will be with us in dear memory, just the same."

Moling, coming up, took away the Judge's attention.

"Picture?" said Mrs. Fenno, low. "How?"

"Frankly —" The rabbi was a leaner, and a whisperer too. "Salt of the earth, those two women. But a cancer of that type, why should a girl on her wedding day be reminded!" Then he stood back. Clearly he didn't want to bless this gathering too firmly. "Frankly, I must be going." He leaned over Mannix. "Come to the vestry, hmm?"

"He used to say 'really,'" the Judge said after him. "I'm coming to love Dr. Aitch — for his uncertainty."

And Warren asked himself whether he couldn't come to love this man, for his.

"About what, Judge Mannix?" said Mrs. Fenno. She would *not* say Simon.

"Eternity, Margaret." He said it deliberately. "As my father used to say: 'A true Jew is never guilty of the phrase "*modern*" life' . . . And now, if you'll excuse me —" He wheeled himself off.

"Does he always talk like that?" said Mrs. Fenno to her husband.

"He was a prodigy."

"Cancer," she said. "The wife. Well, if that's all it was —"

"Was it. Tried this morning. He wouldn't give."

"They always talk about money in the end," she said.

Austin, coming by, grabbed and spun her round, with the peculiar bonhomie of bridegrooms to mothers. Then he held her off. The huge pin on her bosom quivered. He knew it well, but grinned at his sister. "Who died!" Then, craning over the crowd from his height, he saw who the Judge had gone to. Edwin Halescy was here.

He'd been invited of course; that is, he'd been sent the formal announcement with reception card enclosed. Though he'd struggled privately over whether or not *he* wanted to come, it never occurred to him that he was expected not to. He and Simon Mannix now believed the worst of each other. In this guarded business enmity, their column — written alternately, never jointly, but published as the Judge's in entirety, with Edwin billed as assistant — seemed to go all the better for this. They now spoke only of the "law." And Edwin was the charity the money was given to.

To Simon, every subtlety he'd taught this boy was now in service to

Edwin's natural depravity — which had come to the fore to show a Mannix how dangerous it was to be loosely libertarian. He'd brought his benefaction inside the home, and this was what had come of it. It never occurred to him that — except for a vicarious filial emotion, which now made Mannix wince for David's sake (at the waste of it) — all those vaunted subtleties had belonged to the intelligence alone. Or that Edwin had been brought into the house as nowadays intellectual blacks were, to frequent only those influential homes which were culturally safe enough, there to feed on everything they wished except the normal emotions of human intercourse — which it was quietly assumed they practiced somewhere else. All this Edwin now saw. One article he had written with the lyric sob of betrayal in the throat. After that, he merely hated them.

Once so brave, he was afraid of experience now. Like his mother. He would never be stupid. But, in the style of the streets he was born to, he tended to believe the worst of people too quickly, and the better more sullenly slow. In such halls as tonight's, ignorance of the social insincerities kept him awkward — and effectively concealed that he believed the best of nobody at all. He still wasn't afraid to dare — if given the direction. He slept once a week with a secretary, but meant to marry well. His once prideful "reservoir" of instinct, he tried never to think of. The one night it had overflowed, it had made him "ill" — a newer word for murder, rape — or honesty.

He was talking at the moment to a girl. He could tell the story of his early life these days, and too often did. "Oh, he knows his age *now*," said one of his former professors, after his recent visit there in attendance on the Judge. "Uses the catchwords of modernity like the oldest scholar here." A second said, "And we thought he was log-cabin material, when he was here! Guy ought to know for himself, what *is* the best mob. Not ask." The third, who'd never met Halescy before, said "I wonder. Usually I can't stand Mannix's column. Too florid a view of life for me. But there was one beaut on politics, there was. Called 'How Villains Are Made.'"

Austin went toward him in the spirit of the day, until he saw who he was talking with. "Didn't know you knew my cousin Di. Hallo, Di."

"Didn't know she was your cousin Di."

Why should so many gather to these two at once — the Judge, Moling behind him — like fish in an aquarium, behind two up ahead who have seen the same fleck of food? The girl faded back, as women did

before duels they hadn't provoked. Last came the bride herself, followed laggingly by Augusta, in whom the crocus-colored wine, on top
of Borkan's brandy and her own mossy nostalgias, had produced a
positive floral essence of ideas. When she could get Simon alone, she
meant to tell him. That she was ready now, to live in his house.

"Brought this along," said Edwin, handing over the folder which was
his excuse to himself for coming.

"Anything important?" said the Judge. "For now?"

"That's for you to say."

Moling, the foundation man, enormously tall, always listening bent-
headed to other people's conceptions, which he then returned to them
more securely knotted, said, "Ah well, your column, Judge, that's always important."

Inside the folder was a single copy of an Israeli newspaper Edwin
often put there — though the column had never spoken of Israel. To
the Judge's eager glance, it held nothing new — current stories of Ben-
Zwi and Ben-Gurion, pictures of desert military in their protective
beards, Tel Aviv holy men in their consecrated ones, and the usual
diplomats, clean-shaven for the chancelleries of the West. "All the
gossips and accomplishments of a country with God behind and heavy
business ahead," said the Judge. "Edwin's always wanting me to do a
piece on Israel. Or go there." He no longer cared how Edwin had
found him out. To him it was appropriate. That this boy — even in his
way — should be the only one to lend credence to the hope that David
might be alive. A light torture was better than no belief at all. And a
loose end opening out, out into living life.

"Chaim Weizmann," Moling said softly. "How many people remember he created the acetone Britain needed for explosives in World War
One?"

"It's hard to be a lion of Judah," Mannix said.

A waiter offered Edwin a tray. He took a glass. "Filled too full," he
said to Austin. Half-tones he did learn, he never forgot.

"Not today," Austin said. Arm round his bride, he could afford to
view Edwin objectively. If *he* married, Austin thought, it could be
taken for granted — unless his mother's heredity came proudly to the
fore, creating once again some stolid, pleasantly dumb reminder of the
basic human lot — that his children would go to Harvard, or at least
try for Yale. As for a house — it was Austin's surmise that Edwin knew
of one without heirs live or willing — and meant to inherit it.

Edwin drank, held out the glass. "Congratulations," he said to the bride. No telling whether he had innocently mixed up his wishes. "Fenno —" He made it sound like the clan rather than the man — "Good *luck*."

A moment later they saw him halfway down the room, moved there so dexterously that none had seen it done. As he stood there, in horn-rims and a suit too Ivy League only for snobs, glass in hand, a hungry sparkle on his lip, over his head the two palm trees of any ad that now brought environments together, he looked appealing enough — in the modern way. One saw such legions of him everywhere.

"Who *is* that young man?" asked Moling.

"Edwin?" The wheelchair swung itself around. "He's what the world's going to be. And it won't be like us."

"Edwin?" It was the bride, just barely putting herself to the fore, in the softer accents Moling approved. Her hand lay on the back of the wheelchair — dutiful. "My father — was his protégé."

A bowknot of the bride's friends from the troupe hung near, too abashed to approach, in their center an accordionist. Taking sudden heart, they joined arms — surrounding the couple with their lovely, fluctuating barrier. At their edge was Ralston, in the crook of his arm an object of chrome.

"Modern life," said Moling, unable to better the phrase, and stood on tiptoe, all seven feet of him, to go forward to it.

Borkan, coming up, heard him. "Rabbi is selling his story every-where."

"You still say 'Rabbi' direct," said the Judge. "At home we already said 'the rabbi.' Or 'Doctor.' Therein lies a whole history of religious reform. Or social."

"So? Simon — have dinner with me, after this?"

They looked at each other. Two widowers? It was like saying it.

One of the old politicos from the Judge's list, seeing them in confab, came up to them, white-haired and wing-collared, a tottering charcoal of a man, with a little Irish glow left to him, at the long lip. "You look gay."

"Married off my daughter today."

"And you — not so gay."

"I buried my wife, some months ago."

"Ah yes, ah and yes. That takes a long time." He doddered off, away from death, toward Austin's young cousin, who was chatting with Augusta.

"My old cousin looks all the better for a little wear," said the Judge. "Or I need my glasses. Dinner? If you can wait until I can leave. Where'll we go?"

"How about my club?"

"The Harmonie?" Which his own father and Mendes had never joined.

"No. Not the Harmonie."

Something in Borkan's tone alerted the Judge. "Not —?"

Before he could let the august name drop, Borkan nodded, his face carefully grave.

"Why, yes. That would be appropriate." Borkan must have had a willing brother-in-law somewhere. Or times had changed. "That was Chauncey Olney's club."

"Olney? I'd almost forgotten him."

"I suppose it's still the same."

Borkan was proud. "*Just* the same . . . Is that music?"

Another young group ran by laughing, peering into each one of the palmy bowers dotted down the vast parquet. "They're looking for the bride," Borkan said with a smile.

"She went ice-skating this morning," said her father. "You ever think, Borkan, that the present world might be the last to see life as a consecutive story? Or to try?"

"Nope. Who does."

"The Duke of York," said the Judge, feeling the cane which hung by his side. "Not the present one."

"He never was in the courts," Borkan said.

Left alone, Borkan gone to take a leak, the Judge, wanting the same, looked around for Charlie, hidden by people at the buffet. The reception was at its height. He didn't want to see them catch the bride. Neither did anyone else, not yet. This was the city as audience, ninety feet of it, three hundred strong in top form, inside a house but not its own, and it was having a good time.

There was an agreeable freshness of new clothes, and the sugary odor of girls with good legs. Everybody was thinking about sex, in the most polite way. On the question of whether Austin and Ruth had already slept together, one could have ticked off the decades backwards in gradations, from foregone conclusion, through a nineteen-thirtyish "Of course, they'll have had an affair," to those few antediluvians among whom it couldn't be discussed. These stood about the great room like old hands welcoming in new members who were the ghosts.

In the western windows, an extraordinary tumulus of blue winter light held at bay the Turk's-head chandeliers. Hats of any insolence looked well in this peacock light, the dowagers' best of all. Great bows of turquoise velvet and cut steel bent benevolently even to the male dancers sidling among them like pugs. Margaret Fenno's severe coif was likened by a cousin to a common ancestor's — "Annetje van Rijn!" — and amended sotto voce by another: "More like the Indian." This was the only open interracial remark of the afternoon. But in the palm bowers, people managed their owlish hints of it. From each bower, half hidden yet open, the talk fell gracefully, like sprays of a fountain that wasn't there.

Into one of these Augusta had led Ruth. From behind its private chapel of fretted green, swooped into that same high, fin-de-siècle arch through which the new age had been born into these houses, their talk came like dialogue to Rupert outside it.

AUGUSTA: I've always known he had something to conceal. Simon. Will you protect him to the end? (*Her voice weakened, as if to say, "Will we?"*)

RUTH (*in a voice strange even to any passing impresario*): Yes, I will protect him to the end.

AUGUSTA: What I can't forgive —

RUTH: My mother?

AUGUSTA: Whatever there was to conceal later, *she* brought it into the house. I always felt that, it's true. But that's nothing. That's just — jealousy. (*It was said superbly, a throwing down of a life in all its maidenly significance, like an annuity spent in one throw.*) No, what I can't forgive is his — your father's concealment. He should have risen above it. (*It showed grandly, her craving to make him a man of action.*)

RUTH: He would have had to rise above *me*.

AUGUSTA: I've always known you knew — what there was to hide.

RUTH: So it showed?

She must be smiling. If a certain observer very slightly shifted himself, meanwhile lifting another wineglass from the trays being passed under one's nose with the locomotive verve of these Americans, he could glimpse the pair, like two behind the papery lattice of a flower shop.

AUGUSTA: Will you tell me? I don't ask for myself. (*And the other figure was seen to bow, assenting this as true.*) I mean — shouldn't you?

RUTH: For whose sake?

> (*Whose could it be but his?* AUGUSTA's *head said it.*)

RUTH: No, I can't tell you. For *your* sake. And I'm used to it.

AUGUSTA: Or you need it! For your power over *him*.

. . . But there's jealousy. That's how Augusta must know. Whatever she knows. How we know, many things. And why wedding champagne so often tastes of insight . . .

RUTH (*hand over mouth*): I need it . . . I never thought . . . One learns to live a certain way — if one has to . . . But not for power. Not for *that*.

She came blindly out of the greenery, parting the broad leaves with the same dazed, seraglio gesture which came out of balcony windows in sets for operas by Leoncavallo. Or from the wartime flat gray doorways, like a row of broken teeth, in the bombarded stone of Rupert's mother's groveled street in the Midlands. And saw him, hunched there, not cheap enough to move, but like a whippet in the rain.

"I need it? I never knew," she said.

She touched one of his sideburns, as if they'd been talking together for hours. "Then I used them all! Even you."

"Never. Not you."

For answer she took his glass, drained it, and left it empty in his hand.

From behind, he watched her poise on the brink of the crowd, facing the noisy young group coming at her. She was darker, taller, on this side of the Atlantic, or else the shadowy vibrato of her future made her seem so. There was more of her. He had a moment's chance to see it. And then they caught her.

The Judge hadn't seen. Borkan had gone one flight below, to the temporary cloakroom set up there near the old-fashioned elevator. Coming up in that open iron cage, the Judge had seen into another world, piled with coats of the younger Fenno clan come strong and early, such odd shapes of sheepskin and helmets of bright leather, clothing for a race of Berbers to attack the Plaza in — and one flushed girl, hair in sunburst points like a kindergarten cutout, carmining her rosy lips and saying meanwhile with all her heart to another, "Thing is, you have to be sincere." He couldn't get his chair down there now, and didn't want to. In the rear of this "étage," as Ralston called it, there was an ancient lavabo, gone to mop closet, which their host's sharp eye hadn't yet renovated. The Judge had wheeled himself back, and standing up, was making use of the old terra-cotta shell, set in the wall at a height before vitamins had raised the mid-century pubis to the level of the 1870 navel — meanwhile hoping that the pipes still went somewhere. These secret peeings, and the places he found for them, had become the most meditative part of his days, reminding him that he was getting old to a pattern he'd first caught on to as an urchin at his father's soirees — that old men tended to ruminate either with a hand spread pragmatic on their bellies, or horny with intellect, at their flies.

Near the lavabo, there was an oriel window — Ralston, what words you revive! The water tower, invisible, must be at the left, still shedding its light. Wheeling himself toward it, putting his glasses on, he could see across the two backyards, to his house. He saw how well it had maintained itself. His kind, the middle kind, bound tight the ends of life, always tending to resist those looser ends which weren't the better part of existence nor the worse — but the parts that life insistently built itself of. One way and another, each member of his family had denied that heritage. His house was a triple amputee. Yet he wouldn't admit himself or his house to be already history. Empty as it was tonight, a light still burned there, claret-colored as of old, tinged with blood as were all the houses of the earth.

He turned. A pair of shoes was coming toward him — no, they were boots — astrakhan boots, incredibly frogged and tittupping their wearer to a motion not for the tweed above them, more suited to a fan. "Your sisters are looking for you."

"I worry them. They're afraid I won't say the right thing. But I thought I was good with the rabbi. He went."

"You were. But he didn't." She sipped from the brandy she had with her. "He's still *here*."

"What delayed him?"

"Important Christians." She sipped again. "Frankly."

He'd forgotten these old exchanges, brother to clever brother, above the crowd. She came to the window, to see the view. Together they looked at it. A wedding was such a perfect reprise.

"I can see myself over there," he said. "Funny. Walking the top floor."

"The top floor's Anna's."

"So it is. I forget. But I do walk, nights. On the floor above mine." It was totally dark over there. "Sometimes, I stop at David's room. Last night — Ruth wasn't with us, you know, I can tell *you* that — I went into hers. I hadn't, since Mirriam died. But she keeps things. That old dollhouse. Pauli was so hurt when she wanted to get rid of it. And that old engraving Mirriam must have given her. Gave it to *her*, for a joke once. 'Behold Now Behemoth.'"

"'That I have made with thee!'" The brandy shivered in its globe. "No, she took it. Afterwards . . . And you needn't have worried, last night. She stayed — with me."

"Did she." He said it absently, to this younger brother from whom an elder had had to keep a few facts of life. "Middle age —" he said, peering as if he could see himself across there wandering the halls, that luminous night of his inheritance. "It's a time for conspiracy. On one's *own* behalf."

He scarcely saw his cousin's face, blunt, gray bulldog, beside his own neater one, faintly Buddha in the old glass. It was the speech in which he explained his retirement. In his mind, over the past months, he had made it to many — now that he had finished it. He stared at that claret light over there, rosying even his cousin's glass. Music came now from behind them somewhere. The chair held him, a walking confessional. "I was destined to be a murderer, wasn't I," he said. "And was saved."

In his mind, they had all asked who the victim was. Family didn't have to ask. "I scare my sisters," he said. "Though they're proud of it. I'm the man under their beds. But I never worry you, do I. You always know what I'll do, don't you."

A pigeon strutted their garden wall. Was she watching it?

Oh, he knew he shouldn't ask the next question; it was the kind that couldn't be answered except by a blinding flash from the throne of

God. "Augusta," he said weakly. "Stop holding that damn brandy glass. I mean, don't take any more. Answer me. I've done the right thing for her *now* — haven't I?"

The boots moved faintly, missing the Chummies, all that line of dogs male or female who knew he'd always been the man under her bed. *He* had always known, up to now. Cruel, to let her see he'd forgotten it.

"Augusta. What the fuck are you staring at!" He could have bitten his tongue off, of course.

She stared on. The dogs always knew what sex she was, as she knew theirs. And they knew that house; not a one had been fooled. No dog of hers could live there; how could she have thought of it? She always had to walk them stiff-leashed around what couldn't be seen from over here. But was there well enough. They always sniffed and growled at its clawed wood as if another animal had been there before them.

She turned and answered him. "The newel-post."

Too late, as she waddled away from him, he saw the high heels of her boots.

At the party, they'd missed him; even Margaret Fenno smiled. But no one spoke or listened to anyone carefully; the party now was everything. Music of a kind his house hadn't been built on was yearning from an accordion, a harmonica, and from clackets and other baubles that with a jolt in the chest he recognized — they'd raided David's childhood, that sonic, sealed room. It was the kind of conspiracy that came about at weddings. The troupe had joined with delighted Fenno jokesters, here and there even linking arms with an elder — he saw Moling — to hop a minuet. "Get Rupert to get his recorder!" came a cry.

But Rupert, kneeling over the fountain in entente with Ralston, said to the approacher, "Bug off. You've got enough."

Yards away, Mannix could read what was being said.

"Any prop man can fix this thing," said Rupert. "Somebody's made off with the gasket. Got a knife on you?"

Ralston, handing it over, fingered the cut greenery star, now flat on the floor. "Often wish *I* could be Jewish," he said.

"Nonsense," said Rupert. "Come and play the gutbucket with us afterwards, instead." Or that was what he seemed to have said. "Meanwhile, hold your foot out."

Straining for a line of vision, the Judge saw him cutting a circlet from the sole of the other's shoe. "That'll do it."

Ralston took his blue lenses off. "Gutbucket?"

"Eh?" said Rupert. "Oh, it's a washtub got up with foot pedal and arm, makes a fearful racket. Kids made it in the wee hours. Shan't let them bring it in your pretty hall though. It's no 'Harp that once.'"

And Ralston said, "Calypso? Oh, any rhythms and all, dear boy. I sang countertenor once. What part do *you* sing?"

He could see almost everything being said if he wanted to, his distance glasses firm on his nose. Height hampered him less here than it would a giant like Moling; maybe all his life he'd been a coxswain in spite of himself. And maybe should have let himself lipread, on and on, to see how little was being said of the Mannixes even here, when all was said and done.

Taking up his duty as host, he began going from bower to bower, palm to palm, handshake to handshake, breaking into conversation which had nothing to do with the occasion — or everything. Lurid as the secret was, his house had ingested it, and lived by it, the knowledge of others as flowing a part of its being as the actual event — all of which not even he knew. So was the human thickness of a household attained.

Down at the far end of the room, little alcoves set with table and chairs and flickering lamp-candles were empty; people preferred to stand, and he saw how they kept their backs to the windows, only turning to look out of them in wallflower moments of meditation, or in a sense of their own singleness. Dark clots of time and cloud were out there, inscribed with cities. City. Inscribed on it, in living dust — the single family. The city reeled with lives. No wonder they turned their backs on it. For the moment, this was the household.

Suddenly, the music in the room was deafening; the dumbshow of mouths stopped. No one in this part of the room was even known to him. People without noticing it had formed a wall in front of his chair, Two little boys did ogle him, then pushed giggling in front of him — "They're coming!" — and squirmed through the wall.

So they were coming — to no music *he* recognized! Under him was the new patch of floor, obelisk-shaped, like the cut-off explanations of kings. He could lipread anywhere what the households were saying to one another. If he should open his mouth it would be to say it to some coeval in a piping voice — like two survivors on a mid-ocean rock, watching the water come to rescue them. *"What shall we say to it when it reaches us?"* Did other men know? Was anybody ever old enough?

He was sure now of what a great man was — that he had the capacity to be lone through all the purlieus of life, yet walk its actual staircases every day — as he hadn't done — walking it stair to stair, greeting those who tripped it with light breath or propped themselves up by its balustrade, grasping at those who came down it white-faced to their dead, or to their own charnel. A great man saw all of it with a generalized love — and kept his hates clean for progress, clean and young. Maybe the great *were* the young, for a time. Until we — they themselves — got to them. He reached out his cane and touched one of the two round little behinds with it. Generations were nothing; anyone alive got to them. Where was Borkan, Moling, Warren — someone of his own age? Speech was a dumbshow — but his way. *"I meant to speak for the middle,"* he said, to nobody in particular. *"But life moves."* And inching his wheelchair humbly, he made himself known, the walls gave, and a place was made for him.

They had caught them both. Bride and groom were dressed for travel in the new way, that was to say — as they were. A thick circle had formed itself around the borders of the room, no opening anywhere. They had to dance their way out of it. It was a wedding. Anybody could see them perform. The music, kazooing a blues, fluting a Jericho, got itself together. The bridal couple took hands like skaters, put their heads together — was it a waltz? Round and round they went to it, slowly, breast to breast.

"Austin was always a fine ballroom dancer," Margaret Fenno said.

One of the harmonicas snuck into ragtime, was hushed, spread itself again when the couple never faltered — today they would jig to whatever was required of them. "Oh but that other was *Swan Lake!*" Leni wailed, touching a handkerchief to one eye.

The couple paused before her and Pauli, for their blessing. "Joy!" said Pauli, boosting them on, and gazed after them, considering his luck.

"That's the housekeeper she's going to now," someone whispered. "Been with them all her life." Anna, bending over the buffet to embrace her, muttered low her benediction. "No, you don't have to bodder any more."

Edwin, who hadn't stayed to see the rest of it, was told of it later.

"When Austin and she got to the far end of the room where his chair was — why, it was like Lourdes or something!" said the girl he was snuggling with. "He got up and *walked*."

"He walks at night," Edwin said.

"Like a zombie?" she giggled.

"No. Like a ghost."

She snuggled closer. What a lark, to be in the Mannix house, next door! "Honor bright, it was like the Pope getting up," she said. His hand went up her skirt. "They danced!" said Austin's cousin Di.

But that was a Fenno description.

"I see you dance!" the Judge said when she came toward him, breaking from her husband at the sight of him standing without cane, alone. The muscles could do everything.

Too late, he saw that she was frightened of his embrace. Her arm came up. As in a minuet, he grasped high the wrist that might strike him, and brought it down near the floor, his upper arm shivering like a samurai's.

"It should have been me," he said, pride and anguish locking their hands. "You should have chosen me." And she, masking their struggle in the dancer's deep curtsy, unlocked them. "Oh, please, please — *please* —"

Austin came and bore her away from him, like a rival. The dowagers snuffled at his handsomeness.

On that young man's arm, a girl should never again have to wonder whether the smaller life wasn't worthy enough to set beside the larger agonies. Yet her father could see that she was still not sure.

"Oh Warren," said Margaret, "I hope she'll be good enough." Her son was carrying off the girl as if he knew better than she what an heiress he had.

Austin, shielding his wife close against the resemblance he saw in her, tucked her head on his breast. Shielded there, she felt its rhythmic message, that the experimentation of life was over, for her and him. For a truant moment, they stood still again. Each looked sideways, not at anyone. Fluttering out kisses through the aisle that parted for them, they ran down the new staircase and were gone. Nobody knew where they were going. The dowagers approved of that.

"Youth," said Rupert, beautifully drunk, standing up to watch. "Youth is the assoluta." (It was what Ninon often said, to him alone. Because, like so many of her other confidences, he knew it already.

Only good reason for giving confidences, she said. "Which is why I can tell you, Rupert, about her.") Youth is the assoluta. "Then it merges." (Like you, Ninon.) "Or stops." (Like me.) "And the next ones wobble out of the chrysalis even of crime — on trembling pointe."

His companion was crouched over the fountain. Rupert knelt next him, to finish the job. "Hear *that* exchange, dear boy?" whispered Ralston. "Between father and daughter. One does hear the *most*. Was he her lover?"

"No," said Rupert. "She was his work of art . . . oh *blast!*" And the fountain sprang up before he was ready for it, in the true spray.

A hand was placed on the Judge's shoulder. "You married her to a friend," said Miss Augusta. "Now she'll be ready for a stranger." The voice was hard, the gloved hand like a man's. "You can sit down now."

"Come and warm the house, everyone!" Mr. Ralston cried.

⁓⁓

Judge Mannix, when Judge Borkan came upstairs to get him, in the room emptied of all but the caterer's men, was still sitting in his chair. He was thinking of the column he and Edwin rode in tandem, each so kept from knowing for sure the verdict on his strength alone. One day, the Judge meant to tell the world of that authorship. Though already such a system was not a hoax, but "honorable." For honor was changing, unless this was the way decade and decade had always had to ride together. His wife's conscience was no longer here to tell him how badly he'd done in years since her death. Grown almost to be his conscience, tonight it no longer waited up for him. Soon he'd be wearing gaiters, or some later token of time past — and his feet would be dangling from the chair. While those around him waited for him to be dead, so that they could really *listen* to him.

Borkan's huge fur collar was already turned up, his homburg jammed on his head.

"Don't think I'll join you, Borkan."

"Why not?" Borkan's face fell. "I only see you at *public* dinners. And I —"

"My chair'll be too difficult. Charlie's taking Anna out to dinner."

"Oh, if that's all it is." Borkan cheered. "I'm a Hercules on wheelchairs — the past five years, if you want to know."

"Or we could eat here."

They looked over at that funeral feast, here and there a beef still unbloodied, a turkey with the chef's pimiento *légion d'honneur* still on its chest.

"Man's martyrdoms are endless," said Borkan dryly. "For the Jew — it takes a little longer. Good God, Simon, if this is the way a man goes on about a daughter — for once I'm glad even of my son."

The other looked up quickly.

"Come on, Simon. The cuisine at the club is excellent. A good hot meal."

And some cold story, which he must bear with? Borkan's face was quivering ready. If you'll want to know, Mannix; if at the club, among the easy chairs of the widowers, the extortionists, the knotted bowel or the perfect lover extracurricular, all of them sucking the cigar, *fellatio* — if only you'll want to know everything.

"Not sure I can stand the colors of clubland."

"Eh? Oh." Borkan stole a look at the bare rosy walls, in the muted light once more floating the Ca' d'Oro toward them, four hundred years young again, now that the rented palmeries were gone. "Don't worry, no decorators there. To change a napkin there, the board of governors takes a vote. Still the same."

"I know." Red cheeks, yellow skulls. And purple-heart lips. "What *are* the veterans talking about this year. Which war?"

Borkan laughed. "The Huns about have it. How long since you been there?"

Apparently Borkan didn't remember that night especially. So why not see the cycle as it comes round again? Modern life, Mrs. Fenno! — that night all over again, the lamps lit, the city doges slumbering, in the colors of Childe Hassam too. "OK. Why not see the end of it."

"Come on. Why the place is *flourishing!*"

Borkan bundled him into the car. "Brrr, can't be more than ten above. And my God — listen to them!"

All the leftover young ones. They were in the garden of the Mannix house.

"Won't your neighbors mind?"

"It's an institution, on the other side. And on this — "Through a din of sprocket wheels and sour flutes, the mayhem beat of what must be the washtub came steady. " — I think that may be our host."

Sitting inside the car, they were both loath to go. So much starlight, and energy! "What *is* that stuff!" Borkan said gruffly. "I like a little Strauss."

The Judge looked at his watch. Quarter of eight. A few more minutes and they could hear the voices of Our Lady. The façade of his house, never quite dark, looked back at him. Music was its income, or had been once, in Mendes's time. None of any kind ever really embarrassed it. Echoes of *Tiger Rag* climbed to its eaves again, and sat on its chimney pots like paper hats. His house was entrepreneur to anything, in the end. "They're calling it Gutbucket on the Outside. I think it's classical."

Borkan, once the car was in motion, had the grip of a man whose car was his shell, his fine star sapphire suave on the wheel. "Ever think of joining a club?"

"No. My house is my shell."

Borkan laughed, as if he didn't believe this. He seemed all mission now, something more purposeful than dinner or a confidence after. Mannix wondered whether later it mightn't be suggested they go to a house of another order. He wouldn't agree — or only to see what Borkan, in the long trek from Grand Street, had settled on in these matters — what would now be his style.

At the broad steps of the club, he refused the chair. "No, Borkan. I miss my walk." He felt a certain shame at his own style. The occupant of such a chair always had too many such easy little dramas at his command. He wasn't surprised to see Borkan nod, admiring.

On the first of the three steps, he paused, head lifted. "Earmuff weather." He said nothing more until they were inside, their coats taken, and Borkan, all bustle and hesitance, said half to himself. "Now — which room —" Mannix's reply was brusque, almost proprietary. "In there."

Memory was life, of course, plenty of times. From the door, the members' library was quite the same in its long conventions of comfort and gazettes, spaced lamps and servitude, and more confident of enduring than many a cenotaph whose crumblings were of greater concern to the globe. "Note this door," said Borkan. "Solid oak, nine feet high, the carving on it alone must be an inch in — yet see that device on it? Original's in the Adam house the Chase Bank has, in London. No matter what angle that door's left ajar, it'll close."

The Judge made no move to try. "The death of the polite world — I never really did believe in it."

He was ensconced in a chair from which his feet did indeed dangle, until Borkan kicked an ottoman under them. "Now I'll go see the maître dee. What would you like? Steak? Lobster?"

"Shellfish? Why not? Later on, for our sins we can go upstairs and wind on our phylacteries." He glanced up. He was tireder than he thought. "Nathan. I apologize."

Borkan was red. But his eyes were shrewd. This was how he had become a judge, maybe. "You're a fraud, Simon. My father had the *tefillin*. I'll bet yours never did. Am I right?"

"Right." When he glanced up again, Borkan was at the door, looking back at him paternally, his hands rubbing each other. No doubt about it, in these halls Borkan was proud of him. When he left the room, the door did close.

He was content to stay where he was. No urge to stand at the window for perorations, no need. From the club crest — *Ignoti nulla cupido* — stamped on every bit of morocco and in a stone chaplet over the fireside, the membership knew what was outside its windows as well as he. *No desire is felt for a thing unknown* — though their readings might vary to a degree. What he wanted just now must be ever in good supply here. He was looking for a dodderer. To whom he might address himself sentimentally. None came.

Shortly, a younger man, fifty say, did come in, crossed past the Judge with the slightest of nods, and stood at a window looking out. The law was heavy on the roster here. Though surely the cut of this well-steamed one was finance, of the newer sort grown in the suburban breadbasket; that blunt cheek itself would taste like Cornish hen. But he was a *customer*. That was his pose. The window in front of him was open. What was he looking at? It was only 1955, but he too should already be hearing the neo-silence of the new century, its neo-energies, cleansed waters, reined-in planets, and up among those air-brushed ozones, maybe even — strange and multiple — a kind of neo-peace. To which his own age would be a turbulent photograph, awful, but dead.

"Beautiful view," the Judge said.

The man turned, surprised, gave a courteous murmur, and with a bow of the head, turned its back to him. One saw he was used to such quavers and knew best how to deal with them, as part of the responsibility of membership here. Even though, whatever else the club offered within the marble silences of its well-known atrium construction — its windows had no view.

Shortly after, he left. The air came through the window, peaceful with the dust of old wars. When Borkan returned, he was carrying the chair.

At dinner, Borkan said, "Might do worse than here, you know. It does have an upstairs. One of the last. Thinking of living here myself, instead of rattling around in fourteen rooms. Give it a thought, why don't you. If you ever want to give up the house."

So that was his mission. "Oh, they wouldn't have me. We have no outside affiliation — such as the DeKalbs."

Borkan turned red again. But again he looked pleased. Maybe this was the way to make a friend, in the sharp backtalk of the same breed.

Borkan was twisting the cellophane from a modest cigar. A metal-tubed one lay on the cloth for his guest. It was like old times, these gestures of negotiation, often enough between two who didn't smoke. "You have — now."

Mannix stared, then burst out laughing. Two men just leaving gave Borkan's table a passing scrutiny, who again seemed pleased. "Oh *no*," Mannix said. He took up his cigar, wondering how to give Borkan the tone of the Fennos. That he hadn't got it, in spite of today, was the distance a Borkan still had to travel, to be a Mannix. *Cohn?* his mother's voice said. *Abe Cohn?* — he hadn't heard that voice in years . . . *Selig* to you, Mamma, after all. . . .

"My new relations? They're a queer bunch." May God forgive him, or safer still — might they! "They're not society, you know, like your wife's. Not nearly. Oh, a good enough family of course, in its way. But not that upper. And not that rich." He watched a waiter address himself to the angle of a curtain, for activity's sake. In this central room the windows, enormously portiered and with as many underpinnings as a well-made bed, must give out on nothing at all, not even a courtyard. "They're just —" There was no other epithet. "Middle."

Borkan did smoke. "It would be enough."

"You wouldn't propose me yourself?"

"Too new here." Borkan, signing the check, smiled guiltily afterwards. "Can't tip like I like. Have to be careful. Don't want to single myself out."

"Ah yes." I remember.

They leaned back, the last in the dining-room except one old man in a corner sure to be his by right, and no move to dislodge them, none indeed. The dues were high here; one could be sure of that.

"What keeps us Jews, Simon?" Borkan said it softly, a shade too low for Mannix's comfort. "Why don't we take it all on *trust?*" Then he laughed. "Mine own answer!" He was smart enough in his way. And somewhere — maybe in that finger ring, this club, Borkan's marriage to the top without going through the middle — was the story Borkan was ready to tell.

"Haven't thanked you yet for what you did for us today, Nathan. Nathan — tell me about your son."

"Today? A pleasure, Simon." Borkan was flushed with his hot meal, maybe uneasy with it too. "I confess it, Simon, I can tell you know I didn't bring you here for nothing. And it's not the club — though I would like that too. My son?" He shrugged. "Married. Lived in Scarsdale, once. The rest I won't bother you with."

"In the Korean War?"

"Three kids." Borkan himself had been a judge advocate of sorts, in a redistribution office, not of people but of property. "And — well — three kids." He sighed. "Oh he's alive."

"Families behind the lines," said the Judge. "But the kids — maybe *they'll* go. . . . Don't look at me as if I were perverted, Nathan."

"Sorry to hear about your son," said Borkan, not sparing the patronage. "Oh, you'll have grandchildren yet."

"Your son a lawyer?"

"He was. A talented boy."

These particular stories were hard on lawyers. Even to those who had been in the courts. He was silenced.

"Nothing criminal, Simon. Not even a Communist — you hear about Moling's son? Not even women. Or men." Borkan's voice was bitter. "You heard the old saw, 'He's got a great future *behind* him.' That's my son."

"My father used to say that. I always thought it was his." But my mother knew an old saw to answer with. "What did the poor man *do*," she would say — "steal a —"

"For God's sake, Nate, what did the poor boy do — steal a hot buttered roll?"

Borkan acknowledged the phrase with a shrug, a shamefaced smile.

Maybe that was why Jews acted as Trojan horses for their brethren, like Borkan wanted to — in order to swap the old saws they'd left behind. "He refuses to be outstanding," said Borkan virtuously. "In any way. A boy of such talents — only I know what a crime."

And this man could ask the question he just had!

"Maybe he doesn't want to be a Jew any more, Nate."

"What do you mean?"

"We're hooked on future deeds from the moment we're born."

"My wife, a Gentile, felt exactly the same."

"Ah?" That's *your* story, then. Of you and a DeKalb. "Still — *we* —" said the Judge. Still, there's a difference. "What does keep us —?"

Softly the waiter poured another brandy; he might have been wearing special shoes to tread the borders of these stories with, or had taken lessons in the art of their intervals. Still, gentlemen, still? What keeps you as you are?

Borkan, in time to it, rubbed his upper lip.

"We mean to be *judged*," said Simon Mannix, in a harsher voice than he'd ever used on the bench. "And that is enough."

In the same instant, he guessed what Borkan wanted of him. It was in Borkan's sudden stance forward over the table, careless of the ash under his arms, in those full, speaker's lips, ready to tremble and swell a little more, across the good hot meat of another's eminence. It was in the blood whirring in his own ears. His eyes closed now like a prisoner's in the dock, at the sound of the sentence deserved.

"They said you'd never be willing," he heard Borkan say hoarsely. "That you'd *been* asked, once before. I said you might be interested — now. That I'd ask you. Whether you'd be open to it. That's all I'm empowered to do."

He opened his eyes. The jowled, bland face was mottled, nervous. If ever a prisoner needed corroboration on his effect on others, it was there.

"So — by the authority vested in me, Simon — that's twice today. You're to think it over; you're not to say a thing, not tonight. I'll leave; sit here, be my guest, and God bless you. Or you can say — 'Nate, take me home.' I won't say another fucking word. Either way. All I have to do is tell you you're being thought of. And now I do." How it got to them all! Borkan was as moved as if the honor had come to himself. He was nod-nodding the many imperceptible times appropriate to holiness. "Your name is in that high place, Simon. You're being mentioned

for it. Not in vain — I'm not even allowed to hope. That's all I have to
say."

For the Court.

The table silver was crested too. In his mind, before he made himself
look away, he was already shifting spoon, salver, saltcellar, in the way
men scribbled their fortunes on table linen — men who could never
forget how to play chess.

Might have been three minutes or so before Borkan said, tentatively,
"Simon —?" and was motioned to stay. A few more minutes on, he
said, "You all right?"

"I'm looking at the harbor." The portieres were still closed.

Borkan waited a few minutes more before he said, "They put a
tower on this site, you *could* see the harbor. But it's always voted
down."

"Every room in this city has a view of the harbor."

Borkan subsided, clearly anxious to take him home. But he liked it
here. He might well become a member of a club where the most
serious matters could be discussed under no need to act on them —
though he doubted he'd ever come to live in it. Even though he *could*
see the harbor from here. Out beyond far Montauk, beyond Basch's
balustraded corner, and Henderson Place, and the solitary rose-of-
Sharon bush once on the corner of Fifth Avenue and Seventy-ninth
Street, his house was still being built by himself and all the cohorts
beside him, just as he was helping to build theirs — a pyramid not
built by the slave labor of others, Borkan — all of us slaving for ourselves. Out farther, forever translating this into the eternity those
portieres were closed against, the waters exchanged themselves, in the
unrepeatable coda of the waves. Houses were built on such music.

"Excuse me, Borkan. No, stay. I'm — thinking of someone."

Borkan nodded expressively. "Your father was a lawyer." It was
what he would have done.

"My son-in-law." He thought of Austin, who so long ago, at the
beginning of their entente — which now by very relationship would be
closed — had said, "I don't feel private any more." What was "public"
life? The access of each organism into the current, and its submission
to it, held all the dramas of life. But one couldn't stipulate where the
rises and falls might come, early in a particular span, or late. And death
alone, as with David, doesn't finish it. Consciousness is the experiment
which always fails, Walter — and starts again. Is this worthy to be God,

Dr. Hildesheimer. I am wounded, but I live. I am in healing — and shall never get over it.

Chauncey had given him ten years. It had taken him — more than twelve. How long you've waited for me, Chauncey. But I'm here, aren't I, only a little later than Geoffrey Audley-Taylor. I got to you, in time.

What if he should say to Borkan, as Chauncey had said to someone, "I think my private arrangements might not bear scrutiny." I do not wish to bring them into full view.

"Borkan?"

"Yes?"

"If I'd gone to war — and returned of course — my whole life would have been *neurologically* different. After that, I could have been a man of peace."

In the corner, there was a majestic stir, while the old man there rose and was attended to, with the imaginary brushings-off which were so beautifully standard here that the Judge could have wept at the sight — of privilege still not interred. He was close enough to breaking down anyway. "Does the prisoner understand the sentence of the court?" Oh yes, your honor. The prisoner understands everything.

As the old man passed their table, they scrutinized each other. Eighty years to their sixty, his war would have been what? The "Spanish"? The "German"? — connotations blending or almost gone. He was the dodderer. He gave them a look of regal enmity, unsoftened by the sight of the Judge's chair. Modern life!

The two at the table watched. Behind him, the door did *not* quite close.

"War and peace!" said Borkan. "If that were only all of it!"

"The decade to come is always the Hun," said the Judge. "Take me home."

He let Borkan help him into the chair. In full view of the city, the single story took place—and was the full view. This was the only allegory he knew; he had made it himself. He was willing now — to admit his generation into history. Oh, he was willing! There was light for all men in the truly finished life. And it seemed to him that he was at last united with her, the silken, raging woman who knew so much, but had never accepted it — that we were all of us gliding through a history which we would never see.